Parachuting

Parachuting

a novel

by
Leora Freedman

Sumach Press
TORONTO

Parachuting
by Leora Freedman

First published in 2010 by
Sumach Press, an imprint of Three O'Clock Press Inc.
180 Bloor Street West, Suite 801
Toronto, Ontario
M5S 2V6

www.sumachpress.com

Sumach Press gratefully acknowledges financial support for our publishing activities from the Ontario Arts Council, the Canada Council for the Arts, the Government of Canada through the Book Publishing Industry Development Program (BPIDP) and the Government of Ontario. The author would also like to acknowledge the support of the Toronto Arts Council.

Library and Archives Canada Cataloguing in Publication

Freedman, Leora, 1959–
Parachuting : a novel / Leora Freedman.

ISBN 978-1-894549-86-8

I. Title.

PS3606.R44P37 2010   813'.6   C2010-904785-0

Text design by Colleen Wormald
Cover design by Em Dash Design
Cover Photo Copyright © http://www.istockphoto.com/stock-photo-11856107-through-dirty-glass.php

09 10 11 12 13   5 4 3 2 1

Printed and bound in Canada by Marquis Book Printing, Inc.

To my family, Nessiya and Eric,
and to Jean, my teacher and friend

"Your daughter, after renouncing her Hungarian citizenship, joined the British Armed Forces and was a Radio Officer in the Parachute Corps. Last spring she flew from Cairo, via Italy, to Yugoslavia, where she was dropped, and spent a considerable length of time with the partisans. From Yugoslavia she made her way to Hungary, supposedly for the purpose of rescuing Jews and British prisoners of war ..."

After yet another terrible silence he said, "I must pay tribute to your daughter's exceptional courage and strength of character, both of which she manifested until the very last moment. She was truly proud of being a Jew," he stated with undisguised, if puzzled, admiration.

I replied, "I don't know the military laws and whether my daughter has transgressed them, and if she did, what that act was ..."

"Her offence was exceedingly grave," he interrupted.

"But that she stands innocent before man and God," I went on, "I don't doubt at all. Because anyone so gifted, so endowed with talent, could only have volunteered for a great and noble cause."

"True, she was an exceptional human being. But it is just such people who volunteer for unusual assignments. Pity she chose the wrong path ..."

Catherine Senesh
"Meeting in Budapest"

Part One
Jewish Girls

Chapter One

"This is the *suburbs*," Zoe Diamond said, leaning against the brick wall of Temple Beth Israel, hands in the pockets of her army pants. "I can't believe there was almost a rumble."

"Well, believe it," Adam told her. "I heard that five guys got caught carrying knives today." He leaned against the railing, a tall skinny boy with dark hair down to his shoulders. He wore a plaid flannel shirt with a tear in one sleeve, and a button that said "Impeach the President: Do It Now."

A big fight had been planned for that day after school: white kids fighting black kids. It wasn't clear whose side the Puerto Ricans would've been on. Fortunately someone had phoned in another bomb scare right after lunch, and there were so many cops around that the rumble was called off.

"That is so stupid," Zoe said. "Those people are such assholes." Zoe had been a pacifist and a vegetarian ever since she was thirteen and read Joan Baez's essay "OK, So You're a Pacifist." She was sixteen now. Of course, as Joan Baez pointed out, you never knew exactly how you'd react if you were driving down the highway and saw a baby sitting in the middle of the road in front of you and a truck coming in the opposite lane. But picking up a gun or a knife intending to hurt or kill someone was a different matter. Once you'd decided never to do that, becoming a strict vegetarian was the logical next step, Zoe thought.

She watched Naomi take out her film container of pot. Naomi didn't open it, just rolled it back and forth between her palms, her blue eyes checking out the parking lot. There wasn't enough time to smoke a joint before their Hebrew High School class; it was ten to four, and Mrs. Lev would be there any second.

"If everyone just got stoned all the time, there wouldn't be any violence," Naomi said. The long tails of her oversized men's shirt flapped in the cool autumn breeze. Zoe could detect that Naomi's tone was insolent and sincere at the same time, possibly because Nao had been her best friend since the first grade.

"That's naive," said Danielle, who was sitting on the top step looking up at them. Her hair fell across her eyes in ringlets like the hair of an angel in an old painting. "People will always have a capacity for evil."

"Yeah," said Jeff, sitting next to her. Then there was silence. Both of Danielle's parents had been in concentration camps when they were young. Sometimes, Zoe thought, people looked at Danielle as if she herself had been in a camp.

It was early October, and the sun lit the leaves of the trees bordering the parking lot, making them glow an almost psychedelic yellow. Zoe looked at them as she absently adjusted all the things she wore around her neck: a string of heishi beads Naomi had stolen; a gold necklace that said *Chaya*, her Hebrew name; a wooden roach clip on a piece of rawhide; and over it all, a heavy, plated Star of David stamped with the name of a refusenik in the Soviet Union. She watched as a silver Cadillac raced down the back road and turned into the parking lot. It made a quick arc, just missing some other cars, and landed neatly at the end of a row.

"Hey, Nao, what're you smoking these days?" Jeff asked.

"Columbian," Naomi said, handing him the film container. Jeff lifted the lid and sniffed. "Mmm."

Mrs. Lev got out of the Cadillac and walked across the parking lot. Even from a distance you could see how straight she carried herself. She was an Israeli. When she said it, all the vowels were separate: I am an Is-ra-e-li.

Jeff glanced at Mrs. Lev and handed the film container back to Naomi. "Ask her if she wants to smoke a joint before class," he suggested.

"It'd be good for her," said Zoe. "It might make her more human."

Mrs. Lev didn't understand things at all. When the kids talked about what a terrible president Nixon was, mimicking his hunched shoulders and making V-signs in the air, Mrs. Lev just shrugged. But nothing will ever be the same, they'd say, No one can ever trust a politician again. Nixon is good for Israel, Mrs. Lev had told them. They hated her for saying things like that.

"Hey, baby, want a toke?" Adam muttered, not quite loud enough for Mrs. Lev to hear as she came toward the steps.

"What?" she said, stopping in front of them. Zoe and Naomi looked at each other and started to laugh, silently and hard.

"I said, hello," Adam said.

"Hello." Mrs. Lev exaggerated the word. She always smiled at them by frowning, turning down the corners of her mouth, looking amused and contemptuous at the same time. She had black hair cut in layers to her shoulders, grayish-blue eyes, and she was young. If she'd had a nicer expression on her

7

face, she would have been extremely pretty. "I saw what you were doing," she said. "I know what you are laughing about."

Adam shrugged. "We weren't doing anything."

"Sure." She looked at them knowingly with her frowning smile.

"What were we laughing about, then?" asked Zoe. She wanted to test Mrs. Lev's ESP.

At that moment the bell rang for class. "Never mind," said Mrs. Lev. She walked past them into the temple, and they followed her down the narrow hallway. The temple was small, and the hallway near the classrooms swarmed with kids of all ages. When Zoe's mother first brought her here in the third grade, it had startled her: the shabbiness of the worn green linoleum and yellowed walls, the crowds of people rushing around, the noise. It was so different from her shiny suburban public school; there was a hint of the past in it, of a time when people lived more closely together.

Mrs. Lev walked through the crowd with her shoulders back, breasts forward. Adam and Jeff marched silently behind her, lifting their knees like soldiers. They stopped instantly when she reached the door of their little classroom and turned around.

"I know everything about you," she said fiercely, and for a moment they were all silent. It was funny how she could almost make you believe it.

Mrs. Lev had the strongest ESP of anyone Zoe had ever met. About death, for example. Mrs. Lev would dream that someone she knew was calling to her from the bottom of a flight of stairs, while she stood at the top, unable to move. When she woke up, that person would be dead. During the Six-Day

War she was at home in Haifa, and her brother was fighting in Jerusalem. She'd had that dream the night before he was killed. Then her ESP followed her to the United States, where she'd predicted accidents on the Connecticut Turnpike, two unlikely divorces and Watergate. In Zoe's Hebrew High School class, Mrs. Lev had guessed several people's names correctly and come close on the rest. She said she always knew when someone was thinking about her, and if they thought hard about her — even ten years from now — she would know it. She'd chosen to tell them these things about herself during the first few weeks of class.

Now Mrs. Lev sat on top of the scarred wooden desk, her legs crossed and a copy of *Hebrew Today* on her knee. Every Tuesday and Thursday afternoon she showed up wearing one of a series of similar outfits: dark pants, a tight shirt or turtleneck in a solid color and clangy Middle Eastern belts. Today the shirt was dark blue and outlined her breasts — you had to admit, she did have a good figure. All her movements were controlled, deliberate, but when she changed position her belt, made with strands of metal set with blue stones, clattered against the desk. She sat very straight and looked at them intently. "Shalom. How are you?" she said to Charlie in Hebrew.

"*B'seder,*" he said. OK.

"Good. What did you do today?"

He thought about it for a moment. "I study in school. I play soccer."

"Very good," she said. "But you must say I studied, and I played."

Then she looked at Zoe. "What did you do today?"

Zoe looked down at the floor, away from Mrs. Lev's eyes, which could have been reading her mind. "Today I studied in school," she said. "There was a bomb scare." She said the last two words in English. Then, more out of politeness than curiosity, she asked, "How do you say 'bomb' in Hebrew?"

"*P'tzatza,*" Jeff said. His vocabulary was larger than everyone else's because he'd spent the summer in Israel. Everyone laughed and started saying *p'tzatza, p'tzatza.*

Mrs. Lev looked shocked. "There was a bomb in your school?" she said. Her eyes were wide.

"No, there was not a bomb. Someone said on the telephone that there was a bomb." Zoe gave up trying to explain in Hebrew. "There's never really a bomb. Someone just calls in and says there's one, so the school has to call the fire department, and we get to hang around outside while they search the building. It's like a little vacation."

Mrs. Lev looked confused. "That is terrible. They make you think that there is a bomb —"

"No, it's not," Naomi said. "They're doing us a favor."

Mrs. Lev looked at them the way she often did — as if she really didn't understand English. "Nice favor," she said. After this she gave up on conversation and had them open their books to the paragraph they had been assigned for homework. "Anyone feel strong enough to translate this paragraph?" she asked. There was silence.

"We feel really weak," Naomi said, looking down at her book with a regretful expression. Zoe put her hand over her mouth and bit her finger so she wouldn't laugh. Naomi never did the homework; she probably hadn't even opened the book since Tuesday.

"You know," said Mrs. Lev, "in the army they would just

say, Who here knows how to play the piano? Then a lot of people would raise their hands, and they'd say, OK, you — you — you" — her finger pointed out the imaginary volunteers — "can go and wash the dishes." She laughed. She'd been in the army for two years, when she was just a little older than they were now.

"Sounds like a great time," Adam said.

She gave him the hairy eyeball. "OK, Adam, you can be the volunteer."

Adam sighed and started translating. "'I was talking to a very interesting young man who is a student at the university. He told me about his life in the United States. What is there that is good about the life of the Jews in the Diaspora? I did not say anything, but I hoped he would decide to stay in Israel —'" Adam stopped. "This is Zionist propaganda," he said. Everyone laughed.

Mrs. Lev smiled her sarcastic, frowning smile. "It won't hurt you," she said.

"It *does* hurt me." He looked at her steadily, his face a mask of hurt innocence. She shrugged. Adam looked down at his book. "Shit," he said in Arabic. "Bitch." He had taught these and other Arabic curses to the rest of the class last year.

"Adam!" said Mrs. Lev. "Do you know what you just said?"

"Sure. I used to have an Arab girlfriend," he told her.

Mrs. Lev's eyes narrowed. It was semi-true, what Adam said. There'd been a girl from Saudi Arabia in public school with them last year, and Adam had hung out with her — only in school, of course — for about three weeks. Then Adam's mother found out and almost had a heart attack, and the girl's parents sent her away to boarding school.

Adam was now smiling a small, nasty smile. "She also

11

taught me how to say —" He reeled off a long curse that Zoe knew meant something like, your grandmother has shit on her mustache.

"Adam, that's enough!" Mrs. Lev yelled. She slid off the desk and stood up, her belt tinkling. "It's very rude, what you said. And this is a Hebrew school. We don't speak Arabic here!"

For a moment no one said anything. There was a strange feeling in the room, on the edge between fear and hysterical laughter. Everyone was watching Adam and Mrs. Lev. In a way it was mean of Adam to say something about grandmothers, since during the last class Mrs. Lev had told them how her Polish grandmother spit in the face of a Nazi who was putting a noose around her neck, before hanging her in front of her whole village. The Nazi then put the noose on backwards, so that Mrs. Lev's grandmother hanged without dying for as long as possible. At the same time it was funny that Adam could get her so angry.

Adam leaned back in his wooden chair and doodled with his pen on the desk, which like all of them was carved with initials, names and dates, some from as far back as the 1940s. There was something a little scary about the way he kept smiling. "What's wrong with speaking Arabic?" he asked.

"You might like to think how beautifully they treat Jews in Arab countries," she answered, her voice heavy with sarcasm. Her hands held the sides of an empty desk in the front row, and she leaned forward, staring hard at the class. Zoe, two desks away, was close enough to smell her perfume. She leaned back in her chair, drawing away from the scent.

"My brother was killed by Arabs," Mrs. Lev continued. "Every day I am concerned about my sister and her family, every night I hope that I will not have a dream of them at the bottom of the stairs. There could be another war at any time." Her hands gripped the edge of the empty desk tightly. Zoe looked at her smooth polished nails, the three gold rings against her olive skin, and thought about how Mrs. Lev would know how to shoot a gun. She always answered their questions about why she was here by saying that if there was ever another war, she'd go back immediately to help.

The sky was darkening outside the big arched windows, and the classroom was uncomfortably warm, wavering like a dream. It felt like something was pressing in on them and forcing an emotional scene; it was terrible and beautiful at the same time. Then Zoe spoke into the heavy, waiting silence.

"I think the Arabs want peace, too," she said. "I mean, maybe not the leaders, but you know, the regular people." Zoe liked the way her voice sounded, saying these things in the quiet room. She did mean them.

Mrs. Lev glared at her. "You will not convince me," she said. "If I knew who killed my brother, I would like to kill that person myself. I hate them."

Zoe felt her heart pound. She couldn't believe she was in a room with someone who was saying these things. "Hating people doesn't solve anything," Zoe said. "If all you want is to hate them back and get revenge, you'll just have an endless cycle of violence. Why should we lower ourselves to killing people — it's like becoming Nazis."

Mrs. Lev's eyes were bright with anger. "We have to show our enemies that we are strong! You don't know what you are talking about," she said.

"I do so!" Zoe exclaimed. She was furious now; she hated Mrs. Lev. She could feel the whole class watching them. "I just don't want to kill Germans or Arabs or anyone."

13

"You don't care for your people," Mrs. Lev said.

"I do care!" Zoe felt suddenly desperate, as if nothing she said from now on could prove that she cared. "I care a lot," she repeated.

"Well, I also care," said Mrs. Lev. "I care that we should kill a Nazi like Eichmann when we find him."

"You're a real hate monger!" Zoe yelled, louder than she'd intended. The bell rang, like a long guttural scream in the room, but no one moved.

Mrs. Lev picked up her copy of *Hebrew Today* with a swift, angry gesture and stared at Zoe. For a moment Zoe thought she was going to throw it at her. Instead Mrs. Lev stood up very straight and looked down at Zoe with her lip slightly curled, as if Zoe were a specimen of something distasteful. "I know you are not a stupid girl," she said. "But today you show no smartness."

The next morning both Zoe and Naomi felt they needed an Aggravation Day. There were twenty-five hundred kids in their public school, so it wasn't hard not to be missed. The teachers were too busy prowling the halls between classes, making sure no major fights erupted. After homeroom Zoe went out to the courtyard and waited, hoping no teachers happened to be looking out the upper windows. A minute later the door opened, and Naomi tapped her on the arm, saying, "Let's go, kid." They walked quickly across the parking lot and got into Naomi's little blue Datsun. Once they'd backed out and driven around the corner they were safe, but Naomi drove fast and wildly down the big hill anyway. They both laughed, and Zoe opened her window a bit to let the breeze in. "Good timing," she said, and Naomi smiled.

Among adults, Naomi had a reputation for being irresponsible. She skipped school and didn't do her homework; she didn't care about anything they wanted her to care about. Even when her mother grounded her, she found ways to sneak out her window and stay out late. When her mom — her parents were divorced — tried to find out where she'd been, Naomi would look at her with huge, innocent blue eyes, smile happily, and say something like, I told you. We went bowling. It was hard for anyone to punish her since she was never sullen or mean. With her friends, though, Naomi was a very responsible person. If she said she'd skip school with you, she'd be there, right on time. If she said she was going to get you some drugs, you'd get them, and they would be good.

"Bagel King?" Nao asked, turning onto the Post Road.

"No, I think Howard Johnson." The last time Zoe and Danielle had skipped third period and gone to Bagel King, they ran into their two lesbian gym teachers who were having a deep conversation at a corner table. They all pretended not to see each other.

The Howard Johnson was several miles away, down near the Connecticut Turnpike, and it was doubtful they'd run into anyone there. They stopped at a traffic light, and Zoe listened with pleasure to the sounds of the cars all around them, the screeching of a crane lifting a metal dumpster, a siren in the distance. Their school was huge and new; it had won an architectural award for its big ugly gray cinderblocks in weird shapes. Compared to the low-ceilinged classrooms and thick cinderblock walls, the outside world seemed reassuringly real and alive. In school there was no place to go to relax. A few years ago they'd had a student lounge, but it was closed after too many interracial fights and other incidents, like boys catching girls and sticking their hands down the girls' pants, and sometimes, Zoe heard, finger fucking them. Zoe wasn't sorry they'd closed the lounge.

It was a gray day, and a light rain was starting to fall as they drove around, smoking a joint in the car. Getting stoned in the morning always made her sleepy. As they waited for a table at the Howard Johnson, Zoe saw two men at the counter staring at Naomi. So she moved in front of Nao, keeping her back to the men. People often stared at Naomi. She had long, wild, dark blond hair and very full, definite features, like a Greek statue. Her round blue eyes were never still; they always moved, shining, away from your face and then back again when you talked to her. She hid her body beneath enormous men's shirts and baggy torn jeans that were frayed at the bottom, belling out over her feet, which were often bare, though today she wore old basketball sneakers. People always said things like, If she only took care of her appearance, Naomi would be a very pretty girl. They treated her like she was stupid, but she was actually very smart.

Finally they got a table by the window. They ordered coffee and pancakes and then, on second thought, two large servings of french fries. The waitress gave them a strange look, but they didn't care; they were munched out.

Zoe took a pack of cigarettes out of the front pocket of her overalls, on which she'd embroidered a large yellow and orange sun. They both smoked; it was delicious. "Good time for an Aggravation Day," Zoe said. Nao looked at her for a moment, then blew out a stream of smoke and they both laughed. Aggravation Days were preventive: They kept you from getting too weirded out.

Zoe sighed. "I shouldn't have yelled at Mrs. Lev yesterday. I shouldn't have called her a hate monger."

Naomi shook her head. "She's a bitch. I knew it right away."

Zoe put her cigarette down on the ashtray and leaned her elbows on the table. She smoothed her hands over her long dark hair, which was getting frizzier by the minute as the rain fell and the humidity rose. Her own face was the opposite of Naomi's. She had dark eyes, and her thick eyebrows would've met in the middle if she didn't pluck them. Her nose was long and her mouth wide; she thought there was something off balance and secretive about her face. She knew she wasn't pretty, but she didn't hate the way she looked, either. Danielle said she was interesting-looking, and most of the time Zoe was satisfied with that.

"Yeah, I knew it, too," Zoe said. "I took one look at her, and I knew she'd be a bitch." She felt a strange excitement, saying this.

"So why should you worry about it?" Naomi put out her cigarette as the waitress set down their pancakes.

"I don't know, we were pretty rude. Adam was really baiting her." Zoe started to smile, remembering what Adam had said, but she made herself stop.

Naomi gestured to forget it. For a minute they both ate in silence.

Nao poured them each some coffee from the big plastic pot. Two little kids in the next booth were having a fight, pushing each other on the seat. Diagonal to them sat a man in white coveralls spattered with paint, holding a cigarette between his thumb and forefinger like a joint. Zoe was spacing out on the other customers and almost didn't hear Naomi when she said, "Actually, I think all the adults

17

we know are full of shit. I'm tired of everything. I want to become a heroin addict."

Zoe was startled. After a moment she said, "I don't think that's such a good idea, Nao."

"Why not? I think it'd be fun." Naomi smiled at her and sipped her coffee. "It might be better than killing myself. That was last week's plan."

Zoe had never heard Naomi say anything like this before. Usually the ESP between them was pretty strong, but — "Naomi," she said, feeling clear and alert now. "What are you talking about?"

"You heard me." Naomi put her chin up and looked at Zoe through half-closed eyes.

"Are you serious?" A long ash fell off Zoe's cigarette into the crusts on her plate.

"Yeah, I was serious." Nao paused for a moment, then opened her eyes wide again. "For about five minutes." She grinned at Zoe, who tried to smile back.

Zoe didn't know if she should make a big deal about this, since Nao was laughing it off. But she decided to pay more attention to Naomi, to watch her carefully. She knew that Naomi had been depressed on and off since last spring, when her mother caught her with some pills and her parents sent her to the drug rehabilitation center upstate. Zoe didn't think Naomi had really needed rehabilitation; she thought it was cruel of them to send her to that place. Luckily her own parents hadn't found out about it. She told them that Nao was visiting her father in New York. When Naomi got back, she said they watched her with eagle eyes and made her pee in a cup every morning, but that most of the counselors were nice and group therapy was kind of interesting. She'd seemed quieter and sadder, though, since she came back in the middle of summer.

"You're really all right, Nao?" Zoe asked again. She felt confused and anxious, as if her friend had turned around and walked away from her for no apparent reason. It had been that way, on and off, since Naomi started taking stuff like speed and Quaaludes last year. Zoe thought smoking pot was a good thing and made you more aware. She had taken LSD a few times with Naomi and had liked it so much that she'd promised herself not to do it too often. But she thought pills were gross, and you had to draw the line somewhere. Naomi didn't believe in drawing lines. In all other ways, though, they were as close as they'd always been.

"Yeah, I'm fine." Now Naomi looked almost surprised that Zoe had asked, and her voice was reassuring. "Let's get out of here."

"Let's split this scene," Zoe said, and they both laughed at the old-fashioned expression.

The rain had let up and the sky was clearing, so they decided to take a long drive through all the little towns they didn't know very well, the ones with winding roads and mansions along the water. They smoked another joint and the road was beautiful, its wet surface gleaming in the light coming down through the red and gold trees. After a while Carole King came on the radio, and Zoe turned up the volume. They both sang along: "'I feel the earth — move — under my feet — I feel the sky tumbling down —'"

Mrs. Wasserman was out raking the yard. She'd already made three huge piles of leaves, and the scratch of her rake was rhythmical and energetic. On her head was a red scarf that matched the leaves left on the big solid oak trees shading the house. She waved to Zoe and called out in her German accent, "How are you, sweetie? Danielle is upstairs!" Zoe called back, "OK," and waved at her, thinking how Danielle had the nicest parents of anyone she knew. For example, they would never have made Danielle come out and rake leaves. They got her anything she wanted that they could afford, and they always told her to invite her friends for dinner and sleepovers. Sometimes Danielle complained that they were too nice, they were smothering her with niceness, and then Zoe and Naomi would say, "Oh, poor thing," in chorus.

Zoe went up the stairs. "Hey, Danielle," she called.

"Hi, Zoe," Danielle said, not looking up. She sat at an old table in the corner of her room, painting the designs she'd hammered into a leather wristband. She had a whole set of leather tools to make belts, wallets and pocketbooks, which she gave or sold to people. Her paintings and pastel drawings, mostly pictures of the beach or of her friends, were all over the walls. She had a small loom, too, and she'd once woven a wall hanging for Zoe with a design like the cross-section of an enormous seed. Danielle was almost always making something, but she didn't mind talking to you while she worked on it.

Zoe sat down on the edge of the bed. It was a small room, with a sloping roof and a window that looked out onto a patch of woods; it was the nicest room in the house. Danielle was playing a James Taylor record on her little stereo. "Good night, you moonlight ladies," he sang.

"I was going to call you," Danielle said. "You weren't in school today, were you?"

"Nope. I skipped school with Nao. We had a blast." Sure,

Zoe thought, except for Naomi talking about suicide. But she decided not to mention that; there were other things she had to say to Danielle. It was the day before Yom Kippur, and you were supposed to set things right with your friends. She still sort of believed all that stuff.

"I guess I read your mind," Zoe said. This wasn't usually the case with Danielle; they'd known each other only about two years, since the Wassermans had moved here from New Jersey. She didn't always know what to expect from Danielle, not like with some of the kids she'd known all her life.

Danielle smiled without looking up. Her long fingers were still for a moment while she thought about which color to use next. Her skin was very pale, and across the bridge of her nose were light brown freckles, the same color as her eyes and hair. She had a reputation for being creative, of course, and pretty cool. But also aloof. She dipped her brush in the yellow and said, "I went to the movies with Adam last night."

"You *did?*" They'd agreed before that Adam was interesting, but not to be trusted.

"Well, he asked me. But I shouldn't have gone. We drove out to the beach afterwards, and he seemed to think we were going to have some big make-out session. It was dark out there, and no one was around, and I got scared. I had to ask him three times to take me home, and I knew my parents would be really worried because I was supposed to be back by ten." Danielle hesitated. "The thing is, I didn't even really want to make out with him, but I did. I felt so guilty afterwards."

Zoe didn't see why Danielle even hung out with guys — it always turned out that she got scared and wanted to go home. Zoe herself didn't have this problem, since almost no guys she liked or would consider being seen with ever asked her out. She didn't spend much time thinking about them, either, though she knew she wasn't as naive as Danielle. She would have sense enough not to get trapped in cars with people like Adam.

"It doesn't matter if you made out with him," Zoe said patiently. "But maybe you shouldn't do it again, if you didn't like it."

"My parents were really flipping out when I got home. It was after eleven, and they were about to call the police."

Zoe sighed. "You didn't do anything wrong." This was the other side to Danielle's parents: They worried. Zoe had seen them flip out totally one afternoon last winter when she and Danielle went for a walk without telling them. When they got back Mr. and Mrs. Wasserman were sitting close to each other on the couch, and Mrs. Wasserman's lips kept trembling for a long time, even after they'd screamed at Danielle and then apologized almost instantly. It was because of the concentration camp.

"Adam said, 'Oh, I didn't think you were so innocent,'" said Danielle. "'Being a friend of Naomi's.'"

"Oh, tell him to fuck off," Zoe said. She was sick of the way people talked about Naomi. It was true that Nao had slept with people. She said she didn't have to be in love; she just did what felt good. But there was a lot more to Naomi than this.

"That's what I'd like to say to him," Danielle said, sounding more cheerful. "Fuck off!"

"Yeah," said Zoe. After a moment she said, "Danielle?"

Danielle was cutting out another wristband, the razor knife slicing through the damp leather. "Yeah?"

"Listen, remember what I said in Hebrew yesterday?"

Danielle was silent for a while. "You said you didn't want to kill Arabs. Or Nazis."

"Well, I don't. But I'm really sorry about what happened to your parents, and I'd do anything to keep it from happening again. I didn't mean to offend you." Zoe waited, watching Danielle's lowered head.

"I wasn't offended." Danielle was staring at the piece of leather as if she could see a design on it before she'd actually started.

Zoe was so relieved — she felt a rush of love for Danielle. "You really weren't?"

"No, I saw what you meant. But you probably shouldn't ever say those things to my parents."

"I won't," Zoe promised. "Honestly, I'll be really careful."

"It's not that hard." Danielle looked up at her finally, the light brown eyes in her delicate face strangely distant. "They barely ever talk about it."

Once in a while, though, they did. Zoe remembered the time Mr. Wasserman had gathered a bunch of kids around after Friday night services. He told them that he had been in a concentration camp when he was about their age, and he'd shown them the blue tattooed numbers on his arm. Zoe had always imagined the numbers would be large, sprawling over people's forearms, but also faded: She thought you'd have to look hard to see them. Instead, when Mr. Wasserman rolled up his sleeve, the numbers were small and evil-looking, and very dark blue. They looked as if they could have been put there yesterday.

It was often like this on Yom Kippur: bright autumn sun, the smell of burning leaves in the air. Zoe was reminded of certain moments in childhood — riding in the car, running down the street — when she'd felt lifted up by a sudden euphoria that would make the whole world seem perfect, complete. She'd float, unthinking, her body part of the universe. Then she'd be let down again, but gently. She sometimes got this feeling back on the High Holidays, a less intense version of those old moments of floating that she knew, in their purest form, were gone forever.

Zoe thought her family looked all right today. She, her mother and her sister Melanie were wearing short dresses with bright psychedelic patterns; her father had let his hair get longer this fall and had it tucked behind his ears. This was the only time of year her parents went to temple. Zoe's father was an atheist, but her mother believed God was a force and people had souls that could return to earth after death. These beliefs didn't make her observant, though. When Zoe and Melanie had started Hebrew School, they couldn't understand why their house did not seem to be a Jewish home. One Yom Kippur morning they came out to the kitchen after not even brushing their teeth and found their parents drinking coffee and eating English muffins. Zoe had been furious; she hated the calm looks on their faces. You do what you want to do, and we'll do what we want to do, her mother had said.

Now, though, Zoe and Melanie were more like their parents: They'd each eaten a little bowl of cereal this morning, smaller than usual. As they walked across the temple parking lot, they could see people standing out in front, lots of them in white clothes that reflected the sunlight. Zoe looked for Naomi and Danielle but didn't see them.

Then Mrs. Hoffman, a friend of Zoe's mother, came out of

the crowd and walked toward them. She was wearing a white dress, and around her neck was a gold watch on a chain. For some reason the watch was open, and it looked weird hanging there showing the time: ten-thirty in the morning. Mrs. Hoffman's face had a preoccupied, held-in look, as if she were about to give an angry lecture. "You've heard about the war?" she asked.

They all stopped and stared at her. "No," said Zoe's father. "No, we didn't listen to the —"

"They've attacked Israel," Mrs. Hoffman broke in. "Egypt and Syria. On Yom Kippur morning — the holiest day of the year. They knew — they knew it was the best time —"

Mrs. Hoffman was really pissed off about it, and she looked at each of them in turn with her little brown eyes. Zoe wasn't sure how to react. Zoe's parents were saying how terrible it was, but they didn't seem as excited as Mrs. Hoffman.

"I've got to go find Naomi," Zoe murmured, as if she had to be the one to tell her the news. She wandered through the crowd. Everyone was talking fast and loud, and once in a while a voice rose up above the others, saying, "On Yom Kippur! They knew! They knew!" People were saying Israel was unprepared for this war, and it was going to be bad. They said "we'll win"; they said "they'll have to win." We and they both meant Israel. About the Arabs, they said over and over again: "They knew!"

Of course they knew. The Arabs didn't need ESP to know that Yom Kippur was the holiest day of the Jewish year and therefore the best time to attack Israel. Zoe felt disgusted with the Arabs, but also disgusted with the people she heard all around her. Of course it was a dirty trick, but so was every war. She couldn't understand how anyone could pick up a gun and shoot another human being. If everyone was as repulsed as she was by violence, she reasoned, there wouldn't be any.

She stopped near all the Israeli teachers, who stood talking in loud, excited Hebrew, but she could hardly catch a word of it. Mrs. Lev was there, standing next to a man who Zoe thought must be her husband; Mr. Aharon was there and Mrs. Ben-Yakov, and a bunch of kids. Something electric seemed to be radiating from them, an almost visible current. Zoe looked carefully at their faces and realized what it was: They were scared. Mrs. Lev put her hand on a little boy's head and stroked his hair as she talked, over and over without looking down at him, as if she wasn't aware of what she was doing.

Zoe felt sorry for them. But if Naomi had been there with her, she might have laughed instead. After all, Mrs. Lev always said if there was ever another war, she'd fly back immediately to help. But here she was, with a bunch of dressed-up people standing in the sunshine on a beautiful fall day in Connecticut. The truth was, she wasn't going anywhere.

Zoe felt relieved, in a way.

Inside the temple the sun poured through the arched windows and made wide bands of light around Zoe and her family, sitting in an extra row of folding chairs. Zoe held a large red and gold maple leaf in one hand and turned the pages of her prayer book with the other. During a short break she noticed Mrs. Lev and her family moving in along the row of chairs right in front of them.

"Oh, hello, Zoe," Mrs. Lev said loudly. Her voice always seemed to carry too far.

"Hi," Zoe said unhappily. She hadn't seen Mrs. Lev since

Thursday, when she'd called her a hate monger. But she was trapped, now. She introduced her parents and her sister. Mrs. Lev introduced her husband, Natan, and the two boys, Elisha and Eitan, who were twins, seven years old. Then she introduced herself as Rivka Lev. Today she was wearing a tight, knit, purple dress and a chain belt with gold coins hanging from it. Zoe thought it was embarrassing the way she showed off her body all the time.

"Your daughter is a very interesting person," said Mrs. Lev. She glanced sideways at Zoe, who looked down and opened her prayer book to the place she'd marked with the leaf. She touched the delicate veins running beneath its colored surface and felt her face getting warm.

Zoe's mother said, "She can be," and then there was an awkward silence.

"It is such a shock," Mrs. Lev said.

"Yes, it really is," Zoe's mother agreed.

"What's terrible is to just have to sit here feeling so helpless," said Zoe's father.

"We are not *helpless!*" Mrs. Lev exclaimed. Zoe glanced up. Mr. Lev was looking at his wife as if he wanted to calm her down but didn't know what to say.

"No — of course — I just meant there's a certain — uneasiness — being so far away —" Zoe's father was getting tangled up in his words, and Mrs. Lev was looking at him as if he were crazy.

It was a relief to pay attention to the services. The reading and singing were much louder than on a usual Friday night or Saturday; Zoe looked down into her book and joined in. She was not an atheist like her father, but she didn't really *get* her mother's idea of all these souls flying

27

around, propelled by the force that was God. She thought that what they called God was really just the good parts of people. Singing like this, she felt her own good part and the good parts of everyone else in the room float up and join together: That was enough of an explanation. After the adults and the cantor had stopped singing, the voices of the older kids went on, harmonizing, carrying the tune into variations. They knew different, livelier melodies than their parents, and they used the Israeli pronunciation instead of the Eastern European. The rabbi folded his hands on top of his podium and waited, silently, staring at a spot on the green plush carpet.

After a while Zoe looked up and saw Naomi and Danielle in the aisle. Naomi nodded toward the door, where the younger kids were starting to leave for the children's service, which was always held in the basement of the church across the street. Zoe excused herself all along the row and caught up with them. Danielle looked beautiful in her brown dress, which had a pattern like feathers on it. Naomi wore a navy blue corduroy skirt and a baggy blue sweater; her hair was the same as always. When they got outside, she said "Whew." The bright sun made them all squint.

"'We have been stiff-necked. We have dealt treacherously. Exchanged wanton glances,'" Naomi mumbled in a ponderous tone as they walked quickly through the crowd of parents escorting their little kids over to the church. Zoe and Danielle laughed. Nao sighed. "And 'engaged in all manner of perversions'? What the hell does that mean? This is the last year I'm coming." Then she grinned at them and opened her hand a little so they could see the joint she held.

"I don't know, Nao," Danielle said, but she ran across the

street with them anyway. They checked to make sure no one was watching, and then casually went around to the side of the church. "It seems disrespectful."

"You got high on Rosh Hashanah," Naomi said. "What's the difference? You can still pray if you want to."

"I don't know," said Danielle. "I mean, the war and every-thing."

They walked across the church lawn, autumn leaves crunching under their shoes. There was a nice place to sit on a stone wall hidden behind some trees, a spot left from when the area was farms and not a suburb.

"We can't do anything about the war," Naomi pointed out. "It won't stop the war if we don't smoke this."

You couldn't argue with that.

Zoe looked up at the deep blue sky above the trees. On the other side of the street, she could see a Star of David against the sky, and over here, a cross. She looked back and forth, feeling that it was sad and beautiful at the same time. It occurred to her that she was stoned off her ass. Then she looked back at her friends, and the events of the day returned to her in a great rush, like a 3-D movie. "Did you see how freaked out all the Hebrew teachers were?" she asked.

"Yeah, I saw them talking out in front," said Danielle. "I felt sorry for them."

"Do you think any of them are going to go back and fight?"

Naomi let out a snort of laughter. "Can you picture it? Mrs. Lev and Mr. Aharon riding around in a tank? Rrr-mmm-rrrmmm —" She spun an imaginary steering wheel, and Zoe and Danielle went hysterical.

"No," Danielle gasped. "The women don't fight —"

"Mrs. Lev would *make* them let her in the tank," Naomi

said. "'I care that we should keel zem!'" she exclaimed in Mrs. Lev's voice.

"We shouldn't — laugh —" Zoe gasped. "It's serious. People are getting killed."

They stopped and held it in, looking silently at each other for a second before bursting into fresh laughter.

"We should be getting back," Danielle said as they were finishing the second joint. She looked from Zoe to Naomi. Her eyes were very bright; she always got a little paranoid when she was high. "Do you want to go to the kids' service or back to the adults'?"

"Judy Teitelbaum is leading the kids' service," Zoe said. She made Os with her hands in front of her eyes to look like Judy's big glasses, and opened her mouth wide like Judy singing the prayers, except with no sound coming out. Danielle and Naomi collapsed into giggles. Judy Teitelbaum wasn't a bad person; she just did everything she was supposed to and wore her shirts buttoned right up to her neck. There was such a huge difference between the kids who smoked pot and the kids who didn't.

"Oh *shit*," Zoe whispered.

"What's the matter?" said Danielle, wiping her eyes.

"Shh," Zoe said, pointing with her thumb at Mrs. Lev, who was walking across the churchyard in their direction. Naomi put out the roach and stuck it in her shoe. What the hell was Mrs. Lev doing here? She must have brought her kids over to the church basement, and maybe she'd heard them laughing.

Mrs. Lev strode directly over to them, hesitated for a moment, then came around behind the trees to where they sat. "I knew it!" she said loudly. Then she lowered her voice. "You smoke marijuana, don't you." Her arms were crossed and her face showed so much anger — her eyes wide and dark, her mouth frowning — that it was like a person pretending to be angry, except it was real. "How can you do it?" she asked. "On this day?" It wasn't clear whether she was upset that they were being sacrilegious or unpatriotic.

"We're not doing anything wrong," said Zoe.

"We were just having a cigarette." Naomi held up a crushed pack of Marlboros.

Danielle said nothing.

"You are lying," said Mrs. Lev. "I know what it smells like. And I saw you run across the street to hide here. You think no one can see you?"

"We've never done this before. It's the first time," said Naomi, changing tactics. She was obviously desperate.

"Well, I will tell your parents, and then they can decide," said Mrs. Lev. "You will ruin your lives like this." Zoe could hear the satisfaction in Mrs. Lev's voice; she probably cared more about getting back at them for what they — especially Zoe — had said in class.

"Please don't tell our parents," Danielle said. "We'll never do it again." She sounded like she was about to cry.

Naomi's elbows dug into her knees, and her hands pushed through her wild hair. "Shit, oh shit," she muttered.

Zoe realized it was up to her. She got off the wall and took a step closer to Mrs. Lev. Once again she could smell Mrs. Lev's perfume, and it made her feel dizzy and afraid. "Listen, you can't tell our parents," she said. "Naomi already got caught once. If she gets caught again, they're going to send her away to this drug rehabilitation center for a really long time, and it's a terrible place. It's like going to jail."

Mrs. Lev looked at Naomi, who seemed completely

31

hopeless. For some reason Mrs. Lev's lower lip was stuck out as if she were confused or even hurt. You'd think they were threatening to do something to her, instead of the other way around. Zoe had a moment of panic, thinking that Mrs. Lev hadn't understood what she was saying.

"All right, I won't tell them," Mrs. Lev said finally. "But you have to stop this."

Naomi looked up instantly. "Thank you," she said. "I promise we'll stop."

"Thank you," said Zoe and Danielle together. "We won't do it again," Zoe added.

Mrs. Lev was just glaring at them.

"Thank you so much," Naomi repeated.

"I don't understand you," Mrs. Lev said, forcefully and with great scorn, as if this in itself were a terrible condemnation. "You don't act like Jewish girls."

Zoe lay in bed that night with the light on and the book she'd been reading, *Hannah Senesh: Her Life and Diary*, resting on her chest. She looked around her room: the painted boxes from Mexico on her dresser, the seed-shaped wall hanging, the bookshelf filled with many books she knew almost by heart. On the closet door hung a black light poster with a design like a multicolored fire; on the wall across from her was an optical illusion of brightly colored balls that converged to a point in the center. She stared for a long time at the psychedelic balls and then shut her eyes. Bright orange and green spheres floated in the darkness. There comes a time, Hannah Senesh believed, when a person decides she must do something useful. Zoe thought of twenty-three-year-old Hannah parachuting into Nazi-occupied Europe and being captured, tortured, never telling them what she knew. When they shot her, she refused the blindfold and stared at the sky instead. A Jewish girl.

Zoe sighed hard. She didn't know why, but she wished they'd been caught by almost anyone except Mrs. Lev. She started to cry as the bright spheres shrank and then burst into fragments.

Chapter Two

Zoe's two favorite books were *Exodus* and *The Electric Kool-Aid Acid Test*. She'd read them over and over, alternately attracted to the accounts of Zionist pioneers farming the hills and deserts of Palestine and the stories of the Merry Pranksters stoned on acid, careening across the country on their psychedelic bus. The main problem was that both these eras were already past, or would be for sure by the time she was old enough to escape the suburbs. Israel was now a place where kibbutzniks worked in factories and everyone came home and watched TV. As for hippies, everyone said they practically didn't exist anymore and that people Zoe's age were selfish and conservative: the Me Generation. This made her furious; she would not accept it. She knew she would never have the chance to be a Jewish pioneer or a Merry Prankster. She felt extremely impatient, as if there were only a limited time left in which interesting things might happen.

"'Hamlet's tragic flaw,'" Zoe read aloud from her notebook, "'is that he's too self-centered. His egotism makes him spend too much time thinking about himself, which leads to his downfall.'"

Her father sighed and turned a page of *The New York Times*, shaking the paper to make it lie flat. "Is that what you really think?"

"I don't know." Zoe was drawing geometric scribbles in the margin. "I just have to come up with a thesis."

"I always thought Hamlet's problem was his father," her father said, lifting his eyebrows mockingly at her the way you could imagine he'd do with his students. Even though he was a history teacher at the other high school across town he didn't take helping her with her homework seriously; he always used it as an opportunity to tease her. "Hamlet wouldn't've had any problems if it hadn't been for that lousy ghost, his father."

"Be *serious*," Zoe said. "I have to get this done by seven-thirty in the morning."

"I *am* serious," her father said, slumping farther into the couch. He'd just finished grading papers, and he looked tired. Unknowingly, he had rested his forefinger on a picture in the newspaper of two Israeli soldiers clutching machine guns, running against a background of flames. The war had been going on for nearly two weeks now; almost two thousand Israelis were dead.

"The sins of the parents," said Zoe's father, "are paid for by their children." He glanced up at her again, but didn't seem to actually be seeing her. Sometimes she thought her father was a real space cadet.

"What are you talking about?" she said irritably. During the past two weeks, while she was taking out the garbage or dialing the combination on her locker, her mind had been asking unnerving questions. So, were they supposed to hold a sit-in out there in the Sinai? Curl into little human balls? She had to admit she disliked the image of the Israelis curling

35

up into little balls, protecting their heads like marchers being clubbed by the cops at a peace demonstration. As soon as her mind asked these questions, Zoe would bang down the metal lid on the garbage can or slam the door of her locker to shut it up.

"Well, I was talking about Hamlet," her father said in a reasonable tone. "But you can apply it to the present situation, too. You know, the effects of this war are going to last for a long time."

She wished he wouldn't talk like this. She didn't want to figure out how the Yom Kippur War related to Hamlet, so she shut her notebook and leaned her head against the back of her mother's big brown chair, stretching one of her legs out over the arm. Zoe liked to sit in her mother's chair when she wasn't home. Tonight, her mother was out at her consciousness-raising group. From down the hall Zoe could hear a faint drum beat coming from Melanie's room; her sister was always in there with the door shut, listening to the same records over and over. It sounded like, "Come on baby light my fire." Yes, that was it. "Try to set the night on fi-re —"

"So did you figure out your thesis?" her father asked.

Zoe sighed. "I guess I'll go with Hamlet thinking too much about himself. There's more to write." She was finding it hard to concentrate on Hamlet, who kept talking about pointless things like suicide. Her eyes kept returning to the picture of the soldiers running against the flames, her father's finger right in the middle of the fire. While she was wondering if she'd be able to beg her English teacher for an extension, she heard the garage door go up, and she and her father exchanged a glance.

A minute later Zoe's mother stood in the doorway, taking off her coat. She held it over her arm for a moment and looked at them, pushing one hand through her hair, which was brown and frizzy, like Zoe's but cut into a kind of afro. She wore her rectangular wire-rimmed glasses to these meetings instead of putting in her contacts, which she always wore to work. She was a counselor at the unemployment office downtown. For some reason you didn't want to disturb her when she'd just come home from consciousness-raising; sometimes she looked upset and other times she came back happy. But she was always unapproachable for a while, as if she'd drawn an invisible shield around herself that gently but firmly repelled everyone else, like an opposing magnet. So Zoe and her father waited for her to say something first.

"The car's making a funny noise," she said finally. "I think it's the brakes."

"Yeah, I know," said Zoe's father. "I was thinking it might need a brake job soon." Actually he knew nothing whatsoever about cars, but he seemed to feel he had to fake it, opening up the hood whenever the car broke down.

Her mother sighed. "We got pretty heavy tonight," she said.

"Mm. Uh-huh," her father said sympathetically.

"Yeah," said her mother, staring at him in a way that made Zoe feel suddenly uncomfortable.

"Mm," her father said in a less sympathetic way.

She went to hang up her coat, and he went back to his newspaper.

"I'm fed up with this!" Zoe's mother had yelled one evening last summer. She threw the frying pan and its cover clattering into the sink, then dried her hands on the dishtowel and threw that in the sink, too. Zoe, her father and Melanie were still sitting around the table. Zoe's father had spread out a map of New England over the crumbs and placemats, which Zoe's mother hadn't yet cleared away, and was showing them the route they were going to drive for their vacation in Maine. The three of them had looked up, startled.

"I'm fed up to here!" Zoe's mother yelled again, her hand slicing the air above her head. "You expect me to work all day and then come home and cook and then clean up on top of it all. Not one of you even lifts your finger. I'm sick and tired of it!" Her eyes were dark brown and shining behind her contacts.

"Oh, we'll help," said Melanie. She stood up and got the sponge and started wiping the table.

"Never mind! There's practically nothing left to do. I want you to show me you'll help when there's really something to do." She started to cry, strode over to the table near the door to pick up her car keys and slung her leather pocketbook over her shoulder.

"Arlene," said Zoe's father.

"Damn it, Ben," said her mother. She slammed the door hard on her way out. The garage door went up with a roar, and then she drove away. She didn't come back until they were all in bed.

After that there was a new schedule: Zoe and Melanie each did her own laundry, cooked one night a week and alternated cleanup. Their father became more attentive and polite and made pancakes on the weekends. A few weeks later their mother started going to the consciousness-raising group. Zoe didn't really like to think of her mother sitting around in a living room with eight other ladies, telling them undoubtedly private things about herself and her family. It was like her mother was taking off her clothes in front of strangers every Tuesday night.

Occasionally Zoe wondered where her mother went that night she drove away. Did she go to a movie? Or did she just drive around for a few hours? It was difficult and sort of embarrassing to picture one of your parents driving around with no specific place to go.

Zoe's parents always used to get angry about the same things. For example, during the big strike last year, they sat around after dinner and talked about the schmucks on the Board of Education who wouldn't give the teachers a fair contract. Their voices got louder and louder until they were almost shouting, but they were both on the teachers' side. After Zoe's father had been on strike for about two weeks, Zoe's mother and all the other city workers went on strike, too, to support them. Zoe's father was out picketing every day. One day Zoe and Melanie came along with their mother to bring him some lunch. It was still Indian summer, and Zoe's father was sweaty, strands of his dark hair sticking to his forehead. He wasn't marching around as she'd imagined, but just standing in one spot holding a sign that said "We Are Your Children's Future." He smiled when he saw them pull up in the car. Zoe had thought her parents were secretly enjoying the strike; she thought they were pretending to be like garment workers who might get beaten up or thrown in jail. But after watching her father get stung by a bee and then go on eating his sandwich in the hot sun as if nothing had happened, she was somehow more impressed with his courage.

What would happen now that Zoe's mother had been to

consciousness-raising? Would she not even bring Zoe's father a sandwich on the picket line?

Melanie avoided their parents' arguments; right after dinner she'd go into her room, shut the door and turn on her record player. But Zoe always sat with them and drank coffee, waiting to see what would happen.

One night Zoe's mother said, "Tomorrow it's seven years since Dad died."

"Did you get a candle?" Zoe's father asked.

"Yes." She sighed, pouring milk into her coffee. She sat there watching the swirling design. "I felt all tied up in knots about it."

"Why?" Zoe asked.

Her mother held out one hand, palm upturned, as if the answer was obvious. "Well, I'm angry," she said. "I don't like to remember all the things he did."

Zoe remembered Grandpa Lenny as a short, excitable man with thick white hair that would never lie flat. Once, Zoe had made the mistake of taking a fork from the meat silverware drawer and using it to eat a piece of cheese Danish. Her grandfather grabbed the fork away and then leaped across the tiny Brooklyn apartment, turned on the kitchen faucet and shoved the fork under the stream of cold water. Then her grandmother had to wash it several times. She also remembered him letting her sit on his foot while he moved it up and down like a seesaw. But the things her mother remembered were different. She said her father would come home from work to the cramped apartment with five kids, and he wouldn't let them talk. He'd shout, "You sit at the table to eat! So eat! Don't talk!" She imitated his Yiddish accent. If any of them made a sound, he'd hit them.

40

Zoe's mother laughed without smiling. "It's funny how you never get free of them. I mean, I can see him so clearly. 'What you want to marry Ben for? He's a poem? A poem? What good is he?'" They all laughed. That's what he'd said about Zoe's father, who was a history student but also wrote poetry when Zoe's mother first met him at City College.

"I was a poem," Zoe's father agreed. He hadn't written a poem since way back then, though. Zoe wondered what his poems were like and had asked to see them years ago. He said he'd show them to her on the day of the first snow that winter. But on the day of the first snow, she forgot all about it. From then on, every year she'd plan to ask to see his poems on the day of the first snow, and every year she'd forget. He never reminded her, and he refused to show them on any other day. Eventually she realized she wasn't going to see them.

"But you have to give your father a break," he said now to her mother. "Think of it — you work all day in a factory and then come home tired and hungry to a bunch of screaming kids and your wife saying, 'Lenny, this one didn't behave himself, this one did that —'"

"I know, I know," said Zoe's mother. "But he never got any better, not even when he retired. He still wanted to run our lives. He had to tell us where to live, what furniture to buy. And it's all part of the same pattern. Men just want to be in control of every situation."

"Well, I don't know about that," said Zoe's father.

Zoe could tell they were going to have another fight. She also saw, at that moment, how foolish she was to think that her presence would keep them from arguing.

"What do you mean, you don't know?" Zoe's mother said. "It's an obvious fact." She waited to see what he'd say.

He said nothing.

"Well, if you think I'm wrong, why don't you say something?" she asked. "Tell me how you feel, Ben."

He sipped his coffee.

"Well?"

"This isn't going anywhere, Arlene," he said. "I don't know what to say."

The lines around her mouth seemed to deepen. "Typical," she said.

"For centuries men were supposed to pretend they didn't have any feelings," he said. "Then all of a sudden the feminists come along and demand the perfect articulation of every nuance of every feeling. I'd say it's a little bit disorienting."

"I'm just saying, you have to try," she said.

He shook his head. "We don't have the vocabulary for it."

Zoe snickered, and they both looked at her. She'd thought her father was trying to be funny. "I think the problem is that men can't talk *fast* enough," she said seriously. "I remember when all those ladies were here for bridge, Melanie and I couldn't believe how everyone talked so fast all at the same time. It was like, two or three ladies would be having a conversation, but each one would be going on and on, not even listening to what the other ones were saying." The women — all of them Jewish — would gesture wildly, interrupting each other, the noise getting louder and louder.

"At least we were talking to each other," her mother pointed out.

"Arlene, I'm sorry, OK?" he said. "I don't know what to do."

"I'm sick and tired of everything," her mother said through clenched teeth. She threw her napkin on the table, went to the hall closet and put on her coat. They knew that pretty soon she'd be driving away again, leaving them with the dishes.

Zoe washed and her father dried. For a long time neither of them said anything. As she scrubbed the plates, Zoe stared at the wood grain in the cabinet above the sink, and in it she saw a face. She'd never noticed it before: elongated, with wide nostrils and protruding, ringed eyes, like an African mask. She stared at it, letting the hot water run over the plate in her hands. The face frightened her, and she was angry at being forced to stand there in front of it. She wondered if this was how her mother felt.

She glanced at her father, who was waiting silently with the checkered dish towel in his hand. He leaned against the bright yellow countertop, his face very distant. As she looked closely at him, she felt a sharp guilty sadness.

"Dad?" she said.

"Hm?"

"Tell me about that time you almost joined the Beats." She liked hearing him talk about when he was a grad student at City College, writing poems on the hour-long subway ride between Brooklyn and Manhattan. "I forget how you found out about the Beats in the first place," she said.

He glanced at her as if he was irritated, but then seemed to change his mind. "I've told you a million times." But, he was beginning to look more cheerful. "I first heard about the Beats," he continued in his deeper storytelling and teaching voice, "when a friend of mine — I think I may have told you about him, his name was Irv and he had green hair — invited me to a poetry reading. Irv was always going somewhere, up to Harlem to hear jazz or —"

"Wait." She laughed. "How did he make his hair green?"

43

"I don't know. He put some stuff on it in the shower, I guess. It was black to begin with, so it really just ended up with a greenish tint."

"And so was that poetry reading given by the Beats?" she asked.

"No," said her father, wiping a glass vigorously. "We never laid eyes on an actual Beat. They were all in San Francisco. But some people who were at the reading that night were talking about going out there. This place Irv took me was down in the Village and it was completely unmarked on the outside; there were just steps leading down from the sidewalk to a blue door." He paused to make it more dramatic. "Then inside, you had to walk down a dark passageway."

"Why?"

"It must've been fixed up as a speakeasy during Prohibition. So you walked down this passageway and there was another door, and then you were inside. It was really just a very plain bar, with wooden tables and chairs, and it was the sort of place where everyone knew everyone else. So we sat in the back and had a beer, and Irv and these other guys started talking about Ginsberg, Kerouac, all the people out in San Francisco. Then some of them read poems. After that night I decided I had to get out to San Francisco. I thought I'd drop out of school and head west with a little bundle of belongings, you know, and see *America*."

He stopped and laughed at himself, and Zoé smiled, even though she knew this was where the story got sad. She wanted her father to have run away to San Francisco.

"So I went to the head of the history department and told him I was taking off. He listened, and then he said, 'I'm always amazed at how ignorant history students are of the

44

times in which we're living.' I asked him what he meant, and he said, 'Ben, do you realize there's something called the draft? You'll have more chance of being shipped off to Korea than of becoming a Beat.' Then he threw in some disparaging remarks about his poet friends who'd lived on bread and buttermilk. Bread and buttermilk!" Her father laughed, a little hesitantly, as if he was still afraid the history professor might overhear him.

"So you didn't go," Zoe said, turning the coffee pot upside down in the dish drainer.

"Well, obviously, I didn't go," he said. "I stayed in New York, and Irv and I rented an apartment on the East Side. We painted three walls black and one wall orange. It was a fantastic place."

Zoe's mother had often described that place: Her father and Irv threw their dirty laundry under their beds; when they needed something to wear, they just pulled it out. They ate things like peanut butter and onion sandwiches.

"The main thing of course was the draft," he added.

"Yeah," Zoe said. They were both leaning a little awkwardly against the counter; the dishes were done and there was no real excuse to keep talking. "And then you met Mom."

"And then I met Mom," he agreed. "Who was no complacent soul herself. The first thing she told me was that she was on an FBI list, and if I went out with her, I'd probably get on it, too." He laughed. "You know, your mother belonged to this discussion group in high school, just a bunch of bright kids getting together to talk about music, or art, or books — whatever. So the FBI felt they had to keep an eye on this hotbed of potential insurrection."

"Hm," Zoe said. She wondered if he thought high school

kids couldn't be politically dangerous. There was silence for a moment. Then she said, "You know what? Your whole life would've been different if you'd gone out to San Francisco and joined the Beats."

He gave her a strange look, as if he wanted to make a joke but couldn't think of one. "You're probably right," he said.

That's when Zoe saw why he always told her this story: It was the big turning point in his life, the time when he chose to become what he was now instead of having adventures in San Francisco. She realized that her mother was wrong: Her father did talk about his feelings. He talked about them in code.

When Zoe tapped on Melanie's door, her sister opened it just a crack, then all the way, when she saw who was there. "Hi, Zoe," she said, quickly shutting the door again once Zoe came in. Melanie was supposedly studying for a test, but the whole room was strewn with her outfits: jeans and shirts laid out in different combinations on the bed, sweaters piled on the floor. She had on an outfit Zoe had never seen before — a denim shirt with two elaborately embroidered mandalas on the front pockets, right over Melanie's breasts, and a pair of jeans that had flowers and vines starting at the bottom hem and climbing up to her thighs.

"Those jeans are beautiful," Zoe said. "Where'd you get them?"

"Fran just gave them to me. Her sister did all the embroidery, but she's gained so much weight that nothing fits her anymore, and they didn't fit Fran either."

"Great," said Zoe. She knew Melanie was glad to be thinner than both Fran and her sister. Even though Melanie was a year older, Zoe was taller and heavier. Melanie never made her feel bad about it, though; she said that Zoe was voluptuous and not fat at all. Zoe and Melanie had stopped fighting about a year ago, when their parents started to fight, and now Zoe loved her sister. She watched Melanie unbutton the shirt and throw it on the bed, then stand there in her bra, deciding what to try on next. Melanie's breasts were full and her stomach was perfectly flat. She had their father's green eyes, whereas Zoe had gotten their mother's brown ones, and Melanie had a smaller, prettier face and a short nose. She did have the same dark frizzy hair as Zoe, but she straightened it by rolling it up on old orange juice cans fastened with bobby pins. The reason she was so thin was that she never ate anything fattening — she turned down ice cream, bagels, even pizza.

Zoe admired Melanie, but she'd pretty well given up on trying to be like her. If Zoe rolled her hair up on the orange juice cans, it came out with strange kinks in it, weirder-looking than the natural ones; if she tried to diet, she forgot about it within hours and found herself wolfing down cookies. The thing about Zoe was that she lacked willpower, which was why she couldn't diet or plan how her clothes would match. In the public library there was an old porcelain phrenology head, divided into sections like Courage, Intelligence and Amiability. In Zoe's own head she'd discovered an incredible hollow place where Willpower should have been.

"I'm trying to figure out what to wear to West Hartford on Friday," Melanie said.

"For *Barry*. Better wear something sexy."

"Yes! *Barry!*" Melanie said in a dramatic husky voice, thumping her hand over her heart. Barry Weitz was her boyfriend. They'd met last spring at the big Youth for Torah and

47

Israel kinnus. From the very beginning of the retreat you could tell that most of the kids hadn't come for the services or discussion groups on Torah in the Modern World: They'd really come to find a boyfriend or girlfriend. By free time on Saturday it seemed like almost everyone had paired off and headed into the woods bordering the old hotel grounds. Zoe and Danielle — Naomi had refused to come — had caught a glimpse of Melanie and Barry Weitz walking off under the trees, arms around each other. Everyone joked about how sex was a mitzvah, and a double good deed on Shabbat.

Then Zoe, Danielle and three other girls who hadn't found boyfriends sat by the lake and talked about how cliquey YTI was. One of those girls had been to Israel the previous summer, and before coming back she'd hollowed out the wide rubber soles of her Earth Shoes and smuggled back many grams of Israeli hash. Sitting by the lake, they all smoked some of it and felt much better. Zoe didn't remember the rest of that day too well, but she did recall that she, Danielle and their new friends left the dance early that night and went up to their rooms, laughing hysterically. Someone pointed out that kinnus rhymes with penis, and they just got sillier and sillier. There were big double beds in the rooms, and it ended up that all five of them piled, giggling madly, into one bed and eventually slept there.

"You still like Barry, though, right?" Zoe asked. Melanie had changed into a tight ribbed turtleneck that looked like something Mrs. Lev might wear.

"Yeah! Sure. He's a really, really nice guy. We have a lot of fun."

Barry *was* nice, Zoe thought, and he was cute, too: tall and thin, with a big mane of curly dark hair and little round wire-rimmed glasses like John Lennon. Melanie had good taste. "Have you actually slept with him?" Zoe asked cautiously.

Melanie laughed. "Uh-huh." She was quiet for a moment. "It was nice. We've just done it a couple of times." She looked almost shy, saying that, and Zoe was too shy herself to press for more information. Zoe had made out with a few boys at parties and other kinnuses and was grossed out by most of them; they always touched you in a creepy way, like they owned you or something. She had no doubt it would be different with someone really nice like Barry Weitz, only you had to be as pretty as Melanie to even think about flirting with him.

Once she'd jokingly told Melanie about the night she and the other four girls had slept together in the big bed at the kinnus, but Melanie didn't see what was so funny. She said, I don't think that's so good. Zoe said, Why not, it was just innocent fun, and Melanie said, I don't think it was such a smart idea.

Mrs. Lev swam through the ocean wearing her turtleneck, the gold coins of her chain belt miraculously floating on top of the waves. The sea was rough, and it made Zoe, who was sitting on a thin branch overhanging the water, nervous. She was afraid of falling in. There was a roaring in the waves that made it hard to hear Mrs. Lev as she shouted, "You don't care for your people!" But Zoe yelled back with all her might, "I do so! I care! I caaare!" The louder and more desperate her voice got, though, the more the branch shook dangerously over the water; she slipped back and forth on it, scraping her clutching hands on its bark. "What are you afraid of, American girl?" Mrs. Lev taunted her, swimming effortlessly through the waves. "I'm not afraid!" Zoe screamed back. Then the

49

branch shook violently and she lost her balance, slipped off and fell toward the swelling blue waves.

Zoe opened her mouth to scream and woke up with her face pressed against the pillow and her mouth dry, as if she'd been shouting for hours.

"Check this out," Danielle said. She and Zoe were standing in front of The Love Shop in Greenwich Village. The window, which was below street level, displayed velvet-lined cases containing vibrators of different sizes and shapes, packages of colored condoms, black underwear slit at the crotch, leather bras and several small whips.

"Wow," said Zoe. Automatically they both walked down the steps and went inside.

"You might like this one," said the man standing behind the counter, holding up an enormous plastic penis attached to a cord. He was showing it to a couple. "It comes with these —" He fished out some different attachments: round, elongated, some with little rubber massage tips. Zoe and Danielle looked at each other and started laughing silently; then Zoe went over to the display of condoms, biting her hand. Danielle came up behind her and pointed to a purple condom with the head of a little rubber gnome on it, complete with funny ears and a little red rubber tongue stuck out. It was too much; they both shook with the giggles.

"Hey, get outta here, kids." The salesman interrupted his shpiel and pointed to the door. "Out!"

They climbed the steps, laughing so hard their stomachs hurt. There were bunches of people standing on the sidewalk getting high, and some kids hanging out and playing guitars on a bench in a small triangular park. Zoe and Danielle found the entrance to the subway and hurried down the dark steps; Zoe didn't want to be late meeting her grandmother.

On the train they sat close together, swaying back and forth. The car was packed with people but seemed strangely silent, everyone reading or staring off into space, the roar of the tunnel drowning out all other noise. When Zoe and Melanie were younger, they used to stay with Grandma Esther — their father's mother — on school vacations, and they'd ride this same train to Chambers Street. There, up in a big loft, was the wholesale hardware business that Zoe's grandparents had started. Zoe's father never had any desire to take over the family business when his father died; he didn't know one bolt from another and didn't want to learn. Zoe remembered being a little girl and following her grand-mother through the trash flying in the breeze at the dark entrance to the subway, watching her grandmother's black high heels go *click click* across the concrete and through the turnstile, over to the deep black pit where the trains ran. Once Zoe asked Grandma Esther if she wasn't afraid to take the subway alone every day, and her grandmother had given her a strange look and said, This is how I get to work.

Danielle was whispering in her ear. "You know those little men with the tongues? What are they for?"

Zoe cupped her hand around Danielle's ear and said, "Just for decoration, I think." Then she thought about it for a moment and added, "No, maybe it gives the woman an orgasm." Danielle's hair smelled good, like herbal shampoo.

Danielle looked blank for a moment. Then she whispered in Zoe's ear, "I wonder what it feels like."

Zoe shrugged. She settled back into the plastic seat and

thought about how, when they were little, she and Melanie used to have orgasms by riding the arms of the living room couch as if they were on horseback. They'd worn out the fabric, and the couch had to be recovered. She still had orgasms by pressing against her own hand in bed at night, and it felt so good, she thought what you'd feel with a guy would be ten times better. Now, swaying back and forth in rhythm with all the other people jammed into the subway, a feeling came over her, something she was aware of at intervals and then forgot about, only to remember again. It made her clench her teeth and feel a heaviness in her shoulders, her chest and behind her eyes, as if tears were trapped there. This feeling, she knew, was the need for someone to love.

The clock above the water cooler said quarter to five. Zoe's grandmother was still sitting at her desk, her black half-rimmed glasses slipping down toward a pile of papers. It was catalog time; hundreds of little squares of paper with pictures of nails, bolts, drills, sanders, hammers and brackets covered the desk, waiting for Grandma Esther to rubber-cement them to the page. Mary, the secretary, had already gone home, but they could hear sounds from the other end of the loft where Tony was still packing boxes.

"Hi, Grandma," Zoe said, walking over to the big steel desk. Her grandmother was really spaced out on those catalogue pictures.

Grandma Esther looked up quickly. "Zoe! *Ziss maydele*! I didn't even hear you come in." She got up and walked toward them, her heels clicking on the wood floor. She was taller than Zoe, with silver hair puffed on top of her head and deep-set brown eyes. The half-rims had slipped to her chest and dangled on a cord. She hugged and kissed Zoe, and kissed Danielle.

"How are you?" she asked, holding her hand against Zoe's cheek. Without waiting for Zoe to answer, she added, "I'll just clear off my desk and then we'll go."

When Zoe had called to ask if she and Danielle could come for the weekend, her grandmother immediately offered to take the girls to dinner and a movie. Zoe didn't mind this: Grandma Esther was fun to be with, and Zoe's friends always liked her. You did not think of her as an old person at all.

"How's Melanie?" Grandma Esther asked, reaching across her desk and scooping papers into piles.

"She's going up to West Hartford for the weekend to see *Barry*." Zoe batted her eyelashes.

"Good!" Her grandmother laughed. "He sounds like a nice boy."

"He is," Zoe agreed. Her grandmother approved of boy-friends. Zoe had seen the old photos of Grandma Esther and Grandpa Sol when they were young, out at Coney Island for the day, her grandmother with long wavy hair and a nice body, and her grandfather in a funny black bathing suit with holes cut out at the sides. In one picture she was standing while he knelt in the sand with his arms around her waist, looking up at her.

"And what've Mother and Dad been doing?" her grand-mother asked.

Zoe shrugged. "I don't know. Dad's been grading tests all week and complaining about the illiterates. Mom's still into all her women's lib stuff. She gets mad."

Grandma Esther's face became more serious, but her voice was still cheerful. "Well," she said, drawling the word out.

53

She'd grown up in Chicago, and her words often sounded funny to Zoe. "I think she just wants some help around the house."

"Yeah." It seemed like her mother wanted something else, too, but Zoe couldn't explain what it was, and she didn't know if Grandma Esther knew either. She'd never heard her grandmother say anything harsh about anyone, except about her own stepmother, who'd beaten her when she was young and forced her to run away to New York. "We've been helping," Zoe added.

"Good!" said Grandma Esther.

Zoe sometimes thought that her grandmother's childhood had been so unhappy — what with her mother dying and that horrible stepmother — that she could never admit to any unhappiness in their own family now. She just wanted everything to be wonderful with them, and when she was around, it usually was.

Grandma Esther always said, Don't cut your hair. She'd stroke Zoe's or Melanie's hair and say, Men like long hair. She and Grandpa Sol had gotten along extremely well; everyone always said it was a love affair that lasted. She had to elope with him when she was eighteen because he was a traveling salesman and her family didn't approve of that in a husband. Later they started the business: Diamond and Company, Inc. Grandma Esther had graduated from business college before they got married, so she was able to help him quite a lot. Zoe's father said she always had good ideas — the catalog was one of them — and she would present them to Grandpa Sol in such a way that he would immediately see how good they were, and would also think that they were his own ideas.

She let them drink wine with dinner, and they ate fondue, which had more wine in it. After a while Zoe felt flushed and happy.

"So, how's Hebrew High School?" her grandmother asked.

Zoe and Danielle looked at each other and giggled. Danielle's cheeks were red and her eyes were shining.

"What's so funny?" her grandmother asked, smiling.

"Hebrew High's OK," Zoe said. "It's the same. Only we have a new teacher this year, and she's really a — well, she's an Israeli."

"Oh, that's very good," said Grandma Esther. She was much more of a Zionist than either of Zoe's parents, and she'd been on a two-week tour of Israel once. She loved it. When Zoe had asked her parents if they could all go, they'd looked at her as if she were crazy and said, It's dangerous over there.

"She's really hard to get along with," Zoe explained. "She doesn't like American kids. She thinks we're degenerates. And you can't challenge her opinions, it's like she's got everything figured out already."

"Hm," said her grandmother, twirling a piece of bread in the fondue.

"Plus she talks really loud like she's yelling all the time," Danielle said. "It makes you feel like you're always doing something wrong."

"Well, maybe that's just how she talks," said Grandma Esther. "Not everyone has a soft voice."

"Also, she has ESP." Zoe had discovered that she liked talking about Mrs. Lev, even though she hated her. "This kid she'd never seen before came to our class last week, and she guessed his name. And she says she always knows when someone's thinking about her."

"Well, her ears must be burning right now," said her grand-mother. "I think she'll like you once she gets to know you."

Zoe didn't answer; she was thinking of something she wanted to ask her grandmother. After a moment she said, "They really have to do what they're doing, don't they?"

"What do you mean, dear?" asked her grandmother.

"I mean —" Zoe flushed with embarrassment, remember-ing Danielle's presence. All of a sudden her questions seemed childish and their answers obvious. "The Israelis," she said. "They sort of have to — kill people — oh, I don't know."

Her grandmother's deep-set brown eyes looked at her steadily from their hollows. There was a strong connection between Zoe and Grandma Esther on matters like this; her grandmother did not like ugliness and violence, either. Now, she just looked at Zoe and nodded her head without saying a word.

Zoe paced back and forth in her room, then stopped in front of the bookshelf. She opened *Exodus* to the part where the children are rescued, carried down the mountain at night from their besieged village. Then she shut the book, put it back on the shelf and took down *The Electric Kool-Aid Acid Test*. There was a phrase the Merry Pranksters used: *the current fantasy*. It meant, simply, the next crazy thing they were planning to do. Zoe sometimes wished that she too had a current fantasy, a bizarre and wild plan, but she had none. There seemed to be a lot of reality around in her own life.

She opened her door and went down the hall to the kitchen, where she drank a glass of juice. Then she heard a rustle from the living room and went to see who was in there.

The lights were out, and there was a figure in the brown

chair. It was her mother. She was sitting quietly in the dark, and she didn't look up.

"Mom?"

"Yes?"

Zoe wanted to ask her a question but she couldn't find exactly the right words. It had something to do with pacifism and Hannah Senesh and Mrs. Lev, and whether you could be a pacifist and still parachute into an occupied country to save people, and also whether you could possibly like someone who said things you hated.

"Should I turn on the light?" Zoe asked.

"No," said her mother. "I'd just like to sit here for a while."

It wasn't the right time to ask her anything.

"OK," said Zoe.

She left her mother sitting there in the dark.

Chapter Three

"Why didn't you go back?" Susan asked.

"Well, it's difficult. We have a family, jobs," Mrs. Lev said. "It's very difficult."

For some reason no one felt like pressing the issue. The relief that the war had turned around in Israel's favor seemed to extend straight across the world and into their classroom, almost as if there were no distance at all in between. Ever since the war started and she hadn't gone back, Mrs. Lev had been a little nicer to them, too. She had to be: They knew something about her now. Zoe had learned the Hebrew word for people like Mrs. Lev, Mrs. Ben-Yakov and Mr. Aharon. *Yordim:* those who have gone down. In Zoe's dictionary this word was related to other words meaning common, immoral and degenerate.

"During the wars, and afterwards, the Israeli government is telling all the women to have as many babies as possible," Mrs. Lev said.

"Does everyone *do* it?" Naomi asked.

The class snickered.

"No, they don't," said Mrs. Lev.

"How many kids do you have?" asked Carol.

"Only two," said Mrs. Lev.

Zoe glanced at the boys — Adam, Jeff, Charlie and the

rest — who were sitting more toward the back of the room. She could tell they were a little embarrassed by Mrs. Lev.

Naomi said, "How come you didn't have more?"

Zoe could feel disapproval emanating from Judy Teitelbaum, who sat directly behind her. Lately the girls had started asking Mrs. Lev a lot of questions, and Judy said it was rude. Zoe told her that Mrs. Lev was hardly polite herself, and anyway, she didn't seem to mind.

Mrs. Lev shrugged. "I'd rather be doing something else," she said. "But I have two beautiful children. They have black hair and very large eyes, sort of blue-gray color." She gestured in front of her own face. Since she was actually describing her own appearance, too, it was like telling them how beautiful she herself was. She sighed. "It's terrible for the children, this war on TV. Now they want always to play war, they pretend they are making a bomb out of those — Lego."

No one laughed. Zoe asked, as politely as she could, "Why'd you come here in the first place?" She really wanted to know.

Mrs. Lev looked alarmed; then her face relaxed and she shrugged. "Why not? America is the promised land, right?" She seemed to find this very funny. "You know, they told me that when I arrived, I should not walk around in New York looking up at all the buildings." She tilted her head back as if looking up at a skyscraper. "They said I would look like a tourist, but I didn't care. I did it anyway." She laughed.

Zoe didn't see what was so funny. Weren't there any tall buildings in Israel? They always said it was a Modern State.

Zoe and Naomi looked at each other at exactly the same time, and then rolled their eyes toward the ceiling.

At night Zoe switched out all the lights in her room except

the black light and watched the multicolored fire burn on her closet door. She tried to piece things together. A couple of years ago they had an American teacher, Mrs. Horowitz, who had moved to Utah when she was a little girl. Zoe imagined Utah as a long sweep of dry yellow land with a few trees, sort of the way she imagined Israel. Mrs. Horowitz told them how the kids in Utah had cornered her; they'd never seen anyone Jewish before. They pulled her hair out, hunk after hunk, trying to find her horns.

So the Jews needed a place to go, and they kept this place by fighting wars. The thought of Israel not existing anymore was frightening to Zoe.

Did that mean they were fighting *for her?* she wondered.

Did she want them to?

Not that she'd ever have to take responsibility for killing someone herself. Mrs. Lev said they didn't let women fight because of what the Arabs would do to them if they caught them as prisoners. Rape them, Zoe supposed, or worse, but Mrs. Lev never said exactly. Adults were always vague about the really important things. No one ever talked about what this all *felt like*. What it felt like to be a Jew; what it felt like to be an Arab. What would it feel like to be Mrs. Lev? Zoe couldn't imagine. Mrs. Lev was a university professor, a mother and twenty-eight years old, she said. She was naive about New York and she hated Arabs. She was from Haifa. In high school she'd won a prize for being the best runner. A jock, Zoe thought with distaste.

One day Mrs. Lev was late. She came in quickly with her tan trench coat still on, books under her arm. "I was stopped by the police," she said.

"For drugs," Adam whispered in Zoe's ear. She didn't laugh.

"For what?" Susan asked.

"For speeding. He said I was driving ninety miles an hour." Mrs. Lev grinned. Zoe could not imagine either of her parents getting a ticket for doing ninety on the turnpike — or thinking it was funny.

"You trying to kill yourself?" said Charlie. But the boys were laughing; they were starting to respect her.

Zoe had often seen the silver Cadillac screech into the temple parking lot, cutting close to other cars. "You drive like a maniac," she said.

Mrs. Lev smiled her frowning smile. "I know, but usually they don't catch me. It's — how do you say — it's not my day."

"Why not?"

"I don't know. Last night I was sitting on the floor in my living room, with my husband, and I was smoking a cigarette. Then all of a sudden I looked down and there was this big hole —" She gestured to show how enormous it was. "We didn't even notice that part of the rug just burned up! We laughed so hard when we saw it." She smiled an almost satisfied smile. Again Zoe tried to imagine her own mother laughing at a big hole burned in the living room rug, and could not.

"You shouldn't smoke," said Naomi. "It stunts your growth."

She looked at Nao and shrugged. "If I didn't smoke, I'd be fat." Several girls snorted. "I used to be very fat. I could never wear anything that fit." She gestured in the air over her flat stomach.

"Well, you better not tell Rabbi Hersh that you smoke to stay thin," Carol said. Rabbi Hersh taught their Jewish ethics class, and he'd been horrified one day when a girl who was dieting had fainted right in front of him from lack of food. He'd given them all a big lecture on the importance of eating.

"'Breakfast is the most important meal of the day.'" Susan shook her finger at them.

"I never eat breakfast," Mrs. Lev said. "Only coffee."

"Uh-oh. We're going to have to tell him," teased Carol.

"I don't care! I do what I want," she said, frowning.

"She's only kidding," said Zoe. Mrs. Lev sure was touchy. Maybe it was living on coffee and cigarettes that made her nervous as hell. Just being in the same room with her made Zoe nervous, too.

> Blessed is the match consumed
> in kindling flame.
> Blessed is the flame that burns
> in the secret fastness of the heart.
> Blessed is the heart with strength to stop
> its beating for honor's sake.
> Blessed is the match consumed
> in kindling flame.

The words of Hannah Senesh were stuck in Zoe's mind. She had been compelled to memorize the poem. But how could someone be so willing to give up her own life? People glorified dying for a cause, but they never talked about what was lost forever when someone did. Death was the worst thing Zoe could imagine. There was the universe: an expanding black space, eternal, and you'd be completely swallowed up in the nothingness. She was ashamed that the poem appealed to her so strongly.

Zoe was the last one in the coatroom because she'd stayed after ethics class to ask Rabbi Hersh a question. She pulled her gray poncho over her head, and its strings got tangled up in her necklaces: the gold chain with her name, *Chaya*, the hei-shi beads, the heavy Star of David. She stood there untangling them; once, the rawhide holding the roach clip caught the pewter-colored bracelet on her arm, which was engraved with the name of a man who was MIA in Vietnam. She shook it free, then tied the long tasseled strings of the poncho.

Zoe was just about to leave the coatroom when Mrs. Lev came in for her trench coat. She nodded to Zoe. Then, after a moment, she said quietly — for her — "What have you been thinking about?"

Zoe looked at her, startled. "Nothing," she said. The coatroom suddenly seemed very small. Did Mrs. Lev know that Zoe had been thinking about her?

"I can see that you have been thinking," said Mrs. Lev, her fingers with the gold rings on them buttoning the trench coat.

If you're so good at ESP, Zoe thought, why don't you already know what I've been thinking?

Mrs. Lev glanced at her.

"I think about a lot of things," Zoe said.

"Yes? Like what?" She sounded casual and sincere, like a friend who was interested in your answer.

Zoe nervously braided the threads of the tassels on her poncho. Last night she'd lain awake trying to figure out, among other things, why she always looked forward to seeing Mrs. Lev, whom she did not like.

63

"I've been thinking about war," Zoe said finally. "And why human beings perpetuate all this violence, and then glorify it."

Mrs. Lev looked at her with one corner of her mouth turned slightly downward; she seemed almost amused, almost annoyed — maybe both. "Again you are thinking about war? For a girl who has never seen a war, you spend a lot of time thinking about it."

Zoe shrugged.

"I will tell you something," Mrs. Lev continued. "You know, the people you do not like, the ones who kill others. They did not really want to kill other people, and they didn't want to die. They did it because they had to."

"Well, it's disgusting," Zoe said. "The whole thing is completely insane ."

"Of course it's disgusting!" Mrs. Lev's voice was getting louder. In between her words, they could hear men's voices rise from the sanctuary down the hall, singing the evening prayers. "Did anyone say it was not terrible?"

Zoe was silent. She unbraided the tassels and started smoothing them out, over and over. Mrs. Lev stepped uncomfortably close to her. "You thought I said that it was *good?*"

Zoe was about to say, Well, you never said it was wrong, you seem cold-blooded as hell. But something stopped her, and she just shook her head. She looked carefully at Mrs. Lev's face — at the gray-blue eyes, the lines around her mouth — and saw that there was something else there besides anger, or mockery, or disgust. What Zoe had never noticed before was the sadness in Mrs. Lev's face.

Don't you want somebody to love
Don't you need somebody to love

The radio was turned up so loud, Zoe could hear it as she ran down the front walk toward Naomi's car in the driveway. She threw her duffel bag onto the back seat, next to a jug of milk, then got in behind Danielle. "'You better find somebody to love —'" Naomi and Danielle sang out loud, and then Nao put the car into reverse and rolled down the driveway. It was Saturday night.

Ten minutes later they turned into Sleepy Hollow, where Naomi lived. The road circled the apartment complex — a maze of parking lots, curves and two-storey buildings, which Naomi navigated expertly, going fast on the long stretches, slowing down for the curves, then zooming down the next block. She pulled up in front of M-1.

Inside they followed her to the little stand-up kitchen, where she put the milk in the refrigerator. "I'm back!" she yelled. "Got the milk!"

"Thanks, Nao!" her mother called from upstairs.

Naomi smiled slightly and lifted her eyebrows at Zoe and Danielle. "She's got a heavy date tonight. She's in her room getting prettied up."

"Who's she going out with?" asked Zoe.

"I don't know. Some guy she met at Parents without Partners."

Naomi's mother was the youngest mother any of Zoe's friends had; she'd gotten married and had Naomi when she was only sixteen. Nao's parents had been divorced for more than six years now. Ever since they'd separated and the house down the street from the Diamonds' was sold, Nao and her mom and her two younger brothers, David and Michael, had lived in Sleepy Hollow. The complex was full of kids and their divorced mothers — that was just about the only type of family that ever moved in there, so there'd always been other kids like Nao, who had to watch their younger brothers and sisters after school while their mothers were at work. This made Naomi feel a little less terrible about the divorce. Zoe used to go over nearly every afternoon when they were younger and Nao was still watching her brothers every day. They'd hang out with the older kids and smoke cigarettes or play basketball. Sometimes it was like a party inside one of the apartments, everyone sitting around listening to records and some of the kids going off into the bedrooms to make out. Even back then, in seventh or eighth grade, Naomi was practically going all the way with some of the boys. Zoe wasn't. She'd play Seven Minutes in Heaven and let a boy kiss her and feel her up, but she never really liked it. Zoe had decided that she didn't want to be like Naomi's mother, married and pregnant at sixteen. Mrs. Kaplan, surprisingly enough, always wanted Naomi to have a boyfriend. It amazed Zoe how some people never learned.

Mrs. Kaplan came into the kitchen. "Hi, girls," she said. Her light hair was cut into a curly mane, and she wore a soft rose-colored jumpsuit. Her perfume filled the kitchen, smelling like something you could eat or drink. "How're you doing?" she asked Zoe and Danielle.

"Good. You look nice," Danielle said.

"Thank you!" She smiled and turned to Naomi. "David and Michael went bowling with the Millers, they won't be home till about ten. Now where're you off to?"

"We're going to a party." Naomi hesitated. "At this girl's in my homeroom."

"OK," said Mrs. Kaplan, almost too quickly, like she really had her mind on something else. Zoe's mother had asked for the name of the girl, and Zoe had had to think up something fast.

Then Mrs. Kaplan put both hands on Nao's wild hair and kissed her twice. "Be good," she said, sounding like she meant it.

Naomi grinned, glancing at Zoe and Danielle. "I *am* good," she said. Her voice was serious, though.

"I know that." Her mother kissed her again.

"Can we go now?" Nao asked, teasing her mother.

"Go! Go!" she said. "Have a good time. I'll see you later."

"Don't do anything I wouldn't do," Naomi told her mother.

They drove up the Post Road, going nowhere in particular. Zoe leaned forward, an arm on each of the two front seats, her face between them. They passed a joint around.

"*Chaya, Chaya, Chaya,*" Naomi said to Zoe, making it sound like Hiya, Hiya, Hiya. "You're getting all of it."

Zoe handed the roach up front. "That's OK," Danielle said. "You two can finish this." She was probably getting paranoid. An ambulance was coming up behind them, and Nao pulled into the right-hand lane to let it pass. It had one of those new sirens that wasn't the usual long whine, but gave off two alternating notes, one high and one low.

"My mother says they shouldn't be allowed to use that kind of siren," Danielle said. "It's the same kind the Gestapo used. She almost has a heart attack every time she hears one."

"God," said Naomi.

Zoe said nothing, but put her hand on Danielle's shoulder for a moment. Danielle was wearing a soft brown suede jacket and a sweater underneath, but Zoe could still feel her shoulder bone.

Danielle looked back at her, not quite smiling, but she didn't seem unhappy, either. Sometimes Zoe couldn't tell what Danielle was thinking. She was spaced out, like Nao said. But once in a while Danielle came out of her own thoughts and remembered them — like now, she was asking, "So what's new with you, *Chaya-Chaya*? I haven't seen you since Thursday."

"Nobody has," Zoe said. "I've been writing my fucking term paper for US history."

Naomi laughed. "I haven't even started mine yet."

"What're you doing it on?" Danielle asked Zoe.

"American Utopianism," Zoe said. "Did you know there're these people out in Colorado who live up in the mountains in these domes? Like see-through geodesic domes? Everyone lives in it together, men, women, kids, and there's a big fireplace in the middle and a big loft where they all sleep."

"No shit," said Nao. "How'd you find out about it?"

"I read an article. There're people in these underground thingies too."

"Let's *go*," said Naomi. "Let's just keep driving till we're in Colorado."

"God, I wish we could," Zoe said. She put her hands over her face and pressed her fingers against her eyelids. Every once in a while she realized how trapped she was, here in this stupid suburb on the East Coast, imprisoned in school for another two years. In the meanwhile there was nothing to do but get stoned and try to forget how boring it all was.

"I'm serious," said Naomi. "Let's just keep driving. I want to get *out* of here. This town has nothing to do with real life. I want to go have some adventures."

"Tell me about it," said Zoe.

"Well, the minute we're eighteen, we can take off," said

Danielle. "I'd like to have a big van, you know? Something with beds inside, and little tables where you could do artwork. We could make things and travel around, and sell them when we needed money."

"That's a great idea," Zoe said. She was surprised Danielle could be so practical.

"I don't know how to make anything, so I'll just drive," Naomi said. "We'll be free! No parents, no school, no guidance counselors." Mr. Brown, Nao's guidance counselor, was always calling her in to find out why she didn't do her homework, why she skipped so many classes. Last time she told Mr. Brown that she'd skipped gym because she was too old to go bouncing up and down on a trampoline wearing a little stretchy suit. Mr. Brown tried really hard not to even smile, but it ended up with both of them roaring.

"We're here," Naomi said.

"Where?" asked Zoe.

"At Tad's."

"He lives *here?*" Danielle said, peering through the windshield. They'd pulled up in front of one of the old rundown houses that lined the waterfront, about a block from the boatyards. You could tell they used to be really beautiful houses, with columns and scalloped designs around the windows, but no one had ever bothered to renovate them, so they were all peeling and decaying, the gardens overgrown. Tad's house was mostly hidden behind huge shrubs and thick trees; all you could see was a window on the top floor where his apartment was. The yard and the house were dark, lit only by a dim streetlamp. Tad was some guy Naomi had met recently, a friend of this other guy she bought pot from. When Zoe had asked if he was good-looking — meaning was she attracted to him — Naomi said only two things: He's thirty-five years old and he's a Jesus Freak. Zoe took this to mean no.

"I don't see any lights on," said Danielle.

"Well, sometimes he sits around in the dark," Nao said. She got out of the car and they followed her across the yard to the front door. Inside they walked round and round and up, on a narrow spiral staircase. At the top was a door with a bare bulb shining above it. Naomi knocked.

They waited a minute. "Yeah?" a voice said.

"It's Naomi."

After another moment the door opened. "Hi, Nao. Come on in," Tad said in a soft voice. He held the door open for them. Zoe didn't know why, but she felt uneasy when he shut and locked the door behind them; maybe it was just because there were no lights on in the apartment. A short red candle burned on the kitchen counter, and through the doorway to the living room she could see another candle on a table. Music she couldn't identify was playing on the stereo, voices harmonizing nicely. But the kitchen had a funny smell, like no one had cooked or cleaned in there for a long time.

"How are you, kiddo?" said Tad to Naomi.

"All right," she said. She introduced them all: Tad Kearney, Zoe Diamond, Danielle Wasserman, first and last names, as if he were an older relative or a teacher.

"Nice to meet you," said Tad. He had hair down to his shoulders and a bandanna tied across his forehead, dark eyes and a dark, drooping mustache. He did seem pretty old, but he was good-looking, Zoe had to admit. In the dim light his face gave the impression of seriousness and a kind of wise distance from the situation.

"Nice to meet you," Zoe said.

He nodded, but didn't seem too interested in her or Danielle. He looked at Naomi again and said, "Want a drink, Nao?"

"OK," she said. "What're you drinking?"

It was vodka and orange juice. A bottle of vodka stood on the counter, and he poured the juice from a plastic pitcher that sat uncovered in the empty old fridge. Both Zoe and Danielle refused the drinks. Zoe thought drinking was disgusting, just a poor substitute for more decent drugs. In the harsh white pool of light cast by the open refrigerator, Naomi looked small next to Tad, her light hair flying out in all directions and his dark head bent down as he handed her the drink. When Tad closed the door, Zoe noticed two photographs taped to it, of a woman and some kids.

There were only two mismatched chairs in the living room, which Tad insisted Zoe and Danielle sit on. Zoe rested her palms on the arms of her chair, and then took them off again because the material had a strange, waxy feel. Tad and Naomi sat on cushions on the floor. "Hey, Tad, do you mind if I turn on this light?" Naomi said.

"What do you want to do that for?" he asked softly, but she turned on a little lamp that sat on a wooden melon crate.

"You caught me at a weak moment," he said, sipping his drink and then setting the glass beside him on the floor. "I had a phone call from Diane today. She says she *loves* Boston and the kids are *very* happy and she *definitely* wants a divorce."

"I'm sorry," said Naomi, fingering something on the rug in front of her.

Zoe tried to look sympathetic, too, but the way he exaggerated those words — she *loves* Boston — made her uneasy.

Tad looked at Zoe and Danielle. "Diane's my wife," he explained. "She had every right in the world to leave me." He shook his head. "I was a miserable sucker, I was high all the time, it was terrible. But that was before I found Jesus and got my head straightened out. I'm mostly through with drugs now, and I know if she came back, I wouldn't touch a thing. But she just took the kids and split without even giving me another chance."

"I'm sorry." Zoe did feel badly for him. The harmonizing songs continued in the background, and now she began to make out the words: all about Jesus walking the earth and saving people who see the light. She wondered if Diane was staying away because of all this Jesus Freak stuff.

"I don't really deserve any sympathy," Tad said. "I've been a miserable sinner. But I just want people to see that I've turned off drugs and turned on to the Lord. I want them to *see*."

There was silence for a moment, and Zoe thought, This guy is drunk as a skunk. The music went on: "Put your hand in the ha-and of the man from Gal-i-lee."

"Well, maybe they *will* see," said Danielle. Zoe looked at her and could tell that she felt sorry for Tad, too, but that she also didn't like him.

Tad shook his head. "Maybe." Then he looked at Naomi and said, "What about you? You being good these days?"

"Sure, I'm always good," Nao said, but in a quieter, more intimate tone than she had used with her mother.

"Yeah, I know, honey," he said. "I passed you in the car the other day, about ten o'clock in the morning when you were supposed to be in school. You didn't even see me." He grinned at her.

"You did? Oh, I know which day that was. I only skipped algebra, and it was because Rick said he could meet me at ten-thirty. He had some windowpane, and I promised some kids at school."

"Naomi!" He leaned forward, elbows resting on his knees. "You have to promise me you're not going to take acid. That stuff Rick's got now is full of strychnine, it's terrible stuff. You'll ruin your head with it."

She crossed her arms and looked at him with her head tilted back and her eyes half-closed. "How do you know?" she said.

"I know, baby, believe me, I know what acid trips'll do to you —"

"I mean, how do you know specifically about that acid Rick has *right now?*" She was smirking at him.

He uncrossed his legs and slouched back against the wall. "OK," he said. "So I'm not a saint. I'm just trying to keep you from getting all messed up, Nao." He looked at her and she stared back.

Zoe looked closely at Tad's eyes. They were brown and had that same gentle magnetic quality she'd noticed in the eyes of kids at school who'd turned on to Jesus. This was the biggest year for Jesus Freaks yet: They called it Key 73. Every week there were more people at the early morning Bible readings held before school up in the chemistry lab. All those kids stared into your eyes with that same look, trying to pull you into their way of seeing things. It was almost as if they were hypnotized, and they were trying to hypnotize you, too. Now Tad looked like he was silently pleading with Naomi, except with the absolute assurance that she was going to come over to his side any minute. Zoe looked quickly back at Nao, who was still staring at Tad. Oh no, thought Zoe. She didn't want to see Naomi get messed up, either. She'd often wanted to tell her to get her act together and go to class — she was so smart — and stop talking about suicide and heroin. But she didn't want Tad's way to be the answer. She had to get Naomi out of here before she turned into a Jesus Freak.

"Nao," she said softly. Naomi didn't look at her. "Naomi," she said again, more loudly.

"Yeah?" Naomi seemed the same as always; her blue eyes were not magnetic or gentle.

"I think we should get going," Zoe said.

"Yeah, it's getting late," said Danielle, though they all knew it couldn't have been that late.

"OK," said Naomi.

Tad said nothing. He followed them to the door, and Zoe felt relieved when he opened it.

At the bottom of the spiral staircase Zoe and Danielle stopped and looked at each other. "Where's Naomi?" Danielle said. Nao had walked out the apartment door right behind them.

"I don't know." They waited in the dim light for what seemed like a long time. "I'll go see," Zoe said.

Halfway up the staircase she heard Tad saying, in a too-sweet drunken voice, "You don't *have* to go, Nao."

"Yes, I do," said Naomi. "Be nice, my friends are here." She sounded like a mother trying to deal with a difficult child. "I have to go."

"Nooo —"

"Yeees."

Then there was a thump, and Naomi's voice, louder and more desperate now, saying, "Let me go! I have to go!"

"Naomi!" Zoe yelled. She raced up the steps, turning around and around in a sickening corkscrew. "Naomi!" she yelled again as she reached the top.

The apartment door was still open, and Tad was standing in the hall, holding on to Naomi's arm, saying "Please, Naomi, please —" Naomi's whole body was straining to get away, and it looked like her arm wasn't even a part of her anymore; it was just this *thing* between them that Tad held.

"Naomi, we've got to go," Zoe said stupidly, not knowing what to do.

They both stopped and stared at her, and Naomi used the moment of surprise to wrench her arm and get away. "I've gotta go, I'll see you, Tad —"

"Naomi, you don't have to go!" Tad yelled after her.

They ran down the stairs, around and around. It felt like they'd never get to the bottom but would just continue spiraling down into the darkness forever.

"What was going on up there, Nao?" Danielle asked after they'd sped down the street.

Naomi was hunched over the steering wheel, gripping it tightly and peering through the windshield like a tired long-distance trucker. "That's just Tad. He gets like that when he drinks. He just didn't want me to leave."

Zoe was annoyed that Nao wasn't angry. "He's sort of a schmuck," she said, "acting like all he wants to do is help you, but he's really after your ass."

"I'm not stupid, Zoe." Naomi spoke calmly; it was only by the little tremor in her voice that Zoe could tell she'd been scared. "He's someone I can really talk to, but he gets a little crazy when he drinks. I can handle it."

"Yeah, great," said Zoe. "If I hadn't come back upstairs, he probably would've just dragged you back inside."

"He's not a *rapist*," Nao said.

"I didn't say that!" But Zoe wondered if that was what she was saying. "All I mean is, maybe you shouldn't go back there. You don't want to sleep with him, do you?"

"Why not?" said Naomi. "Why should I feel guilty about it?"

Naomi often brought up the idea of guilt when Zoe hadn't said a thing about it. "Because he's old and he's messed up," said Zoe. "You'll get messed up, too, if you keep hanging out with him." She hated the social-worker tone of her own voice.

Naomi sighed. "I know he's not good for me," she said, speaking slowly, deliberately. "But I think there's some kind of evil force controlling my life."

"*Naomi*," said Danielle.

"I mean it," said Nao.

Danielle lay in bed that night with her head propped up on her hand. "I skipped gym with her one day last week — did she tell you?" Zoe, lying in the cot next to her, shook her head. "We rode down to the beach, we were just having a good time, and then all of a sudden she started talking about all these freaky things. Like, she said she was home alone one night, and she took out a bunch of Quaaludes and just stared at them for like an hour. She thought about taking them all at once and seeing if she — if she would die or not. She said if she lived, then maybe it would be a sign that she was meant to live."

"Oh God," Zoe groaned, pressing her face into her pillow.

"So I was getting more and more scared, and then all of a sudden she stopped talking and said, What're you looking at me like that for? as if nothing she was saying should be bothering me. I said, Naomi, you can't do that, it won't solve anything, you've got to talk to someone about it. And then she just laughed and said, Oh, I was only kidding, Danielle. You take everything so seriously. But why would she even kid about something like that?"

Zoe turned her face up from the pillow. "She said the same thing to me."

"She did?"

"Yeah, she joked about killing herself, and then she said she didn't really mean it."

"But do you think she really does mean it?"

"I have no idea," Zoe said. "How can you tell?"

"I don't know," said Danielle, rolling over onto her back and pulling up her covers. "I don't want to think about it."

She jumped out of a plane and she was parachuting, floating gently through the air. Below her, green fields and hills rolled out as far as she could see. When the wind picked up, her parachute billowed out like a sail, and she was flying faster and faster. The hills were such an intense green, and the landscape had such a radiant, mysterious quality; it wasn't like a place in real life except that it looked so strangely familiar. The wind rushed over her body, and she felt exhilarated by the speed. But then, thinking of Hannah Senesh, she wondered where she'd be when she finally came down. She didn't know. As she floated closer to the land, she saw deep shadows cutting between the hills, which were rough and stony, with small, gnarled trees — not at all sheltering.

Rabbi Hersh was talking about love. They'd just finished read-ing the section called "Love and Marriage" in their textbook, *Jewish Ethics for Teenagers*. The rabbi was an old man who'd retired from this congregation. Now he just taught in the Hebrew High School and worried about the girls who starved themselves to be thin. People liked him, and Zoe admired him. He'd told them once how he helped some of the young men he'd known prove that they were conscientious objectors so they wouldn't have to go to Vietnam. He even hinted that he'd stretched some points a little, since they had to prove they'd been very religious since they were children.

Rabbi Hersh sat in a circle with them, in one of the student desks. "What is love?" he asked.

There was silence, and he waited. He wore a dark suit and a white shirt, a tie and a kepah on his mostly bald head. His face was full of crisscrossing wrinkles, and his eyes were small and bright. He looked out at the class directly and kindly. You could tell he liked everyone; he wasn't secretly thinking they were silly and decadent, and he didn't blame them for being born Americans.

"Well, love is a very strong feeling for something, or some-one," Judy Teitelbaum said. "It means you really care, and if it's a person, it means you'd do almost anything for them." In another context Zoe and Naomi might've looked at each other and rolled their eyes, but in Rabbi Hersh's class they didn't.

The rabbi smiled at them. "Well, let's say you've met some-one fairly recently, you hardly know him or her. But" — he looked at them in a more serious way — "for some reason, you have very strong feelings about this person. You sud-denly find yourself thinking about the person all the time, and looking forward to every chance you have to see him — or her. You find this person extremely handsome — or beautiful — and utterly fascinating, even though you don't know what it is, exactly, that fascinates you. Is it *love* you're feeling for this person?"

Zoe stared at Rabbi Hersh. *Was* that love? He'd described almost exactly how she felt about Mrs. Lev.

"It could be," said Adam. Then he shrugged. "On the other hand it could be just infatuation."

"Right!" said Rabbi Hersh.

"If you don't even know them, it's probably just infatuation," Carol said. "If you haven't even known them long enough to know what kind of person they are, or what their family's like, or how they act in different situations."

"Right," he said again, nodding his head. He looked at them and spoke softly, but firmly. "Because before you love someone, you have to *like* him. Or her."

He paused a moment to let that sink in, and Zoe thought, Yeah, right. I don't even like her. We don't agree on anything.

The class went on to talk about interdating and whether that led to intermarriage, and what you should do if you had a sudden and intense feeling for someone who wasn't Jewish. But Zoe wasn't really paying attention. She was fascinated by the distinction the rabbi had drawn between love and infatuation. Maybe she didn't have to worry about having intense feelings for someone she barely knew. It was just infatuation that made her look forward to seeing Mrs. Lev and react so strongly to everything in her presence; it would all disappear when she found someone to love. She felt soothed and happy, as if the rabbi had just taken her hand and offered to lead her to some calm and easy place.

♦ ♦ ♦

"The Galilee is beautiful," said Mrs. Lev. "You look out and there are a lot of olive trees and green rocky hills, one after the other —" She drew her arm in an arc through the air, and her gold rings flashed in the light. "It's beautiful," she repeated.

The class listened, and for once no one said anything sarcastic, like, If it's so beautiful, why did you leave? Zoe pictured the green rocky hills and small trees, thinking they seemed familiar; then she realized it was just like that place in her dream. That was it — the strange landscape she'd been parachuting into. She stared at Mrs. Lev.

I dreamed about that place.

She noticed that Mrs. Lev was looking enthusiastically at her. "You have been there?" she asked. It was the first time she'd ever smiled at Zoe in a non-sarcastic way.

"No." Zoe shook her head. "I haven't been there."

"Oh," said Mrs. Lev. "I thought — from your expression — that maybe you have been there."

Chapter Four

For a few minutes, while Zoe's father said the blessings on the Hanukkah candles and Zoe lit them, it felt like they were a normal family again. Her mother and Melanie stood behind them, and they all watched the two little flames, one on a blue candle and one on a red. No one was arguing with anyone else; in fact, no one said a word, and Zoe felt a rush of gratitude that her parents weren't divorced, like Naomi's.

"Very nice," said Zoe's mother. She waited a moment. "I'd better get going or I'll be late picking up Marilyn."

"Mom, do you dry the potatoes on a towel after you grate them or what?" Melanie had gone back to the counter where she'd been washing and peeling potatoes.

Zoe's mother lowered her eyebrows and shook her head quickly, like she had water in her ears. "I don't remember," she said. "Why don't you just look it up?"

"I can't cook," Melanie complained. "I know they're going to come out terrible."

"Look it up! If you can read, you can cook." Zoe's mother went to the hallway and got her coat out of the closet. Zoe's father was trying to deal with the leg of lamb in the oven; Zoe suspected he didn't dare ask her mother to check if it was done. Her mother had announced two weeks ago that she was going to a conference at the university, which started with a potluck supper tonight. It was called "Marriage and Family: Necessity or Oppression?"

Zoe's father had said, "Friday's a holiday, Arlene. I thought it might be nice if we were all home."

"I know, but how many conferences do I get to attend?" she said. "I'm lucky I can go to this one because it's so close."

He sighed. "But why do they have to hold it on the first night of Hanukkah, anyway? Why couldn't it be some other weekend?"

"That's probably the only time they could get the space," she explained.

"I suppose. But it seems a bit inconsiderate, doesn't it?"

"Oh, for God's sake, Ben," she said. "Since when are you so zealous about Hanukkah? We haven't made a big deal about it since the kids got older. It's not even a very important holiday."

"I just felt like being zealous this year, all right?" he snapped. But the conversation was over.

Melanie's latkes were terrible: limp and greasy.

"These are great," said Zoe's father, covering his with more applesauce.

"They're disgusting," Melanie said.

"No," said Zoe. "They're good." She put another one on her plate, next to the bean salad she was eating instead of lamb. She tried not to judge her family for eating meat even though she could hardly stand to look at it on their plates.

Melanie poked her in the side. "You little liar," she said, and they all laughed. "It doesn't matter," she added, a bit sadly. "My ego isn't involved." She almost sounded as if she wished it were.

What a goddamned depressing dinner, Zoe thought. They might never have another holiday where all of them sat around the table and talked and laughed. She remembered laughing so hard once at a family dinner that she literally fell off her chair. Her father had been talking about the Brooklyn Boys — the boys he grew up with in his ninety-nine percent Jewish neighborhood — who were still his friends. They used to build fires in an empty lot and roast potatoes. Once, when they were pretty young, it was dark by the time they finished eating their potatoes, and they got lost. They were city kids, and the big empty lot was like the wilderness to them; they'd wandered around in it for a long time until someone's older brother rescued them. Zoe thought this was hilarious. That's what family dinners used to be like; you'd laugh hysterically at things that weren't even that funny, but it made everyone happy.

Her father didn't seem to feel like telling stories right now, so instead she asked him something she'd been wondering about. "Hey, Dad," she said. "Why'd you want to make a big deal about Hanukkah this year?"

"I don't know." He took a sip of wine. "I just felt like it. I think it has something to do with aging."

"You're not aging," Melanie said. He did look pretty much the same as always: His hair was black and wavy with a bit of gray in his sideburns; his green eyes were clear and he still didn't need glasses; he'd always had those deep lines in an arc around his mouth. The only difference was that now he talked about getting old.

"Of course I'm aging," he said more vehemently, with a hint of bitterness in his voice. It seemed important to him to insist on it, so neither of them contradicted him again.

It worried Zoe to hear her parents complaining all the time. The only real difference between them was that her mother was angry and bitter and her father was sad and bitter. Her mother had conferences and consciousness-raising to go to, but her father had no one else to talk to. All they'd need to complete the disintegration would be a men's consciousness-raising group, too; then neither of her parents would ever be home, and she and Melanie would be sitting here at the table by themselves. The picture of herself and Melanie alone made her feel even sadder as she picked at the cold latkes on her plate. It felt like someone had sent a sliver of glass, something almost invisible but deadly, into her family, which was slowly bleeding from some place she couldn't see.

Zoe stood in a shaft of bright winter sun coming through the office window at Temple Beth Israel. She'd phoned her mother at work to say she was going to eat over at Danielle's house that night, and her mother had put her on hold. While she was waiting she glanced down at the desk where Dana, the secretary, worked, and saw a mimeographed list of all the Hebrew teachers, their names, addresses and phone numbers. Rivka Lev, 22 Rampart Drive, 853-2096.

Zoe talked to her mother for a few minutes, then put down the phone and thanked Dana, who was typing something about fundraising for the United Jewish Appeal.

"Sure, no problem," said Dana, glancing up. "How's it going, Zoe?" Years ago, when she was in high school, Dana used to babysit Zoe and Melanie. Back then she talked about how she wanted to hitchhike all the way from Canada to Florida, and she'd taught Zoe and Melanie how to sit in the bathtub with a pair of new jeans on so they'd mold to your body right away.

"Pretty good," said Zoe, but as she said it, she wished she had someone to talk to who might be able to help her figure out this feeling she had that things weren't right. Something seemed to be waiting, tricking her, like an image that looks like a reflection on the surface of the water but turns out to be a plant or a huge rock underneath.

"You're a junior now?"

"Yeah, right."

"Oh my God, I feel so old." Dana grinned at her and went back to typing.

No, it wasn't going to be Dana, who'd known her since she was a kid. Zoe turned to go and saw Mrs. Lev walking in the door. Rivka Lev. It was a cold day, and instead of the trench coat she was wearing a gray wool coat and black leather gloves. "Hi, Zoe," she said.

"Hi," said Zoe. They both paused for a moment. Mrs. Lev looked at her as if she expected Zoe to say something more, but Zoe couldn't think of anything. Later it reminded her of the part of the prayer about your tongue cleaving to the roof of your mouth. *If I forget thee*: But that was about Jerusalem, not about a person.

After Hanukkah was over came the first real snow, the day on which Zoe had stopped asking to see her father's poems. Everything had a four-inch coating of white, glittering in the sunlight that seemed to pour down from the entire sky. Walking to school Zoe felt free, like she could do anything she wanted because the world looked so different. Just as she was walking up the steps to school, a snowball hit her in the back.

She turned around and started throwing snowballs back at Naomi, who was hiding behind a sad little pine tree. It was seven-thirty in the morning, and they were laughing wildly, pelting each other with snow, not caring that everyone was looking at them as if they were incredibly immature. When the bell rang they decided they couldn't face going inside, so they hopped into Naomi's car and drove away. The roads were slick and the air felt warm. On their way to Howard Johnson, Naomi detoured toward the water. "I love the first snow," Naomi said. They smoked a joint and then Country Joe and the Fish's song about fighting in Vietnam came on the radio:

And it's five, six, seven, open up the pearly gates
Ain't no time to wonder why

"Whoopee, we're all gonna die!" the girls sang. Nao skidded a bit coming around a corner and then slowed down as they approached a large white church.

"Tad works here," Naomi explained.

"Oh." Zoe hoped they weren't going in.

"Don't be so enthusiastic," said Naomi. She drove slowly past the churchyard and then started waving. Yes, there was Tad out in the middle of the graveyard, shoveling snow off the walks. "He's the maintenance man."

Tad looked so funny standing out there in the middle of all those gravestones wearing an Air Force parka with a big furry hood that Zoe had to laugh. Before she knew it, she was waving, too. Then Tad saw them, stuck his shovel upright into a drift, and waved back. Just as he started to walk across to the car, Naomi honked the horn and they drove away.

◆ ◆ ◆

Zoe often lay awake at night thinking about the wars that had made the permanent sadness in Mrs. Lev's face. She realized the reason peace was so hard to come by was that people didn't see each other as human beings. In war they killed symbols of something they hated, not other people like themselves. Of course part of the reason she didn't see Mrs. Lev as a person was because she was a teacher. You were supposed to call them Mrs. This and Mr. That; you were supposed to believe all the opinions they gave you disguised as facts. But what about your own opinions? Zoe could not ignore the fact that some of the people she admired had held guns in their hands. Hannah Senesh was a *paratrooper*: the military elite.

Zoe turned over and over again in her bed, feeling hot and nauseous.

The next day in Hebrew School, during the ten-minute break between classes, Zoe lagged behind while the other kids went outside for a cigarette. She walked slowly down the hall, stopping to look at the ultra-realistic portrait of a boy at his Bar Mitzvah, smiling shyly over the Torah scrolls. Then she stopped in front of the worn poster advertising pine seedlings that could be planted in the Jerusalem forest. A minute later Mrs. Lev came out of the classroom and started walking quickly toward the library to join the other teachers.

"Hey," Zoe said quietly as she passed. "Rivka?"

"Yes?" Mrs. Lev looked startled, her eyes wide against their background of blue makeup.

Zoe stuck her hands into the deep pockets of her army pants and leaned her back against the wall, feeling slightly foolish. They were standing across from the open doors to the sanctuary; no one had turned on the lights yet for evening services, but the Eternal Light glowed down there like a red eye in the darkness. "Can I talk to you for a minute?" Zoe said.

"Of course," said Rivka Lev. She was starting to look almost amused; she had her arms crossed and was leaning against the wall next to Zoe. There was a brief silence. "What do you want to talk about?"

"Well, I wanted to tell you that I'm sorry about your brother. I wasn't very sympathetic before, but I know" — Zoe took a deep breath — "that someone has to defend Israel." She hated to admit it, but there it was: You could not really say Rivka Lev's brother had died for nothing.

Rivka looked startled again. "I'm glad you say these things to me," she said finally.

There was more silence. Zoe looked down at the green linoleum floor and traced the outline of a tile with her foot. She was wearing her fringed suede moccasins. If she moved her eyes across the floor a little, she could see Rivka Lev's brown leather high heels with small gold-colored buckles.

"He fell when they took Jerusalem," Rivka said. "We were twins, like my sons."

Oh my God. Zoe just barely mouthed the words. She glanced at Rivka Lev, but she was staring straight ahead, not looking at her at all.

"I can never forget it," Rivka said. "I am thinking about him every day."

Zoe felt a kind of tingling in her shoulders and back, as if they'd been asleep. "Is that why you came here?" she asked.

Rivka looked at her quickly. "There are many reasons." She looked away.

"Oh," said Zoe. She almost wished that she had some great

sorrow to reveal to Rivka, but she had none. Then Zoe said, "It's hard to — I mean, nothing that terrible has ever happened to me."

"There will be something," said Rivka, frowning.

Zoe stared at her. What was going to happen? Did Rivka know something she didn't know?

"I don't mean that you should be frightened," Rivka added. She shrugged sadly. "That's just the way it happens in life."

Zoe dialed the combination on her locker, opened it, and a piece of folded paper dropped out. An unsigned message from Naomi: Meet me in the courtyard after second period. Over the past year or so Naomi's handwriting had gotten larger and messier — an almost adult-looking scrawl, except that the letters leaned in all different directions. It worried Zoe. She tossed her books in her locker and slammed the metal door. Walking down the hall, she said Hi, Hi, Hi to different people. The whole high school was divided into cliques: the jocks, the freaks, the student council types, the artists, the black kids, the Puerto Ricans, and each clique had its own courtyard in the ultra-modern building.

Zoe and Naomi were unclassified. Outside of school they mainly hung out with each other and with Danielle. On the other hand Danielle fit right into the artist crowd, so Zoe and Naomi often hung out in the artists' courtyard. This was convenient, since you had to watch where you went to stay out of trouble. You had to avoid certain bathrooms because if you didn't, you'd walk in and a crowd of black girls sitting on the sinks would look at you in a really tough way and say, What're you doing in here, white girl? You couldn't tell them that you had nothing against them, and they wouldn't have believed you anyway.

Naomi was sitting on one of the broad wooden benches at the very end of the courtyard, smoking a cigarette and staring out at the line of bare trees beyond the tennis courts. The artists' courtyard was the only one that opened to the outside world: the parking lot, the tennis courts, the playing fields and then Reality. "*Chaya-Chaya*," Naomi said.

Zoe sat down next to her. "What's up?" she asked. "Besides you." She could tell right away that Naomi was high and that it wasn't just pot.

Naomi smiled and then blew some smoke rings. "Wanna 'lude?"

Zoe thought about it for a moment. She was probably too uptight; she and Naomi would be closer if they did more drugs together. But then, even though she was skipping study hall right now, she meant to make it back to US history — her favorite class — on time. "That's OK," she said.

Naomi smiled again, looking sleepy. "Do you have some time right now?"

Zoe smiled back. "For you, sweetie, I always have time." She patted Naomi's shoulder. They were both wearing their mothers' old suede jackets: Zoe's was brown and peeling at the elbows; Naomi's was dark green with a ratty fleece collar. "It's cold as hell out here. Do you want to go get something hot to drink?"

"Yup." But Naomi didn't seem to be noticing the cold much; her coat wasn't even buttoned.

"Want me to drive?" Zoe asked, and Naomi threw her the keys over the top of the car. When they got inside, Nao settled back in the passenger seat and closed her eyes. "I'll just relax for a minute."

Zoe drove quickly out of the parking lot and down the hill. "Been to any classes yet today?" she asked.

"Nope. I was over at Tad's early this morning."

Shit. Zoe didn't say anything.

Naomi opened her eyes. "I just remembered, they sent a letter to my mother."

"Who?"

"The school. They said my level of truancy is unacceptable, and they're threatening to suspend me."

"Uh-oh," Zoe said lightly. "Better get your ass to class."

Naomi yawned. Then something occurred to Zoe. "Did you get those Quaaludes from Tad?"

"Yeah," said Naomi. "'So, I'm not a saint,'" she added in a perfect imitation of Tad's soft spaced-out voice.

"Do you really like him, Nao?"

Naomi sighed. "He's a hypocrite, but he can be nice. He's too old for me, but I've gone to bed with him, and it didn't seem to make any difference." She glanced sideways at Zoe. "I think his head is on backwards, though. He thinks he wants to marry me and have more kids, start all over again —"

"Like with Jesus," Zoe said. "Like he's all clean now, no drugs, no nothing. Give me a break."

"Well, I might just take him up on it," Naomi said as they pulled into the parking lot in front of Bagel King.

When they were settled in a corner table with their bagels and hot chocolate, Zoe said, "Nao, you don't really want to get married and have kids now, do you?"

"Why not?" Naomi raised her eyebrows over her

sleepy-looking eyes and leaned her head back so she could look down on Zoe, challenging her to come up with reasons.

"Because your whole life would be over, just like that." Zoe snapped her fingers and took a sip of hot chocolate. "D'you know how much *work* it is to raise a family? You'd never get to do anything else."

"You sound exactly like your mother," Nao said.

"Well, you sound like yours!" They both had to laugh. "Besides, you're not the type. I can't even picture you with a bunch of kids. And you don't really want to live your mother's life all over again, do you?"

Naomi's face changed; it was like all the muscles in it suddenly went slack. She put her hands over her eyes. "No, my mother's had a hard life. She got left with three little kids and almost no money, and she only has a high school diploma." Naomi's voice was flat and toneless, and she kept her eyes covered.

Zoe knew Nao's family had a tough time. Naomi's father was occasionally generous, like when he bought Naomi the Datsun. But he was unpredictable, and they couldn't count on him. Sometimes Naomi would see him every Sunday for a while, but then other times he wasn't around for months. Zoe reached across the table and put her hand around Naomi's wrist, covered by the ragged cuffs of her big gray sweater. "Hey, it'll be all right," Zoe said, trying to uncover Naomi's eyes. "You don't have to do those things."

Naomi took her hands away from her eyes. Her pupils were huge. "What else can I do?"

"Well, I mean, if you don't get married and have kids, you've got your whole life to do what you want."

Naomi folded her arms on the table and leaned over, look-ing intently at Zoe. There was almost no blue left in her eyes. "I mean now," she said. "I want to know what I can do right now."

Zoe sighed. There wasn't an answer to that one, and Naomi knew it. "There isn't that much we can do right now," she said. "You have to just hang in there, go to school, get through all the bullshit —" She was losing Naomi's attention, and it annoyed her. "You can hang out with the people you like, you can read some books, you can make things like Danielle does. I mean, my life isn't so great, either —"

Naomi leaned her head on her hand and spoke slowly. "Well, I don't have so much tolerance for bullshit," she said, her words soft and almost slurred. She looked at Zoe and smiled a little, as if none of this really mattered, as if they were talking about someone else's life. "Don't you ever feel that way?" she said gently.

Zoe was frightened for a moment, as if Nao were asking her to do something impossibly dangerous in the name of their friendship. But then she looked away from Naomi's dilated eyes and around Bagel King, which seemed bright and warm, and the feeling passed. "Yeah," she said. "Only I guess I have a higher tolerance for bullshit than you do. Sometimes I can get all involved in something — like writ-ing that paper about the communes — and I forget it's for that alcoholic Old Man Harris. I get interested. It's silly, in a way." Even Hebrew High School had some interest for her now, she thought briefly, but she didn't say it. She pushed away the image of herself and Rivka Lev standing in the hallway talking, as usual, about war and death.

"But I'm just not like that," Naomi said.

"Well, what do you really want? I mean, if you could do anything?"

Naomi was silent for a moment. "I don't know. I mean, what's there to do that's really worthwhile? I can't think of too many things I'd want to be."

Zoe could think of a number of things she'd like to be some-day: a traveling hippie, a foreign correspondent, a civil rights activist. It kept her going, thinking that she could become something. Zoe didn't think it was possible for a person not to want anything. But then Naomi was so much smarter than anyone else Zoe knew. Maybe that was her problem: She always saw the truth, she was never unconscious of how ridiculous things were. Zoe's mother said Naomi had no self-confidence, but Zoe couldn't see how that fit with the way Naomi so fearlessly saw behind all the facades adults put up to make you think that high school classes and school sports and yearbook meetings had some kind of deep meaning. Did it take more self-confidence to see the truth, or to ignore it so you could survive with a minimum of despair? Zoe didn't know.

"Hey —" Naomi waved a hand in front of Zoe's face. "Earth to Zoe."

Zoe smiled and shook her head. "Isn't there some *place* you want to be? Where would you go if you could go anywhere?"

"Colorado. Maybe California. Or Japan. It doesn't matter — I can't run away."

"Why not?" Zoe felt happy just thinking about it. "Maybe we can figure out a way."

"You know what happens to kids who run away?" Nao said. "They become prostitutes. I bet you'd really like that."

"We're sixteen, Nao, we could get other jobs."

"You think our parents would just say so long, have a nice life? Come on! They'd have the cops after us in about two seconds. It's hopeless," Naomi said, but she smiled as if it were a joke. "Life is hopeless."

Zoe looked at her steadily, and Naomi stared back, her eyes very affectionate now. Quaaludes did make people feel loving sometimes. It was just that Naomi was always high; Zoe hadn't seen her straight in a long time.

"It's too depressing to be straight," Naomi said.

Even though she didn't like to hear Nao say that, Zoe smiled because it was always nice when they read each other's minds.

"Want to go to the movies tonight?" Naomi asked.

"I may as well, if everything's hopeless. What movie?"

"Something Tad wants to see. I think it's called *The Hidden Ones*. He said maybe we'd be interested because it's about some Christian people who were hiding Jews during the war."

"Oh, good," said Zoe. "That'll cheer us right up."

Zoe poured some oil in the pan, turned on the heat and then raced back down the hall to her room to finish the last two Spanish exercises. She had to hurry; it was her turn to cook that night, and Naomi, Tad and Danielle were picking her up at seven for the movie. She was standing at her desk, biting on a pencil and trying to remember the uses of the subjunctive when she heard her mother yell, "What're you *doing*?" Zoe turned and raced back down the hallway.

When she got to the kitchen her mother was pouring a box of baking soda over the frying pan, which was smoking like crazy. The whole kitchen was full of black smoke, and the fan above the stove was blasting on high.

"Oh my God, I'm sorry," Zoe said.

Her mother sprinkled out the last of the baking soda and then turned to her. "Zoe, the flames were up to here!" she said, pointing to the hood over the range. "How many times have I told you, you can't just —"

"I know," said Zoe. "I know. I'm sorry —" She felt sick, breathing in all the black smoke. Her mother was wiping down the stovetop now — more work, obviously, than if she'd just cooked dinner herself, and she was right, it wasn't fair. It wasn't fair Zoe's mother was unhappy, it wasn't fair Naomi was depressed, it wasn't fair Rivka Lev's brother had died. "I'm sorry," Zoe said again. She felt she could go on saying it forever: I'm sorry, I'm sorry, I'm sorry, sorry, sorry ...

The Jews were just five shadowy faces, upturned in terror every time the cellar door opened and one of the two Christian ladies appeared with food and water. "Is there any sign of — anything happening?" the one with the long dark beard always asked. "No. I have had no news," the Christian lady said. "Here. Please eat and drink." She'd have to press the stuff on them: The Jews were polite and reluctant. Maybe the food was ham or something. But they'd thank her profusely anyhow. "Thank you. You are a good and kind woman, and God will reward you." She would bow her head. "I am only God's humble servant. Please don't thank me." They thanked her again.

Zoe moved around in her seat, feeling sweaty and itchy at the same time.

Outside in their yard, the Christian ladies — who were sisters — did their chores with occasional sighing glances at the sky. They pumped water, weeded the garden and milked cows, wearing long flowered skirts and kerchiefs like the girls in the Key 73 Jesus Freak movement. In one scene the younger sister suddenly stopped churning the butter and collapsed onto her knees, pressing her hands together and staring at the sky. She prayed to Jesus to give her strength. Pretty soon the other sister fell to her knees, too, and they prayed together. You had to wonder if all this praying out there in the yard was going to tip off some passing Nazis. Then a written message flashed on the screen: *Even in this most trying time in the history of mankind, these sisters called upon the Lord in their distress, and He answered their prayers.*

Zoe scratched her head, then crossed and re-crossed her legs. She looked over at Naomi, who was slouched down in her seat with her eyes closed. Tad was staring straight ahead at the screen, his hand resting on Naomi's thigh, his fingers caressing the inside of her leg.

Danielle, who was on Zoe's other side, leaned over and whispered, "Do you like this?" Zoe drew back from her and curled her lips in disgust. She opened her mouth and mimed poking her forefinger down her throat to induce vomiting.

"Let's get out of here," Danielle whispered. Zoe nodded, and they whispered to Naomi, who kept her eyes closed and put her hand over Tad's on her thigh.

Zoe and Danielle went out into the cold, windy night. The theater was on the edge of downtown and the streets were dark; they started walking faster and faster, as if something were pushing them along.

"I had a feeling it might be like this," Zoe said. She felt guilty about leaving Naomi alone in the movie theater with Tad. But what could happen in a movie theater? It was Naomi's fault for bringing them here, anyway, and they weren't her chaperones. "Fucking Naomi," she said.

Danielle didn't seem to be listening. "God, I wish I hadn't come," she said. "I wish I hadn't seen that."

In a way Zoe was glad she'd seen it. She wanted to talk about some of the specifics, like how could they get away with making a movie that showed the Jews as scared little helpless animals in the dark and only the Christians as strong and noble. And how could they use the Holocaust as an excuse for all this Christian propaganda? But Zoe didn't think Danielle wanted to talk about it. Maybe Nao would've, if she hadn't slept through the whole thing. Zoe tried to imagine what Rivka Lev would say about a movie like this, and she started to feel better. Rivka would be scornful. The whole world wants only that the Jews will suffer, she'd say, they don't even think we should defend ourselves against our enemies. Ordinarily when Rivka said things like that, Zoe felt very uneasy. But thinking of Rivka's anger now made her deeply happy; walking down the dark street she almost giggled. She glanced over at Danielle, walking with her head bent forward into the cold wind, and saw that she was crying.

Of course, she recognized him as the one she'd seen many times before. In between their meetings, she almost forgot about him, but here he was again. A man about her father's age, with deep lines curving around his mouth, shuffling papers on a desk. He looked at her and almost, but not quite, smiled. He never spoke to her, but she understood that he was her relative, that he'd died in a concentration camp. They hadn't gotten this man yet, but they would; they had. She strained her eyes but couldn't see what was written on those papers he held.

She wasn't frightened when she woke up in the middle of

the night — he didn't frighten her. What kept her awake was wondering what she was supposed to understand. Once she'd tried to ask, in the dream, what she should do, and he'd looked at her silently, fiercely, in a way that made her feel washed into insignificance. Once she'd asked her father about relatives who'd stayed behind in Europe, and he said he didn't know anything about them.

It was the shortest day of the year, four days before Christmas. It was already getting dark by mid-afternoon, but no one had bothered to turn on the lights. The class was sitting around in the dim room waiting for Rivka Lev to show up. There was depression in the air — it was just that time of year.

"Well, hey, listen —" Charlie was saying. "I'm having a New Year's Eve party. I've cleared it with my parents and everything — you're all invited."

"All right," said Jeff. "Great," said Adam, but they didn't sound really enthusiastic. A few more people said thanks.

"Which drugs are permitted?" Adam asked.

Charlie laughed. "We're allowed to drink a little, but anyone who gets drunk has to sleep over. That's a deal I made with my mom." Charlie's hair stuck up on his head in a funny way; he was a nice guy but he'd always been goofy-looking.

"It's nice of your mother to help you plan this den of iniquity," Naomi said.

"Well, they're going to be right upstairs having their own party," Charlie explained. "And I said none of my friends smoke pot, so you'll have to do that outside."

"Very cunning," said Jeff thoughtfully.

"Cunning-lingus," said Adam.

"You're a riot," said Carol in a bored tone, her face blank. "I haven't laughed so hard in days."

"Don't be such a prude, Carol," said Jeff. He put his arms around her and started tickling her. She tried not to laugh. "Knock it off!" she yelled.

"Leave her alone!" said Susan. She picked up *Hebrew Today* and hit Jeff on the head with it. He let Carol go.

"Let's give him a wedgie," Naomi suggested, and everyone laughed.

"You guys are so immature," said Charlie in a mock girl-voice.

"He'll never reproduce if you give him a wedgie," said Adam.

"You should know," said Zoe. "We almost made sure you didn't." Adam grimaced at her mention of the time last year when they'd pulled his underwear right up out of his pants, but he put an arm around Zoe in a friendly way.

You had to have at least a little bit of affection for everyone in this class, after knowing them for so long. None of them had changed that much over the years — Adam had gone on being obnoxious, and Judy Teitelbaum was still a goody-goody, silently watching everyone even now. In some strange way, Zoe always felt physically larger in Hebrew School than she did in the outside world; she took up more space here, it seemed. Her voice was louder, and it didn't matter so much what she said.

Years ago the Christmas season was much worse. Their public school teachers said it was a universal holiday and had nothing to do with religion. The kids knew better, though, even in elementary school. Judy Teitelbaum always warned that it was a sin even to say the word Christ, which made it hard to sing Christmas carols. Every time the forbidden word came up, you had to clamp your mouth shut. One year, Mrs. Avery, who'd studied music in Germany, thought it would be nice for the kids to learn "Silent Night" in German. She passed out sheets of paper with blue writing, fresh and damp from the ditto machine, and blew a note into her pitch pipe. It took quite a while to memorize the words. Mrs. Avery made them sing the song over and over, lined up in rows on the bleachers.

Nao still lived in the house on Zoe's street then, and Zoe slept over on the night that was Christmas Eve. On Christmas morning she, Nao and Nao's brother Michael woke up early and made decorations. They taped four socks to the fireplace, and around them hung stars and candy canes cut out of red and green construction paper. Then they waited for Naomi's parents to get up, half expecting that Mr. and Mrs. Kaplan might secretly have gotten some little presents for them. When Mr. Kaplan finally came out in his plaid bathrobe, they all jumped out from behind the couch and started singing "Silent Night" in German. "Sti-i-le Nacht —" they sang.

"What the hell's going on out here?" he yelled over their singing. Abruptly they stopped.

"Merry Christmas, Daddy," Nao said, but from her tone you could tell she already knew she was in trouble.

"I'm sick and tired of all this goddamned assimilation," her father said. When nobody moved he yelled, "Get those things down! Right now!" He came over and hit Naomi and Michael. Zoe just stood there wondering what assimilation was.

Naomi cried while they peeled the socks and candy canes

off the mantelpiece, so Zoe didn't ask her what it meant. Afterwards, upstairs in Naomi's room, Nao had whispered that word again: ass-i-mi-la-tion. She said she thought it was a bad word that meant Christian people were asses. She and Zoe started chanting *ass*-imilation, *ass*-imilation, giggling hysterically and feeling very unhappy.

"Why do you sit in the dark?" asked Rivka Lev, putting her book bag down on the big desk.

"Why not?" Adam said. "It's relaxing."

"We don't feel like doing anything today," said Zoe.

"Do we ever?" said Jeff.

"You don't want to do *any*thing?" said Rivka.

"It's a depressing day," Naomi told her.

"Why is it depressing?" Rivka sat down on the desk. The soft gray light coming through the arched windows made her face look gentler than usual.

"Ah, it's just that time of year," Charlie said. "You know, everyone's getting ready for Christmas, there's nothing to do."

"What does it matter — Christmas?" said Rivka. The word sounded strange coming out of her mouth. "You're Jews."

"We're aware of that," said Charlie.

"It's not that bad," said Jeff. "You can always go to someone else's party."

"Last year," said Susan, "we all walked around the streets near my house and looked in everyone's living room windows to see what they were doing on Christmas Eve. It was hilarious."

"Sounds like a great time," said Adam.

"I'd rather stay home and watch 'Rudolph the Red-Nosed Reindeer,'" Naomi said.

"You know what is the matter with Americans?" Rivka said. "You don't know how to enjoy yourselves." She looked around the room at them. "You don't know how to have any fun, and you are depressed about stupid things."

"Maybe to you. But to us, they're not stupid," Zoe explained patiently.

"What're we supposed to be enjoying?" Naomi asked.

"Well," said Rivka, "what do you want to do? You know some songs?"

A few people snickered. "Oh, please," Adam said. "Give us a break." But his tone wasn't mean; it was as if they'd all decided, without consulting each other, to give Rivka a break. They told her they didn't know any songs and couldn't sing, but they were only joking. Maybe they were all just too tired of things that day to be sarcastic.

"All right," said Rivka. "If you don't know any songs, you can learn one. I'll sing it to you." There was silence for a moment and a few sighs, and then Judy Teitelbaum said, "Sure, go ahead."

Rivka sang "*Yerushalayim Shel Zahav*," a song about Jerusalem, the city of gold, copper and light. Zoe didn't understand all of the words, but she pictured the stones of the city walls turning gold in the sun, and she started to feel more cheerful. By the third verse she'd forgotten about it being winter or Christmas; there was only the image of strong sunlight and the sound of Rivka's voice. It came to her then, as if she'd always known, that Rabbi Hersh was wrong. You *could* love someone you hadn't known for very long, and without knowing much about them. You could even love someone you didn't particularly like. She strained her eyes in the darkening room, trying to see Rivka Lev more clearly.

One needs something to believe in, something for which one can have whole-hearted enthusiasm. One needs to feel that one's life has meaning, that one is needed in this world.

Hannah Senesh, age 17

Part Two
Dream of Snow

Chapter Five

Just as Zoe slowed her bicycle, approaching 22 Rampart Drive, she saw the silver Cadillac coming in the other direction. As the car turned into the driveway, Rivka saw her and waved; the whole family was in there, and Natan was driving. Zoe had hoped that at one-thirty on a Saturday afternoon, they'd all be hanging around inside, scattered in different parts of the house so Zoe would get to talk to Rivka alone. As if they'd stay home on Saturdays just because they were Israelis ... What a fool she was.

Zoe stood in the driveway, straddling her bike, her foot still on the pedal. The two little boys got out of the car and stared at her. Then Natan and Rivka got out, looking surprised.

"You remember Zoe?" Rivka said to Natan. "This is Zoe Diamond."

"Yes, I remember," he said. "Hi, Zoe."

"Hi," she said. Her foot played with the bike pedal; she had a momentary urge to ride away as fast as she could.

"It's a cold day to ride a bicycle," said Rivka.

"Oh, it's not bad," Zoe said. "The sun's out." It was, in fact, streaming down on them, bouncing off the snow on the lawn. It turned out that the Levs lived in a large white colonial-style house; the bare branches of maples and oaks curved over the road and sheltered the front yard. In this neighborhood the houses were older and prettier than Zoe's, and unlike her street, they weren't all built according to the same plan.

"You were just riding by?" Rivka said. "Or —?"

"Well, yeah," Zoe said. "Actually I sort of wanted to talk to you about something." Again she had the urge to ride away, but something stronger compelled her to stay standing on the Levs' driveway, almost wincing under their four stares.

"Sure, why don't you come in?" Rivka looked amused, but she spoke in a nicer way than she did in Hebrew School. "We're just going to have lunch."

Zoe looked at her to see if she meant it, and Rivka nodded her head towards the house as if to say, of course you'll come. "OK," said Zoe.

Natan said she should put her bike in the garage, and he followed her as she wheeled it in. There was a blue sports car in the garage as well. Natan pushed a button that shut the door; as it was going down, he said, "I've heard a lot about you."

"Oh, yeah?" she said, embarrassed. Probably he'd heard that Rivka had caught her smoking pot. Had he also heard that she'd yelled at Rivka, called her a hate monger?

But he smiled at her. He was a thin, small man with dark eyes and eyebrows that arched over them in two curving black lines: the face of someone who was paying attention. "You don't have to worry about anything," he said. She followed him through a door that led into the house.

Their food looked and tasted strange. There was salad chopped up into little bits. The soup had a lemon flavor; the bread was flat. The Levs were all eating chicken, but Zoe just put a lot of salad on her plate and hoped no one would notice. The kids started talking in Hebrew, and she couldn't understand anything.

"Speak English," Rivka told them.

"I liked the brontosaurus the best," said one of the twins — she thought it was Eli.

"It was practically up to the ceiling," said Eitan. "Its bones are as big as a tree."

"I know. It could bend its neck and eat leaves from the top of a tree," said his brother.

"It could even eat a whole tree. It could eat, like, five trees. Or a hundred." Both boys were giggling.

"Eat your lunch," said Natan, but he was just reminding them, not scolding. He looked at Zoe. "They are fanatics about dinosaurs. They went on a field trip yesterday to the museum."

Sitting around the table with them made her remember the warmth and comfort her own family had lost. Everything seemed simpler here; no one was trying to argue a point or use the meal as a time to prove something.

Rivka was looking at Zoe's plate. "You don't like chicken?" she said.

"I don't eat meat," Zoe explained, hoping Rivka would just let it pass. But people could never do that; they wanted to know all the reasons and lecture her about getting enough protein.

"Why not?" Rivka asked.

Zoe sighed. Even Natan was looking at her closely, waiting for her answer. She'd heard through the temple grapevine that he was a psychiatrist, and she wondered what he was noticing. She didn't like that. "I don't believe in killing animals," she said.

"Oh, you don't believe in killing animals," said Rivka, raising her eyebrows. Tell me all about it, her expression said.

"It's no big deal," Zoe said. "I eat everything else. I never liked meat anyway."

"Hm," said Natan. "Well, that's fine."

Zoe smiled at him.

"One of my students at the university told me about an experiment in his botany class," Rivka said. "They have special machines — I don't know how you call it — to tell you what vibrations are coming from the plant. Like electric vibrations. You have heard of this experiment?"

"No," said Zoe. Rivka was wearing jeans and a dark blue sweater today, and small gold earrings shaped like shells, which you could glimpse through her hair when she moved her head. Her face was tense and beautiful. When she spoke, there was no one else in the room; the world dropped away at the edges of a picture that contained only her.

"Well," Rivka continued, "they took two plants and let them grow near each other for quite a while. Then they took away one of the plants. When they did this, they discovered that the one left all alone had vibrations coming from it that are like human vibrations when we are very sad." Rivka stopped and took a sip of tea; she looked like she was enjoying herself. "Then they did another experiment. They cut off part of the plant that was alone, they killed it with a knife. And the vibrations said that this plant was having pain, there was a lot of electricity coming from it." She looked at Zoe. "You haven't heard of this experiment?"

"No," said Zoe. "It's awful."

"You're eating plants," Rivka said, smiling her sarcastic smile.

"I have to eat something," said Zoe, glancing uneasily at the salad on her plate. She could feel her face getting flushed.

"Those plants you are eating probably feel like they're being tortured," Rivka said, laughing now as if she'd just told the world's best joke.

"Oh, leave her alone, Rivka," said Natan. "There are plenty of vegetarians in the world." But he was smirking, too.

"Don't worry, Zoe," Natan added. "Rivka would not tease you so much if she didn't like you. That's the way she is."

Rivka and Natan smiled at each other. Zoe smiled politely, too, but neither of them was looking at her.

After lunch they all spoke a lot of loud, fast Hebrew, and then the kids went thumping downstairs. *L'sakhek*, she remembered. To play. Rivka cleared away the dishes and put the food back in the refrigerator, but she wouldn't let Zoe help with anything, so Zoe stayed at the table, sitting across from Natan. Rivka did everything very quickly and efficiently in the kitchen, like it was nothing.

"Do you understand what we say?" Natan asked Zoe.

"She speaks only a little bit of Hebrew," Rivka told him, but her tone was unusually sympathetic. She was standing at the sink, washing dishes with her back to them.

"You have been to Israel?" Natan asked her.

"No, but I'd like to go. The two places I really want to go are Israel and California."

Natan looked like he was holding back a smile. "We went to California last year. It's very beautiful, you know, the ocean, and the redwood forest I liked —"

"Wow, you did? Were the people really friendly?" Zoe was surprised and impressed.

He was silent for a while, as if she'd asked an impossibly

complex question. "Yeah, I suppose they were. We were staying with friends of ours from Israel who are living in San Francisco."

"Oh." So they had friends in California. They were starting to seem more normal to her, more like real people.

"I was just thinking about this party that our friends took us to," Natan said. "I remember I was sitting on a couch, next to this girl, and she was talking all about peace and how nobody should participate in a war. I said to her, 'Well, I have been in a war.' And then" — he smiled wryly — "she started to move away from me on the couch. While I tried to explain, she kept moving away, little by little, until we were sitting on the opposite sides of the couch." Abruptly he stopped smiling and reached into his shirt pocket for a pack of cigarettes.

Zoe looked at him, this small, thin man sitting across from her, fishing a cigarette out of a near-empty pack, and tried to imagine him as a soldier. She felt ashamed of the girl in California who had edged away from him as if he had a contagious disease, even though she didn't know her. True, Zoe had argued with Rivka, but she hadn't known there were people in the world who wouldn't even want to sit on the same couch with Natan or Rivka.

"That's really unfair," she said. Natan nodded and, after a moment's hesitation, offered her a cigarette. She noticed that Rivka had turned around at the sink and was watching them.

"In Israel everybody eats these," Rivka said. "The shells are all over the bus seat, trails of them on the sidewalk." She smiled, but not sarcastically. They were sitting on the rug in the living room, eating sunflower seeds from a large bag. Natan was downstairs with the kids. The *yeladim*. On one wall was a colorful print of an Oriental-looking design that seemed to turn while you looked at it. Zoe was amazed because it was something a person on a drug trip might enjoy staring at.

"That's a really nice print," she said.

Rivka nodded. "My brother made it for us. He was very talented."

Zoe said nothing, but she was aware of a strange — and not really unpleasant — feeling in the room, as if the space around them had expanded to include the presence of Rivka's dead brother. She sensed that it was necessary for Rivka to mention him at regular intervals. Beneath the picture window where they were sitting, a rectangular patch of sun, crisscrossed by shadows of the moldings around the windowpanes, fell in a bright pattern on the floor. She thought how Rivka seemed incredibly relaxed for someone who'd just finished giving lunch to five people and cleaning up by herself afterward. Zoe's mother would've been screaming bloody murder. "Rivka," she said, "what do you think about consciousness-raising?"

Rivka lowered her eyebrows. "Consciousness-raising?"

"Yeah, like my mother goes to consciousness-raising and she's all into women's liberation. She thinks men and women should be equal, and everyone should have equal responsibilities at home. We all have to cook and clean and wash dishes."

Rivka looked surprised. "And your father — he cooks, too?"

"Sometimes. Not as much as he's supposed to. She gets all upset about it."

"Hm." Rivka cracked a sunflower shell between her teeth. "Well, it's good for you to help your mother."

"Do you think she's right? Do you think women are slaves when they get married and have families?"

Rivka put a shell in the pile on the rug; each of them had a little pile of shells in front of her. "No, I don't think so," she said. "I like my family, and I also like my work. I like especially teaching at the university. I am not a slave."

"But you do all the housework, too, right? And take care of the kids?"

"So what?" said Rivka. "I'm supposed to scream at Natan to wash the dishes?" She made a dismissive gesture with her hand. "It's not important."

"My mother says all these things that don't seem important are actually political problems. She says —"

"*Political problems*? About who cleans the house?"

"Uh-huh," said Zoe.

"I don't think Americans know what is a political problem," said Rivka.

"Well, you know, it's not fair for men and women to be unequal —"

"I know, I know. I've heard of this before." Rivka cracked another shell. "But I just don't think about these things." She looked at Zoe. "In Israel, when a woman marries a man, she does not even know if he will live to be thirty-five years old."

Zoe felt suddenly ashamed that she'd brought up the topic. Women's lib was always like that: You were sorry you'd mentioned it. "I'm glad that my husband is alive," Rivka said. "I don't look for more political problems."

A moment later Zoe gathered her courage. "There's something else I wanted to ask you." But she took a deep breath and let it out again without saying anything.

Rivka reached up and took a pack of cigarettes and an

ashtray off the windowsill. They both smoked in silence for a minute.

Then Zoe said, "You know my friend Naomi?" Rivka nodded, and Zoe thought, No, this is all wrong. You shouldn't talk about Naomi; it isn't what a friend would do.

The sun had moved, and Rivka moved with it, leaning her back against the wall beneath the window, her legs stretched out in front of her. She exhaled a stream of smoke and said, "She's not a very happy person."

"What makes you think that?" Forget this, a part of Zoe's mind said. She tried to ignore it.

Rivka shrugged. "I can tell. Her face looks unhappy. Her eyes." She looked at Zoe. "You are both still using drugs."

Zoe didn't know it was that obvious, but she decided it would be best to ignore Rivka's comment. It was clear by now that Rivka hadn't told anyone that she'd caught them on Yom Kippur; she could be trusted. But why antagonize her by pointing out that, technically, marijuana wasn't a drug?

"She *is* unhappy," Zoe admitted. "I think she's pretty depressed."

"About what?" Rivka asked quietly.

"I don't know. Her parents are divorced, and her father doesn't see them very often — she's practically raised her two little brothers. And she's depressed about school. The main thing is, there's just nothing to do around here that seems really worthwhile —" She stopped, feeling that Rivka wouldn't know what she meant.

"It would be hard to be a young person here," Rivka said thoughtfully. "You have to find your own way for everything."

Zoe wasn't sure what she was talking about.

117

"There is a saying, you know, that Israel is a country that eats her citizens. It's very hard for young people, to know that they will have to be for two or three years in the army. But here is just the opposite — you know you will not be required to do anything. They treat you like babies."

"I know," Zoe said. She felt excited, like something was breaking up inside of her. "They don't even think we're capable of making our own decisions. Everyone talks about how they want you to be responsible, but if you *take* responsibility, they freak out."

Rivka nodded, miraculously agreeing. Then, abruptly, she said, "So what were you going to say about Naomi?" Rivka's eyes were very clear. *I know everything about you.*

She knew, then. Maybe she already knew. Zoe put out her cigarette in the ashtray. Shut up, forget it, that part of her mind said again. When she looked up, Rivka was still watching her. Zoe thought it would sound either terrible or ridiculous to say it out loud; she didn't know which. But maybe it wasn't that way at all. Maybe she wouldn't feel helpless or frightened anymore. Even if Rivka laughed, it would be a relief. Why not tell her? "Naomi keeps talking about suicide," she said softly.

Rivka's stare became sharper. "She does?"

"Uh-huh. She just sort of jokes about it, like you're not sure whether she means it or not. She said something about it to Danielle, too. I mean, I don't really think she'd — kill herself — but, I don't know. It worries me." Now that she'd said it, she didn't feel any better. She waited for Rivka to say something that would make it all right.

"That's very serious," Rivka said.

"How do you know? She could be just joking — she's like that."

Rivka shook her head. "I don't know. But if someone who's very depressed is talking about suicide, it can be that she will try to do it."

"How do you know?" Zoe heard her own voice rise in the quiet room.

"I don't mean that she *will*," Rivka said. "I don't really know. I'm just saying that you have to take it seriously."

"Shit," Zoe whispered. She sat with her knees pulled up to her chest and her arms crossed on top of them. She rested her head on her arms and stared at the blue carpet, feeling panicked. Every minute might be too late — and yet, probably if she pedaled over to Naomi's as fast as she could right now, Nao would look at her like she was crazy and say, What the hell are you talking about? I was only kidding. "I don't know what to do," she said.

"You asked her, did she mean it?"

"Yeah, I did and Danielle did. And both times she said she was just kidding. But then, all the rest of the time she's, like, cynical. She keeps saying that life is hopeless."

Zoe felt somehow that the whole world was changing shape during this conversation. Was it just because of Rivka, with whom she always seemed to be discussing dark things? It was like a bad acid trip, where everything was distorted into the most terrible forms your mind could imagine.

"I'm not sure what you should do," said Rivka. "I have to think about it. I'll talk to Natan."

"No!" said Zoe. "I don't want you to tell anyone."

Rivka gave her a disgusted look. "You told this to me so that I will sit and do nothing about it?"

"No, but I just — Please don't tell him."

"Why not? We won't tell anyone else, I can promise you."

119

Leora Freedman

Zoe was silent. She hated it that Natan was a psychiatrist. Her father always said, If you want to learn how to be really conventional, go see a shrink. She and Naomi would be like specimens of adolescence to him. But there was something else, too: A stubborn part of her mind wanted this conversation to be a secret between her and Rivka.

"You're very foolish," Rivka was saying. "I don't tell him everything that someone says to me. But this is something he knows a lot more about than I do."

Zoe thought maybe she was right; Natan didn't actually seem like such a bad guy, and telling him was more like doing something instead of just sitting around talking about it. She felt sick at the thought of it, though.

"Look, I'm going to tell him," Rivka said.

"OK," Zoe said. "OK." She sighed deeply and looked around the room. It was only then she realized how late it was getting; the patch of sun on the floor was gone, and they'd been sitting in shadow for a long time.

After Zoe put on her heavy sweater, windbreaker, hat and gloves, she stood facing Rivka at the door. From downstairs came thumps and laughter, and the sound of wheels rolling along the floor.

"Are you sure?" Rivka was saying. "I can put your bike in the car."

"No, I'll be all right. It's really not that far." Zoe didn't want to ask her for any more favors. Rivka looked worried, though, or maybe tired. There were little lines and shadows under her eyes; she looked older than twenty-eight, somehow.

"Thanks for lunch," Zoe said. "I'm sorry to cause you so much trouble."

Rivka touched Zoe's shoulder quickly. "You don't," she said. "You know I don't think so."

Zoe rode fast through the dim light, pedaling with all her strength. She felt like she was flying, and she kept thinking of how Rivka looked sitting in the sunlight on her living room floor. Zoe had never known any adults who sat on the floor, but Rivka said it was a habit from her mother's family, who were from Morocco. Zoe had never thought of there being Jews from a place like Morocco; Rivka said there were lots. One thing Zoe loved about Rivka was that you couldn't talk to her for five minutes without being absolutely sure there was a whole world out there beyond the suburbs.

As soon as she got home, she shut the door to her parents' study and dialed Naomi's number, still wearing her sweater and her hat.

"Just a minute, Zoe, I'll get her," Mrs. Kaplan said.

It took a long time. Maybe she wasn't there and her mother only thought she was.

"Hi, Zoe," said Naomi.

Zoe sighed with relief into the phone. "Hi, Nao."

"You sound out of breath."

"I was riding my bike. Are you OK? I mean, what'd you do today?"

It sounded like Naomi was yawning. "Went shopping with Mom. We picked out some birthday presents for Michael. I got a shirt."

"Oh." Well, that sounded OK. "What kind of shirt?"

"A great big used shirt from Goodwill. My mother hates it. Where'd you ride your bike?"

Zoe explained about riding past Rivka Lev's house and

121

running into her outside. She didn't say she'd gone there on purpose.

"I can't believe you went in," Nao said. "Was she nice to you?"

"Yeah, sort of. But I got hassled about being a vegetarian."

"Why you do not eat meat?" Naomi said in a thick Hebrew accent. "Americans don't know how to enjoy themselves."

Zoe started laughing.

"A Jewish girl doesn't laugh like that," Naomi continued, her voice a perfect imitation of Rivka's. "You show no smartness."

"Ah, she's not that bad, Nao." Zoe couldn't stop laughing. "She's just — she's from a different world. Nao, listen, I have to go. I'm supposed to babysit tonight. I just wanted to ask you — is everything all right?"

"Yeah, sure," Naomi said in her normal voice. "Why?"

Zoe sighed. "I don't know. I worry about you sometimes." There was silence on the other end of the phone. "When you start talking about —"

"I know, I know," Nao interrupted. "I just get depressed sometimes, but I get over it. You don't have to worry."

"I can't help it." Nao did sound reassuring today, though. Maybe everything would be all right.

"Listen," Naomi said. "What're you doing tomorrow?"

"I can't do anything. I have to go to Brooklyn and have lunch with Grandma. I'll see you on Monday, though."

"OK. Zoe?"

"Yeah?"

"Thanks for worrying about me. I mean, you don't have to, but thanks —"

"It's OK, Nao."

After she hung up, Zoe thought, What the hell was Naomi

saying? You don't have to worry about me, but thanks for worrying? Goddamn it, Naomi. *Is* there anything to worry about? No, but thanks for worrying. Yes, but I'll get over it. Rivka would say, *Yes, it can be that she will try to do it.*

She'd turned on the small light above the desk, but the rest of the study — the old books, the couch, the TV — was in shadow. Her eyes went over the shelves and stopped where a big swastika stood out: *The Rise and Fall of the Third Reich*, which she had tried to read but couldn't. Her mother joked that her brother Abe was the only person she knew who'd read that book cover to cover. It wasn't really a joke, though. People didn't want to read about all those terrible things for hundreds of pages; they didn't want to get too close to anything having to do with suffering and death. Reading about the Holocaust and knowing it could've been you, easily, if your grandparents hadn't come to America, was like reading about your own death.

How could anyone *want* to die? She couldn't understand it.

Rivka handed her two small, flat stones of an intense blue color, carved with worn, intricate designs; they were so beautiful, they made her gasp. All she could see were Rivka's hands, her hands, and the flat blue stones, their color so deep that it was almost surreal. It was understood between them that these stones were very old, even ancient.

"Have a piece of fruit," said Grandma Rose, setting a white bowl full of apples, bananas and oranges on the side table next to the old brown couch.

Zoe's parents groaned. "Come on, Mom," said Zoe's mother. "We just ate."

Zoe reached over and took a banana, snapping the top open. "Good girl!" said Grandma Rose. Zoe's parents and Melanie looked annoyed, but Zoe and her grandmother grinned at each other as if they'd done something illegal. It was fun to see her grandmother laugh, her old face wrinkling up and her perfect false teeth gleaming. They'd just finished a huge lunch of bagels, lox, cream cheese, herring, chocolate cake and coffee — the same things they always had when they came to Brooklyn for lunch. Zoe's parents would stop to buy the things at the little shops that stood close together under their old signs, all along the main street before the turn to her grandmother's apartment. Her parents always complained about how long it took to drive to Brooklyn — an hour and a half from Connecticut — but then they always opened the paper bags with the lox and bagels in them and sniffed deeply, saying, Ah, that's the real thing.

"You'll never lose any weight like that," said Zoe's mother.

"I don't care," said Zoe, eating the banana. "I'm never going to have Twiggy legs anyhow." She and Grandma Rose laughed again. Her grandmother was short and much heavier than Zoe. She'd had her white hair freshly done up and sprayed at the beauty parlor; she wore a pink dress and black pumps. Zoe's mother always asked, Why don't you just wear comfortable flat shoes? because her mother's ankles swelled over the tops of the black pumps, but Grandma Rose wouldn't wear any other shoes if people were coming, even if it was only them.

To Zoe's right was a large bookshelf, and in front of the books were framed pictures of everyone in the family: graduation pictures of her mother, her aunt and her uncles with strange molded hairdos, and then smaller, older pictures of her great-grandparents and other relatives who'd come over from Russia. Grandpa Lenny had come from Minsk by himself when he was only fifteen. The women, who were usually standing behind their children in the pictures, were broad and fat with big breasts and double chins: solid as rocks, Zoe's father would say. Their big arms were spread protectively over their children's shoulders; they looked like women you would not want to argue with. Zoe finished the banana and went into the tiny kitchen to throw away the peel.

As she looked out the kitchen window at the street, a couple with a dog walked by, and then a gang of boys, shouting and bouncing a ball. She could hear her family in the living room, talking about the state of the apartment. "You have to get the super to look at it," said her mother. Zoe could picture her grandmother's shrug. "You have to do some things for yourself," her mother said. Oh, leave her alone, Zoe thought. Her mother and her grandmother couldn't talk for five minutes without arguing. Probably they were talking about the sink, which was partly stopped up, with a couple of inches of dirty water in it.

"The whole neighborhood's changing," Grandma Rose was saying when Zoe came back into the living room. "They're moving in all over the place."

Oh no, thought Zoe, sitting down in the chair with the flowered slipcover. Here we go.

"Who's moving in?" asked Zoe's mother in an innocent tone.

Grandma Rose jerked her head toward the front window. She'd lived in this apartment for over thirty-five years; Zoe's mother had grown up here. When Zoe's parents were dating, if Zoe's father had to use the bathroom when he brought her home, he'd have to find his way across the crowded living room where her brothers were sleeping on cots. There were only two bedrooms, one for Zoe's mother and Aunt Joan, and one for Grandma Rose and Grandpa Lenny.

"*Who's* moving in?" repeated Zoe's mother.

Grandma Rose looked embarrassed but defiant. Lowering her voice, she said, "the *schvartzes*."

"Oh, *Mom*," said both Zoe's mother and father at the same time. Melanie said, "There's nothing wrong with black people, Grandma."

Zoe's mother clicked her tongue and sighed, shaking her head as if she wanted to say a lot more but was restraining herself. "You're prejudiced, Mom," she said.

"Why don't you want them to move in, Grandma?" Zoe asked, trying to sound kinder than her mother.

Her grandmother sighed. "It won't be long before the whole neighborhood's changed. You'll see. The landlord won't keep up the building, it'll all go downhill. Downhill," she repeated, giving Zoe a little mocking smile. "Then I'll have to move."

"Well, wait and see," Zoe said vaguely. She remembered that Grandma Rose hadn't liked it when the Hasidim moved in across the street, either. In fact, she didn't seem to like Hasidim much better than she liked blacks. Zoe wondered if she hated Israelis, too. Rivka and Natan were both fairly dark; maybe she'd think they were *schvartzes*.

"Izzie already had to move," said Grandma Rose, meaning her brother. "His neighborhood got so bad, he was afraid to walk out on the street."

"Well, we'll worry about it when it happens," said Zoe's father. "Listen, Mom," he said, obviously trying to change the subject, "what've you been doing with yourself lately?"

"Nothing," she said cheerfully.

"Oh, come on," he said.

She grinned at Zoe and Melanie. "I don't do *nothing*," she said again, mocking their father, and, somehow, herself as well.

"Have you seen Mrs. Rosenbaum lately?" asked Zoe's mother. Mrs. Rosenbaum had lived upstairs for about thirty years; she was the one who made all the intricate bead flowers that sat in little vases on the tables and bookshelves.

"Of course I see her," said Grandma Rose. She gave an elaborate shrug. "She doesn't do anything, either."

"You do nothing together," said Zoe. That made her grandmother laugh. Zoe knew that Grandma Rose and Mrs. Rosenbaum actually had long games of cards and Scrabble together, and watched TV. In nice weather she and Mrs. Rosenbaum and all the other old people in the building would sit out on the sidewalk in lawn chairs, sunning themselves and talking.

Zoe's parents always tried to convince Grandma Rose to "do" something; they wanted her to join the synagogue Sisterhood or Hadassah or the National Council of Jewish Women — anything that would get her involved in fundraising lunches and volunteer work. But she wouldn't do it. Zoe didn't blame her — it sounded boring, and besides, Grandma Rose had raised five kids and probably planned enough lunches to last the rest of her life. She'd made everything they ate, right down to the bread. And Zoe knew her mother had given up on those women's organizations herself. Why then did she want her own mother to join? It seemed like there should be something better for Grandma Rose to do, but Zoe couldn't think of anything. Maybe her mother couldn't, either.

◆ ◆ ◆

When Zoe woke up she looked out her window and saw that every branch on every tree was flaming the color of pure light. The sky was deep blue, and the ice-covered trees cut across it in shining patterns. The picnic table and the bird feeder were coated with ice; huge icicles hung from the roof of the house.

"No school today," her father said when she came out to the kitchen. He was drinking coffee and reading a magazine. "It's the biggest ice storm in fifty years," he added happily. Zoe got a cup of coffee and went back down the hall to Melanie's room. The door was open, and Melanie was sitting in bed reading *Vogue* while the brilliant sun poured through her window.

"Hey," Zoe said, "no school today."

"Yeah!" Melanie pulled her legs up under the quilt and made room for Zoe to sit. "This is great."

Zoe sat on her sister's bed and drank her coffee, feeling dazed. In her dreams she'd been screaming at her parents until her throat was sore. She didn't remember what she was trying to tell them. "I had weird dreams," she said. "Melanie?"

"Hm?" She was studying a glossy picture of a girl in a low-cut black dress.

"Do you ever think ... well" — she lowered her voice — "that Mom and Dad might ever get divorced?" The word sounded like it belonged to some other language, spoken aloud in Melanie's room, here in their own house.

Melanie put down the magazine and leaned back against her pillows, closing her eyes for a moment and then opening them again. She looked younger in the mornings, before

128

she'd put on her makeup. "I've thought of it sometimes," she said. "They don't always get along that well. But it's not like some stories I've heard from other kids."

"I know," Zoe said, "like Naomi's parents. She remembers things like her mother throwing plates. She says the whole year before her parents separated she just remembers the sounds of yelling and breaking glass."

Melanie sighed. "Well, Mom gets pretty mad sometimes, and I think Dad doesn't really know what she's talking about. Sometimes *I* don't even know what she's talking about."

"Well, some of it makes sense. I wonder if they'll work it out."

"I don't think they're about to run out and get divorced," Melanie said. "I just can't picture it."

"Neither can I. I think they love each other," Zoe said hopefully. "Don't you think so?"

"Yeah." Melanie didn't sound completely convinced, either.

Zoe looked out the window at the ice-covered houses across the street and wondered what Rivka was doing right now. Was she drinking coffee and looking out at the ice? She'd probably never seen anything like this before. Then Zoe thought of Naomi in her apartment. Nao drank lots of coffee in the morning and ate strange breakfasts that she concocted out of leftovers. Danielle might be sketching the ice-covered trees. Zoe felt them all connected to her, but separate, too, the way objects were made distinct by the ice that covered everything and made the world seem as fragile as glass.

Chapter Six

"— And this is Me-tza-DAH. Masada," Rivka said, as the old fortress on the flat-topped hill flashed onto the screen. She told the story of how the Jews held out against the Roman Empire in the Judean Desert, which looked kind of like the Grand Canyon. "You know what was the date when Masada fell?" For several class periods Rivka had been showing them slides of the ancient sites, and she was shocked at how little they knew. She seemed determined to pound into their heads the names, dates and significance of each place. "Who knows?" she asked enthusiastically, as if she were hosting a game show. "Who knows the date?"

Judy Teitelbaum said, "Seventy-three CE."

"*Tov Me'od*!" said Rivka.

"Cor-rect!" Adam said in a nasal game-show voice, speaking into his fist as if it were a microphone. "Now, Miss Teitelbaum, you're ready to try for the final prize behind curtain number three. A trip for two to Masada, all expenses paid."

"No," said Rivka. "You only get the trip for two if you know what this one is." She flashed on a slide of another site: stone walls and winding pathways blending into a rugged hillside below the Old City of Jerusalem. "Who knows this one?"

It was impossible to know. If Rivka hadn't told you it was the ancient City of David, King of Israel, you'd hardly look twice. Sometimes even after she'd explained it all, the stairs, walls and courtyards, Zoe still had trouble imagining exactly what these piles of rubble had been. It was like Rivka saw something that was invisible to the rest of them.

Zoe watched Rivka in the light from the projector. She was sitting a couple of seats over. Rivka was frowning, concentrating, as if she were seeing the slide for the first time. Absently she adjusted her belt, slipping her thumb underneath the linked bronze triangles; she was wearing earrings, too, made of the same bronze triangles dangling from little chains. From this angle you could see the way her nose curved down slightly and the nostrils flared back above the frown lines that made arcs around the corners of her mouth. Her hair was black and soft-looking. Zoe was close enough to see the mascara on Rivka's eyelashes, and the sparkly green makeup that matched the turtleneck she wore. Her breasts moved very slightly as she breathed.

Zoe leaned in the doorway after the rest of the class had left and watched Rivka slip a tray of slides into its box and close the cover. Then Rivka sat on one of the desks near the projector, which was still cooling down, its fan whirring. "How are you?" she asked in a tone she might use with someone her own age.

"Everything's wonderful," Zoe answered, with what she hoped was adult irony. She was wearing her oldest jeans and a blue work shirt with flowers embroidered on the front. She'd been trying to eat as little as possible for the past three days, and she felt thin.

"Listen, Natan would like to talk to you," Rivka said. "Can you come over and have dinner with us?"

Just then Zoe felt someone playfully grab the back of her neck. "Hey!" She turned around to see Naomi and Danielle in the hallway with their coats on.

"What're you up to?" Naomi asked. She peeked into the classroom, where Rivka had unplugged the projector and was winding up the cord.

"Nothing," Zoe answered. She didn't really care if they knew she was hanging around with Rivka; in a way she wanted them to know.

"I liked seeing those slides," Danielle said to Rivka. "They're really nice."

Rivka looked at Danielle for a moment, as if wondering whether she was sincere.

"It looks hot as hell over there, though," said Naomi.

"It's not *hell*," Rivka said.

"I didn't say that."

But Naomi sounded almost insolent, and Zoe wished she'd shut up. Zoe didn't know if Rivka even liked Naomi. And since Naomi didn't take her seriously, Rivka was unlikely to see how wonderful she was. Had she been right to tell Rivka so much about her friend? Just because *she* loved Rivka didn't mean Naomi did. And now Natan was in on it, too. What a mess, she thought. And I did it all myself.

Zoe poured milk in her tea and spent a long time stirring it. She felt awkward sitting alone in the kitchen with Natan. He tapped a cigarette on the table before lighting it, his dark eyes focused on something else but giving the impression that, beneath those heavy curved eyebrows of his, they would snap to attention if she made the slightest sound. She wasn't afraid of him — there was a kind of delicacy in his manner and appearance that she found reassuring — but he was so quiet that she was afraid of what she might tell him, just to fill the silence.

But then it was Natan who spoke first. "I hope you're not upset that Rivka has told me about Naomi," he said. He pronounced Naomi's name in the Hebrew way, Nah-OH-mee, which almost made it sound as if they were talking about someone else. "You were right to tell Rivka, and she's right to think we should do something."

Zoe looked at him closely. He had dark, fine skin, and the kitchen light caught the oil on his forehead and made it shine. "What do you want to do about it?" she asked, hoping to dissuade him if he had something stupid in mind. He was an adult shrink, and she suspected he didn't know anything about kids.

He crossed his arms and frowned, as if to say, Don't rush me, I have everything under control. She saw that he was going to be just as stubborn as Rivka. "Well," he said, "do you think Naomi has told her mother any of these things?"

It hadn't occurred to Zoe to wonder about this. "I don't think so," she said. "She really tries not to worry her mother. Even though she gets in trouble all the time, she still feels bad when her mom finds out." Her voice sounded to her as if it were coming out of a tape recorder — a surprisingly low voice with a strong Connecticut accent — and she heard the contradiction in what she was saying. If Naomi was really trying not to worry her mom, why was she always getting in trouble?

"Yes? So she's really trying not to worry her mother?" Natan said quietly.

Zoe knew that he'd heard the contradiction, too, and that he knew that she knew. What a strange game this was.

"She seems very depressed to you?"

"I know she is," Zoe said. "I'm worried about her. But I don't really think she'd commit suicide."

"Maybe not," he said. "But it's better to be safe about these things and take them seriously."

Rivka came downstairs and sat down at the table. She looked at both of them quietly. Zoe started to feel jittery inside, the way she always did when Rivka was there.

"I know Rivka made you a promise that we wouldn't tell anyone," Natan said carefully. "But I think that Naomi's mother has to know."

Zoe was suddenly afraid. "You mean you want to —"

"I'm going to call her mother," Rivka said.

"I don't think that's such a good idea," Zoe said. Damn them, they didn't even think enough of her to ask her opinion. Nao would not take kindly to this. "I think *I* should talk to Naomi and convince her to tell her mother."

"OK, sure, you can convince her," Rivka said, her voice becoming more vehement. "But I'm still going to call."

"But —"

"It's the best thing to do," Natan said. "And Rivka has the obligation, she's her teacher."

"Naomi is *sick* of her teachers calling up," Zoe said.

Natan didn't even blink. "You just said she is afraid to worry her mother. But I think you can see that maybe Naomi has been trying to tell her mother that something is wrong."

"If you are really her friend, you will see that I have to call her mother," Rivka said.

Zoe looked back and forth at them. They had it all figured

out. So why didn't she trust them? Maybe because they were foreigners, they didn't really seem to understand the way it was with American kids and their parents. Rivka had been shocked to discover how little Zoe's parents knew about Zoe's real life.

"She's going to kill me," Zoe said. Then she realized the irony of her remark and started laughing, a strange humorless laugh that was like a tense string pulling at the inside of her body.

There were footsteps on the stairs, and then Eitan appeared in the kitchen wearing pajamas with trucks printed all over them. "I can't sleep," he said. "You guys are having fun down here."

"We're just talking," said Natan. He held his hand out to the little boy. "Come on, let's go upstairs. I'll read to you."

After they'd gone, Rivka took out her cigarettes and offered one to Zoe. "I shouldn't encourage you to smoke," she said, "but I feel rude if I don't offer."

"I'd smoke whether you encouraged me or not," Zoe said.

Rivka flicked her lighter and held the flame to the end of Zoe's cigarette. Zoe looked down at Rivka's hand, so close to her own face.

Then Rivka lit her own cigarette. "I know," she said. "But I'm not a very good example to you."

"You don't have to be a good example." Zoe made a couple of smoke rings and watched them disappear. "I'm not trying to be like you — I wouldn't want to be."

Rivka raised her eyebrows, and she looked amused. "No? You would not want to be like me?"

"Nope." Zoe tried not to smile. "When I first met you, I thought you were awful. I couldn't believe anyone like you could even exist."

"Yes, I know," Rivka said. "Someone so loud. So rude. *So*

mean." She pronounced the words *loud, rude* and *mean* in a mincing way that suggested the pettiness of anyone who would use them to describe her.

"Yeah." Zoe couldn't help laughing. "And naive —"

"Naive? What are you talking?"

"Well, there're some things you don't understand," Zoe said cautiously. "For example, you don't know anything about drugs." Zoe leaned forward. It seemed silly to her that Rivka was so straight about some things when she was so cool about others; Zoe felt certain that Rivka had the potential to become a completely cool and knowledgeable person. "Haven't you ever smoked any pot?" she asked.

"No, and I don't want to," Rivka said irritably.

Zoe was glad to see it was getting to her. She felt somehow that the way Rivka and Natan had pushed her around — just announcing their decision to phone up Mrs. Kaplan without even asking Zoe's opinion — gave her the right to be any way she wanted with them. "It's OK, I won't hold it against you," Zoe said.

"But I will hold it against *you*." Rivka said. She had her fierce look on, but Zoe was learning to ignore it.

"Listen, don't say anything about drugs to Mrs. Kaplan, OK?"

Rivka gave her a disgusted look. "Don't worry, Zoe, I won't tell your little secrets." She dragged on her cigarette and looked at Zoe through slightly narrowed eyes. "I'm not a disloyal person."

"OK," Zoe said, looking down at the table. She was afraid to look at Rivka whenever anything serious got said between them. "Actually I've changed my opinion of you," she said, looking up again. "I don't hate you."

"That's very nice," Rivka said. "Thank you for the compliment."

Zoe looked down the long rows of shelves and saw Naomi standing by the card catalog, her hair falling across her face as she wrote something on a scrap of paper. She knew she had to tell Naomi what was happening, but how the hell was she going to bring it up? They'd come downtown together to the public library to work on their research papers for English. Zoe's topic was the causes and effects of the Vietnam War, but her teacher had said that was too broad and she'd have to narrow it down. The problem was that everything that had happened was related to everything else. If the teacher would leave her alone, she knew she could figure out how to do it. If Rivka and Natan had left her alone, she might have figured out how to help Naomi without everyone being so authoritarian about it. But as it was, she was going to have to confront Naomi this afternoon, and then go home and write her paper on some picky little thing.

Naomi's topic was reincarnation. She'd found a pile of books and articles, which she plunked down on her side of the table in the Acropolis Diner, at an angle where Zoe was sure to see the titles. Zoe had put her own books down on the seat.

"Did you know that most people in the world believe in some form of reincarnation?" Naomi asked.

"No," Zoe said.

"Yeah, well, I'm going to write my paper on the Buddhist idea. They believe that if you accumulate a lot of good karma during your life, you're reborn into the world a step closer to nirvana."

137

They were interrupted by the waitress bringing them pie and coffee. Outside the window the sky was slowly turning dark gray, and the storefronts across the street glowed yellow. Cars passed with a whoosh, spraying slush up onto the curb. Inside the Acropolis it was noisy; steam hissed from the grills, and glasses clinked.

"Anyway, the Buddhists believe that death is just another part of this cycle that brings you closer to nirvana, which is this perfect state where you don't have to be reborn anymore because you've reached total enlightenment." Naomi ate a big mouthful of chocolate cream pie, keeping her eyes on Zoe.

"Jews don't believe in that," Zoe said flatly. "We believe you have only one life, so you better just do the best you can with it. You have a responsibility to stay in the world and do what you can to help it, and not because of some reward in a future life, either."

"Buddhists believe," Naomi said, ignoring Zoe's little speech, "that it's actually a good thing to die —"

"I don't think that's what they mean," Zoe interrupted. She felt sure the Buddhists meant ordinary death, not suicide, and she knew Naomi was twisting these ideas. She was frightened and annoyed by Naomi's enthusiastic expression.

"— because if you die," Naomi continued, "you have the chance of making spiritual progress. You might be reborn into a better life."

"On the other hand, you might be reborn as a fly or an ant," Zoe argued. "You'd live for about two days, and then someone would come along and crush you with their foot. Or maybe you'd find out too late that there's no such thing as reincarnation, and it's just something people made up so they'd feel better about having to die. Most people don't *want* to die." She stared hard at Naomi, and Naomi looked away. Zoe realized she was gripping the handle of her fork so hard her hand hurt.

Naomi had stopped eating and was staring into space at something private.

"Nao, I've been really worried about you," Zoe began.

Naomi looked at her quickly. "Why?"

"Because you keep talking about death, and suicide." The words sounded ridiculous, spoken aloud in the Acropolis Diner.

Naomi shrugged, and set her mouth in a smile that was not really a smile.

"Danielle's worried, too."

Naomi said nothing, but she was paying close attention, Zoe could tell.

"I've been really worried," Zoe repeated slowly, "and I was talking to Rivka Lev about it."

"About *me*?"

"Yeah." Zoe hesitated. "It worries her, too."

Naomi was silent, waiting for what was coming. Her face was pale, and her eyes were huge blue stones.

"She's going to call your mother." Zoe's coffee had gone cold and tasted terrible.

"Oh, great, that's just what I need." She looked at Zoe. "I wasn't asking you to do anything about it," she said in a slow, deliberate tone. She seemed almost angry, but her voice also had a funny sound, like she might cry if she wasn't so controlled. "I was just telling you those things as a friend."

"I'm sorry. I know I haven't been a good friend. But I was so worried, Nao," Zoe said. "Maybe I didn't have to be," she added hopefully.

139

"It doesn't matter," Naomi said. "I mean, it's not like they can do anything about it. If I really want to kill myself, no one can stop me." She said this as if she were reciting a boring fact.

"*Naomi*," Zoe said, trying to keep her voice down. "Are you serious? Do you really —" She couldn't finish the sentence.

Naomi shrugged. "Sometimes I think about it. Not all the time. But I planned out a couple ways I could do it."

"Nao, I never even knew if you were serious, you're always turning it into a joke." Zoe heard the hidden tears now, not in Nao's voice, but in her own.

"I don't know if I'm serious or not." Naomi seemed angry now, finally. "How the hell should I know what I'll end up doing? I'll tell you one thing, though. Life is a fucking drag most of the time, and I don't really think anyone would mind if I wasn't around to participate in it anymore."

Zoe had never heard Naomi say so much, so directly. She felt frantic, as if she had only a minute to assemble a convincing argument before Naomi jumped off a cliff. "*I* would mind," she said, leaning over the table toward her friend. "I think it'd be a really, really stupid thing to do. Life isn't that hopeless. You think your mother and David and Michael and Danielle and I would get over it just like that? You can't do it, Nao, it's ridiculous." She stopped, remembering that Natan had told her not to argue or lecture Naomi if she talked like this. He said to be calm and reassuring. So why hadn't she planned what to say? Because she'd been trying to convince herself that Nao just couldn't be serious. Rivka was right: Zoe was a fool.

"That's the way it is with death, though," Naomi said thoughtfully. "People do get over it. I remember when my grandfather —"

"*Naomi!*"

"Well, at least my mother wouldn't be bugged by all these goddamn teachers calling up."

"I'm sorry. But I had to tell someone. Would you rather I told my mother?"

"No, no, no. That'd be worse, for sure." Naomi sighed. "You're right," she said simply. "I'm all fucked up. I know it."

Zoe suddenly felt how much she loved Naomi and wanted to go sit on the other side of the booth and put her arms around her friend, who was looking so lost in a plaid flannel shirt many sizes too large for her. At the same time she felt that Nao would be justified in never wanting to be close to her again. She hated herself for what she'd done. It was disgusting the way Zoe went around thinking she loved Rivka Lev more than any human being she'd ever met, even though she'd only known her for five months. What about Naomi, who'd been her best friend for ten years? Why was it so easy for one kind of love to make you forget about the other people in your life? She didn't know how to separate all the different kinds of love or what to call them.

"It'll be OK," Zoe said. "She promised not to say anything about getting high."

"Well, I wouldn't trust her. She's like a one-woman vice squad. My mother is going to *freak out*."

"Well, Rivka probably won't call until tonight, so maybe you can talk to your mother first?"

"I'm not going to talk to my mother," Nao said. "Why should I be the one to get her all upset? I may as well just let *Rivka* do it."

Zoe knew Naomi was making fun of her, calling Rivka by her first name, and she felt she deserved it.

Then Naomi seemed to relax; she turned sideways on the seat and slouched against the wall, lighting a cigarette. "What're you hanging around with her for?" she asked. "I thought you hated her."

Zoe shook her head. For some reason she was starting to feel all emotional now. Naomi looked calm, but Zoe felt like she wanted to cry or smash things or beg Naomi to forgive her. Naomi was a wonderful friend and she probably didn't deserve her; Zoe was playing with Nao's head and nothing made any sense. "I was wrong about Rivka," she said. "I think she's a really nice person. She says a lot of things that make sense."

Naomi hooted. "She's *nice*? She's *nice* and she makes *sense*? I think you're even more fucked up than I am."

"That's probably true," Zoe said. "I don't know what I'm doing, either."

Danielle was leaning against the machine that contained rows of shiny red apples, each in its slot. She was wearing a leather vest and dangly beaded earrings she'd made herself. Her eyes were wide, but she said nothing.

"... so at least now her mother will know," said Zoe.

She waited for Danielle's reaction. They were standing in the hallway in front of the doors to the courtyards, where everyone was having a cigarette between classes. Danielle was still silent.

"I feel guilty as hell," Zoe said.

Danielle nodded, put a couple of books down on the floor, and started thumbing through the sketchpad she was carrying. Finally she opened it to a place in the middle. "I wanted to show this to you," she said, turning the picture toward Zoe.

It was an elaborate pen and ink drawing of an abstract eye, with intricate designs radiating from its center. The picture was very intense: It was clear it had taken her a long time to draw all those tiny patterns that merged into the one big one. Zoe was reminded of the times she and Nao had taken LSD and she'd noticed that the smooth surfaces of ordinary things were actually made up of incredibly complex designs. Danielle apparently saw these things without taking acid, though. Usually Zoe admired Danielle's artwork, but something about this picture upset her. It seemed to have nothing to do with real life: Danielle was just going deeper and deeper into a place where none of her friends could follow. Zoe knew Danielle would want to know what the drawing reminded her of, but she couldn't talk in metaphors right now. She wanted to know what Danielle thought about Naomi. "It's really nice," she said finally.

"Thanks," said Danielle. She looked pleased with the praise, and kept on holding the sketchbook open toward Zoe.

"Are you angry with me?" Zoe asked.

Danielle looked surprised. "No. Why should I be?" She was still holding out the drawing.

"You haven't said anything about Nao, about what I just told you."

"Oh," Danielle said. "I don't really know what to say." Zoe waited in silence for a moment. Danielle closed the sketchbook. "I just don't like to think about — death, things like that. I don't want to talk about it."

Zoe looked at her helplessly. She noted Danielle's clear brown eyes, the delicate line of her nose, the light brown freckles scattered across it. Danielle looked beautiful and totally unworried. Her jeans fit her slender body perfectly;

her homemade leather vest was snapped closed around her small waist. The vest had tooled flowers around its edges, colored carefully with blue and yellow paint.

"You're so fucking spaced out," Zoe said. "Your best friends could kill themselves and you wouldn't even pay any attention."

She hesitated, then walked away, leaving Danielle standing by the rows of seemingly identical apples lined up in the apple machine.

After school that day, Zoe was lying down across Naomi's bed, which was covered with clothing and books, when the phone rang. Nao went into her mother's room to answer it. Books were all over the floor, too, some on reincarnation, but there were others on Judaism and Christianity. A wrinkled piece of notebook paper said, "The idea of a state where one has no desires or even any feeling of 'self' is perhaps the most difficult for Western minds to understand." There were more words scattered down the page in Naomi's wild scrawl: *Christianity, the devil, karma, Jewish soul: neshama.* Just seeing those words in proximity to each other made Zoe nauseous; she couldn't see how they related to each other or to Naomi's paper. She looked up at the wall where a torn picture of Bob Dylan hung by one thumbtack, next to two of Danielle's drawings taped up at weird angles. One was a pencil sketch of Naomi sitting with her arms crossed, her head tilted back, with that challenging look she often had on her face; the other was an abstract watercolor that looked like a lake with a city underneath it. Zoe felt sick and guilty, so she put her head down on her arms and closed her eyes. Why did life have to be so fucking depressing? A shirt of Naomi's was near her face, and she breathed in the sweet, warm, cigarette-and-soap smell that was Naomi. She pretended for a moment that they were young again; there was no unhappiness, and when Naomi came back into the room, they'd just have fun and not think about anything serious.

"That was Mom." Naomi sat down on a pile of laundry and lit a cigarette. "She wanted to know if I was home. I told her I was just sitting in the bathtub slitting my wrists when she called, but I was being really careful not to get blood all over her pillow."

"*Naomi*," Zoe said, laughing nervously. "It's not funny."

Naomi grinned at her. "She's going to have me punching a time clock pretty soon." Then she stopped smiling. "She made an appointment for me to see a shrink tomorrow afternoon."

Zoe nodded. She felt enormously relieved, but didn't want to offend Naomi by saying so. Naomi had avoided the whole topic during lunchtime in school today and on the drive over here, so Zoe decided she'd just wait and let Nao tell her whatever she felt like, whenever, and that she would be calm and reassuring.

"I know you're greatly relieved," Nao said, opening her blue eyes wide and staring at her, a bit sarcastically.

"Well, you're my best friend," Zoe said, bunching up Naomi's shirt and resting her head on it.

Naomi looked away, drawing on her cigarette. "My mom was on the phone with Mrs. Lev for an *hour* last night."

"She was?" Zoe felt a little stab of panic, but then she remembered the way Rivka had said *I'm not a disloyal person*. She just hoped Rivka hadn't overdone it with the doom and gloom.

"Yeah. But she had the bedroom door closed so I couldn't hear a thing. I was lying on the floor outside with my ear up against the crack." There was silence for a moment.

"Hey, you didn't tell her anything about Tad, did you?" Nao asked.

"Nope. Does your mother know about Tad?"

"Nah. I mean, she knows I have a friend named Tad who's a Jesus Freak. I think she thinks he's someone I know in school."

"Oh, yeah." Zoe tried to make her voice calm and non-judgmental. "Have you seen him lately?"

Naomi looked at her. "Yeah. I was over there on Monday, and we had this big theological argument." She smiled.

"About what?"

"Well, I told him about my theory that there's this evil force controlling my life, like a devil, sort of, and he *freaked out.* He kept saying, 'Nao, baby, you shouldn't tempt him, you shouldn't tempt him.'" She laughed.

Zoe laughed too at the idea of Tad's distress. Then she noticed that Naomi was looking at her like she was waiting for a reaction. Zoe said, "You don't really believe that, though, do you?"

"Sure, I do," said Naomi, but Zoe still wasn't sure if Nao was teasing her or not.

"There's no such thing as a devil, Nao," Zoe said, trying to keep her voice light. "It's just something people like Tad believe in so they can blame all their evil impulses on it."

"Even Jews have believed in *dybbuks,* or disembodied spirits that inhabit a living person," Naomi said, sounding as if she were quoting from a book. "Christians and Jews aren't really that different, when you come right down to it."

"I think they're different," Zoe said bluntly. "I mean, how could anyone believe all that Jesus stuff?"

Naomi blew some smoke rings in the air. "Well, yeah, I

know what you mean. But Jesus was really just this Jewish guy, you know, who went a little bit overboard. The Jewish idea of the *dybbuk* is really amazing."

"Like, what do you mean?" Zoe said patiently.

"Well, there could be a *dybbuk* who had unfinished business in Connecticut, so she comes down and sticks to me, torments me. Maybe she knew Tad. The Kabbalah says we can be reincarnated. And the Jews also believe that everyone is born with a clean soul, your *neshama* is basically good. So if you figure it out, a person who's being controlled by a *dybbuk* can potentially die and be reborn with a clean soul, maybe even better than in their previous life."

I feel like there's some kind of evil force controlling my life. Zoe had thought this was just an idea Nao had made up to be funny, or to bug Tad with. It was beyond Zoe to understand how she could be taking devils and *dybbuks* seriously — if that's what she was doing. "Naomi," Zoe said cautiously, "you don't really believe that, do you?"

"Why not?" Naomi said softly, staring at her.

"Because —" Zoe started to say, but then she felt suddenly helpless and without words. She remembered Natan's warning. She also realized that she knew a lot less about all this mysticism than Naomi did. What especially worried her was that Naomi was obviously doing a lot of reading and thinking for this paper, and it wasn't like Nao to put so much effort into something for school.

"*Why not?*" Naomi said again, still in the soft voice, but more insistently. Her eyes were round and very blue today, the color of the sky when it looks endless.

"I don't know," Zoe said.

Naomi smiled.

Leora Freedman

♦ ♦ ♦

At seven-thirty the next morning Zoe stopped underneath a tree at the edge of the soccer field to smoke a joint. It was a cold, gray day, just barely getting light out. She decided she couldn't face school today; she was starting to feel bad every time she ran into Naomi or Danielle. After smoking half the joint she stubbed it out against the tree trunk, put the other half in the pocket of her army pants, and walked past the high school. She continued up the hill and around the corner past her old elementary school. In the playground a row of empty swings hung from their chains, very still in the early morning air.

In Bagel King, it was beautiful the way the waitress poured her coffee into the cup, a deep brown stream. It smelled wonderful. She drank it, remembered to pay, and then left. It was lighter now, but still gray, the kind of morning when the air seemed heavy and sounds were muffled. She kept walking up the Post Road, past the furniture store, the carwash. It must be eight-thirty or nine already, Zoe thought. She realized she was walking in the direction of Rivka's house. Was it too early to visit an ordinary, civilian human being? You got such a warped idea of time, starting school as early as if you were in basic training.

Zoe went over Rivka's schedule: She taught on Tuesdays and Thursdays, at the university in the morning and at Temple Beth Israel in the afternoon. On Wednesdays she had office hours. Today was Friday, so Rivka was free.

She kept walking, along the back streets now. Once she stopped and sat on a stone wall and put eye drops in her eyes. She blinked rapidly in the cold air and felt deliriously happy.

• • •

Rivka opened the door. "Hi, Zoe." She was wearing a striped shirt with the sleeves rolled up, and she held a blue pencil in one hand.

"Hi." Zoe smiled at her as she shut the door.

"What are you doing? Don't you have to be in school?"

"I'm taking an Aggravation Day." Rivka looked puzzled.

"You know, to keep from getting too aggravated," Zoe explained.

"Oh. Do you want something to drink?" Rivka asked.

"OK." Zoe followed her into the kitchen, where Rivka had obviously been grading a pile of university papers on the table. Zoe glanced at the ones on top; they were all in Hebrew. One had a B and one had a C. It was a good thing they didn't get grades in Hebrew High School; you never knew, maybe Rivka was really hard.

"Don't they know that you are not in school?" Rivka asked, setting a glass of juice in front of Zoe.

"As long as you don't go to homeroom, you're on the absent list," Zoe explained. "It's such a big school, they can't keep track of everyone all the time." Besides, Zoe's homeroom teacher never asked for notes from anyone's parents the next day, as long as they kept their skipping under control. Miss Spear never made them stand up for "The Star-Spangled Banner," either, and she sat and talked with the class while the Pledge of Allegiance rasped over the PA. Everyone liked her. Zoe tried to explain all this.

Rivka was sitting across the table from Zoe, in front of the pile of papers. "Why don't you want to say the Pledge of Allegiance?"

"Because if you listen to the words, what you're pledging is to be completely loyal to the United States, no matter what it does. Even if it means going to a war you don't believe in and killing innocent people."

"Oh," Rivka said. She held her coffee cup in both hands, and looked into it thoughtfully.

Zoe waited for a moment, then said, "Aren't you going to argue with me?"

Rivka looked up. "No." She drank some coffee. Zoe had noticed yesterday in Hebrew School that there were dark circles under Rivka's eyes; they were still there now. "I just wanted to hear what you'd say."

"Well, that's a change," Zoe said.

"Al tachshevi sheat yodaat hakol," Rivka told her.

Zoe lowered her eyebrows, uncomprehending.

"It means, don't think that you know everything." Rivka gave her a hard look. "Maybe one day you will learn Hebrew."

Then Zoe said, "I heard you talked to Mrs. Kaplan for a long time the other night." She wondered if she'd be able to find out what they'd said.

"Well, of course, she was quite upset. But she's glad you told me about Naomi."

"Uh-huh." Zoe knew she didn't deserve any credit. If she hadn't been so crazy to see Rivka, to talk to her about anything, she probably wouldn't have told anyone.

"I felt very sorry for her, you know, as a mother." Zoe nodded, as if she knew what it felt like to be a mother. "Natan and I stayed up late, talking about it. I think I am still not being myself today."

"Naomi's mom made an appointment for her to see a shrink," Zoe told her. "She's going this afternoon."

Rivka looked relieved. "Oh, I'm so glad. I tried to convince her, but she didn't think she could afford it. She had to talk to the father."

Zoe was silent, picturing Mrs. Kaplan on the phone with her ex-husband in New York, telling him Naomi might kill herself if he didn't shell out some money for a shrink. Naomi always said her mother was weird for a week afterwards every time she had to talk to her father. Somehow Zoe no longer wanted to know all the details. She looked at Rivka and said, "Do you think everything will be OK?"

Rivka looked almost startled. "I hope so."

Why hadn't she said yes? "No, but I mean —"

"I can't see the future," Rivka said. "Right now Naomi has a lot of problems. I hope she'll be OK."

Zoe didn't feel so happy anymore. She promised herself to stay close to Naomi, to be a good friend to her. The only problem was, when the adults thought she was being a good friend, Naomi didn't think so; and when Naomi thought she was, the adults didn't. It felt funny not being on Naomi's side.

Then Zoe felt a wave of stoned paranoia. She didn't belong here at Rivka's house, pretending to be her friend. It was too bizarre. Ever since she'd started hanging around Rivka, she'd been more and more at odds with Naomi and Danielle — her real friends. Zoe's mind told her that if she kept this up, Rivka was going to cause her a lot of pain someday.

"Your eyes look really strange," Rivka said.

"I'm going to have to get some different eye drops."

Rivka smiled her sarcastic smile. "Very funny."

"I wasn't trying to be," Zoe said. "You're so moralistic. Tad the Jesus Freak should meet you to find out how it's really done."

Rivka lowered her eyebrows. "Who?"

"Tad the Jesus Freak is this guy Naomi knows. He has a little trouble living up to his own morals."

Zoe watched Rivka narrow her eyes, trying to figure out what she meant. Rivka's face had lost that sarcastic, accusing look; now her curiosity had taken over. Zoe knew she wasn't going to leave. She liked talking to Rivka. And she could not remember any other woman ever seeming as beautiful.

"What does this mean — Jesus Freak?" she asked.

Zoe smiled. "Well, you know, usually a freak is someone who's into drugs, right? But a Jesus Freak is a person who's hooked on religion, instead. They've turned off drugs and turned on to Jesus."

"These Christians think that there are only two choices in life? Religion or drugs?"

"That's what Tad thinks. He's been baptized again and everything."

Rivka looked at Zoe as if she'd said Tad had a habit of eating pig's feet. Zoe got the feeling Rivka thought everything having to do with people who were not Jewish was very weird. "It seems like everyone you know is into drugs," Rivka said.

"Not everyone. But most of them are." Zoe laughed a little, mainly to herself. "Even the threat of hell isn't enough for Tad."

Rivka put her arms on the table and leaned forward, looking intently at her. "Why do you think you need this?"

"I don't *need* anything. I'm not overdoing anything. It's recreational, in my case. And I see a lot of things I'd never notice otherwise. It's like a whole different way of looking at the world."

"It is an escape from reality," Rivka said.

Zoe groaned. "That's the oldest one in the book," she said. "There's another saying, you know. 'Some people think that drugs are for people who can't handle reality. But actually, reality is for people who can't handle drugs.'" She laughed.

Rivka didn't think it was funny.

"Sorry," Zoe said. "I thought you were my friend."

She looked at Zoe a moment before answering. "I am. But I don't understand you. There is something about Americans that I just don't —"

Americans again. "Listen," Zoe interrupted. "You think we're so awful, but I happen to know people in Israel get high, too. This girl I know in YTI smuggled back the most incredible hash in the soles of her shoes — and you know where she got it?" Zoe was almost shouting now, triumphantly. "On the street in Tel Aviv!"

"You don't have to tell the whole world," Rivka said.

Zoe's mother sat in her favorite chair with a gin and tonic in her hand, her feet up on the footrest. Zoe was stretched out on the living room couch. Her father and Melanie were banging around in the kitchen, trying to make spaghetti.

"I told her what you would say," Zoe continued, "and she said, 'She thinks that who washes the dishes is a political problem? Americans don't know what is a political problem.'" Zoe imitated Rivka's accent pretty well.

Her mother smiled and poked the lime in her drink. "Well, you know, you have a country like Israel that's always been threatened from the outside, and people tend to retreat into very traditional behavior."

"Oh, yeah," Zoe said. She considered that for a few moments. "But she doesn't think of herself as traditional."

153

Zoe sat up, straightened her shoulders and looked down at her mother. "'I am not a slave,'" she said fiercely, in Rivka's voice.

It was nice to see her mother laugh — she seemed so serious most of the time. "I think I like this woman," her mother said.

Zoe slumped back down on the couch. "I do, too," she said. It seemed that Zoe was always waiting for it to be Tuesday, or Thursday, or whatever other day she could manage to see Rivka. In between, she thought about her almost nonstop. It was funny, but her mother didn't seem to mind her going on and on with these Rivka Lev stories. Her mother liked them.

Danielle's mother called out to Danielle, and when she didn't answer, Zoe went upstairs and stood in the doorway of her room. There was just one light on over the bed, where Danielle sat with her sketchbook on her lap, drawing with her black technical drawing pen. She still didn't look up when Zoe said hi. Zoe hadn't realized how angry Danielle would be. She normally didn't think of Danielle as capable of real anger.

"Hey, Danielle," Zoe said quietly, sitting down on the edge of the bed. "I have a big mouth."

Danielle drew a long curved line, then little lines curling away from it. "You do, sometimes," she said.

Zoe looked away, at the dark side of the room.

"You act like a crusader," Danielle said. "Like you're the only moral person in the universe."

"I know I'm not," Zoe said.

"Well, you act like you're the only one who really cares. Even if other people have feelings, you don't pay any attention because you think they have the wrong feelings."

"I'm sorry," Zoe said again. Maybe there was some truth in that, she didn't know. "But I just get so mad when people won't face things."

"Naomi's glad there's someone who doesn't want to talk about — those things. She says it's a relief."

Zoe felt like Danielle had punched her. "I guess she thinks I'm a real shit," she said, trying to keep her voice steady. Maybe Naomi had told Danielle that Zoe was being an asshole and was just using her as part of some bizarre thing she had going with Rivka Lev.

Danielle was silent for a moment. "No, she didn't say that. She thinks you're really great." Zoe wasn't convinced. "I really do feel for her," Danielle said. "She's my friend, too." She bent over the sketchbook and started working a new design down from the top of the page, toward the lines she'd already drawn.

This wasn't entirely convincing. Zoe watched the way Danielle's thin fingers held the pen loosely, confidently. The two of them could sit in silence for a long time now, Zoe knew, if she didn't say anything.

"It's just that you seem so distant sometimes," Zoe said carefully. "Like whenever I'm talking to you, you're always doing something else at the same time. You're always drawing, or making things —"

"I can't stand to waste time," Danielle said, without removing her pen from the page.

"You think having a conversation is a waste of time?"

"No, I didn't mean it that way. I'm listening to you. I can talk to you and draw at the same time."

"But why do you have to?" Zoe asked.

"I can't help it. I always feel like there might not be enough time. Like something could happen and I won't be able to do any more artwork."

"You have plenty of time," Zoe said. "You're only sixteen. What could possibly happen?"

"I don't like to think about it," Danielle said for the second time in one week.

Naomi joked over the phone about how everything in her life was breaking down at the same time. Her car was in the garage because something was wrong with the carburetor. When she'd gone to see Tad today, he opened his door a crack and said she'd better go because Diane was in town, staying with him. And yesterday afternoon she'd been to the shrink for the first time, which she wouldn't be doing if her head didn't need serious repair. She seemed cheerful about it all, which worried Zoe, who was beginning to be afraid of Naomi's cheerfulness, her jokes that weren't really jokes. Zoe tried to be reassuring. Tad was full of shit, she said, and she could get her dad's car and they'd go out, since it was Saturday.

When she got to the Kaplans' apartment, Naomi and her mother were sitting at the kitchen table. Mrs. Kaplan smiled at Zoe. "Where're you girls off to tonight?"

"I think we're going to see Craig and Irene," Zoe said. "On their boat." This was Naomi's idea; Zoe hadn't even seen them since they graduated last year.

"They got an old houseboat last summer," Naomi added. "It was a total wreck, but Craig knows about carpentry, and they've fixed it all up. I haven't even seen it since they finished, but I ran into Irene at the record store last week and she said come over any time."

"Sounds like fun," Mrs. Kaplan said, looking doubtful. The lines on her face seemed more pronounced than usual, and her hair looked funny, too. She didn't seem to have a date tonight; she was wearing a sweatshirt and jeans with a tie-dye pattern on them, and fuzzy bedroom slippers. "I want you back by midnight, though, Nao. You've had a hard week."

Naomi stood up and pushed in her chair. "OK." She seemed embarrassed by what her mother had said; she turned abruptly and started up the stairs. "I'll be down in a minute, Zoe."

Mrs. Kaplan still looked uncertain, like she wasn't sure now which parts of Naomi's life she should be worrying about. Zoe couldn't think of anything to say. Finally Mrs. Kaplan looked at her and said, "Thanks, Zoe. I know you really care about Nao."

Zoe was a bit embarrassed. "Well, she's my best friend."

Mrs. Kaplan nodded. Then she said, "This Rivka Lev — is she a young woman?"

"Pretty young, I guess." Was twenty-eight young? Not to Zoe, but to Mrs. Kaplan it might be.

"Well, she seems like a nice lady. She was very sweet on the phone."

Zoe nodded, and tried not to smile. Sweet was not exactly the word she would've expected Mrs. Kaplan to use about Rivka, but maybe Rivka could be a completely different person when she felt like it.

For a while they passed a joint back and forth without saying much, while Zoe drove. "What was it like, Nao?" Zoe finally asked.

Naomi blew out a huge lungful of smoke that she'd been holding in. "It wasn't really intense or anything. It was just like, you know, a pretty normal conversation. He's not a bad guy, but he does have these funny ears —"

"Did he take notes on what you said?"

"No, he just listened, and asked some questions." Maybe he wrote it all down as soon as Naomi was gone.

"And we made this contract," Naomi said, so quietly that Zoe almost didn't hear.

"Huh? A contract?"

"Yeah, the contract is, if I'm planning to commit suicide, I'm supposed to call him first." There was an edge of mockery in Naomi's voice, but she didn't sound really annoyed or anything.

Zoe didn't know about this contract: Would that really be enough to stop someone from killing herself? It seemed like there should be something more the shrink could do, but she couldn't think what it might be.

"What else did you talk about?" Zoe asked.

"Oh, we talked about my family, and about school." After a moment she added, "We talked about you."

They were stopped at a red light, and Zoe glanced over at her. "Yeah?"

Naomi turned her head and looked out the window. "I just told him that you're my best friend and I love you."

Zoe, too, looked straight ahead so that Naomi wouldn't see her eyes, which had tears in them. She didn't want any more sadness between them and she knew Naomi didn't, either.

Craig and Irene's boat was tied up at the very end of the dock. They walked carefully; about a quarter-inch of snow had fallen earlier that evening, enough to make the surface of the long wooden dock slick. The black water of Long Island Sound was all around them, and the lights of buildings — warehouses, a few crumbling old apartment houses — circled the bay. Zoe was surprised at how nice the little houseboat looked, rocking slightly in its mooring. Even in the dark you could see the shiny new paint. At the front of the cabin was a stained-glass window with a design like a mandala, glowing red and purple and yellow from the lights on inside. A stovepipe stuck up through the roof of the cabin, and smoke was coming out of it. Naomi leaned over the railing and tapped on the little door.

"Hey, Nao. Hi, Zoe, I haven't seen you in a long time," Craig said. He looked pretty much the same as he had in high school, except his blond hair was grown out past his shoulders. Irene came up behind him and said, "Hi, hi, come in." They were both very thin, and wore faded jeans and bulky sweaters.

"Welcome to our humble home," Irene said as Zoe and Naomi climbed onto the boat.

"Gee, if I knew you were coming, I would've gone out there and swept the snow off the dock," Craig said. "It gets pretty slippery."

Irene told Naomi and Zoe to sit down on the couch in front of the woodstove. "Just watch out," she said. "You sit down in that couch and you'll never want to get up again."

The couch, covered in red crushed velour like something in an old movie, was comfortable. Irene said they'd gotten it at the Sally Ann. She and Craig sat down on two old chairs that were placed across from the couch, on the other side of a low trunk covered with India-print cloth. Irene smiled at

Zoe, and Zoe thought how pretty she looked, with her small, pale face and long, straight blond hair. She was one of those girls who always looked perfect.

"Did you notice that little kerosene lamp on the wall?" Naomi was saying to Zoe. "It's made especially for boats, so it can't tip over."

"Yeah, that's neat," Zoe said.

"I bought it off a guy down at the other marina," Craig said. He crossed one leg over the other and pulled up his sock with a forceful, almost irritated tug.

"Yeah, Craig's always scavenging," Irene said. "He's good at finding things." Zoe noticed that she looked around the cabin quickly, nervously, as if trying to decide what to point out next. There were posters on the walls — one of a trail through a forest of white birch trees and one a blowup of a Grateful Dead album cover. There was a tiny kitchen with jars of different teas or herbs on the counter, and in the back, a bed.

"Can we light a candle?" Naomi said. She'd taken another joint out of her shirt pocket. "That'd make this the perfect atmosphere."

Irene glanced at the joint. "Oh, yeah, sure." Almost impatiently, she lit all five of the candles — some tall and multicolored, some short and coated with sand — that sat on the trunk table. She also lit some incense and put the glowing cone in a brass incense burner. Craig turned down the kerosene lights.

"Nice," Zoe said. Somehow, though, the silence was awkward, and she wondered if they'd stopped in at a bad time.

"Yeah, well," Irene said. "Actually we just got some smack. Do you want some?"

Zoe felt her eyes widen in the half-darkness. She looked

back and forth between Craig and Irene, who had both gotten out of their chairs. Craig pulled up his jeans, which kept
slipping down over his hips. Zoe said, "No thanks," and then
they all looked at Naomi. It occurred to Zoe that she might
not say no, so she stared hard at her until she did.

"Nah, that's OK," Naomi said. "Save it for yourselves."

"We'll be back in a minute," Craig said. They watched as
he and Irene went to the back of the boat where the bed was
and opened a little cabinet on the wall. The two of them sat
together on the bed, and Zoe saw Craig holding the needle
delicately with both hands and Irene pushing the bulky
sweater up on her arm so her skin caught the yellow light
from all the candles. Then Zoe stopped watching because it
grossed her out. She looked at Naomi, who was watching
Craig and Irene almost without blinking. Zoe felt like she'd
arrived at some kind of border: She could see into this country, but she would never go there. What Craig and Irene were
doing, shooting up heroin, was definitely not recreational.
She'd never been so close to something so dangerous.

Zoe tapped Naomi's hand, which held the unlit joint. She'd
been so busy watching Craig and Irene, she'd forgotten about
it. "Mind if I light this?"

"No, go ahead." Naomi handed it to her. She settled back
into the couch and looked at Zoe. "They're both addicted
now," she whispered.

"Did you know?" Zoe whispered back.

Naomi nodded. "She told me in the record store."

Zoe handed her the joint. "You haven't ever tried it, have
you?"

"No." She grinned at Zoe. "It was generous of them to offer,
though."

"Oh, fuck," Zoe said.

Naomi laughed at her. She was still laughing when Craig and Irene came back. "Hey, that's pretty funny," Craig said, but he couldn't have heard what they were saying.

"I'm going to put on that new Joni Mitchell if I can find it," Irene said, flipping through records in a melon crate. Every once in a while she stopped to look at one of the records, turning it over, reading the cover, then putting it back. She didn't seem nervous anymore, and she looked like she was enjoying the anticipation of the music almost as much as she'd enjoy the record once it was on.

Craig was happy now, too. He was telling Naomi about all the different people who'd fixed up old boats to live in at this marina. It was like a family, he said. In the boat next to them was a guy who'd recently gotten out of jail and spent most of the day practicing his bongo drums. Then there were a few hippie types, and an old couple who'd had their boat moored for fifteen years in this same spot. A lot of the people were on welfare like Craig and Irene, and everyone sort of watched out for everyone else.

Irene put Joni Mitchell on the turntable, singing about a child growing up through the seasons of life. Then she told a story about the first time her brother Danny came to visit wearing a suit and tie. The people living at the marina thought he was a cop or a narc. They refused to tell him which boat was theirs.

Everyone laughed. "That's great," Zoe said. "School is full of narcs now. All these kids who've been busted are working for the cops. You know, 'we'll forget all about your record if you just do us this little favor.' You two are lucky."

"Yeah, we're really well protected here," said Craig.

Irene was slumped down in her chair. Craig threw one leg over the arm of his chair and settled further into the cushions. He yawned. Then they closed their eyes and rested their blond heads. There was a little smile on Irene's face, and Craig looked like he was watching something very interesting behind his eyelids. They looked almost angelic. Maybe it's not such a terrible thing, Zoe thought; they seemed happy enough. She leaned back in the couch and looked at Nao. "They're nodded out," she said. "I think they're gone for the evening."

Naomi smiled. "She said it makes you feel perfectly contented, like you have everything you could possibly want."

"Wow," Zoe said.

She and Naomi sat in silence for a long time. The record had ended, and no one bothered to turn it over, so the only sound was the water gently hitting the sides of the boat, and a faint traffic noise farther away. Zoe kept looking at Craig and Irene and wondering what it felt like; she realized that she herself was very high. The more she looked at them, though, the less angelic they seemed. Craig's hand dangled over the side of the chair, and his fingers were long and bony-looking; Irene's mouth looked small and somehow pinched the longer Zoe studied her face. Actually, she thought, it's like Craig and Irene aren't even here anymore, it's like they're further away than just asleep.

She looked at Naomi, who was still watching them, completely fascinated.

It's a death trip, Zoe thought suddenly. This is a death trip. She was becoming frightened.

They're alive, she told herself. They're just sleeping.

But they weren't asleep. And when they came back from

wherever they'd gone, they'd be edgy again, nervous, like when she and Nao first got here. The inside of this boat, which had seemed so welcoming, now seemed sinister. She wanted to leave, so she looked at Naomi.

Who was still watching.

Naomi, Zoe thought. She was high enough to forget to say it out loud, but Naomi looked at her as if she'd heard.

It looks nice, Naomi said, only she too forgot to say it out loud.

But Zoe heard. *No,* she told Naomi silently. *No. It's not.*

This is what I want, Naomi's round blue eyes were saying. *To be sleeping. Or dead. It looks beautiful.*

No. You can't. Come back, she said — as if Naomi had gone away somewhere. Zoe tried to pull her with her eyes, as if by staring hard enough, she could yank Naomi away from her fascination with this death trip.

Neither of them looked away from the other's face. *No — yes — no — yes.*

I'm probably going crazy, Zoe thought as her head cleared for a moment. I should stop getting stoned all the time. Naomi looked away from her then, back to Irene and Craig.

The boat seemed to rock very gently. Outside all around them was the dark water, the dark winter night. From on shore came a clattering sound and then a loud yell. Zoe got up and looked out the window to see what it was, but none of the other three paid any attention. She thought maybe she was the only one who'd heard it.

Chapter Seven

When he wasn't selling hardware, Grandpa Sol had loved to fish. The biggest one he ever caught was a blue, green and yellow sailfish, off the coast of Key West. It still hung on the living room wall in Grandma Esther's apartment. Zoe thought it was funny the way her father was sitting on the couch with his own father's lacquered fish leaping in an arc over his head. Her father had tried to learn to fish, but it was one failure after the next: eels, huge fish that got away, the bottoms of other people's boats. Parents and children were so different; if you scrambled everyone up in the world, you'd never know who belonged to whom.

Zoe was telling her father about Danielle. "She makes you feel like a lazy slob. She's always drawing or making things — it's like she's afraid to stop."

"She'll probably end up being an artist." He leaned back on the couch and put his feet up on the Sunday *New York Times*.

"Yeah, but she doesn't talk about being an artist. She talks about how something might happen to keep her from becoming one."

"Hm," her father said.

Zoe put her own feet up next to her father's on the stack of newspapers. From the kitchen came the clattering of pots and pans — her mother and Melanie were helping Grandma Esther, who was not much of a cook. Just this year she'd finally learned how to make decent vegetables because they'd come out with these frozen ones in plastic packages that you just dropped into boiling water, package and all.

"What does Danielle think is going to happen?" her father asked.

"I don't know. She doesn't like to talk about — anything negative."

Her father nodded now as if it all made sense. "Well, Danielle is the product of historical forces. Look what happened to her parents when they were young."

"I know," she said. "But that's her parents. Danielle was born right here, she's had a nice life — easier than most kids I know."

Her father sat up on the couch now, turning the watch around on his hairy wrist. "I think that for Danielle, it's just as if the death camp happened to her, too. On some level she doesn't make a distinction between her parents' experience and her own." He looked pleased with himself.

"Uh-huh," Zoe murmured. "But what do you think I can do about it?"

Her father looked surprised. "There's nothing you can do, other than accept her the way she is. You can't alter the facts of history," he said forcefully, as if, being a history teacher, he owned these facts.

"There has to be something," Zoe argued. Her father was always so pessimistic. "I mean, how can she just go around ignoring everything that's really serious —" The minute she said this, she knew she'd gone too far.

"What exactly is she ignoring?" her father asked, but before she could find an answer, the doorbell buzzed, and he got up to let in her cousins. Relieved, she knew he'd forget to ask her again later. That was the way her father was.

Zoe liked her cousins Marvin and Sylvia; they were the same age as her parents, but they seemed younger. They still talked in loud Brooklyn accents because they'd never left Flatbush. When Zoe was a kid, Marvin had a trick of making it look like his middle finger was cut in half and the top was sliding off. Whenever Zoe saw him, even now, she'd say, Hi, Marvin, and then hold up her hands, doing the finger trick. It still made everyone laugh.

"So you had a pretty good time, I guess," Zoe's mother was saying to Joel, Marvin and Sylvia's son, as she passed him a basket of rye bread. Joel was a small guy, but very muscular now, and he had thick curly hair pulled back into a ponytail. His brother, Larry, was away at law school, so all the attention was on him.

"He had a wonderful time," Sylvia said before Joel could answer — but her tone seemed to be saying, If you can believe it.

"Yeah, I did. It was great," Joel said. Last summer, Joel had ridden his bicycle cross-country, which most of the relatives thought was dangerous and unnecessary, like going to Israel. Then, as if that wasn't enough, when September rolled around he'd decided not to go back to college, and instead got a job as a carpenter in Lake Tahoe. Now that he was back, Zoe knew, all the adults would immediately be asking him what he planned to do next.

Marvin poured cream soda into his glass, and then into Sylvia's. "I envy him," he said. "I think I may quit my job and take a bicycle trip, too."

Sylvia gave him a look. "You need that like a hole in the head."

Zoe snickered.

Sylvia reached around behind the chairs and grabbed a handful of Zoe's hair, tugging it gently. "What're you sniggling about? Look at you, with this mop." Sylvia was a hairdresser and always wanted to cut Zoe's hair, particularly after she'd been drinking; Zoe knew better than to let her.

"So what's next on the agenda?" Zoe's mother asked Joel.

"I'm not sure," he said. "I think I might work around here for a while and then maybe head back to Lake Tahoe."

"He had to come back to see his girlfriend," Sylvia stage-whispered behind her hand.

Just another year and a half, Zoe thought, and she'd be able to do whatever she wanted, too. "Your life sounds great," she told Joel.

"Oh, to be young and free," Marvin said. You could tell he didn't mind what Joel was doing as much as Sylvia did.

Zoe took her plate into the kitchen for more quiche. Everyone else was eating brisket. Grandma Esther would not allow the quiche on the table, only on Zoe's plate; for her that made the meal kosher enough.

It was an old apartment on the West Side, and before you got to the kitchen, you went through a narrow pantry with high cabinets painted a shiny light blue. Zoe stood in the kitchen for a moment, looking out the back window to the rooftops and smokestacks. In the summer, people would put plants and lounge chairs out on the roofs, but now they were deserted. She thought of Rivka walking around New York with her head tilted back, marveling at the skyscrapers.

When Zoe came back to the dining room, they were having

a big discussion about whether life was better out west, in California, and Joel was starting to look uncomfortable.

"Well, I ran away to the East," Grandma Esther reminded them. "So now the family's moving in the other direction." She looked calm and pretty today in her sleeveless navy blue dress.

"Did you really run away, Grandma?" Melanie asked. "I mean, did you have to, like, pack your suitcase and sneak out?"

"Yes, dear," Grandma Esther said to Melanie. Then she quickly changed the subject. "There's lots more brisket, everyone."

Nobody said anything else about it. Zoe hadn't known she'd actually had to sneak away from that stepmother. She knew that Grandma Esther's older sister had gotten married and moved to New York the year before, and had sent the train fare. Grandma Esther was sixteen then — Zoe's age — and she'd traveled all the way from Chicago to New York by herself. It was funny how Zoe's parents admired the things Grandma Esther had done, but they'd be furious if she ever did them.

Zoe looked at her grandmother now, an old woman eating a slice of rye bread and talking to her father about mystery novels. She thought again of what her father had said about there being no difference between Danielle's life and her parents'. If what he said was true, if history passed from one generation to the next, then it was just as if Zoe herself had run away at sixteen, eloped at seventeen, and decided to run the hardware business alone after her husband's death. It was just as if she herself had left Minsk when she was fifteen, alone, and just as if she'd brought up five kids in a

169

tiny apartment. It was just as if she'd wanted to run away and join the Beats, and just as if she'd had her consciousness raised. It was in her to do all of these things, but it was more than that: She had done them.

That night Zoe lay in bed and couldn't sleep. She turned over and over, and felt the muscles in her legs tighten as if she'd been running. In her mind was her father's voice saying *there's nothing you can do.* Oh sure, she could tell the adults about Naomi so they'd send her to a nice shrink with funny ears, but *you can't alter the facts of history.* Her father would see Nao's threats of suicide as serious beyond words, almost predictive. It was as if Naomi herself had gotten married at sixteen, and she and her husband had thrown a lot of glass at each other; then he'd left her with three kids and no money. This explained why she thought it might be nice to be a heroin addict, or dead, and why she might be unstoppable.

But they had to be more in control of their destinies than this; she could not accept her father's reasoning. Sitting up, she punched the pillow several times, then lay back, exhausted. She pictured Rivka in the sun on her living room floor. Don't you think we can *do* something? Zoe asked. Rivka thought so. But you're not afraid? No, Rivka would say, in that sarcastic, defiant way of hers, Why should I be afraid? *There will be something. That's just the way it happens in life.* You could hear the sadness in those words, but also the absence of resignation, the anger. Sitting with her in the rectangle of sun on the floor, you could lean against her, and she might kiss you, and you would touch her breasts —

Zoe thought: What am I thinking?

But her mind wouldn't stop. She could see the way the

sun fell across them in strange warm patterns. Everything happened excruciatingly slowly; it was almost like an LSD trip, Rivka's hands leaving trails of light on Zoe's skin. Zoe reached under her flannel nightgown and pressed her fingers into the spot that sent sharp pleasure through her body and mind. It made her want to scream something at Rivka — she didn't know what.

Walking to school against the cold, early-morning wind, Zoe wished she could just empty out her mind and start over. She realized she shouldn't think about Rivka so much. So all through that day, she tried not to think about her — even though just yesterday she'd asked Rivka if she could come see her, and Rivka had said, Sure, come over tomorrow afternoon.

After school, though, she hung around outside, smoking cigarettes with some kids from her homeroom; then they all went downtown to the Acropolis. Sitting there in the booth, listening to two guys talking about the Rolling Stones, she pretended she wasn't going to Rivka's. She wasn't one of Rivka's real friends, the kind who came over for dinner with their husbands and kids. Rivka would probably be relieved if she just left her alone, Zoe thought. But she kept glancing at the clock above the milkshake machine, and when it was three-thirty, she said she had to go meet someone. She put a dollar on the table and left before anyone could ask who. Hurrying up the street, she got nervous; Rivka would've expected her an hour ago, and she had to take the kids to arts and crafts class at the Nature Museum by four. Zoe was supposed to come along. She stuck out her thumb, and luckily got picked up by two senior girls she vaguely knew, who dropped her off just a little ways from Rivka's. Once the car disappeared, she ran, carrying her backpack full of books. She was sweating by the time she got there.

Rivka and the boys were just walking out the door. Eli saw her coming from the porch and yelled, "There she is!"

"Hi, Zoe." Rivka was kneeling at the top of the steps, adjusting the buckle on Eitan's boot. "Hold your foot," she said, and he made a face, which she didn't see. Zoe saw three gray hairs on the top of Rivka's head.

"I thought you were not coming," she said to Zoe.

"I almost completely forgot," Zoe lied. "I was sitting in the Acropolis Diner and then all of a sudden I looked at the clock —"

"But I knew you were thinking about me. It felt like something was not good with you," Rivka said.

In answer, Zoe sent Rivka a silent, fierce ESP message: *I love you, but it's too much.* Rivka went on buckling Eitan's other boot.

Zoe noticed a piece of paper taped to the front door.

Zoe shalom,
   Sorry we couldn't wait longer for you. I hope everything is OK, please to call us.
   See you later, Rivka

Her handwriting in English was very strange; the letters were uneven and almost childlike. Zoe peeled the note off the door, folded it and put it in her pocket.

"Where's your car?" Eitan asked.

"I don't have it today," Zoe said. "I got a ride instead."

"You got a ride?" Rivka said.

"Yeah." Zoe held out her fist, thumb up in the air.

The boys copied her instantly.

Rivka was smirking. "In Israel that will mean the 'f' word," she said, reaching out and covering Zoe's hand with her own. Zoe laughed and, looking at their two hands together, she felt like she received an ESP reply: *It's not too much. It's OK,* Rivka told her silently.

While the kids were at their class, Zoe and Rivka walked through the permanent exhibits: dioramas of native Indian villages, cases full of stuffed porcupines and squirrels and a big screen where you pressed a button and saw a blue wave rise, crest, and fall in slow motion toward the beach that had arrows pointing to its eroded areas. Finally they came to the dark room in the center, where the geology exhibit was. Gems and geodes were cupped in black velvet walls, and in the middle of the room was a large stump from the petrified forest in Arizona. The top of the stump had been sliced flat and polished, and it was lit from above by two spotlights. You could find nearly every color in it — purples and blues, orange, green — all spreading into circles like a tie-dye pattern done in stone.

"Beautiful," said Rivka.

"It's really psychedelic," Zoe said. She stood next to Rivka, both of them looking down at the petrified log. It had always been Zoe's favorite thing in the museum.

"Look at this part." Rivka leaned over and traced, with one finger, an orange squiggle that flowed into blue, like colored water. Zoe leaned over, too, and touched the same part of the stone with her own finger. It felt cool and smooth; at that moment, she became very aware of her own body, the shape of it, the position it assumed in space.

173

"I would like to go there, to see that forest," Rivka said.

"Oh, I would, too," said Zoe.

The kids had made wobbly clay pots, which were all lined up on the table for the mothers to admire.

"— with coils," Eli said. "You make a long, long coil, like a snake, and wind it all around —"

"They are wonderful," Rivka said.

"We're going to leave them here and then paint them!" Eitan said.

"That will be really great," Rivka said enthusiastically. Zoe wondered if she ever got tired of being a mother.

Before leaving they made a quick visit to the animals: rabbits in their cages, snakes sleeping under bright hot lights and Peter the Parrot, who refused to speak and looked mean as hell, staring at them from red-rimmed eyes. What the kids seemed to like best was the big open pool where the turtles lived.

"I like that little one with the yellow spots," Eitan said.

"I like that great big one with the pointy tail," Eli said, leaning over the edge with his hand stretched out toward it.

"That's the snapping turtle," Zoe said.

"Could it bite your hand off?"

"I don't know. But it could make you sorry if you touched it."

"I really wish I had a turtle."

"No way," said Rivka. "Can you see him crawling around the house, getting into your bed with you?" Rivka put her hands on his shoulders and drew him gently back from the edge of the pool.

"Nicky DeTullio, who's in the fourth grade," Eli said, "has

a frog that he caught in a hedge. If we find a frog, can we have it?"

"Sure, if you can catch it," said Rivka.

"Did you ever catch a wild animal, Ima?" asked Eitan.

For a few moments Rivka looked lost in thought, with a sad half-smile on her face. Then she said, "One time our dog caught a rabbit. He was a big dog, and when we were hiking, he used to run in the hills. One day we heard a squeak sound coming from inside his mouth. It was like *squeak, squeak, squeak.* So Yehuda, my brother, made the dog to open his mouth, and on his tongue was a little baby rabbit that was just born. Usually he liked to eat rabbits, but this one he didn't hurt—the rabbit was still alive." Rivka had tears in her eyes, but the kids didn't seem to notice.

"Wow. Did you get to keep it?" asked Eitan.

"Just for a little while," she said. "Then he grew bigger, and one day we looked in his cage, and he wasn't there. He ran away."

Zoe wished she could comfort Rivka, put her arm around her, but she was too shy. She realized this was the first time she'd heard Rivka say her brother's name. Yehuda. Now Zoe knew three things about Yehuda: He'd been killed in the 1967 war in Jerusalem, he was artistic and he once found a baby rabbit, miraculously alive, inside the mouth of his dog.

The reason Naomi kept leaning forward while she talked to people, her hair hiding her face, was that she had a dark bruise slanting across her cheek, right under her left eye. On the way to Lynn's party, Zoe asked how she'd gotten that bruise. Nao said she'd gone over to Tad's apartment yesterday afternoon and told him he was an asshole for letting Diane stay there for a week and totally ignoring Naomi the whole time. At first Tad said he was really sorry and asked her to forgive him. He said Jesus knows he was just trying to keep on good terms with his wife because of the kids. But Naomi knew better; she kept telling him he was a fucking asshole for doing that and lying about it afterwards. Tad said she was just a kid and didn't understand anything about adult responsibility. She kept yelling at him and crying, and that's when he hit her in the face. She punched him back and then ran down the spiral staircase; from the bottom she yelled up that she was never coming to see him again. He said, Good. He said she was a baby and he didn't know why he'd wasted his time with her. So she left, and when her mother got home from work, Naomi said she'd gotten hit in the face with a basketball during gym class.

Zoe was appalled. "You really shouldn't go back there, Nao," she said. "He *is* an asshole."

"Yeah, I know I shouldn't go back," Naomi said, "but I can't help it, I probably will. Unless I can find some way not to," she added in a strange low voice.

"Don't go back," Zoe said, annoyed. She made a fist and punched the door of the Datsun; there was something about Nao's story that made her want to hit someone herself. "Just don't." Then she remembered that yesterday was Friday. "Hey, weren't you supposed to be at the shrink then, anyhow?"

Naomi sighed. "Yeah." She drawled out the word regretfully. "I didn't go, though."

"Why not?"

"I was still fighting with Tad when it was time to go." Naomi drove in silence for a while, as if she'd explained everything.

Zoe tried not to feel angry. "Won't your mom find out?"

"Yeah, she knows I didn't go. But I told her I was lying down at home because of my eye."

Naomi had been going to the shrink for several weeks now, every Wednesday and Friday, and during that whole time she hadn't joked even once to Zoe about suicide. Zoe had thought maybe Naomi was starting to get her shit together — until now. Without saying anything, Zoe punched the door of the Datsun again, hard enough to hurt her knuckles.

Sugar Magnolia, blossoms blooming, heads all empty and I don't care —
Saw my baby down by the river, knew she'd have to come up soon for air —

"You like the Dead?" this guy — his name was Tim or Tom — was asking her. Someone Lynn knew from public school. They were standing right near the speaker, so he was almost shouting.

"Yeah," Zoe said. "I saw them in New York last summer. It was a really good show —"

"Yeah!" he said. "I know, I was there, too." He was wearing a black Skull and Roses T-shirt; he seemed like a typical Deadhead.

She didn't say that "Sugar Magnolia" reminded her of Ophelia floating in the river, flower petals all around her. This guy might think that was disrespectful to the Dead or something. She could tell he'd have all their albums at home and probably a big collection of traded tapes, too. Had he said Tim or Tom? He was sort of cute: dark, wavy hair and a narrow, intelligent face. His eyes were a light amber color and slitty from smoking pot all the time, but they were still alert, aware.

177

They sat on the couch together, drinking beer and smoking cigarettes. He was half-turned toward her, but she slouched against the armrest, watching people on the other side of the room. Danielle and Naomi were over there, laughing and talking, but you couldn't hear anything over the music. When Naomi turned her head at a particular angle, the bruise on her cheek seemed to spread out and darken.

"Hey," Tom was saying — she'd decided it must be Tom. "Is that for a political prisoner or something?" He was looking at the heavy plated star that hung above her breasts.

"Yeah," she said, blowing out a stream of smoke.

"Yeah, that's cool," he said. His voice was low and smooth, almost without inflection.

She looked back across the room because she didn't feel like explaining anything about refuseniks. The suffering of Soviet Jews seemed very far away. What had she been thinking about all these months? Just the people in her own life. Face it, she thought, you've been thinking about Rivka Lev. She realized that the part of her mind that thought about Rivka all the time was alive and buzzing, and the parts that thought about other things were tired and disorganized, as if thinking about Rivka had drained all the energy from the rest of her brain.

"You've got a lot on your mind," Tom said.

"Huh?" His slitty amber eyes met hers. She felt uneasy, as if he could read her thoughts.

"Your mind," he said. "A lot on it." He was smirking. She decided he was not as harmless as he'd seemed at first.

"Not really," she said. "Just listening to the music. Spacing out."

"Yeah, you sure are spaced out," he said, and laughed a

little. She was put off by his laugh and attracted at the same time. "Are you in love?" he asked.

She gave him a Rivka Lev sarcastic smile. "No."

Then his smile became almost genuine. "You act like it."

"Well, I'm not." She wasn't used to drinking, and on top of being stoned it was very strange. Nothing in the room looked solid anymore, and for a minute she forgot what they were talking about.

"That's all right," he said quietly. He put his hand over hers, which was resting on the couch. His hand felt cool and dry. "It's all right if you're not in love."

She looked critically at their hands lying on the couch together. She didn't want to hold hands with him, but she didn't move her hand away because she didn't feel like it belonged to her anymore. She gave Tom a mean look, narrowing her eyes as she drew on her cigarette.

"You're pretty tough, Zoe," he said. His fingers touched her wrist, lightly.

"Oh, yeah?" She had the feeling that he didn't really believe she was very tough, that he thought he could see right through her and that maybe, in fact, he could.

"Yeah. You almost look like you don't want anyone to mess with you or something."

She looked at his amber eyes again, and felt his fingers starting to caress her wrist. It was like being touched by the tentacles of some alien creature. The party was loud all around them, the speakers blaring.

Driving that train, high on cocaine,
Casey Jones you better, watch your speed,
Trouble ahead, trouble behind —

179

She couldn't fix her eyes on any one thing for very long; they slid around the room to the kitchen doorway, where she saw just the backs of Charlie Blum and Judy Teitelbaum, whose jeans fit her in a funny way, sort of bunched up in back under her belt.

"I just do whatever I want," she said coolly. She glanced at Tom again; his arms looked strong where they met the sleeves of the black T-shirt, and there were fine dark hairs on his skin. He wore soft-looking faded jeans that fit well. Her eyes went almost involuntarily to the place on his fly where the denim curved, darker in one spot. Then she looked away.

"Who's been giving you lessons in bitchiness?" he said softly. He leaned over and kissed her lightly on the lips.

He kissed her more when they were upstairs, lying on a couch in what seemed to be Lynn's parents' study — a room with books, a large wooden desk with a covered typewriter and a stack of papers held down by a plaster paperweight with a child's hand imprinted on it. His mouth felt large and wet, and it was good to be lying down. She didn't know how many beers she'd had, but she knew she was drunk by the way she felt so stupid, not at all the way she felt when she was just stoned. She was vaguely curious about what would hap-pen, since she'd never actually been lying down on a couch with a guy before. Walking up the stairs she'd been watching herself, interested in what she was going to do next, and she also had this strange feeling that Rivka was watching her, too, maybe even approving. Rivka had sex with Natan, of course. If Zoe fooled around with this guy, it would make them more the same —

But she'd stopped thinking. Now there were just tongues.

And his hands, more gentle than she'd expected. He unbuttoned her shirt and slid down, lying on top of her, kissing her breasts and at the same time moving his chest back and forth across her crotch. It felt amazingly good. It was so rare for anyone to touch her, even to put an arm around her, and now this. She heard herself breathing and looked down at him. He looked up through his slitty eyes with her nipple between his teeth, almost as if he were laughing at her. Then he caressed her crotch through her jeans. She leaned her head back and closed her eyes, feeling his hand moving back and forth against her. I don't even like him, she thought, and then she came, the quick, almost painful pleasure pulsing out from the center of her body. But she didn't yell or say anything, the way she wanted to when she imagined feeling this with Rivka. She was perfectly silent; she was alone in a whirling dark space.

When they walked down the stairs, Tom tried to put his arm around her shoulders but she shrugged it off. They had nothing to say to each other anymore; it was past midnight, and she wanted to get out of there.

"Do you want a ride home?" he asked.

"No," she said. "I'm going with Naomi."

"Oh. OK." He looked away from her and lit a cigarette. There were fewer people here now, and Zoe felt like everyone was watching her and knew what she'd been doing. Oh, shut up, she thought. You're paranoid.

He looked at her again. "Maybe I'll call you sometime?" he said.

"Maybe," she muttered. Then she said "See you" and walked across the room to where Naomi was sitting. It didn't occur to her until they'd put on their coats and were out the door that her answer to Tom's question hadn't made any sense. She hoped he wouldn't call; she wished he didn't exist. Walking down the stairs with him, she'd thought again of Rivka, and the feeling that Rivka would approve had not come back. Instead she'd thought of how much she loved Rivka, and it made her feel as if she'd been abandoned in some bleak and cold place where she was doomed to stay until she died.

The inside of the Datsun was freezing but Zoe didn't shiver; it felt good to have the cold air drain the heat and confusion from her body. After they'd been driving for a few minutes, the world began to solidify again. The passing black shapes of trees and houses were soothing, anonymous, and then the trees got thicker: Naomi was taking the back roads. Zoe slouched down in the seat and closed her eyes.

"Hey, I saw you hanging out with Tom," Naomi said.

"Yeah." Zoe didn't open her eyes.

"He's a nice guy. He was in my geometry class."

Zoe thought, Your idea of a nice guy, sure. You're full of shit. "I think he's pretty weird," she said. "And possibly mean." Somehow everything Naomi said tonight was irritating her.

"I don't know, I don't think he's a mean guy. He's smart. He knows a lot about the Dead." Naomi's voice was soft, rhythmical, almost as if she were talking to herself.

Zoe felt the car zooming along. She opened her eyes and saw that they were going very fast. The car swerved around a corner, picked up speed, then swerved again, the big dark trees flying past. The road gleamed with a thin coating of ice, and Naomi sat hunched over the steering wheel, holding on with both hands. Her blue eyes were bright, shining. "I was not impressed," Zoe said.

"Oh, I thought you liked him. I thought maybe you were upstairs making out with him."

Goddamn it, Zoe wished she'd slow down. It felt like the car was going to fly off the road. "I was. But I wish I hadn't," she said tightly.

"Oh, well," Nao said. "I always say, if it feels good at the time —" She started singing the Jefferson Airplane song: "'If you feel like love, make it, if you feel like flying — Break china laughing, baby —'" She hummed, driving faster and faster. She had the words all in the wrong order.

Forget it, Zoe told herself. Naomi was never going to understand anything. She wasn't even thinking about her friends; all she thought about were her own fucked-up philosophies of life and death. You couldn't say anything about sex, you couldn't say anything about love. How had they gotten so far apart?

A huge black tree loomed up out of the night, and they were heading straight for it.

"Naomi!" Zoe yelled. "Slow down!" She covered her face with her hands.

The car swerved with a sickening jerk, and they slid from one side of the road to the other, back and forth on the ice. "God!" Zoe said.

But they were still moving. Zoe parted her fingers and saw that they were driving down the middle of the road, straddling the yellow line. "Shit," she said, pressing her fingers into her skull. Her heart was beating so fast it felt like it might explode.

"Sorry," Nao said without looking at her. She got back into the right lane, and they drove in silence for a minute.

Sorry? Was that all she was going to say?

"Naomi, I can't stand it anymore," Zoe said. "Maybe you want to die, but other people want to go on living."

"I said I'm sorry." Naomi glanced at her, but her face was strangely unsympathetic, as if she had her mind on something else entirely. "I didn't do it on purpose —"

"You were going so fucking fast," Zoe said, her voice loud and shaky. "We almost crashed into that tree."

"I told you," Naomi said, "I didn't do it on purpose. There's some kind of evil thing controlling my life."

"That's bullshit! You're the one controlling it!"

"You don't know what I'm talking about." Naomi was still speaking quietly.

"Well, I know that I'm tired of worrying about you all the time," Zoe said. "I'm sick of trying to be a good friend. I feel like I don't get anything in return except maybe I'll get to go through the windshield of your car sometime —" She was surprised at how harsh her voice sounded. Naomi had slowed down and was driving in the exact center of the right lane. Her lips were tightly closed.

Zoe couldn't stop. "I'm scared of you," she said. "I can't do this anymore. Something bad is going to happen to me if I keep on hanging around with you."

Naomi pulled off onto the shoulder and parked. She kept both hands on the steering wheel, but turned her head to look at Zoe. "You don't want to hang around with me anymore?"

A car was coming in the other direction with its high beams on; the lights grew, spreading their jagged rays over the dirty windshield of the Datsun. The tension between them in the car was almost unbearable; it felt like something was going to explode, like the approaching lights would drive right through and smash them, ignite everything, swallow them in flames.

"Oh, God," Zoe said. "I don't know what I mean. I just feel like you're riding for something really bad, and I don't want to be there —" She looked at Naomi, at the purple bruise on her cheek. "I just don't understand it."

"What?"

"Like why you keep going back to see Tad, why you didn't go to the shrink. Just all of it. Tad is such a shit to do that to you —"

The jagged lights exploded in their windshield, and the other car passed with a whoosh. Then it was dark again, with just Naomi's headlights spilling two yellow patches on the bumpy pavement. They both relaxed a little, as if some kind of crisis had passed.

Naomi hugged the steering wheel, resting her forehead on her arms and speaking to the floor. "I know all that," she said. "But haven't you ever known that you didn't really belong in a certain place, but you keep going back there over and over again? Or — or like, there's a person you don't belong with, but you keep getting drawn back to see them?" Naomi's voice went on, as if she'd forgotten Zoe was listening. "It's really bad to be so involved with the wrong things and the wrong people. It's like the worst thing in the world. If you love someone who's the wrong person for you to love. And you don't even know why you should love them so much."

Zoe's eyes filled with tears.

"You've probably never felt like that," Naomi said, but she didn't seem angry. Her voice was soft and distant, as if she were talking about someone else's life instead of her own.

Finally Zoe said, "I'm sorry, Nao."

Naomi didn't answer.

"I have felt like that," Zoe said.

185

Naomi lifted her head from the steering wheel and looked at her.

So this was the truth: She and Nao *both* loved the wrong people. Zoe had always thought Naomi didn't feel love the way she did — how stupid that was! She hadn't realized that Nao might love Tad, maybe as much as she loved Rivka. It was all that talk about sex, about just doing what felt good. But sometimes Zoe did that, too — what about Tom? She and Naomi were still so much alike, but Zoe tried not to see it because it scared her.

Naomi was still looking at her. "You *have* felt like that?" she asked. She seemed interested.

Zoe had never told anyone how she felt about Rivka, though, and she didn't think she could tell Naomi, even now. "Well, yeah," she said reluctantly. Of course, there were differences. Rivka had looked like she wanted to throw something at Zoe that time Zoe called her a hate monger, but she never would. It was a lot safer than being with Tad. Rivka didn't want anything from Zoe other than this strange, teasing friendship, but what if the person you didn't belong with wanted to have sex with you? It would be even more impossible to stay away. Zoe couldn't really imagine Naomi's life — in Zoe's life, sexual desire and love sometimes seemed like America and Israel, two countries separated by oceans.

"Who?" Naomi said. Her blue eyes looked deep and very awake.

Zoe couldn't answer. Why was she so hung up on Rivka? Why? She was going to have to try harder not to be.

Naomi sighed. "Listen," she said, "I'm sorry you've had to put up with so much from me. You've been a good friend to me, and I don't blame you —"

"I'm still your friend," Zoe said. "Honestly, Nao, I still am. Let's just forget about tonight, OK? It's been a really terrible night."

Naomi didn't say anything.

"OK?" Zoe said anxiously.

"Yeah, OK." Naomi pulled away from the side of the road and drove on, slowly. Neither of them spoke again until they were in Zoe's driveway.

Zoe felt unbearably sad. She and Nao had hardly ever fought, and she was afraid it was going to take a long time for this to heal. For some reason Natan's attentive face flashed into her mind, as if he had heard all the shitty and non-reassuring things she'd just said to Naomi. Now that she'd made the wound, though, it was better not to keep pressing on it. "Will you call me?" she asked Nao. "Tomorrow night, maybe?"

"Yeah, OK," Naomi said.

"I'll see you," Zoe said. All her words sounded fake. She leaned over and hugged Naomi, who took her hands off the wheel and hugged her back. But even their hug was awkward; Zoe touched what she thought was Naomi's hair and then realized it was her own. They drew away from each other.

"I know who you mean," Naomi said.

"You do?" Zoe looked at her, one hand on the door handle.

Naomi moved slightly and her face caught the yellow light shining from the front porch. Her expression was so knowing, so old, that for a moment her face seemed like a stranger's, emerging from the dark where it had been watching Zoe, seeing everything. "Yeah, I know who you were talking about," Naomi said.

Zoe hoped Naomi wouldn't say Rivka's name. "I can't help it," she said. "But it's nothing, I'll get over it."

"You're really pretty innocent, aren't you?" Naomi grinned at her suddenly, looking like herself again.

"I don't know." Zoe had opened the door and gotten out of the car, but she was still leaning on it, looking in at Naomi. She was too tired and confused to ask Naomi what she meant; tomorrow night she'd ask her. "I've got to go," she said. "OK? I'll talk to you —"

"Yeah." Naomi stopped smiling and her face was the old and knowing stranger again. "It's all right," she said. "You're better off that way."

Zoe shut the door and watched Naomi back down the driveway. As she climbed the steps to the porch, she heard Nao's car zoom up the street, going fast.

When she lay down, first her bed and then the whole room spun in circles, faster and faster. She had to keep opening her eyes to make it stop. I'm never going to drink again, she thought. The bed kept spinning, but after a while she was too tired to open her eyes. She pictured herself and Naomi sitting in the car, behind Nao's windshield that was so smudged and streaked it was a matter of pride to her that she could still drive. Zoe's bed spun around like Nao's car on the black ice. Right before she fell asleep, she heard one of those horrible Gestapo sirens in the distance.

She was walking through a forest of thin white birch trees covered with snow. Thick flakes swirled among the bare branches of the trees. She walked on, following a path that was rapidly being covered. She was trying to catch up with someone, just a shadow way ahead of her on the path. But the snow came down heavily, piling up on her head, her arms, and obscuring the shadow-person, who finally disappeared between the trees. Everything was totally white.

Zoe tried to yell something, to run forward, but the snow was so heavy she couldn't move.

She woke up with the first really terrible hangover of her life; it felt like knives going sideways through her head. She looked at the clock: It was eight-thirty, and she could hear the phone ringing. Who was calling so early on a Sunday morning? She got out of bed and went to the door. She didn't open it, though; she just stood there waiting, feeling thirsty and sick.

Then footsteps in the hall. "Zoe?" Her mother's voice, her mother knocking painfully right near where Zoe's head was. Slowly Zoe opened the door, but only part way, as if protecting herself physically.

Her mother was standing there in her bathrobe, her hair curling in wild tufts around her face. Her skin was pale from sleep, and there was a strange pulling expression around her mouth, a look Zoe thought she might have seen a long time ago and then forgotten until now. "Honey, Naomi passed away last night. Her mother found her at the kitchen table. She'd been drinking, and she'd taken a lot of sleeping pills."

Zoe stared at her mother. The knives in her head went wild. She didn't cry, but she watched as tears gathered in the corners of her mother's brown eyes — so strange, the way they came from nowhere. *Passed away*. What a strange choice of words.

"Naomi's dead?" she said.

Her mother nodded. "Yes. She's —" She couldn't say the word. "Mrs. Kaplan said she'd been very depressed lately, and she was seeing a psychologist. Did you know that?"

Zoe nodded. "Yeah." Then she felt a big wave of fear: There was so much her mother didn't know.

Tears were sliding down her mother's cheeks now. That faintly familiar expression around her mouth was the beginning of grief, of her starting to cry as if she were a child, not caring how awful she looked. "I wish I had known," she said.

She put her arms around Zoe, but it was really Zoe who held *her*, arms around her mother's shoulders, as if Zoe were the mother and her mother were the kid.

Chapter Eight

There was a roaring around her head like she was flying in the wind. Her body did not exist: She *was* the wind. She was the air. She was nothing.

A crying wind pressed against the windows of her mother's old Plymouth, and Zoe rested her elbows on the steering wheel, covered her face with her hands and cried along with it. She felt totally sick. She hadn't eaten all day because of her hangover.

"It's not your fault," Danielle said, putting her arm around Zoe's shoulders. They were parked in Rivka's driveway, waiting for the Levs to get home so they could tell them Naomi was dead.

"Yes, it is."

"No, it's not," Danielle said.

Zoe took a deep, shuddering breath. "I had a fight with her on the way home from Lynn's. I made her think I didn't want to be her friend anymore."

She looked up and saw Danielle's light brown eyes staring at her, inches away. Zoe omitted the part about Tom, and just told her about Nao driving toward the tree and almost killing both of them. She also told Danielle what Nao had said about loving Tad.

"God, that's so sad," Danielle whispered. Without any warning she cried, too, her pretty face changing instantly into the child's face Zoe had seen on her mother that morning. Zoe turned and hugged her, feeling for the first time that it *was* wrong for Danielle to have to face any kind of sadness.

"I don't think she meant to die," Danielle said into Zoe's shoulder.

"I do," Zoe said grimly. The wind seemed to answer her; a long powerful gust came up outside the car, straining against its seams of metal and glass. Zoe looked up past Danielle's soft hair and saw Natan and Rivka bending down at the window to look in at them, their faces silent and wondering like people in a dream that seems to have no meaning.

Rivka's face didn't become a child's the way her mother's and Danielle's had; when she told her, her face just took on a cold, distant expressionlessness and stayed like that. Zoe and Danielle had a cup of tea at the kitchen table and told Natan what had happened. Rivka almost looked like she wasn't listening.

"It's like something that happens to other people," Zoe told Rivka the next morning. They'd been standing in Rivka's hallway for what felt like a long time. Neither of Zoe's parents had objected when she said she wasn't going to school, and her mother had even lent her the car. Driving through the early-morning rush hour traffic, she'd become aware of a new and vaguely unpleasant feeling of freedom.

Zoe kept glancing at Rivka, and Rivka was just shaking her head very slightly. She was wearing jeans and a sweatshirt, and her feet were bare, but she had on all her usual gold jewelry: her wedding ring, a ring with a diamond, three gold bracelets and the gold earrings shaped like shells. "I'm really sorry," she said finally. "Things like this always feel like they can't happen, and then they do."

Zoe felt sadness creeping up on her slowly and steadily, like carsickness, so she tried not to concentrate on it. She realized she'd been expecting Rivka to say something that would ward it off.

"I don't know what to say to you," Rivka said. There were tears in her eyes, and she touched Zoe's hair quickly, as if it were something she shouldn't do. Zoe wanted to stand very close to her; she wanted to put her arms around Rivka.

"I'll be right back, OK?" Rivka said.

"Yeah, sure." Zoe went into the living room and sat on the couch, and she heard Rivka going upstairs. Zoe was wearing her big green army-surplus sweater, but she still felt cold. Finally she put her hands up inside her sleeves, kicked off her shoes and curled up on the couch. She could barely keep her eyes open — she tried to stay awake, but her mind kept shutting down.

When Rivka came downstairs, Zoe opened her eyes again.

"It's OK, you can sleep," Rivka said. "I have to go out and do some things."

"OK," Zoe whispered. It seemed like she'd never felt so tired. Rivka took a red blanket off one of the chairs and put it over her. The touch of the blanket was light and comforting: It was the kind you get on airplanes, thin but warm. Zoe thought of flying in an airplane under her blanket, the roaring of the engines and the wind blocking out the world far below her, beneath a thick layer of clouds. She fell asleep.

♦ ♦ ♦

When she woke up, the house was very still and the sky outside the living room windows was a solid light gray. She lay on the couch, her mind empty, feeling the sense of dislocation she often had when she skipped school. Then she remembered Naomi. Oh God, how could she have done that? How could no one have stopped her? You stupid asshole, she thought, what a fucking waste. It seemed as if Naomi were going to step into the room at any minute, and Zoe wanted to tell her off. Then she'd tell off all the stupid adults who'd thought they had known what was good for Nao. She pictured herself and Naomi in the Datsun, pulled over by the side of the road on Saturday night, but she pushed it away. Don't think about that.

She rolled off the couch and went into the kitchen. It was only eleven o'clock, but it seemed like about two days had passed. She thought Rivka was still gone, but just to make sure she opened the door that led out to the garage and saw that the car wasn't there. It was cold, and she shut the door quickly.

Then she stood in the middle of the kitchen, wondering what to do. There was a package of Oreos on the counter; she ate three and drank a glass of milk. Then she wandered down the hallway, stopping to look at a painting of boats in a harbor, their masts and rigging overlapping each other, the water a deep gray-blue. The picture looked very New England, and it was reassuring to her that the Levs owned it.

She went upstairs and walked down the hall, stopping in the doorway of the kids' bedroom. Their beds were unmade and had Superman sheets on them. Open books, Magic Markers and Lego were strewn around the floor. Zoe walked over to the bookshelf: Yes, they had *Charlotte's*

Web and *The Twenty-One Balloons*. They also had some other books in Hebrew. She knelt in front of the shelf and tried to read one about the wise men of Chelm, skipping over the words she didn't know. The wise ones of this town, she knew, were really fools. When she finished the book and stood up, her foot came down hard on a sharp little piece of blue Lego. "Ow-ow-ow," she whispered, rubbing the bottom of her foot; it really hurt. She started to cry for her foot, but made herself stop.

A bit farther down the hall she stopped in the doorway of Rivka and Natan's bedroom. They had a low bed with a headboard stenciled with designs of leaves and vines. Their windows looked out onto the backyard: the lawn and picnic table covered with snow, the bare trees, a stone wall. On either side of the bed was a night table, and on each table a lamp and a pile of books in English and Hebrew. She didn't go into the room for a better look.

Next she explored the study: more books, piles of magazines and a desk with a lot of papers — on top was a letter in Hebrew on blue airmail stationery. She sat down in a chair near the bookshelves and pulled out something that looked like a photo album. It was: pictures of Natan and Rivka on the beach, looking younger than they did now; pictures of Eli and Eitan as babies, then playing on an apartment balcony with more apartments in the background. There were several pictures of a young man who looked a lot like Rivka, and Zoe realized after a moment that this was Yehuda. In the bottom left corner of one page was a small picture of Rivka, looking very young with her hair pulled back, wearing an army uniform.

"Holy shit," Zoe whispered. She peeled back the plastic

cover to get a better look. Rivka was standing in front of a wall with a gun on a strap over her shoulder and the funny little army hat on her head; she was smiling.

Zoe looked at the picture for a long time, thinking. Rivka looked young; she must have been eighteen or nineteen. After her two years in the army, she'd gone to university, and then she'd had the twins almost eight years ago. So how could Rivka be twenty-eight years old? No way. More like thirty-one or thirty-two, at least. What a liar!

Carefully she stuck the plastic cover down again, took one last look at the photograph, then shut the album. Why would Rivka lie about her age? She wasn't that old. Zoe could tease her about it: Don't trust anyone over thirty, Rivka. The thought made her smile. But then she started thinking, Why do people lie about their age, anyhow? She put the album back on the shelf exactly as she'd found it. The sad-carsickness was creeping up on her again. People lied about their age because they were afraid of getting old, of course. They were afraid of dying.

For a long time that afternoon Rivka looked through some books and wrote lesson plans at the kitchen table, and Zoe sat opposite her, thumbing through a pile of newspapers and magazines. She didn't read anything more than the head-lines and a few sentences. The thought of Naomi's funeral tomorrow was awful, but she didn't want to talk about it; that would make it worse. She watched as Rivka wrote quickly in her notebook, the same kind of notebook Zoe's father used for lesson plans, only Rivka wrote in Hebrew from right to left. She looked at Rivka's face, her expression of concentration. Zoe wanted to touch her. God, she really wanted to. She thought of the time Rivka had touched her shoulder very quickly at the door the first time she came here. And earlier today Rivka had touched her hair. Zoe usually didn't dare touch Rivka, and she sometimes felt that Rivka was being very careful around her, as if she were afraid of something. At any rate Rivka certainly didn't care about Zoe as much as Zoe cared about her. *You're a liar, too,* Zoe thought. Rivka looked up from her notebook, and they stared at each other for a moment.

"Hey, why're you guys just sitting here being so quiet?" Eitan asked.

Rivka glanced at Zoe, then looked back at Eitan, who was standing by her chair. She put her arm around him. "Remember we told you? Zoe's friend has died," she said.

Eitan looked down at the floor, then back up at his mother. Eli opened a grimy-looking manila folder and took out a drawing of a large green-and-orange dinosaur eating some little trees in front of a house. He put it on Zoe's knee. "You can have that," he said.

"Thanks," she said. "It's really nice. What kind of dinosaur is this?"

He stood close to her and traced the dinosaur with his finger. "It's a kind of dinosaur that I made up."

Zoe bent her head down over the drawing, close to Eli's head. His soft black hair touched her cheek. "Looks a little bit like a brontosaurus," she said.

"Yeah, its neck is a brontosaurus neck ... but its tail is a stegosaurus tail ..."

"Yeah ... right ..." She wanted him to go on talking. He was leaning against her now, telling her about the trees and the house, his body warm and relaxed next to hers. His hair smelled good. She put her arm around him and shut her eyes for a moment.

"Ima, do we know anyone who's dead?" Eitan asked.

There was silence for a moment. "You knew Yehuda. Your uncle. But you don't remember him because you were just a baby."

"Why is he dead?"

"Because he fell in the war, in Israel."

"Oh. I don't want to die."

"You won't," she said. "Not for a long time."

Zoe opened her eyes and looked up. Rivka was leaning her elbow on the table with her hand shading her eyes, fingers pressing into her temples.

When Natan got home, Rivka was already cooking dinner and Zoe was still hanging around the kitchen. She knew she should go home, but she didn't want to — it seemed so bleak, facing her parents at the dinner table. They'd known Naomi almost all her life, and they clearly wanted to know a lot of things Zoe didn't want to tell them.

Rivka put down the knife she was using to cut up vegetables and went out to the hallway where Natan was hanging up his coat. Zoe watched as he shut the closet door and put his arms around her. They kissed and then held each other, speaking softly in Hebrew. Zoe looked away. Oh fuck, she thought. She should have gone home sooner. They didn't really care about her; they didn't care about Naomi. People just cared about their own lives and wanted to be as separate as possible from everyone else. That's why Naomi was dead, because no one had cared enough to save her from herself.

She got up to go just as Rivka and Natan walked into the

kitchen. Natan came over and put his arm around Zoe. She stuck her hands in the pockets of her army pants and looked at the floor. Once again, his quietness made her feel she had to say something.

"Nobody really gives a shit," she said.

"That's not true, Zoe," said Natan, tightening his arm around her. "We did try to help, but it didn't work. You tried, too. You really did care a lot —"

She pulled away and looked at him. "I'm not a baby," she said. "I know what the truth is." She was suddenly furious; she wanted to break something or hit someone. "Everyone always blamed her for everything, and now they're going to be all sorry about it, but it's too late. They didn't give a shit about her when it could've done any good." She wasn't sure who, specifically, she was talking about, but she knew she was right.

Natan kept his dark, calm eyes fixed on her face. He was probably memorizing what she said for future reference, Zoe thought. God, it was annoying. Rivka was looking at her, too, frowning as if Zoe were saying something that made no sense. Then Rivka and Natan exchanged a look, like parents with an unruly child, making sure their reactions would be identical.

"You didn't try hard enough, either. You could've done a lot more," she told them, and went off to find her shoes.

Zoe sat between her mother and Melanie, holding a black prayer book on her lap and rubbing the soft corners of its pages. She tried to look only at the blond polished wood of the seats in front of them, but every once in a while her eyes moved, against her will, to the white coffin at the front of the sanctuary. It rested on a stand, and tall white candles stood at either end. The coffin was the only unfamiliar thing to her in the dim sanctuary, where all the seats were covered with dull green plush and the light filtered through stained-glass windows. Bronze plaques with the names of other dead people lined the walls, and some of them had their little memorial light bulbs on for the *yartzheit*.

She could only think about Naomi's body being in that coffin for a split second at a time, and then she had to look away, this time up at Rabbi Gleuck, the new young rabbi who'd replaced Rabbi Hersh.

"Naomi was well liked by her classmates and her teachers. She was a loving and responsible daughter ..." he was saying, looking out at the congregation.

Wrong, Zoe thought. She annoyed her teachers. She was irresponsible. You're not even talking about Naomi.

She stopped listening to the rabbi. Naomi would not have wanted her to listen; she would've laughed at the wisp of the rabbi's hair flying up off his head with static electricity. When they were younger and used to go to services more often, Zoe and Nao had often spent the whole time in wild silent giggles behind their prayer books, laughing at things like this rabbi's unstuck hair until their stomachs hurt and tears came out of their eyes. Zoe wondered if she'd ever be able to laugh like that again. She glanced at Melanie, who was staring straight ahead, her face very serious. Without looking at Zoe, Melanie took her hand and held it.

Then they were finishing the prayers, everyone was standing up. Zoe shivered; she hadn't eaten anything all day, and it was two o'clock in the afternoon. She felt like there was a sort of film in front of her eyes; through it she saw the white coffin and the Kaplans in the front row. She watched as six men came down the aisle — she recognized two of them as Naomi's uncles — and carried the coffin out the side door. It looked heavy, which was strange when you thought how light Naomi's body would have been for six men. They slid it into a hearse waiting by the door.

People were crying all around her, but Zoe didn't feel like crying. She looked at them: kids from Hebrew School and public school, people's parents and friends of the Kaplans. Naomi hadn't even liked some of these people. When she was alive, a lot of them had shaken their heads and said things like, She could be such a pretty girl. If only she didn't wear those awful clothes. If only she combed her hair. If only she didn't go around with such dirty bare feet. It began to run like a broken record through Zoe's head: *She could be such a pretty girl, pretty girl, such a pretty girl, she could be —*

There was a crush of people in the hallway afterwards; the temple floor was wet and streaked with mud. Zoe saw Adam, then Carol and Lynn and Susan. She saw Mr. Brown, Nao's guidance counselor. She saw Rivka. Then, coming around the corner to the coatroom, she ran right into Tad.

"Hi, Zoe," Tad said. He was wearing wrinkled corduroys and a sports jacket that looked too small for him. Around his neck was a large gold cross on a chain. She felt a rush of hatred for him, and turned away without saying anything, pushing her way into the coatroom. She pulled on her mother's old suede jacket and started making her way back through the crowd toward her mother and Melanie, who were talking to Danielle. When Zoe got there, Danielle hugged her. They hugged each other very tightly while Zoe fought the urge to just push Danielle away.

Zoe shivered, standing by Naomi's grave, looking at the white coffin suspended above the raw hole in the ground. The ropes holding the coffin were dark against the snow. Zoe felt like she'd never been so cold in her life. She looked around and saw that fewer people had gone on to the cemetery: Even Danielle hadn't come. This made Zoe angry with her all over again. Zoe crossed her arms tightly and heard a strange sound, almost like a moan, come from herself. It was very faint, and she hadn't intended to make it.

Finally they said the Mourner's *Kaddish*. After the final amen, Zoe looked up and saw that her mother was watching her closely. My mother knows nothing about my life, she thought. But she loves me. When the burial was over and they were walking down the hill to the car, Zoe linked her arm through her mother's — a gesture she hadn't made for a long time. Only once she glanced over her shoulder, back toward Naomi's grave. It was already out of sight, the fresh hole now hidden behind the little city of gravestones. She kept on walking.

On the stoop in front of the Kaplans' apartment was a pitcher of water and a bowl. Zoe held her hands over the bowl, and her mother poured water on them, then handed her a towel. Zoe poured water over her mother's hands, and Melanie's. What are we washing off? she thought. Death? Naomi? Yeah, everyone washed their hands of Naomi a long time ago.

It was horrible how alive everyone was inside the apartment, all of them talking and eating at the same time. She saw Mr. Kaplan standing by the table, holding a paper plate and eating a bagel with cream cheese and lox. How could you watch your daughter's coffin creaking down into the grave on those ropes and then come back here and eat a bagel? She didn't know. It was so weird to see him inside the Kaplans' apartment. Usually he just pulled up in his car and waited outside for Nao and her brothers to come out.

Over near the kitchen table she saw some kids from Hebrew School — Adam was there, and Jeff, Charlie, Judy, Carol. Adam was saying something she couldn't hear, and everyone else was smiling hesitantly. They all had paper plates of food, too, and plastic cups of soda. Zoe leaned against a wall, not knowing what to do; she watched her mother and Melanie put food on their plates. It was a death-day party. Naomi's relatives swarmed around — bald-headed men and ladies with loud New York accents — but Zoe didn't know half of them, even though she and Nao had memorized each other's family trees when they were kids. These people wouldn't have come to a birthday party for Naomi: Why should they come to her funeral? The heavy smell of perfume, the closeness of all these people, was making Zoe feel sick.

Then her mother was at her side again. "Aren't you going to eat anything, honey?" She was holding a paper plate with pickled herring and rye bread on it.

Zoe shrugged. "I don't know." She was hungry, but the thought of food made her feel like she might throw up.

Susan's mother came over to talk to her mother, and Zoe slipped away. She wandered through the crowd until she saw Rivka and Danielle talking in a corner of the room. She went over to them.

"It really doesn't matter," Rivka was saying.

What didn't matter? They stopped talking as soon as they saw her.

"Hi, Zoe," Danielle said. Rivka didn't say hello. They hadn't said good-bye to each other last night, either: After Zoe found her shoes, she'd just put on her coat and walked out the front door without going back into the kitchen. She hadn't been able to help it.

"You weren't at the cemetery, were you?" Zoe asked Danielle.

Danielle's face changed; she looked sad and embarrassed, and Zoe could tell that's what she and Rivka had been talking about. "No." She shook her head. "I just couldn't."

"Yeah," Zoe said, but her tone was unsympathetic. She tried not to look at Danielle's delicate face, at the freckles across her nose, the long eyelashes.

"I think I'll go in the kitchen for a while," Danielle said, and moved off toward the other kids from Hebrew School.

Rivka was frowning at Zoe again.

"Hey, I'm sorry about last night," Zoe said.

"You made us feel really bad," said Rivka.

Zoe didn't believe her; this sounded like the kind of thing your mother said to you when you were five years old. *You hurt our feelings when you hit your sister like that.*

Before Zoe could say anything, Adam's mother swooped down on them. She was a skinny woman in a blue dress, with an older and more heavily made-up face than most of the other mothers. "I'm so sorry, Zoe," she said. "Naomi was your best friend, wasn't she? This must be very difficult for you." She nodded her head at Zoe in a conspiratorial way, her sharp brown eyes not leaving Zoe's face.

Zoe shrugged and ignored the look. Mrs. Wolfe stood up

straighter and looked around as if she wasn't sure what to do next.

Then Zoe saw Mrs. Kaplan coming and wanted to get away, but it was too late. Mrs. Kaplan's face was incredibly white; she had makeup on but it looked somehow like it wasn't attached to her skin. Her eyes were red all the way around. "Oh, Zoe," she said. She put her arms around Zoe and hugged her very tightly. Zoe's arms hung at her sides; she didn't hug Mrs. Kaplan back. She wanted to feel sorry for her, but all she could feel was that this whole scene was grotesque.

When Mrs. Wolfe and Mrs. Kaplan had both moved on, Zoe turned and saw Rivka watching her from a little farther away, a Styrofoam cup in her hand and one arm crossed. She looked totally unapproachable. She and Zoe exchanged a look as if they were strangers. Zoe turned abruptly and went up the stairs. It was so twisted, all these people, some of them in their forties and fifties, gathering for the funeral of a sixteen-year-old girl. They couldn't possibly understand what it felt like to be sixteen and have your best friend dead, and the rest of life stretching out ahead of you: ruined. Because she knew she'd never be completely happy again; there would always be this loss of Naomi imprinted on her. It was disgusting the way they'd all thought Nao was so bad, so stupid about things, the way they'd gossiped about how she was on drugs and slept with guys. And now they were pretending they'd always loved her.

Shit.

Zoe walked down the upstairs hall. The door to Naomi's room was closed, thank God. She went into Michael and David's room and sat down on one of the beds piled with people's coats. The coats had a funny smell, a mixture of perfumes that was alien and intrusive. The rest of the room, though, was comforting: model airplanes hanging from the ceiling and a poster of Neil Armstrong walking on the moon. Two pairs of hockey skates, a goalie mask and two sticks. It was the world of things that were real. Zoe wished she had a brother so she could sit around in a room like this. Naomi was lucky to have had two brothers.

Naomi was.

After what seemed like a very long time, Rivka appeared in the doorway, as Zoe had known she would. "Hi," Zoe said. She was still sitting on the bed, looking through a copy of *Motorcycle Racer* magazine.

Rivka came in and looked around; then she leaned against the wall with her arms crossed. "Why do you act like this?" she said.

Zoe stared at her. "Like what?"

Rivka just stood there for a moment, looking pissed off and beautiful. She was wearing a black dress with a belt and deep pockets in front. The late afternoon light coming through the curtains was pale and sort of blue, and Rivka's dark hair, her skin and the dress were all blending together perfectly, as if she were in a painting. Zoe could hardly stand to look at her.

"You act like you hate everyone," Rivka said.

"I don't hate you. I said I was sorry."

"I mean all of these other people."

"I can't stand them," Zoe admitted.

"Why? You know, they feel guilty, too. They are wishing that they could have done something."

"They're full of shit," Zoe said. "They *could've* done something —"

"Zoe —" she said.

"I'm allowed to hate people, too, you know. You hate Arabs, I hate phony Jewish ladies. What's the difference?"

Zoe wished that Rivka would just come and sit down next to her on the bed and put her arms around her. She wanted Rivka to do this so badly that for a second she thought it was just about to happen, but then she blinked and Rivka was still standing against the wall.

"You're making it harder for the other people here," Rivka said. "Do you think only *you* are the one who feels anything?"

"Do you think you're the *only* one who feels anything," Zoe corrected her angrily. "Maybe one day you'll learn English." She didn't understand why Rivka was picking a fight with her; it didn't make sense.

Rivka's face became expressionless again. "I don't like you," she said, turning and walking out of the room.

"Fuck you," Zoe said, but she was already gone.

Do you think only you are the one who feels anything?

Zoe lay in bed that night watching the black light shining on her fire poster. The fire looked fierce, the colors deep; she'd never noticed before how some of the flames looked like they were about to leap off her closet door.

But I *don't* feel. Not what I should. I can't believe that was Naomi inside that white box. Under the ground now.

She did it on purpose. It wasn't an accident: She meant to die.

When her mother found her at the kitchen table, head resting on her arms, she might have thought she was sleeping. *Hey, Nao, why don't you get up and go to bed?*

She was suicidal, though. It was more important to her to die than to think of Zoe living on all alone afterwards. But

207

maybe she meant for someone to rush in at the last minute and save her. She'd been drinking that night, too; alcohol and sleeping pills were a deadly combination — but they all knew that. Had Nao just forgotten for a moment? She hadn't left any suicide notes.

It's your fault, her mind said. Nao thought she didn't have any friends left.

Zoe put one hand over her eyes and pressed her temples. It did still her thoughts for a moment, but when she took her hand away, she remembered, instantly: Rivka standing there in her black dress. *I don't like you.*

I don't. Like you.

"*You* should talk about feelings," Zoe whispered. "You act like you don't have any. You probably need Natan to explain every feeling to you." But maybe she did talk about her feelings in code, like Zoe's father. When she said all the other people felt guilty and wished they could have done something, she meant herself. And her feelings about Zoe were pretty clear: Get out.

Of my life.

So now they'd both be gone: one dead, and one because she didn't like Zoe.

Her whole life was falling away. She was falling off the world into space: the permanent darkness where you could never be alive again.

She fell asleep and then woke up instantly, hearing her own voice cry out.

The next morning her mother sat across from her at the breakfast table, drinking coffee and glancing at the newspaper. Her father and Melanie had already left for school. Zoe's whole body hurt, as if she'd done some unaccustomed physical exercise the day before.

Her mother looked up from the newspaper like she was about to say something, then hesitated.

"I can't go to school today," Zoe said. "I feel awful."

Her mother was silent for a moment. "What're you going to do all day?" she asked.

"I'll just go back to bed. I feel really sick."

Her mother rested her head on one hand and looked at her. "You know, sooner or later, you'll have to go back to school and face everyone. You can't put it off forever."

"It's only been two days, Mom," she said. There was an edge of tears in her voice. By now, Zoe was convinced, everyone in school would've heard how she had a big fight with Naomi right before Naomi killed herself. Danielle would have told the whole story.

Her mother sighed. "All right. But what're you going to do? Are you going to go see Rivka?"

"No," Zoe said quickly. "No, I'm just going to hang out here." She knew she was going to see her, but didn't feel like admitting it.

"OK," said her mother. "Are you sure you'll be all right?"

"*Yes*," Zoe said. What was this, anyhow? You'd think Zoe had never stayed home from school by herself before.

They drank more coffee in silence. Then Zoe saw what it was: Her mother was afraid Zoe might kill herself, too. Zoe looked at her mother, who was reading the newspaper again; she had dark circles under her eyes, and she looked tired. In just a few minutes she'd have to get ready to go to work, and she couldn't know what Zoe would do once she was alone. Zoe felt tremendously sorry for her; she felt like

209

bursting into tears. Her poor mother, having to worry like that for nothing.

"Hey, Mom," she said.

Her mother looked up.

"I'm never going to commit suicide," Zoe said. "I couldn't imagine it, no matter how bad things got." The minute these words were out, she wondered if they were really true. She'd never actually given much thought to killing herself.

Her mother smiled and tears came into her eyes. Then she was sort of laughing and crying at the same time, shaking her head. "You have no idea how reassuring it is to hear you say that," she said.

Zoe walked fast because it was cold. She had to get there by the time Rivka got home from her office hours, before she left to do anything else. Zoe had to tell her.

She was sorry for them all now: her mother, Mrs. Kaplan, Danielle, the kids at school, Rivka, Natan, Tad. Even Mrs. Wolfe. They hadn't wanted Naomi to die. Some of them had tried to prevent it. She still thought that they hadn't done enough, but she felt compassion for them now, too.

And shouldn't she include herself? What had she done?

Not enough, either.

When she thought of how she'd told Naomi she was sick of trying to be a good friend, it made her shoulders tighten, and that strange involuntary sound would come out of her throat.

Zoe clenched her fists inside the pockets of her mother's old suede jacket, feeling desperate to get to Rivka, to make her listen. As she walked, it started to snow, big white flakes swirling down. It was just like that dream: the snow coming faster, obscuring the bare trees and piling up on her jacket as she hurried along. The whole world was turning white. Was it Rivka, then, who'd been disappearing on the path ahead of her in that dream of snow?

When Rivka opened the door and saw Zoe standing there, she smiled. "Hi," she said. "Come in." She sounded the same as always, as if nothing had happened. She didn't seem angry at all. The little speech Zoe had worked up on her walk over fell away from her, as she took off her snow-covered jacket.

But of course something had happened. They stood awkwardly in the hall, glancing at each other. "I was just thinking about calling you," Rivka said.

Zoe was astonished. "You were?" Rivka had never called her for any reason.

"But I thought you'd still be in school," Rivka added.

She shook her head. "No, I didn't go to school today. I stayed home to think about things." It was much easier sometimes to talk to Rivka in her mind than it was when she was standing there in front of her.

"Zoe, listen, I'm sorry for what I said to you yesterday. I didn't mean to say that I don't like you."

Zoe stared at her, amazed. "I was sort of being an asshole," she said.

"No, it's just that I have been quite upset. I haven't been sympathetic." Rivka crossed her arms and leaned against the closet door, looking at the floor.

She wasn't angry. She was sorry.

"It's all right." Without thinking, Zoe put her hand on Rivka's arm as if she were Naomi or Danielle. "Forget it," she said.

211

Rivka looked at her quickly and smiled. "OK," she said. She put her arms around Zoe and hugged her.

Zoe hugged her back, more shyly than she had thought she would. She could feel Rivka's breasts against her own, and Rivka's body felt unexpectedly fragile. *You're really pretty innocent, aren't you?* That was one of the last things Naomi had ever said to Zoe, and now she would never be able to ask her what she meant. She'd be dead for the rest of Zoe's life. Zoe started to cry with her cheek against Rivka's fragile shoulder. The smell of Rivka's perfume, which used to seem frightening, was now a comfort, one she had almost lost forever, like Naomi. The tears seemed to start deep in her body and rise up endlessly. She felt she'd never run out of sadness.

Rivka held her and said something quietly in Hebrew — or maybe Arabic — that sounded like a string of swear words. Without understanding them, Zoe knew that Rivka was cursing something large: the whole world, the universe. For a second she wondered if Rivka believed in God.

They sat on the living room floor, their backs against the wall, drinking tea and smoking. Zoe tapped her cigarette in the ashtray and wished briefly that it was a joint; she hadn't gotten high in three days. Neither of them spoke for a long time.

"I don't know why I was so mean to everyone," Zoe said finally. "Especially you and Natan."

Rivka picked up her cup and drank some tea. "You don't have to apologize, OK?"

"I'm just trying to figure it out."

Rivka looked at her without saying anything, but Zoe felt an ESP message: *I still really like you.*

Zoe looked back at Rivka and thought, *I want to tell you.*

It was unbearable just to send her ESP messages about the hardest things. "Sometimes I don't really know what I'm doing when I'm around you," she confessed, too frightened to tell the whole truth but telling as much as she dared. "I get really — I don't know. I feel like I'm bouncing off the walls."

"You didn't do anything that bad," said Rivka. "It's just a difficult time."

"I know, I know, but — there's something that's wrong about me, with you. It's not the way I am with anyone else. I expect too much, or something."

Rivka was smiling a little. "You shouldn't worry. I don't always know what I'm doing, either."

She put her cigarette down on the ashtray and put her hand on Zoe's hair, pushing it gently away from her face. "*Yihiyeh b'seder,*" she said. It'll be all right. As if saying it in Hebrew made it definite, beyond challenge. Rivka's fingers were warm when they touched Zoe's cheek.

Zoe shuddered.

Zoe had the feeling that all twenty-five hundred kids in public school knew, by Friday, what had happened to Naomi. She could imagine everyone discussing it, even if they hadn't known her. *Hey, did you hear there's a girl in our class who died of an overdose? Yeah, and it might've been suicide.* Maybe she was just imagining things, but whenever she turned a corner in the hall or stood by her locker dialing the combination, she heard people say things like, *It's so strange,* or, *I don't understand how anyone could do that,* or even, *Really?* — and each time she was convinced it was about Naomi.

Among the people who'd actually known Naomi, everyone became extremely nice all of a sudden. When one of them walked into the cafeteria for lunch, a dozen others would look up, smile and wave, and invite whoever it was to join their tables, even if they'd never eaten lunch with that person before in their lives. On Friday Zoe bought a dime bag of pot from this guy who'd been in civics class with her and Naomi, and she said she couldn't pay him until Monday. Sure, no problem Zoe, no problem at all, he kept repeating.

On that same Friday Zoe skipped her algebra test, and instead of leaving school, she walked out to the center court-yard where the freaks hung out. She had the feeling she could go almost anywhere now that the school had momentarily stopped being divided into such rigid territories.

Sitting on the wooden benches were two guys Zoe didn't know and a girl named Nicole who'd been in her English class last year. They all looked up and said hi, and Nicole handed Zoe a tiny roach they'd been smoking. "It's almost gone," she said, "but it's the thought that counts."

Zoe smiled. She took one hit off the roach and it burned her fingers, so she dropped it on the ground. She licked her fingers and then blew on them. Then she sat down on the end of the bench, near Nicole. The two of them were silent for a few moments, but Zoe felt that Nicole was getting ready to say something. Nicole had never actually paid attention to Zoe before, but Zoe had admired Nicole. She had long straight hair and large, intelligent eyes; when she spoke in class, everyone listened carefully. The teacher had even read aloud several poems Nicole wrote. Zoe recalled one about colored balloons floating against the sky; the person in the poem discovered that the blue sky itself was actually made up of many different colors.

Nicole was still staring thoughtfully at the ground. She was wearing a long India-print dress, and over it a down vest. "I don't know," she said. She spoke in a quiet, low-pitched voice, so that Zoe had to strain to hear some of the words. "It's strange how something really terrible can happen and everything just goes on the way it always has. You keep expecting things — I mean physical things, like the trees, or the benches, to look different. Do you know what I mean?"

"Yeah," Zoe said, but it occurred to her that things weren't going on the way they always had. For her, anyway, everything did look different; things had a faded look, as if she were seeing them from a great distance. But maybe in order to notice this, you had to have been close to Naomi.

"Yeah," Nicole repeated in the same quiet voice, still not looking at her. "It's really a bummer, Zoe." She sounded like she meant it, and for just a moment, Zoe felt close to her, as if they were going to become friends.

"I know," Zoe said, trying to make her own voice quiet. "It's really a drag." She looked up, then, at the large window in front of them and saw Danielle walking down the glassed-in hallway. Danielle came closer, and when she was almost in front of them, Zoe waved to her. Danielle stopped and looked out, and for one terrible moment, Zoe was afraid she wasn't going to wave back.

She waved back, though she didn't smile. Then she walked on.

"Hey, you know this dude Bill Esposito?" Nicole was asking her.

"Yeah, sure." How could you not know Bill? He was practically the cutest boy Zoe had ever seen.

"I ran into him on Wednesday night," Nicole said, "at the Acropolis. We were both really freaked out about what happened to Naomi." She paused. "So we just sat there and talked for a really long time, and then I went over to his house, and we talked until almost midnight." Zoe wondered what they'd said about Naomi but didn't feel she should ask. Instead she said the first thing that came to her mind about Bill, which was, "Is he still going out with Eleanor, I forget her last —"

"Yeah, he is," Nicole said. "And I'm going to be screwed if I don't watch out."

Zoe looked at her. She didn't really care whether Nicole had a crush on Bill or anything, but Nicole wanted to talk about it. Zoe realized Nicole was only being friendly because of Naomi. She couldn't help being flattered and irritated at the same time. Zoe looked up again and watched Danielle come back down the glassed-in hallway. Again, they waved solemnly to each other.

You can't just replace them, Zoe thought.

"I really like that dude," Nicole said softly.

I'm so fucking lonely, Zoe thought. She couldn't believe now that she'd been so mean to Danielle at the Kaplans'. She couldn't believe that Naomi was dead and that she'd been able to think, even for a minute, that Nicole might replace her.

Zoe and Danielle drove to a bar up Route Seven on the Saturday night two weeks after Naomi's death because Mark Brauss, a guy Danielle liked, was playing the piano there. Zoe was turned off by the idea of bars and drinking — she would've preferred to drive around and get high — but she went because Danielle wanted to, and she wanted to be all right with Danielle.

They showed their fake IDs — driver's licenses with the birthdates changed — then sat at a corner table and drank white wine. The place was paneled in dark wood and there were plants hanging from the ceiling. Danielle talked about Mark, how he'd taught himself to play jazz piano, how he had to lie about his age in order to play here. Danielle said she really liked him a lot. She said he was sensitive. He was Jewish, too, luckily for her.

"Yeah, well," Zoe said. "I've been thinking a lot about — sensitivity."

"Yeah?" Danielle's face was half lit by the yellow candle in the center of their table. She picked up her wine glass and Zoe noticed, as if she'd never seen them before, how long and thin her friend's fingers were, curved around the glass.

"Uh-huh. Like, it's funny how you can feel sensitive inside yourself and still be a real shit to other people." She hoped Danielle would understand the apology.

Danielle smiled a little. "You're not a shit," she said.

"I feel like one. I've done almost everything wrong that anyone could do —" Zoe looked at the liquid pattern the candlelight made on her glass and tears came into her eyes.

"That's not true," Danielle said. "You were a lot better than I was about Naomi. I'm not good at people's problems." Danielle spoke calmly; her face looked regretful but not really upset.

Again Zoe wondered if Danielle was feeling anything at all. She felt the impulse to say something sharp to her. But she didn't want to do that again. So what if Danielle wasn't perfect — she was her friend. There was a strange distance between them, though, as if Danielle were edging further and further away from Zoe so she wouldn't be within range of all this emotion. Stop it, Zoe told herself. You're so fucking insensitive. She does feel things; she feels a lot of fear.

217

It was so hard to talk to Danielle now. What did they used to talk about — before? She couldn't remember. All Zoe could think about every time she looked at Danielle was Naomi, and maybe Danielle felt the same way. It was like each of them reminded the other of some failure or — worse — some crime.

"Well, I haven't been good about you. I didn't try to understand how you must feel about — death," Zoe said. "I didn't see why you wouldn't talk about painful things. I wasn't even thinking how you'd feel about what your parents went through." Danielle was staring at her. "Shit, it's coming out all wrong, but you know what I mean?"

Danielle's face was still calm in the candlelight. She shook her head. "No, it's not that," she said. "I don't feel anything really intense about what my parents went through. I don't even remember most of what they told me about it."

"You don't?" Zoe found this hard to believe; she remembered everything she'd read about it in those books, and she knew that for the rest of her life she'd have occasional — but terrifying — nightmares about it. "Well, it's probably just too deep to put into words."

"No," Danielle shook her head slightly, as if she'd forgotten some obvious but not very important fact. "I don't get that freaked out about things. I miss Naomi, but I haven't really felt that sad since her funeral. And I don't feel anything really awful about my parents."

"Why?" Zoe said bluntly. This was completely beyond her.

"I don't know," Danielle said. She glanced over at Mark, who was between songs. He smiled and nodded at her. "I think it's because I'd rather not dwell on things I can't change."

Something seemed to be missing in Danielle, some lack Zoe'd always suspected but could never really put her finger on. "Danielle," she said, leaning forward. She waited until Danielle looked away from Mark and back at her. "You should think about it. If you think really hard —"

"Why should I?" Danielle said quickly. There was a trace of anger in her manner now. "It's not going to help. You can't bring back six million people, and you can't bring back Naomi. You just have to go on with *life*."

"I *know that*," Zoe said. Don't be impatient, she told herself. Don't.

"Why do you always have to dissect everything?" Danielle asked.

Zoe sat back in her chair and took a swallow of wine. "I don't know," she said. Was that what she did? It was like being told she had a gross way of eating or something.

"It's not healthy," Danielle said.

Zoe looked at her, and she realized that Danielle felt just as put off by her as she did by Danielle.

"So you'd told Rivka Lev about Naomi?" Zoe's mother asked. "She knew that Nao was suicidal?"

"Uh-huh." Zoe's parents weren't exactly sitting close to each other, but her father was resting his arm along the back of the couch and his hand was dangling near her mother's shoulder. It was Friday night, almost three weeks since Naomi died, and for that whole time Zoe's parents hadn't argued, at least not in front of her or Melanie, who was sitting on the footstool close to Zoe's chair. Melanie was wearing her tightest jeans and her hair was damp and smelled good; she was waiting for a friend to pick her up to go to West Hartford. She'd invited Zoe to go along, but Zoe was tired of everyone being so nice.

Her parents had neatly avoided the question of why Zoe hadn't told them about Naomi. To be honest, she no longer knew exactly why she hadn't. Well, it had seemed dangerous at the time; she was afraid of getting caught with drugs, or getting caught skipping school. She'd thought that any bit of information would give them the key to a whole lot more: the domino theory of parental knowledge. By now she didn't care so much what they knew, though she wasn't going out of her way to tell them things. Naomi's whole life was an example of how helplessly adults could fuck things up; you had to feel a little sorry for them. "Well, people talk, and I'm not sure what to believe," her mother said. "But I heard that Naomi was on drugs for quite a while." Zoe and Melanie looked at each other, but kept their faces expressionless. "Do you know if that's true?"

Her mother looked worried but not accusing. It was strange to hear that phrase come out of her mouth: *on drugs*. It sounded like something from the six o'clock news, the way she said it, and that made Zoe feel sort of embarrassed for her.

"Well, that depends how you define being 'on drugs,'" Zoe said. "I'm not sure exactly what you mean." She looked at her parents, feeling tired of lying all the time about what she did. At that moment she was one step away from saying, Hell, I don't know how to define it, either. Sometimes lately I get high, and then I wish I hadn't. But I always do it again. Then she realized it was miraculous enough that she was here with all her family, that they were still together in one room. There was no reason to risk ruining the calm.

The doorbell rang. "Marcie's here." Melanie put on her coat, grabbed her duffel bag, and was out the door.

Then there was silence. Zoe's mother did not attempt to

define being "on drugs." Instead she looked at Zoe's father and smiled somewhat wryly. "Off to see Barry," she said.

Her father sighed, but didn't look really unhappy. "Barry," he said. "Well, I like Barry, actually."

Yeah? Well, that's good, Zoe thought somewhat sarcastically. Melanie was supposed to be staying at Tova Wallerstein's house, but Barry's house was so big, he could sneak Melanie in at night and out again in the morning, back to Tova's, and no one ever knew. Didn't her parents ever imagine things like this? She looked at them, slumped closer together on the couch now. They didn't look as if they were imagining anything. She understood that this was their choice: They weren't stupid, but there were a lot of things they preferred not to know.

"We were thinking of what we could do as a sort of remembrance for Naomi," Carol said. The classroom got very quiet. Rivka closed *Hebrew Today* and put it down on the desk.

"Yeah, something from the whole class," said Charlie.

"That's what we were thinking," Lynn said. Then she explained about how the Sisterhood was fundraising to expand the temple library, and how their class could contribute money for books in Naomi's name.

"That's a great idea," said Adam. He was completely serious for once. Zoe said "Yeah," along with several other people, even though she couldn't get really excited by the idea. She'd already heard, earlier this week, how the new yearbook committee at public school was planning to give a full page to a picture of Naomi with some kind of quotation underneath it. Someone had told Zoe she should think about making a suggestion for the quote. So far she hadn't thought of anything except the Rolling Stones song that kept going through her head when she thought of Naomi:

> You can't always get what you wa-ant
> You can't always get what you wa-ant
> You can't always get what you wa-ant

But this wasn't appropriate at all, if you thought that what Naomi had wanted was to die. In life, Naomi hadn't known what she wanted. Zoe had an uneasy feeling that she kept singing this song inside her head as a kind of revenge against Naomi.

"You will have to earn the money for this, right?" Rivka was saying.

"Yeah, we were thinking about that," said Carol.

"Maybe a bake sale?" Judy suggested. "You can make a lot of money at even one bake sale."

"Yeah, we could have it on, say, a Sunday morning right at the beginning of Hebrew School, catch all the parents and kids just when they get here. People are usually hungry then," Lynn said.

Step right up and get your Naomi Kaplan Memorial Brownies, Zoe thought. She tried not to smile since everyone else was being so earnest. Maybe they could sell hash brownies instead — more in keeping with Naomi's character. Or to hell with the brownie part: They could finance the whole library by selling just the hash. She couldn't help it; for the first time since Naomi died, she started to laugh hysterically, the way they used to laugh together.

Everyone looked at her.

Zoe covered her face with her hands and laughed some

more, completely out of control. The other kids smiled at her uncertainly or gave her weird looks and shrugged their shoulders. Danielle was staring at her from across the room.

"Are you all right?" Rivka said.

Zoe looked at her and nodded, still laughing.

"That's good," Rivka said. She gave Zoe a big smile. "I'm glad to hear that." Then she shook her head and started laughing along with Zoe, as if she were sure she'd think the joke was funny if she knew what it was. This was touching to Zoe, because Rivka would not have found the joke about hash brownies really funny.

She trusts you, Zoe's mind said suddenly.

"So you can't logically take all the blame," Natan said, squinting at her as he drew on his cigarette. It was a dark Saturday afternoon, pouring rain outside. Zoe had been sitting around the kitchen table with Natan and Rivka, eating sunflower seeds and smoking cigarettes for over an hour. The kitchen was dim — no one had turned on the lights since the storm started — and filled with smoke. "Even if you did have this argument with her. She also had a fight with her boyfriend." He made a gesture of futility with his hand. "She had a lot of problems that went back a long time in her life. Whatever happened this year was just like — you know — the last straw on the camel."

"It may have been an accident, too," Rivka said. "Who knows?"

Zoe knew none of them really believed that, though Natan said it was likely that in some way Naomi hadn't really wanted to die. And it did mean something that Naomi had had a fight with her boyfriend — if you could call him that — one day, a fight with her best friend the next day and had killed herself that night. It made Zoe want to throw up every time she thought about it. She kept waking up in the middle of the night wishing harder than she'd ever wished anything that she could undo that conversation in the car. Zoe cried because she hated herself more than she'd ever hated anyone, and then she cried because she felt so sorry for herself. But in the daytime she said none of this; she was logical.

"Logically," Zoe said, "I am at least partly to blame. I mean, as much as anyone who was close to her. You can't go around saying, Oh, it's just self-destructive to feel guilty. There's a lot to be guilty about, and if we don't take the responsibility, who will?" She looked at Natan, who was looking at her, she thought, with more respect. "Know what I mean?"

"Yes, of course," he said.

That frightened her momentarily. Everyone else had been saying for weeks, You can't blame yourself, Zoe.

"So we *can* blame ourselves," she said slowly. She felt frightened but oddly relieved at the same time, and she knew that this was the truth.

"We can each blame ourselves just a little bit," he said, "but not for the whole thing. And you especially did a lot of good, many more good things than bad things for Naomi."

They were all quiet for a while. Then Zoe said, "Well, I just keep hearing all this stuff about how no one should feel guilty. Like feeling guilty is stupid and ridiculous."

"No, I don't think so," Rivka said. "You can learn a lot of the truth about things if you feel guilty. As long as you don't get too guilty."

"I feel guilty, too, actually," Natan said.

Zoe looked at him, and for the first time felt the sympathetic part of her mind expand to include him as closely as anyone who was really her friend.

Rivka walked out onto the front porch with Zoe before she drove home. It was still raining hard, but it wasn't quite dark yet, and you could see that the light was lasting longer each day.

"I wanted to ask you —" Zoe said. "Did you ever have that dream? Before Naomi —?" She meant the dream Rivka always had before someone died, when they called to her from the bottom of the stairs.

Rivka looked out at the rain pouring in a little river down the driveway. "I did," she said. "But I had it a long time ago. When you came over here the first time and we were talking about her — you remember? I had it that night. But then nothing happened for a while, and so I thought, it's just a worry. I never had that dream such a long time before a person died."

Zoe stared at her. The rain was loud in the silence; it sounded like something breaking next to her ears.

"I wasn't going to tell you," Rivka said. "It doesn't help."

It's so unfair, Zoe thought. What good is ESP if it doesn't allow you to help anyone? Whatever it is, you get just enough information to confuse you and scare the shit out of you. It made her angry and sad, like when she was much younger and blamed God for human suffering.

"I had a weird dream the night she died," she told Rivka, "and I think it was about you."

Rivka looked at her. "Tell me what was that dream."

"Well, in the dream I was walking through a forest of white birch trees, and there was a snowstorm. I was following someone on the path ahead of me, I was trying to catch up to them. But the snow kept coming down harder, and I couldn't see very well. Everything was white, the snow was like this white veil, and the person ahead of me just disappeared behind it. I tried to run after them, but the snow piled up on me and I couldn't move. Then I woke up."

"Who was that person?" Rivka's eyes were wide.

"In the dream I didn't know who it was," Zoe said. "But then, you know, the next morning I found out that Naomi was dead, and a couple days after that at her funeral you and I —" She didn't want to mention their fight at the funeral; it was an ugly memory.

"Yes, I know what happened," Rivka said.

"Yeah, so then the next morning when I came over here to see you, I had to walk through a snowstorm. It just kept snowing harder, exactly like that dream. And I was afraid the dream was symbolic." Zoe wanted to say, *I'm afraid I'm going to lose you.* "That you were going to, like, disappear from me somehow and we wouldn't be friends anymore —"

"That was not a dream about me," Rivka said. "That was a dream about Naomi."

"No," Zoe said automatically. "No, I —"

"Yes," Rivka said. "You knew it was going to happen, too. That was a dream of death."

The thunderous roaring of the engines killed conversation. I studied the faces of my comrades, all deep in thought, and felt our hearts must be pounding in fateful unison. My eyes rested on Hannah. Her face was aglow, and she exuded happiness and excitement. She winked at me, waved her hand encouragingly, and a delightful, impish smile enveloped her features. Below her paratrooper's helmet her face seemed smaller, her expression almost elfin, and her luminous smile reminded me of a little girl on her first merry-go-round ride. Her excitement was contagious; we were all infected by it. Gradually tension relaxed, and the air seemed lighter. Fears and black thoughts receded, finally disappeared, and we began feeling peacefully confident.

Reuven Dafne, "The Last Border"

There are events without which one's life becomes unimportant, a worthless toy; and there are times when one is commanded to do something, even at the price of one's life.

Hannah Senesh

Part Three
Parachuting

Chapter Nine

Zoe sat in the kitchen of her grandmother's apartment one Saturday afternoon, drinking tea and eating chocolate blackout cake. "I think he was saying that life is such a drag and people are such fools, all you can do is laugh about it," Zoe said.

"Maybe," said her grandmother, who wasn't big on analyzing things like plays. "I'm glad you liked it," she added.

Zoe's father had said that "Endgame," by Samuel Beckett, was a good play, but it had turned out to be almost incomprehensible to both Zoe and her grandmother. They didn't mind; they liked the parts they understood. In the play were two cynical people who lived in garbage cans and popped out to talk to each other. The man would say something like, May I scratch your back for you? And the woman would shout, No! Then she'd say, Well, maybe a little scratch might be nice. Zoe felt cheered by it.

The windows were open and the sounds of traffic and people talking on their rooftops drifted in. It was nice to know there was all that life out there. Zoe had begun to make a distinction between live things and dead ones. Winter was a dead thing, and so was school, and so were parties where everyone got drunk. Spring was a live thing, and other live things included New York City, long walks on the beach and even spending days alone sometimes. Her friendship with

Danielle was a dead thing, but when she was with Rivka, she felt alive. She also felt alive with her grandmother.

Later, when they were both sitting on the living room couch looking through a photo album Zoe'd seen a million times, she tried to explain this life-death difference.

"I know what you mean," said Grandma Esther. "Work is what makes me know I'm alive. I don't know what I'd do if I couldn't work."

Zoe turned the page to pictures of her grandparents on the beach at Coney Island. She could tell that her grandmother felt deeply for her, in the sense that Zoe's hurt was pain to her, too. She knew from the way she watched her, and from the way she invited her for the weekend and acted as if everything were perfectly normal. She didn't expect any big displays of emotion; Zoe had noticed it was mainly people who were emotionally distant from her who did.

Grandma Esther put her hand on Zoe's hair and drew her fingers through it — it was down to her waist now — until they came to a big knot. Then she started separating the knot with her fingers.

"My hair's a mess," Zoe said, turning the page to a big graduation picture of her father wearing his robe and flat cap with the tassel. Zoe worried briefly, thinking of all the classes she'd missed this spring. So far she'd successfully intercepted all the warning letters addressed to her parents, but she'd ignored the threats in them. The teachers said her work was good when she did it, but that she'd done progressively fewer assignments and had missed more classes than was acceptable. It was only a matter of time before they'd be calling her mother at work, but things had been sliding away from Zoe so fast lately that she couldn't find enough energy to stop them.

Her grandmother was having trouble with the knot. "Wait, I'll get a comb," she said. When she came back with it, Zoe sat sideways on the couch, the photo album still on her lap, and Grandma Esther sat behind her, combing out the knots. Her hands were gentle, and Zoe could feel her whole body relaxing, the tension going out of her shoulders.

"That feels good," Zoe said, her eyes shut.

"You'll have to get a boyfriend who'll do this for you," said Grandma Esther.

Zoe was perfectly content to have her grandmother do it, but she said nothing. Probably Grandma Esther thought it was strange that Zoe didn't have a boyfriend; even Zoe was starting to wish sometimes that she did. It seemed that since Naomi died, she'd wanted more than anything else to be physically close to other people. If she had a boyfriend she'd have someone to be close to, in the way Rivka was close to Natan, the way Grandma Esther had been close to Grandpa Sol. It didn't seem likely, though. Every time a boy did get interested in her, like that guy Tom at Lynn's party, her instinct was to get away as fast as possible. They seemed desirable from a distance but dangerous up close. She could not imagine any guy she knew combing out the knots in a girl's hair.

"Did Grandpa ever comb your hair?" she asked.

"Yes. He used to like to brush it."

"That's really nice," Zoe said.

They were quiet for a long time while Grandma Esther worked on another big knot at the nape of Zoe's neck.

Suddenly Zoe opened her eyes and said, "A lot of bad things happened to you, too, when you were my age."

"Yes," said her grandmother. "But that was a long time ago."

"Well, I know you had to run away and all that," Zoe

said. "But you weren't happy when you got to New York?"

Grandma Esther was silent for a moment. "No. I wasn't happy."

"How come?" Zoe asked softly, trying to keep her talking. "Weren't you living with your sister?"

Her grandmother sighed. "I lived with her, but it wasn't much of a life."

"No?" Zoe kept very still, as if by not moving she could make her grandmother forget she was there. Her grandmother was combing her hair, over and over, even though all the knots were out of it. "What happened?" Zoe asked.

"Well, I was living with my sister and her husband," Grandma Esther said in a resigned tone, and Zoe knew she'd decided to tell her the whole story. "Going to business college. But they had a very small apartment. Her husband worked nights, so he would come home late, and we'd both be sleeping. And he — didn't make much of a distinction between us."

"Huh?" Zoe said.

There was another silence. "He acted as if we were both his wife."

"Oh," Zoe said. What exactly did her grandmother mean? Did he rape her, or just try? Zoe didn't want to ask; she didn't really want to know. Instead she said, "What'd you do?"

"I'd sit up in a chair all night."

"God," Zoe said.

"But that was a long time ago," Grandma Esther said. "After I met your grandfather and got out of there, I was very happy."

"Yeah," Zoe said, feeling dazed. The story reminded her of something, but she couldn't think what it was. "I'm glad you were happy," she said.

Her grandmother stopped combing and ran her hand over Zoe's hair, which was smooth now and felt lighter without the knots. "You'll be happy, too," she said.

How can you be so sure? Zoe wanted to ask, but you didn't say things like that to your grandmother.

As the train clacked through Harlem on Sunday afternoon, Zoe looked out the window at the broken-down buildings, the kids playing in the streets, and she remembered what Grandma Esther's story reminded her of.

It was an afternoon after school in the eighth grade, when she and Naomi were hanging out together in Naomi's room. The style then was to wear tight-fitting leotards with your jeans; she had a magenta one and Naomi's was electric blue. They'd taken off their jeans and were lying on the floor, doing exercises in their leotards. There was a dusty, perfumed smell to the orange shag carpets in that apartment — a leftover smell of people who'd lived there before. Naomi was playing 45s on a little record player she had, and she and Nao lay on their backs, riding bicycles in the air. Then they got bored with that and started to dance in front of the mirror, moving in slow motion to the Beatles' "Strawberry Fields Forever," stretching their arms and legs dramatically.

Then Naomi said, "Have you ever gone all the way?"

"No, have you?" They were both still moving in slow motion.

"Yeah," said Nao.

"You have? With who?" Zoe had stopped dancing and was just looking at Naomi. "You mean with Carl?" Carl was Naomi's boyfriend at the time; she wore a silver-plated ID bracelet with his name on it.

"Yeah." Nao had stopped dancing, too, and was sitting on the edge of the bed. Zoe sat down on the floor in front of her. "In his apartment when no one was home."

"Oh," Zoe said. She hadn't wanted to seem too surprised or ask too many questions; she was afraid Naomi would think she wasn't cool.

"Do you think that's bad?" Nao asked.

"No," Zoe said. "I don't think it's bad. I mean, not if you like him." Other girls in the eighth grade had gone all the way with boys, usually at parties. Those girls bleached their hair and acted tough. But Naomi didn't hang out with them, and she dressed in work shirts and army pants like Zoe and the other girls in their crowd. She didn't try to look sexy. Zoe thought that Naomi was truly a cool person; she felt instinctively that whatever Naomi did must be all right, because although Naomi was tougher than any of the other girls in their group, she was also smarter than the peroxide-hair girls. It was only once in a while that Zoe worried about Naomi turning out like her mother: pregnant and married at sixteen.

"Well, I do like Carl," Naomi said. Then she'd said the strange thing: "But I have fucked people I didn't like. I fucked some boys when we were in fifth grade."

"You did?" Zoe was confused, but tried not to let it show. "Who?"

"Some boys who used to live in D-3. They were in junior high. They moved away a long time ago."

"Did you want to?" Zoe asked.

"No," she said, "I didn't want to. But — I don't know. I don't remember how it happened."

Zoe hadn't asked any more questions.

Watching the people hurry by at the 125th Street Station, Zoe remembered more and more. After Naomi's parents had gotten divorced the summer before fifth grade, there'd been a space of a year or so when Zoe hadn't seen Naomi that often outside of school. She wasn't old enough yet to ride her bike over to the apartments. But was that the only reason? She pressed the thought further, past some reluctance in her mind. Yes, that was the year Naomi was weird. She wasn't that much fun to be with. When Zoe was over, Naomi would always want to stay inside rather than go out to the playground. When Zoe asked why they couldn't go out, Naomi would say, I hate those kids. Even on sunny days she kept the curtains in her room drawn and only wanted to look at her collection of Beatles and Monkees paraphernalia. That year she had bored Zoe.

That was the year she fucked the boys in D-3?

Zoe had pushed that conversation in the eighth grade completely out of her mind. Now she knew what it meant: Those boys had used Naomi, the way Grandma Esther's brother-in-law had used her. It occurred to Zoe now that this was when Naomi had changed. She'd never stopped being her best friend, but she'd started always taking things further than Zoe and her other friends. If everyone was fooling around during class, Naomi would be the one to get sent out of the room. Later on, if they were all smoking pot, she'd be the one to get caught with pills and sent away for rehabilitation. If other girls had boyfriends and slept with them, Naomi had to find a thirty-five-year-old Jesus Freak. She'd started talking about suicide only a few months ago, but she'd been living on that edge for years. Way back in fifth grade, when her parents got divorced and she moved to Sleepy Hollow, she'd started to slide into that other world where Zoe never really followed. And Zoe had ignored her when her problems got

237

to be too much, like in the fifth grade, or when she had better things to think about, like this year. She'd spent the whole year trailing around after Rivka Lev when her best friend was threatening to kill herself. Now it would seem like a miracle if Naomi had turned out like her mother: better pregnant at sixteen than dead.

Zoe got out of her seat quickly, startling the man reading a newspaper next to her. She stumbled out into the aisle and then made her way down the car, holding on to the seats. Inside the cramped smelly bathroom she locked the door, sat down on top of the toilet, and held on to a metal handle above the roll of toilet paper while the train lurched back and forth. For the first time she cried bitterly not for her own pain, but for Naomi's.

Zoe sat alone in the courtyard and turned her face toward the sun. First she rolled the sleeves of her white men's T-shirt up over her shoulders like a 1950s greaser, then she rolled up the bottoms of her green army pants and kicked off her sandals. She lit a cigarette, leaned back against the concrete wall and shut her eyes, feeling the warmth seep through her skin down to the cold center of her body, to the sadness that was like black ice inside her.

The courtyard was perfectly silent because everyone was supposed to be at the assembly to give the outgoing princi-pal an award. Zoe couldn't see what this principal had done that was so wonderful, if you considered all the violence in the hallways and the general boredom. But when it was rumored that the school board wanted to ditch him and hire a black principal, lots of kids discovered how much they respected him and passed around a petition saying he should be kept on. Zoe refused to sign it. But she thought the school board's plan had only a slim chance of making the black kids feel less alienated; quite possibly they'd see the black principal as simply another Oreo. Black on the outside, white on the inside.

She heard the door open and, hoping it wasn't a teacher, kept her eyes shut for one more moment. But it was just another kid skipping the assembly. She looked more closely and saw it was this guy named Philip Glass. She didn't know him, but Naomi had pointed him out to her once. She said he was gay and that a bunch of guys had beaten him up last winter. He was in her psychology class, and he'd come in with a lot of bruises. She'd also said he was a nice guy. Zoe watched as Philip sat down on a bench across the courtyard from her and lit a cigarette. He had blond hair and was very thin; as he settled himself down, leaning back with his arms crossed, his body looked nervous and energetic. Zoe shut her eyes and turned her face toward the sun again.

A moment later she was startled by the sound of someone sitting down at the other end of her bench. She opened her eyes and there was Philip, setting a notebook and some books down between them. His face was expectant; it looked like he was smiling, even though he wasn't, exactly — something about the curve of his mouth. "Hi. You're Zoe, right?" When she nodded, he said, "Naomi pointed you out to me once." He said Naomi's name as casually as if she were still alive.

"You're Philip," she said, and he nodded. "She pointed you out to me, too."

There was silence, and Zoe realized after a few seconds that she'd been waiting for him to say the usual things: that he was sorry about Naomi, that it was a real drag. But he wasn't saying any of it; he was just smoking quietly, giving her that same expectant glance, then looking off across the fields. She lit another cigarette, feeling greatly relieved, and also curious about what Philip was thinking.

"I suppose," she said, "you're not exactly heartbroken over the departure of our esteemed principal."

He made a motion with his right hand as if he were tossing away a piece of garbage. Then he looked at her over his shoulder and said in a hushed, dramatic voice, "I don't give. A flying fuck."

She smiled.

He stood up and held an imaginary plaque. "We will all deeply miss," he said in the exact nasal tone of the student council president, "your presence in our peaceful and scholarly institution. You have made this school what it is today —" Then suddenly Philip jumped up and down, waving his arms and screaming, "— A pile of shit!"

Zoe laughed and Philip sat down again, closer to her this time. His hair was thick and wavy and a gold-red color, like autumn leaves in the sun. When he looked at her again, she noticed his eyes were very bright blue and he had long eyelashes that curled. There was definitely something effeminate about him; she wondered if he had been born gay and simply couldn't help it.

He finished his cigarette and tossed the butt on the ground. "Hey, do you want to get out of here?" he asked. "Go out to breakfast or something? I've got a car."

"Sure," she said.

As they stood up to go, Philip looked around at the blank windows circling the courtyard from above. "Whenever I'm out here, I feel like someone's spying on me," he said. "I think that's why they built the school this way."

"Yeah, Big Brother is always watching." She glanced up at

the windows and felt relieved that there weren't any other kids around to see her leaving with Philip.

She stopped in front of his car: a blue Datsun. He opened the door on the driver's side and then looked at her over the roof before getting in. "It's not much," he said cheerfully, "but it goes."

"Naomi had the same exact car," she said. "A blue Datsun."

"Oh, really? I didn't know that," Philip said in that same casual tone, as if Naomi were still driving around in hers.

"Yeah." She couldn't stop looking at the car; it gave her a strange feeling of having circled back on her own life, as if time had been suddenly compressed. She had the feeling that something significant was about to happen.

Philip made a quick motion with his hand. "Let's boogie before the thought police catch us," he said. He got behind the wheel and closed his door.

Again she felt relieved. It was what Philip didn't say that was comforting. In the spaces between the words, he seemed to be grasping her thoughts and taking them in whole, the way they were before she messed them up with words.

Zoe opened the door on her side and got in.

"I've started to really hate school and everyone in it," she confessed. "It's so hypocritical. I mean, it doesn't even seem worth it to make any effort."

"Yeah, I know what you mean." Philip looked over and signaled the waitress to bring them more coffee. They'd been sitting in the Acropolis for over an hour, and neither of them had suggested heading back to school, even though the assembly was long over. "Someday high school will seem just like a bad dream," he added.

"More like a nightmare. And it seems like it's going to go on forever. I wish I could just get out."

Philip dragged on the end of a cigarette, holding it between his thumb and forefinger like a joint, his face thoughtful. Watching, Zoe was pretty sure he got high; she should've suggested it on the way over here. Next time, she found herself thinking, and she realized they were going to become friends.

"A good friend of mine dropped out last winter," Philip said. "Did you know Randy McHugh?" She shook her head. "Yeah, well, he dropped out of school at the end of second quarter, and after Christmas he went out to LA."

"Really? What's he doing out there?" She didn't know anyone who'd actually dropped out.

Philip sighed. "He's working as an extra in Hollywood. Twenty-five dollars a day. And at night he waits tables, same as he did here." He shook another cigarette out of the package and offered it to Zoe. "He's dismally poor, and he never gets any sleep."

"He sounds pretty brave."

Philip shook his head and smiled wryly. "I can't figure out if he's being really brave or really stupid."

"Does he want to be an actor?"

"Uh-huh. I met him last year in the drama club, and we got to be really close friends. I learned a lot from him."

Zoe looked out the window at the cloudless sky, the sun making even the old dirty brick buildings of downtown look cheerful. When she looked back at Philip, he was rolling the end of his cigarette around in the ashtray and his face was serious. She felt pretty sure that he intended her to understand that his relationship with Randy had been sexual, and she was a little surprised at how natural that seemed, with him sitting across the table from her.

"You must miss him a lot," she said.

"Oh, yeah." He looked up at her, and his face, which was usually so expressive, was still for a moment. It occurred to her that this was probably the most important thing that had happened to him so far in his life.

"Did you ever think about going out there with him?" she asked. "Or —"

He nodded. "I thought about it. But I could never drop out of school, my parents would kill me."

Zoe sighed. "Mine too."

Philip shrugged. "I can stick it out for another year. If it wasn't for the drama club, though —" He seemed to be regaining his usual enthusiasm. "Did you know we're putting on a play next month?"

"No," she said. "Well, maybe I did hear about it." She was vague on all extra-curricular activities.

"It's going to be really good," Philip said, and then he smiled. "That sounds like I'm being a braggart because I've got one of the leads, but really, the whole cast is great. We wrote the play ourselves and everything. You'll have to come see it."

"I will," she said. For a moment she envied him; he looked so happy when he was talking about the play. She didn't have anything in her life that she really put her whole heart into. But whose fault was that? She was starting to think there was something lacking in her, that the loss of Naomi she'd been mourning all these months was actually symbolic of an even bigger emptiness in herself that had nothing to do with Naomi. Together she and Naomi and Danielle had created their own little world; they'd driven around and smoked pot, had adventures. But what did it add up to? Now that Naomi was dead and she and Danielle weren't getting along, there was nothing from that time she could continue doing on her own. Maybe the reason Danielle had always been a little apart from Zoe and Naomi was that she did have something else that mattered to her. Zoe had to admit to herself that she and Naomi hadn't really had much that mattered to them. The only thing they'd believed wholeheartedly was that there was nothing worthwhile in this environment, and you just had to suffer through it. Of course they'd had a lot of fun suffering through it together, but that was all over now.

She noticed that Philip was just watching her while she thought. If she spaced out like this when she was with Rivka, Rivka would ask, What are you thinking about? as if being quiet or reflective was strange. But Philip seemed to find her silence natural. It occurred to her that he would have a lot of sorting out to do in his own mind. His life, too, could not have been easy this past winter, not with Randy leaving for LA, getting beaten up at school and who knew what else.

"You're lucky you have something you're really into," she said, meaning the play.

"Oh, I know," he said fervently. "I would've died this winter if I didn't."

For a while after Naomi's death, Zoe had the feeling that all the fixed roles people played had suddenly become more fluid. For a brief time, anything seemed possible. Then after a while the world solidified again, but in the meantime some hidden things had floated to the surface. One of these was Rivka's decision that Zoe was really her friend. She never said anything about it, but Zoe knew. Rivka talked more about herself, and Zoe got a better picture of Rivka's life, strange as it seemed to her. Rivka hung out mainly with other Israelis; she said they didn't drink or smoke pot, and they drove out to different state parks on weekends with their kids: Good Clean Fun. What interested Zoe more were the times she glimpsed something darker — more mysterious and less resolved — beneath the niceness of Rivka's American life.

One afternoon that spring Rivka announced to Zoe, "Shoshanna Ben-Yakov just got her American citizenship." They were drinking tea at the kitchen table; Rivka put down her cup and raised her eyebrows, as if this were something really momentous.

Zoe didn't know what she was supposed to say. Mrs. Ben-Yakov had been their Hebrew teacher two years ago; she was nice enough, but boring as a teacher. Zoe knew she and Rivka were good friends, though, so she said, "Oh yeah? That's good."

"Yes, and Shoshanna's husband got his citizenship, too."

"What'd they have to do — to get it?" Zoe asked.

"Well, first you have to live here for five years. Then you write in a lot of papers, and wait to see what will be decided," Rivka explained. "And then you have to take a test in American history and English."

"Is it a hard test?"

"Well, you have to memorize all of this history. When did Washington become president, and the Civil War, and Lincoln's speech — I forget what was it called —"

Zoe smiled to hear those very American words coming out of Rivka's mouth. "The Gettysburg Address."

"Oh, right."

245

"The Great Emancipator," Zoe added. She was enjoying teaching Rivka things, instead of the other way around.

"That was Lincoln, too?"

"Yeah, that's what they called him."

"Oh, I didn't know."

"Well, stick with me and you'll learn a lot. I'm a storehouse of useless information."

Rivka looked thoughtful. "I have learned a lot of things from you."

"Everything you never wanted to know about American kids," Zoe said.

Rivka smiled.

"Hey, so why did you want to become an American citizen?" Zoe asked.

Rivka gave her a look. "To be honest, I sometimes don't know."

Zoe thought about that one for a few moments. Then she said, "What've you learned from me, really?"

Rivka was quiet for a moment. "Some things about myself."

That wasn't what Zoe had expected. "About yourself?" Rivka didn't answer; she looked like she didn't want to explain. "Like what?" Zoe said very quietly, in the voice she used to keep Grandma Esther talking.

"Well, it's not very nice to think about," Rivka said.

Some corner of Zoe's mind was afraid Rivka was going to say that Zoe shouldn't be hanging around her so much.

"I don't mean that you should be frightened," Rivka said, and Zoe realized that Rivka certainly was good at detecting fear. Even just a little of it in you, and she'd see it. "It is just a very sad thing." Rivka put her arms on the table and leaned forward confidentially. "You know, the reason I was so angry with you at Naomi's funeral is that you reminded me of myself."

"Of yourself?" Zoe still didn't understand.

"When Yehuda —"

"Oh," Zoe said softly.

"Yes," she said, "I was just like you. I hated everyone. I acted like I was the only one who had lost somebody in the war. I had so much hate for other people, I thought no one could know how I felt." She paused, and her face had that same lack of expression it had had the day Zoe came over to tell her Naomi was dead. "I know in my mind that he did not waste his life," she continued. "He gave it for his country — he had to do it." She hesitated for a moment, then added, "But I feel in my heart that it was a waste. He wanted to be an artist, he was doing those — I think in English it's etchings? Yes. So after a while you start to see that no one will ever do the things that person would have done."

Zoe was sitting very still, hardly breathing. *I feel in my heart,* her mind repeated, *that it was a waste.*

The moon made curls of light on top of the waves rushing in between the rocks. Behind them the beach was dark, the houses and snack pavilion just vague forms in the night. They were sitting at the end of the breakwater, and the air smelled so good it seemed to be blowing in from some distant, untouched place. Zoe lit a second joint and passed it to Philip.

"— so then," he said, "my mother found out that Randy and I were — in love —" He hesitated; it was the first time he'd said something so direct.

"You told her?" Zoe tried to keep her voice perfectly smooth.

"No! She just figured it out by herself. It was really terrible."

"What happened? Did your dad find out, too?"

"Oh, yeah," he said. "Yeah, she told him. It was really awful. They feel like they did something wrong with me. My mother kept saying she was going to kill herself."

"Oh my God."

"I know. It was terrible." He shook his head and took a long hit off the joint. His hair was standing up off his forehead; it was the brightest thing in the night.

"Well, if she did, it wouldn't be your fault —" Zoe stopped, feeling overwhelmed by the weight of the situation. She should've had some wisdom to offer on the subject of suicide, but actually she had none. Instead it was as if she'd had only so much energy in the part of herself that could deal with these things, and it was all used up now.

"But I honestly don't think she would," Philip added quickly. "She was just really freaked out. I think she's getting over it now." He lay back on the rocks, one arm under his head. "God, it's such a beautiful night. It feels like we're moving through the water."

"I wish we were." Zoe leaned back, too, and looked at the stars. "If you could be anywhere right now, where would you want to be?"

"God, I don't know. Where would you want to be?"

"On a boat," she said, "going someplace I've never seen. It wouldn't even matter where. Just someplace far away, where I wouldn't know what it was like until I got there."

"That sounds pretty adventurous." He turned to face her, lying on the rocks.

"Or I wouldn't mind being in California." As soon as she

said this, she remembered Randy and wished she hadn't mentioned that particular place.

"That'd be all right," Philip said calmly.

"What about you?" she asked. "Isn't there any place you want to go?"

He looked thoughtful for a moment, and she watched the way his Adam's apple moved up and down when he swallowed. "I don't know," he said. "I mean, it's funny, but if I had the chance to be anywhere in the world right now, I think I'd still want to be here. It's not that my life here is so great or anything. But I have this feeling that I'm meant to be here, like I'm supposed to go through certain things before I can go on. I don't know how to explain it."

"You're so optimistic." She was amazed by Philip's optimism and enthusiasm, which she would have found obnoxious in anyone else. But in Philip, given his circumstances, they became stubborn and unexpected qualities, and cheered her.

"I don't know why," he said. "But I am. I'm really optimistic."

The long beam of a flashlight intruded, lighting up their bodies. They sat up and got the flashlight in their eyes.

"It's the fucking cops," Philip whispered.

"It's OK, I don't have anything else on me," Zoe whispered back, even though the cops were too far away to hear.

"It's illegal to be on the beach at night, though."

"Why? What right do they have?" The flashlight played back and forth, first on his face, then on hers. She put her hand over her eyes. "Oh, go away," she said.

"I guess we better get back to the car," Philip said. They walked back along the breakwater toward the beach, the flashlight tracking them every step of the way. When they got close to the end, the light dropped to the ground and they could see two cops standing on the sand. Zoe was glad it was dark; she was so high, she felt like they'd taken an hour to walk over the rocks.

"It's against the law to be out on the beach at night," one of the cops said in a monotonous, almost bored tone, like he was reciting from the rule book. The light reflecting off the sand was so bright, it hurt Zoe's eyes. "Oh. We didn't know," she said stupidly.

"You didn't know?" His voice became snide. "There's signs everywhere." He looked at Philip. "I guess you can't read, either. What were you kids doing out on that breakwater?"

"Oh, I'm really sorry," Philip said, sounding embarrassed and contrite. "I just wanted to take my girlfriend out there." His act was perfect. He was holding on to her arm now as he talked to the cop, looking confused and innocent.

"Well, you'll have to do your necking somewhere else," the cop said.

"OK," Philip said. "We will." He took Zoe's hand and started to back off before the cops had had a chance to decide whether to dismiss them or not. "Have a good night," he said.

They looked at him doubtfully, and then Philip and Zoe turned around and started walking up the beach to the parking lot, still holding hands. "Whew," Philip said when they were far enough away. They walked quickly across the parking lot, and still he didn't let go of her hand.

"That was great, Philip," Zoe said.

They both started snickering softly, even though no one was around. When they got to the car, Philip put his hands on Zoe's shoulders and jumped up and down. "We fooled those bastards!" he hissed. Gradually their laughter died down and Philip stopped jumping. He put his head on Zoe's shoulder for a moment and groaned out into the night. "Aaaarrrrgggghhh!"

They drove away fast. Philip loved his car as much as Naomi had loved hers; he could drive around all night without getting tired. He'd bought it with money from his job waiting tables at a restaurant downtown. "Thank God for the getaway vehicle," he said, making a sharp right-hand turn and zooming up a hill.

"Yeah." Zoe patted the dashboard. She was enjoying herself; she hadn't felt this happy in a long time. Philip was driving fast, but she wasn't afraid.

"What do you want to do now?" he asked.

"I don't know." They were driving past her old elementary school, and she looked at the playground on top of the hill, the shadows of swings and jungle gyms. "Let's go on the swings," she said, and he pulled into the parking lot immediately, driving in a fast arc.

They were the good kind of swings: sturdy, wide seats, hanging from thick chains attached to long unmovable metal poles. It was as if the person who designed them had thought of the kids who might want to come back to their old playground ten or twelve years later. For a while Zoe and Philip pumped their legs, swinging higher and higher. The air was cool on Zoe's face, and she could see down the sloping hill where she and Melanie used to go sledding when they were kids. After a while Philip and Zoe were swinging really high in unison, so they could look across at each other as they went up, down and then up again, forward into the night.

"I always wonder what it'd be like to just fall through the air," she said.

"I know some guys who went sky diving once," Philip said. "They said it was the most incredible rush —"

"Yeah!" she said. "Imagine that second right before your parachute comes out."

"It's not on my list of the ten things I most want to do," Philip said.

"Oh, me neither. I'm a physical coward, actually. But I read this book once, about this girl who learned how to parachute, and she — well, she was Jewish, and she parachuted into one of the Nazi-occupied countries, I forget which one, to try and save Jews. I read it last year, and I just kept thinking and thinking about it."

"That's amazing," Philip said. "What happened to her? Did they catch her?"

"Yeah, they caught her and tortured her, but she wouldn't give them any information. Then they shot her."

"Jesus. We certainly are wimpy, compared to that."

"I know."

They swung in silence for a moment. Then Philip said, "Are you Jewish?"

"Yeah, sure." She was always surprised when anyone asked; she thought it was obvious. On one hand, it didn't seem to matter that Philip wasn't Jewish because they were just friends. On the other hand, he was a guy, and it *had* seemed strange when he picked her up, standing in the hallway with her mother. Surely her parents would object sooner or later.

"Oh, I didn't know that," he said. "Did you have a — what are those things called again?"

"A Bat Mitzvah. Yes, I did." That was always the first question they asked, for some reason.

"Wow. Do you go to the synagogue, still? I hope you don't mind me asking all these questions. I'm just your average WASP, I don't know anything about it."

"It's all right," she said. "I don't go to temple very much. But I go to Hebrew School." She explained what Hebrew High School was.

"Do you like it?" he asked. "Or do you just go because your parents want you to?"

"No, my parents wouldn't care if I stopped going," she said. "But my friends are there. And this year I've gotten to be good friends with my Hebrew teacher. It's sort of a strange thing." She told him about how she'd talked to Rivka about Naomi, how she'd started going to see Rivka all the time.

"She's from Israel?" Philip said. "What's she like?"

Zoe hadn't expected him to be interested in this part of her life. "Well, she has pretty strong ESP, and she just seems to know a lot of things. And she always says what she's think-ing, even if it isn't what you want to hear."

"Yeah?" he said. "So you can talk to her?"

"Yeah, we talk a lot. It's funny, at first I thought she wasn't the kind of person you could talk to at all — I thought she was really cold and insensitive. And actually, we are really different from each other. But it doesn't seem to matter."

"It's like you have some kind of psychic connection?" Philip asked.

Exactly, Zoe thought, glancing at him in admiration. But all she said was maybe. She didn't know how much she wanted to tell him; she felt on the edge of telling him every-thing. She almost forgot it was Philip and not just some dis-embodied voice speaking into the rush of air around her head.

Philip said, "It's amazing how those things can happen with people who are so unlike each other."

"Yeah," she admitted. "It is." Zoe had the feeling that nothing would surprise him or be too weird to tell him.

"What does she look like?" he asked.

Zoe described Rivka: her dark hair and skin and gray-blue eyes, the way she smiled sarcastically, the kind of clothes she wore. Philip asked what colors she tended to wear. Zoe couldn't help admiring him; he was the only guy she'd ever talked to who seemed aware of the details of a person's appearance and what they might mean. She hesitated for a moment, and then added, "She's really beautiful."

Zoe felt happy. She leaned her head back each time her swing went forward, so she was hanging upside down for a second. Her hair touched the ground.

"Have you ever been in love?" Philip asked.

Zoe sat up straight again. "No," she said, feeling dizzy and confused. She never used those words herself: *in love*. She thought of either loving, or not loving — of course you could love people to different degrees, or in different ways.

"Oh," Philip said. "I just wondered."

"Well, I've loved people, if that's what you mean," she said. "I *love* Rivka —" She stopped, hearing those words go out into the night.

"Uh-huh," he said encouragingly. They swung in silence for a while. Then he said, "I have a couple of good friends who are lesbians."

Zoe felt afraid, knowing why he'd said that word. She couldn't explain that it did not apply to her and Rivka at all because any sexual part was only in Zoe's mind, and anyway, she would probably get over it. As Rabbi Hersh taught them, thinking about a thing and doing it were two separate issues. So how could you know whether you were a lesbian if you hadn't even kissed a girl?

"I don't know any lesbians," she said. "Except the gym teachers, of course." She avoided mentioning the mystery surrounding the gym teachers, who were both taking early retirement at the end of this year and moving away to Florida. There were rumors that some kids had complained about them in a meeting with the principal — Zoe thought it all sounded incredibly stupid.

"Yes, you do," he said. "You know some other ones."

"Who?"

"Pamela and Cindy."

"Oh," she said. Pamela and Cindy were good friends of Philip's; they were in the drama club play with him. She'd met them once or twice in the courtyard with Philip. They certainly didn't look like the gym teachers, who were both fat and had super-short hair. Pamela and Cindy were both thin and pretty; they acted like Philip, speaking dramatically all the time, exaggerating everything. Zoe wondered if they were really lesbians or if they were just trying to shock people. She had the uneasy feeling that Rivka wouldn't even like being talked about in the same conversation that included them.

It was late when Philip drove her home; all the houses on her street were dark. The car sounded loud, idling on her driveway. "I had a great time tonight," Philip said, smiling at her.

"Oh, I did, too," she said.

"We'll have to do something again soon."

"Definitely." She had already turned away and was starting to open her door when she felt his hand on her shoulder. She looked up at him, and he leaned over and kissed her on the mouth.

For a moment they stared at each other; Philip looked almost surprised, as if someone else, and not himself, had kissed her. "Good night," he said, and took his hand off her shoulder.

"Good night." She shut the door and went quickly up the front walk.

When she was lying in bed, she thought about what they'd told each other, about how he'd kissed her. There didn't have to be a reason for it, she told herself. They'd had a good talk; he liked her. That's all. She was tired of trying to figure out the reasons for everything. When she shut her eyes, she felt as if she were still swinging back and forth.

Between second and third period Zoe walked out to the courtyard and saw Philip talking to Lisa, a girl from her homeroom. Philip was already gathering his books. "Hi, Zoe!" he said when he saw her. "Can you meet me out here during lunch? I've gotta make it to class on time or the bastard's going to lock me out —"

She laughed and said "Yeah, sure," and watched him run into the building. Then she said hi to Lisa and sat down next to her on the bench. Another guy from their homeroom, Greg, came over and said to Lisa, "I saw you talking to Philip." He batted his eyelashes and grinned.

Lisa flipped her hand in the air and said, "*Yes*. He was telling me how I *must* come and see their *play*."

Greg laughed and shook his head, his upper lip curled. "That guy's such a flaming faggot."

"I know," Lisa said.

Then why were you talking to him? Zoe wanted to ask Lisa.

You were smiling, you didn't look like you were in such a big hurry to get away.

"He probably can't help it," Lisa said to Greg, and they both laughed.

Zoe pretended to be busy taking out a cigarette and searching for her matches, her head down. You're a fucking hypocrite, she wanted to say to Lisa, but she knew that she was one, too, for not sticking up for Philip. Inside she felt a little seed of fear. If Lisa and Greg knew how she loved Rivka, they'd think it was gross. And what about her and Philip? When they were alone together, he acted like he was attracted to her. He'd kissed her twice this week, he was always putting his arm around her. For the first time she admitted to herself that, for some reason, Philip wanted her to be his girlfriend, and that maybe it was what she wanted, too. But the two of them as a couple would be seen as totally bizarre, like a strange mutation. She looked at Lisa and Greg, who were talking about something else now, and felt that little seed of fear begin to swell and send out roots.

Zoe was naked on a large rock, kissing and embracing Philip, who had soft skin and breasts. Their lower bodies were curved and muscular, shaped like seals instead of people. They rolled back and forth, and the excitement between them reached a peak. But they were wordless, like seals coupling in the wild. Then a long beam from a flashlight illuminated their bodies, and Zoe saw that she was actually holding Rivka very tightly. Rivka said, "I have to think about it. I'll talk to Natan." "No!" said Zoe. "I don't want you to tell anyone."

"I think that if we look very carefully," said Eli, "we may find some kind of small animal."

"There must be some turtles in here," Eitan agreed.

"Why don't you look over there?" Rivka pointed to a spot near the stream where a patch of skunk cabbage grew. She looked at Zoe and winked as the kids walked away along the edge of the water, looking intently for anything that moved. Rivka and Zoe sat down on the plank bridge that went over the stream, dangling their legs and resting their arms on the lower railing.

The Nature Museum trails seemed far away from town this time of year; the leaves blocked out the traffic noise, and there was a feeling of being in the deep woods. Zoe looked down at the submerged stones splotched with brown and black algae, and watched the designs quiver beneath the moving water. Then she looked up at the trees, full and green against the sky. She'd been dying for summer to come this year, but now that it was June, she was overwhelmed by the physical beauty of the world, as if it were an inappropriately generous gift. It made her think of Naomi, and of the contrast between the outer world and the cold dark spot she carried inside herself.

"I always get really homesick at this time of the year," Rivka said.

Zoe leaned her head on her arms and looked at her. "You do?"

"Yes. But it will be OK, we're going to Israel in July."

"You are? For how long?"

"The whole month, I think. It will be good, we haven't been there for a few years."

"Really? You mean you don't go back that often?"

"No." Rivka glanced sideways at her, smirking as if she were talking about some illegal and pleasurable activity. "Our families usually visit us here."

"Well, that'll be nice," Zoe said, though she couldn't work up much enthusiasm for Rivka's being away. "I have no idea what I'm going to do this summer."

Zoe and Rivka got up and walked farther along the trail with the boys, who had made their way back from the stream. Eli and Eitan walked ahead, covered with mud and dragging long walking sticks. There was a smell of earth and leaves, and it was dim and cool under the trees. The spot of bright sun at the end of the trail slowly got larger, and finally they walked out of the woods and into the upper field. Zoe hadn't been here in years, but she remembered exactly this feeling of emerging from the thick woods into the open meadow, the way your skin was cool until the sun gradually sank in.

Rivka was standing on the trail with her hands in her pockets, looking across the meadow, while Zoe kicked the ground, thinking about how her parents were nagging her to get a summer job. Philip had wanted his job so he could save up and buy a car, but Zoe didn't really care if she had a car or not. "I can't figure out what to do this summer," she said.

Rivka walked a few steps away and sat down on the grass. She took out her cigarettes and offered one to Zoe, who sat down next to her. "What do you usually do?" Rivka asked. "What did you do last summer?"

Zoe shrugged. "Read books. Hung out at the Jewish Center pool. But this year I have to get a job, I guess. Mom and Dad want me to learn responsibility and the meaning of work and the value of money," she said in a pompous parental tone.

Rivka started laughing. "They are very cruel people," she said.

Zoe felt irritated. "Well, I don't want to just do some dumb job," she said. "I want to *do* something." She paused for a

259

moment, thinking. "You know, the other night I was talking to a friend of mine about Hannah Senesh, and he said it's amazing how wimpy we seem compared to her —"

"What?"

"It means, like, weak," Zoe said impatiently, "or cowardly, good for nothing. And I started thinking how negative Naomi and I always were. I mean, she really thought there was nothing worth doing in life. I always thought maybe there was, but as this distant thing. But maybe I'm wrong."

"Of course you're wrong," Rivka said, flicking the ash off her cigarette.

"Well, it's not that simple," Zoe said. "I mean, I have friends who do things they're really into, but —" She stopped, not wanting to tell Rivka about Philip. This whole train of thought was really about Philip, and how his optimism and his enthusiasm about his play had become connected in her mind with Hannah Senesh farming in Palestine, then parachuting to save her people. Philip had something, Hannah Senesh had had something; she herself had nothing. "I've just never found anything around here that seems worth doing. It's all always seemed like so much bullshit."

Rivka looked at her. "There are a lot of things you could do that would be meaningful."

"Like what?"

"I don't know," Rivka said. "You'll have to find it by yourself."

Zoe sat hugging her knees, thinking how Rivka's life had probably never been as boring and pointless as her own sometimes seemed. She heard the kids shrieking across the meadow; they were picking buttercups and tickling each other's chins with them. "What were you doing when you were my age?" she asked.

Rivka looked startled, as if she'd forgotten she had a past. "You mean, in the summer?"

"Yeah, when you were sixteen, seventeen. What'd you do?"

Rivka thought about it for a moment. "I was a volunteer. My brother and I both went with a man who drove around to these — how do you say — like immigrant camps. We had a truck with a lot of things in it, and every day we drove from the city and went to a different place in the *Galil*. Yehuda would connect the movie projector, and we showed movies —"

"What kind of movies?" Zoe asked, momentarily forgetting her own life.

"Oh, about sanitation. Hygiene. Then the man would talk to them for a while."

"What'd you do?"

"My job was to teach them some Hebrew with a film strip. You know, I'd show a picture of something, and then everyone had to repeat the words."

"Hm." Zoe was transported into this other world now, picturing Rivka and her brother riding around in a truck in the Galilee, having adventures together. "What'd those places look like?"

"They were living in tents, most of them. The government sent them out there, and they were supposed to build their own houses and make farms."

"That sounds hard."

"Well, it was better than the ones who stayed in the immigrant camps in the city. We went to one of those once and it wasn't very nice. Just little shacks made out of metal like this —" She showed Zoe what she meant with her hand.

"Corrugated, yeah," said Zoe.

"And a lot of people doing nothing, just sitting outside on the ground in the shade from the — corrugated shacks. It was a very depressing place."

"Why didn't they leave?"

Rivka smiled. "They didn't want to be farmers. The government tried to convince them, but they didn't want to go. They didn't farm where they came from."

"Where'd they come from?"

"Different places. India. Morocco. Algeria."

"Wow." Zoe became aware of the meadow around them again. For a moment it felt like something was missing, and then she remembered her sadness. "There's nothing that interesting to do around here," she said.

"Oh, stop it, Zoe," Rivka said, getting to her feet and brushing off her jeans. She started walking down the trail toward the kids, who were heading into the woods on the other side of the meadow. She yelled, "Eli! Eitan! Wait for us!" Then she looked back at Zoe, who was following her. "I'm sure you can find something useful to do. You think there are no people around here who need help?"

"No," Zoe said, suddenly ashamed. She felt a wave of self-loathing; she knew she'd never been useful in her whole life. She caught up to Rivka and said, "You must think I'm a real wimp."

"That's not what I think," Rivka said, walking more quickly. "What I think is, you can be very good at anything you want to do. You are just spoiled. But I think you can get over it."

Zoe looked at her in total amazement. "What are you talking about?" She was deeply offended; no one had ever called her spoiled before. Rivka didn't even know what spoiled meant. She should see those girls from West Hartford; she should see Tova Wallerstein's clothes. Zoe wasn't even rich.

Rivka looked at her. "I mean that it won't hurt you to be a little more tough about things. You could stop thinking always about yourself, and think about other people." She kept walking fast as she said this, and ran the last little way to where the kids were.

Zoe stopped where she was and sat down on a stump. The others kept walking, and she let them get farther down the trail until they were out of sight.

Who did Rivka think she was, anyway? She wasn't some kind of Zionist pioneer draining the malarial swamps. She wasn't even the young woman in the army uniform in that old photograph Zoe had seen, and she hadn't been for a long time. She was a university professor who lived in a big house in the United States and drove around in a Cadillac. Did she think that just being Israeli gave her some kind of immunity to becoming spoiled?

Finally Zoe got up and started walking, but she followed them at a distance for the rest of the hike, which led in a circle back to the museum parking lot. Her thoughts went in circles, too, but always came back to the question of what she should do this summer. When she emerged from the woods, she saw Rivka and the kids waiting for her in the big silver car, and she thought, Yeah, tell me all about it. But she couldn't shake an unpleasant feeling that Rivka might be right.

The opening night of the play was the perfect opportunity to watch Philip for two hours straight; Zoe had never had the chance to observe him so closely and so anonymously. She sat near enough to the stage to see his forehead shining with sweat. The play was about two young men — played by Philip and another boy — trying to make it as actors in New York. They were thwarted by heartless directors who didn't see their talent, greedy landlords who objected to unpaid rent and farty parents who disapproved of their ambitions. What saved it from corniness, Zoe thought, was the absolute sincerity of the whole cast; they believed in what they were doing so much that you started to believe in it, too. The boys in the play did not lose hope. In the last scene they were auditioning again, jazz dancing, and Zoe leaned forward in her seat, fascinated, as Philip and the other boy snapped their arms and legs in and out, whirled around and leaped across the stage side by side.

At the cast party afterwards they were all high on success; everyone crowded into the drama teacher's living room and congratulated each other again and again. Myra, the drama teacher, was arranging the flowers they'd given her. Philip introduced Zoe to her, and then to a lot of other people whose names she instantly forgot. Everyone kept saying things like, "You were fantastic!" and "I thought I'd die when we made that big crash backstage!" Mark, the guy who'd played the other lead, came up to them and shook hands enthusiastically with Philip. Then they both laughed and hugged each other quickly.

Zoe left Mark and Philip talking about the play, and wandered through the crowd by herself. She got a Coke, and walked out the glass doors that opened onto a patio. It was cooler out there, and small groups of people were sitting around. She sat down by herself on a lawn chair near a large planter with a shrub in it and drank some of the Coke. In the dim light she spotted Philip's friend Pamela on her right, talking to another girl whose name she couldn't remember. She heard the other girl say, "That's exactly how it is!" and then they both lowered their voices. Zoe was still close enough to hear, though.

"Last year it was Myra," Pamela said. "I liked her so much. I thought about her all the time. Cindy and I used to wander over here sometimes on the weekends. Once she and John were upstairs when we got here, and the dogs started barking really loud. Finally they came down, and I mean, it was obvious what we'd interrupted."

"Ohh," the other girl groaned.

"It was awful," Pamela said, but she was laughing.

They were silent for a moment. Zoe didn't look at them; she didn't want them to notice her. Then the other girl said, "Well, there's no way I could see her on a weekend. She lives too far away, and I don't have a car. All I do is sit around and think, and wait for the weekend to get over so I can see her."

Pamela sighed. "I know how that is," she said. "That's how I failed French last year, just thinking all the time like that."

"And you can forget about them liking you," said the other girl.

"Well, I know Myra likes me," Pamela said.

"Oh, I know, but —"

"Yeah, not the way you want them to."

They were quiet, then, but Zoe kept listening, wanting to know what they'd say next.

"Hey, Zoe," Pamela said. "Is that you over there?"

Zoe turned around quickly as if she were surprised to see them. "Yeah," she said. "Hi, Pamela."

"You look lonely," said Pamela. "Come on over."

"I'm OK," Zoe said, but she went over to where they were sitting.

Pamela smiled at her; she looked very excited and pretty, her long hair loose on her shoulders. She still had traces of eye makeup on from the play, which made two greenish-white half moons above her eyes. "When Philip introduced us, you looked really familiar to me," she said to Zoe.

"Maybe you met her in some other life," said the other girl, whose name, Zoe remembered now, was Holly. They all laughed.

"Wait a minute," Zoe said. "Did you ever take swimming lessons at the Jewish Center?"

"Yes!" Pamela said. "Oh my God. With that girl who used to make us go off the diving board? You were there?"

"Yeah, it was like walking the plank," Zoe said. "She'd *make* you just go out there, and then she wouldn't let you turn around. She'd make you dive, head first —"

"Yes! That's the one!" Pamela shouted, putting her hand on Zoe's knee. "What a bitch she was. I can't believe you remembered me from there."

"Yeah, it's kind of strange," Zoe said, looking at Pamela's face but mainly aware of her hand on her knee. No girl had ever done this to her before.

"Good memory," said Holly.

"Philip says really nice things about you," Pamela told Zoe.

"He does?" Zoe glanced down at Pamela's hand on her knee, and Pamela took it off.

It was different with her and Rivka, Zoe thought while she was driving home. It wasn't just a big fantasy where she sat around thinking about it all the time; their friendship actually existed.

But not the way you want them to.

266

It made her uncomfortable to find out that the pattern of her own life was being repeated in other people's lives. Everything she'd thought was so weird, so particular to herself and so private was obviously familiar — with minor variations — to Pamela and Holly, and who knew how many other people as well.

So what?

Well, she still couldn't believe that their feelings would be exactly the same; the way she was drawn to Rivka was so powerful and Rivka's intuitive knowledge about her so complete that it seemed unlikely anyone else could experience something like it. Yet apparently other people did. Zoe didn't need to hear the conversation between Pamela and Holly go on any further: She knew what things their words stood for.

The question was still, what did it matter? Just because Pamela was a lesbian — or said she was — didn't mean anyone else had to be.

Didn't mean her.

You're really pretty innocent, aren't you?

Naomi, I know what you were getting at. You thought I didn't know what I was doing with Rivka, and you were right. I still don't know what it means. Alone in the car, driving downhill through the night, Zoe spoke to Naomi as if she were sitting right next to her. She felt Naomi's presence so strongly; for the first time since she died, Zoe had an absolutely clear picture of Naomi's face, heard the exact tone and rhythm of her voice as she said the word *innocent*. Zoe held the steering wheel tightly, but she was almost unaware of the road winding out ahead of her.

It's all right. You're better off that way.

She glanced over to the passenger seat and was almost surprised to find it empty.

♦ ♦ ♦

"It's great you stopped by, Zoe," said Mr. Brown, the guidance counselor. He smiled warmly at her over the cluttered desk. His graying hair stood out in tufts, like David Ben-Gurion's. "How're you doing these days? Your teachers say you're honoring them with your presence."

"Yeah, I'm all right," Zoe said. "I'm going to class."

"I'm glad you're OK. It's not easy."

"I just try not to think about myself," she confided. You couldn't help liking Mr. Brown, as Nao had, and wanting to explain things to him. "It's better to be tough about things."

His face looked serious. "I'm not very tough," he said. "I feel so bad, still. I wish I could've helped her more."

They looked at each other in silence for a moment. Then Zoe, pretending she was Rivka, insisted, "I'd rather think about other people. What I feel isn't the most important thing in the world." Before Mr. Brown could object to that, she added, "Listen, what I came to ask you about is the Jobs for Students program."

"Right!" Mr. Brown, obviously glad to be helpful to her, started rummaging through a pile of papers on his desk. "I've got all kinds of listings here, somewhere."

"I don't want to do just anything," Zoe said. "I want to do something useful."

"Let's see, something useful," he repeated, reading down his list. "Well, OK. How about girls' counselor for Summer Fun at the YMCA? 'Would be in charge of twenty-five to thirty girls, ages nine through twelve, to work with inner-city children on values clarification, lead recreational activities. Responsible, mature high school junior or senior —"

"OK," Zoe interrupted. "I'll do that one."

◆ ◆ ◆

"It sounds like heavy-duty exploitation to me," Philip said, lying on his back next to her on the beach. "Cooped up with thirty inner-city kids in that crumbling old YMCA building — do you know what that's going to be like? The twelve-year-olds'll be carrying knives, and all the little nine-year-olds will be smoking pot in the locker room."

"Oh, come on," Zoe said.

"Really! Why do you think Mr. Brown still had that job open? How much are they going to pay you?"

"Two hundred dollars."

"Uh-huh. How often is that?"

"That's for the whole summer."

"Oh Jesus," Philip groaned. "You could make that in three weeks of waitressing."

"Philip, that's not the point —"

"I know, I know, you want to make yourself useful. It's that Israeli friend of yours, she's giving you a complex. She's convinced you that you must put on the hair shirt."

She scooped up a handful of sand and poured it on his chest.

"Aggh!" He sat up.

"How about a sand shirt?" she said, pouring more sand on his shoulders, which were bare and white and covered with suntan oil so the sand stuck. She laughed.

"You bitch!" he yelled, and ran toward the water. She followed him more slowly, then stood at the edge and watched him wade in. He was wearing blue track shorts; his legs were covered with curly gold hair. Two large wings of sand were stuck to his back and shoulders, and it made her laugh again. He turned around and said, "It's freezing!" but he went on wading in. She looked down at her own legs, still white below her new purple bathing suit, which she thought made her look fairly thin. Philip finally dove in and swam out a ways, fast, then swam back.

He came charging out of the water toward her, dripping. "It's so fucking cold," he gasped. "My heart almost stopped."

Zoe laughed.

"Really, it did. You think I jest?"

"Poor thing." She put an arm around his waist for a second and patted his skin, which was freezing cold.

He put both hands on her shoulders and she shivered. "You're nice and warm," he said.

She started to move away but then stopped and looked up at him instead. He put his arms around her and drew her close to him. She put her arms around his waist and leaned her head against his chest. His body felt skinny and tense, very alive, and its cool touch now felt good against her skin, which was starting to burn from its first exposure to the sun.

Chapter Ten

The kids had already left when Zoe noticed that the X-Acto knife was missing. She searched the whole room, brushing scraps of leather off the tables and into her hands as she walked by. The tables were old and scarred, their tops made of dark sticky wood that blackened her hands. She looked in all the corners, pulled aside the heavy venetian blinds to check the windowsills, and went through the cabinets carefully, rearranging jars of poster paint, balls of yarn, piles of paper and drawings.

The knife wasn't anywhere. She squatted in front of the cabinet, sweaty and tired. "Oh, fuck," she whispered. The knife was supposed to be returned to the box in Marshall's office that held the hammer, hole-puncher, shears and other tools considered risky to leave around. Well, she'd deal with it tomorrow. She stood up and started pushing the chairs, which were scattered wildly, back toward the tables. She didn't know how you were supposed to get the kids to clean up. They never finished their projects on time and always wanted to work on them until the last minute, and anyhow they messed the place up so fast, it would've taken half the arts and crafts hour just to clean up.

She picked up her blue backpack, which held her damp bathing suit and towel, and her notebook and clipboard, and turned off the lights, waving to Marshall as she walked quickly past the reception area. He sat behind the glass at his desk in the director's office, a short, muscular guy with no neck and thick dark hair matting his arms and any other part of him that was visible.

Outside, her father was waiting for her in the parking lot. The car was cool with air conditioning, and classical music thundered from the radio as they drove away. Zoe waited until they were heading toward the turnpike to tell him about the missing knife.

"Ah, shit," he said sympathetically, shaking his head. He turned down the music. "Are you sure you looked everywhere?"

"Yeah," she said sadly. "It's not there. Marshall's going to have a fucking heart attack." She usually didn't use expressions like that with her father, but she was too upset to care. "What if he fires me?"

Her father said he didn't think that would happen, and told her to look again tomorrow, when she was calmer. "But if you don't find it," he said, "mention it to the kids first. I mean, don't accuse anyone —"

"Yeah, I know, I know." She leaned back in her seat and shut her eyes. Tomorrow was Friday, thank God, and then she'd have worked there for one week. She'd thought about nothing but Summer Fun at the Y for the past four days. At home she could hardly pay attention to anything anyone said, and every night before she fell asleep, images from the day flashed through her mind. So far, they'd made gimp key chains, then wristbands from leather scraps, and they'd written a continuous story about a flying girl hero. Every afternoon they played kickball in the gym. At the pool, Janice, the

lifeguard, taught them, and Zoe just encouraged the reluctant ones to get in the water and keep going. Most of them
couldn't swim, and it was strange to see some of the bigger
girls of eleven and twelve, who seemed so tough out of the
water, hanging on desperately to the sides of the pool.

The next morning Zoe stood in the big dusty room with her
clipboard and her whistle — which she was determined never
to use — and called out the girls' names. Almina, Juanita,
Sandy, Carmella, Denise, Katrina. There were thirty-two registered but only about twenty showed up on any given day.
They were all sitting around on chairs or tables, holding bags
with their bathing suits, towels and lunches. Once everyone
was quiet, Zoe mentioned the missing knife.

There was a brief silence. Then Denise, who had long
stringy hair and a loud voice, said, "Maybe somebody stole
that knife."

"Shut up, girl," said Juanita, one of the black girls, in a high
voice. "You don't know that, you just talking."

"I'm not saying anyone stole it," Zoe said. "I don't know.
But if anyone did, it's too bad because there'll be a lot of
other projects we won't be able to do. It's hard enough to
get things —"

She stopped herself from telling them how limited the budget was. When Zoe had pointed out to Marshall that there
were only five pairs of scissors for thirty-two kids, and that
three of the pairs were left-handed, he had done an elaborate shrug, lifting his hairy arms off the desk as if she'd said,
You're under arrest. He told her that the Y gave hardly any
money to this program because the kids hardly paid anything for it — unlike the regular day camp. That's not fair,

Zoe said, and Marshall said they'd already spent the money for this summer and there was none left for scissors.

"You could kill someone with a knife like that," said Carmella, swinging her plastic bag, which had the name of a hardware store on it. She swung it in a circle in front of her until it wound around her wrist; then she swung it the other way, narrowly missing the face of the girl sitting next to her.

"Yeah," said Monique, one of the older girls, who had a huge afro with a yellow pick stuck in it. "I be afraid for my ass if there be somebody walking around here with that knife —"

"All right, all right," Zoe interrupted, sorry she'd even mentioned the knife, "it's time to go." She made them line up for the walk across the building to the gym.

Once, Monique looked back at Zoe, her forehead wrinkled. "You not worried?" she asked.

"No!" Zoe said lightly, feeling sick inside. "There's nothing to worry about."

"That's what you think," Monique said, shaking her head like an old lady who'd seen it all.

"So whoever it was put back the knife but not the razor blade that goes inside it," Zoe told Rivka. They were sitting on the picnic bench in Rivka's backyard, watching the kids play Wiffle ball on the lawn. It was late afternoon on Friday; on Monday, which was the Fourth of July — and Zoe's birthday, too — the Levs were leaving for Israel.

Zoe was glad to have found the knife and fitted it with a new blade — Marshall would never have to know. But the incident had made her care less about how well she did her job; next week she wouldn't knock herself out trying so hard to make things nice for those kids. "Those little shits," she said.

Rivka laughed. "It sounds like you are doing all right." Then she looked more closely at Zoe. "You seem different," she said. "You're growing up."

Somehow that didn't offend Zoe, because she knew it was true. "When I'm at the Y, I feel a little bit like you."

Rivka's eyes were as clear as a child's; they had none of the slittiness or tiny red veins Zoe could see in her own if she looked closely. It made her seem vulnerable in some way Zoe couldn't define.

"It's true, that is like me," Rivka said. "But just because you have something to give, it doesn't mean the other people will want it. I thought last year that I should give something to the Jewish community. Everyone said it would be awful to teach Hebrew to the kids here —"

"We were little shits, right?" Zoe said. But she couldn't help it; the memory made her smirk.

Rivka made a dismissive gesture. "You wanted during this year a lot from me. And you think I'm very strong and I can always help you. But I wasn't prepared for what was needed."

For the first time, Zoe understood what it might mean for Rivka that Naomi had killed herself just when Rivka was trying to give them something. Instinctively she didn't say anything but just waited for Rivka to say more. *She wants to talk to me*, Zoe thought.

"You know, a person who leaves Israel doesn't feel like a very good specimen of a human being," Rivka told her.

"You are good," Zoe said.

Rivka looked over to where the kids were playing. "No, I'm

just a mother who doesn't want to send her sons to the army. I'm not sure you can understand all these things. If you knew Hebrew, I could explain to you better."

There was silence for a moment. Zoe took something out of her pocket and held it tightly in her hand.

Rivka looked at her.

"Hold out your hand," Zoe said.

Rivka held out her left hand.

Zoe rested her clenched fist on Rivka's hand for a moment, and then opened her fingers. When she took her hand away, there was a dark blue cylindrical bead in Rivka's palm, about two inches long. It was glass and had minute yellow and orange designs melted in. Beads like this were usually used as roach clips but Rivka didn't have to know that.

"It's very pretty," Rivka said, rubbing her thumb and forefinger over its smooth surface. "It's from North Africa?"

"I don't know," Zoe said. "Maybe."

"It looks like it's from there," Rivka said. She seemed pleased; she smiled at Zoe. "Thank you," she said.

"Thank *you*," said Zoe.

Sunday, the day before Zoe's seventeenth birthday, was such a beautiful day — sunny and warm already at ten in the morning — that she almost forgot where she was going. She rode her bike happily through the quiet streets toward the Kaplans' apartment. She wore a pair of denim cut-offs and a faded T-shirt from a Solidarity Day march for Soviet Jews; you could just barely make out the faded blue Star of David with the black chains running through it. As she coasted along beneath the full trees that shaded the road, the warm wind on her bare arms and legs made her feel incredibly free.

It was only as she came around the last corner and saw the entrance to Sleepy Hollow that she started feeling nervous. Mrs. Kaplan had called when Zoe was at Rivka's on Friday night and told Zoe's mother she wanted to give Zoe something of Naomi's for her birthday.

"Hi, Zoe, come in," Mrs. Kaplan said when she opened the door. She spoke very naturally, as if she saw Zoe every day. Zoe hadn't been inside the apartment since the day of Naomi's funeral. Everything looked pretty much the same; even the feel of the shag carpet under her bare feet was the same as it had been every summer, as if nothing had changed.

"How are you? Your mom said you're working at the Y." Mrs. Kaplan had poured her a cup of coffee and pushed aside the Sunday *Times* she'd been reading when Zoe knocked.

"Yeah, it's a pretty good job. I mean, it's hard, but at least I feel like I'm doing something worthwhile." She stopped, feeling that she might've said the wrong thing, but Mrs. Kaplan nodded and smiled at her from across the couch. Her hair was a darker blond than it used to be, and she was wearing it drawn back from her face in a loose ponytail. Zoe had expected her to look older, even haggard, but she didn't; if anything she looked younger. She wore very little makeup, and she looked calmer and more serious than when Naomi was alive. She looked — yes — better. A few months ago this would have made Zoe furious, but she wasn't angry now. Mrs. Kaplan had been through enough: Why shouldn't she try to be happy? On the table to Zoe's left was a large photograph of Naomi in a silver frame. It was her school picture from last fall; her round blue eyes looked straight out, and her smile was wry but generous, as if the photographer had been saying something stupid.

Zoe had expected to feel sadder coming here, but looking around the apartment at Naomi's picture, at Naomi's mother, she realized that her memory of Naomi was starting to exist as something apart from all the details of Naomi's actual life. Naomi was becoming more of a feeling, a way of looking at things, than an actual person connected to a family, an apartment and a blue Datsun. So it no longer mattered so much what other people said about her. For Zoe, she was changing into a reliable inner sensation that would always be Naomi no matter what anyone else said, no matter what evidence of her actual life remained.

Mrs. Kaplan picked up a small brown velvet-covered box that Zoe hadn't noticed was sitting on the coffee table. "Zoe, I wanted you to have something of Naomi's, and this seemed like a good time."

"Thanks," Zoe almost whispered, taking the box. Of course Naomi wasn't here, she wasn't really connected to these things anymore, but still it was so strange. Inside the box was the gold *chai* Nao had gotten for her Bat Mitzvah. Slowly Zoe took it out and put it around her own neck.

Mrs. Kaplan was watching her. When Zoe thanked her again, she just nodded her head quickly without saying anything, and her smile was more like a grimace.

Zoe snapped shut the brown velvet box. The chai meant Life, of course: It was a charm, a protective. The fact that Mrs. Kaplan had chosen to give it to her made Zoe feel a little resentful, as if it were a symbol of some unfair accusation.

"It doesn't seem like she's been gone only five months," Mrs. Kaplan said. "It seems a lot longer."

"I know," Zoe said. She hoped Mrs. Kaplan wasn't going to get all emotional.

She didn't. She just shook her head quietly for a moment and then looked up, gave Zoe a genuine smile, and said, "I'm glad you came. It's good to see you."

Zoe didn't know how to answer, but it didn't seem to matter. Mrs. Kaplan said she was meeting someone at noon, and she led Zoe to the door, wishing her a happy birthday. Then Zoe was back out in the sunny morning.

She rode quickly past the kids on the playground, up the hill onto the street. There was more traffic now, and the day was getting hot. As she rode, it became an ordinary Sunday in summer again, and she started hoping Melanie had waited for her before going to the pool. She was sweating by the time she pedaled up her own driveway, and when she reached the top, she felt totally exhausted. She wheeled her bike into the garage, breathing hard, and thinking how Naomi would never be seventeen. Zoe didn't touch the gold *chai* or even look at it, but she felt its slight weight against her chest, its delicate chain around her neck.

"Pull in right here," Zoe said as she and Philip were driving down Beach Road on their way to the fireworks. She pointed to the Jewish Center parking lot.

"Here?" Philip said. "The Jewish Center?"

"Yeah, yeah, it has the best view of the fireworks. It's up on that hill, you know? We can sit out on the beach wall." She knew she'd run into people she knew, but what the hell. Her parents had opened a bottle of wine for her birthday dinner, and she felt warm and safe, happy to be out with Philip.

He turned into the big lot and circled around looking for a space. "Are you sure they'll let me in?" he asked.

"Of course they'll let you in!" She was vaguely offended by

the suggestion that they wouldn't. "There's no one checking cards at night," she explained as they walked through the big open gates, "but you could come as my guest, anyhow. You can come with me to the pool sometime."

"OK," he said, sounding uncertain.

Zoe made a welcoming gesture with her hand and said in a thick Yiddish accent, "You're een, you're een."

Philip laughed, and seemed to relax. "What?"

Then she explained about the old man who sat at a card table all day in the shade of the big tree near the gate, checking membership cards and letting people in, his tone suggesting they were entering some secret and privileged society instead of just the Jewish Center pool.

They walked up the steps and past the darkened snack bar; lots of people were heading toward the beach wall, whole families carrying blankets and thermoses, kids running ahead. At the wall, Zoe and Philip stood looking out over the sound, and every once in a while a familiar face emerged from the darkness, saying hello to Zoe. Mrs. Rabinowitz, wife of the president of Temple Beth Israel, said, "Hello, Zoe, how are you?" in a loud Brooklyn voice and looked with interest at Philip. She knew Mrs. Rabinowitz didn't like her; she'd thought Zoe and Naomi were degenerates because she'd caught them lying on top of her car once in the temple parking lot, smoking cigarettes and laughing.

They headed further down along the wall until Zoe heard someone say, "Hey, Diamond!" and turned to see Jeff and Adam, Lynn, Carol and Susan standing around with two other guys she didn't know.

"Today's your birthday, isn't it?" Susan said. "I always remember — the Fourth of July." They all took turns kissing

Zoe and saying happy birthday, and then Adam started hitting her lightly on the ass, saying "One! Two!" but they stopped him. "We're too old for birthday spankings," Susan said.

"We are getting so fucking old," said Jeff. "Next summer'll be the last summer we'll all be here, probably —"

"Shut up!" said Lynn.

"This is nice," Carol said, leaning over and touching Naomi's *chai*. "Did you always have this?"

"No, it was Naomi's. Mrs. Kaplan gave it to me for my birthday." There was an awkward silence, the way there was any time you mentioned Naomi, and Zoe said quickly, "You know Philip, right?" She was proud of Philip tonight. He was wearing old Levis and a white shirt; he had a tan and looked good.

"It's nice that the whole country's celebrating your birthday, huh?" said one of the guys Zoe didn't know.

"Yeah," she said. "I always tell them not to make such a big fuss, but they do it anyhow."

"I wish we had a boat," said Carol. "That's the best thing — being out on the water for the fireworks." The sound was crowded with hundreds of boats, and people were sending up rockets and white flares that fell softly in flaming balls of light.

"I was out on a boat last Fourth of July," Philip said, taking a drag off his cigarette and blowing the smoke out in an energetic stream. "It was great."

"Yeah? Do you have a boat?" Carol asked.

"No, no, it was my friend's." It had been Randy's cousin's boat, Zoe knew, though Philip didn't say. "There was a full moon with like four rings around it, just lighting up the whole sky and making rings on the waves. It was gorgeous."

"Wow," said Susan.

"Yeah, it gave you this really magical feeling," Philip said.

"Really?" said Adam, with unfriendly sarcasm in his voice.

There was silence for a moment, and then Philip said "Uh-huh," very quietly, and lit another cigarette. Zoe looked at him in the flare from his lighter, and all of a sudden he looked too tall and too blond, and his voice was too dramatic. When she was alone with him, she forgot how strange he seemed in a crowd of other kids, especially if there were other guys around. Adam's hostility made her uneasy. She was glad when the fireworks started and they all sat down in a row on the beach wall to watch.

As the fireworks exploded in the sky, Philip moved closer to Zoe on the wall, and she felt a flash of annoyance toward him. She couldn't stand the thought of her friends talking about them afterwards — but why blame him? It was irrational, she told herself, as chrysanthemums burst in the sky, raining down red, white and blue light. Then Philip rested his hand on her thigh, and she was alarmed at the way the explosions were echoed in the darkness of her own body.

Today's topic was Responsibility. The girls and Zoe made an uneven, sprawling circle of bodies on the floor of the big gym. It was dim and cool in there, but through the windows up near the ceiling, you could see how bright it was outside. It felt unnatural to Zoe to be indoors all day in summer, but the Y was right in the middle of a city block and there was no space outside. She would try to organize a field trip to the beach, but in the meantime they were supposed to be hanging out in the building, doing things like this Values Clarification, which Zoe thought of privately as brainwashing hour.

"So, uh, let's say you have a friend, and you know this friend is doing something dangerous," she said, glancing down at the *Values Clarification Handbook* and then up at the girls, who were quieter than usual. "Something that could hurt him or her."

"Like what?" asked Denise.

Zoe sighed. The handbook did not go into specifics. "Well, just something that you —"

"You mean if, like, your friend be shooting up smack?" said Monique. A few of the other girls giggled, but there were a couple of gasps around the circle, too. All their eyes were on Zoe.

"Yeah, that could be classified as something dangerous," she said as calmly as she could. "But it could be other things, too. The point is, what should you do about it, as their friend?"

"You could talk to them and convince them to stop doing it," Almina suggested. She was a serious-looking girl with wide dark eyes and her hair in neat French braids around her head. For a moment they all considered what she'd said.

"Yeah, but what if they won't —" said Juanita.

"— Stop?" Zoe said. "Are you being responsible if you tell an adult — someone you can trust?"

No one answered right away, and with awful clarity Zoe saw herself in the car that last night with Naomi, who was singing, "If you feel like love, make it, if you feel like flying —"

"— You feel sick, girl?" Monique was saying.

In a split second Zoe was back in the gym, and all the girls were looking at her. "No," she said, but her voice came out hoarse. She had a moment of panic trying to remember what they'd been talking about, but then she thought, Oh yeah, Responsibility.

"You look like you seen a ghost," Monique said.

Zoe laughed and shook her head, but she knew Monique wasn't fooled. If you showed the slightest sign of weakness in front of these girls, they picked up on it right away, like Rivka. Looking at their curious faces, she had a wild urge to tell them about Naomi, to confess how hard it was to be responsible for anyone else and how badly she'd done at it. But instead she smiled and said, "No, no ghosts around here. I don't think so, anyway," looking with mock concern around the gym and up at the high ceiling, which made them laugh.

"How old are you?" Juanita asked suddenly. Again, the circle of expectant faces. They looked half-shy, like they thought she might yell at them, and half-amused, because even if she did yell, they wouldn't take it too seriously.

"Seventeen," she said. There were a few giggles, and someone said, "My sister be seventeen."

"You got a boyfriend?" Juanita asked.

"No," said Zoe, but she couldn't help it, she started to laugh.

"She does have a boyfriend!" said Monique. "That's why she laughing!"

Zoe let them go on like this, speculating, trying to tease information out of her, talking about their sisters' boyfriends, until it was time to go down to the locker room and get ready for swimming. She didn't want to talk about responsibility any more than they did.

Zoe wandered into the living room and found her sister sitting on the edge of the couch, turning the pages of the *New York Times Magazine* furiously, the thin newsprint crackling in the quiet room. Usually Melanie would carefully study all the ads; she could tell you which outfits were nice and which were tacky, and she'd figure out how to put her own clothes together in new ways to look like the nice ones. But now it seemed like she was barely looking at them. She muttered, "Oh, fuck," as she turned another page so fast that it ripped.

Zoe sat on the couch and put her feet up on the pile of newspapers. "What's the matter?" she asked.

Melanie stopped turning pages and bit her nails for a moment. Then she sat very still as if listening for something. The only sound in the house was their mother's faint voice talking on the phone in the bedroom. Their father was in the study grading papers for summer school. "Shit," Melanie whispered.

"What's the matter?" Zoe repeated. This was the first time she'd been alone with Melanie since before she had left to spend Fourth of July weekend in West Hartford, at Tova Wallerstein's house.

"Fucking Mrs. Weitz," said Melanie. "I knew she was going to call. I knew it."

"What *happened*?"

Melanie shook her head and bit her nails. "She caught me and Barry coming down the stairs — it was about four o'clock in the morning and I was trying to sneak back to Tova's." The absurdity of the situation seemed to hit Melanie and she started to giggle unhappily. "'All right, you two, the game's over!' she said, like we were in a gangster show or something." Zoe laughed, too. Melanie's green eyes were very bright, and on her lids were rainbow stripes of makeup: green shading into turquoise and then white, right up to her eyebrows. She was working in a department store this summer, and she still had on her work clothes — a pair of tight white corduroys and a silky turquoise blouse, so sheer

285

you could see her bra through it. Zoe thought she looked gorgeous. Zoe herself had been trying to look a little better lately — probably Melanie's and Rivka's influence — but so far she'd only gotten to the stage of tucking in her shirts and wearing mascara on her eyelashes. She knew she didn't really know how to do any of it the right way and lacked the discipline to learn.

Abruptly Melanie stopped laughing and lifted her head, listening. They heard their mother's quick footsteps coming down the hall.

She came into the living room and stood glaring at them both for a moment. She and all the other ladies in her con-sciousness-raising group had started to wear jeans and baggy sweatshirts all the time. Zoe thought it was cool, but Melanie said it made them look dowdy. Their mother's eyes looked angry, magnified behind her glasses, and her hair was frizzed out, standing up off her forehead. "I'd like to talk to Melanie alone," she announced.

Zoe glanced at Melanie, who looked scared. "Why can't I stay?"

"Because I don't want you to," her mother said.

Zoe got up and went down the hallway into her room for a minute; then she sneaked back out and stood outside the liv-ing room doorway where her mother couldn't see her.

"Well, Mrs. Weitz says it wasn't the first time she thought she heard you and Barry sneaking down the stairs at night," her mother was saying. "I want to know what you've been doing up there."

"Nothing," Melanie said. There was a short silence. "We were talking."

"You really expect me to believe that?" Her mother's voice

was louder and her Brooklyn accent was coming back — it always did when she got angry.

"Mom," Melanie said. "I'm eighteen years old. I'm going to college in less than two months. Why can't I just live my own life?"

"Because it's not just your own life! You're part of a family, too, you know. You're still my daughter, and I don't want you going around all made up like a raccoon and doing God knows what with your boyfriend."

Melanie was silent.

"All right, fine," their mother said, her voice rising even further. "It's your own life you'll ruin, not mine. You're the one who won't get to go to college if you get pregnant. You're the one who's going to wind up living in some shack with a bunch of screaming kids and your husband out digging ditches all day. You'll see how you like it!"

"Mom," Melanie said wanly. "It's not going to happen."

Tell her there's such a thing as birth control, Zoe thought. It might make her mother feel better to know that Melanie was on the pill. But she remembered that Melanie hadn't actually confessed to making it with Barry, and probably didn't want to. Still, it was so stupid, Zoe couldn't just stand there —

"Listen," Zoe said to her mother in a calm, reasonable voice, as she walked into the living room. Melanie had her head in her hands; it looked like she was crying, or about to.

"Zoe, I told you —" her mother said, but Zoe cut her off.

"Just listen to me for *one minute*. You're all opposed to us getting married and living our lives around men. Well, we're not! Melanie's not getting married, she wants to go to college and become something. But when did *you* get married?" Her mother looked like she'd rather not think about that. "You were only two years older than Melanie!" Zoe said triumphantly. "So don't you think she can have the same — the same desires — as anyone who does get married? I mean —" She stopped, because Melanie was giving her a warning look.

But this had momentarily shut their mother up. She looked tired and old.

"No, she doesn't think we have any feelings," Melanie said, starting to cry now. "She wants some other kind of daughters, she'd rather we didn't even kiss a boy. Maybe she wants us to be lesbians."

Startled, Zoe looked at her mother.

"That is *not* what I want," her mother said. She was silent for a moment, and then she looked at Melanie. "You're my responsibility until you move out of this house. Do you understand? After that, you'll make your own decisions." She spoke more quietly, though; she'd been semi-defeated.

"OK," Melanie said. She'd stopped crying and there were dark smudges under her eyes. Zoe knew, as her mother probably did, too, that Melanie would go right on sleeping with Barry.

"God Almighty," her mother said, shutting her eyes. "Give me strength." They all sat in silence for a minute, and then her mother opened her eyes and looked at Zoe. "And the same thing goes for you, too. I've decided I don't want you seeing Philip more than two nights a week."

Zoe felt her heart start beating fast at this new injustice. She and Philip had been hanging out together a lot more than two nights a week. Without Naomi, with Danielle practically a stranger to her now, and with Rivka in Israel, who else was there? She and Philip were good friends; he sometimes kissed her or held her hand, and he also put his arms around her when she needed to cry about Naomi. She didn't really know what was going on with Philip, but it wasn't heavy sex, that was for sure. "He's not my boyfriend," she said.

Her mother and Melanie both looked surprised. "No," said her mother sarcastically, "just your constant male companion. Look, Zoe, I'm not playing games —"

"You just don't like him because he's not Jewish," Zoe said.

"Well, I think I'm being fairly reasonable," her mother said. "You know, a lot of parents wouldn't even allow you to go out with him. I'm saying it's OK for you to go out with him, but not more than twice a —"

Zoe was shaking. "I'm not going out with him!" she yelled. "He's gay!"

She saw the look of confusion on her mother's face, then turned and strode out of the room, down the hall and into her own room, where she slammed the door and locked it. Then she was lying on her bed, crying hard.

Zoe shalom,
    We're having a good time, visiting family and friends. Hope it's a good summer for you too. I miss our strange talks.
    Rivka

On the front of the postcard was a picture of a Yemenite girl working at a loom. She looked about Zoe's age; she had long dark hair and a serious, concentrated expression. Zoe sat on the edge of her bed, looking at the picture and trying to imagine what Rivka was doing at that moment. Everything she could imagine was based on the pictures she'd seen in their photo album: They were sitting on the beach, maybe, or out on someone's balcony.

It was a warm evening, still light out. Zoe was wearing her shorts and YMCA staff shirt; she smelled of chlorine and the mustiness of the Y building. Through the open window she could hear the shouts of kids playing softball in the street. She looked closely at the picture of the Yemenite girl and wondered why it gave her a vague feeling that something was wrong with her own life. I should go to Israel, she thought. But after a few minutes she decided no, she was where she belonged and she was making herself useful. She could still go to Israel sometime, but it wasn't important right now. What then was wrong? Had something happened to Rivka? She turned the postcard back over to the note from Rivka and touched the words with her fingertips, as if doing so would make an ESP message come through.

Yes, 'n' how many times must the cannonballs fly?
Before they're forever banned?
The answer, my friend, is blowin' in the wind,
The answer is blowin' in the wind.

"Louder!" said Jim, the boys' counselor. "Can't hear you over the traffic!" The kids sang it again, and Jim strummed his guitar as if his life depended on it. He was the one who'd finally convinced Marshall that the kids should be allowed to go outside for an hour each afternoon. There was barely enough room for all of them to sit on the patch of prickly brown grass between the building and the parking lot, just a few yards away from the street. It was a muggy, hazy afternoon, and Zoe felt limp and hot. Marshall had said they'd better grow eyes in the backs of their heads, because they had to make absolutely sure no one slipped away. Zoe didn't know about the boys, but there wasn't much chance of the girls running off — she could hardly get them to sit even a few feet away from her anymore. Right now, Monique had her arm around Zoe's neck and was singing into her ear, Denise and Almina were lying on the ground with their heads in her lap, and Juanita was behind them all, gripping Zoe's shoulder to balance herself as she danced on her knees to the music. All the other girls were pressed in close around them, just waiting, Zoe knew, for a chance to crawl up next to an unoccupied part of her body.

She'd realized a few weeks into Summer Fun at the Y that the main thing these girls wanted was affection. If you were friendly, it was easy to get them to do most things. They'd started cleaning up the arts and crafts room, and there hadn't been any more bad incidents like the knife.

But she'd never seen people so hungry for attention, and sometimes on hot days it was too much. Today she felt like their sweaty bodies were pressing her down into the prickly ground. "God, I'm suffocating," she said, and started peeling the sticky arms and hands off her shoulders, then moved over a few feet and sighed with relief.

When the song ended Monique said, "You don't like us no more."

"Yes I do," she said. "It's just hot." It was the first time she'd pushed them away.

"It just be too hot for y'all climbing all over her," Juanita said.

"Fan her," suggested Denise. The other girls joined in, fanning Zoe with their hands and giggling, making a little warm breeze around her head.

"The Queen of Sheba," said Jim. The boys glanced at them and then went back to thumb wrestling and shoving handfuls of grass down each other's backs; they thought the girls were stupid.

Someone came up behind Zoe and clamped strong damp fingers over her eyes. "Guess who?" The girls giggled. "Don't tell her!" This seemed to signal that things were back to normal and they could start hanging all over her again; they'd forgotten what she'd said a minute before and pressed in around her.

Damn, she thought. She was about to peel the hands off her eyes, but then she thought suddenly of Rivka. God, she missed her. She'll be back in two weeks, she thought. Instead of pushing the girls away, Zoe went on patiently with the game, saying, "I don't know. Almina? Sandy?"

"Wrong!" they shouted happily.

It was cool and calm in the Water Lilies room at the Museum of Modern Art. Zoe and Philip sat on a padded bench, their backs to a big window overlooking the sculpture garden. Monet's paintings took up the other three walls, the soft blue-green patterns with flecks of pink. If we could see this every day, Zoe thought, life would be different. She concentrated on the places where the shapes of water lilies emerged most clearly from the abstraction, and after a while she could see their movement, how they floated on the water. But there was still, inside her, a place of uncertainty that kept unfocusing her eyes from the painting and focusing them on her own mind.

She felt Philip's hand on hers and turned to look at him. "Are you all right?" he whispered.

Zoe looked away, back toward the Water Lilies. No, she thought, I'm nervous as hell. I'm about to lose my virginity.

But the thought made her want to snicker; that was such an old-fashioned way to describe it. Naomi probably would've found it funny: a seventeen-year-old virgin about to seduce this gay guy, or half-gay, whatever he was. Bisexual. *Why do you always have to dissect everything? Just do it.* Well, she would. Since Naomi died, Zoe felt like she should step out boldly into life and grab hold of whatever was worthwhile. She had a condom in the bottom of her backpack now, stolen from her parents' night table drawer last week. And there was the fact that Philip's parents went out every Saturday night with their same friends and never came home before midnight. It seemed inevitable: Sex was the logical next step that had to happen before anything else could.

Before *what* could? Before she could love Philip?

She would not answer that question.

Then she remembered him sitting next to her on the bench. "Yeah, I'm fine," she said.

He swallowed, and his Adam's apple moved up and down. "You're missing your friend a lot, aren't you?" He didn't mention Rivka's name, though of course he knew what it was.

Zoe hadn't known it was so obvious. "Well, I don't have anyone to talk to."

He looked sideways at her, making his eyes into slits and smirking. "Thanks."

She laughed. "No, I mean —"

"I know, I know. No girls."

"Yeah." She had, in fact, been spending most of her free time with Philip. Ever since the night Zoe yelled that Philip was gay, her mother clearly wanted to avoid the subject. Twice this week Zoe had cried when she was with Philip, and he probably realized it wasn't only the usual cycle of grief about Naomi. She hadn't told him she was worried about Rivka, though. Her ESP said *danger*; she was afraid there would be another war, or a bomb that would kill Rivka before she could make it back to Connecticut.

"I don't know," she said. "Nothing feels normal lately."

Philip dropped her hand and did an elaborate shrug. "Normality?" he said, speaking like a thoughtful stage character. "You think all these artists were normal? God, look at those Mondrians out there. Did you see how every time he varies the color in one of those little squares, you feel a slightly different emotion? He must've been really wild just to think of that. If people could see inside the mind of someone like him, they'd probably think he was completely insane."

Zoe smiled; he did know how to make her feel better sometimes.

He took her hand again and looked at her more seriously. "I'm really glad to be here with you," he said, almost shyly.

Zoe looked at his eyes and felt certain that Philip was trying to tell her something without saying the words. He had never done more than look at her like this, or hold her hand, kiss her. Either he wouldn't, or couldn't, do more. She realized that he was waiting for her to lead them into normality.

They sat on the couch in the den at Philip's house, smoking a joint. He was burning a yellow cone of incense on a little Oriental-looking metal tray that Randy had given him, to mask the smell. In front of them was a large blank TV, and lined up neatly on the shelf above it were his parents' bowling trophies. Philip sat slumped on the couch next to her, leaning his head against the fake leather cushions. "God, that was a great day," he said. "I can't wait till I can move to New York."

"Yeah," Zoe said, passing him the joint. "I wouldn't mind living in the city for a while."

"That'd be great. I mean, if we were both there. We could have a blast."

Yeah? she thought. Really? She wondered if he meant maybe they could live there together after graduation. It excited her to think of how pissed off her mother would be. But you could go to college and still live with someone, couldn't you? "It'd be great," she agreed, but Philip just nodded and said nothing further about the exact arrangements.

Then he said, "You can just be free there, you can be any way you want. That's what I like about it."

"Yeah, like that girl we saw today just walking down the sidewalk and singing like she was in an opera? I thought she was great." They both laughed, but Zoe had the feeling Philip meant something else when he said you could be any way you wanted. It had to do with him and Randy, with that other part of his life she knew almost nothing about. She'd never asked him about being gay, what it meant, what he wanted, and he'd never told her much. Whenever he mentioned Randy, which wasn't often, he talked as if it were an incident in his distant past; yet Zoe felt it was part of who he was in the present, too. Sometimes she thought maybe he was using her to prove to himself that he wasn't gay. Other times she thought he was keeping things from her, and she'd imagine him and Pamela talking, laughing at her behind her back.

Well, she didn't know. He curved his hand gently around the back of her neck and kissed her, lightly and hesitantly, the way he usually did. Feeling almost angry, she reached up and pulled his blond head toward her, kissing him back hard, her tongue inside his mouth. She felt him stiffen for a second as if she'd hurt him, but then he leaned forward and kissed her back with an intensity that was not like Philip, or not like the Philip she knew. They kissed for a long time.

Then they were lying together sideways on the couch, half undressed. She caressed his skinny shoulders, his smooth chest, his ass, and he touched her breasts lightly, his hand making circles on them, but he didn't kiss them. She thought briefly of that guy Tom at that horrible party, sucking her nipples and exciting her so much. She wondered if Philip had ever made out with a girl before — surely he had? But they couldn't seem to get comfortable on the couch, now; Zoe was on the outside edge, balancing.

"I'm falling off," she murmured.

"No you're not, I'm holding you," he said.

They moved closer to each other, and she could feel that his penis was hard. His hand was inside her underwear, his fingers moving gently against her crotch. With Tom, she'd had an orgasm, but she didn't now. She wondered at what stage she should get the rubber out of her backpack, which was on the floor next to the couch. Closing her eyes, she concentrated on feeling something. She rested her face against Philip's chest, and her mind produced the old fantasy of Rivka holding her, Rivka's quick kiss on her cheek when they parted turning into something more passionate.

Philip's eyes were shut, his long eyelashes a red-gold fringe on his cheeks, and he was breathing deeply. Maybe he's thinking about Randy, she thought, and for the first time she saw that being gay was something real. She imagined

Philip and Randy lying together on this same couch, with incense burning on the little plate. And Philip and who else, and where else? Somehow she felt that if she reached over and got that rubber out of her pack, and they did it together, the fact would be definite, sealed, certain: She would have a boyfriend who — maybe — had a boyfriend.

He was pushing his penis against her vagina, holding her tightly. "Zoe," he whispered. She pulled away from him and sat up.

"What's the matter?" He raised himself up on his elbow and looked at her, his eyes very round and blue.

"Nothing. I don't know, I just don't want to —"

"Oh, I'm sorry," he said, sounding embarrassed and sincere. "I didn't mean to. We don't have to go all the way." He reached over and caressed her arm, and tried to pull her down next to him again.

She stayed where she was. "No, I just don't want to," she said miserably, feeling as if she couldn't stand for him to touch her even one more time. "I'm sorry." She leaned over and got her shirt, put it on and felt instantly calmer. Reaching under her collar, she pulled out Naomi's gold *chai*, which had moved around on its chain while they were making out.

Philip sat up, his penis now limp against the fake leather couch. Zoe felt a terrible loneliness coming over her. Why did taking off their clothes wreck their intimacy? It was somehow unfair. *I wasn't prepared for what was needed,* she thought sadly, seeing the hurt starting to show in his face.

Chapter Eleven

"Come on! Keep going! Good!" Zoe walked along the edge of the pool while five of her girls — the worst swimmers — thrashed through the water. They seemed to use up so much energy and make hardly any progress. "Stretch your arms way out!" she said, her voice and the voice of Janice, the lifeguard, who was with the rest of the kids down at the deep end, echoing back and forth in the tiled room. "That's good, Sandy, keep kicking!" If she stopped shouting, she felt they might drown.

She'd been throwing herself into her job like this ever since that night at Philip's house, which she tried not to think about but found herself marking time by. It hurt even to think around the edges of what had happened, and she knew things were never going to be the same; neither of them had called the other for two weeks now. In a way she wanted never to see him again, but she caught herself imagining scenes with him talking to her, touching her, persuading her to change her mind. In reality, he had seemed to take her rejection that night as total, complete — even expected — and somehow just knowing this made her unable to call him up and say that it wasn't.

It just went around and around like that, and she was better off not thinking about it. "Good, Denise!" she yelled. "Don't forget to breathe!"

Across the room one of the double doors swung open; at first she thought it would be Marshall, but it was Rivka, Eli and Eitan. They'd come to see her at work! She'd told Rivka to stop by when they got back, but hadn't really thought she would. They'd only been home for two and a half days.

"Keep going!" she yelled at the girls, and then walked around the pool to the door. Rivka and the kids were grinning at her, looking shy and out of place.

"Hi, Zoe," Rivka said. "They told us we could come and say hello to you — I hope it's all right —"

"Hi! Yeah, it's fine." Zoe hugged the kids and, after a moment's hesitation, Rivka. They all had dark tans and their hair was shorter. Zoe asked if they'd had a good time, and they said yes. After a few minutes Eli and Eitan moved away from Rivka, their eyes large and serious as they watched the other kids in the pool.

Zoe thought Rivka looked younger — or happier, maybe. She was wearing shorts and a blue shirt with silver embroidery around the neck. Zoe felt shy standing in front of Rivka in her purple bathing suit, arms crossed over her breasts. "Does it feel strange to be back?" she asked.

"Yes, it's very strange. I went to the supermarket the other day, and I had such a — culture shock —" Her hands described big fireworks going off. "Everybody looks so plastic," she said, laughing.

Zoe laughed, too, though she didn't really know what Rivka meant. "I guess so," she said. She felt the pain she'd been in since that night with Philip starting to lift. Rivka said they could come back and pick Zoe up after work, and they'd all go to the beach. Apparently everything was all right, after all; she shouldn't have worried.

"OK," Zoe said, backing away a few steps. "So I'll see you later —" She was about to turn around when she saw Rivka's eyes move down and then up again, over her body.

"You look good," Rivka said.

"Thanks," said Zoe, feeling the compliment slide over her skin like a pair of hands.

When she turned around, she saw all five of the girls hanging on to the side of the pool, watching from across the water. She walked around to them, feeling incredibly cheerful. "Hey," she said, "you guys are supposed to be swimming."

They looked up at her, their faces wet and their legs foreshortened by the water, which made them look somehow vulnerable. "Who's that?" Sandy asked.

"A friend of mine."

There was a brief silence while they tried to figure it out. Finally Monique said, "She pretty," and everyone agreed. They left it at that, as if all their unasked questions were answered.

Zoe and Rivka sat on a large beach towel covered with a design of anchors, while the kids dug a big tunnel down near the water. The boys' and Rivka's bodies were so dark, it looked like the sun in Israel had surrounded them from every possible angle, more powerful than any sun Zoe could imagine.

"I'm going to keep working there over the winter, if they get enough money to pay me," Zoe was saying. "Marshall says he'll know by next week."

"*Mazal tov!*" Rivka said, smiling at her. "That's really great, Zoe. They like you."

"They ought to, I've worked my ass off all summer," Zoe said, but she really was pleased. She felt like she was float-ing in some kind of liquid happiness this afternoon, sitting here on the beach next to Rivka, with still another month of summer left, and knowing she would probably have her job for the winter, too. She looked at Rivka, who was wearing a bathing suit with a bright geometric pattern. When she leaned forward, you could see where the skin on her breasts was lighter. Zoe watched her breathe.

Rivka was looking out at the sound, where boats with white sails traveled slowly between the islands. "We are going to move back to Israel," she said.

Zoe wasn't sure she'd heard right at first. She felt like some-one had hit her in the chest, right between her breasts. "You are?" she said stupidly.

"Yes, Natan has a job in Jerusalem," Rivka said, turning to look at her. "He's going to work with students at the univer-sity." She looked calm and far away, and she spoke as if she didn't know how her words were affecting Zoe.

"Jerusalem," Zoe repeated. "Wow." She wanted to shout No! No! No! Why the hell would Rivka want to live in Jeru-salem? So she could walk down the street where Yehuda was killed? It was sick, it must be Natan's idea. Instantly she hated him.

"We both want to go back very much," Rivka said. "We were thinking about it for a long time before we went, but we couldn't know how we would feel."

A person who leaves Israel doesn't feel like a very good specimen of a human being. Obviously Rivka hadn't explained what that

301

really meant because Zoe was next to nothing to her. "When are you going?" Zoe asked, feeling sick.

"At the end of August, the end of this month. I have still to find a job there."

Zoe looked out toward the water, but what she actually saw was Rivka walking down a street in the ancient city, surrounded by a maze of yellow walls, closed off from her forever. She noticed that Rivka certainly had picked about as public a place as possible to tell her this wonderful news. That must be because she didn't want a scene. *It wouldn't hurt you to be a little more tough about things.*

"Why do you want to leave?" Zoe said finally. "I thought you liked it here."

"I do like it," Rivka said. "I'm not saying it was easy to decide. But this place is not really my home. I'm an Israeli."

Good for you, Zoe thought. She hated the way Rivka said Is-ra-e-li, pronouncing each vowel distinctly. "So, you're an American, too," she said. "If you stayed here longer, you'd feel like this was your home." She knew it was childish to argue, but she couldn't help it.

Rivka smiled a little and shook her head. "At least then you wouldn't have to worry about your kids getting killed in any wars," Zoe added.

Rivka's face became angry; Zoe could see that she wanted to say something sharp — about Zoe, about Americans, it wouldn't matter what — but that she was controlling herself. Then she just looked away, and Zoe realized that Rivka had no obligation to her anymore; she didn't have to be nice to her just because Zoe was her student, and she wouldn't have to keep in touch with her after she left. Zoe wanted to move over and sit close to Rivka, put her arms around her as if she could hold her back, keep her from going. Rivka kept staring out at the sound. Zoe looked down and traced one of the anchors with her finger.

Finally Rivka said, "Well, of course I will worry. But it's a very different place, children grow up in a different way. You will have to go there to understand it."

"Yeah," said Zoe. "You don't want your kids to turn out like me." She half meant this as a statement of the bitter truth, but it made them both smile and Zoe could tell Rivka wasn't angry anymore. "They must have laid a lot of guilt on you over there," Zoe said. "I think you're on a big guilt trip."

"*Zeh loh nakhon*. That is not correct," Rivka told her. "In Israel I felt something more deep than guilt. I felt like my heart wasn't closed anymore."

How disgusting, Zoe thought. It was like Rivka had fallen in love not with a person but with a place, and one where terrible things had happened to her. "You can come to visit us," Rivka pointed out. "It's your place, too, and you can stay there as long as you want to. It will be nice."

Zoe thought how Rivka was always full of these little reassuring statements. *It will be all right. It will be good.* All Zoe's friends were now either dead or estranged from her or about to move thousands of miles away. *It will be nice.* "Actually I'm planning to go to California," Zoe said.

"All right, so go to California," Rivka said. "I don't care what you do."

Zoe smiled sarcastically at her. "I know that," she said.

Zoe woke up in the middle of the night and wondered what was wrong. But all she heard were just the usual sounds in the house — the refrigerator humming, a car passing in the distance. Then she remembered that Rivka was leaving. She cried until her eyes burned and her nose ran. Sitting up in bed, she switched on the light and reached for a box of tissues. Then she just sat in the middle of her bed, arms wrapped around her knees, feeling the beating of her own heart. Rivka was leaving, Naomi was dead, Danielle and Philip weren't her friends anymore, and even Melanie was going to college in a few weeks. But at that moment the part of her mind that knew these things suddenly stopped knowing. Her pulse beat in the sides of her head; she felt like she was falling through space, everything she knew rushing away from her. She realized that tears were a luxury: They presumed that someone was there to perceive your sadness.

Zoe's mother tried to be nice; she went out of her way to ask Zoe if she'd come swimming with her one evening, just the two of them together. Usually her mother liked to go to the Jewish Center pool and swim laps alone, in the evenings when there weren't many people there. She said it was how she got rid of her aggressions.

So the two of them swam back and forth, passing each other in the middle of the pool. Their paces were very different; Zoe's mother swam slowly and steadily and never stopped, while Zoe swam as fast as she could for as long as possible and then stopped, completely out of breath, her heart pounding as she held on to the side and looked at the sky gradually darkening over the sound.

Finally her mother stopped, too, and they floated next to each other, holding on to the side. The air was getting cool but the water was warm. Her mother looked funny with her hair tucked into a white rubber bathing cap — Zoe would never wear one — that made her seem strangely anonymous, until you looked closely at her face and saw who it was.

"I'm sorry that Rivka's leaving," her mother said. "It's really too bad for you."

"Yeah." She was grateful for her mother's sympathy but didn't really know what to say. She couldn't tell her mother that the thought of Rivka's leaving made her feel so lonely that it seemed like she herself wouldn't exist anymore after Rivka was gone. Zoe sighed. "Well, she says I can come visit them."

"Sure, if you're working this winter, you can save up for it."

"She says, 'It's your place, too,'" Zoe said in her imitation Hebrew accent.

Her mother smiled, and Zoe held her breath and pushed herself down under water. Her feet touched the bottom of the pool, and then she pushed off and surfaced again, water streaming from her hair over her face. "It's funny," she said, wiping water away from her eyes, "but all the bad things I thought might happen this year never did, and all the things I never expected just hit —" She thumped the concrete side of the pool.

"What things did you expect to happen?" her mother asked.

"I don't know." She thought about how to put it delicately. "Once I got worried — I thought you and Dad might get divorced or something."

Her mother moved away from the side of the pool and started treading water, her arms and legs circling slowly, rhythmically. "No, we're not going to get divorced," she said, and if her voice sounded strange it might have been because she was moving around in the water. "I think it's more revolutionary to try to make your family over into something different than to become just another divorce statistic." She sounded almost as if she were talking to herself, but then she looked at Zoe and seemed to remember that she was talking to her daughter. "Actually your father and I love each other," she said.

Zoe was shocked, though, because she'd never heard either of her parents talk about divorce as if it were anything remotely like a real possibility. She had suspected, in a vague way, that it could happen, but she hadn't understood how close it had come. Her mother implied that she'd actually weighed the possibilities; she didn't say Zoe was wrong to have worried.

Zoe pushed away from the side of the pool, too, and then both of them were treading water. As her own arms and legs made circles in the warm water, she tried to imagine what it would be like to survive a shipwreck and be treading water in the middle of a freezing cold ocean. How long could you do it? How long would your will hold up your body, which got heavier every second and wanted to sink?

It was the last week of Summer Fun at the Y. One week until Rivka left. Zoe sat on a wooden bench in the section of the locker room reserved for counselors and stared at the cockroaches scuttling over the wet floor, up the lockers and into the little air vents in the metal doors. The room was dim because one tube in the fluorescent light had burned out and they hadn't replaced it yet. Zoe noticed the familiar smell of chlorine mixed with something like mildew. The girls had already changed and were on their way down to the pool where Janice was waiting for them. Zoe had told them to go ahead, she'd be there in a minute, but now that they'd left and she was alone, she felt like she didn't even have the energy to get up off the bench. She watched as a big, fat, ugly cockroach crawled right up to her foot, unafraid. Usually she hated them and banged the floor with her sneakers to chase them away, but today she didn't care.

Naomi would have understood about this — Zoe hadn't even realized how well until after she was dead.

You're just feeling sorry for yourself, Zoe thought, and it's disgusting.

I could just lie down on this bench and go to sleep, right now.

Then Zoe heard a bunch of kids shouting, a loud yell and the sound of someone crying. She was off the bench and out the door so fast she didn't even remember running down the hall toward the kids.

Denise was crying, hunched over against the wall with her arms across her stomach; some of the other girls were standing around her looking scared, and a couple of boys from Jim's group were hanging around the door of the boys' locker room, watching. "What happened?" Zoe asked, quietly and urgently. She put one arm around Denise, and with the other tried to pull Denise's hands away from her stomach. Denise was sobbing and making a sound like she might throw up. "What *happened*?" Zoe repeated. The girls were standing around like mutes, their towels draped around their necks.

Monique looked up and down the hallway before finally answering. "It was Eugene," she said quietly. "He punched her. That boy is crazy."

"Eugene is nasty," Carmella said, and a few people agreed with her. "He bothers Denise and her sister when they're walking home, right Denise?"

Denise nodded silently.

Zoe knew the kids had all kinds of feuds from their neigh-borhoods that they brought here with them, and sometimes things exploded. This was the worst so far, but Denise looked like she'd be all right; she said she could breathe and it didn't hurt so much anymore.

"OK, why don't you guys go down to the pool," Zoe said. "Tell Janice we'll be there in a minute." As they were walk-ing away, she heard Carmella say to Monique that Denise should've called Eugene something worse than blubber-belly fathead.

"Come over here and sit down," Zoe said, leading the girl over to the wooden bench in the hallway. She sat next to Denise, who looked pale and seemed smaller than usual. Well, she was only eleven years old — Zoe forgot sometimes that they were so young. Denise's long light-brown hair was tangled and looked like it hadn't been brushed lately, and her eyelashes were dark and pointed from her tears.

Zoe leaned forward to look at the girl's face. "You'll be all right?" she asked, feeling awkward.

Denise stared straight ahead for a moment. Then, abruptly, she started crying again.

"Denise, it's all right," Zoe said. "Jim's going to talk to Eugene. We won't let him bother you anymore."

Denise sobbed and then caught her breath. "My mother's in the hospital," she said.

Zoe was stopped for a moment. Then she said, "What for?"

"I don't know," Denise said. "But she's been there for two weeks." She cried harder, her face a sad contorted mask.

Zoe put her arm around Denise and sighed. "I'm sorry," she said. "It'll probably be all right." Denise glanced at her, not hopefully, but as if startled and amazed that Zoe could be so stupid. Zoe thought angrily, How the hell do I know it'll be all right? Maybe it'll be like Judy Teitelbaum's mother, who went in the hospital last year and died of breast cancer. How do I know? I sound like Rivka, pretending that it will all turn out for the best. *You can stay there as long as you want to.*

Fuck you, Rivka.

"I'm so sorry, that's really a hard thing," she said to Denise, who was trying to stop crying now. But Zoe knew she was sorriest for herself; what she was really sorry about was that the person she loved most in the world was going away. *You could stop thinking always about yourself. Think about other people.*

I don't want to think about other people. You can't help them, anyhow. I couldn't save Naomi. I can't do anything about Denise's mother.

In fact, she didn't want to think any more about anything at all. She would prefer not to do anything or be anywhere. She would prefer *not to be.* She realized that what she was actually wishing was to be dead, and for the first time she understood exactly how Naomi must have felt.

Naomi honked the horn of her Datsun in Zoe's driveway, and Zoe ran down the front walk, screaming her name. "Naomi, Naomi, Nao!" she yelled. Her friend rolled down the window and stuck her head out, her long messy hair curling over the car door. Naomi had a huge smile on her face, but she was actually very angry. Zoe asked her, "What took you so long to get here?" Naomi replied in an annoyed tone, "I just fell asleep for a while, that's all." In horror, Zoe realized that all the time they thought

Naomi was dead, she was only sleeping. Guilt went through her like knives.

"I love these," Zoe said to Grandma Rose as she picked up her glass of tea that rested inside one of the silver tea-glass holders that Grandma Rose's mother had brought over from Russia. Grandma Rose had gotten them out specially because Zoe and Melanie had driven to Brooklyn alone for the first time — a terrifying experience — to visit her.

"Take them. You can have them," Grandma Rose said.

"No way. My mother would kill me if I came home with these. She'd kill you, too." It infuriated Zoe's mother the way Grandma Rose gave everything away. For years now, if Zoe or Melanie said they liked something — even if it was something she used every day — she'd say take it.

"I'll be gone, anyway," Grandma Rose said, waving her hand in the air. "I don't need that Arlene should kill me. I'll be gone."

"*Grandma,*" said Melanie, sounding exactly like their mother.

Grandma Rose smiled her mocking smile that showed her false teeth. "It's the truth, my darling," she said.

"What do you mean?" said Zoe. "You're going to be around for a long time, Grandma."

"That's not what they tell me," said Grandma Rose.

"Who?" Zoe said.

"What are you talking about?" Melanie had put down the half of a bagel she'd allowed herself, and her pretty face was scrunched up, half curious and half annoyed.

"Well, I saw Grandpa Lenny not too long ago, and my sister Evelyn, and they told me I'll be with them soon." Grandma

Rose shrugged, her old wrinkled face serious but not worried. She spooned lots of sugar into another glass of tea, which she wasn't supposed to have because of her blood pressure.

"I saw Naomi, too," she said to Zoe. "Your friend Naomi, I remember her from when you were little girls. She's very happy with you, she says you were a good friend."

Zoe looked down at her plate and moved a piece of pickled herring around with her fork. "Did she say I'll be with her soon, too?" she asked.

"*Zoe,*" Melanie said. "You shouldn't joke about things like that."

"No, she did not," her grandmother said, her voice more vehement than usual. "But you be careful." She tapped Zoe on the arm with her old soft hand until Zoe looked up at the magnified blue eyes watching her sharply from behind her grandmother's glasses. "You listen to me. You be careful," she said. "You hear?"

"Yeah," Zoe said quietly. She wondered what Naomi had told her grandmother in the dream. Maybe Naomi knew that Zoe was beginning not to care much whether she lived or died. Zoe had never really considered the possibility that she might see Naomi again in some other life — but of course Naomi had believed in reincarnation. Maybe they could both be reborn together as something better and easier than two teenage girls in Connecticut, Zoe thought. Even if there was no such thing as reincarnation, death wouldn't be so bad if her soul could talk to Naomi's as they flew around out there in the dark.

Zoe hadn't told anyone because it wasn't really happening. She'd never wanted to die before; it was an emotion she did not approve of. There was no way she could tell Rivka that not only was she not at all tough, and not only did she think about herself all the time, but she thought about Rivka all the time, too, and wanted to die because she was leaving. There was nothing Rivka could do about it, anyway. It wasn't her fault that Zoe had messed things up with Danielle and Philip — not to mention Naomi — and now had no friends left. It was, quite simply, a hopeless situation. Like Nixon had given up and resigned from the presidency, she could resign from life. If she was just going to keep losing and losing and losing everyone, there wasn't much point in living.

That's not true, said her mind.

She tried to think of everyone who would be genuinely freaked out if she died. Her parents, her sister, her grand-mothers, her friends — but they all looked to her like card-board people pasted into another world that was far away, like a fake diorama of life on the other side of this thick, heavy sadness of her own. It was unfortunate, but she simply didn't have enough grief left over to feel any for them.

But it was strange how you could go around thinking about killing yourself and no one even noticed. All week Zoe had been helping Melanie get packed for college, driving around doing errands with her, and the subject of what Zoe thought was her own obvious sadness never came up. Instead Melanie talked on and on about college; she had decided this week to major in Radio and TV.

"Barry's brother says that at college you have the best times of your life and the worst times of your life," Melanie told Zoe as she was folding her new underwear and putting it into the big blue trunk.

"Yeah?" was all that Zoe said. She felt as if she'd forgotten how to talk; she couldn't seem to put her thoughts into words and sentences. Her words were all lost somewhere deep inside, and she didn't think she'd be able to have a real conversation with anyone ever again.

But Melanie seemed to think she was just sorry about her leaving. Looking up from the trunk, Melanie gave Zoe her nicest smile. "I'll really miss you," she said in a generous and sentimental tone, as if she were giving Zoe a present.

"I'll miss you, too," Zoe said, but she felt nothing when she said it, except a kind of emptiness that kept getting bigger. It was the place all her words had disappeared into, and all her feelings, too: She had become just the outer layers of a person. She had already almost died and disappeared, so there wouldn't be much for anyone to miss.

It was a Wednesday morning at the end of August when Zoe's father drove Melanie up to college for freshman orientation. Summer Fun at the Y was over, and Zoe still had a week of vacation before school and After-School Fun at the Y started. Rivka was leaving in three days. These were the facts of where she was in time and space, but none of it seemed real.

Her father looked at her as they all stood out on the driveway next to the loaded-up car. Her mother had already said good-bye to Melanie and left for work. Stuff was piled right up to the windows in the back seat; Zoe could see a lamp and a white pillow, and Melanie's posters rolled up on the back ledge. Her father smiled, and Zoe could see that he was sad and proud of Melanie. "I should be back by around six," he said. "And she'll" — he pointed to Melanie, who was leaning against the car, wearing cutoffs and a white halter top — "be back for Rosh Hashanah."

313

Leora Freedman

He didn't know, of course, that the whole family might never be together again. Zoe was almost convinced that if she didn't kill herself, something else was going to kill her: She'd be hit by a car while crossing the Post Road or drown while swimming in the sound. Doing it herself would just eliminate the waiting. She certainly couldn't go on like this until Rosh Hashanah — a month away. Either she would be dead, or time would simply end.

She stood at the top of the driveway and waved good-bye to Melanie as her father backed the car down.

By noon it had already turned into a very hot day, overcast and muggy, the humidity like something pressing down on her shoulders. Zoe had been sitting on the edge of her bed staring at her fire poster for what felt like a long time. She could not seem to make a decision, and it just got later and later. The house was incredibly quiet. If she wanted to kill herself, this would be the perfect time. It seemed so easy. She could get up off this bed and ride her bike down to the boat-yard where Rick — the guy Naomi used to buy drugs from — worked. She had money now from Summer Fun at the Y; she could get whatever she wanted. Pills and alcohol, that's how Naomi had done it: easy. It wouldn't hurt.

She would not want to die in a way that hurt, like Hannah Senesh had. She didn't want any more pain; she was already so depressed that it almost hurt to breathe.

She wondered if the *desire* for death had ever crossed Hannah Senesh's mind. Zoe felt vaguely ashamed of the thought. At least Hannah Senesh had kept on being useful right to the end of her life, teaching Hebrew to other prisoners in the Nazi jail. She didn't cop out like Zoe wanted to. Yet Hannah

Senesh, too, had been lonely out there in Palestine before she left on her mission. She couldn't find a boyfriend, and Zoe got the feeling she'd been tired of raising chickens on the kibbutz and having no chance to be a writer. She didn't have too many friends.

Like me, Zoe thought, she had trouble with love.

Zoe's arms and legs were tense with the need to just make a decision. Yet she felt hypnotized by the heat and the psychedelic flames that were climbing her closet door. Sometimes she almost felt that the fire might speak to her, that a voice might come out of nowhere like Moses at the burning bush. The comparison made her snicker, and yet she still sort of believed it might happen. The day was so hot, so still; it felt like the world was waiting for something. Probably it would rain this afternoon — they needed a thunderstorm.

Who needed it?

What do I need?

Zoe whispered, "I don't know."

She thought of Rivka sitting on the beach in her geometric bathing suit. *All right, so go to California.*

I don't care what you do.

Rivka would not be glad if she died, but it wouldn't really change things that much for her. Naomi was right when she said life just goes on without you. It was one of those nasty truths that everyone was too hypocritical to admit.

Decide, said Zoe's mind.

She looked away from the fire and down at the flowered rug, which she'd picked out when she was twelve and now hated. She thought of Melanie and her father driving away on the turnpike in the loaded-up car.

Do something. Say something. Decide.

315

She thought of calling someone; she thought vaguely of calling Rivka, whom she was supposed to see tomorrow afternoon. But what could she possibly say? There were so many things Zoe had never said to anyone — about Naomi, about Philip, about Rivka — and the things had just gotten bigger and more complicated until they were too large for any words to get around them. It was this huge mass of unsaid things that had pushed on her and made this big dead empty space where all the things and all the words she might have used had fallen, gone forever.

Don't just sit here.

"OK," Zoe said. She got up off the bed with sudden, impatient energy; she knew she was going to do something now, though she didn't know what. She put some money and her fake ID into her back pocket, and then went out to the garage to get her bike. This was what it felt like to watch yourself doing things without knowing what you were going to do next. *I feel like there's some kind of evil force controlling my life.* Zoe knew now what Naomi had meant. She understood a lot of things about Naomi now.

At least she was moving, rolling down the driveway, pedaling up the street. But it felt like being under a spell, or caught inside a big wave that was spinning her forward and would toss her out someplace she couldn't yet see. Riding up the streets that paralleled the Post Road, she could have been going to Bagel King, she could have been going to the boatyard, she could even have been going to Rivka's — they were all, ironically, in the same general direction.

She crossed the street carelessly, not waiting for the light, but there wasn't much traffic and she didn't get hit. She still hadn't decided for sure what she should do, even after she'd passed Bagel King and the turn toward Rivka's and was riding toward the water. What could she say to Rick — what exactly did she want to get? How many would it take? She had no real idea. She felt overwhelmed by the complexity of the whole thing. *What do you want?* her mind screamed.

"I want Rivka to stay," she whispered. "I want Naomi to be alive."

She wished so hard that Naomi had not died that she found her fingers clenched almost painfully around the handlebars of her ten-speed. Right then she got a picture in her mind of Naomi, as vivid as that night when she'd been driving home from the cast party. Naomi's blue eyes and strong, definite features were so clear that for a moment Zoe didn't see anything else. On Naomi's face was the small, satisfied smile that meant they were about to do something forbidden and fun. Then she was gone.

"Naomi," Zoe whispered as she rode past the rows of small houses, quiet and hazy in the muggy afternoon. She was sweating; she was soaked underneath her T-shirt. "You asshole."

Because it was really Naomi who'd started all the bad things happening — at least, her suicide was the beginning of this time when nothing seemed to work out right. Like the domino theory again: Nixon would've been right if he'd applied it to relationships between people. The road leading down to the water had been repaved, and her bicycle bumped onto the smooth new tar. It was easier to ride now, and the air was cooler down here. She took a deep breath and her head felt clearer.

What she really wanted, she had to admit, was not death. Dying was easy and possible; Naomi had proven that. But

317

she wanted things that were impossible: She wanted her dead friend to be alive again, and she wanted each of her other friends — Philip, Danielle, Rivka — to be something they were not. She especially wanted Rivka to be something she was not.

Zoe saw the blue sound ahead, the masts of boats at the marinas, and still thinking of Naomi, she realized she was riding right by the place where Tad lived. The old house really didn't look as ominous in the summer afternoon; it was just an old house that needed a paint job and its bushes pruned back. She rode slowly past it, feeling less panicked than she had all day. She still didn't know what to do, but the wave was going to drop her off soon, she could tell. Something had to be decided. She turned the corner and rode up another street, feeling very close to Naomi, as if Nao were still driving around here in her blue Datsun and Zoe was going to see her any minute.

Instead, riding past the big white church, she saw Tad.

She hadn't seen him since Naomi's funeral, and without thinking she braked and then stopped, one foot on the curb. He was mowing the church lawn, pushing a small noisy lawnmower around the gravestones. A red bandanna was tied around his head, and beneath it his hair fell to his shoulders. She was surprised at how harmless he looked, how attractive, even, and she momentarily forgot how much she hated him.

Then he looked up and saw her. She put one foot back on the pedal to ride away, but he'd already recognized her and had turned off the mower. He was walking between the gravestones toward her. She would've felt stupid riding off.

"Hi, Zoe," Tad said, stopping just a few feet away from her. She looked at him without getting off her bike. His face was tanned and sweaty, and his brown eyes still had that gentle, hypnotized look. There were blades of grass sticking to his work boots and his jeans. "Hi," she said finally.

"How are you?" he asked softly, meaningfully, as if he really wanted to know.

Looking at him confused her. He seemed so harmless, and yet she knew what a shit he'd been to Naomi. He was old and he was fucked up, but looking at him now, she could see how Naomi might've been scared at first even to kiss him, but would have done it, and then done more, because there was something about him that kind of drew you in.

"I'm OK," she said, picking at the tape on her handlebars.

"Are you sure?" he asked. "You don't look too happy."

How ironic that he was the only one who'd noticed. But she stopped herself from telling him anything, because she didn't like him and didn't want his sympathy. "Yeah, I'm fine," she said, and as she said it, she really did feel a little better. "How're you doing?"

He smiled very slightly, but his eyes remained the same — sort of glazed over and sad-looking. "I'm doing all right," he said. "God's taking care of me. I don't deserve it, but — I won't complain." Then he gave her a real smile, as if they'd shared a joke.

She couldn't smile back, but she felt strangely comforted, just standing next to this person Naomi had been close to. At the same time, she wanted to say, Why did you hit Naomi that day? Why were you such a shit? She stared hard at him, asking the questions in her mind. Then they both looked down awkwardly at the sidewalk.

"Zoe," he said.

She looked up at him again.

"I think about her all the time," he said. "And I pray to Jesus to forgive me for what I did."

That won't help you, she thought nastily, but she didn't say it. Instead she felt tears coming into her eyes, and she blurted, "Well, I mean, we'd all like to be forgiven. I'd like to be forgiven for how I treated her." She felt sick after she said this, hating herself for being sincere with Tad.

For a moment she thought he was going to tell her to pray to Jesus, but he did not. He just shook his head and said, "You have a lot less to be forgiven for, Zoe. You were a good friend to her."

She shook her head. "I don't know."

"You were."

"I just can't stand it that she's never going to be here again," she heard herself say. "All these terrible things keep happening one after the next, and I feel like I just can't stand it anymore —" She stopped, disgusted with herself.

Tad sighed and looked down the street as if he too expected Naomi to pull up any minute, honking her horn. "You've got to learn how to live with a lot of bad things, babe," he said. "It's the only way."

Yeah, she thought, you should know. You have to live with being a jerk. But she didn't really feel much hate for him anymore; unwillingly she was feeling comforted by what he'd said.

"But I guess we'll both be carrying her around in our heads for the rest of our lives," Tad said.

"Yeah." That was a creepy thought, but it too made her feel better. It sounded like it might be true. Both of them could go on living, and go on thinking about Naomi, and go on wanting to be forgiven for what they'd done. She could go on thinking about Rivka, too, and Danielle, and Philip, and wishing things had been different. *For the rest of our lives.* At that moment Zoe started to feel more like living.

Tad was looking at her, waiting to see if she'd say more, but she wanted to get away from him now. The sky was darkening, and a few drops of rain fell on her. The spots they touched felt cool, relieved. There were big cracks of thunder. The whole world was cooling down, opening up, and she knew now that she was going to ride home fast, trying to beat the storm. "I've got to go," she said, and Tad nodded.

"God bless you," he said.

For a second she didn't know how to answer. Then she said, "Same to you."

She rode off down the street, but this time she felt like she was riding the bike, not being shoved along by some other force. Pedaling harder, she went faster, and the speed felt good. She was moving her own body through space.

Acknowledgments

I am grateful for the financial support of the Toronto Arts Council, and for the moral and financial support of my late mother-in-law, Dr. Florence B. Freedman, may her memory be a blessing. Also, I warmly thank Catherine Dorton, my editor.

RED CHINA BLUES

My Long March From Mao to Now

Jan Wong

Anchor Canada

First published in paperback in Australia and New Zealand in 1997 by Anchor
Hardback edition 1996 by Doubleday
First published in Canada in 1996 by Doubleday Canada Limited
105 Bond Street, Toronto, Ontario, Canada M5B 1Y3

Library and Archives Canada Cataloguing in Publication has been applied for.

ISBN 978-0-385-66566-7

Cover design: Kelly Hill
Cover image: (bicycles) © Reuters/CORBIS
Text design: Heidy Lawrance Associates
Printed and bound in the USA

Published in Canada by
Anchor Canada, a division of
Random House of Canada Limited

Visit Random House of Canada Limited's website: www.randomhouse.ca

BVG 20   19   18   17   16   15   14   13   12   11

CONTENTS

To my parents
and
Fat Paycheck Shulman

Acknowledgments

John Pearce, editor-in-chief of Doubleday Canada, first approached me with the idea of writing a book, and stayed enthusiastic for five more years while I finished my posting in Beijing. He read several very rough drafts, and with great tact and grace, helped steer me in the right direction. Charles Conrad, editor-in-chief of Anchor Books, New York, made invaluable suggestions and kept me true to the spirit of the book. Shaun Oakey did a masterful job of copy-editing the manuscript. Michael Cohn, my agent, was always there when I needed him.

I thank Norman Webster, former editor-in-chief of the *Globe and Mail* (and former Beijing correspondent), and Geoff Stevens, former managing editor, for sending me to Beijing. I also thank William Thorsell, my subsequent editor-in-chief, for keeping me there, and John Cruickshank, my subsequent managing editor, who saw to it that I got a year's book leave upon my return. I thank the Canada Council for providing a timely grant.

In Beijing, my fellow journalists Catherine Sampson and Lena Sun gave me their indispensable friendship, valued insights and professional expertise. Later, Cathy read several early drafts and made numerous helpful suggestions and corrections from Ann Arbor, Michigan, and Hong Kong. Lena read later drafts in Washington, D.C., helped me with queries and saved me from myself many, many times. Thanks also to my matchmakers, Zheng Peidi (Betty) and Xu Shimin (Saiman Hui), who helped me render the title into Chinese. They also read a draft and corrected several errors. Any remaining mistakes, of course, are my own.

Many friends taught me so much about China. They include the old revolutionaries who went to work there: Pat Adler and her late husband, Sol, Betty Chandler, Ruth Coe and her late husband, Frank, Isabel and David Crook and their remarkable sons, Carl, Michael and Paul, Israel Epstein and his late wife, Elsie Fairfax-Cholmeley, Kathy Chiu and Bill Hinton, Joan Hinton and Sid Engst and their children, Fred, Billy and Karen, Ione Kramer, Sidney and Yulin Rittenberg, the late Julian Schuman, Sidney Shapiro, Bertha Sneck, Jane Su, Ruth Weiss, and Gladys and Yang Xianyi and their daughter and my classmate, Yang Zhi.

They also include former classmates and friends, now diplomats, aid workers, businesspeople and sinologists: Patricia Alexander, Anu Arponen, Timothy Brook, Neil Burton, Anders Hansson, Peter and Chris Gilmartin, Pat and Roger Howard, Ellen Judd, Frank and Dorothy Kehl, Britta Kinnemark, Nick Menzies, Sandra Sacks and Ola Svensson.

My fellow Overseas Chinese, with whom I could discuss anything, include Norman Bock, Maria Fang, David Hsieh, George Leung, Ben Mok, Bing and Bonnie Thom and Wenlan Peng. I also thank the MSG Club members, the Macho Sino Girls of our elitist, racist, sexist club in Beijing, whose founders included journalists Charlene Fu, Lena Sun, Mary Wong and Sheryl WuDunn.

Diplomats and other professionals working in China who gave me friendship and generously shared their knowledge include: Mary Ann Burris, Daniel Dhavernas, Earl and Monica Gruder Drake, John Hecht and Laura Sabin, Normand Mailhot, Don Myatt, Michel Riberdy, Judith Standley and Tse Hau-sing.

I especially thank these journalists and colleagues in China and Hong Kong: Jim Abrams, Zorana Bakovic, Daniel Biers, Diana Bishop, Louise Branson, Michael Browning, Sandra Burton, Mike Chinoy, Robert Delfs, Seth Faison, Jaime FlorCuz, Edward Gargan, Caroline Gracie, David and Fumio Holley, Susan Lawrence, Lee Yee, Julia Leung, Simon Long, Timothy Luard, Robert MacPherson, Jim and Cathy McGregor, James Miles, Jim Munson, Judy Polumbaum, Caroline Straathof, Mia Turner and Kathy Wilhelm.

Among the Chinese friends who have left China and can be thanked are Chi Ching, my indispensable news assistant Yan Yan and her successor, Stella Wu. There are many, many others to thank who cannot be named. They include several classmates, a filmmaker, a novelist, two journalists, a laid-off factory worker, an office worker, several dissidents, student activists and a seamstress.

Professors Ella Laffey and Paul Lin of McGill University gave me an appreciation of the complexities of China's history. Many more people have guided and influenced my career as a journalist. I especially thank: *The New York Times*'s Fox Butterfield and James Sterba, who showed me how much fun being a foreign correspondent could be; Professor Melvin Mencher of Columbia's Graduate School of Journalism for teaching me the nuts and bolts of reporting and how, above all, to keep that fire in the belly; Joseph Gelmon, my copy chief at the Montreal *Gazette*, who fed me dinner while I watched "Lou Grant," and valued colleagues Jay Bryan, Janet Brooks, Jennifer Hunter, David Pinto and Shirley Won; my editors and colleagues at the *Boston Globe*, Gordon McKibben, Lincoln Millstein, Steve Bailey, Jane Meredith Adams, Kathryn Tolbert and Jonathan Kaufman; and my bureau chief and colleagues at the *Wall Street Journal*, June Kronholz, David Wessel and David Stipp.

I owe a great debt to my editors and colleagues at the *Globe and Mail*. Timothy Pritchard hired me as a business reporter and didn't mind when I ran off to Beijing soon after. Sue Andrew of the foreign desk always kept the money flowing, even when I was five months behind in my expense accounts during Tiananmen Square. Ann Rauhala, my foreign editor, was unfailingly encouraging, as were her two deputies, Jane Gadd and Larry Orenstein. Colleagues Alexandra Eadie, Stephen Strauss and Elinor Reading always kept the in-house gossip flowing so I would not feel completely isolated in Beijing. Amanda Valpy, the chief librarian, and her colleagues helped me retrieve photos I had taken in China for the *Globe* and obtained permission for me to use them in this book.

In Toronto, my Aunt Ming and Uncle Ying, now both in their eighties, and my cousin Colleen Parrish Yao, helped me trace the family history My Uncle Yao provided the Chinese calligraphy for the jacket. My sister, Gigi, provided computer advice no matter what time of the day or night and helped me recall some of the funnier incidents in China. My parents, Bill and Eva Wong, instilled in me an abiding curiosity about the country of my ancestors and put up with my Maoist phase unfazed.

In Beijing, my Chinese staff did everything so I could concentrate on journalism. In Toronto, Mercedita Iboro took over the housework, the cookie baking and the care of my sons, making it possible for me to write this book. Ben, then four, learned that a chair placed in front of the entrance to the living room, which led to my sunroom office, meant No Entry, and soon taught his brother, Sam, then one, the same. My husband, Norman, has been unfailingly supportive and loving, giving up his career to follow me back to Beijing, changing the majority of the diapers for our sons and correcting my drafts while taking the subway to his new job in Toronto.

A Note About Names

To help readers cope with a plethora of Chinese names, wherever possible I have tagged on titles, such as Chancellor Zhou or Professor Ding or Cook Mu. Mao's radical wife, Jiang Qing, becomes Madame Mao. I also have translated the names of a few characters who figure prominently in the book. Some might argue that this renders them cartoonish or unnecessarily exotic, but it is intended primarily as a memory aide. Translations are also interesting because political movements influenced the choice of many parents. My classmate, Gu Weiming (Future Gu), was born just after the Communist takeover when Chinese were optimistic about the future. My first roommate changed her name to Scarlet during the Cultural Revolution, when anything red was good. Chinese speakers will notice I sometimes take liberties. The name of Mao Zedong's grandson, Xinyu, for instance, literally means New Universe, but in English I think the meaning is more faithfully rendered as New World.

In a very few cases, I have altered names and place names to protect people. I do not always make this clear because I do not want to tip off the Chinese authorities.

I have used pinyin, the official system of romanization in the People's Republic of China. It has been adopted by the United Nations and other world agencies, many governments, journalists and scholars. Pinyin is generally pronounced as it looks, with the following exceptions: *c* is pronounced *ts*, *q* is pronounced *ch*, *zh* is pronounced *j* and *x* is pronounced *hs*. In pinyin, Peking becomes Beijing, Mao Tse-tung becomes Mao Zedong and the Kuomintang becomes the Guomindang. In the interest of clarity, I have made a few exceptions where alternative spellings are well established in English: Canton, Nanking, tai-chi, Sun Yat-sen and Chiang Kai-shek.

The vernacular term for the common people is *lao bai xing*, or Old Hundred Surnames. With only about a hundred family names in common use in China, some are more ubiquitous than the commonest Western surnames. The 1995 Toronto phone directory, for instance, lists three pages of Joneses, eight pages of Smiths and seven pages of Wongs, even though ethnic Chinese account for less than 7 percent of Toronto's population. Chinese minimize confusion by dubbing acquaintances Big Wang, Little Wang, Old Wang, Mama Wang, Old Man Wang, Granddad Wang, Uncle Wang, Auntie Wang, Granny Wang and so forth. The reader should never assume that people with the same surname are related unless that is specifically stated. Family names, by the way, precede personal names in Chinese, just one indication of the paramount importance of the family over the individual.

Finally, all dollars are U.S. dollars.

PROLOGUE
Brave New World

Preceding page: Chairman Mao's grandson, Mao Xinyu (New World Mao), in his private room at 307 Military Hospital.

Photo: Jan Wong

Chairman Mao's grandson was the fattest Chinese person I had ever met. At twenty-three years old, Mao Xinyu (New World Mao) had the same moon-shaped face, the same jowls, the same Buddha-like bulk as his famous grandfather. But his features were coarser, and he lacked Mao's elongated Mona Lisa eyes and inscrutably pursed lips. And instead of slicking back his hair, he had a bristling brush cut.

In 1993, the one-hundredth anniversary of Mao Zedong's birthday was just seven weeks away when I slipped into a military hospital in Beijing to see New World Mao. I had tried for months, without success, to interview someone from Mao's family. Then I heard that New World was here. Brandishing a bouquet of yellow roses, I talked my way past an armed sentry and three checkpoints.

New World was watching television in his private room. I introduced myself as a reporter for Canada's *Globe and Mail*. "Come in," he said, with a cheery smile, as if we had known each other for years. "It's a Chinese opera. Mind if I keep watching?"

His hospital room reeked of unwashed socks. Rumpled and unshaven, he sat, his belly bulging, in a striped hospital-issue pajama top, which he wore like a jacket over a full set of street clothes. His fly was half unzipped. His brown nylon socks, visible under blue plastic shower flip-flops, had gaping holes. New World had inherit-ed the family disdain for bourgeois hygiene. His grandfather Mao Zedong had been a crotch-scratcher, once dropping his pants to search for lice during an interview in the 1930s with the American reporter Edgar Snow. After Mao took supreme power and moved into a golden-roofed imperial palace in Beijing, he never bathed; attendants rubbed him down nightly with hot towels.

New World was born in 1970, at the height of Mao's personali-ty cult. He grew up thinking it perfectly normal that people sang ditties glorifying his grandfather as "the red, red sun in our hearts." Or that everyone wore a Mao badge, and that some of the more fer-vent believers even pinned them to the flesh of their bare chests. Although Mao was no model grandfather, he had taken time out from the revolution to choose a name for the only son of his only surviving son. The Great Helmsman understood the Orwellian importance of names. The choice of "New World" was a reminder to all that Mao was creating a Brave New World.

There were three other grandchildren, but they were the off-spring of Mao's daughters and by Chinese tradition didn't count. New World was the only grandson with the magic surname. He grew up in a hillside villa on the western edge of Beijing, with a dozen nannies, chauffeurs, cooks, maids, private secretaries and aides catering to his every whim. No adult or playmate dared cross him. That world fell apart in 1976, when his grandfather died. New World was still a little boy when Deng Xiaoping began dismantling Mao's personality cult. New World's father, already mentally inca-pacitated, sank into depression. His mother quickly toed the new Party line.

When New World was a toddler, his mother both indulged and disciplined him. She sometimes hit him so hard she broke sticks on his back. At other times, she stuffed him with sugar, pork and fried foods, hoping he would gain weight. Still fretting that New World was too thin, his mother ordered compliant doctors to dose him with hormones.

Mao Zedong never cuddled him, never held him, never played with him. Instead, New World worshipped his god-like grandfather from afar and tried his best to emulate him in the only way he knew how. New World's favorite dish became the one the Great Helmsman loved best – Red-Cooked Pork, chunks of glistening pork fat, gelatinous skin still attached, stewed in a lip-smacking sauce of soy, anise, rice wine and brown sugar.

Over the years, New World ballooned to three hundred pounds. To lose weight, he tried everything from diet teas to herbal medicines to slimming creams. By the time I met him, thirty-seven days of enforced crash dieting in Military Hospital Number 307 in the western suburbs of Beijing had cut his weight to 250 pounds. At five foot nine inches tall, he wasn't off the scale by Western standards of obesity. But in a land where his grandfather's utopian policies had sparked widespread hunger and even famine, New World's ham-like thighs stuck out in China like Roseanne's at the Boston Marathon.

He lived in his own dream world. When a college classmate once asked what he'd like to be one day, New World replied, "A leader," as if that were a job category, like electrician. He harbored secret hopes that someone, someday, might see fit to anoint him general secretary of the Chinese Communist Party. In 1989, he had been a student at People's University. When the Tiananmen protests started and his classmates flooded the square, his mother had her chauffeur drive her to the campus. She bundled her son home for safety until everything was over. The tragedy hadn't touched him at all. He seemed scarcely aware that the People's Liberation Army had shot thousands of ordinary Chinese in cold blood.

When I met him, New World had graduated, just barely, and was now studying for a master's degree in Mao Zedong Thought at Beijing's Communist Party School. He dreamed of going abroad. "My mom wants me to go to the United States because they do a lot of research into Mao Zedong Thought there. I've heard that in the U.S. Chairman Mao is held in higher regard than George Washington. Is that right?"

"Not exactly," I said.

New World didn't seem to notice. He sighed, his belly heaving. A school in Mississippi – he couldn't remember the name – had offered him a scholarship, but the Central Committee had nixed it. "The government won't let New World Mao out of the country," he said. "They're afraid I'll go out and my thinking will change. Or I won't come back."

He turned back to the cacophonous opera on TV. I asked him how long he planned to stay in the hospital. "I don't want to go home," he confessed. "I don't want Mama to tell me what to do. I'm afraid of her. The time passes quickly in here. I can watch television day and night."

Mao's grandson a couch potato? Mao's grandson dreaming of studying Maoism in the States? Mao's grandson a prisoner of communism? My head was reeling. So the dynasty of Mao Zedong had come to this.

And to think that I originally came to China as a Maoist.

Part I

FOOL'S PARADISE

1

Montreal Maoist

Top: A normal upbringing: president of the Canadian Girls In Training, a church version of the Girl Guides.

Bottom: The only brunette among five "freshette princesses".

"What am I going to do in China at night?" I wailed. It was 1972. I was nineteen, on my college summer vacation, and I had a coveted visa to the People's Republic of China. It was a silly question, but I really had no idea what Communists did at night. I already had lopped off my waist-length hair because my mother warned there would be no hot showers. I had reviewed the few hundred words of Mandarin I had learned in Chinese 101 at McGill University. And I had filled my suitcase with toilet paper, color slide film and blank notebooks for keeping a journal. Now the night before I was supposed to leave Montreal, I had a panic attack. Irrationally, I felt I could face the days alone, but what about the nights?

My father, who owned several Chinese restaurants, was sitting on our basement floor playing solitaire. He had been to China on a visit with my mother nine months earlier. He looked up at me, took a puff on his Cuban cigar and frowned, mentally calculating how much he was going to have to shell out for my air fare, hotels and meals for a summer in China. "Don't go," he growled.

That did it. As a teenager, I was duty-bound to do whatever my parents didn't want me to do. The next day, I boarded a plane for Hong Kong, then virtually the only gateway to China. At a fluorescent-lit emporium that sold only mainland goods, I spent $15 on two pairs of black cloth shoes, two pairs of baggy gray trousers and three plaid blouses. I gazed at my authentic revolutionary self in the hotel mirror, and was pleased. The best way to see China was as a Chinese.

In 1972, China was radical-chic. Beijing was a beacon of hope. Maoism was mesmerizing. Growing up in the rebellious sixties at the height of the Vietnam War protests, I had scant faith in the West. Friends my age in the States were being drafted and sent to die in a Southeast Asian jungle in the name of national security. Draft dodgers streamed into Canada, proclaiming their opposition to the war. Millions joined peace marches. For me, the turning point came in 1970 when I was a seventeen-year-old college freshman in Montreal. That year the Ohio National Guard opened fire at Kent State University, killing four student protesters and wounding nine others.

For my generation, the credibility of the U.S. government – and, by extension, my own – was at an all-time low. Washington had lied about virtually everything to do with the Vietnam War, from the secret bombing of Cambodia to the Pentagon Papers to the My Lai Massacre. State Department types cited the domino theory. If Saigon fell, all of Asia would go Communist, and somehow our own way of life would be threatened. For his part, Mao had called on "the people of the world" to "unite and defeat the U.S. aggressors and all their running dogs." In Canada, many in my generation thought our own country was one of those running dogs of U.S. imperialism.

Knowing nothing about the world, I thought Western society was a hopeless mess of racism, exploitation and shopping malls. The natural human impulse was to hope, to believe, that somewhere there were answers. I reasoned, with the naive logic of the young, that if our own governments were lying to us, their enemies must be telling the truth. That China was the biggest domino only enhanced its credibility. I imagined only harmony and perfection in China.

Growing up in Montreal in the 1950s and 1960s, I had a comfortable middle-class life. (Translation: I was pretty damned spoiled.) I went to church and summer camp, figure-skated and skied, and took ballet, piano and flute lessons. My parents took my siblings and me on vacations all over the States, Europe and Asia. On rainy days at the summer cottage we rented in Magog, Quebec, I embroidered pillowcases and ate jelly donuts, a national pastime. (For some unknown reason, Canadians consume more donuts per capita than anyone else in the world, five times more even than our American junk-food-eating cousins.)

In high school, as a straight arrow, I was voted head prefect and elected to the student council. In college, I was thrilled to be selected as a "freshette princess" – along with four blondes. But after the experience of being interviewed about my "favorite flower" and my "favorite color" I quickly embraced feminism. At seventeen, I tossed out my *Seventeen* magazines and had a rubber stamp made that said, "This Exploits Women." Heart pounding, I would stand at the back of city buses and brand offending pantyhose ads before getting off. It was the perfect warm-up for making friends with Mao's youthful storm troopers, known as the Red Guards.

From feminism, it was a natural step to Maoism. I believed women were oppressed. Workers were oppressed. Teenagers were oppressed. I thought, to quote Mao, that "all reactionaries are paper tigers." I thought peace and love would solve all the world's evils, including pantyhose. I thought candles were better than electricity, and that if only I made my own candles, the world would be a better place. I thought I could hitchhike anywhere and nothing would happen to me – until the first time I did and a very friendly man offered me $5 for a blowjob.

I went to Beijing partly to search for my roots. My Canadian-born parents always told me I was Chinese, and certainly, the mirror did not lie. They emphasized that I had to be extra good, extra smart, extra nice, because whatever I did reflected on my race. My grandparents had paid the head tax and my parents had lived through the humiliation of the 1923 Chinese Exclusion Act, which barred Chinese from Canada. At age four, my father had to register with the Department of Immigration and Colonization. At the bottom of the form, which we have kept to this day, it says: "This certificate does not establish legal status in Canada." When my uncle was a little boy in Victoria, British Columbia, people pelted him with lumps of coal and taunted, "Ching chong Chinaman, washee my pants."

The nursing school in London, Ontario, where my mother was the first Chinese-Canadian graduate, rejected an earlier applicant with this remark: "A sick person doesn't want to look up and see a yellow face." Ottawa stripped my aunt, the third Chinese-Canadian woman in Canada to earn a medical degree, of her citizenship in the 1940s when she married a Chinese. She discovered the loss three decades later when she applied for a passport to go on a vacation to Spain. When the government restored her passport, it gave her a pamphlet entitled *How To Be A Good Canadian*.

The lingering effects of the Exclusion Act, which was repealed in 1947, froze the size of the Chinese community in Canada. When I was born five years later, in 1952, Montreal had only about a thousand Chinese, about the same as in 1915. But already I was growing up in a different Canada. Attitudes had changed so dramatically that, in the 1950s, discrimination was something that upset francophone Quebeckers, not someone like me. In the 1970s, under Prime Minister Pierre Trudeau's multi-culturalism, I became proud of my ethnic heritage. Not that anyone would let me forget. Where are you *really* from? other Canadians wanted to know. They meant well, but weren't satisfied until I caved in and uttered the magic word: China.

Their curiosity about my ancestry made me feel ashamed that I couldn't speak Chinese and knew so little about China. I began to read everything I could about the People's Republic. To my delight, it seemed to be one of the few places in the world doing something right. Led by a charismatic genius named Mao Zedong, the Chinese were building a better world, or so I thought. The chosen few allowed inside reinforced my view of utopia. Writers as diverse as Eurasian novelist Han Suyin (*Love Is a Many Splendored Thing*) and American journalist Edgar Snow (*Red Star Over China*) reported that the Chinese were happy as clams. When President Richard Nixon visited China in 1972, the hardened, cynical U.S. press corps accompanying him went ga-ga. If you threw out a razor blade, the reports went, it would be returned to you at a later stop.

In the more cynical nineties, it's hard to believe China had established such a glowing image abroad. After all, Beijing made no secret of being a "dictatorship of the proletariat." But back then, only a beleaguered minority talked about human rights, dissent and megalomania. The 1957 Hundred Flowers Movement, in which Mao enticed intellectuals to speak their minds, then shipped them off to labor camps as rightists, wasn't understood until later. The economic disaster of the 1958 Great Leap Forward, which sparked one of the worst man-made famines in Chinese history, was blamed on bad weather and the Soviet pull-out of aid. Mao used the Cultural Revolution to purge his enemies within the Communist Party, but many China-watchers portrayed it as his brilliant strategy to prevent the emergence of a new class of party bureaucrats. Who could argue with that?

For some reason, the Chinese were the good guys of communism. The Russians were the bad guys. They had gulags and a menacing secret police called the KGB. The Chinese had pandas and an army in sneakers. Mao was cute, a cultural icon, like Marilyn Monroe. Andy Warhol had never made a silkscreen of Brezhnev. And if there were excesses, well, Mao had a quote to deal with that, too. "A revolution is not a dinner party, or writing an essay, or painting a picture, or doing embroidery; it cannot be so refined, so leisurely and gentle, so temperate, kind, courteous, restrained and magnanimous. A revolution is an insurrection, an act of violence by which one class overthrows another."

The West's own cultural revolution of the 1960s predisposed a whole generation to being sympathizers. To conform in the late sixties and early seventies was to be anti-establishment, anti–Vietnam War, anti-antediluvian – and pro-China. I didn't trust anyone over thirty, and couldn't imagine ever being that old one day myself. I didn't shave my legs or my armpits. I read Frantz Fanon, Eldridge Cleaver and Betty Friedan. I absorbed Sartre and de Beauvoir, and *enjoyed* being alienated. I parted my flowing hair down the middle, tie-dyed T-shirts, took pottery lessons and listened to Joan Baez and Bob Dylan.

But unlike my peers, I never got into drugs or alcohol. Maoism was all I ever needed to get high, although in hindsight it's questionable which would have inflicted more brain damage. In the

1960s and 1970s, I thought I was a hard-nosed revolutionary, but I was really a Montreal Maoist. I never joined any radical group, let alone considered setting off bombs. At one university sit-in, I quickly lost my nerve when helmeted riot police arrived to clear us from the chancellor's office. I gave one leather-jacketed cop a tentative punch in the shoulder, but backed down immediately when he whirled around to arrest me. "Excuse me, how do I get out of here?" I asked, all law-abiding Asian sweetness. He allowed me to leave unscathed.

As part of their relentless insistence that I was Chinese, my parents somehow managed to instill the Confucian work ethic in me. As a third grader I lay awake worrying about how I would ever earn a living. Unlike the stereotypical Asian, I was terrible at arithmetic. But I won spelling bees and enjoyed gossip, so journalism seemed the natural job for me. My role model came straight out of Superman comics. Who cared about the Man of Steel? I wanted to be Lois Lane.

As I grew older and idealistic, I didn't have to modify my grade-three dream. A journalist seemed the perfect do-gooder job. A reporter could help change the world, someone once said, by comforting the afflicted and afflicting the comfortable. Even when I took a left turn, it was easy to stay on the same career track. Just the way Jane Fonda became Hanoi Jane during the Vietnam War, I could be Beijing Jan, aiding China's cause. As a misguided Maoist, I saw nothing wrong with propaganda. Telling people only the positive side of China was morally justified. Shouldn't everyone support a nation that was trying to improve the world?

If I was ever to become a correspondent in Beijing, I figured I'd better learn the language and study the history. In 1971, I enrolled in Asian studies at McGill University and was immediately plunged into an academic world that mirrored the cold war. Pro-China professors taught me that Mao was creating a New Man. Anti-China sinologists were derided as U.S. government stooges. There was no middle ground in studying the Middle Kingdom.

I longed to see the country for myself. That summer, an Australian classmate and I applied at the Chinese Embassy in Ottawa for tourist visas. After a month of suspense, the word came back. She couldn't go – she was white – but I could because I was an "Overseas Chinese." It seemed odd to me that we should be separated into categories, and I was apprehensive about a solo journey, but I wouldn't dream of turning down the chance. That was why I was having last-minute jitters about being all alone in utopia.

Silly me. By 1972, there were already 800 million Chinese.

The 7 a.m. train from Hong Kong deposited me across from a sleepy border town called Shenzhen. As I walked over a small footbridge, wearing my new mainland Chinese outfit, I heard the strains of revolutionary opera blasting over the loudspeakers. Above my head the Chinese flag, red with five yellow stars, fluttered in the hot breeze. A handsome young People's Liberation Army sentry stood at attention. I stared at him in awe and thought to myself, "My first Communist." Another PLA border guard checked my passport and politely waved me through. I was in! It was June 1, 1972, exactly one hundred days after President Nixon had arrived in China.

After a glass of hot jasmine tea in a waiting room, I boarded another train for Canton, where a young woman my age met me at the station. With her round pink cheeks and glossy braids that she tossed briskly over her shoulders, my guide, Bai, looked as though she had popped right out of a propaganda poster. Genetics dictated that I stay at the Canton Overseas Chinese Hotel. The Stalinist-style sandstone building teemed with compatriots from Indonesia, the Philippines and Malaysia who lounged around the lobby in flowered polyester pantsuits and solid-gold jewelry, picking their teeth and shouting to one another in village dialects.

I liked the lobby decor. In 1972, China was smack in the middle of the Cultural Revolution. Student Red Guards, who specialized in ransacking temples and burning books, had slathered the lobby walls with red paint and emblazoned the Chairman's quotations everywhere. My tiny room continued the class-struggle motif. The interior designer had chosen the prison-cell look – whitewashed walls, quite a few mice and no windows. Someone had brilliantly solved the ventilation problem by cutting a circle the size of a bicycle wheel high in the wall separating me from the next room. At night, I listened to the shouts, and later the snores, of the family next door as I wrote in my diary. So few people had the chance to visit China in 1972 that I felt obliged to record everything I saw.

Had I been deemed a genuine foreigner, I would have been charged twice as much for a room in the East Wind Guest House, which offered luxuries like interpreters and rooms with windows. At the Overseas Chinese Hotel, service was exclusively in Chinese. I closed my eyes and let my finger land at random on the Chinese menu. The hotel waiters assumed I was a deaf mute who liked poached innards.

Guide Bai, who spoke almost no English, rarely accompanied me anywhere. Each morning, she stood on the steps of the hotel to ensure I got into the right car. One day, she told the driver to take me to the Canton Trade Fair. To my disappointment, it looked like a clearance sale at an army and navy surplus store. I couldn't understand why the crowds passionately jostled and shoved for a glimpse of a clunky refrigerator or a pair of leather shoes. I didn't know these were the best goods China produced, and that even if they had the money, the window-shoppers couldn't buy anything. Everything on display was exported for hard currency.

With my visa good for three months, I didn't want to waste a moment. I explored the streets, wandered into shops and peered into people's courtyards. Everyone seemed tanned and fit compared with the scrawny, pasty-faced Chinese I had seen in Hong Kong. Male and female alike wore identical loose white shirts and navy blue or gray or tan pants. No one wore any jewelry, not even a wedding ring. To my idealistic eyes, they looked beautiful. The women used no makeup and wore their hair in braids or in simple blunt cuts. I had nothing to stamp "This Exploits Women."

The only billboards had either Mao quotation's – huge white characters on a glossy fire-engine-red background – or else propaganda paintings of happy workers, peasants and soldiers. Busts of Mao, usually in pure white, decorated office lobbies and meeting rooms. Outdoors, towering Mao statues, portraying him with his right arm outstretched to acknowledge homage from the masses, dominated university campuses and city parks. In contrast to the neon lights of Hong Kong, store windows here displayed only red flags and Mao's works. If this was the Cultural Revolution, I approved. It didn't occur to me how annoying it must have been to live in a place where you couldn't buy Scotch tape or take-out Chinese food.

My professors had told me the Cultural Revolution was also Mao's attack on feudalism. I thought that it was all about getting rid of superstitions, trashing musty operas and eliminating bad habits like selfishness, dishonesty and shopping. I had no idea that so many people were being hounded to their deaths. I took everything at face value, and when it didn't add up, I still didn't get it because virtually everyone I met enthused about the Cultural Revolution. In 1966 when it first began, most Chinese were genuine believers. By 1972, many had stopped believing, but only a very few were unwise enough to share their thoughts with a loose cannon like me. Having grown up in Canada, I had no idea an entire nation could be cowed for years into saying what few believed any more.

When the rare person tried to set me straight, I tried to set *them* straight. At the Canton Zoo one afternoon, I struck up a conversation of sorts with a slim twenty-two-year-old worker with high cheekbones and finely shaped eyes. His name was Chen. We talked mostly in sign language. When he fingered his worn denim work jacket, he meant he was a worker. But what kind? He went through the motions of driving a car, then fixing an imaginary engine. An auto mechanic! He must be happy, right? I smiled broadly, pointed at my grinning mouth, then at him. He shook his head, and turned down his mouth in a Chaplinesque expression of sadness. He thrust out his hands and made me feel the calluses. Then he rubbed his fingers together and shook his head. He meant the pay was meager.

How could a worker in China be unhappy? Wasn't this the dictatorship of the proletariat? I couldn't exactly say that in Chinese, so I tried to pantomime a happy worker. I pretended to repair a piece of machinery, all the while smiling broadly. He thought I was crazy. He pulled a card from his pocket. I studied it carefully. Slowly I understood. Chen could not travel freely in his own country. The pass stated where he was from (Guangxi province) and where he was authorized to travel (Canton). It specified exactly how long he could stay (two weeks) and the purpose of his travel (visiting relatives from overseas).

I told him I was from Canada (*jia na da*), and he immediately said he wanted to go there. I was shocked. You want to go to a *capitalist* country? I had been in China exactly four days, so I was an expert. I told him, in my fractured Chinese, that China was much better than Canada. Granted, we had more money (I rubbed my fingers together), but look at how *happy* people were here. On cue, a line of singing schoolchildren marched past. He looked dubious.

For three and a half hours we walked around the zoo, gazing at tropical fish, dusky brown elephants and sleepy pandas. We got caught in a tropical downpour and huddled in a bamboo grove until we were driven away by bloodthirsty mosquitoes. Chen asked shyly if I'd like to go rowing the next day. I agreed instantly. What better way to find out about China than to hang out with a gorgeous auto mechanic? He told me ordinary Chinese weren't allowed in the Overseas Chinese Hotel unless they were visiting relatives, so we agreed to meet on the steps the next morning.

Bai tracked me down at breakfast in the hotel dining room. "You're going to see Chairman Mao's school," she said, beaming. My face fell. I tried to explain I was going rowing, and pulled my arms back and forth, but she couldn't figure out what I meant. I motioned her to follow me outside. I went over to Chen and asked if he preferred to join the tour of Chairman Mao's school. By then Bai was at my elbow.

The change in her was startling. The sweetness was gone. Her face hardened. She looked older and meaner. "Who are you?" she demanded roughly, planting herself in front of Chen. His neck flushed in anger, but he said nothing. He slowly pulled out his travel pass. She snatched it from him and frowned. She barked something. I couldn't understand the words, but the meaning was clear.

I walked through Mao's school in a daze. (I couldn't understand a word anyway.) Why couldn't a Chinese go rowing with a foreigner? Was I the problem, or was it Chen? I scarcely understood what had happened, but I felt like crying, at the ugly change in Bai, at the humiliation Chen had suffered and at my shattered illusions.

2

Revolutionary Tourist

Top (from left): Grandmother Fong Shee, First Wife and Grandfather Chong Hooie, in a photo taken just before my grandparents left for Canada, leaving First Wife behind in China.

Bottom: Grandmother Ma Shee and Grandfather Ark Wong.

Bai decided to do what Chinese authorities had been doing to young people since the beginning of the Cultural Revolution: she sent me to the countryside. "How would you like to visit your ancestral home?" she asked me later that day, all sweetness again. After the ugly episode with Chen, getting away from Bai seemed like a good idea.

Returning to one's village was a time-honored tradition for Overseas Chinese. Having made good abroad, they swaggered home as big shots. They bowed ritually before ancestors' graves, threw banquets for all the villagers and handed out red envelopes of cash to the unfortunate ones who had stayed behind. I had no intention of doing anything as uncouth as that; I wanted to be as deprived as they were.

By tradition, I traced my ancestral village through my father's side to Taishan county in the fertile Pearl River delta. My paternal grandfather, Ark Wong, had left China in 1915, and there was little sentimental draw for me there. But rural China was usually off-limits to foreigners in the early 1970s, and I was anxious to see anything of it that I could. Being a high-fashion radical, I also took to heart Mao's dictum that physical labor was good for the soul. Of course, my mother told me the same thing, but I never cleaned up my room. I told Bai that I would go to Taishan if I could spend the time working in a factory or on an agricultural commune. She smiled sweetly.

I was awoken by a Third-World wake-up call – a 4 a.m. knock on my door. It could have been high noon for all I could tell in my windowless room. I stumbled outside into the humid dawn to await the hotel shuttle to the regional bus station. Bai had bought me a first-class bus ticket, which meant I got to squeeze in with caged chickens, sacks of rice and other first-class human beings. Second-class humans – and chickens – rode another bus to preserve the fiction of a classless society. When the first-class bus arrived, we surged on in a cacophony of shoving and grunting. Every seat was taken. In fact, every seat was taken one and a half times. Three people squashed into a seat that in North America would hold two. I was beginning to see the advantage of food rationing.

We pulled out of the bus station and tore, horn bleating, through a sea of bicycles. Beyond the city limits, we drove smack down the center of the unpaved road, our wheels sending up clouds of reddish dust. My aisle seat in the front row jutted out so that when the bus veered to the left, my two seatmates lurched right, and I had to brace myself on a hump in the floor next to the driver. The hump, which covered the engine, grew steadily hotter. With each lurch, I had to choose between falling on the chickens or burning my fingers. The ninety-mile, six-hour journey included three ferry rides. At 9 a.m. we stopped at a restaurant, my first experience with ordinary food in China. The only dish on the menu turned out to be boiled noodles in greasy broth. I stuck to tea, or so I thought, and was surprised when only plain hot water came out of the chipped teapot. The peasants called the water "white tea," I learned later. Decades of poverty and central planning had made tea a luxury in China.

Comrade Bai had betrayed me. How was I supposed to remold my thinking here? My hotel room in Taishan was huge, with seven big windows, a patterned blue tiled floor and a balcony overlooking a pretty lake. My bed was equipped with a clean mosquito net and a woven bamboo sleeping mat. On the desk was an old-fashioned brown radio the size of a hotel minibar. I even had my own bathroom toilet and sink.

I seemed to be the first "returning" Taishanese who didn't know a word of the local dialect. My three guides promised me that an interpreter would arrive that evening. Taishan, unfortunately, had no interpreters. After dinner that night, the seventy-year-old vice-chairman of the District Revolutionary Committee knocked on my door. Tan Wei looked like a Chinese Colonel Sanders, except he didn't have a bucket of fried chicken under his arm. He had golden brown skin and thick white hair and was wearing a shiny black silk shirt and heavy cream-colored pants. He settled into one of the old-fashioned armchairs in my room and, in perfect English, announced he would interpret for me – when he felt up to it. He had learned English in New York in the 1930s as a member of the American Communist Party, and had returned to China because he was afraid he would be arrested. I had heard of Chinese trying to escape to Hong Kong, but I had never thought of anyone seeking political asylum in *China*.

"You are an Overseas Chinese," he said. "You have come such a long way. We welcome you back to the motherland. Besides, your parents must really love Chairman Mao and have faith in China to let you come all alone." I managed not to roll my eyes. *I came because my parents wanted me to come?* How retrograde. I told Tan that my chief purpose in coming to Taishan was to do manual labor to reform my thinking. His smile remained unchanged, and so did my itinerary.

The Taishanese thought I was nuts. Avoiding hard labor was precisely why everyone left in the first place; hence it was dubbed the Ancestral Home of Overseas Chinese. People whose roots were in Taishan and its three neighboring counties, Kaiping, Enping and Xinhui, dominated the Chinatowns in North America. The exodus began in the 1860s, when American labor contractors anchored off the South China coast to recruit peasants to build the great transcontinental railways across Canada and the U.S.

My maternal grandfather, Chong Hooie, was one of those coolies. He was born in Kaiping, the county next to Taishan, on December 18, 1860, "an auspicious day in an auspicious month," according to the Chinese characters carved on his gravestone in Toronto's Mount Pleasant Cemetery. Before he left home, his family married him off.

He arrived in British Columbia in 1880 when he was nineteen, the same age I was when I headed in the other direction nearly a hundred years later. I wondered if he had had any last-minute fears. Did *he* wonder what Canadians did at night?

Grandfather Chong joined a construction gang blasting tunnels through the Rockies, at less than half the pay of white workers. As the Canadian Pacific Railway neared completion in 1884, the contractors reneged on their pledge to provide passage home for the Chinese workers. Chong Hooie faced the choice of spending all his savings on a boat ticket back to Kaiping or paying a $10 "unemployment tax." He paid, and stayed. In Esquimalt, British Columbia, he found work as a houseboy at a dollar a month for Col. Josiah Greenwood Holmes, the deputy adjutant-general of the Pacific Station, the Canadian west coast military base then under British command. With Colonel Holmes's blessing, my grandfather boosted his meager salary by providing a laundry service to the fort's soldiers, and eventually to civilians in nearby Victoria.

Family lore has it that Grandfather Chong became the tenth Chinese in Canada to take out citizenship, a fact now hard to check because Ottawa's extant records date back only to 1917. But the national census of 1901 shows that he became a Canadian citizen in 1899. Under race, it described him as "y" for yellow, under religion a "Confucian" and under "trade" a "laundryman." The census showed he was forty years old and, rare among Chinese at the time, able to read, write and speak English. Under marital status, it listed him as "m" for married.

Perhaps Grandfather Chong took out citizenship so he could return to Canada without hassles. Soon after the census, he sold his laundry business and booked passage back to China. He had been away for two decades. Back in Kaiping, his wife was considered past child-bearing age. They adopted a teenaged boy, who was already married, to ensure continuation of the family name. Then, because his wife didn't want to leave China, he bought her ten *mu* (one and a half acres) of land – so much that the Communists later charged her with being a rich peasant. Leaving his wife in charge of the family holdings, Grandfather Chong began looking for a concubine to take back to Canada to have his children. Second (and third and fourth wives) were common among the well-to-do at the time. Grandfather was now a good catch, a Canadian citizen and a prosperous Overseas Chinese, and his wardrobe included a silk top hat and tuxedo. A matchmaker introduced him to a sixteen-year-old girl from Canton.

Like most Chinese females of her generation, the girl had no name of her own. She was called Fong Shee, or *née* Fong. When she was a baby, her father had walked into Canton carrying her and her infant sister in two wicker baskets suspended from a shoulder pole. Standing on a street corner, he offered them to passersby. He couldn't afford to feed them, he said. A housekeeper took pity on the tiny sisters and brought them home, where her master, a judicial official surnamed Yin, agreed to raise them. Yin must have been an enlightened man because he refused to bind their feet and saw to it that they were each given a year's education. From that base, Fong Shee eventually learned to read and write, and even compose poetry.

As an abandoned girl, she had few prospects. But she had smooth black hair, large eyes and clear skin, and spoke elegant Cantonese, a more refined dialect than the Kaiping patois my grandfather spoke. Westernized by his long sojourn in Canada, Grandfather Chong was undeterred by my grandmother's big feet. He gave her several pieces of jewelry as a dowry – a bracelet of gold threads twisted into a thick rope, a solid-gold brooch fashioned into the characters for wealth and good fortune and a pair of gold hoop earrings studded with iridescent opals.

In 1902, just before my grandfather and grandmother left for Canada, they posed for a photograph with First Wife. At forty-one, Grandfather Chong in his three-piece suit was lean and handsome, like a Chinese Paul Newman. First Wife sat in the middle, her expression morose, wearing a stiff, embroidered silk robe, one hand reaching out so that she was almost touching Grandfather. She clearly out-ranked my grandmother, the second wife, who sat to one side, her face coolly blank; her hands demurely folded in her lap.

Grandfather Chong and my grandmother boarded the ship accompanied by his newly adopted son and his own wife. At sixteen, Number One Son was the same age as my grandmother. Grandfather Chong paid their head taxes, $100 each, and spent the rest of his savings on equipment from a bankrupt shoe factory. He went into business making leather boots in Victoria for British Columbia's miners. He invested the profits in real estate, and the family prospered and multiplied. By the time she was thirty-five, Fong Shee had given birth to six boys and five girls. In English, the children called her Mother, but in Chinese they called her Big Sister because their official mother was First Wife back in Kaiping, some-one they had never laid eyes on. Each time a son was born, Grandfather Chong sent money back to First Wife to buy another cottage and a plot of land so that each heir would have something to fall back on in China in case of emergency.

As a leader of the fledgling Chinese community, Grandfather Chong headed the Chinese Freemasons Society of Canada, which pragmatically combined anti–Qing dynasty activities with gam-bling. When a firebrand named Sun Yat-sen came to Victoria to drum up support for his plot to overthrow the Qing, my grand-father was an early sympathizer. He had already boldly cut off his queue, in defiance of a Qing law that was designed to distinguish the subjugated Han Chinese from the ruling Manchus. Now rais-ing funds and hiding dozens of rifles under his front porch. Grandfather Chong also founded the *New People's National Journal*, a Chinese newspaper in Victoria that backed Sun's Guomindang Party. In 1911, Dr. Sun succeeded in overthrowing the Qing dynasty and became, briefly, the first president of republican China.

With the outbreak of World War I, Grandfather Chong's proper-ties in Victoria plummeted in value. Then newfangled rubber galosh-es wiped out his leather boot business. In 1923, he moved east, where he organized a self-help credit union for the Chinese community in Hamilton, Ontario. When he knew he was near the end of his life, he wanted to return to China. He got as far as Toronto, where he died of pneumonia on June 2, 1937, at age seventy-six.

Grandmother Fong Shee moved to Woodstock, Ontario, where she opened a restaurant called the Food-Rite, serving roast beef, mashed potatoes and homemade apple pie. I hardly knew her – I was one of more than two dozen grandchildren, and she died when I was seven – but I inherited two things from her. One was her opal earrings. The other was a Chinese robe of fragile, nearly threadbare rose silk. It was like the one she wore in her photograph with First Wife, with flared sleeves, hand-knotted buttons of silk and a strip of delicate embroidery in cream and blue and black. As a kid, I carelessly wore it as a bathrobe, never understanding why it was so soft and warm. Years later, when I had to weather my first Beijing winter, I realized my grandmother's robe had been padded with the finest silk floss. I bought myself a padded jacket in Beijing, but it wasn't the same. Grandmother's had been luxuriously warm and light. This one was chunky, and made me look like turnip.

A century later, those who stayed behind in the Pearl River delta lived off remittances. Why sweat in the fields for socialist work points when a cousin in Toronto or Toledo could send back a few hundred dollars a year to keep you in style? My father, who had been to Taishan county on a visit nine months earlier with my mother, returned to Montreal muttering that nobody there seemed to do an honest day's work.

Taishan's other official nickname was the Ancestral Home of Volleyball – there was a big sign on the main road boasting of that – and it was an apt moniker. As the beach bums of south China, the Taishanese dominated China's national team. But I felt ashamed of my ancestral villagers whiling away the Cultural Revolution by spiking volleyballs and sipping thimbles of Smoky Black Dragon, the espresso of Chinese tea.

Tan Wei and I spent the next day touring the local dam-building feat. When I asked again about physical labor, he assured me I could work "for a short while" at a factory. The next morning, after a quick tour of a farm machinery workshop, we stopped in front of a woman squatting on the floor in a white cap and blue work jacket. As I watched, she took apart a lump of machinery and reassembled it, smiling at me at each step. Then she dismantled it again, and with another smile, shoved the pieces at me. This was hard labor? This was how I was supposed to reform my bourgeois mind? This was nothing more than Communist Lego. A small crowd had gathered. As everyone stood around giggling and pointing, I sheepishly reassembled the parts.

I repeated to Tan Wei that I wanted to do *physical* labor. He nodded again, smiling. The next day, at a small porcelain factory, after another ritual walk through the workshop, we stopped before a young woman waiting patiently with several unfired clay teapots. She showed me how to dip them into a vat of vanilla-colored glaze. *A piece of cake*, I thought, having taken one pottery course at my local YMCA. I donned an apron, sat down and picked up my first teapot. As I plunged it into the liquid, it cracked. Embarrassed, I looked up just as someone snapped a picture. The smiling young woman motioned for me to try again. I did, more cautiously this time. Again it cracked. On my third attempt I managed to dunk one without destroying it. Everyone applauded with relief. A few days later, the factory delivered a souvenir to my hotel. It was two tiny cups and a teapot, trimmed in gold and inscribed in Chinese and English: "Jan Wong learns from the workers of the Taishan Porcelain Factory."

I *had* learned my lesson. I quit visiting factories. I caught up with my diary or spent the morning in the lobby with the hotel staff, eating bags of luscious lichees. Whenever I went out for a stroll, my guides insisted on accompanying me. At the time I was paranoid that it had something to do with the incident involving the hapless mechanic, but I guess they thought that anyone crazy enough to volunteer for physical labor needed close watching.

During our walks around the lake, dug by corvée, or unpaid labor, during the Great Leap Forward, my guides kept bumping into people they knew. "Have you eaten?" they asked one another, in the standard rural greeting. I finally understood my own preoccupation with food. I was born with Chinese starvation genes. When I first arrived, the question always stopped me in my tracks. I had to think twice. Was I just about to eat, so the answer was no? Or had I recently finished a meal? What about snacks? Did a chocolate bar count? By the time I opened my mouth to answer, the other person was halfway down the street. Eventually I learned no one actually cared. The polite response was always to say, "Yes, I've eaten," to avoid the appearance of angling for a dinner invitation.

For some reason – perhaps I shocked everyone by not knowing the Chinese names of my brothers (to me, they were just Earl and Ernie) – the hotel segregated me from other Overseas Chinese.

While they ate in the dining room, I dined alone at a table set up in the hall. Which was just as well, since I wasn't yet acclimatized. Until I lived in China a long time, and learned to eat (but not love) white worms, pig esophagus, scorpions and donkey penis, I was as squeamish as the next Canadian. Or maybe worse. I used to recoil when I had to reach inside the cavity of a supermarket chicken to remove the paper bag of gizzards. One lunch in Taishan, as I picked my way through a platter of wok-fried chicken, one lump seemed particularly bony. I worked it around in my mouth for a while, then spat it out on my plate for a better look. It was the chicken's *head*, complete with dead eyes, a rippling cock's comb and a sharp beak. For a long time after that, I stuck to scrambled eggs.

The guides could not believe I didn't know the name of my ancestral village, either. All I knew was that it was in Taishan, which was a bit like saying you were from New York without knowing if you were from the Bronx, Manhattan, Queens or Brooklyn. Because my parents had been there so recently, someone remembered it was Xinzhangli, or New Jade Tablet, a short drive from the county town. That Sunday, we set out in an ancient British car. The road was narrow, and at times non-existent except for a squiggly bicycle path of rust-colored earth, bordered by fields of green rice seedlings, squat peanut plants and skinny corn stalks. At last we came to a few stone cottages in a bamboo grove beside a brook.

My father's cousin's wife, the only relative I had left, had been alerted in advance and came running out at the sound of our car. Smiling nervously, she grasped me by the hand and led me into her stone cottage. Several villagers followed us inside. Ren Meirong, fifty, with blunt-cut hair, was wearing a blue print cotton suit buttoned, Chinese-style, down one side. I looked around the two-room cottage, which had once belonged to my grandparents. It looked even more primitive than the eighteenth-century pioneer homes I had seen on school outings in Montreal. There were a few wooden stools, a table and a plain bed. The floor was stone. In the blackened roof was a hole so the smoke from the kitchen fire could escape. I was surprised to see a Buddhist shrine with fresh sticks of incense on one wall. I thought religion was banned, and was chagrined my relatives were so backward.

Overseas Chinese returning in the early 1970s usually brought gifts of color televisions or at least a nice Swiss watch. Unlike me, they didn't believe the propaganda about how happy everyone was. I assumed no one would want anything so bourgeois as a watch. On my mother's advice, I had brought a few packets of bobby pins as emergency gifts. Cousin Ren thanked me profusely. Everyone else tittered in embarrassment.

We sat awkwardly. She knew nothing about my grandfather, who had left years before she was born, or maybe she was miffed at not getting a watch. But an old peasant dressed in rags, one of a dozen who crowded into the cottage, told me my grandfather's nickname had been Half-Belly. "His stomach was always empty," he said. A wave of relief flooded over me. Hooray! Grandfather Wong suffered!

For me, it was merely a sick case of trying to be politically correct. But my feelings were not much different from those of many Chinese at the time. During the Cultural Revolution, Chinese lived and died by their class backgrounds. They boasted about ancestors who had starved to death. But if a banker or landowner lurked in their background, they dropped their voices low and disclosed the shameful fact as if they came from a long line of pedophiles. Those with "bad" pedigrees were barred from university or sensitive government jobs. In extreme cases, they were beaten, jailed or even killed. During the Cultural Revolution, having *any* relatives overseas was suspicious. My aunt's sister-in-law, too frightened to communicate with her Chinese brother in Canada, yet worried she would lose contact with him, wrote his address inside a chemistry textbook and memorized the page number.

The harsh story of the first generation of Chinese immigrants to Canada is almost impossible for someone in the third generation like me to understand. While Grandfather Chong endured twenty years of enforced bachelorhood in Canada, and eventually left his first wife in China to marry my maternal grandmother, my paternal grandparents endured a bleak separation that lasted all but the first few years of their marriage.

The youngest of seven sons, Ark Wong knew he would inherit very little and so decided to seek his fortune in Canada. Before he left in 1915, he married, intending to take his wife with him. But they lost all their savings when the bank collapsed. After they bought the two-room cottage in New Jade Tablet (where Cousin Ren now lived), there was only enough money for one steamship ticket and one head tax. Grandfather Wong was twenty when he boarded a Canadian Pacific steamship for Vancouver. He paid the head tax, which by then was $500, the equivalent of several years' earnings. In Montreal, he found a job with a fellow villager who owned a grocery store in Chinatown.

By saving every penny he could, he was able to send money back for my grandmother's passage and head tax. She joined him a few years later, squeaking in just before the 1923 Exclusion Act, a discriminatory law that barred Chinese immigration and virtually ensured that the Chinese already in Canada – almost all men – would remain bachelors. (Inter-racial mariage was extremely rare, and was considered by the Chinese community a betrayal of the motherland.) Like Grandmother Fong Shee, my paternal grandmother had no personal name. Even her gravestone in Montreal's Mount Royal Cemetery lists her as Ma Shee, or *née* Ma. Like most Chinese women her age, she had bound feet, a process that broke her toes and arch so the resulting stump was a few inches long. Although she later undid the bandages, she remained half-crippled. During Montreal's brutal winters, she tottered on the icy sidewalks in Chinese black cloth shoes – the only kind that didn't hurt her feet.

As a result of the Exclusion Act, Ma Shee and Ark Wong were a rarity, one of only about ten Chinese couples in Montreal. They had a daughter, who died in infancy, and three sons. The family was prosperous enough to hire a maid to help look after the children, but everything collapsed in the Great Depression. In 1929, Ark Wong took his young family back to Taishan.

"It was cheaper to starve in China than in Canada," my father recalled. "We had a little bit of land. We could grow our own sweet potatoes and vegetables. We didn't have to pay rent, and we didn't have to pay for heat." Ark Wong stayed a month to settle his wife and sons in Taishan, then took a ship back to Canada.

As the oldest male, my nine-year-old father, who until then had known only the streets of Montreal, suddenly had to learn how to farm. His most vivid childhood memory was of hunger; war, revolution and invasion had made rice a luxury in the Chinese rice belt. At Taishan Middle School, he learned he could earn a few squares of fried beancurd by doing the homework assignments of his better-off classmates. For years, the family survived on yams. To this day, my father refuses to eat sweet potatoes, even at Thanksgiving.

In 1937, during the Japanese invasion, my father, then seventeen, returned to Canada alone. His younger brother Gordon had died several years earlier of dropsy at age eight. Ma Shee, who couldn't obtain a visa, stayed behind with John, the youngest, who was twelve. When the Canadian Pacific steamship from Hong Kong to Vancouver docked in Yokohama, a Japanese doctor boarded the ship. "You," he barked at my father, the only young Chinese male on board. "You're sick. You get off the ship here." With Japan and China at war, the order meant certain prison camp, and probable death. The Canadian ship doctor intervened. "He's not sick, just malnourished. He stays." My father sailed on.

After eight years in Taishan, my father had forgotten all his English. In Vancouver, he flubbed a question about his birthdate, but was able to produce his Canadian birth certificate. He found his father still working in a grocery store in Montreal, still unable to support his family. In 1945, Ark Wong died of a heart attack in the hallway of an illegal Chinatown gambling parlor where he was moonlighting as a guard. He had not seen his wife or youngest son in the sixteen years since he had left them in Taishan.

"My big regret was that my father did not see me graduate," said my father, who put himself through engineering at McGill. "I was the first person in my village to graduate from university." In Montreal, my father toyed with the idea of returning to help rebuild China, but changed his mind after the Communists won. Instead, he guessed that Canadians would like fried rice and egg rolls, opened the first Chinese restaurant outside Montreal's Chinatown and made his first million by the time he was forty.

My sister, my two brothers and I grew up speaking English and learning French. My tenuous links with the old country consisted of the Taishan chefs my father hired in his restaurants and Chinese classical dance, where I learned to whip silk ribbons in the air and jingle tea cups while taking mincing "cloud steps." My mother provided the only other exotic touch; when we misbehaved, she whacked us with chopsticks.

Our quiet street, Rosedale Avenue, was otherwise entirely Jewish. We lived between the Gersovitches and the Shaare Zedek Synagogue. Impressed with the synagogue school's rigorous academic standards, my father tried to enroll us there – until the principal politely informed him you had to be Jewish. Instead, my siblings went to elite private schools, my sister to Miss Edgar's & Miss Cramp's, my brothers to Lower Canada College. I alone opted for public school. I had no desire, I told my father, to hang out with rich kids.

While my playmates on Rosedale Avenue learned Hebrew, I suffered through weekly lessons in Cantonese, the dialect of the Pearl River delta. In 1950, two years before I was born, my father brought Ma Shee back to Montreal. We saw her on weekends, but I never learned enough Cantonese to speak to her. All I remember was a silent old woman with gold earrings and gray hair knotted in a bun. Every Christmas, she bought two toy guns for my brothers and two dolls for my sister and me, even when I was too old to play with them. Ma Shee died in 1963, when I was eleven.

After two weeks in Taishan, I returned to Canton. Bai had decided the deaf-and-dumb approach to revolutionary tourism wasn't working and had signed us both up with a group of ten American students. They were mostly from Berkeley and, like me, were budding ethnic Chinese Maoists in search of their roots. They also spoke no Mandarin but, unlike me, they had been allocated an interpreter who wasn't seventy years old.

We hit all the revolutionary hot spots. In Shaoshan, China's Graceland, we gazed reverently at Mao's scarred kitchen table, the tiny vegetable patch he once weeded and the trapdoor to the attic where he conducted subversive meetings. In Dazhai, the Disneyland of Maoist agriculture, we spent three days peering into cooking pots, trampling the maize crop and attending *yi ku si tian*, or remembering-the-bitterness-of-the-past-to-savor-the-sweetness-of-the-present lectures. One evening an old peasant told us a harrowing tale of how the local landlord had killed his father and raped his mother. He started crying, and pretty soon we were all sobbing so loudly no one could hear. Somehow, he recovered, so we quieted down, and he told us how wonderful life was now under Chairman Mao. Only later, after I had lived in China for a year and had attended a dozen such lectures, did I realize he had to cry on cue several times a week.

Propaganda was the sacred duty of Dazhai's peasants. The village was on the revolutionary tourism circuit not because it was scenic or historic but because Mao had chosen it as the national model of agricultural development. At its peak, twenty thousand visitors a day came to ogle the eighty-three families who lived in yellow loess caves dug out of the barren mountains of Shanxi province. Practicing collectivism and self-reliance, Dazhai's peasants had reshaped their accursed land of dried gullies and steep hills into neatly terraced fields. To accommodate all the tourists, the state built an auditorium, a block-long dining hall and a hotel with real plumbing. As Mao's chosen ones, its peasants traveled all over China giving testimonials. Although the village was battling a five-month drought that summer, the peasants never lost their photogenic smiles.

Chen Yonggui, Dazhai's Communist Party secretary, was one of Mao's homespun heroes. The son of beggars, Chen joined the Politburo and became a vice-premier during the Cultural Revolution. A prolific author who didn't learn to read until he was forty-three, he composed articles with catchy titles like "Study and Creatively Use Mao Zedong Thought to Achieve a Bumper Harvest," which became required reading across China. Everyone, from steelworkers to intellectuals, was supposed to adopt the terraced-field approach to daily life.

Chen Yonggui received us on our last day. With his trademark white terrycloth turban and week-old stubble, he looked like an amiable Chinese Yasser Arafat. While he droned on about Maoist agriculture, I watched as he literally chain-smoked. To consume every bit of tobacco, he would fit a fresh cigarette into the unfiltered smoldering butt of the old one. Rumor had it he used one match a day.

After Mao's death in 1976, critics charged that Dazhai's production figures were faked and accused the model commune of receiving millions of yuan in state aid. Chen himself was purged in 1980 and died several years later of lung cancer. After his death, loyal friends would light a cigarette in his honor and implant it, like a stick of incense, in front of his grave.

Our revolutionary tour seemed designed to prove that socialism was superior to capitalism, something we already believed anyway. One steamy July afternoon in northeast China, our guides announced we would watch workers repair 220,000-volt wires without shutting off the power. That seemed to surpass walking on hot coals for the revolution. As an emcee excitedly announced a young woman's name and age over the loudspeaker, she climbed nimbly up a rope ladder suspended from the wire. Sparks crackled as she approached the electrical field. I held my breath as she reached the wire and began to repair it. We all clapped wildly and snapped pictures.

"We were scared at the beginning," the young woman said later, as I eagerly jotted down her words in my notebook. "But we slowly are tempering ourselves." There were three more like her, all fresh-faced and earnest, in Mao caps and denim work suits. Another spoke up. "Before when there was something wrong, we had to cut the power," she said. "But after thoroughly studying Mao Zedong Thought, we were able to make technical innovations." We were all duly impressed. Years later, I found out that what they did was a standard technique in the West. As long as they used a ladder that didn't conduct electricity, the women were fine, just as birds and squirrels can land on high-voltage wires without getting fried.

The Chinese were always searching for ways to impress gullible foreigners. They claimed that acupuncture, the ancient practice of inserting needles into various points of the body, could treat everything from paralysis to mental illness. Patients looked like voodoo dolls, but many swore by its results. I tried it for colds, and it seemed to work, but who really knew?

Acupuncture anesthesia was an innovation of the Cultural Revolution. In one city, we watched doctors precede a cesarean section by inserting long thin needles into the patient's ankles and swollen belly. As the patient waved and smiled to us up in the observation dome, the surgeon sliced her open. The woman showed no reaction, although some in my group nearly lost their lunch. It seemed miraculous when the doctors lifted out a baby girl, all wet and blue, from the red sludge below. We watched as doctors sewed the woman up. "I felt nothing at all," the patient said afterwards. "Acupuncture anesthesia is marvelous." Despite success stories like this, acupuncture anesthesia was in fact unreliable, and was largely abandoned by the 1990s.

After several weeks, the non-stop rhetoric wore down even wannabe Maoists like us. The only acceptable way to let off steam in China was to roll stones up a hill, Sisyphean-style, when what we really needed was a Rolling Stones concert. When a guide droned on too long about how many slave days it took to construct the subterranean Ming Tombs in Beijing, I started tap-dancing on the marble floor, until Bai gave me the evil eye. Another time at dinner, someone in my tour group began parodying an acupuncture operation. We all joined in. Chopsticks twirled as mock needles over someone's stomach. Leftover buns became tumors. The skit soon deteriorated into an all-American food fight – in a country where people had died of starvation not so long before. Our guides sat on the sidelines and looked grim.

Because I had studied a little Mandarin, I was often designated the official thanker. Each time I got up to make a speech at the end of a visit, the Chinese beamed expectantly. Their smiles faded when they couldn't understand a word. After several excruciating performances, I began to lobby for a chance to study Chinese. Bai told me most colleges were mothballed because of the Cultural Revolution, and assured me no one in China was interested in tutoring for money. Undeterred, I pestered officials and bureaucrats in every city. On July 18, 1972, Bai took me aside in Beijing and whispered that I had been granted permission to study. She wouldn't say what school I would attend, when I would start or what it would cost, but if I accepted, I would have to drop out of my tour group at once. I asked for ten minutes, walked once around the block, took a deep breath, and said yes.

3

Welcome You!

Top: Hamming it up with Erica Jen, right, at the Forbidden City.

Bottom: My first roommate, Scarlet Zhang.

After a week of suspense, an official told me I would begin studying at Beijing University in early August. I was thrilled and a bit in awe to learn that an American named Erica Jen and I would be the first students from the Western world to study in China since the Cultural Revolution. Although my visa was good for only three months, it appeared there would be no problem extending it for a year. With a few weeks to kill, I explored the capital. Almost every tourist attraction was closed, including the Fine Arts Museum, the imposing Beijing Library and the Temple to Confucius. At the Summer Palace, one of the few sites still open, Red Guards had daubed whitewash over thousands of decadent floral murals.

For the first time in years, I felt safe walking the streets alone. Dark shadows didn't scare me, the way they did at home. I never had to look behind me or quicken my pace. I knew no one would leap out at me and conk me on the head. China had no pickpockets, no muggers, no rapists. I was in paradise, and I was secure. Or so I believed.

Desperate for something to read, I browsed through the New China Bookstore, a Chinese Barnes & Noble, except it was a state monopoly with only one bestseller, the *Selected Works* of Mao Zedong, available in Chinese, Japanese, Arabic, English, French,

Spanish, German and Esperanto and in several editions, from pro-letarian to deluxe. I chose a hardcover set in faux leather. When I wearied of reading Mao's "A Comment on the Sessions of the Kuomintang Central Executive Committee and of the People's Political Council Sessions," I read an authorized biography of Kim Il-sung, the Great and Dear Leader of North Korea.

To prevent breakage and shoplifting, and to keep surly people fully employed, all goods, including books, soap and socks, were kept behind counters policed by nasty salesclerks. I watched as the masses beseeched them to pass over items, then quivered with inde-cision until the clerks snatched them back and barked at the cus-tomers to make up their minds. While I was delighted to see that no makeup or hair curlers were for sale, I was less thrilled to learn there were no tampons. Chinese women folded coarse gray toilet paper into rubberized belt-like holders. A six-cent roll came stud-ded with fragments of still-legible recycled newsprint, which also neatly solved the problem of reading matter in the bathroom.

The Cultural Revolution had trashed both quality and taste. The quality of china – in the country that invented it – was so bad that salesclerks tapped each porcelain bowl with a spoon to check for an off-tone indicating a flaw. Silk, another Chinese invention, came in hideous prints. I bought a garish blouse just so I could defy anyone to name a color it didn't have. No one ever could. I later learned that Finnish diplomats piled all their official gifts in a room at the embassy they dubbed the "chamber of horrors."

I toured the city by randomly hopping trolleys and buses. When I tried to buy a bicycle at an ordinary store, I discovered I needed special ration coupons. Although it offended my Maoist sensibilities, I had no choice but to buy one at the Friendship Store, an Orwellian-named shop that barred Chinese and catered to foreign-ers – and sold them bikes, rice, oil and other rationed items with-out requiring coupons. I began noticing that in China some people were more equal than others. The masses squeezed onto wheezing trolleys; meanwhile, top officials glided around in gleaming Red Flag limousines (which were black, not red), shielded from curious eyes by shirred taupe gauze curtains.

Food stores were sparse and the lineups long. Produce was

strictly seasonal. At one time, the only fruit available was soft yellow apples, too sweet and mushy to my taste, but beloved by the Chinese. Then the apples disappeared. When the first perfumed peaches, golden pink and fuzzy on the outside, white as jade on the inside, came on the market, people greedily filled their net bags with them.

I noted in my journal that the skies were a startling azure, but it didn't occur to me that the lack of pollution was due to lagging industrial production. As I biked down car-free streets, I thought happily that China had chosen the right path for development. I didn't think about how the very old, the very young, the handicapped, the sick, not to mention entire families, got around the vast city. Everyone glowed with health. China resembled a Colorado health spa. There was the same low-cholesterol vegetarian diet, known as meat rationing. There was the same early-to-bed regimen, known as power outages. And instead of working out with a personal trainer, the Chinese just plain worked. The only difference was you could never check out.

On August 8, 1972, a Soviet-made car picked me up at my hotel and headed for the university area in the northwest. Of the dozens of institutes clustered here – aeronautics, politics, law, forestry, agriculture, foreign languages, rocketry, Communist Party history, electronics, diplomacy, pedagogy, telecommunications, national minority cultures and spying – only Beijing University and Qinghua University had reopened. They were China's two top universities, its Oxford and Cambridge, its Harvard and MIT. The campuses were side by side in the loveliest, coolest part of Beijing. Qinghua focused on applied sciences and turned out the country's technocrats and engineers. Beijing University specialized in basic sciences and liberal arts and was favored by the elite. It was where Mao Zedong once worked as a librarian, Deng's third wife studied physics and both families had sent their children.

Over the years, Beijing University produced a disproportionate share of China's troublemakers. In 1919, its students led the May 4th Movement, demonstrating in Tiananmen Square for democracy. In 1966, Red Guards at Beijing University took the lead in denouncing

Deng Xiaoping as a "capitalist roader." They incarcerated his eldest
son, a Beijing University physics student, who jumped from a fourth-
floor dormitory window and ended up paralyzed from the waist
down. In 1989, Beijing University students would again take the lead
in organizing pro-democracy protests at Tiananmen Square. How
could Deng not remember, when he gave the order to fire, what the
earlier group of rebels had done to his son?

I knew very little about Beijing University's turbulent history
when my car entered the white granite gates of the campus and
stopped in front of the antiseptically named Building Twenty-five.
Two teachers in Mao suits, their hair neatly combed into long braids,
rushed out. One grabbed my suitcase. The other took me by the
hand and led me to the third floor, where an honor guard of a dozen
young women waited in the hall. I grinned self-consciously. They
smiled back and said in English, "Welcome you!" a literal translation
of the standard Chinese greeting, *huanying ni!* At room 330, a young
woman with impossibly thick braids and a shy smile stepped forward. She was my new roommate, Zhang Hong (Scarlet Zhang).

The school had briefed her on the Western habit of handshaking,
but had apparently neglected to tell her how long it should last. She
grabbed my left hand and shook and shook and shook and shook.
When I tried to shake loose, she interpreted that as enthusiasm and
renewed her handshaking with vigor. If I was taken aback at holding
hands with my new roommate, she was equally surprised with me. "I
was expecting someone with blue eyes and blond hair," she told me
later. "You looked like a Chinese, but you didn't speak any Chinese."

Like me, Scarlet was nineteen. She was a head taller than I and
serious-faced, with a tendency to furrow her thick brows whenever she was perplexed. She was also voluptuous, and slouched self-
consciously most of the time – the Cultural Revolution was not the
best time in Chinese history to look sexy. "Welcome you!" used up
one-third of her English vocabulary. She knew four other words:
"Long live Chairman Mao!" Scarlet was a world history major, chosen to match my major at McGill. In fact, the entire female section
of her class had been moved into Building Twenty-five to keep me
company. Erica Jen, who arrived the same day, got the entire female
section of the freshman Chinese linguistics class.

Although I didn't know it until later, the decision to accept the first two students from the wicked West had been made by Premier Zhou Enlai himself. In hindsight, we were a logical sequel to the Nixon visit. If China was planning to resume student exchanges in a year, what better, safer way to start than with a couple of friendly Overseas Chinese? Erica and I both thought the Cultural Revolution was wonderful. And we were willing and eager to spend a year subjecting ourselves to virtually anything the Chinese threw our way.

Erica, a math major at Yale, was the daughter of C.K. Jen, a Chinese-born physicist at Johns Hopkins University in Baltimore. Beijing, then locked in a struggle with Taipei for international recognition, loved him because he had just given the regime tremendous face by leading a delegation of eminent Chinese-American scientists to China. When Dr. Jen asked if his daughter could study at Beijing University, Premier Zhou himself okayed the request. It helped that Dr. Jen's roommate in the 1920s at the California Institute of Technology was now chancellor of Beijing University.

The Chinese must have figured I was the perfect companion for Erica. I was the same age, sex and ethnicity, and was eager to learn Chinese. Better yet, I wasn't from the U.S., with whom Beijing didn't even have diplomatic relations. Among Western nations, Canada was considered less disgusting than former imperialist powers like Britain and France. Canada had never invaded China. It was one of the earlier Western nations to establish diplomatic relations with Beijing, in 1970. And Ottawa had backed Beijing's bid to oust Taiwan and reclaim its United Nations seat. Canada also supplied China's only authentic Western martyr, Dr. Norman Bethune, a swashbuckling surgeon who died in 1939 while caring for wounded Chinese Communist soldiers.

Besides, I seemed a good bet: a stark, raving Maoist.

In an earlier incarnation, the campus had been an imperial preserve of He Shen, a corrupt eighteenth-century Manchu prince. In the 1920s, American missionaries transformed the site into Yenching University, which specialized in journalism and sociology. After the

Communist victory in 1949, Beijing University, founded at the turn of the century, expropriated the campus. During the noon siesta that fall, when the hum of cicadas was so loud it blanketed the city in white noise, I would cycle on the curved paths, past marble tortoises as big as hot tubs, ponds of pink lotuses and Ming-style buildings with red lacquered pillars and spectacular curved roofs. I could read undisturbed beneath the weeping willows that rimmed No Name Lake, and look across at the graceful pagoda that doubled as a water tower. Farther north, beyond the campus boundaries, were the ruins of the Garden of Perfect Brightness, a pleasure ground of the Summer Palace that once eclipsed Versailles in scale and grandeur.

In 1972, the campus was virtually deserted. Scarlet's class, the second batch to arrive since the Cultural Revolution began, brought the student body to a few hundred, compared with a normal enrollment of ten thousand. Many buildings were padlocked. Lecture halls were empty. Until we arrived, Building Twenty-five, a gray brick structure with a curved-tile roof, had been vacant for six years.

The small room I shared with Scarlet was luxurious compared with ordinary Chinese dorms, where students slept eight to a room on metal bunk beds, stashed their clothes and books under their quilts and studied wherever they could. Scarlet and I not only had space, we had furniture. Our fifteen-by-twelve-foot whitewashed room, overlooking an athletic field, had two wooden desks, two chairs, two beds, a small bookcase and a wooden armoire. Erica and I also had our own classrooms and a reading room, which the school stocked with Mao's works and the scores of the so-called Eight Model Operas, the only works Mao's wife allowed to be performed during the Cultural Revolution.

Even in Building Twenty-five, we had no hot water. We sluiced our faces in primitive stone troughs using icy artesian well water. During the hottest days, I fought an urge to drink the water straight from the tap, a sure invitation to Beijing Belly. Our only drinking water came from a boiler several buildings away. We filled our thermoses there, but I sweated even more when I tried drinking hot water to cool off. Our communal bathroom was a row of porcelain squat toilets, which I found somewhat daunting to use. I was always afraid of falling in, and when I finally stood up, I would have a moment or two of dizziness and have to clutch the swinging doors to steady myself. I also had to wash all my laundry by hand, including my sheets, in a small enamel basin. I would have given my Mao button collection for a washing machine or a laundromat, but none existed. Although Grandfather Chong had begun his new life in Canada running a Chinese laundry, such services were considered bourgeois during the most fanatic years of the Cultural Revolution.

Twice a week, Erica and I patronized the campus bathhouse. For a two-cent ticket, we learned to jockey, soap stinging our eyes, with hundreds of other women and girls for a moment under the communal spigots. Because it was our only chance to get clean for several days, like the Chinese, we scrubbed ourselves and each other until we were all as red and shiny as tomatoes. I hated the days when I couldn't have a shower, and planned my entire social life around Beijing University's bathhouse schedule. To this day, I never take a shower without giving silent thanks for hot running water.

If Beijing University was treating us like revolutionary royalty, then the Chinese students who moved in with us were our ladies-in-waiting. Under orders to be nice to us, they tried to make our beds, do our laundry and even urged us to cut in line at the canteen. In short, they did everything except tell us what was really going on. The university uprooted about forty people in all for our benefit. Besides our dorm-mates, the school assigned us a house-keeper-guard, six administrators, three language professors, a cook and a typist. When we asked for tai-chi lessons, a coach from the athletics department took us through the paces of the languid exercises. When we expressed an interest in Lu Xun, China's greatest modern writer, a literature professor gave us a private lecture. When we went on tours of model factories, the school provided a car and driver. The university bought a ping-pong table for our dormitory and installed a telephone in our hall. I didn't realize what a big deal that was until I learned that only the university chancellor had a home phone. All we paid for was the food we consumed, which came to a few dollars a month.

The housekeeper-guard, a white-haired elderly woman whom we respectfully called Granny, mopped the bathrooms and screened our visitors. The typist, who also moved into Building Twenty-five, mimeographed our lessons and vocabulary lists. The six administrators, who worked out of the newly opened Foreign Students Office, had nothing better to do than challenge us to ping-pong matches at recess. It was the only time we weren't treated like revolutionary royalty. They put devilish spins on the balls and delighted in beating us to a pulp.

The main administrator in charge of us was Huang Daolin, a brittle man with an elfin haircut, brown-rimmed glasses and cheekbones as hard and round as the ping-pong balls he loved to smash into our faces. In his mid-thirties, he was self-righteous, zealous and dogmatic, a typical Communist Party member without a shred of self-doubt. When embarrassed or upset, he laughed as if he were having a nervous breakdown, coyly shielding his bad teeth with his hand in a strangely feminine gesture. Cadre Huang had majored in radio physics at Beijing University but had been assigned to the Foreign Students Office after graduation. As my "handler", he would try to imbue me with Maoism, criticize me for my bourgeois lapses and ruin my love life.

The best part of being revolutionary royalty was getting our own cook. Chef Liu was a grizzled old man who had cooked for John Leighton Stuart, the China-born head of Yenching University and the last U.S. ambassador to pre-Communist China, immortalized by Mao in an essay sarcastically titled *Farewell, Leighton Stuart!* When the Communists expropriated Yenching's lovely campus, Chef Liu came with it. His Western repertoire included homemade potato chips, donuts, apple pie and shortbread cookies. His Chinese specialties included steamed buns stuffed with savory minced pork, crispy pancakes studded with chopped scallions, stir-fried chunks of eggplant in a spicy soy sauce, and plump little *jiaozi,* the ravioli northerners eat dipped in dark rice vinegar. For my twentieth birthday, the week after I arrived at Beijing University, Chef Liu made me a huge bowl of extra-long noodles symbolizing long life. When he discovered I loved spicy food, he tossed chili peppers into my fried rice at breakfast. And when Erica and I became homesick for hamburgers, he improvised by mincing some pork by hand and tossing in an egg, breadcrumbs and spices.

I soothed my guilty conscience by cleaning up after meals. To my dismay, Erica didn't think washing dishes atoned for living well. She fought to be allowed to join Scarlet and the other students in the Big Canteen. "The Chinese revolution is all about ending special privileges," Erica said to me.

"What if we put Chef Liu out of work?" I asked in a tiny voice.

Erica rolled her eyes and changed tactics. "By eating with the other students we can improve our language skills, and get to know them better," she said. Personally, I thought it was better for my Chinese to gorge on homemade apple pie and chat up Chef Liu for recipes afterwards. But how could I argue with truth and justice? When Erica confronted the cadres in the Foreign Students Office, I stood shoulder to shoulder with her and tried to look sincere while wondering what Chef Liu was making for dinner. Cadre Huang broke into his whinnying laugh when she finished. When he picked himself up from the floor, he assured us our constitutions weren't up to it.

"You'll never *xi guan*," he predicted, using a Chinese verb (pronounced *see-gwan*) that means to get used to something unpleasant. In all the years I lived in China, people never stopped asking whether I was *xi guan* or not to the lack of meat, or central heating, or night life, which I always thought out-Canadianed Canadians at making self-deprecation a national sport. The polite answer, the only possible answer, was to shout heartily, "*Xi guan!*" ("I'm used to it!"), even if one had to say so while chewing on a particularly tough piece of dried yak penis.

Eventually, Erica's rhetoric won the day. Three times a week, all that we were allowed, we joined the other hungry students massed around the canteen's padlocked doors. When a cafeteria worker finally unlocked them, we burst through with anxious shouts. The Big Canteen looked like the prisoners' mess in Solzhenitsyn's *One Day in the Life of Ivan Denisovich,* a dark sea of plank benches and rough tables. Clutching our own enamel bowls, we lined up at a tiny window for a ladleful of slop. Three miserable meals in the Big Canteen, while cheap for me, were the equivalent of about half a day's pay for the average Chinese worker.

As the daughter of a restaurateur, I never dreamed Chinese food could be so bad. Breakfast and dinner were identical: tasteless cornmeal mush, with a teaspoonful of inedible salted vegetables. Lunch, the only time my classmates ate meat, was a sliver or two of pork fat mixed with stale cabbage. The rice was dry and tasteless, broken grains, more gray than white, polluted with tiny fragments of gravel and coal. I learned to chew carefully to avoid breaking a tooth. We were lucky to get the rice, classified as fine grain. Several times a week, we also had to eat our share of coarse grain, usually in the form of *wotou,* which were baseball-sized conical lumps of steamed cornmeal that looked and tasted like damp sawdust.

My classmates were so undernourished that they usually ate every scrap, and, after a while, even I found the morsels of pork fat pretty tasty. One day, I saw a blackboard propped on a central table, displaying three half-eaten yams and a small pile of salted vegetables. The canteen workers had chalked a blistering message: "The students lack class feeling for the workers in the kitchen! Each piece of food is the result of the sweat and blood of the workers and peasants. The students don't respect the labor of the workers! What is worse, the students are losing touch with their class background. Before when you were all workers, peasants and soldiers, you never would have wasted any food."

Erica was a Maoist with sparkling eyes and pink cheeks who loved Miles Davis, admired the Black Panthers and hated the Vietnam War. We each were eternally relieved to have the other's company for the moments when homesickness struck. She was something of a celebrity in China, having stolen the show during the four-and-a-half-hour audience her father's delegation had had with Zhou Enlai. Intrigued by the chance to talk to an American teenager, the premier had quizzed Erica about everything from the youth movement to Chinese politics. He wondered out loud whether young people abroad were aware that two of Mao's closest associates "betrayed the original goals" of the proletarian revolution.

"I ask you," Premier Zhou said to Erica. "Would you care to tell us who these two people were?"

"One is Liu Shaoqi and the other is Lin Biao," Erica said, standing up respectfully.

"You are so right!" Zhou said delightedly, bounding out of his seat to shake her hand.

Thanks to Erica, I spent the year being the class dunce. While I could hardly say "I'm from Canada," she was already fluent, having grown up in Silver Spring, Maryland, speaking Chinese at home. Sadistically, the Foreign Students Office once invited a professor from the math department to lecture us on some new theory about something. At the end, he tossed math problems at us like peanuts to chimpanzees. My basic arithmetic skills were shaky in English, never mind Chinese, never mind *sans* paper, pencil and eraser, calculator and multiplication tables. I sat there glumly while Erica, the Yale math major, figured out all the answers in her head. The math professor was so excited he clapped heartily at each correct answer.

Erica was not only better at math, she was always more politically correct, too. With her again leading the charge to remold our minds, we petitioned to join our Chinese roommates in physical labor. I felt it was important not just to witness the Chinese revolution but to live it. According to a famous Mao quotation: "Whoever wants to know a thing has no way of doing so except by coming into contact with it, that is by living in its environment ... If you want knowledge, you must take part in the practice of changing a reality. If you want to know the taste of a pear, you must change the pear by eating it yourself ... If you want to know the theory and methods of revolution, you must take part in revolution. All genuine knowledge originates in direct experience."

Again Cadre Huang laughed hysterically and predicted we would not *xi guan*. He finally gave in, only after Erica laid some heavy Black Panther-style rhetoric on him. From then on, every second Saturday, we dug ditches and hauled bricks to help build a new university library. Cultural Revolution dogma held that by getting dirty, we would become better human beings. During the breaks, I wiped my sweaty face and checked my world outlook. To my chagrin, I felt little change. But I thought it was kind of smart of school authorities to make us dig ditches. The subliminal message was: *Study hard! Or else this could be YOUR life!*

At the time, I didn't understand that Beijing University was a stronghold of Mao's wife and her radical cohorts (who would be

labeled the Gang of Four after their purge). Madame Mao's campaigns directly affected the school – and our lives. In 1972, for
instance, the university responded to the campaign to "deepen the
revolution in education" by scheduling more and more physical
labor. One rainy Sunday authorities announced that we had to dig
a hole for a new swimming pool. Only I objected. "Why not wait
until it stops raining?" I said. "Even peasants avoid working in the
rain." Everyone politely waited for me to finish speaking. Then we
all went out into the rain.

Although all my classmates were classified as worker-peasant-soldier
students, few were actually children of the proletariat. Scarlet, the
daughter of a nurse and a mid-level administrator in Beijing, was classified as a peasant because she had worked for several years in Yanan,
the Communists' dusty wartime capital. To my surprise, she was not
a Party member. "Too obvious," she told me years later. "You would
have felt like you were being watched." Of course, we *were* being
watched, although in my innocence I didn't realize that at the time.

Scarlet's job was to tattle on me to Luo Ning, who *was* a Party
member. A self-assured young soldier of the People's Liberation
Army, she had freckles and wore her thin brownish hair in wispy
braids tucked into her red-starred army cap. Luo Ning reminded
me of a bossy mother hen, and with her pear-shaped figure, she
even waddled like one. Her air of authority came naturally. Her
father was Marshal Luo Ronghuan, a Politburo member and one of
China's ten marshals, the nation's highest military rank.

I didn't know that Luo Ning had been raised as a Red Princess,
with servants, bodyguards and limousines. Nor did I realize that her
playmates included Deng Xiaoping's daughters, who moved in
temporarily to console Luo Ning and her sister after Marshal Luo
died in 1963. Her father's early demise – he had served with both
Lin Biao and Deng Xiaoping – apparently saved Luo Ning from
persecution during the Cultural Revolution. Instead of being sent
to a farm for hard labor, she joined the army, then a prestigious
assignment. From there, she easily got into Beijing University.

As secretary of the class Communist Youth League, Luo Ning
was often so busy remolding other students that Scarlet gave her

reports to another party member, Wang Lizhi, who was both class president and chairman of the history department's student association. Wang hadn't won any popularity contests; the Communist Party had appointed her to these posts because she was tough and reliable. Built like a bull, with coarse features and a husky voice, Wang knew how to use a gun and could wrestle someone to the ground. The daughter of a steelworker, she had been a security guard at Daqing, the oil refinery in northeast China crowned by Mao as the national model for industry. "My job was to protect Daqing Oil Fields from class enemies and saboteurs on the inside, and from imperialist attacks from the outside," Wang told me.

Erica and I had no idea our roommates were reporting on us to Wang Lizhi. Of all my classmates, she was the only one to persist in practicing English with me. "Long live the friendship between the Chinese and Canadian peoples!" she would shout, her face reddening with the effort. So when we heard that Wang was about to turn twenty, we decided to buy her some birthday presents. But what? We feared anything too good might be construed as an attempted seduction of an upright Party member. Erica bought her walnuts and, as a joke, composed a Chinese limerick praising her virtues. I settled on a bag of candies and a Double Happiness ping-pong ball. That evening after supper, we knocked on her door and pranced into her room, singing "Happy Birthday." When we gave her the presents, Wang went white, then beet red.

"Happy Birthday," Erica and I shouted.

"No! No!" Wang shouted in her terrible English, recoiling as if we had given her a copy of Richard Nixon's quotations. "Bad! Bad!" she cried, wagging a finger in front of our noses. Erica and I were mortified, but there was no graceful exit. We had to finish what we started. Wang read the limerick aloud and frowned, remonstrating Erica for the fulsome praise. "A Party member must be modest!" she said.

We smiled weakly. Even Erica's fluent Chinese failed her; she didn't know how to say limerick in Chinese and couldn't explain it wasn't meant literally. Wang pinned me against the wall and tried to shove the ping-pong ball back in my pocket. Finally, perspiring with embarrassment, Erica and I managed to escape.

Just before National Day, on October 1, 1972, my classmates decided to have a party. "Let's *wanr*," Scarlet said, using the verb *to play*. *My first Chinese college bash!* I thought excitedly. It turned out to be more like a birthday party for four-year-olds. We gathered in one student's room, under full-strength fluorescent lights. Half a dozen of us – all females – sat demurely in a circle, crunching sunflower seeds and sipping tea. Everyone giggled. Even though I couldn't see what was so funny, I found myself having a good time. No one had anything as fine as a cassette player, so we had to provide our own entertainment. We went around the circle, browbeating each person into singing operatic arias and revolutionary songs. They were all accomplished singers, a skill drummed into them in nursery school. But when it came my turn, I forgot the words to "O, Canada" the only Canadian song I could muster. Erica, who carried a tune as badly as I did, decided there was safety in numbers. Together we chirped our tuneless way through "Row, Row, Row Your Boat" and "Kumbaya, My Lord," but neither of us knew how to translate "Kumbaya." For an encore, we performed a country hoe-down square dance, which needed no translation. Then we all went back to our rooms to study. The next day no one had a hangover.

4

Pyongyang Panty Thief

Top: (From left) Erica, Luo Ning and Forest Zeng.

Bottom: Striking a pose at Beijing University.

Learning Chinese was tough at the best of times, but the Cultural Revolution had trashed every existing dictionary and language textbook. My teachers wrote my lessons on the fly, the typist churned them out, and I learned them warm off the mimeograph machine. Like every schoolchild, I memorized the three most famous Maoist homilies: Serve the People, The Foolish Old Man Who Moved Mountains and In Memory of Norman Bethune. I soon was reading Stalin in Chinese. Nobody thought this strange. Mao, who was studying English at the same time, used the *Communist Manifesto* as *his* textbook. No wonder he never learned to speak English. I, on the other hand, became fluent in Maoist lingo. Phrases like "Down with imperialists and all their running dogs" rolled off my tongue. But I couldn't say, "May I please have a tube of Bright and Glorious toothpaste?"

By the time I arrived at Beijing University in August 1972, the worst factional fighting of the Cultural Revolution was over. For the moment, the most radical faction, New Beijing University Commune, dominated the school, and two of its most stalwart members, Fu Min and Dai Guifu, became our teachers. Back in 1966, Beijing University had become a battlefield. "It was dangerous just walking around campus," said Teacher Dai, a soft-spoken beauty who had helped carry out the reign of terror. "Students used slingshots and catapults to ambush their enemies. People fought each other on the sports field." Sleep was impossible as loudspeakers blared day and night. Each faction claimed to be the true believers of Maoism and took its own prisoners and fortified its own buildings. But Beijing University was civilized compared to Qinghua University. There, the technically inclined students and faculty made rocket launchers and cannons.

In the spring of 1968, authorities sent six hundred elite troops from Chairman Mao's own palace guard to Beijing University. Squads of hand-picked workers called Propaganda Teams of Mao Zedong Thought took over the campus administration. That summer, the faculty and staff were packed off for hard labor at Carp Island Farm in Jiangxi province in the south. Teacher Fu, who was married but childless, drove a tractor. Teacher Dai, who had a young child and an absentee husband, pleaded single parenthood and was allowed to remain on campus. In 1970, when the university again ordered Dai to the farm, she was pregnant with her second child. Fu helpfully leaked the news to the Workers Propaganda Team, and Dai was excused again, a debt to Fu she never forgot.

At first Erica and I had classes together, but we soon split up because of our vastly different levels. I got Teacher Fu, and took an instant liking to her warm smile, golden skin and waist-length braids. A former soldier and Red Guard in her early thirties, she had grown up in Henan province in central China where her father, the commander-in-chief of the Xinyang military region, had eccentrically named all of his six children Fu Min, using different ideograms for *min*. It was a stunt comparable to naming your six kids Leslee, Lesley, Leslie, Lezlee, Lezley and Lezlie.

But I soon began to regret I didn't have Erica's teacher – and not just because Fu spoke with a Henan accent. Dai was less strident, less dogmatic, less gung-ho. Whereas Fu was a Party member, Dai had been repeatedly rejected by the Party. Dragging her heels about going to the countryside during the Cultural Revolution had apparently sullied her record.

I suppose I got Fu because she was the most politically correct teacher they had and I was the most politically suspect student in the whole of China. My father's string of Chinese restaurants land-ed me squarely among the blood-sucking exploiting classes. "Erica has a higher level of consciousness than you," Fu said to me one day. "Her parents are intellectuals, so they tend to criticize her more. But yours are bourgeois, so they aren't as close to their children." When she saw my stricken look, she hastily added, "All the teachers, including myself and Dai Guifu, love both of you equally."

Fu's pedagogy courses hadn't included lectures on Your Students' Self-Esteem. She often praised Erica's fluent Chinese and mocked mine, and wondered aloud if I was stupid. She measured me against Erica in other ways, too. "You look just like a boy!" she exclaimed one day when I was undressing at the bathhouse. "Erica's chest is much nicer."

I secretly dubbed her Fu the Enforcer. Like a good Party mem-ber, she analyzed everything through the prism of class struggle. When I, a veteran of college sit-ins, balked at standing respectfully whenever she entered the room, she blamed my boorishness on my bourgeois background. When Erica was given a text on a cruel restaurant owner, Fu skipped over it for fear I would feel hurt. She had zero sense of humor, especially when it came to socialist moral-ity. During a lesson about Norman Bethune, who had died of blood poisoning contracted while operating on the battlefield, we dis-cussed blood types. When I joked, "Luckily I'm type AB. I can take anybody's blood, but hardly anybody can use mine," that only con-firmed to Fu the selfishness of the capitalist class.

Without a dictionary, I often was stymied by new words. She would glare and say, rather unhelpfully, "*Ni bu dong!*" ("You don't understand!") When she felt inspired, she scribbled brief sentences on the blackboard, but "I like chairs" did little to clarify the mean-ing of *chair*. She would have been great teaching the hearing impaired: her last-ditch desperation technique was to shout the mystery word louder. As she turned up the volume, I learned to rap on the wall. "*Shenme?*" Erica would call from the next room. *("What?")* Fu would bellow out the word, and Erica would yell back a translation.

Despite her university degree, Fu the Enforcer knew next to noth-ing about the outside world. She was deeply suspicious, for instance, of Western culture, and told me she had been disgusted by a 1950s performance of *Swan Lake*. "The women's skirts were too short and the men looked as if they weren't wearing any pants," she said with a grimace. "Chinese don't like to see that." Another time, after a lengthy lecture, it dawned on me she was trying to explain the concept of a verb. When I told her English had verbs, too, she was astonished.

"They didn't know how to teach Chinese," Erica recalled in 1994 when I telephoned her in New Mexico to reminisce. "They thought we were retarded. They would say, 'Raise high the red flag,' and tell us, 'We don't *really* mean a red flag.' Or they would teach us, 'Take the correct road,' and add, 'It isn't really a *road.*' "

Chinese were great believers in rote learning, which developed from the need to commit to memory thousands of written characters. For two hours each morning, six days a week, Fu the Enforcer stood at the front reading from notes while I sat mutely at a desk. Although I wanted to ditch the audiotapes and lectures and find real people to converse with, Fu ordered me to memorize my textbook. Whenever I interrupted her monologue with a question, she was taken aback. The tradition of rote learning had eroded the ability of many Chinese to think independently, a failing the Communists encouraged. If you were going to cram Marxist dogma into people, you needed unquestioning docility.

Fu meant well. She tried so hard to teach me she had nightmares. One morning she told me she had woken up in a sweat the night before. She had dreamed I was speaking so softly she couldn't hear me, and all my tones were off. Despite our fights over pedagogical technique, Fu the Enforcer somehow managed to cram a hundred and twenty new words into me each week.

I was learning Mandarin, the official dialect, spoken in the capital, taught in schools nationwide and broadcast on state television and radio. Mandarin has four distinct tones, a characteristic that many Westerners have trouble grasping. "Ma" on a flat tone meant mother, a rising tone meant hemp, a dipping tone meant horse, and a sharp falling tone meant to curse. The Chinese written language is uniform throughout the country, but is pronounced differently in various regions. In all, China has eight major dialects and hundreds of minor ones, many of them mutually incomprehensible.

Chinese was actually fun. The written characters were aesthetically pleasing, the grammar minimalist, the phrases vivid. A whirlwind tour was rendered as "gazing at flowers from a galloping horse." And they really did say things like "Long time no see." I memorized Chairman Mao's pithiest quotations, such as "Shit or get off the pot." People actually recited this pearl of wisdom to one another, which Mao had once barked at a meeting when he grew exasperated at colleagues who were all talk and no action.

The more I learned, the better I understood the psyche. Communism was the holy grail, unattainable, pure, otherworldly. China was still a "socialist" country, not yet perfect enough to be a "Communist" one. Words such as *privacy* didn't exist. Honorifics like Miss and Mrs. had been replaced by the unisex Comrade. Still other words, like *please* and *thank you*, had disappeared under decades of Communist influence. If I said, "Please pass the soy sauce," I would get the same look I would if I curtsied to a bus driver in Montreal. "Thank you" was now appropriate only for big favors, such as when someone saved your life.

What really surprised me was that a Mao suit was called not a Mao suit but a Yat-sen suit, apparently because Dr. Sun Yat-sen had originated the fashion craze. Nor was there a word for Maoism. Instead, the Chinese modestly called the ruling theology Mao Zedong Thought, to indicate it was a notch less lofty than an -ism like Marxism-Leninism. Even more surprising, there was no word for Maoist. That was because *everyone* was a Maoist, at least at the beginning. And when they stopped being Maoists, there was only peril in advertising the fact.

Sometimes Chinese was too convoluted for my western mindset. For some reason, the language didn't differentiate between *he*, *she* and *it*. There were at least eight words for rice in its various stages on the way to the table. I could never get straight the five words for aunt (or uncle or cousin), which depended on your position and theirs in a hierarchy of age, sex and matrimony. Colors especially perplexed me. Virtually the only word for brown was "coffee-colored," which struck me as odd since coffee was a recent import. *Huang* meant anything from yellow to brown. *Bai* sometimes meant white, sometimes colorless. The color *qing* (pronounced *ching*) could mean, depending on context, black, indigo, sky blue, grass green or celadon. A *qing mian* was a green pallor. But *qing jin* meant blue veins. When used to describe the color of cloth or a girl's hair, *qing* meant black.

Like me, Scarlet and her classmates studied Marx, Engels, Lenin, Stalin and Mao exclusively and were taught only by politically correct teachers. As Madame Mao and her cohorts increased their influence over educational policy, Scarlet's class was encouraged to debate whether English classes were necessary. A male student said, "I'm a peasant. When I graduate, I'm going back to serve the peasants. Why do I need to know English?" Another declared: "English is useless to us. Our time would be better spent on studying class struggle, Marxism, Leninism and Mao Zedong Thought." English classes soon became voluntary. Scarlet stopped trying to speak English to me and dropped out of the course.

It wasn't easy for us to adjust to each other. When I tried to pass the two-hour siesta by writing in my diary, the rustling pages kept her awake. Being my roommate was all risk and no reward. In addition to having to report on me, she had to obey *waishi jilu*, or disciplinary rules of foreign contacts. One slip of the tongue could have plunged her in trouble. I was too naive to know these rules existed. All I knew was that she was driving me crazy with her revolutionary zeal.

Scarlet took the burden of being my helpmate very seriously. The school had secretly told her that Premier Zhou Enlai had personally approved my studies at the university. For some reason, they had also told her that my father had played a major role in the establishment of diplomatic relations between Canada and China, which wasn't true. In Scarlet's eyes, therefore, we weren't just two college roommates; we were a mini-summit. If she messed up, China would lose face.

Scarlet insisted on giving me the armoire all to myself, tucking her own clothes under her pillow. I once had to lie on my bed to prevent her from washing my sheets. And she monopolized the chores. At 5:30 a.m., she'd roll out of bed and mop our floor. Paralyzed by pre-dawn pain, I listened guiltily to the slap, slap, slap of a wet mop against the concrete floor. If I staggered down the hall to the toilet, she folded my quilt before I got back. If I left my roll of toilet paper on my bed, she tucked it under my quilt. If I flung my damp towel across my chair, she hung it straight. If I left my comb on the bookshelf, she straightened it so that it was parallel to the edge of the shelf. I returned from class once to find that she had reorganized all my books by size and color. I had come to see a revolution, and I was stuck with a dull conformist.

Although she was a history student, she couldn't believe that the Picasso-like rubbing of a nude I tacked on our wall was from the Han dynasty, which had begun in 206 B.C. "Ugly," she said flatly. To my irritation, she rarely questioned anything and sat at her desk memorizing her lessons. When I asked for help with my homework, she would stare at my textbook for a moment, shake her head dejectedly and reply, "Haven't learned that yet." I felt like shaking her. By the time my Chinese was good enough to manage a conversation, we were barely on speaking terms. I confided my frustration to Erica, who offered to help. That evening, she stopped by our room and opened the floodgates with a simple question: "How were you able to leave Yanan and come to Beijing University?" Scarlet began talking so animatedly that she missed a meeting, and I skipped my shower at the public bathhouse.

"I was fourteen when the Cultural Revolution started," she said. "When the schools shut down a year or two later, I became a Red Guard. Everyone did. In 1966, I marched in Tiananmen Square, waving the Little Red Book. When I saw Chairman Mao, I cried. In 1969, we were sent down to the countryside to remold our thinking. I was one of about thirty thousand students sent to Yanan from Beijing that year."

I had always thought it was wonderful of Mao to let Chinese youth help transform the countryside, and themselves in the process. Scarlet painted a different picture. At first, enthusiasm was high, she recalled. But chronic hunger, grueling conditions and homesickness took their toll. The urban Red Guards couldn't understand the local dialect. And they didn't know how to farm.

"I despised the peasants," said Scarlet as she curled up on her bed. "I thought they were so ignorant and dirty. And I hated Yanan. It was a miserable little place. I had to live in a cave. I had to carry water from a well. I got lice. Every day we had to walk a long way to our fields. I would rather have done anything in the city – sweep floors in a factory, anything – than stay there.

"Some students begged their parents to get them out. Others went back to visit their families and stayed there a whole year. The city kids were so upset that some started getting married without the leadership's permission. They weren't actually married, but they lived together. Some even started stealing. The situation was so bad that some students were put in jail.

"Authorities in Beijing were really concerned because it looked as if the experiment would fail. They sent three thousand cadres to Yanan, many of them veterans of the Long March. They told the students stories about the revolutionary tradition of Yanan and they criticized the people of Yanan for their selfishness.

"We students gradually began to change. We thought the peasants were ignorant, but it was they who showed us how to cook our food, they who taught us how to farm. That summer there was a flash flood. The peasants made it safely down the hill, but we were stranded on our mountain plots. The peasants climbed back up and led us by the hand down the hill. We were deeply moved. The peasants said they considered us sent to them directly by Chairman Mao, and so they felt responsible for us. The peasants really, really love Chairman Mao. With their help, we gradually changed."

In my naiveté, I had never dreamed there were problems sending young people to the countryside. What I didn't realize then is that from 1967 to 1972, after Mao no longer needed their stormtrooper services, ten million teenagers, clumsily dubbed going-up-to-the-mountains-and-down-to-the-countryside intellectual youth, were abruptly sent into rural China. To call them intellectuals was a joke, but next to the illiterate peasants, they were indeed educated.

"When some students were offered a chance to come to Beijing University, they refused, saying their responsibility was to build up Yanan. And some even asked for the worst pieces of land," she said. Scarlet, never a fanatic, jumped at the chance to escape and was easily chosen. "No Yanan girl my age had any education," she said.

"They stayed home to help with the cleaning and cooking. By the time they turned eighteen, they were already married." Scarlet wanted to study science, but central-planning czars put her in history. "You have to study what you are told," she said. I was shocked. What if someone had ordered me to major in math? No wonder she sat at her desk each night frowning over her books. It turned out Erica's roommate wanted to study history and had been assigned to linguistics. Scarlet looked at me as I digested all this information.

"You didn't know I only have a grade-six education?" she said. I felt a rush of shame. Barely literate, she was struggling to cope with first-year college courses, and I was exasperated with her for not helping me analyze Stalin. At the rate I was learning new vocabulary, my reading level was soon going to equal hers.

After that, we began confiding in one another. A few nights later, just as I was about to drop off to sleep, she asked why I hadn't talked much before. I was surprised – and remorseful. I thought she hadn't noticed. I muttered a half truth – that my Chinese wasn't good enough. Something happened to her, too, because she stopped mopping the floors every morning. Now we took turns mopping, and only every two or three days, *if* we felt like it. She even stopped going out to fill our hot-water thermoses with her former unbroken regularity.

Years later, when we became real friends, Scarlet remembered none of the early tension. In 1994, I invited her and another classmate to the newly opened Hard Rock Café in Beijing. We shouted to one another over the din of a Madonna song and gawked at the Sistine Chapel–like mural in the domed ceiling – Mao and the Rolling Stones at the Great Wall. I looked at Scarlet with affection. Her youthful voluptuousness had melted into heaviness around the hips. My other classmate, Zeng Lin (Forest Zeng), who had briefly been Erica's roommate, still looked svelte in a figure-hugging black dress. When she scanned the menu and mentioned she was afraid of gaining weight, Scarlet and I both chortled. We stopped laughing when she told us she had been diagnosed with hardening arteries in her brain.

We were all forty-one years old, and feeling it. As I watched Scarlet squint at the menu because she needed bifocals, I reflected that she and my other classmates were part of Mao's Lost Generation. Scarlet hadn't finished high school because of the Cultural Revolution. In Yanan, she spent years toiling in the fields before getting into university on the strength of her political correctness. At college, ongoing campaigns wrecked her last chance at an education. After she graduated, a mere formality since no worker-peasant-soldier student could ever be allowed to fail, Maoism was discredited, so nobody wanted to hire someone like her who had spent her time doing heavy labor instead of studying. By the time she married, new population-control rules limited her to a single child. Recently, Deng's education czar had downgraded her university diploma to a technical school certificate, a move that affected housing, salary, promotions and perks. And now, she was stuck in a dead-end job at the Beijing Library. Due to a surge in unemployment, she faced involuntary early retirement in just four years. I shuddered. Retirement? I had just weaned Sam, my second son, a month earlier.

"I've changed my name," Scarlet announced after we finished ordering. Although the pronunciation was unchanged, it now meant deep water. She explained, "That was my original name. I changed it to Scarlet during the Cultural Revolution."

I asked if she was now a Party member. She told me that she had applied many times but always was rejected. "I really wanted to join, but they told me I was too simple, too naive." As she dug into a plate of ribs, she sighed. "I was really stupid. I missed such a good chance to speak English with you. I was afraid of all the consequences." I asked why she had been chosen as my roommate. She frowned as she considered the question. "I was such an idiot. Whatever they told me, I believed," said Scarlet. "Whatever they told me to do, I did."

Forest agreed. "You were picked because you were the most obedient," she said. "You were the most trustworthy person in the whole class."

I was surprised that Beijing got very cold but rarely had snow. That winter of 1972 the temperatures plunged, freezing the canals and

lakes. People had no skates, but still they frolicked, slipping and sliding. Little boys, and the rare girl, knelt on makeshift wooden sleds,
no more than boards, really, on metal runners, and pumped and
pushed themselves ahead using two tiny poles, like legless cross-
country skiers.

On December 11, Kim Il-sung's *Selected Works* suddenly appeared
on the shelves of our reading room. The next day, several black
Mercedes-Benz limousines disgorged nine neatly dressed North
Koreans. We met them that noon when they marched single file
into our private dining room. Ignoring Chef Liu, they stared at
Erica and me as if *we* were the interlopers. We all sat down in silence
at the same long table as the cook nervously brought out the food.

There were two women and seven men, all in their early twenties. Three were going to study Chinese, three English and three
French. I pitied them. It was bad enough studying Chinese in China
during the Cultural Revolution, but English and French? The
North Koreans had little choice. They literally weren't on speaking
terms with most Western countries.

Unlike Erica and me, who tried our best to blend in, the North
Koreans had no intention of slumming. The last thing they wanted
to be mistaken for were Chinese Communists. They felt infinitely
superior. All children of senior officials, they didn't want Chinese
roommates and used their dormitory rooms only for the noon siesta. Each day after classes, they were driven back to their embassy. I
suppose neither country wanted their nationals getting too friendly. What if they compared notes on personality cults? Ostensibly
friends, about all the two Communist nations agreed on was the
evils of U.S. imperialism. Behind the scenes, they quarreled over
everything else: the Soviet Union, agricultural collectivization,
nuclear weapons and whose great leader was greatest.

The women reminded me of Salvation Army matrons in their
prim navy suits. The men looked like Star Trek extras in their high-
necked Kim Il-sung suits. Although the Chinese had mostly
stopped wearing Mao badges by 1972, the North Koreans each
wore a discreet Kim badge just above their hearts. Back in 1972,
Erica and I must have been the only Westerners in the world lunch-
ing daily with North Koreans. I was surprised they never helped

clean up after meals and even more shocked when they dumped out their food if something wasn't to their taste. Perhaps it was a clever new tactic in the psychological warfare simmering between China and North Korea – conspicuous non-consumption among food-rationing nations. "We have more food than you do, nyah-nyah." That North Korea could not feed its own people was still a state secret. Certainly, the limos and tailored wool suits impressed the Chinese.

The North Koreans treated Erica and me as if we had a contagious disease. Even though I spoke English, Chinese and some French, they rarely spoke to me. Only one was friendly, but maybe he was crazy. His English teacher told me that during classes he made facial contortions, then burst out laughing for no apparent reason. Of course, anyone would go a little nuts with the strain of finally getting out of Pyongyang, only to land in the midst of the Cultural Revolution.

I nicknamed him Skirts because he kept making passes at Erica and me. Once, while I was washing the dishes after supper, he invited me for a stroll. I pointed to a dish towel and told him to start drying. He patted me on my behind and left. Whenever the school took us to model operas and hockey games, Skirts maneuvered to sit next to Erica or me. I learned to give him a sharp elbow when he leaned across the armrest, trying to paste his face against mine. Once, he dropped into my room and said with a leer, "I think you are beautiful." Scarlet was shocked.

When I registered a protest, the school was not interested. As a socialist sibling, North Korea was untouchable. What's more, Skirts's parents were both on the North Korean Central Committee, which I assumed out-ranked my dad's presidency of the Montreal Chinese Restaurant Association. "The Korean and Chinese peoples are like lips and teeth," said Cadre Huang, my handler at the Foreign Students Office. It was his inscrutable way of telling me to get lost.

One day, my favorite lace undies disappeared from the communal clothesline in the women's washroom. I reported the theft to my teachers. They suggested I was mistaken. Did they think I was trying to stir up trouble? The following week I lost another pair. A few days later, I was relieved when Erica lost a pair of *her* underpants.

When we reported the latest panty raid, my teachers looked dismayed. "Perhaps a class enemy is sneaking into Building Twenty-five," said Teacher Fu.

Two months later, I had lost my fifth pair of underpants and was getting desperate. Western underwear was unavailable in China. It was one thing to "go native" with a Mao suit, but I drew the line at the luridly printed homemade boxer shorts my female classmates wore. Then they began losing their underwear, too, half a dozen pairs of boxer shorts in all. I began to suspect the Koreans when I realized the panties disappeared only during the daytime, never at night when they were back at their embassy. My suspicions, of course, focused on Skirts.

One day during the noon siesta, Erica caught one of the North Korean men lurking in our washroom. It wasn't Skirts. It was Im Changjoo, who was studying French. He quickly regained his composure and washed his hands as if that was why he had popped into the ladies' room. My teachers were worried when Erica told them, but still they did nothing. The chance encounter wasn't proof, they said. We continued to lose underwear.

In April, the mystery was solved. A PLA soldier student caught Im with a pair of panties. I never got the precise details, but school authorities went to the trouble of searching through the sewer pipes, where they found most of our underpants. No one told us, of course. One day we noticed Im was missing at lunch. I asked the other Koreans where he was. "Serious nervous disorders," said one curtly. Im was treated for a breakdown in a Beijing hospital, then sent back to Pyongyang.

As for Skirts, he later became a senior official in North Korea's defense ministry. I think of him whenever I hear about the latest nuclear-inspection crisis in Pyongyang.

5

Rationing Friends

Top: Beside Beijing University's No Name Lake: second from left is Fu the Enforcer; third from left is Cadre Huang; fourth from left is Erica Jen; sixth from left is me; on far right is Teacher Dai.

Bottom: Chancellor Zhou Peiyuan, who passed away in Beijing in 1993 at the age of 91. At his death, he was vice-chairman of the Chinese People's Political Consultative Conference, a rubber-stamp governing body. This photo was on the cover of a propaganda magazine called Peace.

Fu the Enforcer wordlessly handed me a printed note. I immediately picked out the words *fan geming*. "Counter-revolutionary" was the Chinese equivalent of "Run, Spot, run," among the first words I had learned to read. It was a form letter from the post office. Three old issues of *Newsweek* my mother sent me had been confiscated as counter-revolutionary propaganda.

I was living in a hermetically sealed Maoist bubble. I had no shortwave radio, no newspapers and now, not even a stale *Newsweek*. There were no Western movies or plays. Satellite television didn't exist. And thanks to Madame Mao, I couldn't even listen to classical music, never mind rock 'n' roll. China was in the midst of a campaign against Beethoven, whose chief crime was "composing bourgeois music." I couldn't exactly see how Beethoven could rot your mind, but I persuaded myself that China had the right to restrict influences it considered harmful. I contented myself with playing Mozart concertos on my flute in the privacy of my room. But just how private was that? Erica assumed authorities bugged us and opened our mail. I scoffed – until two of my letters were opened. The school had translated them and passed them around for everyone to read. Fu the Enforcer thought this perfectly normal.

One day I stumbled upon a secret library. Inside an old campus building, locked in glass cabinets, were some of the most subversive material in China: the *New York Times*, the *International Herald Tribune*, the *New York Review of Books*, the *Guardian*, the *Times* of London, *Atlantic*, *Time*, and yes, even *Newsweek*. The librarian grudgingly let me in when I explained I wasn't Chinese, but warned the next time I would need a letter from the Foreign Students Office. As I hungrily scanned a month-old copy of the *New York Times*, two Chinese students presented their letter of introduction. As they browsed through a British newspaper, the librarian planted herself next to them and peppered them with questions until they gave up and left.

I raced back to my dorm and excitedly asked Cadre Huang for a letter of introduction. "Concentrate on reading Chinese books," he advised. I was crushed. He wouldn't budge. As a sop, he said I could read old issues of *National Geographic* and *Reader's Digest* hidden away in another locked reading room in the department of Western languages. I couldn't understand why *Reader's Digest* was less objectionable than the *New York Times*, but anything was better than *China Pictorial*, a monthly that specialized in bumper harvests. I wondered how many of these secret reading rooms existed. Was there one that offered *Glamor* magazine, the *National Enquirer* and *Penthouse*? As a special privilege, Huang also allowed me to borrow banned books from the university library, including Veblen's *Theory of the Leisure Class* and novels by Mailer, Proust, Hemingway, Bellow and Dos Passos.

With little else to do but study Chinese, I made fast progress. By mid-December I was attending history lectures with Scarlet's class and understanding about half. As a visible minority in Canada, I always assumed I was Chinese. But in China, the more Chinese I learned, the less Chinese I felt. I had expected to find my roots here. Instead I discovered that the harder I tried to be Chinese, the more I realized I wasn't Chinese at all. On days when the sun shone and Fu the Enforcer didn't compare me to Erica, linguistically or otherwise, I felt a bit at home. On days when everything seemed to go wrong, I felt like an alien from another planet.

One Sunday morning in January 1973, I watched a speed-skating competition at No Name Lake. Two men stood out in the sea of Mao suits. They were wearing knee-high leather boots, ponchos trimmed with fur and embroidery and exuberant grass green silk bonnets. Intrigued, I walked over to chat. They turned out to be Tibetan students at the nearby National Minorities Institute. To my surprise, they were instantly hostile. Perhaps they were sick of Chinese gawkers. We spoke stiffly for a few moments. I asked how they found life in Beijing. Apparently, they had been patronized once too often. "All of China is the land of Chairman Mao," snapped one of them. "We're just fine wherever we go."

I sympathized. I myself tried so hard to fit in, even learning Chinese body language. To indicate "me," I learned not to crudely thump my chest the way Westerners did but to delicately point my index finger an inch away from my nose. I adopted the slack-armed shuffle of the local populace. I stopped gesticulating. And I learned never, ever to eat with my fingers. But China was so relentlessly conformist that all lefties were forced from childhood to eat and write with their right hands. My left-handedness attracted instant crowds. "Look, she's writing with her left hand! Maybe she's retarded?" or "Look, she's eating with her left hand! How weird!"

A couple of times, I inadvertently violated the strict Cultural Revolution dress code. Back then, it was okay to wear a blouse in summer, but exposing your sweater to public view in winter was the Chinese equivalent of being topless. "Everyone laughed at you. It looked so ugly," Scarlet said, reprimanding me for going out without a jacket over my sweater. When Beijing's tiger heat set in, I couldn't bear wearing long pants, but skirts, dresses and shorts were unheard of in the early 1970s. I bought some fabric and ordered several pairs of baggy shorts at a local tailor shop at a cost of about ten cents each. The staff looked doubtful until I assured them I was a foreigner. Only after I bicycled around wearing them did I realize my mistake. Beijing truck drivers honked their horns, leaned out their windows and yelled, "Thighs!" I also stumbled when it came to footwear. All Chinese women wore standard plastic sandals, but my feet were much too wide to squeeze into them.

So I wore plastic flip-flops to class. Fu the Enforcer denounced me for being disrespectful. Apparently flip-flops were another sign of near-nudity.

So why did I want to stay for a whole year? China was like a never-ending Outward Bound course; I knew I would never forgive myself for quitting. I also took to heart all the Maoist tenets about improving myself as a human being. I really believed that if I worked hard and reformed my "world outlook," one day I would be worthy of joining the Chinese revolution. I dismissed the culture shock as character-building. The deprivation seemed minor compared to the chance to watch history in the making. Erica and I had committed ourselves to stay until the following summer. After some agonized debate – we really missed rock 'n' roll but we also desperately needed remolding – we even applied for an extension into second year, until the summer of 1974.

As the only two Westerners studying in China, we felt a heavy responsibility not only to live up to the rigors of physical labor but to spread the word about the revolution. We sent carefully worded letters to the *New York Times*, the *Los Angeles Times*, the *Washington Post* and the Toronto *Globe and Mail* offering to write articles about our student life at Beijing University. The *Los Angeles Times* wrote back immediately and assured us any article would be published without distortion. The reply from a *New York Times* editor came shortly after. "We are primarily concerned with accuracy, with absolutely no bias and with complete freedom from official censorship. Without knowing more about you, and without being able to check further into your credentials, I see no way to proceed." We felt insulted, even though our intent was propagandistic. When the *Post* and the *Globe* failed to respond, we lost interest. We never did submit an article to the *Los Angeles Times*. My career as Beijing Jan was getting off to a slow start.

We were most homesick during Western holidays. At Halloween, Erica picked out the seeds from a sunflower to create a passing resemblance to a grinning jack-o'-lantern. At Christmas, the Canadian Embassy invited me for roast turkey and cranberry sauce. On December 25, Erica and I couldn't resist humming a few carols at recess while playing ping-pong. At noon, I went for a stroll to Haidian, the town beside the campus. If I closed my eyes, I could almost believe the tinkling bicycle bells were sleigh bells. The next day was Mao's seventy-ninth birthday. I was surprised that despite a massive personality cult, it wasn't a public holiday and went unacknowledged even in the *People's Daily*. I later learned that Mao, at one point before the Cultural Revolution, had given a specific directive not to celebrate his birthday or name anything after him. That was why there were no Mao Zedong avenues or squares or parks or ships.

Erica and I weren't the only Westerners in China. There were a few foreign correspondents, a small diplomatic community and a handful of "foreign experts" working as teachers and propaganda text polishers. When I split from my tour group in August, I didn't know a soul in Beijing. Out of sheer pity, the Americans left me the phone number of a former classmate of theirs who was working at the Swedish Embassy as a cultural attaché.

While I waited to begin classes at Beijing University, Anders Hansson took me on bicycle tours of the city. In those xenophobic days, people gaped at us as we pedaled by. Anders, who was twenty-eight, worried that the authorities might be upset. I was unconcerned. After all, neither of us was Chinese. Later, after I started at Beijing University, I occasionally dropped by his apartment, sometimes with Erica, for some Camembert and forbidden Beethoven.

But our visits did not go unnoticed. Once, after Anders dropped Erica off in Tiananmen Square, a PLA sentry accosted her.

"Who were those people?" he demanded.

"Friends," said Erica.

"Which embassy?" he barked. She told him.

"How do you know them?"

"My friend's friend," said Erica stubbornly.

"Who's your friend?"

"A foreign student."

"Who are you?"

"I'm also a foreign student."

"Oh," he said, not quite believing her. "From which country?"

"America."

In those days, no Chinese would have dared lie about being an American. The soldier looked embarrassed, and apologized.

Such encounters were common. Erica and I often were treated rudely until people realized we weren't Chinese. Neither of us found this pleasant, but at first we accepted it without complaint. Didn't China have a right to be careful? Hadn't Mao warned that there were many spies trying to undermine the regime?

One day Anders invited us to tag along while he applied for a visa at the Soviet Embassy. There wasn't much entertainment in those days, and Erica and I were curious to see the mission, reputedly the biggest in Beijing. As we drove through the ornate wrought-iron gates, the Chinese sentries stared at us in astonishment. No Chinese ever came here, the enemy's lair. I knew vaguely about the Sino-Soviet split. I knew that Moscow had recalled its technical experts working on Chinese development projects. I also knew that Mao had launched the Cultural Revolution to purge "China's Khrushchev," the insulting codename for President Liu Shaoqi. But how could anyone keep a straight face with Chinese slogans like "Down with the new czars!" and "Boil Brezhnev in oil!" And after all, weren't China and Russia both Communist?

While Anders went inside, Erica and I scampered delightedly around the manicured grounds. Neither of us had seen grass since we had left North America. Mao, believing grass harbored mosquitoes, had mobilized Chinese schoolchildren to uproot every shoot. In Beijing, trees grew out of plain dirt patches. Even the parks were just expanses of dusty earth, punctuated with a few bushes. Back at the university, we gaily recounted our escapade to Erica's roommate. She looked upset, but said nothing.

I was developing a crush on Anders and the feeling was mutual, but we were both too shy to do anything about it beyond going for bike rides. About a week after our visit to the Soviet Embassy, I decided to invite him onto the campus. Beijing University was off-limits to most foreigners, so I asked Fu the Enforcer for permission. She was startled, but stammered that she had no objection. When I innocently asked if she wanted to meet him, she blushed. I had no idea that in China an introduction like that was the penultimate step to nuptials. A few days later, Fu abruptly informed me that any visit from a foreigner first had to be cleared through the protocol department of the Foreign Ministry.

Fu decided enough was enough. She complained to Erica, "No one knows what kind of person he is." Erica, who had a much better grasp of the nuances of Chinese culture than I did, understood at once that she was expected to act as intermediary. She took me aside. "All diplomats here are considered spies," she said. "Just seeing one casts suspicion on us." I was ambivalent. I knew the Chinese were paranoid. I had deliberately avoided the Canadian Embassy. But though complete immersion was good for my Chinese, I felt I'd go crazy if I didn't have the occasional chance to talk to another Westerner. I postponed a decision. I knew that Anders had just left on the Trans-Siberian for a six-week holiday in Sweden.

That Saturday night, the chancellor of Beijing University, Erica's father's old roommate from Cal. Tech., summoned her to his house. Two hours later, she came back to the dormitory with a long face. We were both in the doghouse, but mainly, I was. College students back home were getting into trouble for smoking grass. We were in trouble for walking on it.

"I hear you two went to the Soviet Embassy," Zhou Peiyuan had said to her angrily. "The Soviets could have taken you in and reported that you were seeking political asylum. Since you are not Chinese citizens, China could not have done anything about it. Bright Precious Wong at least could have been rescued by the Canadian Embassy," he said, using my Chinese name. "But not in your case. There is no American embassy here. The Soviets have no scruples in matters like these."

Erica listened contritely. Chancellor Zhou (pronounced *Joe*) then took up the matter of Anders. Why, he wanted to know, had he taken us to the Soviet Embassy? "What were his motives? What was he trying to accomplish?" he demanded. Erica explained that Anders needed a Soviet visa. Chancellor Zhou thought that was clear evidence he was a spy.

"Why does he want to come to Beijing University?" he asked, alluding to my invitation to show him around the campus. Chancellor Zhou noted grimly that many diplomats were anxious to find out anything they could about China. Some even rummaged through garbage dumps hoping to find a scrap of a *neibu*, or "internal" newspaper, which foreigners weren't allowed to read.

"Is Hansson nice and considerate?" he asked. Erica said he was. Chancellor Zhou took this to be highly suspicious, too. "Why can't he find someone else? There are plenty of Swedish girls in Sweden. And why can't she find some Chinese friends? There are many nice Chinese here."

Zhou was adamant. "Are they in love?" he demanded. Erica, in whom I confided everything, responded with a resounding no, bless her soul. He ignored her. "If they are in love, then Bright Precious Wong should go back to Canada and marry him there. Otherwise, she should break it off completely. Just tell him she's busy if he calls."

Chancellor Zhou said authorities were worried about Anders's influence on me. "The Communist Party and Premier Zhou Enlai are deeply concerned about the foreign students at Beijing University," he said. As Erica told me this, I could picture the cadres sitting around in their shabby Mao suits discussing my non-existent love life. "We want you to come in contact only with correct ideologies," he finished.

So there it was. Erica and I were guinea pigs in a Chinese experiment to dump friends and influence people. Anders's Camembert was ruining their grand plan. Erica faithfully reported all this to me, and it set my head reeling. I remembered Chen, the Chinese mechanic. It hadn't been an aberration. The Communist Party was telling me who could be my friends. I had found my roots.

I knew everyone would be relieved if I stopped seeing Anders. After mulling it over for several weeks, I convinced myself that was the only course. It was what any Chinese would do, and I was trying to be Chinese. The question was how to break it off. I went to see Chancellor Zhou, an urbane, silver-haired physicist who spoke excellent English. He ushered me into his comfortable living room, where we sat side by side in tan slip-covered chairs.

"Let's have a frank discussion," he said, beaming at me in a grandfatherly way through his rimless spectacles. I took him at his word.

"I feel partly Western," I began, with dumb Canadian candor. "It's hard to explain to you, but I find China a bit strange. When I can

be with someone like myself, I feel like I've had a break, a holiday."
It wasn't very tactful to tell someone you needed a holiday from his
country, but that was how I felt. Immersion in any language is hard,
but immersion in Cultural Revolution China was very hard.
Chancellor Zhou noted that I already had a friend in Erica. That
was true, I thought to myself. I couldn't have survived without her.
But I didn't realize that in China friends were rationed.

"Why can't I have two friends?" I asked. I didn't seem to be getting through. Chancellor Zhou was seventy years old. He had a
hearing aid, which he turned down when he began speaking and
didn't turn up again unless he felt like listening. In his view, we were
there to discuss not whether I could have a foreign friend but how
to break off the friendship. To my astonishment, he suggested we
role play. "Suppose I'm your young Swedish friend, and I call.
'Hello?' Now you say: 'Please call the Foreign Ministry.' It's easy.
That's all you have to say."

I had already resolved to stop seeing Anders, but I had no intention of doing the deed over Beijing's scratchy telephone system. It
was bad enough to dump a friend at someone else's behest. At least
I would do it my way. Poor Chancellor Zhou. He had survived
Red Guard interrogations, but he wasn't used to rebellious North
Americans. By 11 p.m., we had been talking for three hours and it
was way past his bedtime. "You're dogmatic!" he cried in exasperation, calling me the worst thing he could think of. I felt like
retorting that he wasn't exactly Mr. Flexible, but I bit my lip. I
finally left, with him urging me to talk things over with my classmates and Erica.

Anders called a few days after he returned from Sweden. Because
he was not allowed on campus, I met him by the road. He told me
his father had died of a heart attack a week and a half after he
arrived in Stockholm. I didn't know what to say. At his apartment,
when I broke the news that I was forbidden to see him again, he
said sadly that he found it difficult to live in China. We sat there
silently, feeling sorry for ourselves. Then he drove me back. We had
never even held hands, let alone kissed.

I kept my word and stopped seeing him. Chancellor Zhou soon
forgave me for being dogmatic and invited Erica and me to New

Year's dinner at his home. To my surprise, a maid cooked and served the holiday meal; no one else I knew had help. We sat at a round table and stuffed ourselves with food the masses could only dream of eating: sausages, meatballs with gravy, a whole chicken boiled for soup, crunchy hothouse green beans, sweet garlic pork, tender bamboo shoots, chunks of pork stewed with fresh chestnuts, creamed hothouse cauliflower and thousand-year-old duck eggs. "Eat, eat," his wife urged everyone. Their grandson, who was eight, lit some firecrackers to usher in the New Year. Chancellor Zhou, who was dressed in an expensively tailored dark wool Mao suit, gave me a photo album and Erica a red chiffon scarf. As his wife served cream pastries and a huge cake, he stood up. "To everyone's health," he said, raising his thimble-sized glass of sweet clove wine. Erica and I stood up, too, and raised our glasses. "Happy New Year," he added.

"Happy New Year," I echoed, taking a sip.

In February 1973, just before the Spring Festival holiday, Anders happened to drop by the apartment of a newly arrived British teacher I was visiting. Happy to see him, I chatted with him for half an hour. I foolishly thought the chance encounter didn't matter. But we were all under surveillance. On the first day of classes after the holidays, Fu the Enforcer and Cadre Huang came into my classroom. They weren't smiling.

"Your studies at Beijing University are over," Cadre Huang said. "The leaders from the Foreign Ministry called us on Saturday. You have to exit the border by February 28."

I was stunned. Why? I asked. Cadre Huang didn't change his expression. "Your father went to the Chinese Embassy in Ottawa and requested that you stay only this long," he said. Fu the Enforcer nodded. "That's right," she said. "Your father requested this."

In fact, my mother had just written saying she and my father approved of my staying on another year. She also said she planned to visit me that May. Could they have changed their minds in less than a week? When I told Cadre Huang about the letter, he giggled without smiling and changed tactics. "You yourself requested to stay only six months when you first came in August." That wasn't true. Both Erica and I had asked to stay a year – at least until the summer. What would I have done with myself in Montreal in the middle of the academic year? But Cadre Huang was adamant.

In shock, I started drawing up travel plans. It was February 12. I had sixteen days to leave the country. I decided to take the train down the coast via Nanking and Shanghai, and then on to Canton and Hong Kong, a journey that would take at least a week. That afternoon, Fu went downtown with me to help me close my bank account and send a telegram to my parents to warn them I would soon be home. On the bus, a man hunched in the seat in front of me ground his teeth and laughed eerily to himself. Dressed in a grimy blue Mao suit, he alternately frowned and grinned. I couldn't make out what he was muttering, but whenever we passed a huge red and white billboard emblazoned with Mao's quotations, he would read it aloud and cackle. Fu ignored him, but I felt a spark of solidarity with him.

By evening, the word had spread. My classmates dropped by as I began packing. I searched their faces for some sign that I wasn't crazy. Didn't they realize that school authorities were lying? But no. They closed ranks. Everyone was as friendly and warm as before. No one disputed the official version.

The next morning, Fu brought a plate of homemade dumplings to cheer me up. I just felt worse. Suddenly Cadre Huang came bounding up the stairs to say my parents were calling on the office phone.

"We got your telegram," my mother shouted. The line was so bad I could barely make out what she was saying. "What happened? Did you do something wrong?"

"I don't know!" I bellowed back.

"What?"

"I DON'T KNOW!" I screamed.

"Professor Paul Lin is here with us. He wants to speak to you." Professor Lin was the head of McGill's Asian studies center. He was a Chinese-Canadian who had worked for China's Central Broadcasting Administration in the 1950s and who maintained close ties with the Beijing government throughout the Cultural Revolution. In Canada, he was considered to have the best contacts with China.

"Hello, Jan," said Professor Lin calmly. "Perhaps you should see Chancellor Zhou."

My father got on the phone next. "We're all going to the Chinese Embassy in Ottawa tomorrow," he yelled.

"Okay, thanks," I said.

"What?" my father said.

"OKAY!" I screeched. "THANKS!"

After the phone call, the news finally hit home: I was being expelled. My mother had made me feel as though I had committed some horrible crime, and perhaps I had. After all, hadn't I broken my word by failing to bolt as soon as I saw Anders? I felt guilty and ashamed. I gulped, trying to keep my tears back. Everyone in the office was watching me, so I ducked into my private classroom for a brief cry.

That afternoon, Scarlet lay on her bed, wordlessly staring at the ceiling. Fu the Enforcer stopped by. "So sudden, really sudden," she murmured. The other girls in the dormitory dropped in. Erica could tell that I was on the verge of tears again. "Do you want to be alone?" she whispered. "Go to my room." I ran into her room and cried. Erica was my only link to sanity. No, I was not crazy, she assured me. Of course I was supposed to study at Beijing University until the summer. She reminded me that we both had even applied for an extension for a second year and we were still awaiting an answer.

So this was thought control, I realized. I had arrived believing everything the Chinese told me. Even after I began to have doubts, I still believed most of what they told me. What didn't make sense, I blamed on my own lack of understanding and my bourgeois world outlook. Now I understood that you not only weren't free to do what you wanted but you weren't free to *think* what you wanted, either. The Communist Party said black was white and white was black, and everyone agreed with alacrity. There was not a single murmur of dissent. It was the beginning of my real awakening, a long, painful process that would take many years more. I was not falling out of love with China, but I was beginning to understand it better.

On February 15, the Municipal Revolutionary Committee summoned bewildered Canadian diplomats to a meeting and informed them I was leaving the country. One of the diplomats told Anders.

At Beijing University, the Foreign Students Office held a farewell criticism/self-criticism session for me, a Cultural Revolution ritual. "Dust will accumulate if a room is not cleaned regularly," Mao had said, reminding me of my mother. "Our faces will get dirty if they are not washed regularly. Our comrades' minds and our Party's work may also collect dust, and also need sweeping and washing ... To fear neither criticism nor self-criticism ... is the only effective way to prevent all kinds of political dust and germs from contaminating the minds of our comrades and the body of our Party."

To me, criticism sessions, like a visit to a therapist in the West, seemed a good way to take stock of one's life. As Cadre Huang and my teachers settled into chairs, I knew I was supposed to speak first and that self-flagellation was *de rigueur*. "I didn't make the best use of my time," I said humbly. "I read too many English books instead of concentrating on Chinese. And I didn't speak Chinese with my classmates enough." I wanted to add that Fu the Enforcer's teaching methods were pigheaded, but clearly something had worked: I was fluent after just six months. "Teacher Fu showed great concern about my welfare, whether I ate well, dressed properly and rested enough." She beamed and nodded.

Then I took a deep breath. "I came to China for two reasons," I said. "I wanted to learn Chinese. But I also wanted to transform my ideological outlook. I regret that I didn't have time to do manual labor in a factory. The decision that I leave is very sudden. It is obvious that my teachers have not been consulted. That is commandism. It is against the mass line, against Chairman Mao's practice of always consulting the masses." Today, I can't believe I actually said that, but there it is, in my journal. That was how everyone talked back then, and you have to remember that I learned Chinese by reading Stalin.

My teachers giggled uncomfortably. Cadre Huang cleared his throat, shielding his unshaven jaw with a bony hand. He completely ignored what I had just said. "You are earnest, hard-working and you generally complete your homework on time," he said. "Of course, you are not as diligent as the Vietnamese students we had before the Cultural Revolution. But your attitude is good. Your goal in life is not to make money. You want to go back to Canada and further the understanding of China in that country. Although you have been deeply influenced by the bourgeoisie, your attitude is one of wanting to change. You are enthusiastic about manual labor and studying Chairman Mao's writings. But you should read Marx and Lenin more. You shouldn't read so many English books."

Fu the Enforcer nodded enthusiastically at everything Cadre Huang had said. When he finished, she spoke briefly. "You are a very independent female," she said. "I hope that when you go back you will make revolution among women."

The criticism session was over. As I left, Cadre Huang remembered something. "Your textbooks are experimental. You may take them, but please don't pass them around." I managed not to roll my eyes. Stalin in Chinese was now a state secret.

As Professor Lin had suggested, I went to see Chancellor Zhou to make a last-ditch plea to stay. He greeted me with great warmth and ushered me into his living room, where he poured tea and offered me caramel candies. "Well, what can I do for you?" he said, his eyes twinkling behind his glasses like a Chinese Santa Claus. I was in no mood for chitchat. I said bluntly that I was really upset at being expelled.

"The plan was always that you would study here three to six months," Chancellor Zhou said, the twinkle fading in his eyes. "Now the six months are up, and you must go. It was the plan all along. You yourself are very clear."

Chancellor Zhou began to talk about the weather. Clearly, the meeting was over. I was supposed to accept his version of events and leave, politely, without banging the door behind me. But my Canadian forthrightness kept rearing its head. I asked if I was being expelled because I had done something wrong. He recited a synopsis of Chinese history since the Opium War. I repeated my question. He stared at the wall and launched into a list of China's major cities. Five times I asked him, and five times he changed the subject.

"Well, if I'm not being expelled, then could you put in a request for an immediate extension for me?" I asked.

"How many brothers and sisters do you have?" he replied.

Seeing that I wasn't going to give up, Chancellor Zhou summoned his wife to rescue him. She entered the living room, her face wreathed in smiles. Each time Zhou and I were on the verge of shouting at one another, she smoothed us both down with gentle clucking noises. After more than an hour of this, I finally asked outright if my expulsion had anything to do with my Swedish friend. Chancellor Zhou looked deeply annoyed and repeated irritably, for the umpteenth time, that I was leaving because my father had previously requested a term of three to six months.

I must have looked like I was about to cry. His wife said gently, "Yes, that's the only reason. It's none other."

Zhou looked uncomfortable. "I'm just passing on what they told us to tell you. This is the reason they gave us," he said. When I asked who "they" were, he replied, "I don't know who is in charge of you. When the leaders give us an order, we just accept it and implement it."

Chancellor Zhou knew the importance of toeing the Party line. His brilliant career had nearly been derailed soon after the Communist victory. After obtaining his doctorate from Cal. Tech. in just one year, he worked under Einstein at Princeton. In the late 1940s, he returned to Beijing but got cold feet on the eve of the Communist victory. He quietly left for the United States, where he worked on rocket-launching systems for the navy. Then he changed his mind again and returned to China. Two years later, when Beijing began investigating his American connections, Zhou made a complete confession. He had worried, he said, that China would not permit free scientific research. He blamed "U.S. government special agents" for luring him to the States. As a reward for his public denunciation of Washington, Zhou was confirmed as chairman of the Physics Society of China. When I met him in 1972, he was earning 300 yuan a month, the same as Mao. He had joined the Communist Party. And in addition to being chancellor, he was vice-chairman of the powerful Revolutionary Committee, which ran Beijing University during the Cultural Revolution.

Chancellor Zhou might have been vice-chairman of the Revolutionary Committee, but he was no revolutionary, I realized with disillusion. He had prospered all these years because he was a yes-man who accepted orders without question. At home, I would have staged a sit-in at his office. But I had been in China too long. I felt defeated. As I was leaving, I remembered that he had called me a dogmatist. I tried to think of something equally cutting. Mao had criticized Party members who carried out orders blindly without regard to actual conditions, calling them bureaucratic.

"That's a very bureaucratic way to run a country," I said.

He burst into gales of laughter.

"Please come again," his wife said politely as I forced myself to smile on my way out.

Once outside, I felt trapped. I couldn't go back to my dormitory, where everyone was waiting to hear the outcome. I got on my bicycle and rode furiously, taking deep gulps of cold air to prevent myself from crying.

The rest of the week went by in a surreal blur. Fu the Enforcer took me to get a cholera shot. I sold my red Phoenix bicycle, most of my clothes and my desk lamp at the second-hand store in Haidian. Erica lent me a hundred dollars because I still didn't have enough money to cover my trip to Hong Kong. As I packed last-minute items, she suggested, in a surge of paranoia, that I burn my notes because many of the lectures we had been allowed to audit were considered "internal" and not for foreign consumption. I got rid of everything except my precious diary and my Stalin texts. I wasn't very experienced at spy stuff, and I dropped the flaming sheets into our squat toilet too early, cracking the porcelain. I confessed the damage to Teacher Fu, who assured me it was no problem. Just as she thought it normal that my mail was opened, she thought it perfectly natural for me to burn my vocabulary lists.

Everyone but Erica tried to maintain the fiction that my departure was a planned and happy event. Chef Liu baked a cake. My classmates showered me with the kind of gifts they liked – a doll, a plastic panda, postcards, a green silk diary, papercuts of horses. Only Erica, who had been reassured she could stay until August, understood me. She gave me six Mao badges and a Red Guard armband. Her roommate forced us to sing, but no one's heart was really in it. Everyone refused to eat the cake.

Chancellor Zhou went along with the charade. Despite our acrimonious encounter, he invited me to a farewell dinner at his home that Sunday, my last night at Beijing University. On Saturday night, Cadre Huang dropped by my dormitory. "The time for going to Chancellor Zhou's home has changed," he said, staring at me through his glasses. I stared back in astonishment. He cleared his throat and giggled nervously. "You will not be leaving Monday morning as planned. The reason is the procedures have not yet been completed." He said he had no other information. I was instantly hopeful. Erica groaned. She couldn't take any more surprises.

That Sunday I spent in agonizing limbo, afraid to leave my room for fear of missing a message. On Monday, I should have been on a plane. On Tuesday, Cadre Huang and Teacher Fu walked into my room. He cleared his throat and giggled. "Number one. Because you have requested an extension. Number two. Because your parents have requested an extension at the Ottawa embassy. Number three. Because Professor Paul Lin sent a telegram to Chancellor Zhou. Therefore you can stay until the end of August." They all left the room, leaving me with my mouth agape.

Perhaps someone in the Chinese government decided an expulsion wasn't the right technique for winning the hearts and minds of Chinese-Canadians. Perhaps they decided my meeting with Anders really was an accident. Who knows? Again, everyone closed ranks. Only Erica refused to pretend the past week hadn't happened. The new Party line was I could stay because I had asked for an extension. Fu began teaching right where we had left off. Was it all a bad dream? Then where was my desk lamp? My bike? All my clothes?

My near-expulsion was a turning point for me. Everyone had gone to such trouble to show me a Potemkin China. I had visited model factories, lived with a model roommate and studied under a model teacher. But the past week had been an eye-opener. I had tasted the Chinese pear. I had learned first-hand about the real China. And I now understood, in a very small way, but with a clarity I would never forget, what every Chinese person endured.

6

Snitching

Top: Master Liu, to whom I was apprenticed at the Beijing Number One Machine Tool Factory.   Photo: Jan Wong

Bottom: Cutting wheat at harvest time, hoping to reform my bourgeois thinking.

Ten days after my reprieve, Cadre Huang surprised us by announcing we were going to the Beijing Number One Machine Tool Factory for fifty days of labor. Erica and I let out a cheer. We had been lobbying for months for a chance at thought reform. For foreign students like us, hard labor was an honor. In my case in particular, it meant I was no longer *persona non grata*.

According to Mao, everyone needed physical labor. For class enemies, it was a punishment. For ordinary people, it was an inoculation against bourgeois thinking. For intellectuals, sweating with the proletariat was both a punishment and a prophylactic. In one year, Scarlet's class had already been through mandatory stints of *kaimen banxue*, or open-door schooling, at a farm, a factory, a seaport and a military base.

The Number One Machine Tool Factory, which made lathes, was one of six model factories directly under the political control of Mao and his radical wife. In 1950, Mao had sent his eldest son there to work incognito as deputy Party secretary. In 1966, Number One was the factory considered politically reliable enough to send Workers Propaganda Teams into Beijing University.

Erica, our teachers and I shared one small room in a dingy workers' dormitory. The toilet stalls down the hall were so disgusting I learned to breathe through my mouth. Each morning, we ignored the first, ear-splitting 5 a.m. bell and got up with the 6 a.m. one. We washed in groggy silence, then donned coarse work suits, stiff denim caps and canvas work gloves with seams so thick they gave me blisters. It was still dark when we stumbled outside to board a city bus for the fifteen-minute ride to the factory.

Number One, a sprawling collection of low-lying ugly brick buildings in southeast Beijing, was originally a munitions factory. The Chinese government saw to it that the proletariat lived better than intellectuals. As "workers," we now could shower every day, instead of just twice a week. And unlike the slop served at the Big Canteen, the factory dining halls provided a wide selection of dumplings, noodles, breads and stir-fried dishes.

I was "apprenticed" to Master Liu, a fortyish man with a perpetually anxious look on his face, probably because he was supposed to teach me how to use a lathe. According to socialist etiquette, I called him Master Liu and he called me Little Wong. He had typical class-enemy looks – sallow skin, shifty eyes and a scrawny build – but in fact he was a kindly man with a mania for playing basketball. Under his influence, I joined the women's team, where my towering five-foot, three-inch height was an asset.

In the middle of the first afternoon, Master Liu told me to start tidying up to get ready for a political meeting. Wiping the gunk off my hands with oily rags, I was beside myself with excitement; Beijing University had always barred me from political study. I joined about a dozen workers sitting in a circle on little folding stools. A middle-aged worker cleared his throat. "Today we are going to discuss with what attitude we should receive the opening of Beijing's Sixth Labor Union Congress. Please, everyone actively speak out."

I looked around expectantly. Granted, it wasn't the world's sexiest topic, but what would the proletariat have to say? Nothing, it turned out. There was an awkward silence. Finally, a young worker in stained denim spoke up.

"Uh, uh, the proletariat, uh, um, the dictatorship of the proletariat, er, the proletariat is the leading class. It must lead everything." He stopped, unsure of what to say next. He reddened slightly.

"Speak out," said the middle-aged worker, nodding encouragingly.

"Uh, well, I think the way we should receive the opening of Beijing's Sixth Labor Union Congress is to, ah, um, study Marxism! Study Marxism-Leninism! Yes, to correctly receive the opening we must study Marxism-Leninism," he said. He sat back, looking relieved. Others, all men, began to talk in monotones. Many stared at the patch of concrete floor in front of them. The first worker had set the tone. Each speaker exhorted everyone else to study Marxism-Leninism. Even I felt my eyes glazing over. When the discussion leader finally announced the meeting was over, people bolted for the door.

That first night, waiting in line in the canteen, I spotted a commotion ahead of me. Two young men had faced off, their noses inches apart.

"You turtle's egg!" one of them screamed, using the ancient Chinese word for bastard.

"I fuck your mother's cunt!" the other yelled back, using a more contemporary phrase.

At that, the motherfucker slapped the turtle's egg, who responded by heaving a bowl of steaming dumplings in the other's face. Someone threw a punch, and they began fighting in earnest until bystanders pulled them apart. I had a feeling my Chinese was going to take a great leap forward at the factory.

Fu and Dai took careful notes of everything I said at political meetings. Self-conscious, especially after my near expulsion, I tried hard to live up to their expectations. I wasn't yet aware that Zhou Enlai had personally approved my studies in China. In hindsight, it was obvious: I hadn't been given a deluxe scholarship for nothing. Someone very high up wanted to know how their investment was doing. What kind of questions was I asking? What was I thinking? In China's eyes, I wasn't just a misguided Montreal Maoist coming back to find her roots. I was a secret weapon in training, a propaganda tool to further China's cause in the West.

No one dared point out that political study cut deeply into production time. On Mondays we held "production meetings" to whip up enthusiasm for output quotas. On Tuesdays, Wednesdays and

Thursdays, we held "discussion meetings" to express support for national policies such as birth control. (At one such meeting, workers publicly stated, giggling and blushing, the kind of contraceptives they used.) On Fridays we studied Marxism-Leninism and Mao Zedong Thought.

My initial excitement subsided. I quickly learned that most meetings were excruciatingly boring. For once, everyone disregarded one of Mao's more useful quotations: "Meetings also should not go on too long." Political meetings often lasted several hours, and some the entire day. In a typical two-hour meeting at the factory, the discussion leader read Lenin, then posed two deadly dull questions: What are the differences between a dictatorship of the proletariat and of the bourgeoisie? And how do you consolidate the dictatorship of the proletariat? I watched an older, overweight worker next to me make superhuman efforts to stay awake. He was so sleepy, his eyes seemed to droop shut of their own accord, and he soon nodded off.

The work was equally boring. Once, we spent the whole day counting boxes and boxes of screws to see if there were 451 in a box or just 450. With Master Liu's help, I also learned to read simple blueprints. We scored lines on metal to guide the cutters, using a stinky liquid that looked dull green in the bottle but changed to iridescent purple on metal. Master Liu had joined Number One in 1953. During a lull one afternoon he told me his family history.

"My mother died of lung disease when I was twelve because we didn't have any money to see a doctor. My father was a tenant farmer who came to Beijing to look for work just as the Japanese invaded China. He was a messenger at the Academy of Science, and didn't earn enough. We never ate rice, just a fodder of husks mixed with the residue of peanuts which had been pressed for oil. Life was very bitter. We scavenged through garbage. My father was unable to take care of both me and my little sister, so we gave her away to be a servant. I have no relatives left except my little sister, and I don't know if she is dead or alive. Now my life is very good because Chairman Mao liberated our country. If only I could see my little sister again I would be so happy. I won't say any more because I see that you already have tears in your eyes."

It was true. I cried when he said that his father had given away his only sister. China was like that. Ask someone about their past, and the average person had horrific tales. It was why the Communist Party had been so popular in the 1950s, and why people were willing to forgive so much, despite the excesses of the Anti-Rightist Movement, the Great Leap Forward and the Cultural Revolution.

Not all the workers at Number One were bona fide members of the proletariat. One afternoon, a thirty-four-year-old fitter came up to me and hesitantly tried out a few words of English. He told me that I was the first native speaker he had ever met. Fu the Enforcer had gone out for a meeting, and Master Liu was busy with his work. At first the worker was nervous, but he relaxed when nobody paid us attention. We huddled in a corner of the workshop. I asked him about himself, and I thought he said he was surnamed Wang, but he meant it literally, as in "monarch." He was a Manchu, he said, and his grandfather was the younger brother of Pu Yi, the last emperor of China. "Everyone in the workshop knows my past," he said quietly, adding that his wife was Manchu, too. I thought how different his life would have been if he had been born a century earlier. What was it like to be a prince among the proles, I wondered. When I asked how others treated him, he was silent. "We haven't told our son and daughter anything about our family history," he said finally. "It wouldn't be good for them to know."

Perhaps because the proletariat was considered more politically reliable than intellectuals like our teachers, the workers at Number One were authorized to invite us home. A worker named Master Shi invited us to dinner to meet her mother, a shrunken woman with cropped gray hair who chain-smoked and looked much older than her sixty-six years.

"I used to wear my hair knotted in a bun in the back, but during the Cultural Revolution I made ideological progress," said Granny, as we politely addressed her. "I cut it off, and now it's much more convenient." She had a wry smile that revealed she had no upper teeth. She dressed like all old Chinese ladies, in a simple white blouse, buttoned Chinese-style down the side, and pressed gray cotton trousers. Her ankles were appallingly thin, one-third the size of mine. I couldn't help staring at her tiny feet, encased in black velvet slippers. I had been too young to understand that my paternal grandmother had had bound feet. When Granny saw I was interested, she planted her cigarette in her mouth, slipped off her velvet slipper and let me feel her foot. Under a thin nylon sock, it felt like the hard and bony claw of some prehistoric bird. The front part had atrophied. All the toes except the big one had been completely bent underneath the ball of her foot.

"It's impossible to buy shoes for bound feet because everyone's shape is different," said Granny. "Everyone has to sew her own slippers." She rarely went out because her feet ached so much. Having bound feet was like walking on permanently broken bones. To walk, she tottered on her heels, arms akimbo, legs stiff. For all the pain and mutilation she had undergone, her feet were still too big – at least twice the ideal of three inches. It was hard to imagine why men had ever found this to be a turn-on, until I remembered the whale-bone corset.

Until then, the only Chinese home I had been to was Chancellor Zhou's comfortable campus residence. In comparison, the workers lived in slums. None had running water, let alone a toilet, in their home. Their single rooms had whitewashed walls, bare cement floors, no closets and windows covered not with glass but with cellophane. Their only heat came from smoky stoves that burned lumps of waste coal mixed with dust. One worker shared a bed with her husband *and* a teenaged son. She was better off than another worker: he and his wife lived in a single room with their two sons, aged twelve and fifteen. "It could be worse," he said. "We could have had a son and a daughter."

Another night, Erica's master invited us home. Teacher Fu, to whom I looked to unravel the complexities of Chinese protocol, warned me there would be no food and instructed me to eat first at the factory. I did as I was told. We arrived to discover the worker had prepared a dozen dishes: fried cabbage, boiled peanuts, vinegared sliced lotus root, noodles with a savory dark bean sauce and platters full of dumplings stuffed with minced pork, ginger and napa cabbage. Like a proper Chinese hostess, she piled the choicest

morsels on our plates. I could always eat two suppers when etiquette demanded, so I polished off the plate. As I sat back with a
satisfied sigh, Erica's master piled it high again, despite my protesta-
tions that I was truly stuffed. I politely ate everything, again. She
filled my plate a third time.

Just then another worker who lived next door insisted we pay a
courtesy call at *his* house. He had prepared a similar feast. I managed
to force down another plateful. Erica, noticing my greenish pallor,
finally leaned over and hissed, "You're supposed to leave something
on your plate!"

How was I to know that in China, a country that suffered
through millennia of famine, an empty plate was a rebuke to your
host, an indication that there had not been enough to eat? My
mother, who had grown up in Depression-era Canada, insisted we
never waste a morsel. Besides giving us the standard Western lecture
about "all the starving children in China," she had a uniquely grue-
some technique guaranteed to make you eat up. Anything my siblings and I left, she served on the same dirty plate at the next meal.
Until we finished the previous meal, we wouldn't be allowed to go
on to the next. Whenever we didn't like something, we only had to
imagine how even more disgusting it would taste six hours later,
cold and dried out, and then we ate it up.

After several weeks, Erica and I said farewell to Master Liu's workshop, performing a ghastly duet of "Swing Low, Sweet Chariot." The
next day, we reported for work with the foundry's Iron Women's
Team. As lithe and leggy as a Bryn Mawr field hockey team, its seventeen members were all socialist labor heroines. They were the first
females in China to take on the grueling job of blasting away the
sand and metal scraps stuck to freshly cast pieces of machinery. One
of the Iron Women was a slender beauty with chiseled features and
an aquiline nose. Another, with her self-assured, ramrod-straight pos-
ture, reminded me of a young Katharine Hepburn. When she sang,
she had perfect pitch and a haunting vibrato.

I finally understood why our dormitory had two wake-up bells:
the first was for fanatics. To display their revolutionary fervor, the
Iron Women started work an hour earlier than other workshops.

The first morning, we wandered bleary-eyed into their private locker room, decorated only with a proletarian pin-up calendar. Miss April, a steely-eyed beauty in a militia uniform, aimed an assault rifle at an unseen enemy. As we stepped into heavy boots, the Iron Women warned us that anything left exposed would be black with soot by the end of the day. I tucked my hair inside my denim cap and donned a surgical mask and safety goggles. I looked like a coal miner about to perform an appendectomy.

My master was a young woman my age surnamed Shi. She handed me a pneumatic drill that must have weighed sixty pounds. I'm the type who gets nervous feeding carrots into a Cuisinart. *What if I missed?* I pounded away with no discernible results at one ornery lump of steel and sand. Master Shi finally took over. Wielding her drill like it was no weightier than a mascara wand, she blasted off the sand with two well-aimed blows.

Perhaps the problem was I couldn't see clearly. The workshop was dark. And the surgical mask fogged up my glasses. I dangled a bare lightbulb inside the freshly cast shells, but my drill kept bouncing off the target and into the bulb, which exploded in a shower of sparks and glass. By midmorning, I had destroyed half a dozen bulbs.

Over lunch, with my ears still ringing, I asked Master Shi how she had learned to use a drill. "When we first started, our wrists were so sore we couldn't even comb our hair. But then we studied Chairman Mao's writings on the youth movement. We overcame many difficulties. No women had ever done this work before. That's why they call us Iron Women."

At a pep rally the second morning, Master Shi praised me for my performance the day before. "Bright Precious Wong isn't afraid of fatigue or dirt," she gushed. I glowed, even though I knew I had already used up my quota of lightbulbs for the whole week.

At the Iron Women's Team, we quit at two-thirty in the afternoon for political meetings. To pump up morale, we first sang an ode to Mao, "Sailing the Seas Depends on the Helmsman." On the third day, we were supposed to discuss the *Communist Manifesto.* No one wanted to speak. After half an hour of awkwardness, the team leader told us we could go home.

I was surprised at how jaded the workers were. At a meeting with the Communist Youth League, I asked my first cynical question. A young cadre had just spoken glowingly of the effectiveness of remembering-the-bitterness-of-the-past-to-savor-the-sweetness-of-the-present.

"What happens in twenty years," I said, "when all the old people die who remember the past, and the standard of living gets better and better?" There was silence. People looked at each other. The Youth League secretary, a young woman, brightened. "People's consciousness will get higher and higher."

The Communist Youth League invited Erica and me to make a speech. The night before, Fu the Enforcer took us aside. She smiled at me, searching my face through her thick eyeglasses. "Remember that these young people have no idea at all what capitalism is like," she said. "So you mustn't give the impression that it's good. Everything you say should be a criticism. And if you say anything positive, you should put it in the context of the bad system."

Both Erica and I felt insulted that she questioned our revolutionary purity. Of *course* there was nothing good to say about the West. The next day, a hundred young workers listened intently as Erica talked about racism and labor strife and I spoke about Canada's neo-colonial relationship to the U.S. It was pure radical college stuff, and when I read my diary now, I cringe.

Then someone asked how much a factory worker earned in a year. They gasped when we told them. I could feel Fu the Enforcer's disapproving look.

Beijing in the springtime was a welcome reprieve from the harsh, dry winter. Overnight, willows along the edge of the road became tipped with the palest of tender green leaves, and the breeze was sweet with the scent of locust blossoms. One afternoon in mid-April, the entire factory shut down early for a struggle meeting. A huge black and yellow banner across a warehouse proclaimed: "A meeting to firmly attack criminal elements." With great excitement, I joined five thousand other workers sitting outdoors on little folding stools. After a brief wait, security guards led out three men, yanking them by their clothing. An emcee shouted, "Down with criminal elements! Firmly attack the criminal elements!" People around me half-heartedly joined in, but some didn't even bother to look up.

The men, all former workers at Number One, stood on a platform, bent at the waist, heads bowed. The first, in handcuffs, was about my age. He was accused of raping a co-worker in the factory daycare center. He had also stolen her watch, one of the most valuable possessions a Chinese at the time could own. Those around me thought he would be executed.

The second man, who was not in handcuffs, was twenty-eight. He had bought and sold unused ration coupons. Today, he would have been praised as an imaginative entrepreneur, but in 1973, he was an enemy of the people. As a co-worker screamed anti-capitalist slogans into the microphone, he looked suitably chastened. I whispered my second cynical question to Teacher Dai: "Does this mean some people don't have enough to eat?" She shook her head at me, and turned back to the proceedings. I felt embarrassed that I had asked.

The last worker was also in handcuffs. He had murdered his one-year-old child. According to the accusation, he was estranged from his peasant wife and didn't want to pay child support. I was horrified. I didn't even think there was pickpocketing in China, let alone infanticide. Nor did I realize how Maoist China locked people into marriage and jobs as surely as if they had been chained. Stringent rules kept workers in the cities and peasants on the land. Workers who married peasants were often doomed to live apart their whole lives.

Divorce was for the party elite, not hoi polloi. Mao divorced his second wife; Deng's second wife divorced *him*. But the masses were supposed to use Mao Zedong Thought to work out their problems. That sounded good in theory. In practice, couples were subjected to humiliating pop psychology sessions with nosy co-workers and neighbors. Even in the most egregious cases in the 1970s, divorce was rarely granted. A friend of mine whose husband was a convicted bigamist petitioned authorities for more than a decade before they granted her a divorce.

The foot-dragging was partly due to a desperate housing shortage. If authorities permitted a divorce, as the sole supplier of housing they would also have to cough up an extra apartment. As a result, estranged couples occasionally brought their new love interest home. A famous pop singer, Li Guyi, told me she shared a single room with her ex-husband, from whom she had been "separated" for three years. "I've had to draw a chalk line down the middle of our room. That side is his. This side is mine," she said.

On that blustery afternoon, it didn't bother me that rapists and murderers were punished, or even executed. Hadn't Mao said, "A revolution is not a dinner party"? I still believed in absolutism. If you were wrong, well, then off with your head. I hadn't yet begun to question the Chinese justice system, or lack thereof. Although I was surprised that trading ration coupons was a serious crime, I still yearned to be a true believer. That night, I tried to rationalize it in my diary, jotting down some nonsensical musings about how trading in coupons might upset China's carefully planned economic system.

That April afternoon, I was surprised again at how listless that crowd was. "Long live Chairman Mao!" the emcee at the microphone screamed. People mumbled the slogan under their breaths. But when he announced, "Meeting dismissed!" everyone came back to life. They rushed off to buy cabbage or chatted with their friends. Nobody seemed interested in talking about what they had just seen.

On April 10, 1973, Erica and I were recalled to Beijing University to hear an important Central Committee document. In the Big Canteen, a party official solemnly read aloud the announcement that Comrade Deng Xiaoping had been restored to all his posts. I was stunned. For as long as I could remember, Deng was the enemy. His most infamous quotation was the epitome of opportunism: "Black cat. White cat. As long as it catches mice, it's a good cat." In other words, who cared if stock markets were capitalist? Communists could make use of them, too.

The son of a Sichuan landowner, Deng Xiaoping left home at fourteen and never returned. In France two years later, he worked in a Renault auto plant, acquired a taste for coffee and baguettes, and joined the Chinese Communist Party. He went on to the Soviet Union for a year of Marxist studies, then returned to China, where he joined the Communist guerrillas. His first wife died in childbirth. His second wife dumped him during a 1930s purge and later died in the Soviet Union. In Yanan, like many Party leaders, he acquired a new wife, Zhuo Lin.

After the Communist victory, Deng rose swiftly, first running Sichuan province and eventually becoming a vice-premier. In the early 1960s, the diminutive leader – he was less than five feet tall – began implementing some capitalist-style reforms to help pull China out of the disastrous Great Leap Forward. In 1966, at the start of the Cultural Revolution, Deng confessed before a frenzied mob of Red Guards that he had deviated from Mao's revolutionary line. He and Zhuo Lin were exiled to Jiangxi province in the south. For the next seven years, he operated a lathe while she cleaned rust off scrap metal. In 1971, their paralyzed eldest son joined them. Deng gave him daily sponge baths and begged Mao for medical treatment. The Great Helmsman ignored his pleas. But in 1973, when Mao needed to jumpstart China's ailing economy, he restored Deng to his old post as vice-premier, and Deng had to say publicly how grateful he was.

I didn't understand that his surprise rehabilitation signaled the beginning of the end of the Cultural Revolution. All the document said was, "His crimes were serious, but of a different nature from Liu Shaoqi's" (the now-dead former president). "Historically he has always adhered to a correct line." The *People's Daily* printed Deng's name and photo without explanation, as if the past seven years of being a non-person had never happened.

On our fiftieth and last day, the factory Communist Party secretary received us. Every Chinese workplace, school and government office had one, and the more important the organization, the more powerful its Party secretary. Like my bossy classmate, Luo Ning, Ye Xuanping was the child of one of China's ten marshals. He bore a striking resemblance to his powerful father, Ye Jianying, who was destined to change the course of Chinese history by arresting Madame Mao. Despite his simple cotton clothes, Party Secretary Ye's pedigree as a Red princeling gave him an unmistakable air of authority. An able administrator and an agile politico, he would later become a Central Committee member and governor of his native Guangdong, China's richest province. By the early 1990s, he would amass a personal fortune said to be in the millions of dollars. And when Beijing would try to clip his wings by "promoting" him to vice-chairman of the Chinese People's Political Consultative Conference, a largely ceremonial post that required him to reside in the capital, he would resist for more than a year, refusing to vacate the governor's mansion.

In his presence, Teacher Dai was breathless. Fu the Enforcer kept giggling and saying the wrong thing. The rest of the workers present kept a respectful silence. We sat in a vast meeting room filled with rows of sofas covered with snowy antimacassars. As a young woman poured steaming tea into mugs, Party Secretary Ye, who was then forty-nine years old, said he would not make a speech.

"I'm more interested in what you have to say," he said. "You come from Canada and the U.S. You have known capitalism. Now you are seeing socialism. You must use a comparative perspective to view our factory. What are your impressions of China? How would you compare socialism to capitalism?"

All eyes turned toward Erica and me. I spoke up. "The Chinese proletariat has great class feeling," I began. "One day, during a sudden downpour, the incoming shift gave their raincoats and umbrellas to the departing shift. Then the next incoming shift gave *their* raingear to that shift. I doubt," I concluded, "that would have happened in a dog-eat-dog capitalist society." Party Secretary Ye seemed pleased. Fu the Enforcer beamed.

Encouraged, I embroidered my theme. "Workers at home are badly exploited. Workers in China are working for themselves, and for socialism. I only hope I can rid myself of my bourgeois leanings, and one day join the true proletariat."

In June 1973, Erica and I excitedly joined our classmates for the wheat harvest. We arose at 4:30 a.m., splashed water on our faces and stumbled over to the Big Canteen, where we bought double rations of tasteless steamed bread and extremely salty pickles. After lining up in military formation for a roll call, we climbed into the back of damp army trucks for the bumpy ride to the commune. My classmates cut the wheat with small sickles. Since I was left-handed, my job was to bundle it, making "rope" by twisting shanks of freshly cut wheat.

Stupidly, I had forgotten my straw hat. By eight the sun had vaporized the clouds. Because of a storm the previous day, the ground was literally steaming. When I finally stopped to straighten my back, the wheatfields shimmered like a sea of molten gold and the sky was so brilliant my eyes hurt. I thought I was about to pass out when the class leader called a break. I checked my watch and was depressed to see it was only nine-thirty. At noon, I collapsed on a straw mat and dreamed of iced coffee. My hands were lacerated from the straw, my back hurt, and my throat and tongue were thick with thirst. I couldn't eat the steamed bread and salted pickles. Scarlet was ravenous, and ate her lunch and mine. We finally quit at five in the afternoon, after half a dozen classmates had fainted from heat exhaustion.

In July I prepared to leave China. For more than a year, I had been subjected to a relentless barrage of propaganda and had absorbed many of the values. Maoism suited the absoluteness of youth. I was so self-absorbed. I knew so little about human suffering. And I was always being judged myself. I wanted to prove that despite my "bad" background, I could be as "good" as the next person.

I also had studied Mao's famous essay *On the Correct Handling of Contradictions Among the People,* in which he promised that only the worst class enemies would be treated harshly. Ordinary people who made mistakes would be encouraged to reform and clasped to the bosom of the motherland. Only class enemies would be sent off to the gulag. I did not know that the reason I enjoyed biking down the empty streets of Beijing was because so many of its seven million residents had been sent down to farms and communes for thought reform.

During one school break, I visited the aunt who had been so frightened of losing touch with her brother in Canada that she secretly jotted his address down in a textbook. Aunt Yuying was a chemistry professor in Tianjin, a two-hour train ride from Beijing. She welcomed me to stay in her campus apartment even though it meant hassling with the university bureaucracy. Every morning, she made me omelettes for breakfast, an unheard-of luxury that also used up her monthly ration of eggs. For lunch, she made spring rolls, which wiped out her meager cache of cooking oil. When I left, she gave me her vast collection of Mao buttons, including a hand-painted porcelain one and another made from the tip of a toothbrush.

But Aunt Yuying never talked frankly to me. More than twenty years later, when I was forty and she was seventy, I asked why she had never hinted at the problems in China back then. "You were so radical," she said gently. "You believed everything. We didn't dare tell you. It was too dangerous."

I am not blaming anyone but myself for what I did next. Just a few weeks before I was scheduled to leave Beijing University, a student I knew only slightly approached Erica and me. Yin Luoyi was in the year ahead of us, in the very first history class of worker-peasant-soldier students. She was pretty, with large, expressive eyes. "Let's go for a walk around No Name Lake," Yin suggested. Since most people avoided us, Erica and I were pleased, and readily agreed. Yin seemed nervous. As we strolled around the lake, she peppered us with questions about the West.

"Do you have refrigerators?" she asked. "What kind of class background do you need to attend university?" Erica and I were annoyed. Why was she so fixated on the West? Didn't she understand it was capitalist? She did. Yin paused, and took a deep breath.

"I want to go to the United States," she said. "Can you help me?"

We decided Yin did need help. The Communist Party would save her from herself. After my experience with Chen the auto mechanic, I knew what would happen. Nothing permanently unpleasant. She would be reprimanded, and that would be the end of it. And this way she would be rescued from the dangers of the U.S.A. After all, Mao had said: "Persuasion, not compulsion, is the only way to convince people. To try to convince them by force simply won't work. This kind of method is permissible in dealing with the enemy, but absolutely impermissible in dealing with comrades or friends."

Although Erica and I still had misgivings about the ethics of snitching on people, we suppressed them. We were just twenty years old, with a quite undeveloped moral sense. Like millions of Red

Guards our age, we were trying to do the right thing for the revolution. And we knew that Mao frowned on soft-hearted liberals. "Our aim in exposing errors and criticizing shortcomings, like that of a doctor curing a sickness, is solely to save the patient and not to doctor him to death ... In treating an ideological or a political malady, one must never be rough and rash but must adopt the approach of 'curing the sickness to save the patient,' which is the only correct and effective method."

After talking it over, we reported Yin to the Foreign Students Office. "I remember ratting. I really hate myself for that," said Erica, when I asked her two decades later what she recalled. "We actually thought we were doing the right thing. It was for her sake. We weren't trying to get points for ourselves."

Unlike Aunt Yuying, who knew me better, Yin Luoyi never dreamed Erica and I were True Believers. Two decades later, I mentioned the incident to my classmate Forest, the one who had briefly roomed with Erica. "We all would have done the same," she said. "That's what was wrong with the Cultural Revolution. It didn't just ruin the economy and industry or keep us behind in scientific research. Look what it did to personal relationships. We were all reporting on each other and meddling in each other's affairs under the guise of being revolutionary and patriotic." She reminded me that I had been completely naive back in 1973. When I grimaced, Forest confessed that in 1966, when she was fourteen, she had denounced her own father, then the deputy minister of propaganda. "The Communist Party taught us, 'Love your dad and love your mom, but not as much as Chairman Mao.' "

Chen Kaige, whose evocative *Farewell My Concubine* won the 1993 Palme d'Or at the Cannes Film Festival, also betrayed his father, a successful movie director. At a mass rally during the Cultural Revolution, Chen denounced his father and shoved him around, then stood by as his Red Guard classmates ransacked the family home and burned their books. Chen's three-hour epic, about the tragic fate of three actors during the Cultural Revolution, was partly intended as a tribute – and an apology – to his father.

Luckily for *my* father, he was safe in Montreal, because Yin wasn't the only person I betrayed. During my last week at Beijing University, a woman named Liu Yimei showed up at my dormitory.

Granny, our normally pleasant housekeeper-guard, brought her to my room, then walked out, slamming the door behind her. Liu giggled nervously. Her eyes darted around my room, taking in the precious armoire, the bookcase, the desks. She was short and thin, with old-fashioned rimless glasses and hair prematurely streaked with gray. She explained that her husband, Zhao Lihai, a law professor at Beijing University, was a friend of my McGill professor Paul Lin. She insisted I dine out with her family that night.

They took me to the Moscow Restaurant, which had real tablecloths, thirty-foot-high ceilings and a Western menu that offered borscht, bread and jam and Chicken Kiev. Their shy fifteen-year-old daughter never said a word and could scarcely bring herself to look at me all evening. Professor Zhao seemed neurotically insecure, and reminded me of a Chinese Woody Allen. He ordered shrimp and duck, the two most expensive dishes. When the waiter brought the food, Zhao clucked his tongue and apologized for the poor quality. I bristled; it was far better than most ordinary people ever ate.

During dinner, he and his wife kept their voices pitched at a conspiratorial whisper. They both talked a steady stream of counter-revolutionary thoughts. Nothing in China was as good as in the West; the education system was in a shambles; people didn't have enough to eat or wear. I was shocked and disgusted. In an entire year of living in China, they were the first people I met who disagreed with almost everything the government was doing.

"Why on earth does the Foreign Students Office make you take part in physical labor?" Professor Zhao asked sympathetically.

"I want to," I replied stiffly.

"What does your father do?" said his wife, changing the subject. When I told her he owned several restaurants, she uttered a small cry of approval, the first person in China to admire my blood-sucking background. She asked how much money he had. I was deeply offended, but she didn't seem to notice.

"I was an accountant at the Beijing Library," she said. "But I don't work now. Because of my health." She laughed unnaturally. "Why don't I go to Canada and work in your father's restaurant as an accountant?"

I was stunned. I couldn't believe that a person who lived in paradise would forsake it all to be exploited by a capitalist.

"How long has it been since you worked?" I asked her coldly.

"Since my daughter was born," she said.

A parasite for fifteen years, I thought with self-righteous revulsion. Had I had any brains, I would have figured out that she had stopped working around 1957, the time of the Anti-Rightist Campaign, when 550,000 people, mostly intellectuals, were labeled rightists and fired. But even if I had, it wouldn't have changed my low opinion of her. At that point, I had no inkling that China's rightists were almost all honorable men and women.

Professor Zhao got to the point. "We want to send our daughter abroad to study. She has zero chance here. Can you help us?" His wife began to beg me to help, flattering me and groveling. So that was why they had spent a month's wages on dinner. I felt sick. I muttered something non-committal. Back in the dormitory, I told Erica all of my doubts and suspicions. The next morning at class I asked my teacher about the Zhaos.

"They're evil people," Fu said instantly. "Zhao Lihai sold secrets to the Guomindang and the Americans. He's famous for his crime." She added that he hadn't dared contact me directly because he was on lifelong parole and had to report all his actions to the Communist Party Committee. So he sent his wife. She had come over many times in the past year, and the Foreign Students Office had always turned her away. No one had ever told me. Now that I was leaving, Fu said, they agreed to let the couple see me once, but only because they knew my professor at McGill. Without another moment's hesitation, I reported to Fu the Enforcer that Professor Zhao and his wife had asked me to get their daughter out.

Many years later, I learned that Yin Luoyi was hauled before her classmates and denounced for her "traitorous" thoughts. Scarlet, who had introduced Yin to Erica, was asked to make a speech attacking Yin. To her credit, she refused. Yin was expelled from Beijing University and sent in disgrace back to her home in northeast China. I have no idea what happened to her. Nor do I know what befell Professor Zhao and his family. I only hope that eventually they were all able to join the exodus to the West. May God forgive me; I don't think they ever will.

Part II

TROUBLE IN PARADISE

7

Big Joy Farm

Top: Arriving at Big Joy Farm.

Photo: Jan Wong

*Bottom: My second roommate, Fragrance Zhou, harvesting rice; and Party
Secretary Pan making dumplings at Big Joy Farm.*

Photo: Jan Wong

I left China on August 31, 1973, both sad and relieved. I felt I hadn't transformed myself enough, but I also had had just about as much thought reform as I could take in a single dose. At Shenzhen, customs officials went through my bag, examining a roll of undeveloped film, a Red Guard armband and my collection of Mao buttons. Scarlet had given me the Little Pioneer scarf she had worn in primary school, and after some consultation with his supervisors, the inspector let me keep it.

After fifteen months in China, I succumbed to severe culture shock in Hong Kong. Waiters assumed I was a mainland refugee because I ate three bowls of rice at a sitting. I, in turn, was shocked by the women in their hip-hugging bellbottoms, the glittering shop windows crammed with gold, jade and diamonds, the gleaming Rolls-Royces and Mercedes-Benzes, the displays of pornographic magazines, the obscene abundance of fruit and cakes and meat. The doormen thought I was crazy when I tried to open doors for myself. Maybe I was. I stared at the banks of fresh-cut flowers in the outdoor markets. I had not seen a rose in more than a year.

Back in Montreal, I lived by rules of self-imposed austerity. I still thought I had to toughen myself in case the revolution demanded

I one day settle among China's peasants. So I lived in the McGill student ghetto, in a $15-a-week garret, made all the more virtuous because it had no bathtub or shower. (I cheated by going to the university pool for a daily shower and swim; the lifeguard, impressed with my dedication, gave me private diving lessons.) I ate mostly rice and chicken – the cheapest meat – consciously limiting my ration to one bird for the entire week. After I invited my sister, Gigi, for dinner one night, she went home and ate supper all over again, complaining that I had fed her just three mouthfuls of meat.

My parents were thrilled I had learned Chinese, but deep down, they thought I was going a little overboard. My father said to me, in as reasonable a tone as he could muster, "People don't work very hard under the communistic system." I wouldn't allow anyone to criticize China. He gave up trying to argue. Gigi, who had visited me in China, told my parents my incredible response when she complained that whites were given better hotel accommodations. "It's because *we're* closer, like family," I had said. "Like when guests visit, we give them the bed, but family can sleep on the floor."

By this time, I thought I was Chinese. I got myself a Chinese-American boyfriend. I went to Chinese movies and read every book I could about China. I took courses in Chinese history, philosophy and politics. That spring, I ran for president of the McGill Chinese Students Association. I won, even though I campaigned in Mao suits. I looked like Honey, that character in the Doonesbury comic strip. I talked like her, too, except I never called anybody Sir. In that persona, I joined the university lecture circuit, speaking to receptive audiences in Canada and the U.S. I didn't mention anything negative, certainly not the Pyongyang panty thief, or my confiscated *Newsweek*s, or my near-expulsion for seeing another foreigner. Instead, I spoke glowingly about shoveling pig manure and combating selfishness. I didn't think it was wrong to present a one-sided picture. I was just trying to muster public support for China, which I still believed was the only place in the world doing anything right. The audiences reinforced my convictions by hanging on every word and rarely asking a critical question.

McGill University gave me full credit for my pneumatic drill work at the Number One Machine Tool Factory. After graduating in honors history in May 1974, I knew the only place I wanted to be was China. I had caught the bug, and it would take years to get it out of my system, if ever.

Erica and I had indeed been guinea pigs. Formal government exchanges began soon after I left Beijing University. Students arrived from almost every country except the U.S. and the Soviet Union, neither of which had normal relations with China. After graduation, I won a Canadian government scholarship that included airfare, a monthly stipend equal to Chairman Mao's salary and an annual invitation to the embassy Christmas dinner.

In the fall of 1974, I arrived back in Beijing. This time around I felt smug, and much more revolutionary than the other seven Canadians in my group. I already knew all about class struggle, Chinese roommates and physical labor. By now, I also could pass for a local Chinese without any difficulty. So I avoided the growing foreign student community and took advantage of my passable Chinese to enroll in an undergraduate program in history with ordinary students. By December, I was back in Building Twenty-five, four doors down from where I used to live with Scarlet.

This time, my roommate was a bossy peasant named Zhou Sufen (Fragrance Zhou) who had a severe bob, ruddy cheeks and small dark eyes that smoldered resentfully at anyone who crossed her. Physically tough, she took first place in the women's long-distance race that fall. Unlike Scarlet, a gentle girl from Beijing, Fragrance rarely smiled, even when posing for photographs. She snapped like a crocodile when people teased her. Fragrance blamed her moroseness on her strict upbringing. "My mother still has some feudal thinking. When I was young, she never wanted me to go out and play with others," she said.

At her commune, near the ancient capital of Xian in central China, Fragrance had joined the Communist Party, something that fewer than one percent of peasant girls did. As head of the local Communist Youth League, her job had been to persuade disgruntled urban youth – like Scarlet – to sign on for a lifetime of deprivation and hard work. "Many young people boycotted the Youth League activities," said Fragrance. "I was supposed to get them to sign pledges. It was hopeless."

Obeying Mao's exhortations, the Red Guards had flooded into the countryside in the first flush of the Cultural Revolution. But as time passed, they felt betrayed. The most disaffected formed gangs, practiced martial arts and raised vicious dogs. The youth gangs roamed the countryside, terrorizing peasants. Part of Fragrance's job as Youth League secretary was to organize dog-beating squads. I could picture her kicking dogs. She certainly made it refreshingly clear that rooming with me was a cross she had to bear. Like my old roommate, Scarlet, Fragrance rose before dawn to dust and mop, and even tried to wash my sheets when I was out. But I had learned my lesson. I retaliated by washing *her* laundry, and she finally gave up.

After my experience at the Number One Machine Tool Factory, I should have known lathe operating didn't do much for one's world outlook. After seven years at it, Deng Xiaoping lost little time embarking on the capitalist road. One of the first things he did when he returned to power in 1973 was reinstate university entrance exams. A former Red Guard toiling in the countryside promptly derailed those plans. Zhang Tiesheng showed up late for the test and scrawled across the top: "Life is too hard in the countryside – I had no time to prepare for the exams." Defiantly, he handed in a blank paper. Madame Mao, Deng's fiercest rival, dubbed Zhang a hero. The newly revived exam system bit the dust.

As a result, my thirty-six Chinese classmates got into the best university in the country on the strength of "recommendations from the masses." My classmates ranged in age from late teens to early thirties. Some were semi-literate. Others had finished junior high school. About half were the offspring of Beijing officials. Many were of genuine peasant and worker stock. One classmate's father stoked our boilers on campus. The rest included eight soldiers and four members of China's national minorities. Without objective standards like entrance exams or even high-school graduation marks – almost none had finished high school because of the Cultural Revolution – connections inevitably helped. One boy's father was a general. Another was the top recruiter for the Beijing Military Region. Still another headed the Communist Party Organization Department in Guizhou province.

Normally only unmarried people could enroll in university, so all my classmates were single, with three exceptions. At twenty-seven, for instance, Fragrance had already rejected several arranged marriages her parents tried to foist on her.

"I've decided to get married when I'm thirty," she told me.

"Do you have a boyfriend?" I asked.

"No. But when I'm thirty, I'll go out and find one," she said with finality, ending the conversation.

Dating was strictly forbidden, but that didn't stop Fragrance from surveying the field. In our class, where the ratio of males to females was a favorable two to one, she quietly set her sights on a PLA soldier with a slight stutter and the right demographics. He was from a poor peasant family in Fragrance's home province of Shaanxi and he, too, was a Communist Party member. At one point, he studied so hard he had a nervous breakdown. A buxom peasant from Sichuan competed with Fragrance to wipe his fevered brow, bring him hot meals and wash his socks. By the time he got better, it was clear that the soldier preferred the Sichuanese. Fragrance retreated in defeat but stuck to her game plan. After graduation, she married a worker-peasant-soldier student from her hometown.

If Chinese students couldn't date one another, there was an even greater taboo on liaisons with foreigners. During the entire xenophobic 1970s, the handful of marriages between Chinese and foreigners had to be personally approved by Premier Zhou Enlai himself. I developed a crush on Ma Li, a Communist Party soldier-student with flashing eyes and a quick wit. He and another PLA classmate spent a Sunday morning repairing my steamer trunk, which had been damaged in transit. I poured them endless cups of green tea while admiring their biceps as they hammered and tightened screws.

If I was naive, Ma Li, whose name literally meant Horsepower, had few illusions. Had he gotten involved with me, he would have been expelled from school, kicked out of the Party, dishonorably discharged *and* sent to Chinese Siberia. He restricted our contact to pick-up games of basketball. We held hands only when I challenged him – and my other soldier classmates – to left-handed arm-wrestling contests. (I always won.)

When two of our classmates conducted a clandestine affair, punishment was swift. Our class president, another PLA soldier, promised to help a female classmate join the Party if she slept with him. She did, but when he refused to marry her – and she discovered he was already betrothed to the daughter of his commander back in the provinces – she was so enraged she reported him to the Party Committee. He was expelled, and she received a permanent black mark in her dossier.

In January 1975, Chairman Mao promoted Deng Xiaoping to vice-chairman of the Central Military Commission, chief of staff of the PLA, vice-chairman of the Central Committee *and* standing member of the powerful Politburo. At the same time, Mao gave his wife the green light to launch a hard-line campaign against Deng. Mao wasn't schizophrenic. He had read the *Art of War*, the third-century B.C. classic by Sun Zi, and was merely playing off one side against the other.

On campus, the new campaign's fallout was immediate. A university official made a four-hour speech about an obscure school in northeast China. Chaoyang (Facing-the-Sun) Agricultural Institute had canceled classes and sent its students to farm barren land. "The question for Beijing University is, how can *we* learn from the revolutionary experience of Facing-the-Sun Agricultural College?" the official said. He paused dramatically. "The answer is simple. We already have a farm of our own."

Mao's dictum "Oppose book worship" was going to be taken literally. Big Character posters went up overnight. I had trouble deciphering the brush-stroke calligraphy – very different from printed Chinese - so Fragrance read them aloud while I took notes. "Our teachers want us to be important big-city editors while what is needed are propaganda workers to go to the lowest levels," complained one poster put up by students in the journalism department. Another accused teachers of denigrating the time language students spent at factories and farms. "The new intellectuals must be able to wield a hoe as well as a pen," the poster declared.

The next day, Horsepower and a Communist Party official named Pan Qingde paid me a surprise visit.

"Why were you reading the Big Character posters?" Party Secretary Pan demanded. "Do you think the campus is in chaos?"

"No," I said earnestly. "Big Character posters are good. They show that China is democratic, that people can say what they think."

"Why were you taking notes?" he asked.

I looked at Horsepower for help, but he studied the floor. "I can't remember anything unless I write it down," I said lamely.

Pan was our class Communist Party secretary, a salaried job that involved molding us into hard-line Maoists. He was a bit older than we were, a recent graduate of the first class of worker-peasant-soldier students. At first I liked him. He was a peasant from Manchuria, lean and muscular, with strong white teeth, an earnest gaze and a ready smile. But over time, I realized that Party Secretary Pan was a male version of Fu the Enforcer. He was both ignorant and despotic, the kind of cadre everybody hated. His name, Qingde, meant Celebrating Virtue. After many run-ins with him, my classmates secretly nicknamed him Pan Quede, or Lacking Virtue Pan, a classic Confucian put-down.

"I am a peasant," he once boasted at a meeting. "I have no skills. I'm not smart at my studies. My political consciousness isn't high. But there is one thing I do well. I loyally, fervently obey the Party's orders."

Our classes were canceled for a full week so we could debate how to emulate Facing-the-Sun Agricultural Institute. A Party official spoke first, reminding us that only 4 or 5 percent of young people had a chance at a college education. Someone else said that seven peasants had to toil full time to cover the expenses of just one student. I personally was all for hard labor in the countryside. Coming from the West in the 1970s when everyone was questioning the intrinsic value of exams and grades, I saw China as daringly progressive. I thought work-study would be a great way to teach young people about their society.

To my surprise, more than half my class balked. "What's the point of reforming, reforming, reforming!" a student exploded in frustration at one meeting. "I've worked as hard as anyone. I've already spent five years in the countryside. When am I ever going to be reformed? I'm supposed to be studying now." While I was naive, my classmates knew that the Movement to Learn from Facing-the-Sun was a well-orchestrated campaign. They also knew, with a sense of impending doom, that no matter how the debate wound up, we, too, were going to the countryside.

In early March 1975, seven departments, including mine, were ordered down to Daxing (Big Joy), the university's farm. The goal of the program – grandly called "half-work, half-study" – was both thought reform and economic self-sufficiency. My classmates despaired. After losing so many years to the Cultural Revolution, they didn't want to waste another moment. Our three-year under-graduate degree was already a year short of the traditional program. Now, after a mere five months at university, they were going to be peasants. I watched Fragrance brood. She looked mad enough to punch someone.

I was upset, too, but for the opposite reason. The school announced that foreign students would stay on campus and attend private lectures, much to the relief of the Japanese, Romanian and Ugandan in my class. Unlike me, the other three foreign students had no desire to dirty their hands. Undaunted, I launched a one-woman campaign to go to the farm. Using my by-now large Maoist vocabulary, I wrote passionate letters to the Foreign Students Office, the history department chairman and the Communist Party secretary of the university. My missives fell on deaf ears, but bursting into tears at one or two strategic moments brought grown men to their knees. Forty-eight hours before my class was to leave, Beijing University gave me the green light. Once I set the precedent, my hapless foreign classmates had to go, too. They didn't dare say they didn't want to go, because they were afraid everyone would think they were hopelessly bourgeois, which, of course, everyone thought anyway.

Masochistic Maoism meant no gain without pain. Someone decided we had to *hike* the thirty miles to Big Joy Farm, supposedly to emulate the Red Army's epic Long March of 1934–35. To increase the hardship quotient, the school announced that we would walk at night. On March 20, 1975, Fragrance and I fortified ourselves with a lavish lunch at the appropriately named Long March Restaurant across from the campus. We washed down a double order of sweet-and-sour pork with cups of *bai jiu*, the 120-proof sorghum-based liquor. Then we staggered red-faced back to our dorm, popped a couple of sleeping pills and slept off our excesses.

We awoke that evening with raging hangovers. After a gala, head-splitting send-off, complete with firecrackers, drums and speeches, we marched out the school gates, three abreast, behind a fluttering red flag. By midnight, my headache had disappeared. To boost morale, we sang revolutionary songs. Chinese literature majors, in charge of "propaganda," stood by the side of the road performing rap-like comic dialogues to the rhythmic clack of bamboo clappers.

Every two hours, we stopped for a break. Sitting in the cool darkness, we munched cold sausage and sweet bread and smoked terrible Albanian cigarettes. My soldier classmates passed around their canteens of rotgut, and we all took swigs. Periodically, my professors urged me to ride the bus that trailed behind us to catch the weak and the faint. I was exhausted, but after all my whining, the loss of face would have been too great. At 3:30 a.m., Fragrance and a teacher tried to drag me onto the bus. I didn't have the energy to resist, so I resorted to my now-hackneyed weapon. As my eyes filled with tears, they dropped my arms instantly. No one ever mentioned the bus again.

The last seven miles were the hardest. A few students cried. Some gave up and took the bus. Others, with bloody socks from broken blisters, hobbled painfully along. Fragrance and I were fine because I had sprinkled Johnson's Baby Powder on our feet before we left. Whenever we felt ourselves flagging, we shouted Mao quotations like "Be resolute! Fear not martyrdom! Surmount ten thousand obstacles to win victory!" At dawn, after an eleven-hour march, we staggered into Big Joy Farm. An advance team had already laid out our quilts and poured mugs of cool boiled water for us. We washed our blistered feet in basins of warm water, downed a quick break-fast of salted pickles and steamed buns and went to sleep, not wak-ing until late that afternoon.

That first evening, my class gathered in a military tent to sum-marize our thoughts. I got up to speak. "I'm so happy to be allowed to take part in this great work-study experiment," I gushed.

"Perhaps one day, as Marx predicted, we will eliminate the gap between mental and manual labor. Perhaps we eventually will create the conditions where everyone who wants to can go to university." I must have been the only starry-eyed person in the tent. My Chinese classmates knew we were wasting precious time that should have been spent in the library and lecture halls.

Our first task at Big Joy was to dig latrines for the men. They were primitive, but at least they were open-air. The women's toilets, a line of concrete slits in an adobe hut, reeked with accumulated ammonia gases that burned my eyes. The revolting task of bailing out the toilets was assigned to Big Joy's resident counter-revolutionaries. We met them at a Communist version of the Welcome Wagon.

On our second evening there, Big Joy hosted a class-struggle meeting to introduce the counter-revolutionaries to the newcomers. Marx forbid that we might smile at one by mistake. We sat on folding stools in a dirt clearing that doubled as our basketball court. The first counter-revolutionary was a history professor in his fifties named Yuan Liangyi. Someone yanked off his cloth cap so we could see him clearly (and remember his face for future glares). He was unshaven and wore dirty patched clothes. He blinked nervously through lopsided yellowing plastic glasses.

Professor Yuan was a grandson of Yuan Shikai, the infamous general who tried to subvert the fledgling republic in 1916 by crowning himself emperor, a "reign" that lasted just three months. Professor Yuan's crime was joining Chiang Kai-shek's Guomindang Party, which lost the civil war to the Communists in 1949. Accused of "continuing his reactionary activities, especially in his teaching," Professor Yuan was sent to Big Joy Farm for hard labor. He had escaped the previous spring and wandered through central China until he was caught in Zhengzhou, more than six hundred miles away. I often saw him walking around Big Joy, his eyes downcast. He might as well have been in solitary confinement. No one ever spoke to him.

Professor Yuan cringed as various students, including Horsepower, read out denunciations. As each accuser's voice rose to a high-pitched frenzy, two people at a side microphone led the audience in chanting slogans. "Down with the counter-revolutionary element Yuan Liangyi!" Everyone joined in. I felt self-conscious. How could anyone shout such ridiculous phrases and keep a straight face? But remaining silent was a political statement, too. Hadn't I nagged them to let me take part in political study? As I stared at Professor Yuan's ashen face, I was fascinated and repelled and a little afraid. I wondered about the fine line dividing him from us. We were all living on the same farm, doing the same backbreaking labor, eating the same terrible food. He had to reform his thoughts. So did we. What was the big difference?

The emcee interrupted my musings by announcing that another counter-revolutionary was a con artist. Xiao Yinong, a student in the Chinese literature department, had passed himself off as the son of Xiao Daosheng, the deputy Party secretary of Jilin province, which bordered North Korea and the Soviet Union. Xiao Yinong's real father was a counter-revolutionary, but in a system where class background was paramount, the only way Xiao could change his lot in life was to reinvent himself. He managed to charm everyone for a long time, including a clerk at the Dang An Chu, the powerful dossier register that maintained lifelong files on all Chinese. Incredibly, he managed to doctor his own dossier.

As Party Secretary Xiao's son, he was able to get into Beijing University. There, he impressed everyone by casually offering to pick up friends in government sedans. No one minded when he phoned at the last minute to explain the cars were needed on urgent business. He told classmates he was due to tour the United States. They nodded understandingly when his trip was canceled because of increasing Sino–U.S. tensions. Beautiful women chased him. Officials wined and dined him. But his elaborate fraud began unraveling when someone asked Party Secretary Xiao about his illustrious son.

"I have no son at Beijing University," the Party secretary harrumphed.

Xiao Yinong coolly replied that his mother had been a private nurse to Party Secretary Xiao and that he was their bastard son. "Of course," Xiao Yinong said, "he would deny the relationship."

Finally, though, he was caught. He stood stoically as his former classmates read out denunciations. Just as I didn't understand what was so wrong about selling ration tickets, I actually found it funny that Xiao had managed to fool so many for so long. But something about the scenario bothered me, too. I had seen the curtained limousines. I had eaten the New Year's feast at Chancellor Zhou's home, cooked by a servant. But I had no idea there was an entire organized system of privilege. The official propaganda, which I was only just beginning to question, urged Party members to "combat privilege" and "unite with the masses."

By the late 1970s, during a period of relative openness following Mao's death, a drama titled *What if I Were Real?* played to packed houses in Beijing and other cities. Based on the true story of a youth who had pulled a similar con job, the protagonist's last line, as police led him away, was: "What if I were real?" Audiences loved the play because it asked why the proletariat should be arrested for enjoying the same privileges as the Party elite. Was the real crime fraud, or influence peddling? Xiao Yinong survived his ordeal at Big Joy Farm and, by putting his fertile imagination to work, eventually became a famous novelist in China.

At Big Joy Farm, we seemed to be surrounded by counter-revolutionaries. Next door was the Paradise River Labor Reform Camp for petty thieves. On walks, I stared from afar at the inmates, their heads shaved, in dark blue prison uniforms. I was told never to talk to them. "They are full of hatred for society," warned one of my teachers. But when I saw them toiling in the fields, I wondered again what the big difference was between us and them.

We had arrived just in time for the spring dust storms. At the first gust, choking clouds of fine yellow Gobi Desert sand, blown all the way from Mongolia, coated everything – our beds, our shoes, our dishes. My teeth felt gritty. I had to shake out my diary before I could write. Ten minutes after I shampooed, my hair was dirty again. I gave up wearing my contact lenses.

My class was organized, military style, into three squads, each headed by a PLA classmate. We slept in shacks or khaki tents on bunk beds, ten to a room. Our lighting was a single fluorescent strip. We had no chairs or desks or even a shelf for our rice bowls. At 6 a.m., when reveille sounded, everyone pitched in to do the chores. Someone swept the floor, while others polished the windows with old newspapers, fetched buckets of cold water from an outdoor tap or lugged thermoses of boiling water for tea. At night, we poured half a bottle of pesticide into a washbasin, diluted it with water, and sprinkled it with our bare hands over the floors and walls until our room reeked. I watched the mosquitoes die in mid-flight and tried not to think what it was doing to my descendants.

Everyone's appetites had increased dramatically. At mealtimes, each squad carried galvanized steel buckets of rice and the stir-fried slop *du jour* back from the collective kitchen and dished it out at our dorms. There was never enough food to go around. At lunch, I had to hunt through my portion of cabbage to find the postage-sized scrap of pork fat, with the skin and coarse black hairs still attached. It was my daily protein, and after a while I even found it delicious. To drown out the taste of the stale cabbage, I adopted my class-mates' habit of munching cloves of raw garlic and sprinkling hot chili powder over my rice. At night when hunger kept me from sleeping, I relied on a cache of Chinese caramels to still the rum-blings in my stomach. After several months of inadequate rations, my classmates finally complained to authorities. It turned out that we *were* being underfed; a canteen worker had been embezzling our food money.

I began to dream about food – fresh peach pie, strawberry short-cake, greasy french fries and T-bone steaks slathered in a cognac and black pepper sauce. Once, I had a rare chance to go back to the city. I stopped at the Long March Restaurant and got a double order of sweet-and-sour pork, which I packed into an aluminum lunch box. When I got back to Big Joy, Fragrance and I sneaked behind our dormitory and devoured the cold, soggy mess, feeling as guilty as escaped convicts from the Paradise River Labor Reform Camp.

It wasn't enough that we had abandoned our classrooms and were toiling in the fields. As part of the Revolution in Education, Mao's radical lieutenants ordered us to write our own textbooks. Even I would be expected to write a chapter, although I still had trouble reading and writing Chinese. My classmates reacted to this latest project with dismay. Only one or two could read original source material in classical Chinese, as different from modern Chinese as Latin is from English. One teacher set the official tone: Mao Zedong Thought would help us conquer all.

"You are the revolutionary pioneers," he told us. "In the past, only the most eminent professors revised material. They would retreat to some scenic site and live in luxury hotels while they wrote in grand isolation. What you are doing is a *xinsheng shiwu,* a New-Born Thing. You will farm by day and rewrite history by night." Our deadline for this project? A mere fifty days, including our time in the fields. For my chapter, I chose the Taiping Rebellion, a massive peasant uprising with neo-Christian roots that lasted from 1851 to 1864 and resulted in 20 million deaths. As "research materials," we relied on a recently published set of simplistic monographs, heavy on rhetoric and light on facts.

Our professors were supposed to be ideologically bankrupt. The more book learning they had, the more polluted their thinking. In contrast, we were pure. Our ignorance was a virtue. To ensure the textbook would have the correct revolutionary spin, we would show our draft not to our teachers but to the local peasants, the motherlode of political correctness.

Many of our professors hadn't been with their families for years. After long stints of thought-reforming labor at the start of the Cultural Revolution, they now had to accompany us to Big Joy. We weren't especially appreciative. One elderly scholar came in for particular scorn. "Professor Fan pays attention to the brighter students and ignores those of us with primary educations," complained one of my classmates at an organized criticism session. Someone else accused Professor Fan of looking down on peasant students. "He secretly makes fun of their accents," she said angrily.

Our teachers couldn't win. When they emphasized manual labor, a Big Character poster accused them of neglecting our academic studies, thereby sabotaging the half-work, half-study experiment. When Professor Fan praised his students for studying past midnight, a student said, "Such habits are detrimental to the health of worker-peasant-soldier students."

In May, Beijing University chose the six brightest students in my class to attend a meeting of five universities on textbook rewriting. Not one of the chosen was a female, a peasant or a worker. My classmates were furious. At dawn the next day, Party Secretary Pan called an emergency meeting and laid out the ground rules. "We will not discuss who should be sent, but whether the correct line in education has been carried out," he said. We hurriedly washed our faces and gathered in one of the tents. Horsepower hadn't been chosen, and was smarting. He raised his hand first and accused our teachers of being obsessed with image. "Beijing University is afraid of losing its big-name reputation if it doesn't send its most brilliant students," he said, as everyone nodded. "The teachers are afraid that sending average students will reflect badly on them."

A peasant classmate remarked poignantly that, even if he were picked, "I wouldn't dare go." Yet another said that the chance to attend such a conference was a learning experience. If the best students were always picked, the gap between them and the poorer students would widen. "We're like an army unit. Not one foot soldier must be left behind," the student said.

A female classmate weighed in. "The standards of the class must be raised together. Every time a selection is made, I can't help but think, 'Are there any peasants among them?' " In the end, the same six students went to the seminar. Even the Revolution in Education had its limits.

We nicknamed our experiment Tent University. At first, we had classes in tents for half a day, then toiled the other half. But under Madame Mao's hard-line influence, half-work, half-study soon became all work and no study. Sixteen days after we arrived, we abandoned our classes completely.

School officials decided that Big Joy Farm was such a great idea it should become a permanent fixture of university life. They ordered us to build real housing for next year's freshman class. In fifteen years, they confidently predicted, Beijing University would be self-sufficient in rice, meat and vegetables. Who would have guessed that by then, even the peasants would be fleeing their farms?

Overnight, we became full-time construction workers. When the reveille blasted over the loudspeakers, we jumped out of bed, rolled up our padded quilts and ran to the latrine. After a quick breakfast of salted vegetables and cornmeal mush, we began sifting sand and gravel, mixing concrete, clearing land, digging foundations, unloading bricks and moving rocks. We had no machines. Like ants, a dozen of us dragged slabs of prefabricated concrete with our bare hands. We hauled loads of dirt in rusty single-wheeled carts that were devilishly hard to balance. Many times, I spilled my load, and then my weary classmates had to shovel the dirt all over again. We transported bricks in baskets suspended, coolie-style, from bamboo shoulder poles. Using an old tree stump, we pounded the dirt floors smooth. Peasant carpenters helped us install the windows and doors.

Classmates who weren't very good academically restored some of their self-esteem by out-performing everyone else at manual labor. During the noon siesta, one peasant student always swept the yard and even washed his classmates' socks. My left-handedness, until then a badge of my Western penchant for female domination, became a valuable asset. I became the chief bricklayer for the right sides of all the doors, windows and corners. After a day of hard labor, my arms shook so badly at supper I couldn't hold my spoon to eat.

After twenty-three days of grueling work, we finished building two rows of simple brick dormitories. We planted poplar saplings in front, then set up concrete slabs under them for al fresco dining. I don't think any palace ever looked so beautiful. By May, the dust storms subsided. My classmates, I thought, were accepting me as an equal for the first time. I joined the propaganda troupe as a flautist, taught my classmates to square dance and cajoled my female classmates into forming a basketball team. During one momentary lapse of sanity, I signed up for the broad jump at an athletic tournament, and placed sixth.

I was allowed to participate in everything except Party meetings, which were restricted to members. One afternoon, I attended the "rehabilitation" of the "most stubborn rightist" in Beijing University's history. The son of a landlord, he had enrolled in the history department in 1951, said something wrong – exactly what was not made clear – and had never been allowed to graduate. Now, after eighteen years of forced labor, he was deemed to have finally reformed himself. With a flourish, a school official announced that he would finally be allowed to graduate. My classmates guffawed at the idea that someone in his fifties was getting a diploma. I was shocked that an imprudent comment was enough to ruin his life.

"He now is one of the masses," the official said, "and he can enjoy all the rights and duties of other citizens." The former rightist made a short speech politely thanking the Party and the people for being so patient and giving him a way to redemption. "In the last half of my life that remains, I will dedicate myself to serving the people," he said. And that was that. Everyone considered him lucky to be pardoned.

At another meeting, a five-woman team from Beijing lectured us on the need for population control. As the team began reciting Mao quotations, my bored classmates chatted and giggled. Suddenly, the women whipped out charts with full-color illustrations of the female reproductive organs and began talking about vaginas and wombs. Then they flipped to a huge drawing of a penis and testicles. The male students stared at the ground. The female students buried their burning faces in their laps. Only Fragrance kept her head high. "I looked at everything," she told me proudly.

In early May, Party Secretary Pan called a meeting to sum up the ideological fruits of our first two months of hard labor. He scheduled me to speak for the first time. "Everyone warned me how terrible the conditions would be," I said. "They said I would never *xi guan*. After I got here, I began to understand who I really was. I have been able to have a university education, music lessons and the leisure time to read partly because my father exploits the workers at his restaurant in Montreal." At that point, I was overcome with guilt. My eyes welled up with tears. Mortified, I tried to collect myself, but forgot most of my speech.

The next day, a PLA classmate asked in a kindly tone, "Why did you cry last night?" I told him I felt terrible about my good life.

"The most important thing is to remember that slaves create history," he said, quoting Marx. "The working class created the university where you study." He clucked sympathetically when I said I hated being part of the capitalist class. Neither of us had any idea that in less than five years everyone in China would be dying to get *into* the capitalist class.

8

Chairman Mao's Geishas

Top: My favorite classmate Future Gu, the philatelist.

Photo: Jan Wong

Bottom: My geisha classmates at the Great Wall, Center (in straw hat) and Pearl.

That summer, Chairman Mao summoned to his side two of my classmates from Big Joy Farm. Ying Shuizhu (Pearl Ying) and Feng Jizhong (Center Feng) were southern beauties from Hangzhou, a place Marco Polo described as "the greatest city which may be found in the world, where so many pleasures may be found that one fancies himself to be in Paradise."

Pearl was a contralto with a golden voice and a curvaceous figure. Center was a petite, fragile beauty who played the *guzheng*, or Chinese zither. They were conspicuous among my classmates because they were a decade older and married. I didn't know that Mao had personally intervened to get them into Beijing University. In the summer of 1975, when Pearl and Center disappeared from Big Joy, Mao was eighty-two years old. He had just been operated on for a cataract, and his health was declining rapidly. In a year, he would be dead.

The Great Helmsman had been seeing them secretly for years. They were his geishas in the classical Japanese sense, accomplished professional entertainers. Center, for instance, was a graduate of the prestigious Zhejiang Provincial Music Academy. Were sexual favors part of the equation? As China's last emperor, Mao could have had anyone he wanted. But as far as people knew, the chairman's private life was above reproach. Not even Pearl and Center knew that relations with his third wife, Jiang Qing, had been deteriorating for years. Mao already had a mistress, Zhang Yufeng (Jade Phoenix Zhang), fifty-one years his junior. The masses would learn of her existence only after Mao's funeral, when a list of his personal staff was published.

A primary-school drop-out, Jade Phoenix was fourteen when she began working on the railroad in her hometown of Peony River, a small city less than a hundred miles from the Soviet border. At sixteen, she became an attendant on Mao's private railcar. Nine years later, in 1969, when she was already married and the mother of a baby girl, she joined Mao's personal staff in Zhongnanhai, the vermilion-walled former imperial palace in Beijing. In 1974, Mao asked the Central Committee to appoint Jade Phoenix his confidential secretary, in charge of his personal documents.

By then Mao had Lou Gehrig's disease, a fatal motor-neuron condition. Could he have remained sexually potent into his seventies and eighties? In 1973, when Mao was eighty and Jade Phoenix gave birth to a second daughter, people whispered that it was Mao's. "By some accounts," Harrison Salisbury wrote in his book *The New Emperors,* Mao liked to fill his indoor pool with "bevies of unclad young women." In *The Private Life of Chairman Mao*, Mao's doctor described orgies and harems. But if these accounts were true, where are all the kiss-and-tell stories? And where are all the illegitimate Mao babies? In the 1990s, Jade Phoenix was the only one petitioning to get her two daughters recognized as Mao's children, and that's if you believe a certain Hong Kong magazine. Mao's doctor asserted that he was sterile in later life. To get a sperm sample, however, Dr. Li Zhisui conducted a rectal examination and based his diagnosis on a single test from that. "His prostate was small and soft. I massaged it to extract the secretion for laboratory tests," he wrote.

Although Dr. Li wrote about Jade Phoenix, nowhere in his 682-page biography did he mention Pearl or Center, even though they both saw Mao regularly over a period of nine years. More than a decade after the chairman's death, when rumors surfaced about his wild sex life, Pearl and Center denied to other classmates that they ever slept with Mao. Everyone believed them, and so did I. But, then, I always believed everyone.

Pearl and Center always struck me as prim young women who loved Mao in the same worshipful way that millions of other Chinese adored the Great Helmsman. They first met him in 1967 in Hangzhou, the lakeside capital of Zhejiang province in the south. At least once a year, the Chairman would arrive at his private retreat, Liu Manor, the former lakefront residence of a wealthy tea merchant. At this Chinese Camp David, Mao composed poetry, gazed at the mist, held meetings and plotted strategy. When he wanted to relax, the Zhejiang Provincial Army Cultural Troupe staged private concerts. After one command performance, the seventy-four-year-old chairman sent word that he wanted to see the contralto and the zither player in his quarters. Still clad in their baggy green army uniforms, Pearl and Center poured tea and chatted shyly with the Chairman. Pearl had a lovely smile. Center had a fine bone structure, dewy skin and hair like black silk. After that meeting, they often performed for Mao. When the Great Helmsman held dance parties, they were his favored partners. Nor were they the only young women to catch his eye. One evening when another regular failed to appear, Mao asked after her.

"She's gotten into trouble," said an aide hastily, stepping forward.

"What do you mean?" Mao asked with concern.

"She was criticized and punished," the aide said.

"What happened?" said Mao.

The aide hesitated. "She got pregnant before marriage. So she was forced to go to a village for hard labor."

Mao exploded. "*Hu nao!*" ("Bullshit!") he yelled, as Pearl and Center listened, more fascinated than frightened. "She's pregnant so you make her do hard labor? Get her back at once. Say that I said so."

The terrified aide apologized, but Mao was not mollified. "Are you that clean yourself? Confucius – *he* was an illegitimate child," he raged, referring to lore that the ancient Chinese sage was the fruit of his father's roll in the hay with a servant girl.

Pearl and Center became Mao's frequent companions whenever he was in Hangzhou. They often sat quietly with him while he worked. As supreme leader, Mao thought nothing of overriding central government decisions. He was perusing a stack of documents when a Chinese proposal to build a railroad from Tanzania to Zambia caught his eye one day. He scanned it and looked up at Pearl.

"Shouldn't we give more to our African brothers?"

Pearl was startled. "How should I know?" she blurted out.

Mao stared at the ceiling for a moment, then crossed out the amount. He scribbled a note in the margin, doubling the size of the aid.

In 1973, Pearl and Center were demobilized and assigned to dull factory jobs. Both yearned to go to college, but they were already married with children. The next time Mao visited Hangzhou, he asked how they liked being workers.

Pearl, a Party member, took a deep breath. "We love being workers and taking part in production, but we would really like to go to university," she said.

"Studying is a good thing," Mao said approvingly in his thick Hunan accent. "Let me see if I can't open a back door for you. I'll talk to Comrade Dongxing." Mao's former bodyguard, General Wang Dongxing, was director of the Central Committee General Office, a powerful position akin to chief of staff. Among his many responsibilities, which included summoning Center and Pearl whenever Mao wanted to see them, he also headed 8341, the elite PLA palace guard that Mao had sent into Beijing University to run it during the Cultural Revolution.

"What you say might not count later. Put it in writing," Pearl said boldly.

The Chairman laughed, but did as she asked. "It's good to study at Beijing University for three years," Mao scrawled. "Arts. I'll send you there. If you don't go now, it will be too late. Go see Deputy Chief Zhang today. I will pay your tuition." The handwritten note is now in the Communist Party Central Archives.

The summer of 1975 was a time of growing tension in China. As Mao's health declined, the power struggle intensified. He had become incoherent to everyone except Jade Phoenix and two female aides, Nancy Tang, his English-language interpreter, and

Wang Hairong, his grandniece. Knowing time was short, Deng Xiaoping frantically reorganized the PLA, restructured basic industries and sped up the political rehabilitation of thousands of Party officials purged during the Cultural Revolution. Madame Mao retaliated by launching a thinly veiled attack on Deng's main backer, Premier Zhou Enlai.

One evening, Mao asked General Wang Dongxing to summon Pearl and Center from Big Joy Farm. Mao wanted to listen to music after a particularly grueling meeting. When my classmates arrived at Zhongnanhai, they found Jade Phoenix, Deng Xiaoping and several Chinese leaders still there. Center performed the zither. Then she and Pearl posed with Mao and Deng for photographs in color, a rarity in those days. Although Mao could no longer stand without aid, his mind was still alert. He was curious to hear about the Revolution in Education.

"How's it going at Big Joy?" Mao asked.

"We eat *wo tou* there," said Pearl. Mao laughed. Only prisoners and poor peasants ate those baseball-sized cones of cornmeal.

Mao wanted my classmates to stay on, so Director Wang installed them in a guest house run by the Central Committee General Office. Back at Big Joy, all we knew was that Pearl and Center had left for "health reasons." Pearl soon went back to Hangzhou because she really was ailing. Center stayed on alone, spending most of June and July waiting for summonses to Mao's side.

"What is work?" Mao said. "Work is struggle." We took this quotation to heart. The school canceled our summer vacation as our teachers drove us to do more and more hard labor. On June 10, we started our Three Struggles of the Summer: harvesting wheat, rebuilding our land into paddy fields and transplanting rice. Time was of the essence. The later we planted the rice seedlings, the lower the yield. That first morning, we rose when the sky was still dusted with stars and marched to our fields. We were armed with primitive sickles, and it seemed frighteningly easy to lop off a finger in the dark. But by noon we had finished harvesting forty *mu* of wheat, about the area of six football fields, without serious injury. After a quick lunch, we hauled the wheat to our basketball court. One group fed the wheat into an electric thresher while another flung the grain into the air with shovels to separate the wheat from the chaff. I joined a third group crawling across the fields on our hands and knees, gleaning the last bits of precious grain.

If harvesting wheat was backbreaking, growing rice was ludicrous. I was sure we were expending more calories planting it than we could ever hope to recoup. I wondered why Chinese civilization hadn't died out long ago. After three hours' sleep, we got up at midnight to spread chemical fertilizer by hand over every inch of our land. The next day, we had to transform the flat wheat fields into paddy fields, which meant building an earthen ridge around each patch of land until it looked like a square wading pool. I carried basket after basket of earth suspended from a gently bobbing shoulder pole. Although it looked so graceful in the propaganda movies, it nearly killed me in real life. I tried padding myself with a small towel, but it still felt like someone had plunged a knife into my shoulder. Finally I used a tiny pillow. I looked like a wimp, but at least I managed to keep working.

Using hoes and shovels, we leveled the paddy fields, then flooded them from our irrigation ditch. Standing ankle deep in mud, water and leeches, we began transplanting. Just as a cook knows instinctively how much rosemary to put in a dish, I learned to grab the proper-sized clump of rice seedlings. With a sharp twist of the wrist and a downward thrust of three fingers, I shoved the seedlings into the ground, like an oven thermometer into a raw roast. Like cooking, transplanting rice was an art. Too low and the seedlings would drown; too high and they would list; too close together and they wouldn't thrive; too far apart and precious land would be wasted. We worked ferociously, bent at the waist in the blazing sun, yet it still took eight days for my forty classmates to plant seven acres.

I had already stopped menstruating for several months by the time we started the Three Struggles of the Summer. Now, I was bone-tired. Each time I shoved a clump of seedlings into the ground, the sandy soil tore my cuticles. The strain of bunking with nine others, the disruption of sleep cycles caused by work shifts that started at 4 a.m., midnight or 6 a.m., and a constant fear of failing at physical labor converged to give me insomnia. In desperation, I started popping sleeping pills prescribed by Big Joy's resident "barefoot doctor," a paramedic with a couple of months' training. Even Fragrance, my take-no-prisoners roommate, was in bad shape. The doctor diagnosed her swollen right hand as an inflammation of the wrist and warned she would not recover unless she had a complete rest.

We finally finished the Three Struggles of the Summer after ten days of round-the-clock toil. As a reward, Big Joy officials gave us three days off. I was sleeping soundly on the first day when the reveille shrieked at 6:30 a.m. We arose in confusion, splashed water on our faces and stood at attention in squad formation. A teacher broke the news to us as gently as she could. "We must work another day," she said, and our faces fell. "The department of Oriental languages hasn't finished transplanting their rice. It isn't right for one department to take its holidays earlier than the others simply because it has finished. We have a collective responsibility to the whole farm."

I fought back tears of self-pity. Our summer vacation had already been canceled. We had three lousy days off, and now we'd be lucky to get one. It wasn't fair. I had already passed their stupid test. Now I had folded up my revolutionary ardor and packed it away. I couldn't face another day in the fields. A flood of reactionary thoughts filled my mind. What was I doing working like a coolie? Hadn't my grandparents emigrated to Canada precisely to avoid this?

Some of my homesick classmates were already heading for the long-distance bus back to Beijing when our teachers stopped them. None, of course, uttered a word of complaint, and neither did I. The department of Oriental languages gave us their easiest chores – uprooting seedlings from nursery beds. I cheered up slightly when I got to work next to Horsepower all morning. But my muscles were screaming and my blistered hands – not to mention my ideology – were a mess. At noon, I pushed myself to volunteer for a team repairing some of the earthworks around the paddy fields. I worked in a stupor. Twice, I stumbled and fell. When people spoke to me, I couldn't understand them. Everything they said had to be repeated twice.

By midafternoon, I was hot and irritable. I verged on hysteria when a blood-sucking leech stuck on my leg in the paddy fields.

(Never pull them, slap them hard and hope they fall off, I was advised.) But when even the ladybugs began to bite me through my shirt, I felt I was going to burst into tears. My PLA squad leader sensed this and suggested we both take a break. I had never stopped working before while others were still at it. This time I didn't hesitate. I meekly followed him back to our dormitories, where I started crying from a mixture of shame and fatigue. After trying so hard, I had failed. I was too weak to be a True Communist. He didn't understand. "Did someone criticize you?" he asked. That only made the tears fall harder. "Did you get a letter from home that upset you?" I shook my head. He gave up and left me alone.

The history department was downright cushy compared to the philosophy department, which taught only hard-line Marxism. Like philosophers everywhere, they elevated the most mundane events to cosmic levels. Hauling pig manure wasn't just a smelly job but a test of one's moral fiber. During the overnight march to Big Joy, their female students had carried backpacks to out-macho women in other departments. And to show it was the most advanced ideologically, the philosophy department spent more time than anyone else in manual labor. By June, they were two months behind their class schedule and were forced to cancel an entire course in Communist Party history.

But the philosophy department's most idiotic ruling was a ban on candy. I knew that my caramels were all that stood between me and a nervous breakdown. After several months of hard labor and candy deprivation, one-third of the philosophy department students at Big Joy were diagnosed with *shengjing shuai ruo*, a common ailment during the Cultural Revolution that is best translated as "depression and nervous debility."

My favorite classmate was a Maoist with a sense of humor. Gu Weiming (Future Gu) was the only one I knew who recited slogans like one-liners. A slim guy with a brush cut and thick black-rimmed glasses, he was a health nut who swam every day after lunch. I admired Future because he was so selfless. When there wasn't enough to eat, he shared his meager rations with others. When we needed someone to monitor irrigation levels overnight, he volunteered, then stuck to the same grueling daytime schedule as we did.

Like all my classmates, Future had been a Red Guard. In 1966, he formed a faction of two at his high school in Beijing and mimeographed his own newspaper. "Exams are a reactionary, bourgeois tool," he thundered in his maiden editorial. His instincts were purely pragmatic. "I had failed math and I was afraid to show my marks to my father," he explained to me. "I was so relieved when the Cultural Revolution began. I just threw the exam results down the toilet and wrote the editorial."

That summer, Future, then fifteen, led his classmates in vigilante-style patrols. They slashed tight pants and changed the traditional names of stores and roads. The Soviet mission's street became Oppose Revisionism Road, forcing the embassy to do a self-criticism every time it wrote its return address. The following year, Future joined the exodus of teenaged Red Guards to the countryside. In 1973, after several years of herding sheep in Inner Mongolia, he passed the entrance exams to Beijing University, but was forced to defer a year to applicants with more exploited ancestors.

An avid philatelist, Future lusted after foreign stamps. At Big Joy one hot July afternoon, he showed me his precious collection, which included some of the first Communist Chinese stamps ever issued. My three foreign classmates and I quietly gave him stamps. One day, a letter arrived for me with an eye-catching stamp commemorating the Montreal Olympics. A peasant classmate asked for it. Without thinking, I said I had promised it to Future. Word spread and, within a day, the gung-ho roommate of my Romanian classmate reported the incident to Party Secretary Pan, who confronted Future. Pan demanded to see the stamp collection.

"What's this?" Pan said, pointing to a generic Canadian stamp.

"The Queen of England."

"It's reactionary to put a queen on a stamp."

Future thought, *Who else would Canadians put on their stamps? They can't use Mao.* Party Secretary Pan flicked through the Soviet stamps with equal contempt.

"The worst thing is to have Chinese students fighting over foreign stamps," he declared. "That is a great loss of face for the motherland." He demanded to know if anyone else was collecting them. Future had in fact shared some of his foreign stamps with two other classmates, but he wasn't about to turn them in. He said he was the only one. Party Secretary Pan sighed and shook his head.

"What should be done?" he asked rhetorically, expecting Future to grovel for mercy. My classmate knew he had no defense, so he decided to be bold. The old Red Guard spirit rose in him.

"Burn my stamps, confiscate them or send me back to the countryside," he said, looking steadily at Pan. "I can become a peasant again. I'm not afraid." That took the Party secretary by surprise. He left, leaving the stamp collection with Future. Pan later warned me to stop passing on my "imperialist" stamps.

During ditch digging the next day, the Romanian's roommate came over to us. Tang Mingzhu (Bright Pearl Tang) tried to explain that she had simply done her duty. Future stared hard at her, then continued digging furiously. "Forget it," he snapped. "What difference does it make if I have to become a peasant again? It will all be clear one day if I'm a counter-revolutionary or not." And he stomped off.

We finished rewriting our textbook just before our June 30 deadline. Grandly called *A General History of China*, it would be printed by People's Publishing House. We were guaranteed a national bestseller; all other history textbooks had been removed from the shelves.

We juggled several political campaigns at once. Besides Learning from Facing-the-Sun Agricultural Institute, we also carried out a From Society Back to Society Movement. The latest campaign dashed my classmates' dream of using a university education as a stepping stone out of misery. Instead, they would all return to their original work units after graduation. At meetings, they fervently pledged to return to their farms, factories and army units. I naively took them at their word, and was deeply moved. I wondered if I would ever be good enough to renounce hot showers.

Neither I nor my classmates knew that the Back to Society campaign was the latest skirmish in the fierce battle between Madame Mao and Zhou Enlai. Premier Zhou, trying to remedy the desperate shortage of graduates, urged universities to concentrate on learning. Madame Mao attacked this as reactionary. As her campaign heated up, Beijing University took her campaign to an extreme, decreeing that each class had to send a "volunteer" to Tibet. At a meeting in the Big Canteen, there were tears and revolutionary hymns as students in the graduating class a year ahead of us grabbed the microphone and pledged to work in Tibet.

Having gone through so much hard labor at Big Joy, my own classmates were in revolt. Returning to the hellhole you came from was one thing, but they considered Tibet the worst hardship post of all. To them, the altitude was debilitating, the food terrible and the society unspeakably primitive. To lure Chinese cadres to the Roof of the World, the government paid a 40 percent premium on salaries and gave them three months off every year and a half to go home. Even so, there were few takers.

Party Secretary Pan was desperate, for an unfilled quota affected his chances for advancement. He lobbied all the Party members in our class. Each one made excuses or refused pointblank. Then Future shocked everyone. He knew the episode over his stamp collection had ruined his prospects. "Probably I'd be sent to some mountain gully just as poor as Tibet, and I'd have to be grateful because it was near Beijing," he said. "Why not go to Tibet? This way, they could do nothing, I wouldn't have to be grateful, and I might have fun."

Party Secretary Pan was astonished. Future's application to join the Party was promptly approved, the only one of my classmates to have that honor while at Beijing University. But Pan never talked to Future about his choice, never thanked him, never praised him. It was as if he couldn't bring himself to acknowledge the fact that Future, one of the few students who had ever stood up to him, was the only one revolutionary enough to volunteer for Tibet.

9

Matchmaker

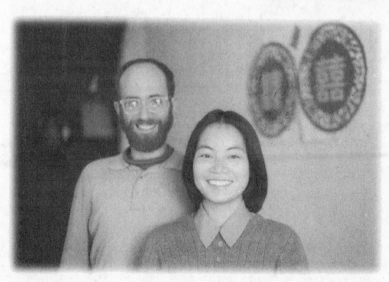

Top: My matchmaker, Betty Zheng, preparing for an English lecture.

Photo: Jan Wong

Bottom: With Norman, soon after our "marriage," in front of the Double-Happiness symbols on the whitewashed wall of our room at the Foreign Languages Press.

An English professor named Zheng Peidi, afraid her English would get rusty, approached me at Big Joy Farm. I was thrilled to talk to anyone who dared talk to me; many of my classmates still kept their distance in this era of xenophobia. We soon became good friends.

Like many who studied a Western language, Zheng Peidi had adopted a foreign name, Betty. Slender and vivacious and in her early thirties, she was one of the most relaxed, self-assured Chinese I had ever met. Her father was chief engineer of the Beijing Public Works Department. A great-uncle was Taiwan's defense minister, and his son later married Chiang Kai-shek's granddaughter. Her mother's cousin had been a Central Committee member and mayor of Tianjin, the third-largest city; his wife was vice-mayor of Beijing *and* editor-in-chief of the *People's Daily,* the official Party mouth-piece. But the most interesting connection of all was that this same cousin had romanced an aspiring starlet named Jiang Qing, long before she became Mao's third wife.

Betty attended the best girls' school in the capital, the Beijing Normal University's Girls' Middle School, where her schoolmates included Mao's two daughters. "Li Min was very quiet and gentle, with waist-length braids. Li Na was a tomboy, tall and arrogant,"

Betty recalled. "They had Mao's features. Both were smart and hard-working, and they always dressed simply. Li Min even wore patched clothes. They were very sensitive about who they were. They never took a private car to school, always public buses. In those days it was safe for them to travel that way."

At Beijing University, Betty studied English literature and picked up a British accent from rooming for a year with Bonnie McDougall, a sinologist who coincidentally later married my Swedish friend Anders Hansson. When Betty subsequently moved back to a Chinese dormitory, she regaled her roommates with late-night tales about the love affair her mother's dashing cousin once had. Four years later, when the Cultural Revolution began, one of the roommates ended up in the same radical faction as Teacher Dai and Fu the Enforcer. The roommate remembered the gossip and accused Betty of launching a "counter-revolutionary attack on Comrade Jiang Qing."

That faction's Red Guards arrested Betty, by then a professor in the English department, and locked her up in an empty classroom, dubbed a cowshed because it held "cow-devil and snake-spirit counter-revolutionaries." Betty had just given birth to her first child, and she begged the Red Guards to let her return home to nurse him. "They refused, and gave me an injection to dry up my milk," she recalled. "I was in agony for several days. My breasts were hard with milk. They felt like rocks. I was in terrible pain."

The Red Guards beat her with sticks and ordered her to confess. They wanted her to retract her scandalous story. Betty rashly decided truth was the best defense. She dredged up every explicit detail she could remember. She told them that her mother's cousin, Yu Qiwei, first met Jiang Qing in 1933, when he was a hero of the Communist-led student movement and she was a twenty-year-old librarian and wannabe film starlet. Yu not only initiated Jiang Qing into love but approved her application to join the Communist Party. When he was arrested a year later, his powerful uncle, Yu Ta-wei, the one destined to become Taiwan's defense minister, bailed him out. After the Communist victory, Yu Qiwei changed his name to Huang Jing. He died in 1958 at the age of forty-six, apparently of heart disease. If he was long dead and all this happened before

Jiang Qing met Mao, Betty reasoned, what was all the fuss about?

The Red Guards didn't see it that way. The Maoist personality cult required that Comrade Jiang Qing be pure as jade. For the next one hundred days, Betty remained in the cowshed. Her mother-in-law fed the baby rice gruel. Betty's husband, who was working in Tibet as an army translator, managed to get back to Beijing once. In his military uniform, a sign of political reliability during the Cultural Revolution, he strode purposefully past the Red Guards and found Betty sitting on the concrete floor among the other prisoners. When their whispers aroused suspicions, he thrust a book of Mao's quotations at her and said loudly, "Make sure you study this." Then he left. There was nothing he could do.

When Betty's brother protested her treatment, the Red Guards locked him up, then exiled him to Sichuan province in the southwest. They jailed her mother, then forced her to clean office toilets for a year before sending her off to Henan province in central China. Betty's father was put under house arrest after his driver accused him of preferring American can openers. As part of his punishment, her father had to scrub the front steps of the Department of Public Works with a toothbrush.

In the cowshed, Betty was the youngest and the lowest ranking of the approximately one hundred prisoners, who all slept together on the concrete floor. The others were all top Party officials and scholars, including Chancellor Zhou. "I felt quite out of place," she recalled. Years later, after the cowshed alumni regained power, they remained friends.

But not all survived. Every morning, the Red Guards forced the prisoners to play an insane version of Trivial Pursuit. Each Mao quotation was assigned a number. When the Red Guards barked out a number, the inmates had to shout back the correct quotation. "Luckily I was young and had a very good memory," said Betty. "But the older professors stumbled. The Red Guards beat them with whips and bicycle chains. One professor was beaten every day until he died."

In 1970, just as her husband was demobilized, Betty was sent to Beijing University's Carp Island Farm. She was supposed to toil under the supervision of the faction persecuting her, which included

Fu the Enforcer. But despite her political handicap, Betty soon won a coveted slot on the farm's propaganda team. "Fu Min was jealous because I didn't have to do any work on rehearsal days, and because my skin was so fair," said Betty. "*Her* nickname was Old Blackie because she tanned so easily."

At Carp Island, people knew Betty had committed a crime that was literally unspeakable. A few bold ones inquired discreetly, but she was too frightened to tell them. Shunned by nearly everyone, Betty was heartened when a young lab assistant sometimes smiled at her. Eventually, she confided in him. "I thought it was much worse," he said, shocked. "Everyone knows that Jiang Qing had many lovers. I can't believe you're in so much trouble for saying that."

Betty felt happier than she had in a long time. He was the first person who had spoken kindly to her in more than two years. In a bitter sea of betrayal, they became fast friends.

It was Fu the Enforcer's turn for guard duty. She hadn't found any class enemies, but late that night when she returned, hot and sticky, from routine patrol, she noticed that Betty was not in her bed. Her suspicions aroused, she went out to hunt for her. She found Betty and the young lab assistant sitting side by side on the riverbank. Fu the Enforcer rushed to report the juicy news to the army representative in charge.

"We were just chatting," Betty told me many years later. "She added soy sauce and vinegar, and started a rumor that I was having an affair with a younger man." The army representative interrogated Betty, who denied any wrongdoing. He didn't believe her. "Those who make political mistakes are doomed to mess up their personal lives," he said. Fu the Enforcer gloated.

"She called me a *po xie*," said Betty, using Chinese slang for a whore, literally a broken shoe, worn out from so many feet trying it on. Betty, who had already weathered two years of Red Guard beatings, was defiant. But the young man went to pieces. "He was really scared. He was a bachelor. He thought he would never be able to get married after that," she said. Under interrogation, he denounced Betty for "taking the initiative." She was furious.

She saw the young man only once or twice after that. On September 13, 1971, he followed her out the campus gates, his face partly hidden by a surgical mask that Beijingers don during dust storms. "Lin Biao has just died in a plane crash," he whispered. "He was trying to flee the country."

Betty recoiled in fear. Mao's heir apparent? His closest comrade-in-arms? She biked home and told her husband. At first he, too, was disbelieving. Then he was elated. The young man came from a well-connected military family; Betty's husband figured he felt guilty about betraying her and hoped the news would help reverse her case. Madame Mao and Lin Biao were allies. If Lin Biao fell, could she be far behind? Marshal Lin Biao, who once extolled Mao as a genius, had indeed died less than twenty-four hours earlier when his plane crashed in Outer Mongolia. Ordinary Chinese wouldn't learn about the stunning event for months. But despite Lin Biao's literal fall from grace, Madame Mao would remain in power for five more years.

Who became a victim and who became a tormentor during the Cultural Revolution seemed completely random. People who knew something was true might still end up persecuting the person who made the mistake of saying it out loud. Teacher Dai, who knew Betty from high school, told me, "It's such a pity what happened to Betty. In fact, Fu Min and I knew the same stuff about Jiang Qing, but nothing happened to us. I said to Fu Min recently, 'Luckily neither of us betrayed the other.' "

When Betty finally was reunited with her three-year-old son, he no longer recognized her, for which she blamed herself. Her love of gossip had devastated her entire family. In 1971, she gave birth to her second child and named her Na, or Silence. Betty hoped her daughter would learn to keep her mouth shut.

Like many Chinese dislocated by the Cultural Revolution, Betty and her husband counted their time together in days and weeks, not years. They had already been separated for eight years while he served in Tibet and she was in the cowshed. After he was demobilized, he was assigned work as an English translator at *China Reconstructs*, a propaganda monthly aimed at foreigners. Just as Betty returned from Carp Island, *China Reconstructs* ordered her husband to do hard labor on a farm in Hebei province. By 1975, he had returned, but by then Betty had to go to Big Joy Farm with her students.

We were sitting under the poplar saplings that my class had planted when she told me about their long separations. She sighed. Then I sighed. I was lonely, too, I said. She glanced sideways at me. "I know a very good American comrade," she said. "He works with my husband." She told me the American had refused to accept the perks reserved for foreigners and fought to get the same low pay as other Chinese. His name was Norman, she said – and I realized I had met him at a party eight months earlier.

I thought Norman Shulman was Chinese the first time I met him. At a Merry Marxmas party thrown by a fellow Canadian Maoist on New Year's Day, 1975, I noticed a pathetic figure huddled against the radiator. He was wearing a padded Mao suit with a faded cap pulled low over his yellowing, plastic-frame glasses. He had a lot of stubble on his chin, but back then many Chinese men didn't shave for days for lack of decent razor blades. The Mao cap camouflaged his Big Nose and hid a shiny pate encircled by curly brown hair. I spoke to him in Chinese, and he replied with a flawless accent. Only when someone else joined us, and he broke into fluent English, did I realize he was a foreigner. Norman, in hindsight, did not look remotely Chinese, but then I had not yet honed my journalistic powers of observation.

Norman was the only Vietnam War draft dodger to take refuge in China. In those days, Washington banned Americans from traveling to Communist countries. For its part, China normally refused visas to Americans. But because his father was already working in Beijing, Norman was granted a Chinese visa. After a circuitous journey from New York to London, Karachi, Colombo, Dhaka and Canton, he arrived in Beijing in February 1966, at the age of twenty-two. He might as well have gone to Vietnam. By the time I met him nine years later, he looked as if he had just gotten out of a Viet Cong prisoner-of-war camp. Years of Chinese canteen dining had pared his wrists and ankles to the size of mailing tubes. And speaking of prisons, he was now marooned in China. His U.S. passport had expired long ago, and he was under indictment back home for dodging the draft.

Both sets of his Jewish grandparents had fled the pogroms of czarist Russia, settling in Rochester, New York, and New York's Lower East Side. His parents, both card-carrying members of the Communist Party U.S.A., eventually quit the Party. They divorced when Norman was four. During the Sino–Soviet dispute, Jack Shulman sided with Beijing and in 1965 moved to China with his third wife, Ruth. There he worked as a propaganda-text polisher at Xinhua, the official Chinese news agency, and she taught English at Beijing's Institute of International Relations, a school that secretly trained spies. When Norman arrived, his father picked the Chinese name Shu Yulu for him after some model Party secretary then being extolled in the *People's Daily*. Yulu literally meant Fat Paycheck, an ironic moniker for someone who insisted on being paid as badly as his Chinese colleagues.

Strangely, many foreigners living in China, even those who resided there for decades, never learned to speak more than pidgin Chinese. One reason was the difficulty of the tonal language. Another reason was that China generally refused to provide tutors. Instead it made it very easy for foreigners to avoid speaking Chinese, supplying them with free interpreters and restricting their jobs to language teaching or text editing. Keeping foreigners ignorant and dependent was an ancient barbarian-control policy. The Qing dynasty caved in to Western demands that it rescind a ban on language lessons only after it lost the 1840 Opium War.

Norman, who had been a software programmer in New York, hoped to help develop China's non-existent computer industry. Although he abhorred teaching and text polishing, he had a talent for languages and already spoke Spanish and some Portuguese. Determined to learn Chinese systematically, he had enrolled at the Beijing Language Institute. Before the school shut down for the Cultural Revolution, he managed to squeeze in two and a half years of lessons. He could read and write, and became one of the best Chinese speakers in Beijing's foreign community.

By 1968, Jack and Ruth were fed up with the murders, the chaos and the ceaseless, ear-splitting broadcasts as the factional fighting of the various Red Guard groups in the schools surrounding the Friendship Hotel where they lived continued for a second year. They decided to go home. Then they discovered China wanted them to stay permanently and join the tiny band of sympathetic Maoist China Hands. Beijing's method of persuasion was to refuse to issue exit permits. Jack grew a beard in protest, but everyone just assumed he had run out of razor blades. He and Ruth and another American couple, who were also refused exist permits, began to picket Premier Zhou's office. The sight of foreign detainees pacing dejectedly outside a government office touched a nerve. After six months, Jack and Ruth were allowed to leave. (The other couple, David and Nancy Milton, were able to leave only in November 1969.)

With Jack gone, Norman had nowhere to live. An American couple, Joan Hinton and Sid Engst, invited him to sleep on their living-room couch. Cultural Revolution infighting had paralyzed Joan's and Sid's work units, so to pass the time they worked as volunteers pruning grapevines at the Sino-Albanian Friendship Commune and cutting ice from a frozen lake for summer storage. Norman's school had shut down, so he joined them. The sight of the three foreign devils astonished the peasants. A few tried plucking the hair on Norman's arms to see if it was real. Later, authorities assigned him a temporary job at the Beijing Number Two General Machinery Works. There, too, he was the first foreigner some of the workers had ever seen. A young female worker chatted with him in the canteen for several minutes, in Chinese, of course, when she suddenly broke off and looked puzzled. "Do you speak Chinese?" she asked.

If you believe draft dodgers are a lower form of life, then there *is* justice. In January 1970, Norman was transferred to *China Reconstructs,* where he was doomed to spend the next eight years in propaganda boot camp translating drivel like "advance in the wake of glory" or "promote proletarian and eradicate bourgeois ideology." *China Reconstructs* was part of the Foreign Languages Press, a gargantuan publishing house founded in the 1950s to churn out novels, travelogues and periodicals. But while the avowed aim of the press was to win friends and influence people, it wasn't a very friendly place. On Norman's first day there, the

Party secretary coldly told him, "We don't need anyone, and we haven't asked for anyone."

One reason people weren't very friendly was because a dozen people had been murdered there recently, and the killers were still all working at the Press. Initially, the cause of death in each case had been listed as "suicide by leaping from fourth-floor windows." An emissary sent by Premier Zhou Enlai ended up dead after he made the intriguing discovery that not a single corpse had a broken bone. By the time Norman arrived, an army investigation had concluded that the victims had all been wrapped in padded quilts and beaten to death.

Of the one thousand employees at the Press, about half were politically suspect people who had lived overseas or attended missionary schools and were fluent in foreign languages. The other half were politically correct hotheads whose total foreign-language expertise stemmed from a six-month crash course in the Fragrant Hills, near Beijing. The latter group was young, xenophobic, impressionable and completely indoctrinated. The members of the Fragrant Hills faction, as they were known, were all Communist Party members, all demobilized soldiers and all former Red Guards. It did not take much to ignite this volatile mix, and soon the press was the scene of torture, beatings and bloodshed.

Most people in the English section of *China Reconstructs* worked together in one large room resembling an old-fashioned insurance office. Scarred wooden desks lined the walls. Employees wore sleeve protectors over their jackets. When the lunch bell rang one day, several young staffers jumped out of their seats in order to be the first in line at the canteen. As they raced out the door, Norman couldn't help joking, "When thunder claps, the wind follows," a Lin Biao quotation exhorting Chinese to react instantly to a command from Chairman Mao. The lunch bunch, all members of the Fragrant Hills faction, was not amused. They did not appreciate quips about the sacred words of Mao's "closest comrade-in-arms." Nor did they like their enthusiasm for lunch compared to their fervor for Mao, least of all by a young American.

The Fragrant Hills faction decided to teach Norman a lesson. The English section chief of *China Reconstructs*, Liu Zongren, organized a criticism meeting. But what was there to criticize about a guy who hardly ever said anything and demanded to be paid as badly as a Chinese? The only incriminating thing they could find was Norman's disconcerting habit of removing the pants of his Mao suit in public. It wasn't that he was a pervert. At the meeting, Norman explained that he got too hot wearing so many layers while biking to work in the winter, but that he needed to dress warmly once he got to the barely heated office. That was why he always donned his final layer of padded clothing beside his desk. To do so, he had to take off his outer pants momentarily. "Whenever I do that," he assured everyone, "I always have three more layers on underneath."

But Section Chief Liu was undeterred. He had had the foresight to enlist the help of a plump, jolly woman who had lived in the States for many years. He turned to Liu Yifang and played his trump card. "Is it true," he asked, "that in American offices men don't change their pants at their desk?" Comrade Liu, who was at risk herself for her U.S. connections, solemnly assured everyone, "No normal American would do such a thing."

Section Chief Liu glared at Norman. "You are insulting Chinese women!" he thundered.

"I'm very sorry," said Norman, giving up. "I won't do it again. I apologize for offending everyone."

Four months later, Section Chief Liu, accused of "brazenly attacking Mao" for a remark he made about Madame Mao, was led away in handcuffs. But after she was toppled, Liu was considered prescient and returned to *China Reconstructs* a hero. One day, he bumped into Norman in the stairwell. His own ups and downs had taught him a lesson, and he apologized.

In 1972, the army investigation blamed the Fragrant Hills faction for most of the deaths. Six of the worst offenders were paraded at a huge denunciation meeting. They were never sentenced, but each spent about five years in prison. By the late 1970s, they were back, working beside their victims' next of kin. In the meantime, *China Reconstructs* continued to publish happy stories about dam-building feats.

By late fall, our stint at Big Joy was nearly over. We harvested our rice crop and ate it for supper that first night. The grains were pearly and amazingly sweet. I closed my eyes as I slowly chewed a mouthful. It was the first time in my life I had tasted fresh rice instead of stuff that had been warehoused for years. I thought of all the hours and days we had sweated in order to get this bowlful, and I took another mouthful. After we harvested the last of our peanuts, tomatoes and eggplants, it was time to return to campus.

Back in Beijing, I began seeing Norman regularly. Did we date? Go to discos? Take in a revolutionary opera? No, we joined a study group and read all three volumes of *Das Kapital*. When I telephoned his office, *China Reconstructs* went on red alert. Whoever answered would cover the receiver and mimic my girlish voice: "Is Fat Paycheck Shulman there?" They loved to watch Norman blush after nine years of bachelorhood.

Beijing University was less tolerant. By late 1975, it was trying to cope with an influx of several hundred foreign students. Even though many were earnest Maoists like me, they still hated the 6 a.m. reveille. One morning, someone hooked up a cassette player to the public address system. Instead of "The East Is Red," we got Mick Jagger belting out "Satisfaction." The Ministry of Propaganda couldn't have dreamed up anything better to illustrate Western decadence. The foreign students didn't just sleep around; they slept *in*.

I was slightly more restrained, having spent so much time reforming myself at Big Joy Farm. Still, I was twenty-three by then, and interested in guys, even skinny ones who resembled Viet Cong POWs. During physical labor on campus one afternoon, I accidentally dropped a brick on my foot and broke my toe. My roommate began fetching my meals from the Big Canteen, and they tasted much worse cold. Norman knew that the way to my heart was through my stomach. He introduced that New York staple, Chinese take-out, to mainland China, which meant taking an aluminum lunch box to the Long March Restaurant across the street and having them fill it up with the daily special. It was love at first bite.

Cadre Huang looked grim. I knew Norman had been caught the night before as he left the campus. "What do your parents think about Fat Paycheck Shulman?" he said, with an unpleasant giggle. Only Cadre Huang could giggle and look grim at the same time.

My parents, who were vehement about not marrying outside the tribe, would be upset, of course. *She went all the way to China and found a Big Nose! She wasn't even in Montreal and she still married a New York draft dodger!* But I wasn't about to admit anything to Cadre Huang.

"What do you mean?" I asked.

"We are supposed to take good care of you on behalf of your parents. We don't think they would want you to make friends with Fat Paycheck Shulman," he said. "Make friends" was a Chinese euphemism for getting engaged.

"You don't tell the other foreign students what to do. Why are you telling me?"

Cadre Huang looked at me as if it were obvious. "You're an Overseas Chinese. You're one of us."

But I had changed. I had once obeyed the Chinese when they ordered me to break off a friendship. I had no intention of doing so again. I stared belligerently at Cadre Huang. He looked confused. This was not the Bright Precious Wong he knew. He tried another tack.

"Fat Paycheck Shulman," he said, "was breaking the rules." This was a serious charge. China was a country of rules.

"What rules?" I said, as disingenuously as I could.

Cadre Huang was getting flustered. He did not want to be specific. "People who aren't students here aren't allowed to spend the night," he said finally.

I thought of all my Italian friends who were enjoying *la dolce vita*. I thought of my Japanese classmate who was besotted with an Icelandic student, whom she would later marry. *They* hadn't been called in for criticism.

"Post the rules for everyone to see! And enforce them for everyone!" I yelled. I was sick of the double standard. How dare Cadre Huang discriminate against me. How dare he interfere in my life. I had changed. I no longer felt that because I was "family" I should have to sleep on the floor, so to speak. I refused to endure the same kind of humiliation every Chinese endured. I told Cadre Huang to go to hell. We started shouting at each other. I burst into tears and stomped out.

Cadre Huang telephoned *China Reconstructs*. Betty's husband, who had become Norman's group leader after Section Chief Liu's arrest, took the call.

Huang dispensed with the chitchat. "What is Fat Paycheck Shulman's behavior like at *China Reconstructs*?" he demanded.

"He's a very serious person," said Xu Shimin, whom we all called Big Xu. "He doesn't like his job. He talks very little." It was a brilliant fourteen-word summary of Norman.

Huang wasn't satisfied. "Does he have any problems in the male-female area?" he asked.

"No," Big Xu replied. "Fat Paycheck Shulman is very serious and hard-working. He doesn't have this problem. What is your purpose in asking this?"

"He spent the night in the foreign students' dormitory," said Huang. He paused. "And he didn't register at the front gate." It was hard to tell which he thought was worse. Norman had long ago ceased filling out the detailed visitor forms at the gate, which were supposed to screen out all class enemies willing to write down their names, work units and exactly whom they were planning to murder.

"Was he with Bright Precious Wong?" asked Big Xu.

Cadre Huang was taken aback. "Yes. How did you know?"

"We introduced them. My wife and I want them to become friends. As foreigners in Beijing, they are quite lonely. We wanted to see if there was any possibility the relationship would develop." Like Huang, Big Xu was a master of euphemism. "Develop" was a catch-all phrase for dating, fooling around, getting married, having babies.

There was silence on the other end. Cadre Huang said, "Oh, so that's the way it is. I just wanted to know his political background and his behavioral record."

Big Xu hung up the phone. After work that day, he pulled Norman aside. "The university called today to check whether you are a decent guy. They also wanted to know why you stayed there for the night." Norman blushed.

"Don't worry," said Big Xu. "I told them you were a good comrade." Then he winked.

10

Peasant Under Glass

Top: In the early 1970s, the entire Chinese leadership, except Chairman Mao, would turn out at the Beijing Airport to greet a visiting dignitary. In the center in the light coat is Jiang Qing (Madame Mao). To her immediate right is Vice-Premier Deng Xiaoping, then Premier Zhou Enlai, and Gang of Four member Wang Hongwen. To the left of Madame Mao (who was a Gang member herself) is Foreign Minister Qiao Guanhua (a Gang sympathizer), an unidentified woman, Gang member Zhang Chunqiao, and Gang member Yao Wenyuan.

Photo: John Burns/ *Globe and Mail*

Bottom: Classmate and snitcher Bright Pearl Tang (far left) washing her laundry under a slogan exhorting us to attack Deng Xiaoping's policies: "Enthusiastically develop a massive criticism in academic fields!"

Photo: Jan Wong

The swelling chords of China's state funeral dirge boomed from the campus loudspeakers. It was January 8, 1976. Premier Zhou Enlai had died of cancer at 9:57 that morning. His health had been a state secret. We had been vaguely aware that he was sick, but there had been no television reporters doing stand-ups outside his hospital, no day-by-day bulletins.

I had never seen such universal grief. It seemed everyone was weeping, men and women, old people and children. Some were almost hysterical. Bus drivers, street sweepers and shop clerks all went about their chores with swollen red eyes. My professors especially mourned his passing. My classmates wept on each other's shoulders. I cried, too, overwhelmed by the reaction to his death.

Of the top Communist leaders, only Zhou had tried to mitigate the suffering of the Cultural Revolution, to stem some of the madness and to protect some of his old comrades from Mao's wrath. Although Zhou was a yes-man who never crossed Mao, many Chinese loved him because he was the best of the lot. What they didn't know was that he was so politically weak that he had failed to save his own adopted daughter, who in 1968 was tortured to death in prison at the age of forty-seven.

Every heir apparent had come to grief. President Liu Shaoqi died naked on the cement floor of his prison cell during the Cultural

Revolution. Marshal Lin Biao perished in a plane crash in 1971 while fleeing allegations that he had tried to assassinate the Great Helmsman. A few months later, when Mao caught a bad cold and thought he was near death, he impetuously crowned Zhou Enlai his successor. "Everything depends on you now," Mao told Zhou, according to Mao's personal physician, who was present. "You take care of everything after my death. Let's say this is my will."

Mao soon changed his mind, appointing instead Wang Hongwen, a member of Madame Mao's radical and powerful clique, subsequently known as the Gang of Four. The move was vintage Mao. By playing off Zhou against the Gang, Mao ensured no faction was strong enough to challenge his authority. With the premier's passing, many Chinese felt they had lost the last voice of reason in the government. Everyone was apprehensive about what would happen next.

My classmates began making white tissue chrysanthemums to wear as a sign of mourning. One PLA classmate, Liang Haiguang, was so upset that he composed a poem in the premier's memory. Liang, who came from an elite family, was privy to inner-circle gossip. Unlike the rest of us, he knew that Zhou had been under attack for months by Madame Mao and her cohorts. He was not surprised when the Central Committee instructed Chinese embassies around the world to lower flags to half-mast for just one hour. And he knew why Beijing University banned black armbands. Madame Mao was determined to suppress public mourning for her arch enemy.

When Party Secretary Pan heard about Liang's sudden burst of creativity, he dropped by the dormitory. "A poem in memory of Premier Zhou is inappropriate," he declared, and ordered Liang to hand over the poem. My classmate refused. Pan repeated the order. Liang rolled the poem up into a little ball, glared at Pan and popped it in his mouth. Pan grabbed Liang by the arm. Liang, the tallest soldier in our class, gave him a shove that sent him flying across the room. As Pan lunged at Liang, other students rushed forward to separate them.

The day of Zhou's funeral, Vice-Premier Deng Xiaoping read the eulogy. Madame Mao scandalized everyone by wearing a bright red sweater, the symbolic color of happiness, which could be glimpsed under her dark tunic. Mao did not attend. The university forbade my classmates to go into the city that overcast day, but a million weeping Beijingers braved icy winds to line the Avenue of Eternal Peace as his cortege made its way to the crematorium.

Mao kept both Deng and the Gang off balance by picking a nonentity named Hua Guofeng as acting premier. "With you in charge, I'm at ease," Mao scribbled shakily to Hua in a note that wasn't made public until later.

That winter, we threw ourselves into another political campaign. Whereas I naively thought we were attacking bourgeois thinking in the abstract, by now most Chinese understood it was a veiled attack on Deng. I had no idea that my classmates and I were bit players in the power struggle. Over and over again, the Gang of Four had used Beijing University to score political points against Zhou. Our stint of hard labor at Big Joy, for instance, was really a broadside at the premier's moderate educational policies.

As Qing Ming, the Festival for Tending Graves, drew near that spring, many people, angered at the earlier suppression of mourning activities, began placing homemade paper wreaths in Zhou's memory at the Monument to the People's Heroes in Tiananmen Square. It was the first time that wreaths for an individual had ever been laid there. Others tied so many white paper chrysanthemums to the shrubs that by early April, it looked like an unseasonable snowfall had blanketed the square. I didn't realize I was witnessing the first spontaneous anti-government protest in Communist Chinese history. By commemorating Zhou Enlai, the Chinese people were indirectly expressing their anger at Mao and the Gang of Four. Under a dictatorship, commemorating a dead Communist premier was the safest, perhaps *only,* way to stage a protest.

My classmates had been warned to stay away from Tiananmen Square. Few dared disobey. Liang Haiguang, my poetry-eating classmate, slipped down and took snapshots of the mountains of wreaths. But he lost his nerve and exposed the film – the only place to develop it was in a state store. No one had told *me* not to go to the square, so I began biking there every day. The Monument to the People's Heroes was plastered with handwritten poems, and the floral tributes were piled ten feet high so that they covered the top plinth. The wreaths bore signed banners such as: "The Revolutionary Masses at the Number Seven Ministry of Machine Building" or "Your Sons and Daughters of the Border Region." People were no longer afraid, it seemed, to stand up and be counted.

On Sunday, April 4, the Festival for Tending Graves, hundreds of thousands of people flocked to the square. As I pushed my way up the steps of the monument, I realized people were copying down the poems. I pulled out a notebook and began jotting them down, too, without quite understanding why.

> *In front of the Monument my tears fall unabated,*
> *The flowers and shrubs leave memories in my heart*
> *Your loyal bones are scattered over the rivers and mountains*
> *Your brave soul and red heart will light a thousand autumns*
> *Your sweat and blood brought springtime to the entire nation*
> *And happiness to the entire world*
> *Let us wave the flag and carry on your cause*
> *Let your last will be enacted in China.*

It was signed Wei Zhou, a pun for "Protect Zhou." Other poems attacked Empress Wu Zetian, a seventh-century Tang dynasty empress who reigned after her husband's death. Still others criticized the first Qin emperor, who executed scholars, burned books and built the Great Wall with corvée labor.

> *Devils howl as we pour out our grief*
> *We spill our blood in memory of the hero*
> *The people are no longer embraced in ignorance*
> *Gone for good is the first Qin emperor's feudal world.*

As I copied them down, I could not figure out why thousands of perfectly normal people had developed a sudden passion for melodramatic Chinese poetry. I did not understand that Empress Wu and the first Qin emperor were surrogates for Madame Mao and Mao himself and that the poets were using the hoary Chinese technique of using the past to attack the present. Similar outpourings occurred in other cities – Hangzhou, Zhengzhou, Nanking – but I knew nothing of this at the time.

A middle-aged man with hard eyes stopped me as I tried to leave. He must have seen me copying down the poems. "Who are you?" he demanded, gripping the seat of my bike so I couldn't get away.

"I'm a worker," I lied nervously.

"Where?" he persisted.

"The Number One Machine Tool Factory," I blurted, wondering if he would believe I was a member of the Iron Women's Team. But he didn't ask further, and let me go. Thoroughly rattled, I bicycled the hour back to the university. Only a plainclothes agent would be so aggressive. What was going on? Why were police in Tiananmen Square? Why had my classmates been forbidden to go to the square? What was wrong with putting up some wreaths in memory of Zhou Enlai? And what if the agent had jotted down the license number on my bicycle? Would I be expelled – again?

The next morning in class, word spread quickly that I had some of the contraband verse. As our professor droned on for four hours about Engels's analysis of Crete as a slave society, my classmates surreptitiously passed the poems around. Unlike me, they understood the literary allusions. But none of us realized that by then the original poems had already disappeared.

On Sunday night, a few hours after I left the square, the ruling Politburo had met in emergency session in the Great Hall of the People, a hulking Stalinist structure that bordered the west flank of the square. Madame Mao peered out at the sea of wreaths and ominously labeled them "the work of class enemies." Wang Hongwen, the Gang member who had briefly been anointed Mao's successor, advocated a showy burning of the wreaths. Acting Premier Hua Guofeng recommended quietly clearing them away and hosing down the poems. With the Politburo deadlocked, a messenger was dispatched to seek Mao's opinion. The Great Helmsman concurred with Hua. In the middle of the night, security forces scraped off the poems and trucked away the wreaths.

On Monday morning, the news that the wreaths had been removed spread like wildfire through the city. Tens of thousands of citizens began flocking to Tiananmen Square. Police cordons prevented anyone from pasting up new poems or delivering new wreaths. When plainclothes agents began snapping photos of the crowd, scuffles broke out. Inside the Great Hall of the People, the Politburo watched the protesters with growing alarm.

"People are trying to burn down the Great Hall of the People," Madame Mao screamed, according to later accounts. The Politburo debated whether to bring in troops or militia and whether to use live ammunition. Deng Xiaoping kept silent. Hua Guofeng sent Mao's nephew to Zhongnanhai to seek the Great Helmsman's guidance. Mao Yuanxin, a Gang of Four ally, told his uncle about the growing protests at Tiananmen and pinned the blame on Deng. In a panic, Mao issued three directives. He ordered that Deng be "isolated and investigated." He labeled Tiananmen a "counter-revolutionary rebellion." And although he explicitly forbade the use of guns, he authorized the use of "necessary force."

The nephew rushed back to the waiting Politburo and read out Mao's directives. The vote, of course, was unanimous. Deng Xiaoping knew his fate was sealed, but asked permission to go outside to persuade the crowds to go home. Zhang Chunqiao, another Gang member, retorted, "It's too late."

Norman called me at noon just after I got out of my four-hour lecture on Crete. We agreed to bike to Tiananmen after we finished our regular Monday-evening study session of *Das Kapital*. At ten-thirty that night, we got to the square, only to find it cordoned off and completely empty. All the floodlights were switched on. The milling crowds, the tiny white flowers, the huge floral wreaths had all disappeared. A recorded statement by Beijing mayor Wu De blared over the loudspeakers. Parroting Mao's line, Wu called the protests counter-revolutionary. We watched work crews hosing down the square, which glistened under the bright lights. I assumed they were cleaning up debris.

I was wrong. They were mopping up blood. Had Norman and I arrived an hour earlier, we might have had our heads bashed in, too. I later found out that around dusk, when the floodlights in the square suddenly snapped on, people began drifting home, nervous that something bad would happen. By 9 p.m., only a few thousand die-hards remained. At 9:25 p.m., security agents sealed off the square. Suddenly, the gold-studded red gates of the Forbidden City swung open, and thousands of militiamen, many of them workers from Capital Iron and Steel, poured into the square. Backed by police and five battalions of soldiers, they waded into the crowd, clubs swinging. Soldiers forced the crowd toward the north end and shoved them into waiting trucks.

Several weeks later, China's vice-minister of public security reported that hundreds were beaten and four thousand were arrested. He did not mention any deaths. But rumors persisted. A year later, a well-connected Chinese friend told Norman that about sixty people had died that night. The friend, who was the sister of Zhou Enlai's chief English interpreter, a man who later became ambassador to Britain, said that sixty protesters had been dragged into the Forbidden City and beheaded – because Mao had expressly banned guns. The corpses had been shipped by train to Shanghai, a Gang stronghold, where they were cremated. Shanghai had adequate cremation facilities, the friend explained, and was one place where silence could be ensured.

Beheadings? Shanghai cremations? It seemed incredible to me, but so many incredible things in China eventually turned out to be true. The friend had a neighbor whose son had disappeared from the square that night. A few months later, a stranger knocked on the door and told her that her son had been labeled a counter-revolutionary. The son had been beheaded in the Forbidden City, then cremated in Shanghai, the stranger said. He showed her an urn containing the ashes and demanded payment for the urn before he would release it.

On Tuesday, the Politburo met again, in Deng's absence. The meeting swiftly accomplished three items of business. Hua Guofeng was formally appointed premier and first vice-chairman of the Central Committee. The Tiananmen Square protests were labeled counter-revolutionary. And Deng was dismissed from all his posts. Mao, in another balancing move, ruled that Deng could retain his Communist Party membership.

The witchhunt began. The doughty old Marshal Ye Jianying gave Deng, who feared for his life, asylum in Canton, where the Gang's influence was weak. At Beijing University, Party Secretary Pan began interrogating my classmates. Everyone had to account for their movements on the Festival of Tending the Graves. Had anyone gone to the square that Sunday? Had anyone copied down poems? As a foreign student, I was exempt. Pan concentrated his investigation on Horsepower, Future and Liang Haiguang.

It is eerie to see how closely the 1976 Tiananmen incident foreshadowed the Tiananmen Massacre thirteen years later. Both protests began as disguised mourning for a senior Communist official. Both crackdowns coincided with purges at the top. Both times, the victims were labeled counter-revolutionary and the death toll was a state secret. The only difference was that, in 1976, Deng was the victim; in 1989, he gave the order to shoot to kill.

The school ordered everyone to write Big Character posters attacking Deng. My classmates were ambivalent. Criticizing him was an act of self-preservation for every worker-peasant-soldier student who had spent their university years growing rice. Yet I noticed the denunciations were less than passionate. Some even copied chunks from the *People's Daily* verbatim.

Bright Pearl Tang, who had snitched on Future for collecting foreign stamps, was an exception. She threw herself into the anti-Deng campaign, copying dozens of Big Character posters, which she mailed to her old work unit to post all over the city of Kunming, in southwest China. An ambitious Party member, Bright Pearl had no intention of going back to her boring old job as a high-school teacher.

As spring turned into summer, we all looked forward to a break. Then, for the second year in a row, we were told our summer vacation was canceled. The continuing Revolution in Education needed us. On July 7, 1976, Zhu De, China's greatest marshal, died at the age of ninety.

Nineteen days later, I was in the port city of Dalian when I awoke to feel the hotel shaking. The next day, I watched the ceiling lamps sway as the aftershocks continued. As always with disasters in those days, not a word was reported in the Chinese media, which mentioned only good news, to demonstrate the superiority of socialism. But it was obvious that an earthquake had occurred. What no one seemed to know was how powerful it had been and where it had struck. I was on a Beijing University tour for foreign students, and our Chinese teachers were desperately worried about their families. My roommate on the trip, Margaret Small, was the daughter of the Canadian ambassador in Beijing. Only after she phoned her father did we learn what happened.

It was the most powerful earthquake in modern Chinese history, registering 7.8 on the Richter scale. It had flattened the northeastern coal-mining city of Tangshan, two hundred miles away from where we were staying, killing nearly half a million people and leaving one million others homeless.

When the International Red Cross offered assistance, the Chinese government haughtily rejected aid, citing its policy of self-reliance. Overwhelmed rescue workers began dumping decomposing corpses down abandoned mine shafts. We made our way back to Beijing by a circuitous train route to avoid the stricken area.

We arrived to find Beijing, 125 miles from the epicenter, resembling a giant refugee camp. Many buildings had been destroyed, but there were miraculously few casualties. Millions were living on the streets in makeshift shelters. At the Foreign Languages Press, the staff slept in cars, buses and tents. No one was allowed inside the offices or dormitories, which were deemed unsafe in an aftershock. Camping out in the courtyard of the press, where fresh water was at a premium, Norman quit shaving and grew a beard. In fact, delighted to be liberated from dull Chinese razor blades, he never shaved again.

In Zhongnanhai, the earthquake rattled the tin roof of the pool house where Mao was sleeping. His panic-stricken doctors and nurses wheeled him in a gurney to Building 202, a gray brick residence they believed was more solid. Ordinary Chinese began to mutter that the Tangshan earthquake was a bad omen. First Zhou Enlai had died. Then Marshal Zhu De. Important deaths came in threes. Who would be next?

I was cycling to Norman's office on the afternoon of September 9, 1976, when I heard the now-familiar chords of the state funeral dirge. I jumped off my bike to listen to the broadcast emanating from an office building's loudspeakers.

"We announce with the deepest grief that Comrade Mao Zedong, our esteemed and beloved great leader, passed away ten

minutes afer midnight." The other cyclists who had stopped to listen looked shocked, but not sad. As I biked to the Press, people were
already donning black armbands. I arrived as Big Xu was calling a
meeting of the English section. "Chairman Mao passed away early
today," he announced. "Anyone who wants to say something should
feel free to speak." There were no gasps or tears, just a sense of relief.
"Everyone had been waiting," Norman recalled.

I raced back to the university, where I found my classmates
already making white paper chrysanthemums, black armbands and
paper wreaths. Pearl and Center were devastated. Some of my peasant classmates cried, too. The youngest in the class, a semi-literate
member of the Yi minority, was inconsolable. Without Mao, they
would never have had a chance to go to university. To my surprise,
most of my other classmates remained dry-eyed. I remembered the
tremendous outpouring of grief at Premier Zhou's death. Now my
roommate lay on her bed and just stared at the ceiling. Future told
me he was on a bus when he heard the news, and thought, *So, he's
only a man in the end. So much for shouting 'Long live Chairman Mao!'*

Mao Zedong, the eldest son of a prosperous grain merchant, had
led China for more than a quarter century. Born in 1893 in the
waning years of the last imperial dynasty, he was a coarse-spoken
man with a love of elegant poetry. Obsessed with physical culture
as a youth, he bathed in icy water even in winter and toughened the
soles of his feet by climbing rocky cliffs barefoot.

In 1921, he became a founding member of the Chinese
Communist Party. As the Communist forces gained strength and
holed up in the mountains of Jiangxi province, Chiang Kai-shek's
Guomindang troops tried to annihilate them. In 1934, Mao led the
Communist armies to break through a near-fatal Guomindang
encirclement. Hundreds of thousands of Red troops began the desperate six-thousand-mile-long tactical retreat that came to be
known as the Long March. By 1935, nine out of ten soldiers had
perished. But the legendary trek ended in triumph when the ragtag forces stumbled into Yanan, a parched village in Shaanxi
province about sixty miles from the Yellow River. There, the
Communists regrouped and went on to found the People's
Republic fourteen years later.

Mao's death was not a turning point for me. That would come later. But I found I had no tears, either. It was strange. His charisma had lured me halfway around the world. Instead of getting a law degree or an MBA or, for that matter, a job, I had happily spent four years of my life hauling pig manure, harvesting wheat and reading Marx. And yet, when I faced things honestly, I could no longer turn a blind eye. China was a country where it was a crime to ask for a used Canadian stamp.

For reasons of crowd control and because everything was organized in China, including who may go to public parks on national holidays, viewing Mao's body lying in state in the Great Hall of the People was by invitation only. Norman put on his best wool Mao suit and joined the *China Reconstructs* contingent. Again, because so many people wanted to attend the state funeral a few days later, each unit sent representatives. In our class, only Pearl and Center were allowed to go. The rest of us held our own memorial service in a grimy room in the history department. As a small tape recorder played the funeral dirge, we bowed low three times before a crepe-draped poster of Mao.

On September 18, the official ten-day mourning period was capped by a massive rally in Tiananmen Square. Again, my classmates and I were not invited, and we watched the proceedings on a television in the Big Canteen. With the glaring exception of Deng, the entire Chinese leadership attended, the last public display of unity before the big showdown. Hua Guofeng used the occasion of the funeral address to exhort the nation to continue attacking Deng. At precisely three o'clock, Hua announced three minutes of silence. Across the nation, factory workers downed their tools. Buses stopped. Cyclists dismounted. Silence fell like a shroud over the capital. Everyone was waiting. What would happen next? Mao had controlled the world's most populous nation for more than a quarter of a century. A China without him was hard to imagine.

Then Wang Hongwen, the Gang member, called out, "First bow! Second bow! Third bow!" A million people in the square simultaneously bowed three times before the giant portrait of Mao hanging from the rostrum. In the Big Canteen, we bowed, too, before the television. As the majestic strains of "The East Is Red" boomed over the loudspeakers at Tiananmen Square, Premier Hua declared the rally over.

Immediately, the competing factions began jockeying for control. Mao's radical nephew positioned troops on behalf of Madame Mao. Her allies armed the militia in Shanghai and Beijing. Marshal Ye Jianying planned a counter-attack. His co-conspirators included Premier Hua Guofeng and Mao's former bodyguard, General Wang Dongxing, who controlled the elite palace guard.

On October 6, less than a month after Mao's death, Premier Hua called an evening Politburo meeting at Huairen Hall in Zhongnanhai, ostensibly to discuss the publication of the fifth volume of Mao's *Selected Works*. He and Marshal Ye arrived ahead of time. General Wang and several army officers hid in a side room. Zhang Chunqiao was the first Gang member to arrive. As he walked in, Premier Hua announced his arrest. General Wang and his men emerged from the side room. Zhang, fifty-nine, did not resist.

Wang Hongwen arrived next. The forty-one-year-old former textile-mill worker put up a fight but was quickly subdued. Accounts differ over the arrest of the third Gang member. Yao Wenyuan was either arrested in Zhongnanhai or at his home. Madame Mao must have guessed something was up. She stayed away, and was arrested in her residence, the Spring Lotus Chamber in Zhongnanhai. Later sentenced to death in a spectacular televised trial, she was granted a stay of execution and spent nearly fifteen years in solitary confinement before committing suicide in 1991.

That the arrest of the most powerful woman the Communist world has ever known could remain a secret was a measure of how tightly things were controlled in those days. Taking advantage of the total secrecy, Marshal Ye and General Wang continued rounding up the Gang's key supporters, even luring some to Beijing where they were arrested as they stepped off the plane.

To the outside world, it was business as usual. Mao had requested cremation, but within hours he was pumped up with formaldehyde and displayed under a crystal lid, a peasant under glass. Two days after the Gang's secret purge, Premier Hua blandly announced that a memorial hall would be built in Tiananmen Square. All major construction in Beijing ground to a halt as "volunteer" crews worked day and night. Li Ruihuan, a senior Party official and former carpenter, was rewarded with a Politburo seat after successfully ramming the massive project through in time for the first anniversary of Mao's death. The hall, a neo-Stalinist structure topped by a mustard-yellow roof, was built to withstand an earthquake ten times the force of the Tangshan one. It was an edifice complex, bigger than Lenin's tomb in Moscow, bigger than Ho Chi Minh's tomb in Hanoi. The mausoleum loomed just south of the Monument to the People's Heroes, ruining the sweep and symmetry of the world's biggest square, like a garish brooch on a classic black dress.

General Wang Dongxing tipped off my geisha classmates about the purge six days after the fact. They whispered the stunning news to Future, who didn't believe them. Three other classmates, all children of senior officials, separately got word a day or so later. By late October, the Communist Party began transmitting the news down the ranks. As word spread, slogans hailing the "downfall of the Gang of Four anti-Party clique" appeared in the streets. The Chinese were accustomed to abrupt reversals of policy. But Mao's widow arrested? Her radical faction overthrown? People literally danced in their offices. Firecrackers exploded all night. Liquor store shelves were emptied as people rushed to drink toasts. Still in exile in Canton under Marshal Ye's protection, Deng Xiaoping downed twenty-seven celebratory shots of 120-proof *maotai*, according to a family friend. Everywhere, I saw people wandering around with broad smiles and big hangovers. It seemed that the entire capital was marching deliriously to Tiananmen Square. Artists who had suffered under Madame Mao's cultural fascism sketched devastating caricatures and pasted them up in the square. Ordinary people took turns spitting on them to see who could score the most direct hits.

On October 22, sixteen days after the arrests, the Chinese press officially dubbed her faction the Gang of Four and airbrushed them from all photographs. Their purge was the turning point for me. Although great efforts were made to portray a wide gulf between Mao and the Gang of Four, I just couldn't make another great leap of faith. Mao and Madame Mao were on the same team. Whatever she had done, it was with his blessing.

I looked around me with newly skeptical eyes. Was the public rejoicing genuine? Or was I being duped again? My faith in Maoism had been eroding slowly, but I had always wanted to believe, always kept trying to believe, that there was a better place in the world. Now it was my turn to lie on my bed and stare at the ceiling. What had I been doing with my life? I had turned people in. For what? I had struggled to dig ditches in the countryside. Again, for what? I had tried to reform my bourgeois mind by reading Mao's *Selected Works*. Who cared? Nobody believed in the revolution any more. They hadn't for a long time, and I had been too stupid to see it.

One stunning, immediate change was an end to xenophobia. In Mao's time, it took nine years for the first Chinese person to dare invite Norman home. At the university, many classmates had shunned me because they were afraid of foreigners. Suddenly, I was able to meet all kinds of people. I made friends with a ninety-year-old gourmet, hung out with avant-garde artists and attended my first underground disco dance. People began revealing their honest opinions. I had lived in China for four years, and I realized that my understanding had just begun.

The celebrations over the fall of the Gang of Four ended the mourning period for Mao. Norman and I decided it was a good time to get married. But our nuptial plans were derailed when we discovered Norman needed a *wei hun zheng*, a document only a Communist bureaucrat could have dreamed up. It was literally a "not-yet-married certificate," and was required before authorities would issue a marriage certificate. Alas, no Chinese work unit was willing to vouch for Norman because he had arrived in China at the possibly-already-married age of twenty-two. We gave up the idea of getting married. Then we discovered that only newlyweds were issued ration coupons to buy a double bed. We cleverly beat the system by pushing together two single beds. The Foreign Languages Press sympathized with our lack of a not-yet-married certificate and turned a blind eye, allotting us a studio apartment, anyway. But friends insisted we couldn't just live together; we had to have a traditional wedding to mollify the neighbors. We set the date for the following weekend without realizing we had picked Halloween.

I invited my whole class, taking care to go through the proper channels, namely Party Secretary Pan. Our wedding lasted two days and cost $15, a bargain considering we had more than a hundred guests. In the waning days of the Cultural Revolution, most bridal couples offered only "happiness candy" and tea, since traditional feasting was still considered bourgeois. I compromised. Besides tea and a bag of the delicious caramel candies that had sustained me through Big Joy, I bought peanuts, sunflower seeds, a jar of Chinese-made dill pickles, several loaves of brown bread, a hunk of liver pâté and a bottle of *maotai*. A cook at the Press fried a huge batch of pastel-colored shrimp chips.

Norman wore the same Mao suit he had worn to the Great Helmsman's funeral. I, of course, had nothing to wear. Chinese brides in the mid-1970s wore gray pantsuits. I went to the corner inconvenience store to hunt for something more … bridal. Next to the gaudy enamel spittoons and wooden washboards, I found the perfect item: a bright red floral-print peasant's jacket of thick cotton fleece that only a country bumpkin would deign to wear.

On our wedding morning, Norman and I prepared for the reception by lugging a dozen thermoses of hot water from the boiler across the courtyard to our third-floor walk-up. His colleagues in the art department of *China Reconstructs* stuck red Double-Happiness papercuts on our whitewashed walls. Someone had composed a poetic couplet in beautiful calligraphy, which they pasted down the sides of our closet door: "Today you fulfill an old wish to plant flowers of happiness. Love binds like minds, traveling a thousand *li* to raise revolutionary crops."

By midafternoon, our room was packed. The little children of Big Xu and Betty, our matchmakers, walked in dangling a pole of lit firecrackers, a good luck symbol. Our wedding presents included a Chinese cleaver, two flowered porcelain dishes, a wooden chopping board, an aluminum kettle and a wok, all decorated with more papercuts of the red Double-Happiness character. No one gave us Mao's *Selected Works*, luckily, because we already had eight and a half sets. I loved the papercuts so much I left them up the entire time we lived at the Foreign Languages Press, like the dreaded neighbor who never takes down the Christmas lights.

Chinese wedding guests traditionally try to humiliate the bride and groom by asking them to recount their courtship. Liu Yifang, the jolly woman who had helped attack Norman for changing his padded pants in the office, started off the proceedings by asking how we had met. As a Chinese bride, I was supposed to cast my eyes demurely downward and giggle a lot. But I didn't know that. When Norman remained silent, I thought I'd better speak up.

"I met him at a party – not a Communist Party," I began. "I thought he was Chinese." The room fell silent in amazement as I proceeded, in my red peasant top, to give a blow-by-blow description of our courtship, including how Norman had brought me take-out food when I broke my toe doing hard labor. They thought I was the funniest foreigner since Khrushchev. Liu Yifang laughed so hard she cracked one of our beds.

The next day, dozens more friends came for a second round of tea and sunflower seeds. But as I swept up the mess at the end of the second night, I realized with a tightness in my chest that not a single classmate had shown up, not even my roommate. Many weeks later, when I overcame my hurt to ask Future why no one had come, he looked surprised. "I didn't know about your wedding," he said. Party Secretary Pan, it turned out, had never passed on my invitation.

Our *China Reconstructs* room had wooden floors painted a reddish brown. The sunlight poured through our single window. At night, we heard drunken cyclists weaving their way home, singing snatches of Beijing opera. I hung tea cups on hooks from our small bookcase as an earthquake warning system. When they tinkled during an aftershock, we ducked into our closet, rumored to be the safest place if the building collapsed.

Our single room was once part of a four-room apartment. A surly Chinese family now occupied two rooms on one side of us. Three single Chinese women, with whom we shared a kitchen and a bathroom, lived in the room on the other side. We had hot water only twice a week, for exactly one hour each time. That made it logistically tough for the three of them and the two of us to each undress, bathe, dress, empty and refill the tub before the water shut off. I struck a deal with the women. They could take the whole hour providing the last one managed to refill the tub at the end. I learned to toss an old plastic sheet over the tub to keep the water hot for hours. Norman and I could then wash at our leisure. The downside was we had to share the bathwater, but at least we were newlyweds.

After the Gang's purge, our long bouts of physical labor stopped. But the political campaigns continued. Instead of attacking Deng, we now denounced the Gang of Four. No one was very enthusiastic. The more we criticized the Gang for their botched education policies, the more we were admitting we had learned nothing. But at least it meant that, after years of persecuting others, the hard-liners in our class were now the target. Party Secretary Pan soon took to his bed and stayed there for six months. Some students suspected he was feigning illness to avoid being criticized. In fact, he had the flu and, later, tuberculosis.

Bright Pearl spent her days glumly writing self-criticisms. After she graduated, she was punished with a year of hard labor and later went back to Kunming in disgrace. In 1978, she was assigned to teach high school, the very fate she had hoped to avoid. Eventually, she became a professor at the Yunnan Provincial Minorities Institute.

Bright Pearl never married. She had to be single to attend university. At graduation, when she should have married, she was mired in political problems. By the time she extricated herself, she was nearly forty. Years later, even Future felt sorry for her. Spinsterhood or bachelorhood was a horrible fate in China. A single person was a social misfit, doomed to a life sentence in a collective dormitory with smelly latrines and no kitchen. Even gays, who had no choice but to remain in the closet because homosexuality was, and still is, illegal, married the opposite sex, often without revealing their secret to their spouses. They did this partly for camouflage and partly because staying single was socially unacceptable. In all my years in China, Bright Pearl was the only person I knew who had never married.

With only a few months left before graduation, everyone hit the books. But it was clear we had learned very little history or classical Chinese. In acknowledgment of that dismal situation, the school dispensed with final exams. Cadre Huang insisted, however, that *I* take one.

"I have done everything the Chinese students have done. Why change at this point?" I said. The double standard infuriated me now.

"Don't worry. It won't be difficult," he said.

"That's not the point. Why bother with an exam? It's hypocritical. Everything we learned has been discredited."

"If you don't write the exam, you won't graduate," he said flatly.

"Fine," I said. I wasn't about to cooperate with a last-minute charade.

True to his threat, Huang saw to it that Beijing University gave me a certificate saying I had *yi ye*, or completed the courses, as opposed to *bi ye*, or graduated. (Many years later, I discovered that in fact the university had recorded me as a graduate.)

We were the first class to graduate after the purge. The propaganda machine accused my classmates of having used personal connections to get into university. The once-glorious label "worker-peasant-soldier student" became a badge of shame. Toward the end of term, we gathered for a speech by a school official. "We hope you will make a contribution wherever you are sent," he said. "What happened at Beijing University was not your fault. We were all caught in the forces of history."

Graduation day that July was the most depressing moment of our university experience. It was unmarked by a ceremony of any kind. It was as if we were a collective embarrassment, as if the university just wanted to get rid of us, to put its crazy Cultural Revolution phase behind. Already the school was focusing on the incoming batch of freshmen students, the first class in a decade to take proper entrance exams. My demoralized classmates gathered in the same dingy room where we had once mourned Mao. Party Secretary Pan began to read out the assignments. By then the Back to Society campaign had bitten the dust. Except for Bright Pearl, most classmates got decent jobs. Not one went back to being a peasant or a worker. When Pan finished reading, he passed around a stack of small red booklets, our graduation certificates. When the last one had been passed out, people drifted away. And that was it. We had graduated.

11

True Lies

Top: Marching to celebrate the purge of Madame Mao's Gang of Four.

Bottom: Demonstrating how to make Christmas punch to a television audience of 400 million, with a British friend, Peng Wenlan.

A month after my worker-peasant-soldier class graduated, the Chinese Communist Party formally declared an end to the Cultural Revolution. One announcement, and we were consigned to the dust heap of history. That, I suddenly realized, was how dictatorships worked. Overnight, every single person I knew made an abrupt ideological switch. Now, everyone told me, the Cultural Revolution had been a bad, bad thing. They said they had been waiting for years for the madness to end. And unlike before, they assured me, they meant it.

I felt betrayed, like the victim of a massive practical joke. Everyone had lied to me – my classmates and teachers, my friends and relatives. I knew it was not personal. They had had no choice. But it didn't alleviate my sense of being suckered. I vowed I would never again wholeheartedly suspend my disbelief. I believed them now only because it finally made sense. But from here on in, I promised myself, I would question everything. I wouldn't just listen to what people said, I would observe what they did and their body language while they did it.

For a long time, I had been living inside a real-life propaganda movie. I loved it because I thought it was reality. I felt so lucky to reside in utopia. I took seriously Boy Scout–like slogans such as Serve the People. I remember squeezing onto buses where young PLA soldiers would spring to their feet and offer their seats to an older comrade or anyone with a child. Only gradually did I realize that the sets were fake and people were just speaking their lines with less and less conviction. After Mao's death, when everyone stopped play acting, I rarely saw anybody help anyone else, not even to hold a door for someone with a baby.

That August, Deng Xiaoping emerged from his safe haven in Canton to join the new five-member Politburo Standing Committee. Only two men ranked above him. One was his protector, Marshal Ye Jianying, who had no ambition to run the country. The other was Chairman Hua Guofeng, whose claim to power rested on a scribbled note by a doddering Mao. Acutely aware of his vulnerability, Hua stepped up a personality-cult campaign, uttering Mao-like quotations, posing in stuffed armchairs for Mao-style photos and staging Hua-Was-Here exhibits. He even grew out his brush cut and slicked it back to resemble the Great Helmsman.

By now, I was enough of a China watcher to realize that Chairman Hua would not last. Ignoring Hua as irrelevant, Deng concentrated on dismantling the cult of Mao. Overnight, the official media began to portray the Great Helmsman as a man who made mistakes. And the decade-long Cultural Revolution, they said, was one of his biggest.

Deng boldly declared that old-fashioned Marxism no longer met China's needs. "Engels did not ride on an airplane. Stalin did not wear Dacron," he remarked as he threw open China's doors to foreign investment for the first time since the Communist victory. He disbanded Mao's agricultural communes, reinstated college entrance exams and linked workers' bonuses to performance. Although Deng had been Mao's chief hatchet man in the 1957 Anti-Rightist Movement, he rehabilitated most of its victims.

All these flip-flops made me feel schizophrenic. What did the Chinese people believe in? And what did *I* believe in, if anything? The political sands were shifting under my feet. After my graduation, I filled in as a script polisher at Radio Beijing, no experience necessary. Each day, I tried to transform turgid Commie-prop into recognizable English. It was hopeless. When the state-run English-language broadcasting station attempted to give me just half what it paid the white Canadian male I replaced, I fought for and won, equal pay. But I realized I no longer had any desire to shore up a propaganda machine for a bunch of racist, sexist Communists. Instead of Beijing Jan, I wanted to be a real reporter.

That fall, when a start-up magazine in Hong Kong recruited me to be their editor – again, speaking English was the only requirement – I jumped at the chance. Although it was my first trip to the capitalist world in three years, this time the transition was easy. I wasn't even perturbed when I discovered my next-door neighbors were running a brothel. Culture shock was minimal, I discovered, when you are no longer living in paradise. To be sure, I still felt a comradely, or perhaps a Canadian, urge to thank all the doormen. And I still mistakenly believed I should support China's fledgling attempts to industrialize. I bought only Chinese-made products – but gave up in disgust after the wheels on my new Golden Monkey suitcase failed to survive their first trip.

Norman faithfully wrote weekly two-line letters. "Dear Jan, How are you? I'm fine. Love, Norman." In 1977, President Jimmy Carter made good on his campaign pledge to pardon draft dodgers, and Norman was able to obtain a new U.S. passport. He arrived in Hong Kong for a three-month visit in February 1978. Even though he hadn't been outside China in twelve years, he also suffered little culture shock. We arrived at my apartment lobby in time for a police raid on the brothel.

China's new open-door policy meant foreigners could now work in fields other than language teaching or propaganda. After Norman returned to Beijing, he was finally transferred out of the propaganda gulag to the Chinese Academy of Science's Institute of Computing Technology. The Hong Kong magazine I went to work for with such high hopes turned out to be secretly backed by the Beijing government. Although it was less heavy-handed than the stuff churned out by Radio Beijing, I now knew I definitely wasn't cut out to be a propagandist. Besides, I missed Norman a lot. And with so much happening in China, I decided that Beijing was the place to be.

By 1978, all China was in ferment. Thousands who had been wrongfully imprisoned during the Cultural Revolution were set free. Millions of former Red Guards, disgruntled at wasting a decade in the countryside, streamed back to the cities. In Beijing, Big Character posters went up on a dusty expanse of brick wall next to a bus depot. Dubbed Democracy Wall, it quickly became a magnet for crowds to debate politics and read posters. People flocked there in part to ogle – it was the first time since the ill-fated Hundred Flowers Campaign of 1957 that China's leaders and policies were openly criticized. Some posters demanded to know why there were no jobs. Others blamed Mao for China's troubles. "Ask yourself: How could Lin Biao reach power without the support of Mao? Ask yourself: Did Mao not know that Jiang Qing (Madame Mao) was a traitor?" One called on China to adopt "Yugoslav-style democracy." Another advocated adopting the American system. One long-winded poster called on President Carter to support the drive for human rights in China. "The Chinese people do not want to repeat the tragic life of the Soviet people in the Gulag Archipelago," it said.

At first, Democracy Wall suited Deng Xiaoping's political agenda. After he called it "a fine thing," copycat walls sprang up in other cities. In Beijing, the posters became bolder and brasher. I joined crowds jostling for a glimpse of the large sheets of pink, green and yellow paper filled with black brush strokes, which I could now read without difficulty, having lived through so many political campaigns.

On December 5, 1978, a twenty-eight-year-old electrician named Wei Jingsheng put up a long poster titled "The Fifth Modernization – Democracy," the first to criticize Deng Xiaoping by name. "How excited people were, how inspired, when Vice-Premier Deng finally returned to his leading post. Deng Xiaoping raised the slogans of 'being pragmatic' and of 'seeking truth from facts' ... But regrettably, the hated old political system was not changed. The democracy and freedom they hoped for could not even be mentioned ... When people ask for democracy they are only asking for something they rightfully own ... So aren't the people justified in seizing power from the overlords?"

A former Red Guard, Wei earnestly signed his real name and wrote his phone number at the bottom. Several young men contacted him. Together they launched *Exploration*, China's first samizdat, or Soviet-style underground magazine. "Democracy is our only hope. To reject democracy is as good as shackling one's own body," Wei wrote in the inaugural issue, mimeographed in his girlfriend's apartment. Emboldened by Deng's silence, other samizdat publications emerged, with such names as *Enlightenment, Today* and *Beijing Spring*. Filled with political essays, poetry and philosophical musings, they constituted the first dissident press in nearly thirty years of Communist rule.

That winter, a ragtag army invaded Beijing. Impoverished peasants, following an ancient tradition of petitioning the emperor for justice, flooded into the capital. It was the first time I had seen true misery in China, and I knew I had to talk to them. As they poured out their tales of woe, I was shocked. The peasants were seeking redress for murders, thefts, rapes. Their oppressors were invariably Communist Party officials.

They camped outside government offices. By January, a shantytown had mushroomed in southwest Beijing. For the first time, beggar children waited behind my chair in restaurants, lunging for the leftovers the moment I got up. I began ordering extra food. Weren't beggars part of *Old* China? Wasn't everyone in New China supposed to be well fed and happy? I remembered, during the struggle session against the ration-coupon dealer, how I had timidly asked Teacher Dai if people had enough to eat, and how she had ignored me. As I watched the ragged petitioners, some on crutches, others with wounds and festering sores, I realized I had no clue what had been happening in the rest of the country. The Cultural Revolution wasn't a radical-chic game. It had wrought untold suffering.

The petitioners added their posters to Democracy Wall. As I read them, my horror grew. According to one poster, a Communist Party secretary had raped a construction worker named Fu Yuehua. After she dared report him, she was fired from her job. On January 8, 1979, the third anniversary of Zhou Enlai's death, I watched her lead a ragtag demonstration against "hunger and oppression" through

Tiananmen Square. A rape victim had organized the first protest march in Communist Chinese history. Police arrested Fu at her brother's home in Beijing ten days later. Her trial that fall was mysteriously recessed. According to one spectator, she startled the court by describing the body of her attacker in intimate detail. Fu Yuehua, the first casualty of China's fledgling democracy movement, was later imprisoned.

In February, Deng Xiaoping became the first Chinese Communist leader to visit the States. As he wowed Americans by donning a ten-gallon cowboy hat at a Texas rodeo, security police stepped up surveillance at Democracy Wall. China's paramount leader returned from his triumphant American tour to find that Democracy Wall had become a hotbed of dissent – against him. Fu Yuehua's daring demonstration had sparked others. One group of unemployed youths even tried to storm the gates of Zhongnanhai, the home of the Central Committee. An angry Deng ordered the arrests of Wei Jingsheng and other activists. On March 25, in an emergency edition of *Exploration*, Wei published his now-famous denunciation of Deng. Entitled "Democracy or a New Dictatorship," it branded Deng "a fascist dictator." A few days later, he and thirty other dissidents were rounded up. The crackdown had begun.

As I made the transition from true believer to objective observer, I decided to see if I could get a real news job. I had once regarded the Western media as running dogs of imperialism. Now I brashly wrote letters to the Beijing bureaus of the L.A. *Times*, the *New York Times*, the Associated Press and the *Washington Post*. It turned out they all wanted to hire me, but the *New York Times* replied first. It wasn't that I was brilliant. I didn't even have any journalism experience. But I was a scarce commodity – a foreigner who spoke Chinese, who looked Chinese and who had lived there longer than any of the American correspondents.

I got a flat tire on my way to the *New York Times* interview. After repairing it and pedaling hard to make up for lost time, I arrived, wild-eyed and sweaty. Ignoring my Red Guard demeanor, the correspondent, Fox Butterfield, suggested we stroll across the street to the Beijing Municipal Revolutionary Committee, where some petitioners were staging a sit-in. I began talking to a young woman. When I realized we were gathering a crowd, I slipped her Fox's business card and told her to contact us if she could. Fox was delighted that it was so easy for me to approach ordinary Chinese. As we went up the elevator to his office in the Beijing Hotel, he began giving me more assignments.

"Are you going to hire me?" I asked timidly.

"Of course," he said. "How much do you want?"

I was ecstatic. The *New York Times*! Who cared about getting paid? "Money," I said, like a Maoist idiot, "is secondary. I just want to learn how to be a reporter."

Fox took me at my word and paid me $800 a month, a salary the *Times* foreign editor, whom I later met in New York, apologized was "coolie wages." (It was about one-fourth what *Times* assistants were paid in New York, but in China, it was a small fortune as long as you lived like a native, as I did.) At the time, I honestly didn't care. And Fox kept his side of the bargain. He was an excellent teacher. He taught me to "answer all the questions" so readers wouldn't be left dangling. And he showed me the value of capturing the telling detail. In a taxi on the way back from an interview, I watched in awe as he scribbled a story long-hand on a sheet of paper. Deep down, I felt I could do the same.

In those days, it was hard for foreign journalists to learn the most basic information. Officials didn't grant interviews. Press conferences didn't exist. Except for the Party mouthpiece, the *People's Daily*, most Chinese newspapers were still classified as secret. When a Western reporter asked an innocuous question, the Old Hundred Surnames, as the Chinese called themselves, froze or fled. Fox once went up to a queue and, in fluent Chinese, asked what everyone was waiting for. They stared silently back at him. I went over and repeated his question. "We're waiting in line to buy televisions," a woman said.

I scrupulously warned people I interviewed that I worked for the *New York Times*. Few believed me. After six years of living in China, I had perfected the local baggy look, a passable accent and the slow, foot-scraping waddle. Once, when I identified myself to some students at Tiananmen Square, a smart aleck in the crowd jeered, "Sure, and I work for the *Times* of London." Even when they believed me, they still assumed I was Fox's government interpreter and that it was all right to talk to me.

I was especially modest when foreigners complimented me on my English. One morning in October 1979, the entire foreign press corps was staking out the courthouse at Wei Jingsheng's closed-door, one-day trial. Naturally, everyone was desperate for the oblig-atory man-in-the-street comment. Naturally, no sane man-in-the-street was there. Aline Mosby, a veteran UPI reporter whom I had met on several occasions, rushed up to me. I was about to say "Hi" when I realized she didn't remember me at all. Aline, who spoke no Chinese, was thrilled to discover I spoke decent English. She began firing questions. Wickedly, I answered as best as I could, comment-ing on the effect Wei's trial would have, admitting I'd heard his speeches at Democracy Wall and predicting the courts would find him guilty. I hated to disappoint her at the end when she finally asked me my name and work unit.

Working for the *Times* made me begin to view China through dispassionate eyes. Although I felt like a renegade and traitor when I helped Fox Butterfield dig out dirt on a country I had once want-ed to be perfect, I also felt that exposing the darker side might help right some wrongs. Twice a day I stopped at Democracy Wall to scan new posters. After the government passed a decree banning them and municipal workers hosed down the wall, I slipped into private homes to watch dissidents mimeographing their latest samizdat. I would bump into some of them eight years later, when I returned as a *Globe and Mail* reporter, and they were still fighting for democracy.

As I became a skeptic, I found myself changing in other ways. I was no longer as tolerant of China's problems as before. I was crab-by, irritable, short-tempered. Perhaps the average Chinese dealt with the population explosion by tuning out, but I got heartily sick of people walking smack into me as if I didn't exist. I learned to point my elbows outward, became expert at crowding onto buses and snapped back at people whenever they snapped at me. At the Beijing Hotel, where I didn't realize the staff was learning about the mysteries of Western etiquette, I got into a tug-of-war with a young waiter who grabbed my chair just as I was about to sit down. I snatched it back, glaring at him.

"This is *my* chair," I barked. "You can go find another one."

"I was trying to pull it out for you," he said.

I think I finally crossed some invisible line in early 1980, when my matchmaker friend Betty asked me to appear on national television to tell the Chinese people about Christmas. Chinese Central Television wanted to broadcast an hour-long English special during the Lunar New Year holidays, when it had its biggest audience of the year. "Four hundred million people will be watching," she said. "Can you help?"

By then, Madame Mao was in solitary confinement, and Betty was no longer in trouble for discussing the Dragon Lady's past love life. In fact, Betty had become the most famous English teacher in China. To meet the huge demand for education following the end of the Cultural Revolution, authorities had launched "Television University," a series of televised credit courses for the masses. Three times a week, Betty explained the mysteries of English grammar on national television to an audience of millions. A companion textbook she co-authored sold 1.6 million copies and could easily have sold more if it wasn't for a paper shortage. Alas, Betty got zero royalties and earned only about a dollar per broadcast. But fans sent her sacks of potatoes and oranges, porcelain tea sets and bags of rice. In crowded restaurants, admirers jumped up to give her their tables. Wrote one Shanghai devotee: "I have switched from the day shift to the night shift so I can catch your program." A soldier on the Soviet border who received an autographed copy of her textbook promised in a fan letter, "Tomorrow at the riflery competition, I'll fire in the air as a salute to you!"

My plan had been to tell the West about how great China was, yet I found myself agreeing to tell China how wonderful the *West* was, and not just explain but do unabashed propaganda, complete with Christmas carols. Betty recruited Big Xu and their two young children. Norman claimed he was too busy at the Academy of Science to have anything to do with the project. I talked an American, Peter Gilmartin, into donning a Santa outfit lent by the U.S. Embassy. A China-born British friend, Michael Crook, mystified the audience with an erudite lecture on the historical origins of Christmas. On a set decorated with a fake tree, also courtesy of the U.S. Embassy, we all sang "Jingle Bells." I played "Hark! the Herald Angels Sing" on my flute. Another friend played the guitar. And we made up some really bad jokes. They had nothing to do with Christmas, but were supposed to help viewers practice English.

Sample: What is black and white and red all over?

Answer: A blushing panda.

Stuffing and roasting a turkey seemed ambitious, so I decided, for reasons I now can't fathom, to demonstrate holiday punch. I completely fabricated the recipe. In an enamel wash basin, I dumped the contents of a bottle of sickly-sweet orange syrup and two varieties of plonk, China Red Wine and China White Wine (their real names). With the cameras rolling, I briskly diced a couple of apples and pears with a Chinese cleaver, talking up a storm *à la* Julia Child. Punch with diced fruit? Perhaps I should have demonstrated the Heimlich maneuver, too. Fatalities weren't reported in those happy-face media days, so I'm not sure how many viewers subsequently choked to death. But I certainly began to respect the power of propaganda. The day after the show aired, as I wandered around the Temple of Heaven, I kept hearing people humming "Jingle Bells."

In May 1980, the Academy of Science assigned Norman a brand-new two-bedroom apartment with real kitchen cupboards. I thought it was the most beautiful home in the world. After a fourteen-year wait, he was at last working in computers. I was having a great time working for the *Times*. And although we still had no hot water, we had a real bathtub. What more could we want? But I was already changing. I knew I could not spend the rest of my life in China.

Many of our foreign friends had done just that — committed themselves to working for the Chinese Revolution. They were the modern, Maoist inheritors of a Western missionary tradition that dated back to the eighteenth century. They came to help save China, and they did not flinch at personal sacrifice. These veteran

China Hands had arrived in the 1940s and 1950s, abandoning careers in the West as doctors, lawyers, labor organizers, journalists, sociologists and economists. Many had witnessed the founding of the People's Republic of China on October 1, 1949. Almost all had met Mao.

By the Cultural Revolution, there were only two dozen of these "lifers" left from English-speaking countries. Half ended up in jail or under house arrest on spy charges, spending an average of four or five years in solitary confinement. At least one of them had betrayed others. None had trials. And all were exonerated after their release. (One American, Sidney Rittenberg, spent ten years in solitary during the Cultural Revolution, and that was his second prison term. His first stint in solitary, in the 1950s, lasted six years.)

Two of our good friends among the old China Hands were Joan Hinton and Sid Engst, the American couple who had taken Norman in. They wore faded Mao suits and spoke fluent Chinese with a Shaanxi accent, picked up in the central province where they had first settled as farm technicians. Norman and I spent most weekends with them, biking two and a half hours to the Red Star Commune, their home during the last half of the Cultural Revolution.

By the time I met Joan and Sid in 1975, they had been in China for more than twenty-five years. I admired them because they were so dedicated and selfless. Yet in some ways, they were frozen in time. Joan once used the word *Chinaman* with me. I froze. How could someone who had devoted her life to China be racist? She saw my face, and realized something was wrong. Later, she explained that when she was growing up in Boston in the 1920s, *Chinaman* was the common term for a Chinese. She never used it again.

Joan was an atomic physicist who had helped build the Bomb. An independent-minded beauty with bright blue eyes and blond hair that had faded to silver, she'd had a proper New England upbringing that included violin lessons, her own pony and Bennington, a women's college in Vermont. Somehow, in the ensuing years, she had learned to burp after her meals just like a Chinese peasant.

Sid, a thin, balding man with bushy eyebrows and a ski-slope nose, was a farmer from Gooseville Corners in upstate New York.

After majoring in agriculture at Cornell, he went to China in 1946 with the United Nations Relief and Rehabilitation Administration. While investigating a famine in Hunan province, the shock of seeing destitute women selling their dull-eyed children for a sack of rice as fat officials drove by in fancy cars converted Sid overnight to communism. At twenty-seven, he made his way to Yanan, the communists' wartime capital, where he was assigned the task of keeping a precious herd of imported Holstein cows out of range of Chiang Kai-shek's bombers. He met Mao there and was impressed by his charisma. "Mao shook hands and looked at me," recalled Sid, who didn't yet know Chinese. "You got the idea he was looking right into you."

Joan and Sid first met through Joan's brother, Bill, who had roomed with Sid at Cornell. When Sid left for China, Joan was working on the atom bomb in Los Alamos, New Mexico. She wrote regularly, not ordinary love letters but lyrical essays about the black hole, the beauty of atomic physics, the life cycle of stars. "He wiped his ass with my letters because he didn't have anything better while they were evacuating Yanan," Joan remembered with a laugh. As one of the few female physicists working with the renowned Enrico Fermi, she had the world at her feet. But she quit when the bombs she helped create were dropped on Hiroshima and Nagasaki. "We had this illusion that if this was in the hands of the scientists, we might be able to control it," Joan later told a British documentary film producer. "One hundred and fifty thousand lives, each a living human being – all gone – and I had held that bomb in my hand. I knew what I was against. I wasn't at all sure what I was for."

Joan decided to go to China to find out. Normally, a scientist of her background needed clearance to leave the U.S., but on her passport application, Joan said she was going overseas to get married. That made sense to the bureaucrat who stamped her application. "They always think that women run after men," said Joan. "I wouldn't have left nuclear physics except for the Chinese revolution, but Sid made it that much easier to leave." At age twenty-seven, she took a slow boat to China and made her way past the Guomindang blockades, arriving in Yanan in March 1949. She married Sid a few days later.

Their Chinese comrades gave them new names: Joan became Cold Spring and Sid became Morning Sun.

It took three years for the U.S. government to realize that one of its top atomic physicists had slipped over to Red China. At a peace conference in Beijing in 1952, Joan caused an international sensation when she publicly apologized for her country's bombing of Japan. Headline writers in the U.S. labeled her "the spy that got away." Magazines printed wild rumors: Joan had flown to the peace conference on Mao's private plane; she had given the blueprint for the atom bomb to Red China; she was setting up top-secret installations in Inner Mongolia. The truth was more prosaic. Joan and Sid were working on a dairy farm in Shaanxi province. To get to the peace conference, she hiked seven days to Yanan, hitched a ride on a truck to Xian and from there caught a train to Beijing. Joan was never allowed to work in physics in China. Beijing considered all foreigners, even friendly Maoists, potential spies. The closest she ever got to a Chinese laboratory was helping unpack some imported equipment at a university in Xian.

Joan and Sid had renounced the capitalist world. They saw no reason why their three children, Fred, Billy and Karen, needed English, and spoke only Chinese to them. In 1965, at the height of the Vietnam War, Joan and Sid volunteered to work in North Vietnam. "After we sent the letter to the Hanoi government, we called a meeting with our three children," said Sid. "We told them, 'You will probably have to live without your parents. You will probably be adopted by the Chinese government.'" Three decades later, I asked Karen, who was nine at the time, how she had felt. "I wanted to volunteer as well," she said with a chuckle. Hanoi politely thanked Joan and Sid for their offer, but explained they weren't accepting foreign volunteers.

In April 1966, on the eve of the Cultural Revolution, authorities transferred Joan and Sid to desk jobs in Beijing. In the capital, which was much tenser than the provinces, their young children suddenly found themselves ostracized. Karen's teacher warned the class that the little American girl might be a spy. When the ten-year-old realized she was the evil imperialist she had been taught to hate, she had a mental breakdown. She recovered only after Joan and Sid fought to have her treated like an ordinary Chinese kid, which included going, with her brother Billy, for several years of labor on a tea plantation in Anhui province.

Despite the intense xenophobia of those years, Joan and Sid were two of the happiest people I knew. But I could no longer believe in monotheistic Maoism as they did. So many people had suffered, and so many had died, for such trivial reasons. Both Norman and I still cared about what would happen next and we both wanted to spend more time in China – but not as Maoist missionaries. We decided to go back to school. Norman applied to graduate school at New York University and planned to work again in China's computer industry after earning a Ph.D. I applied to Columbia's Graduate School of Journalism and dreamed of returning as a foreign correspondent. We left behind virtually all our belongings, including our eight and a half sets of Mao's *Selected Works* and a brand-new Snowflake refrigerator, which had cost a year of Norman's pay.

We left China in August 1980. A year earlier, Billy had gone to the States and had gotten off the plane in the wrong city, unable to tell the difference between airport signs that said San Francisco and Los Angeles. Karen was now about to leave to study molecular biology at Yale, her first trip out of China, and we decided we'd better take her with us. Karen was the mirror image of me when I first crossed the border alone into China in 1972. Although she had blue eyes, blond hair and an American passport, for all practical purposes she was Chinese. At twenty-four, she had just spent four years picking tea leaves and knew only a few words of English.

At Chicago's O'Hare Airport, a U.S. customs official was immediately suspicious. *Whaddaya mean, she speaks only Chinese?* He tore apart her luggage. Just as I had filled my suitcase with toilet paper when I first went to China, so Karen had crammed her suitcase with wrinkly gray stuff because I had warned her American toilet paper cost almost 50 cents a roll. Karen was upset as she saw her belongings piling up on the inspection table. It had taken her a long time to squash all that toilet paper into her suitcase. With a triumphant snort, the customs official held up a small box full of plastic vials of dark brown liquid.

"What's this?" he said.

"*Ganmao shui*," Karen said.

"Chinese herbal cold medicine," Norman translated.

That did it. The customs official had had enough. Here was an American who looked like a *Seventeen* magazine cover girl, pretending she couldn't speak English. And a skinny guy with a beard was translating her mumbo jumbo. They were putting him on, he figured. He announced curtly he was taking a vial to the lab for analysis. A few minutes later he returned. Whatever the Chinese put in their cold medicine, it wasn't heroin, thank God. The customs official held out the vial. The tip had been snipped off.

"You keep it," said Norman. "It's really good stuff if you get colds."

"I don't get colds," he said curtly, tossing it in the wastebasket.

Karen got angry. She couldn't understand why he had destroyed the vial in the first place and was now throwing it away.

Norman shushed her up and turned to the customs official. "She's an American who was born in China. This is her first trip back to the United States. You realize that you're not giving her a very good impression."

In China, such a comment would have merely goaded the border inspectors on. National pride would have been at stake. The historic struggle between the proletariat (them) and the bourgeoisie (hapless travelers) would have to have been settled on the spot. The Chinese inspector would have had to find *something* and declare it contraband in order not to lose face. But the American customs official was silent. He stared at Karen for a long moment. He didn't crack a smile, but he also stopped checking her luggage. Norman and I relaxed. We were back in the West.

Part III

PARADISE LOST

12

Dancing With Dissidents

Top: Interviewing a dissident, Gao Xin, in the Altar to the Sun park in Beijing. Imprisoned following the Tiananmen Massacre, he was never sentenced and eventually was released. He left for the United States where he attended Harvard University.

Photo: Mark Avery

Bottom: Millionaire Zhao Zhangguang, holding a bottle of Formula 101, which he claims will cure baldness.

Photo: Jan Wong/*Globe and Mail*

The FBI was on the telephone. "Can I come over and talk to you?" a female asked politely. It was February 5, 1981. I covered the mouthpiece and whispered to Norman. He shrugged. "Sure," I told her. "Why don't you come tomorrow morning?" Our many years in China – six for me and fourteen for Norman - naturally aroused suspicions. We assumed that we had been under surveillance since our return. But I no longer viewed police as pigs. In fact, they seemed downright nice after Chinese State Security agents.

FBI Special Agent Barbara Ann Dennis arrived the next morning at our studio apartment on Riverside Drive in Manhattan. She was in her late twenties, attractive and black. She showed us her badge.

"How many black female special agents are there?" I asked.

"Eight on the whole force."

"Do you carry a gun?"

She laughed. "Yes."

"Where?"

She laughed again, and didn't say. She was wearing a navy blue pantsuit. Maybe her gun was strapped to her ankle, just like in the movies. Or perhaps it was inside her roomy handbag where, we assumed, a tape recorder was whirring.

Her questions about China were as naive as mine were about the FBI. She wanted to know our housing conditions. She asked about *China Reconstructs* and the Institute of Computing Technology. Then she asked us to write down our names, birthdates, birthplaces, the schools we had attended and where we had worked, none of which seemed like state secrets. She gave us her phone number and asked us to call if we remembered anything else.

Perhaps it was hard for the FBI to realize that people could successfully recover from the sixties. Jerry Rubin, the former yippie and wild-haired member of the Chicago Seven, became a yuppie Wall Street banker. P.J. O'Rourke, the acid-tongued humorist of the right, was once a member of a "collective" putting out an "underground" newspaper in Baltimore; he ducked the draft with a doctor's note listing three and a half pages of drugs he had abused. Even Hanoi Jane was peddling exercise videos promising thinner thighs, and would eventually marry media mogul Ted Turner. If I was ever a security risk, I certainly wasn't one any longer. At any rate, we never heard from Barbara Ann Dennis again.

The previous time I had come back from Beijing, I had run around in Mao suits. This time, I avoided anything to do with mainland China, especially the U.S.–China People's Friendship Association. I couldn't stand being among Maoists who reminded me of how dumb I once was. At Columbia, I honed my skills at investigative reporting ("Question authority") and learned incisive interviewing techniques ("There is no such thing as a dumb question"). In between classes, I went to Broadway plays and the Museum of Natural History and Beethoven concerts on a barge beneath the Brooklyn Bridge. I bought bagels at Zabar's and shopped for coffee mugs at the Pottery Barn – such a pleasure after so many years of culture schlock.

After graduating from Columbia, I got married to Norman again, this time with paper, so we would no longer have to explain "not-yet-married certificates" to immigration officials at the U.S.–Canada border. For the next seven years, decked out in bowties and dressed-for-success suits, I worked as a business reporter at the Montreal *Gazette*, the *Boston Globe*, the *Wall Street Journal* and the *Globe and Mail* in Toronto. As I covered container shipping in Montreal and banking in Boston, I followed events in China with mixed feelings. The economy was growing at double-digit rates. Politburo members began riding in Mercedes Benzes. And beauty pageants were making a comeback. In Toronto, I wrote about tycoons and miscreants, and lobbied for the next opening in the *Globe*'s Beijing bureau. A little over a year later, in 1988, I was on my way. Twelve white male *Globe* reporters had gone before me. I was the first woman, the first of Chinese descent and the first to speak the language. I was also the first with a complete Cultural Revolution wardrobe.

I panicked as my plane hit the runway in Beijing. I had airily told my predecessor, James Rusk, not to bother meeting me at the airport. I was, after all, an old China Hand. But as the Canadian Airlines plane landed, I realized I had no idea how to say Sheraton in Chinese. Luckily, Rusk had ignored me and was waiting at the airport.

In the eight years I had been away, Beijing had changed dramatically. Its population had jumped 50 percent to eleven million, including one million "visitors" on any given day, many of them peasants living in shanty huts and searching for work. The smelly horse carts hauling sloshing tanks of human excrement had disappeared. A new six-lane limited-access highway ringed the capital. Bikes still clogged the roads, but now some had speeds and gears and came in reds, purples, blues and yellows. I bought a green Flying Pigeon, which was stolen within a week. This wasn't the China I remembered.

I was not the same, either. Eight years as a business reporter had turned me into a professional skeptic. The corporations I had covered were scarily close in organization and outlook to the Chinese Communist Party, with their hierarchies of power, propagandistic press releases and penchant for extreme secrecy. Just like China, they were dominated by an omnipotent chairman, complete with personality cult and sycophantic aides.

The Great Wall Sheraton, where Rusk had reserved me a room, was Beijing's newest luxury hotel. My cramped single cost $140 a night, up from the $2 a night the Overseas Chinese Hotel had charged me sixteen years earlier for my windowless cell. The Sheraton had high-speed elevators, liveried doormen and gift shops that didn't sell Mao's *Little Red Book*. At breakfast, I had orange juice, croissants with Australian butter and Swiss jam, bacon with scrambled eggs, and real coffee.

Norman was still in Toronto and wouldn't join me until the end of the year, so I explored the city alone. Having once sweated to grow eggplants and peanuts, I was happy to see food was plentiful. Besides an abundance of watermelons, once so scarce you required a doctor's note to buy one, street stalls sold strawberries, pineapples, sweet melons, cherries, purple grapes, peaches, plums, apricots, tangerines, broccoli, oyster mushrooms, golden thread mushrooms, white button mushrooms, fresh shiitake mushrooms, bitter melon gourds, green onions, carrots, yams, tomatoes, potatoes, lettuces, peppers, beans, snow peas, celery and slender green asparagus. There were crabs, shrimp, carp, eels, chickens, ducks, pheasants, geese, partridges, eggs, bean curd and all kinds of pork, lamb and beef for sale. The only thing that had disappeared were the lineups.

The government had bulldozed entire neighborhoods of picturesque courtyard homes to build hundreds of featureless eighteen-story apartment buildings in hospital green, dead tan or gray. Some foreigners thought that was cultural genocide, but many Beijingers preferred the highrises, which had central heating, plumbing and piped-in cooking gas, amenities lacking in the traditional homes. The highrises also had automatic elevators, which seemed a metaphor for modernization, Chinese-style. You could have technology, but forget about freedom. Ordinary people weren't trusted to operate the elevators. Instead, special staff, sitting in chairs, stabbed the buttons, using rubber-tipped chopsticks so they wouldn't have to over-exert themselves. The operators also moved in desks, telephones, tea thermoses, knitting, stacks of newspapers and, in summer, electric fans or, in winter, space heaters, not to mention their lunch. When they went to the toilet or on a break, the operators would lock the elevator and hang up a sign: Back Soon.

Although most buildings had several elevators, I rarely saw more than one in use at a time. The Chinese believed that elevators needed regular rest periods and that complete rest was the best. Typically, the operator locked the elevator for an hour at a time, about four times a day, and too bad if your aunt forgot the schedule and came visiting at the wrong time, or you were out shopping and didn't make it back in time. Most elevators shut down for the night at ten-thirty. At the theater, it was not uncommon to see people bolt before the final curtain to catch the last elevator home. A man who suffered a late-night heart attack had to wait until six in the morning, when the elevators reopened, to go to the hospital because his wife couldn't carry him down seventeen flights of stairs.

In Mao's day, bikes so outnumbered cars that at night motorists were required to drive with their headlights off to avoid blinding cyclists. Now, the number of cars was growing so fast that most drivers were rank beginners. Imagine having to live and work and go for a relaxing Sunday outing in one gigantic, never-ending Chinese driving school. (As for the six million manic cyclists in Beijing, their motto seemed to be: Better dead than red.) The *Globe*'s old Toyota was a manual shift. Unfortunately, I only knew how to drive an automatic. At first, I stalled every time I stopped, so until I got the hang of it, my technique was to slow down for red lights, without actually stopping. The other drivers used their horns, not their brakes. And it seemed that no one had told them it wasn't safe to change four lanes at a time. Nor had anyone warned families not to let their one and only child learn to walk on the expressway.

Amidst this chaos, siren-wailing military-style motorcades became a daily plague. Swollen with self-importance, senior officials hogged the already crowded roads. Their fleets of Mercedes-Benzes barreled through busy intersections without regard to life or limb, as traffic police frantically shooed the rest of us aside like so many gnats. The highway to the Great Wall even had a special VIP lane right down the center. One day, a southbound convoy collided head-on with a northbound convoy. That's when the masses saw the value of giving senior officials their very own lane.

All the Mao portraits were gone, except for the giant one in Tiananmen Square; virtually all had been replaced with neon signs advertising French cognac and Japanese televisions. The first real bars had opened. Stores sold Chinese-made tampons and decent toilet paper, but I was pleased to see the gray wrinkly stuff was still available. There were even padded bras, false eyelashes and the kind of underwear that had undone the Pyongyang panty thief.

The standard of living may have risen dramatically, but not everything was an improvement. The brilliant blue skies I so loved had disappeared in a yellow smog, the result of an unbridled industrial revolution and no unleaded gasoline. Once, I had been able to see as far as the Fragrant Hills, twenty miles away. Now I couldn't see clearly beyond the next block. Even on days when I stayed indoors, my nostrils were black with grime. Plastic bags used to be so scarce they cost half a day's pay. Now one way to measure the ferocity of a winter dust storm was to count the number of dirty bags stuck in the tree branches.

A lot more people smoked, including many young women. By the late 1980s, China had become the biggest consumer of cigarettes in the world, averaging seventy-five packs a year for every man, woman and child. That added up to 1.7 trillion cigarettes annually, or more than Eastern Europe, the former Soviet Union, Latin America and North America *combined*. Nobody seemed to be aware of the dangers of lung cancer. The government certainly wasn't saying. Its tobacco monopoly, after all, produced more than one-quarter of all taxes and state profits.

The relaxed atmosphere, however, delighted me. Compared to the old Maoist days, when people were afraid of their own shadows, China now seemed free and open. Instead of bumper-harvest reports, newspapers printed frank stories about rude salesclerks, spoiled children and the rising crime rate. Ordinary citizens seemed remarkably blasé about being interviewed. They rarely requested a pseudonym and didn't mind having their picture taken.

People laughed when I told them I had been a worker-peasant-soldier foreign student back in the 1970s. They laughed harder when I said I had worked on a farm. Even my language was archaic. No one called anyone Comrade, any more. I found it so hard to say Miss, Mrs. and Mr. in Chinese, titles that were once unspeakably bourgeois. When I referred to Norman as my *ai ren*, the Maoist word for spouse, people tittered because it literally meant lover. Now everyone had "husbands" and "wives." I had to learn a whole new vocabulary: *generation gap, inflation, human rights* and *Sprite*.

I wasn't certain how much surveillance I was under. I knew my mail was being checked because the post office still confiscated my magazines. I warned contacts not to use their real names over the phone. "Just keep talking," I urged, "and eventually I'll figure out who you are." But most Chinese thought the bad old days were over and that I was being paranoid. Younger Chinese, especially, thought they were untouchable and blurted out their names every time.

Sex was no longer a taboo topic. I attended the first nude art show in the history of the People's Republic of China. And one of my first interviews was with a Chinese Ann Landers who breezily dispensed advice on unrequited love, frigidity and extra-marital sex.

"My husband has been impotent for years," one reader wrote to the *Chinese Women's Journal* (circulation: 500,000). "I can't have the warmth and happiness a woman should have. I want a divorce and my husband agrees. But the officials object, citing Marxist-Leninist principles." It was signed "Hoping for Springtime."

Qiu Ming, the columnist, replied: "Dear Springtime: I've tried my best to search through the works of Marx and Lenin, but nowhere do I find any discussion of whether divorce is permissible if a husband and wife can't have a normal sex life. If you and your husband want a divorce, that's entirely your own business."

But I knew things had really changed when I got my first obscene phone call, in *English*. After all, in the old days people didn't even have phones.

"Do you want to sex intercourse?" a young male voice said. He clearly knew he was dialing a phone number belonging to a foreigner; we were restricted to a special exchange.

"Hello? Hello? What do you want?" I said. "Sorry. What do you mean?"

There was a long pause. "Do you want to sex intercourse?" he repeated, this time more uncertainly.

"I'm so sorry, but I don't understand," I said.

After a few more tries, he gave up. An hour later, the phone rang again. He obviously had been consulting a dictionary. "I mean I love you," he said.

"Thank you very much," I said politely, before hanging up.

Part of me remained an unrepentant Maoist. When I had first arrived in 1972, everyone seemed proud to be Chinese. Women braided their hair. Men looked confident in Mao suits. But by 1988, China seemed to be having a national crisis of self-esteem. I hated seeing people ape Westerners. One of Beijing's newest millionaires had grown rich peddling an expensive hair tonic he claimed could cure baldness. Many women, and even some men, permed their hair into a frizzy mass. They bought "skin-whitener" creams so they wouldn't be mistaken for sunburned peasants. And everybody wanted to be taller. As a short person with straight hair who tanned easily, I felt quite offended.

Mao (himself five feet eleven inches) once disparagingly referred to Deng Xiaoping as "that stump." Official photographs never showed the four-foot nine-inch leader standing shoulder to waist with other world figures. Then I discovered there were height requirements for teachers' college ("The students at the back won't be able to see you") and for television cameramen ("You have to be able to film over other people's heads").

When, in 1993, the government inexplicably issued "standard" heights – five foot three for women, and five foot seven for men – I breathed a sigh of relief. I had just squeaked by. Then I was depressed to learn I had failed the minimum height requirement to waitress at the Beijing Hilton coffee shop. (Norman, at five feet eleven inches, was an inch too short to be a Hilton doorman.) Insecurity swept the vertically-challenged nation. Height-disadvantaged female peasants wore high heels to work in the fields. Young urban toughs tottered on stacked heels while they played pool. Anxious parents invested in "growth medicine" and "stretching machines" for their pipsqueak offspring.

I found myself missing the old blue-gray days. Only Deng still clung to Mao suits. Tourists raved about how well dressed everyone was now but, to me, the Chinese had no sense of Western style. They combined plaid with chintz, chartreuse with burgundy, and wore long underwear under pantyhose. PLA soldiers goose-stepped around in banana-republic uniforms encrusted with stars and cardboard epaulets. To prove their suits were store-bought, men never cut off the labels stitched to the cuffs, a fashion statement no sillier,

I suppose, than paying more for a shirt with a polo-player logo on the pocket.

Yan Yan, my perky news assistant, wore big earrings and tiny jeans. She pierced seven holes in one ear and once dyed a burgundy swath through her short-cropped hair. Occasionally, she bared her trim midriff, shocking the rest of the staff. Once when the two of us arrived at an airport in the provinces – she in a stonewashed denim miniskirt and I in my L.L Bean drab – the comrades assumed *she* was the running-dog reporter. They shook her hand, grabbed her suitcase and left me behind in the dust.

Yan Yan was the new wife of my old friend Julian Schuman, a China Hand from Brooklyn. At various times, Yan Yan had been a PLA soldier, a factory worker and a Communist Party member. The Party had expelled her a few years earlier for her wild lifestyle, and because she refused to snitch on an equally wild friend. She met Julian at *China Daily*, where she was a typist and he was polishing the sports page. *China Daily*'s own version of Cadre Huang had opposed the marriage, in part because Yan Yan was in her early thirties and Julian, who had lived in China on and off since the 1940s, was nearly seventy. Yan Yan, the cadre warned Julian, was a heartless gold-digger and a woman of loose morals. When Julian married her anyway, *China Daily* fired her. Their loss was my gain. She was brash, street-smart and enthusiastic.

As a foreign journalist, I was now officially one of the enemy, except that I still looked like one of the people. Like other reporters, diplomats and spy types, I had to live in special guarded compounds that were off-limits to ordinary Chinese. One day, as I strolled through a compound gate on my way to lunch at a Canadian diplomat's apartment, the security guard snapped out of his noontime stupor.

"Where are *you* from?" he said.

"Canada," I said, in Chinese, as I passed him.

He grabbed my arm. I shook him loose. He grabbed my other arm.

"I am Canadian," I yelled, again in Chinese. As an afterthought, I screamed it in English, too. But the guard assumed I was a "fake foreign devil," a Chinese putting on airs. I broke loose and ran across the parking lot. He was faster, and blocked my way. Unfortunately,

I happened to be suffering from a severe handicap. Not only had I put on an unaccustomed dress, but on my last home leave I had discovered Stay Puts (which came, like salted nuts, in a pop-top can). Invited to lunch with a diplomat, I decided the moment had come to try on my boobs-in-a-can.

The guard chased me around a Mercedes. I ducked behind a jeep. I wasn't sure which worried me more: getting cattle-prodded at high noon or literally falling to pieces. Just then, the Canadian diplomat appeared. He had heard my screams six floors up. In fluent Chinese he informed the guard that he would be filing a formal complaint with the Chinese Foreign Ministry. "You see her?" he said, pointing to my face. "She's Canadian. That's what a Canadian looks like."

It was invaluable, as a journalist in a totalitarian country, to look just like all the other second-class citizens. Sometimes, to fend off security guards, I even pretended I was mentally ill. One afternoon, a guard made a bee-line for me in an office lobby.

"Who are you seeing here?" he demanded.

"I don't know," I told him politely.

"Well, what company are you going to?"

"I don't know."

"Well, what are you doing here?"

"I don't know," I said softly, staring vacantly into space. He backed off.

Looking like a local also helped me avoid the Deng-era surcharges levied on foreigners for everything from park admission to a cup of coffee. At first I voluntarily paid more to expiate my thank-God-my-grandparents-left guilt feelings. Eventually, I resented economic apartheid and sneaked through as a Chinese whenever possible. But because I was forced to live in a foreigners-only compound, I had to pay more for phones, electricity, cooking gas and even a subscription to the *People's Daily*. The final indignity came when I recycled my old newspapers. The scrap dealer paid less, pound for pound, for the *Globe* than for the *People's Daily*.

I decided my first reporting trip should be to the countryside, where three out of four Chinese lived. The retired wife of Norman's former boss at the Institute of Computing Technology suggested I go to coastal Zhejiang province, to a village called Gaobei (North Marsh), so isolated that I would be the first foreigner ever to visit it. When she offered to go with me to help translate the local dialect, I grandly announced the *Globe* would pay her expenses.

I took 500 yuan, or about $100. In the old days, it would have been worth a small fortune. Alas, I underestimated the effect of inflation, which didn't exist in the old centrally planned, fixed-price economy. In Shaoxing, the closest town with running water, I gulped when they quoted me the price of rooms in the foreigners' wing. We settled for mildewed quarters in the Chinese wing. By the fourth day, we were reduced to eating Sichuan pickle soup and plain rice for dinner. I grew desperate as I watched my friend, a ninety-pound woman with a history of stomach ailments, waste away before my eyes. She was too polite to say what she really thought about expense accounts at Canadian newspapers, but she cabled her husband, who promptly wired us a pile of yuan.

The ancient town of Shaoxing was threaded with picturesque canals. Our hotel's foundation was even submerged in one, which resulted in a great view, lots of mosquitoes, and a rainforest-like atmosphere in my bathroom. But after I tried the village privy at North Marsh, the centipedes and cracked tiles of my hotel bathroom seemed positively sybaritic. Nestled amidst mirror-like ponds and feathery groves of bamboo, North Marsh (population: 12,054) was so bucolic it didn't have running water.

The first time – and last time – I used a North Marsh outhouse, I was attacked by a zillion flies and mosquitoes. For some reason, the filthy seats were unusually high. I couldn't imagine how the average substandard Chinese female could hoist herself high enough to avoid brushing against it. When I opened the door and a shaft of sunlight shot in, I discovered white pin-like maggots crawling all over the place. My Chinese friend resolved not to drink anything after we left our hotel each morning.

Deng Xiaoping's economic reforms seemed to be working. North Marsh was so far off the beaten track that it had built its first road only a year earlier. Now it was planning to install traffic lights. In a few months, it would replace its two battery-run, hand-cranked telephones with direct-dial ones. Seven factories had already sprung up along the road's dusty edges, churning out everything from Dacron thread to diet pills to quartz crystals. I watched peasants in long denim aprons lifting brittle sheets of manganese out of acid baths. Another group stamped out plastic parts for television sets. The village now paid factory-level wages to a small group of peasants to handle all the farming.

As an ex-Maoist, I couldn't help but note that the gap between rich and poor was widening. The poorest peasants lived in adobe homes and rarely ate meat. The richest man in the village, who owned the Dacron-thread factory, feasted daily on pork, shrimp and crabs and lived in an eleven-room house with air-conditioning, a breakfast nook, a formal dining room and an indoor fish pond. He even had two bathrooms with Western-style toilets. And it would not be long before he would be able to flush them, too. By year's end, North Marsh planned to install running water.

None of the many books I had read about China talked honestly about what might be delicately called the toilet problem. The Chinese themselves were self-conscious about the disgusting state of their privies because they felt it reflected badly on their image as a civilized country. In 1994, Beijing even ran a contest to find "the best blueprint for a public toilet."

To be sure, Westerners and Chinese approached toilets differently. Once, after a couple of peasants left my apartment in Beijing, I noticed footprints on the toilet seat. I'm sure they thought Western-style toilets were stupidly, dangerously high. *I* was puzzled when the Bean Flower Restaurant, which had the best Sichuanese cuisine in Beijing, posted a sign in the bathroom that warned, "Those who defecate will be fined ten yuan." I never learned why they had a rule like that, or how they knew when anyone broke it.

Traveling through the Chinese countryside was an exercise in bladder control. An enterprising peasant who wanted extra fertilizer might sometimes build a roadside privy. Most of the time, there was nothing. Overpopulation and ankle-high crops meant the bush option didn't exist. My personal desperation method for rural roadside relief was to ask the driver to pull over and leave for a couple of minutes, which he always did with alacrity once I told him my plan. Then I'd open both doors on the side closest to the road's edge, creating my own three-sided latrine.

While hotels in Beijing catering to foreigners had spotless wash-rooms with fresh flowers, crisp linen finger towels and obsequious attendants who did everything but zip up your fly, the average Chinese toilet wasn't made for lingering. In Bengbu, a city of 700,000 on the mighty Huai River in Anhui province, I was inter-viewing a dissident in a small restaurant when nature called. I asked a waitress where the ladies' room was. She looked me over.

"Poo or pee?" she asked.

"Well, pee, actually," I said, with as much dignity as I could muster.

She took me back toward the kitchen and motioned to a room. There was no door, just a grimy cotton sheet tacked over the entrance, and it was pitch black inside. When my eyes adjusted, I realized I was in the coal-storage room. The floor was packed earth. I looked around.

"There's no toilet," I yelled to the waitress, who was hovering outside.

"You said it's just pee, right?" she yelled back, so the entire restau-rant could hear. "Just use the floor!"

So I did.

Although toilets weren't improving much, life in general was get-ting better for many, many people. Just as I had assumed people were happy in the 1970s, I thought people were content under Deng's reforms. I was wrong. That point was driven home to me when I visited my old roommate Scarlet. She had two refrigerators, a freezer, a washing machine, a fan, a toaster oven, a stereo, embossed wallpaper, blue-and-white linoleum floors, a microwave, a big color television and a Panasonic cordless phone. On her dining-room table was a pair of candelabra with dripping white candles.

"Everyone has so many appliances in this building that we keep blowing the fuses," she explained.

"What's that?" I asked, pointing to a contraption I didn't recognize.

"A machine to sterilize dishes."

218 RED CHINA BLUES

I remembered the days when Scarlet didn't even have a plastic bag. To my surprise, she couldn't stop complaining, about her daughter's minuscule chances of getting into university, her own dead-end job, her low wages. Deng Xiaoping had thrown a lot of rice and bikes at people, but expectations kept outstripping economic growth. The old demands he had crushed a decade earlier at Democracy Wall were beginning to bubble up all over again.

The first rumblings began in late 1988. I bumped into Ren Wanding, an activist I had known at Democracy Wall a decade earlier. When he had made speeches back then, I noticed people eagerly gathered around, then drifted away as he entangled himself in his own convoluted train of thought. Ren, who was arrested during Deng's 1979 crackdown, had emerged from jail in 1983, a rebel without a cause. By 1988, authorities didn't seem to consider him much of a threat. When Ren wrote a letter to the *International Herald Tribune* calling on other nations to withhold aid and investment until China's human rights record improved, the government responded, not with cattle prods or handcuffs, but by writing its own boring letter to the editor.

To be sure, China in 1988 wasn't a bastion of liberal democracy. The police still detained and tortured dissidents. But the atmosphere had relaxed considerably. On a trip to Chengdu, the capital of Sichuan province in southwest China, a police chief burst out laughing when I asked if he had arrested any counter-revolutionaries lately. "The only people we arrest now are pickpockets and prostitutes," he said.

Ren Wanding ignored the pleas of his nervous wife, who was afraid he would be jailed again, and made the rounds of Western reporters. When I didn't call him, he called me. He was then forty-four, a delicate-boned man with a bad haircut and glasses that slipped down his nose, giving him a distracted air. Torn between a mania for secrecy and a desire for publicity, he passed out business cards but insisted I turn up the stereo while we talked to thwart electronic bugs. He missed the heady days of Democracy Wall and gloomily admitted that the government wasn't the only one ignoring him. "I don't think many people support me," he said. It seemed that the China Human Rights

League he founded in 1979 hadn't expanded much beyond its original membership of one.

But a handful of other dissidents had emerged during the years I had been away. One of the most prominent was Fang Lizhi, a distinguished astrophysicist. Two years earlier, as vice-president of the University of Science and Technology in Hefei, the capital of Anhui province, Fang had supported some student demonstrations. Enraged, Deng expelled him from the Communist Party and dismissed him from the university.

I first met Professor Fang on the dance floor at a 1988 Christmas bash thrown by the Beijing Foreign Correspondents Club. A few weeks later, when I rang his doorbell it played a full verse of "Happy Birthday to You." I remarked to him that it didn't seem like he dreaded a midnight knock.

"If they don't let me out for a long time, it becomes *their* problem," he said, bursting into his trademark laugh that started with a gentle chuckle, escalated to a high-pitched whinny and ended with an infectious roar. He felt free after his expulsion from the Party. "Now I can say exactly what I think," he said, a short, rumpled man of fifty-two in horn-rims and a tan windbreaker.

"The other dissidents must look up to you," I said. "Are you in touch with any of them?" In fact, he was, but denied it to avoid the charge that he was organizing an opposition group to the Communist Party. "I'm not looking for its downfall," he insisted. "I would just like it to be more democratic. Why is the Party so corrupt? Because it answers to nobody. We should have freedom of speech, an independent press. A multi-party system is the final step."

Professor Fang had recently attacked a vice-mayor of Beijing for usurping a precious slot on a scientific delegation to New York. "I just want to ask him what he knows about synchrotrons," he said coyly at the time. "Is he willing to take a test?" The vice-mayor was not amused. A former construction worker who had never gone to college, he retaliated by canceling a trip Professor Fang had been planning to make abroad.

"Ten years ago, maybe even two years ago, we couldn't even mention human rights. Now it's not such a sensitive subject. More and more people are concerned about human rights." Dubbed

China's Sakharov, Professor Fang was the third most productive scientist in China, measured by the number of scientific papers published a year. He rose at seven, breakfasted on a boiled egg and a cup of coffee, then biked five minutes to the Beijing Observatory, where he taught graduate students. At home in the afternoon and evening, he did his research and answered letters. He and his wife lived in two adjoining flats cobbled into one, a luxurious amount of space by Chinese standards.

I asked Professor Fang why the government treated him so well. He laughed his trademark chuckle again. "They're getting smarter," he said. Noting that 1989 was the tenth year of Wei Jingsheng's incarceration, he had just sent an open letter to Deng, calling for the release of all political prisoners. The letter would soon galvanize other intellectuals and university students and help spark the biggest demonstrations in modern Chinese history. "In my opinion, Deng Xiaoping belongs to Mao's generation," he said. "He allows some change in the economy, but he's just like Mao in terms of ideology."

In February 1989, China announced that Deng would hold a summit with Soviet General Secretary Mikhail Gorbachev, capping the end of nearly three decades of hostility between the two Communist superpowers. Given the golden opportunity for international attention and the relatively liberal atmosphere in China, many dissidents felt the time was ripe to push for improved human rights. Like Professor Fang, they began circulating petitions and holding meetings.

That same month, President George Bush held a glittering state dinner at the Great Wall Sheraton. Among the five hundred guests he invited were Professor Fang and his wife. But the Chinese police and plainclothes agents refused to let the couple near the hotel, and tailed them on foot for several hours, even preventing them from boarding a bus or hailing a taxi. When we reporters realized Fang was missing, we ditched the banquet and ran off trying to find him. His son finally announced his father would hold a press conference at the temporary White House press center on the other side of town. Professor Fang finally arrived at 1:30 a.m. to pandemonium.

"From this incident we can see what the human rights situation is like here in China," he said, blinking owlishly under the harsh television lights. That night, he was interviewed by the three U.S. networks and made the front page of every major paper. *Time* magazine put him on its cover with the headline "Guess Who Isn't Coming to Dinner?"

After months of permissiveness and inaction and writing letters to the editor, China had unsheathed its claws. The invitation to Fang was made "without consultation," the Foreign Ministry snapped, and "the Chinese side resented this." The Chinese were so angry at what they saw as U.S. meddling in its internal affairs that they were willing to embarrass the American president, a sycophantic friend of China. Deng was signaling he would brook no more dissent.

Four months after I spoke to Professor Fang, authorities issued a warrant for his arrest. Fleeing for their lives after the massacre at Tiananmen Square, he and his wife became the first – and only – Chinese dissidents to obtain asylum in the U.S. Embassy. Their exact location in the embassy, which was divided among three separate sites, was a secret from all but a handful of American diplomats. With gun-toting Chinese soldiers pacing outside the embassy walls, the Americans were afraid the Chinese might stage a commando-style raid to seize Professor Fang. For a year, the couple hid in the embassy clinic and ate meals smuggled inside a diplomat's briefcase. Beijing finally permitted them to leave China for "health reasons" in 1990.

13

People Power

Top: Student protester at Tiananmen Square with a caricature of a bloodthirsty Li Peng, after the Chinese premier declared martial law.

Photo: Jan Wong

Bottom: The giant portrait of Mao Zedong which overlooks Tiananmen Square after three men splattered it with paint during pro-democracy demonstrations. They were later sentenced to life, twenty years and sixteen years, some of the harshest sentences meted out during the subsequent crackdown.

Photo: AP/Mark Avery

Hu Yaobang died on April 15, 1989, at age seventy-three. At first, I shrugged off the news. He was a political has-been, purged two years earlier as Deng Xiaoping's heir apparent after failing to contain the same student demonstrations that had led to Fang Lizhi's dismissal. His death seemed unlikely to change the political landscape.

So I was surprised when Big Character posters immediately went up on the campus of my alma mater. Why would anybody mourn Hu? He was a buffoonish character who once advocated that Chinese, for sanitary reasons, use knives and forks instead of chopsticks. The joke went that Deng had chosen him because at four feet eight inches, Hu Yaobang was the only person on the ruling Politburo who looked up to Deng. His fall from grace began when he made the fatal mistake of looking enthusiastic when Deng made a bogus offer to retire. To me, Hu was just another Party hack who proved once again that being heir apparent was bad for one's health.

So why were the students rushing out to lay wreaths? Then I remembered how mourning Premier Zhou Enlai had been the only way to attack the Gang of Four in 1976. Was mourning Hu the only way to criticize Deng, the man who had purged him? For several months now, people had observed how dissidents like

Professor Fang had circulated petitions and held news conferences – all without reprisal. Many felt the government was weak and that it was time to take further action. Rumor had it that former Party chief Hu had suffered a heart attack during an unusually acrimonious Politburo debate on educational policy. Within hours of his death, the students had adopted him as their fallen hero and were calling for a city-wide boycott of classes.

A few days later, a million Beijingers joined in the biggest spontaneous anti-government demonstration in Communist Chinese history. I remembered how gloomy Ren Wanding had been about finding any supporters just a few months earlier. And I remembered how Professor Fang marveled how, only a few years ago, people didn't even dare speak of human rights. I assumed they were as stunned as I was at how rapidly the protests gathered steam.

That evening, a crowd gathered in front of the Central Committee headquarters, yelling for Empress Dowager Ci Xi to step down. Ci Xi, who had been dead for eighty years, was infamous for controlling politics from behind the scenes. Screaming for her abdication was just another thinly veiled attack on Deng. Thank goodness I had majored in Chinese history.

Tiananmen is gargantuan, the biggest square in the world. It is a hundred sprawling acres in all, flatter and bigger than the biggest parking lot I have ever seen. I used to get tired just walking from one end to the other. Moscow's Red Square was intimate in comparison. Tiananmen could simultaneously accommodate the entire twenty-eight teams of the National Football League plus 192 other teams, each playing separate games. It could stage an entire Summer Olympics, with all events taking place at the same time. Or if you put a mountain in the middle, you could hold a Winter Olympics there instead.

Tiananmen Square made me feel tiny, insignificant, powerless. That was no accident. As the geographic and political center of Beijing, it was enlarged after the Communist victory to celebrate the grandiosity of Red China. In 1949, the Great Helmsman stood on the rostrum, in front of the Forbidden City, to proclaim: "The Chinese people have stood up." He returned during the Cultural Revolution, waving majestically to a crowd of a million hysterical Red Guards that included Scarlet, Future and many of my classmates.

Tiananmen, which means Gate of Heavenly Peace, is also one of the least hospitable squares in the world. There is no bench or place to rest, nowhere to get a drink, no leafy tree to offer respite from the sun. Only the one-hundred-foot high Monument to the People's Heroes punctuates it, and, after 1977, Mao's white and gold mausoleum. Tiananmen is also one of the most heavily monitored squares in the world. Its huge lampposts are equipped with giant speakers for crowd control and swiveling videocameras. The commercial photographers, with white pushcarts and colorful shade umbrellas, are actually plainclothes police. For a modest fee, they snap photos of Chinese tourists posing in the square and mail you the pictures a week later. That way, they have your name and address, too.

On April 21, 1989, thousands of students began gathering in Tiananmen Square in anticipation of Hu's state funeral the next day. By then, the criticism of Deng had burst into the open. "Down with dictatorship," read one banner. "You've fooled the people too long," said another. A Big Character poster titled "The Nine Crimes of Deng Xiaoping" accused him, among other misdeeds, of refusing to retire and of protecting his eldest son from a corruption inquiry.

Police videotaped the students on the steps of the Great Hall of the People on the western side of the square. As one youth made an impromptu speech about democracy, a dozen PLA soldiers burst through the hall's massive bronze doors and took karate kicks at the students. The panic-stricken crowd fled. I was angry and upset. It was the first time I witnessed the PLA attacking the people. Had China changed that much in the years I had been gone?

Authorities planned to close the square for Saturday's funeral, but the students outsmarted them by camping out the night before. In a massive procession that Friday, more than a hundred thousand students marched into Tiananmen Square. As passersby applauded, the students sang the Communist "*Internationale*," and for a moment I felt like I was back at Big Joy Farm. Then the demonstrators chanted, "Down with dictatorship!" and "Long live freedom!" and I knew things were not the same. Sixty truckloads of soldiers arrived that evening to seal off the square, but it was too late.

Saturday, April 22, 1989, dawned cloudless and warm. The police belatedly sealed off the square. The tens of thousands of students who had spent the night there remained on the inside. Members of the public, excited and curious, gathered on the edge of the square. At seven, a single line of unarmed police formed in front of the Great Hall of the People. Undaunted, the students advanced toward them until they faced them, nose to nose, less than a foot away.

Remembering my own student demonstrations from the sixties, I expected a full-scale riot. Instead, the students chanted an old Maoist flower-power slogan: "The people love the police! The police love the people!" When the funeral started at nine, five thousand soldiers massed behind the single line of police. We could all follow the proceedings through the square's loudspeakers. When the national anthem began, the students joined in lustily. If I hadn't lived through the Tiananmen incident in 1976, I would have thought they were a bunch of polite college kids. But I knew they were really demanding Deng's abdication.

When the funeral ended forty-five minutes later, I watched from the sidelines as China's aging leaders paused on the broad granite steps of the Great Hall to stare in disbelief at the sea of students. Symbolically, the gulf between them was filled with soldiers. Some students began to shout, "Dialogue! Dialogue! Dialogue!" Three knelt on the steps, holding a petition aloft. Deng slipped out a side entrance.

At first, I couldn't understand why the government didn't just accept the petition and defuse the situation. I learned later that the Politburo was badly split. The latest heir apparent, who played golf and had a penchant for Western suits, firmly believed that doctrinaire Marxism was hindering rapid economic development. Only by keeping ahead of people's material demands, Party Chief Zhao Ziyang contended, could the Communist Party remain in power. No civil libertarian, Zhao (pronounced *Jow*) nonetheless wanted to use the pressure from the students to ram through further reforms – and perhaps force Deng into real retirement. But by even *thinking* of using the anti-Deng protests to advance his own agenda, Zhao had sealed his fate. Heir today, gone tomorrow.

After demonstrations flared in at least six other Chinese cities, a banner headline on a front-page editorial in the *People's Daily* screamed, "Take a Clear-cut Stance Against the Instigation of Turmoil." In normal countries, a newspaper editorial is just the opinion of some pointy-headed editor. But in China, it is a directive from the top. This editorial accused the students of conspiracy and sabotage, which left them vulnerable to retaliation and possible prison terms. Deng had spoken. There would be no compromise, no dialogue.

The students – and the populace – understood the significance of the editorial. But its fighting words only gave them a shot of adrenaline. Outraged at the hard-line labels, tens of thousands of students poured into Tiananmen Square once more. For the first time since the demonstrations began, ordinary residents joined in, too. The protesters demanded a retraction and, for good measure, the resignation of hard-line Premier Li Peng. Emboldened by the outpouring of public support, the students came up with three new demands: an open dialogue with the government, an apology for the police beatings, and unbiased media coverage of the student movement. If they didn't get an immediate response, the students brashly warned, they would retake Tiananmen Square.

Deng was apoplectic. "We are not afraid to shed a little blood since this will not seriously harm China's image in the world," he said, according to reports that leaked later. With exquisite bad timing, Ren Wanding, the old Democracy Wall activist, chose this moment to speak out. "If there are people who force us to shed blood, then let our blood flow," he said.

By early May, it seemed that everyone had joined the demonstrations. Police officers, Foreign Ministry aides, steelworkers, bankers, even *People's Daily* reporters, in a rebuke to their own editorial writers, waved the banners of their organizations and marched with their work IDs pinned to their shirts. The biggest silent majority in the world was no longer silent. For the first time since my misguided Maoist days, I could relate again to being Chinese. I felt a surge of pride. The Chinese people didn't accept being downtrodden. They had real backbone.

But as the days passed, and the mercury hit the nineties, the crowds started thinning. Then the protesters got another shot of adrenaline. A thousand journalists, including CBS's Dan Rather and CNN's Bernard Shaw, began descending on Beijing for the Sino-Soviet summit. With so many journalists rattling around in search of a story, the students decided to reignite public opinion by staging a hunger strike in Tiananmen Square. It was a brilliant tactic. The move would win them immense sympathy, the leadership would be distracted by the summit, and the world's media would go ga-ga over a David-and-Goliath story.

Gorbachev was due in Beijing on Monday, May 15. Two days before, several hundred students indulged in a last lunch. After downing beer and sausages on their campuses, they donned white headbands emblazoned with red slogans and marched enthusiastically for two hours down to Tiananmen Square. By midafternoon, the initial crowd of hunger strikers had ballooned to more than one thousand, or about one per visiting journalist. I squeezed my way to the front of the crowd as a slight, slender woman began reading a "hunger-strike declaration." Chai Ling, a twenty-three-year-old graduate student in psychology, looked like a Gap model in her slim tan pants and white polo shirt, a pair of folded sunglasses dangling from the open collar. The television cameras loved her because her curtain of silky hair was always falling in her eyes, and because she tended to weep at the slightest provocation. After the crackdown, the government's Most Wanted List of Student Leaders would describe her as having "single-fold eyelids, high cheekbones, short hair and rather white skin."

"Comrades!" Chai Ling began, her breathy voice barely audible through a bullhorn. The crowd sitting cross-legged before her quieted down immediately. "We protest the government's uncaring attitude! We request a dialogue! Don't label us as fomenters of disorder!" Everyone cheered. She led the crowd in slogan-shouting, a skill drummed into Chinese kids since nursery school. "Immediate pardon! Immediate dialogue! No delay!" she shouted in her delicate voice, and the crowd screamed back. "I love my homeland more than rice! I love truth more than rice!" she cried. The crowd went wild. Chai Ling then announced it was time to take a collective oath. Raising her delicately clenched right fist, she recited the hunger-strike oath, pausing at every phrase to let the students repeat after her:"I swear, that to promote democracy, for the prosperity of my country, I willingly go on a hunger strike. I will not give up until I realize our goals!"

I looked at my watch. It was 5:20 p.m. Gorbachev was due to arrive in less than forty-eight hours. The students looked grim and determined, a sense of destiny on their faces. I wandered over to a large knot of people where a bookish young man with olive skin was giving an impromptu press conference. The foreign press wanted to know whether the students would try to approach Gorbachev. Wang Dan, who would become Number One on the government's Most Wanted list, smiled coolly. "We're not trying to use foreign influence to pressure the Chinese government," he replied, speaking through a battery-operated bullhorn. It was, of course, a transparent lie, but everybody went along with the fiction, applauding as he spoke. He continued, "I think China's leaders can learn a lot of good things from the Soviet Union." Someone asked if he was afraid of going to jail. Wang Dan smiled inscrutably. The press conference was over.

Overnight, the square was transformed into an urban Woodstock, without the mud and psychedelic drugs. Red silk banners fluttered from flagpoles. Shabby tents of plastic sheeting sprouted from the pavement. Lovers snuggled. Students strummed guitars and sang terrible Hong Kong pop songs. Some debated politics. And they smoked like fiends. I choked even though we were outdoors. "I can give up food and drink," said a twenty-three-year-old engineering student in stonewashed jeans, puffing away. "But not cigarettes."

The hunger strike resonated deeply in China, where the standard rural greeting was still "Have you eaten?" People fretted that the students, esteemed in Chinese society because the chance at a university degree was so rare, would ruin their health. Many Chinese, who defined hardship as anything less than three hot meals with rice a day, were moved to tears. And in an agrarian nation where everyone wanted to get as far away from nature as possible, camping out, even in the middle of a city of ten million, was also viewed as a terrible privation.

Parents accused the government of intransigence. Office workers leaned out of windows to scream support and shower confetti on the marchers. Government organizations, sensing a power struggle in the offing, hedged their bets. The Commerce Bureau of Beijing supplied six thousand straw hats. The Beijing Military Command offered a thousand cotton quilts. State pharmaceutical companies donated medicine.

Wide-eyed students began arriving from the provinces, swelling the already huge crowds at Tiananmen Square to several hundred thousand. There were so many different demonstrations that the marchers sometimes good-naturedly crisscrossed in the square. Several hundred motorcyclists, calling themselves Flying Tigers, roared through the streets like Chinese James Deans, waving flags and screaming slogans. The sit-in sparked copycat hunger strikes in more than thirty other Chinese cities. Workers in Beijing and elsewhere began joining the strike, giving the government nightmares about a Solidarity-style workers' movement.

Tiananmen Square itself was a mess. Students guzzled beer and hurled the bottles, chanting "*Xiaoping wan sui!*" which meant "Long live Deng Xiaoping." I thought it rather odd, not to mention uncomfortable, that anyone staging a sit-in would want a lot of broken glass on the ground, until someone told me that the slogan also meant "Smash Little Bottle" – a pun on Deng's name – "into Ten Thousand Pieces!" The deeper significance of the discarded cigarette butts, newspapers and plastic juice bottles escaped me.

That weekend, Politburo members, anxious to clear the square before Gorbachev arrived, met repeatedly with student representatives, but neither side was truly interested in compromise. As the hours ticked by, the students escalated their demands. They now wanted live television coverage of their talks *and* a public apology from China's aging leaders.

The Sino-Soviet summit was supposed to be Deng's crowning glory. He wanted normalization as much as Gorbachev did, but the wily Chinese leader had hung tough until Moscow withdrew its soldiers from Afghanistan, reduced troop levels on the Sino–Soviet border and pressed Vietnam to withdraw from Cambodia. Playing hardball was China's style. The Middle Kingdom always made barbarian devils kowtow for the chance to make fools of themselves using chopsticks to pick up a slippery quail's egg in the Great Hall of the People.

But instead of arriving as a flunky from a vassal nation, Gorbachev landed in Beijing to a hero's welcome. That Monday, homemade banners along his motorcade route hailed him in Chinese and Russian as the "true reformer." Said one: "The Soviet Union has Gorbachev. Who does China have?" Protesters held up signs that said, "Hello, Mr. Gorbachev," and "Democracy is our common ideal," and "Deng, your health may be good but – is your brain?" One poster simply stated their ages: "Gorbachev, 58; Deng Xiaoping, 85."

At Tiananmen Square, ambulance sirens wailed. White-coated medics rushed around with bottles of glucose, jabbing anyone who looked pale. As bedlam reigned, the Chinese were forced to cancel a wreath-laying ceremony and a twenty-one-gun salute. More than sixty students fainted the first day. Having experienced a surfeit of faked fervor in the old days, I suspected histrionics. Indeed, one person was hustled into an ambulance before he could explain he was a local television reporter covering the story.

To my amazement, for the first time in Chinese Communist history, the state media began reporting the real story about dissent, an indication of the widespread support for Party Chief Zhao within key areas of the government. Until then, I had been contemptuous of my local colleagues for their docility and turgid political reports. But for a brief week that spring, I watched as they scooped the rest of us. "We feel we are finally being journalists," said a friend at *Beijing Youth News*, her eyes sparkling. She was so excited that she began living at her office.

By Wednesday, the fifth day of the hunger strike, 3,100 people had fainted and required medical treatment, the official Xinhua News Agency reported. Many people were incensed by the special privilege and corruption of the elite. One parent carried a placard alluding to corruption in Deng's family: "A question, Mr. Deng. Our son is on a hunger strike. What is your son doing?" Along the pedestrian walkways underneath the square, protesters had pasted caricatures depicting Deng's children driving Mercedes-Benzes.

During Gorbachev's three-day visit, Beijing traffic wasn't just snarled. It congealed. One out of every ten residents, or a million demonstrators, jammed the streets at any given time. Everyone seemed hysterically happy that their leaders were losing face big-time. Authorities were forced to cancel the rest of Gorbachev's public schedule, a humiliating admission that they were no longer in control of their own capital. The Soviet leader never did see the square. To enable his motorcade to reach the Great Hall at all, the Chinese had to dispatch more than a thousand soldiers to seal off the streets. He didn't make it to the Forbidden City, either. An evening at the opera also was canceled. Nor could reporters reach the official Soviet spokesman for comment; he was marooned after police sealed off the area where the Soviet press center happened to be located. I couldn't even get a copy of Gorbachev's banquet speech. The center's photocopier broke down and the Chinese repairmen were all off demonstrating.

For a man used to the limelight, Gorbachev had been complete-ly upstaged. At night, his aides had shown him videotapes of the amazing scenes. At his only press conference, Gorbachev seemed a bit shell-shocked. One reporter asked what he would do if students occupied Red Square in Moscow. "I would use democracy," he said, with a glassy-eyed smile, "to solve the confrontation."

The day after Gorbachev left Beijing, Premier Li Peng agreed to a televised meeting with the student leaders. Li was livid that the Sino-Soviet summit had been ruined. Dressed in a rumpled Mao suit, he thundered: "We will not sit idly by, doing nothing!" A chub-by twenty-one-year-old hunger strike leader named Wu'er Kaixi was not intimidated. Clutching an oxygen bag and dressed in hos-pital-issue pajamas to underline the point that he had come straight from the hospital, he sat sprawled in his stuffed armchair. At one point, he reprimanded Premier Li.

"We don't have much time to listen to you," said Wu'er Kaixi, wagging a finger. "Thousands of hunger strikers are waiting. Let's get to the main point. It is we who invited you to talk, not you who invited us – and *you* were late." The astonishing meeting ended when he clutched his oxygen bag and made as if to faint. Medical personnel rushed on camera to care for him. Maybe because I was now well past the once-loathed age of thirty, my perspective had changed. I almost felt sorry for Li Peng. It was no surprise to me when Wu'er Kaixi ended up Number Two on the Most Wanted List of Student Leaders.

Later, Chinese television would smear the student leader by airing footage of him happily chowing down with friends at the Beijing Hotel. His supporters, though, insisted the meal took place after the strike had ended. Whatever really happened, I knew that during the hunger strike Wu'er Kaixi sneaked off for at least one meal with John Pomfret, an Associated Press reporter. At night, Wu'er Kaixi also surreptitiously slurped noodles in the back seat of a car, bending over to hide his face, according to Andrew Higgins of the British *Independent*. The hunger striker told a friend that he needed to eat to conserve his strength because he was a leader and because he had a heart condition.

In fact, a lot of students were cheating during the hunger strike. The second day, I spotted bottles of sweetened yogurt in a student's knapsack. When I asked about it, he replied airily, "Snacking is okay. It's not really food." I reported the yogurt in my story that day, but I never conveyed the sense that the hunger strike was like a game at first, with students dramatically fainting on cue and the world's media pretending they really were starving themselves.

Yan Yan, my flamboyant news assistant, went to Tiananmen Square as an extra pair of eyes and ears for me. After the first couple of days, she stopped coming back to the office to give me reports. I finally spotted her, wearing a headband and a fatalistic expression, sitting cross-legged among the hunger strikers. I asked with some exasperation what she was doing. "Hunger striking!" she said cheerfully, admitting in the next breath that she never actually missed a meal. One day she asked if she could expense some milk for her comrades in the square. Sure, I said, assuming she meant a bottle or two. When she presented me with a bill for a whole case, I was appalled. I told her the *Globe* was supposed to report on the hunger strikers, not *feed* them.

I could hardly blame Yan Yan. Everyone else seemed to be feeding the hunger strikers. A soft-drink cart did a roaring business in the square. Entrepreneurs, seeing a chance to weaken Communist controls, donated food and blankets. State food companies sent bread and drinks, ostensibly for emergencies, which usually meant whenever anyone got a bit hungry. Even the Communist Youth League donated twenty cases of drinks. Then I discovered the students were hunger striking in shifts. They'd sit out a few meals, until a classmate came to replace them. And every day hundreds of newcomers would buckle down in the square for a few hours' deprivation.

But who wanted to hear that the students were just ordinary kids, trying to be heroic by day but nibbling on snacks at night? It made for much better copy to show them as earnest waifs fighting against Evil. The protesters and the media fed on one another. The demonstrators felt their cause was validated by the intense international attention. No sooner had they issued a statement than they heard it broadcast back on the BBC World Service and the Voice of America. For our part, we reporters loved getting our stories on page one. Who wanted to let a few unromantic facts get in the way of a good story?

Tiananmen was telegenic. The majestic backdrop, with its fluttering red silk flags and huge portrait of Chairman Mao, was a television producer's dream. And the cast of millions, who couldn't speak a word of English, quickly learned to flash a V-for-victory sign that needed no translation. The students understood the importance of sound bites and played Beethoven's *Ode to Joy* over their loudspeaker system again and again. I saw one young man on the roof of a bus vigorously wave a red banner, a fiery look of determination in his eyes. As soon as the cameramen finished the shot, the young man sat down and lit a cigarette.

With Gorbachev gone and the foreign media packing up, the students astutely claimed victory and called off their week-long hunger strike on May 19. But it was too late. That evening, Premier Li Peng, wearing a black Mao suit and punching his fist angrily in the air, declared on live television that the capital was in chaos. The Party, he said, was being forced to take "resolute and decisive measures." The next morning, he signed the order imposing martial law. As more than a hundred thousand troops ringed the capital, my Chinese friend at *Beijing Youth News* stopped sleeping at her office – and stopped being a journalist.

The army swiftly took over the Xinhua News Agency, Central Radio and Central Television. The only way soldiers could get into the *People's Daily*, by now a hotbed of dissent, was by pretending they were medics, disguising themselves in white coats and driving ambulances. Abruptly, the coverage of the protests changed. There was no more news, only polemics. Beijing issued a series of restrictive regulations to try to muzzle the foreign press. Martial Law No. Three, for instance, declared, "Foreign correspondents are prohibited from issuing provocative reports." Another rule banned all unapproved interviews and photographs.

Perversely, martial law gave the protesters another shot of adrenaline. The students defiantly vowed to continue their sit-in. A fanatic new Dare-to-Die Squad swore to protect the student leaders to the death. A hitherto unheard-of workers' alliance handed the government an ultimatum: satisfy the students' demands within twenty-four hours or face a general strike.

Watching this melodrama unfold, I couldn't decide who was more childish, the students or the doddering gerontocracy. An experienced mediator could have solved things so easily. But the students were drunk with their new-found celebrity, and Communist dictators weren't used to negotiating. The Communist Party also had an internal power struggle to settle.

But martial law? I sensed China had turned into a banana republic in my absence, but this was ridiculous. Apparently, many Chinese felt the same way. Instead of cowering in their homes, they took to the streets in an exuberant, crazy affirmation of people power. When military helicopters dropped copies of Premier Li Peng's martial-law speech over Tiananmen Square, people gleefully ripped them up as soon as they touched the ground.

The first evening of martial law, the number of students staging a sit-in swelled to fifty thousand. To thwart the square's videocameras, everyone donned gauze masks. A rumor swept the crowd that the soldiers would attack at 2 a.m. Nervously, I interviewed an officer on the edge of the square who promised that the military would never hurt the students. I watched the students holding hands, sitting cross-legged on the ground, trying to breathe through their masks, and wondered how it would all end. By 3 a.m., someone declared victory, again, and tossed on the tape of *Ode to Joy.*

That night, more than a million Chinese of all ages blockaded the streets, vowing to protect the students. They threw up a protective cordon around Tiananmen Square and barricaded virtually every key intersection, using concrete cylinders, dumpsters, cement mixers, city buses, trucks and construction cranes. Beijing police tried using truncheons and cattle prods to clear a path for the army, but their heart was not in it. After all, the police had been demonstrating, too.

I teamed up with several other reporters. Working all night, we counted seventeen tanks, sixty-nine armored personnel carriers, an entire trainload of fifteen hundred soldiers at the main train station downtown and numerous military convoys on the edge of the city. At an intersection near my apartment, some students excitedly dragged a military attaché over to see a large tractor-trailer. "Look," exclaimed one student. "The government wants to use tear gas on us." The military attaché was stunned. The cargo wasn't tear gas but six ground-to-air warhead missiles.

But the soldiers were no match for the people. Elderly women lay down in front of tanks. Schoolchildren swarmed around convoys, stopping them in their tracks. After the first tense night, the soldiers began to retreat as the crowds cheered and applauded. Some bystanders flashed the V sign. Others wept, and so did some of the soldiers. One commander shouted, "We are the people's soldiers. We will never suppress the people."

The next night, in a southwest corner of Beijing called Liu Li Bridge, I came across a dozen military trucks engulfed by five thousand emotional civilians. Three hundred rifle-toting soldiers sat in the immobilized trucks, their fuel lines cut, frozen like bugs in amber. Mindful of the martial-law ban on interviewing, I approached a middle-aged Chinese woman and identified myself as a reporter for Canada's *Globe and Mail.* I took out my notebook and pen and said, "According to the martial-law rules, I'm not allowed to ask you any questions." She understood.

"The government underestimated us," she said, with a sad, proud smile. She gestured at the crowd. "Look at all the people who have come out to protect the students. The government is wrong." I scribbled in my notebook and thanked her. It was two in the morning and the moon was full. A young man hoisted himself onto one of the truck's wheels. "Have a cigarette," he said, politely trying to break the ice in the classic Chinese way. The crowd good-naturedly urged the soldiers to smoke. Finally, two soldiers lit up. People cheered.

This was martial law? The soldiers, many of whom looked too young to shave, seemed bewildered. The slogan "The army loves the people! The people love the army!" had been drummed into them in basic training, which hadn't included how to deal with smiling civilians who cut your fuel lines. Kept incommunicado, the soldiers had not seen the brief, but extraordinary, Chinese media coverage of the demonstrations. They had been told only that they were going on military maneuvers.

Someone lifted a case of soft drinks onto the truck. An old woman in an apron came out to collect some empty bowls. "You see," a woman in the crowd said to no one in particular, "we give them food and drink. They've been sitting here all day. The government hasn't given them anything." People tossed the soldiers old protest leaflets to read. Housewives told them about the week-long hunger strike. "The students were very well behaved," said one old worker. "All they want from the government is an official apology." Several people distributed Popsicles to the soldiers, who finally climbed down from their trucks and began fraternizing with the enemy. It was hard to feel threatened by a soldier sucking on a Popsicle. This was the PLA I knew and liked. The fresh-faced troops reminded me of Horsepower and my other soldier classmates. When people swarmed over the trucks, proclaiming they loved the army, I felt I was back in Maoist times.

The first twenty-four hours of martial law was a huge defeat for the authorities. For the next ten days, hundreds of thousands of ordinary citizens manned the barricades. People brought their children to Tiananmen Square for shish kebabs, ice cream and a little dissent. The swashbuckling Flying Tigers acted as messengers and scouts, and zoomed around on their motorcycles gathering intelligence on troop movements. One student leader celebrated the "people's victory" by getting "married" in the square. Chai Ling was bridesmaid.

The massive display of civil disobedience fed on itself. Seven top generals, including a former minister of defense and another who was a hero of the epic Long March, signed a petition opposing martial law. Protesters marched up and down the streets laughing and chanting: "Li Peng, step down, or we'll be back every day!" One afternoon, a crowd of several thousand gathered in front of Zhongnanhai to watch a sit-in of several dozen students. A minstrel settled into the crook of a tree branch and, strumming his banjo, began singing satirical folk songs about Deng and Premier Li Peng. Then a drummer led a parade by, singing this ditty in Chinese to the tune of "Frère Jacques":

"Down with Li Peng, down with Li Peng,
Yang Shangkun, Yang Shangkun [a PLA general],
There's still another hoodlum,
Still another hoodlum,
Deng Xiaoping, Deng Xiaoping."

The people had called the government's bluff. Martial law was marshmallow law. Each day I roamed the city in the Globe's old Toyota, which I had finally learned to stop without stalling. During the two-hour traffic-clogged drive out to the university area, I often picked up hitchhiking student protesters to interview so I wouldn't waste time. At one barricaded intersection, I inched along while student marshals in red armbands waved through cars on each side. Finally, it was my turn. Then someone noticed my foreigner's black license plates. A marshal put up his hand to stop me and motioned the jeep on the other side to go through first.

"Chinese before foreigners," he declared. I hated the old days when China let foreigners go before Chinese. Now I was damned if the next generation was going to let Chinese go before foreigners. Anyway, it was *my* turn. I eased forward until my Toyota was nose to nose with the jeep. "Back up!" people screamed at me. Then I did something really stupid. Which was nothing. Before I knew it, the mob was trying to flip our car. One of my hitchhikers stuck her head out the window and yelled, "We're students. She's a good person. She's a foreign reporter. She's giving us a lift home." Then she screamed at me to back up. The crowd hesitated just long enough for me to reverse. The jeep went through first, its driver grinning at me.

I was becoming more than a bit cranky. The outside world thought the demonstrators were disciplined, and marveled. But having lived through the Cultural Revolution myself, talents like slogan shouting and mass marching didn't impress me. Maybe it was sleep deprivation – I was working nineteen hours a day – but to my jaundiced eye it seemed that the students were merely aping their oppressors. They established a Lilliputian kingdom in Tiananmen Square, complete with a mini-bureaucracy with committees for sanitation, finance and "propaganda." They even adopted grandiose titles. Chai Ling was elected Supreme Commander-in-Chief of the Tiananmen Square Unified Action Headquarters.

Like the government, the students' broadcast station sometimes deliberately disseminated misinformation, such as the resignation of key government officials, which wasn't true. They even, indignity of indignities, issued us press passes. Using transparent fishing line held in place by volunteers who simply stood there all day, they carved the huge square into gigantic concentric circles of ascending importance. Depending on how our press passes were stamped determined how deeply we could penetrate those silly circles. We reporters had to show our passes to half a dozen officious monitors before we could interview the student leaders, who, naturally, hung out at the very center, at the Monument to the People's Heroes.

One night, a rumor swept the square that the students had captured some assault rifles. If true, it meant they possessed weapons for the first time. I tracked down the tent where the guns were supposedly stored and asked the wild-eyed student guard if I could take a peek. He refused, but assured me the guns were inside. For an allegation that serious, I had to see the guns for myself. But he wouldn't budge, and I finally stomped off in frustration, never reporting it. Later, I found out it was true, and was perhaps a reason the government decided to shoot to kill on the fateful night.

Others had more serious run-ins with the baby bureaucrats. On May 23, three protesters lobbed bags of ink at the giant portrait of Mao hanging from the rostrum. Student marshals hustled the trio to the command center, where a slender young woman named Huang Qinglin took charge. She was the unlikely leader of the Dare-to-Die Squad, the one thousand fanatics who had sworn to protect student leaders like Chai Ling and Wu'er Kaixi with their lives. She ordered the ink throwers interrogated. They turned out to be democracy activists from Hunan, Mao's home province. To my shock, she then turned them over to the police. It was something I might have done in my stupid Maoist years. But the Cultural Revolution was long over, and Beijing was under martial law. I happened to be interviewing Commander Huang when this happened.

"Why turn them in?" I asked, as evenly as I could, remembering that I had no right to moral superiority.

"We don't want the government to have an excuse to attack us," she said. "They might be government agents, provocateurs. They had no identification papers on them."

I thought to myself: *Would you carry ID if you were going to vandalize the biggest Mao portrait in the country?*

Perhaps Commander Huang, a student in public relations at China Social University, took her major too seriously. She told me she feared the incident might turn public opinion against the students. Even though Mao had been dead for thirteen years and his policies had been completely dismantled, he remained an icon. When a heavy rainstorm began moments later, some of the more superstitious students thought the heavens were signaling their displeasure over the ink-tossing incident. Someone quickly threw a khaki tarpaulin over the vandalized painting and within a day, authorities had hung a fresh Mao portrait in its place.

Commander Huang was beautiful, with flashing almond eyes and soft dark hair. She wore a double strand of pearls at her neck and a plain wedding band on her finger. A wide-brimmed straw hat was her only protection from the downpour. Her running shoes and bulky green corduroy jacket were soon soaked through. Two volunteer nurses tried to throw a sweater over her, but she shrugged it off, telling them to give it to someone who needed it more. Her hands were like ice, and she seemed to be running on pure adrenaline. She said she had been up for five days and five nights, ever since the premier had declared martial law. She stole catnaps in corners but otherwise was constantly on duty. That day, all she had eaten was a cucumber and two boiled eggs. She couldn't keep her food down anyway. She was two months pregnant.

"I didn't want to be the head of the Dare-to-Die Squad," she said, "but somebody has to take the responsibility." Her husband was out of town on a work trip, she said, and didn't know that she was squad commander – or that she was pregnant. Commander Huang spoke rapidly, her delicate hands fluttering. She personally thought the students should leave the square, but said she was bound by an "iron" discipline. "If the majority votes to stay, then the minority must obey them," she said. She seemed to be achingly earnest about her first try at democracy. Then I remembered she had just turned in three protesters.

The ink throwers – a factory worker, a small-town newspaper editor and a rural schoolteacher – had been inspired by the hunger strike in Beijing, according to an account later published in the *Legal Daily*. Before hopping a train to Beijing from Hunan, they had plastered the railway station with democracy slogans. During the eighteen-hour journey, they composed a manifesto calling for the end of the Communist Party and the adoption of Western-style democracy. In Beijing, they made a bee-line for the huge portrait at Tiananmen Square, scoring direct hits just above Mao's left eyebrow, his right temple and his neck. From a distance, it looked like the Great Helmsman was weeping. A Chinese court later sentenced the worker to sixteen years, the editor to twenty years and the schoolteacher to life, three of the harshest terms meted out to the Tiananmen protesters.

(On the night of the massacre, I couldn't stop worrying about Commander Huang. At first I was afraid she had been killed. Later I feared she had been arrested and executed. The first chance I had, I searched out China Social University, which I had never heard of before. It turned out to be a small, privately run school down a dusty alleyway in the east part of the city. I sneaked past the guard at the front gate and approached a friendly-looking young woman. "Do you know Huang Qinglin?" She looked blank. I tried several other students. Finally, I asked a young man if he could point me to anyone majoring in public relations. "This school doesn't teach public relations," he said.

I went back and double-checked my notes. There was no mistake. That's what she had said. Had she given me a false identity to protect herself? Or was she a government agent? Was that why she betrayed the ink tossers? I had no idea.)

By the end of May, the square had become a smelly squatters' camp. Heaps of garbage baked in the hot sun. Makeshift latrines – municipal buses with their seats removed – stank terribly. Many Beijing students had already drifted back to campus. The only new faces were students arriving from the provinces. For a week, the student leaders debated whether to stay or go. Chai Ling, the most radical leader, was against retreating, but even she finally agreed.

For a farewell rally, the students commissioned a thirty-foot-tall plaster statue from the Central Academy of Fine Arts. On May 30, tens of thousands watched a midnight procession of four pedicabs, each loaded with a few segments. In Tiananmen Square, using a bamboo scaffold, the protesters assembled the pieces into a statue they dubbed the Goddess of Democracy. She held a torch aloft and wore a flowing robe, and looked like a Chinese Statue of Liberty. No one could miss the symbolism as she stared north at the huge new portrait hanging from the rostrum. She was facing down Chairman Mao.

14

"Safeguard Your Lives"

Top: Mutilated body of Liu Guogeng, a platoon leader. After he shot four people, Liu was beaten to death, set on fire and disemboweled by enraged crowds as the Chinese army shot its way into the capital on the night of June 3–4, 1989. Chinese authorities released this photo — and showed footage of the corpse on the evening news — to demonstrate that the soldiers were the victims.

Bottom: A rare shot of soldiers after they regained the square around dawn on June 4, 1989. The tents and bicycles belonged to the student demonstrators. The photo was also released by the Chinese government in a propaganda brochure.

On Friday night, June 2, I stayed up all night to chronicle a ridiculous invasion of six thousand unarmed foot soldiers. Some thought the government was trying to position troops near the square. Others believed it was a last attempt to retake the square without violence. Still others thought the soldiers were under orders to topple the Goddess of Democracy. In any case, the mission failed miserably. I watched as irate citizens upbraided the soldiers, who cowered in bushes across from the Beijing Hotel while radioing frantically for instructions.

After sleeping three hours, I gulped down some yogurt and ran out to see what was happening on Saturday. At noon, soldiers fired tear gas on demonstrators who had waylaid an ammunition truck. That afternoon five thousand troops confronted even more demonstrators outside the Great Hall of the People. But except for a beating or two, the showdown was uneventful. At one point, the two sides – soldiers and protesters – even competed to see who best sang "Without the Communist Party There Would Be No New China."

The government had lost all credibility. It had buzzed the square with military helicopters – and people laughed. It had tried to send in armored personnel carriers – and old ladies lay down in their path. The night before, it had dispatched foot soldiers – and civilians trapped them in the bushes. Many thought the battle of Beijing was over and the people had won. Most expected the army to go home and stop bothering them. Everyone, myself included, forgot one of Mao's most famous quotations: "Political power grows out of the barrel of a gun."

That night around six, on the northeast edge of the city, I spied another military convoy stopped on a road littered with broken glass. The *Globe* didn't publish on Sunday, but by force of habit, I got out of my car and counted eighteen truckloads of soldiers toting AK-47 assault rifles. I noticed their faces. They weren't green recruits but grim-faced, seasoned troops. I also noticed they were no longer wearing canvas running shoes.

"They're wearing boots," I told Jim Abrams, the AP bureau chief, when I called to swap information.

"I know," he said. "The army is coming in from every direction."

It was clear something would happen tonight. Had the government any finesse, it would have aired a trio of James Bond movies, and everyone would have stayed glued to their television sets. Instead, it broadcast this warning: "Do not come into the streets. Do not go to Tiananmen Square. Stay at home to safeguard your lives." The government might as well have issued engraved invitations.

"History will be made tonight," I said melodramatically to Norman. He was tired of all-nighters.

"That's what you said last time," he reminded me. I had said the same thing a week earlier when the AP's John Pomfret put out an urgent bulletin, which turned out to be false, that troops were marching down the Avenue of Eternal Peace clubbing anyone in their path. But Norman grudgingly came along for the second time. On the way, we stopped by the Reuters office, where they were frantically trying to confirm the first death, reportedly at Muxidi, a neighborhood on the far west side of the city. I volunteered to call the Fuxing Hospital in the area. The phone rang and rang, but no one answered, an ominous sign.

I did not know that the massacre had already begun. That Saturday evening, Deng Xiaoping had ordered the army to take the square by using "all necessary measures." At Muxidi, the troops found their way completely blocked by enormous crowds. As they tried to press forward, some in the crowd began stoning the soldiers in the front lines, People's Armed Police troops armed only with truncheons. The People's Armed Police, a huge paramilitary force that Deng had split off from the PLA in the 1980s, specialized in quelling domestic dissent. Yet their fiberglass helmets cracked under the torrent of stones. Some soldiers were injured. Behind them, their officers, armed with pistols, panicked and began shooting. Behind the People's Armed Police was the 38th Army, toting AK-47s. As all hell broke loose, they also began firing into the dense crowds. Soon soldiers were chasing civilians down alleyways and killing them in cold blood.

Residents screamed curses and hurled dishes and tea cups from their windows. The army units, from the provinces, probably had no idea those buildings housed the Communist Party elite, and raked the apartments with gunfire. Several people died in their homes that night. The nephew of the chief justice of the Supreme Court of China was shot in his own kitchen.

In the confusion, the army even shot some of its own soldiers. Behind the 38th Army was an armored personnel carrier unit belonging to the 27th Army. Driving in the darkness with their hatches down in an unfamiliar city, they inadvertently crushed to death soldiers from the 38th Army.

Norman and I got to the Beijing Hotel around 11 p.m., just as several armored personnel carriers whizzed by. So as not to advertise my presence, I parked the *Globe*'s car on Wangfujing, a busy shopping street adjacent to the hotel. Catherine Sampson, a reporter for the *Times* of London, offered to share her fourteenth-floor room. Simon Long, a BBC reporter, was also there filing a story. I needed quotes, and persuaded Norman to go with me to the square. Before I went out, I ditched my notebook so I wouldn't attract the attention of plainclothes police and, as a precaution against tear gas, stuffed a hankie in my pocket.

The square felt like a cross between a New York street festival and a British soccer riot. All the floodlights had been switched on, presumably for the benefit of the videocameras. Several hundred thousand people milled around, students in T-shirts, women in flowered dresses, roughly dressed peasants with unkempt hair. Parents snapped photos for the memory book of their children posing in front of the Goddess of Democracy. Western tourists in pedicabs filmed the raucous scene with videocameras. Since mid-April, Tiananmen Square had been a bigger tourist draw than the Great Wall.

The night before, the invasion of the foot soldiers had been harmless fun. With the radio and television warnings on Saturday evening, people were quivering like excited rabbits waiting to see what would happen next. Every ten minutes or so, a panic rippled through the crowd, sparking a mass stampede. After regrouping, another wave of hysteria hit the crowd, and they fled in a different direction. You had to run with them or risk being trampled to death. Once, I tried to take refuge behind a skinny lamppost, but a dozen others had the same idea.

No one had any idea how bad the situation was. Some had heard that the troops had begun to shoot, but the true magnitude of casualties wasn't yet known. People were indignant, not afraid. "It's unspeakable," said one young woman, her hands on her hips. "Worse than fascists." A young man stood on a traffic kiosk with a bullhorn, a small supply of bricks at his feet, shouting, "Down with fascists!" Others like me clutched their hankies. A couple of young men readied Molotov cocktails.

Norman and I walked toward the north end of the square, where an armored personnel carrier was burning. "Are there any soldiers inside?" I asked a student in a red headband. "We pulled them out first," he said. In the distance, I saw another armored personnel carrier in flames just in front of the Communist Party headquarters at Zhongnanhai. I had to pinch myself to make sure I wasn't dreaming. I looked at my watch. It was just past midnight on Sunday, June 4, 1989.

Some people claimed to hear gunfire. I strained to listen, but the din of stampeding humans was too loud. Someone whispered that the soldiers were holed up inside the Great Hall of the People. An Italian journalist grabbed my arm and told me the troops were inside the Forbidden City and would come pouring out any minute. By 12:50 a.m., I was frightened and tired. I had my quotes. "I'm not a cameraman," I said to Norman. "I've got what I need. Let's go."

We made our way back to the Beijing Hotel. Someone had fastened the wrought-iron gates shut with steel wire. We clambered over them and scurried across the parking lot. Plainclothes agents were frisking foreign reporters on the main steps. I walked around them and into the lobby, where a reporter for *USA Today* was filing a story on a pay phone. An agent armed with a pair of heavy shears cut the cord in mid-sentence. The reporter was so astonished his jaw dropped. Without a word, the policeman methodically chopped the wires on the rest of the lobby phones. Norman and I took the elevator up, still unnoticed.

That night, many reporters like myself used the Beijing Hotel as a base of operations. This was not the proverbial wartime-reporting-from-the-hotel-bar-stool-by-jaded-hacks syndrome. The Beijing Hotel had direct-dial telephones, bathrooms and an unparalleled view of the north end of Tiananmen Square. It was so close, in fact, that we were within range of the guns. A small number of reporters, like Andrew Higgins of the *Independent*, stayed among the crowds on the street. And an even smaller number, including UPI's Dave Schweisberg, remained in the center of the square all night with the students. Still other reporters never left their offices in the diplomatic compounds, relying on reports from their news assistants and wire service copy to write their first stories.

Back in Cathy Sampson's fourteenth-floor room, I moved a chair onto the balcony and began taking notes. Norman and I had left the square in the nick of time. Ten minutes later, the troops rolled in from the west side, the armored personnel carriers roaring easily over makeshift barricades. Protesters hurled stones. A cyclist gave impotent chase. I could hear the crackle of gunfire clearly now. I watched in horror as the army shot directly into the crowds, who stampeded screaming and cursing down the Avenue of Eternal Peace. At first, some protesters held blankets and jackets in front of them, apparently believing the army was using rubber bullets. Only after the first people fell, with gaping wounds, did people comprehend that the soldiers were using live ammunition.

I could not believe what was happening. I swore and cursed in Chinese and English, every epithet I knew. Then I realized I was ruining Simon's tape of the gunfire for his BBC broadcasts. I decided the only useful thing I could do was to stay calm and take the best notes of my life. A crowd below frantically tried to rip down a metal fence to erect another barricade. When it wouldn't budge, they smashed a window of a parked bus, put the gears in neutral and rolled it onto the street. They did that with a second and then a third bus. The rest of the crowd shouted, "*Hao!*" ("Good!").

The troops and tanks began closing in from all directions. At 1:20, I heard bursts of gunfire from the south, then another burst five minutes later. At 2:10, several thousand troops marched across the north side of the square. At 2:15, they raised their guns and fired into the dense crowd. I timed the murderous volley on my watch. It lasted more than a minute. Although the square was brightly lit, the streets surrounding it were dark. I couldn't see clearly if anyone had been hit. I assumed they must have been because of the angle of the guns, the length of the volley and the density of the crowds. A few minutes later I knew I was right as five ambulances raced by the hotel through the crowds. Cyclists and pedicab drivers helped evacuate the wounded and dying. I hadn't even noticed that a man had been shot in the back below my balcony until an ambulance stopped to pick him up.

At 2:23, tanks from the east fired their mounted machine guns at the crowds. At 2:28, I counted five more ambulances racing back to the square as people frantically cheered them on. In the distance, I saw red dots trace perfect arcs through the sky. "Fireworks?" I asked, turning to Cathy. Neither of us knew they were tracer bullets, and even if I did, I had no idea they were real bullets, coated with phosphorus to glow in the dark. In my first story, I called them "flares."

Cathy heard a bullet hit our balcony and pointed it out to me at the time. I have no memory of it. I should have realized the lead was flying, but I was so completely absorbed in taking notes. Nor did it occur to me that, as soldiers advanced across the north side of the square, pushing back protesters toward the hotel and beyond, our balcony was in the line of fire. The next day, when I examined the bullet hole, I felt nothing. It was insignificant compared to all the death and destruction going on around me. Besides, the hotel felt so normal, with its twin beds, blond-wood furniture and lace curtains. I learned only later that a tourist in the hotel had been grazed in the neck and the neon sign on the roof had been blasted to smithereens.

As the soldiers massacred people, the loudspeakers broadcast the earlier government message warning everyone to stay home. I leaned over the balcony to watch some people cowering in the parking lot. The crowd ran away after each heavy volley, then to my amazement crept back slowly, screaming curses and weeping with rage. Perhaps like me, they couldn't believe that the People's Liberation Army was shooting them. Or perhaps the decades of propaganda had warped their minds. Perhaps they were insane with anger. Or maybe after stopping an army in its tracks for days, armed only with moral certitude, they believed they were invincible. By now, I was recording heavy gunfire every six or seven minutes. It occurred to me that was about as much time as it took for people to run two blocks, calm down, regroup and creep back.

In the darkness I could make out a double row of soldiers, approximately one hundred and twenty men across. At 2:35, they began firing into the crowds as they marched across the square. With each volley, tens of thousands of people fled toward the hotel. Someone commandeered a bus, drove it toward the soldiers and was killed in a hail of gunfire. The crowd began to scream, "Go back! Go back!" The soldiers responded with another hail of bullets.

By 2:48, the soldiers had cleared a wide swath at the north end of the square. The crowd had thinned a bit. At 3:12, there was a tremendous round of gunfire, lasting several minutes. People stampeded down the Avenue of Eternal Peace. Some hopped the hotel's iron fence. I saw someone hit in the parking lot. Three minutes later, thousands of people were still running and bicycling and screaming hysterically past the hotel.

The soldiers strafed ambulances and shot medical workers trying to rescue the wounded. Some cyclists flung bodies across the back of their bicycles. Others just carried the wounded on their backs. Beijing's doughty pedicab drivers pitched in. Between 3:15 and 3:23, I counted eighteen pedicabs pass by me carrying the dead and wounded to the nearby Beijing Hospital, diagonally across from the hotel, or to the nearby Beijing Union Medical Hospital. I realized that I had seen the same driver in a red undershirt several times. The straw matting on his cart was soaked with blood.

At the Beijing Union Medical Hospital, someone had the presence of mind to photograph each corpse. The hospital put out an emergency call for all staff to return to work. In the next six hours, they treated more than two hundred victims, cleaning the wounds and stanching the bleeding. The staff sent home every victim who could possibly leave. Every bed was needed, and doctors feared the soldiers might come to the hospital to finish off the wounded. "It was terrible," said one surgeon, who operated without a break for twelve hours. "We are used to handling industrial accidents. We had never seen gunshot wounds before."

A Western military attaché told me the army used Type 56 semi-automatic rifles, a Chinese copy of the Soviet AK-47, which fires copper-clad steel-core bullets. The bullets cause terrible wounds because their soft copper jacket often flowers on impact, tearing through the first victim like a jagged knife. At close range, the steel-core bullets are powerful enough to rip through one or two more victims. The Chinese army also fired anti-aircraft machine guns that night, apparently loaded with armor-piercing bullets as thick as a man's thumb. Designed for use against light armored vehicles, their high-tensile carbon-steel bullets have a range of three miles and can easily pass through ten victims at close range.

Across Beijing, supplies of blood, plasma and bandages ran out that night. Red Cross workers stood on the sidewalk outside the Children's Hospital and appealed for blood. Chinese, who normally are afraid to give blood even when offered large cash incentives, streamed in to donate. "As soon as we went on the street at 3 a.m., we got a hundred volunteers," Xing Lixiang, director of Beijing's Blood Donation Squad, told me later.

I sat on Cathy's balcony and wrote in my notebook: "The people are all unarmed. The army has been firing on them for two hours." Over the loudspeakers, a cultured voice repeated: "The People's Liberation Army has a duty to protect the great socialist motherland and the safety of the capital." Soldiers were now shooting their way into Tiananmen Square from every direction. The barriers people had spent so long making did not stop the tanks at all. I looked at the wounded and dying below, at the pavement chewed up by tank treads, at the smashed barricades and the smoke rising from the square. Amidst the carnage, the traffic lights kept working perfectly, switching from green to yellow to red, and back to green.

Beijing was burning. I later learned that enraged protesters killed a number of soldiers with savage ferocity. After an army officer named Liu Guogeng shot four people, he was pulled from his jeep and beaten to death in front of the Telegraph Building, near the Central Committee headquarters. The crowd doused his corpse with gasoline, set it on fire and strung his charred remains, clad only in his socks, from a bus window. So everyone would know he was a soldier, someone stuck an army cap on his head and, in a chilling attempt at levity, put his glasses back on his nose. The furious mob still wasn't satisfied. Someone yanked him down and disemboweled him.

A twenty-year-old soldier, Cui Guozheng, met a similar fate just across from Pierre Cardin's swank Maxim de Pekin restaurant. Eyewitnesses said that he and another soldier got out after their truck got stuck on a piece of pavement. When the mob attacked the other soldier, Cui jumped back in the truck and fired his machine gun into the crowd, hitting an old woman, a man and possibly a child. The mob stormed the truck. Cui tried to flee and made it as far as the sidewalk before he was tackled. His charred corpse swung from a pedestrian flyover for several days. The government later said that Cui never fired, "in order not to wound the masses by accident."

Outside on the hotel balcony, I continued taking notes as bullets flew. At 3:45 a.m. there was another mass panic. This time, the crowd raced all the way down the street, until I was sitting in the middle, between them and the soldiers. Some young men wanted to toss Molotov cocktails. I saw others restrain them. At 3:56, the soldiers let loose another thunderous volley that lasted twenty seconds. I wondered how many other massacres had occurred where a journalist could sit on a balcony with a notebook and record the event down to the minute and the second.

At exactly 4 a.m., the lamps in the square snapped off. My heart froze. I could still see the students' tents near the edge of the square.

Inside the Great Hall of the People, the lights blazed. I wrote in my notes: "This is it. They're going to kill all the students. Are China's leaders watching from inside the GHOP?" I concentrated on counting a convoy of more than five hundred trucks as it rumbled into the square from the west. I could hear the thunder of distant gunfire to the south. By now, I was too tired to sit in the chair, so I slumped on the cement floor of the balcony, wrapped in a hotel blanket. By 4:30 a.m., the soldiers had sealed off the northeast corner of the square. Below me, a few thousand die-hards lingered. I couldn't believe my ears when they began singing revolutionary songs and chanting slogans. Some cyclists biked back and forth in the killing zone in front of the hotel.

I learned later that about five thousand students, many from the provinces, huddled that night around the Monument to the People's Heroes. Chai Ling led them in singing the "Internationale." Many had joined the hunger strike as a springtime lark. Now they were sure they were going to die on a cool night in June. When the lights went out, many students started weeping.

At precisely 4:40, the lights snapped back on. A new broadcast tape started. "Classmates," said a metallic male voice. "Please immediately clear the square." The message was repeated. I heard shots ring out in the square. Were they killing the students in cold blood? I later found out the soldiers were blasting away the students' sound system.

The students took a hasty vote and decided to leave. At 4:50, I recorded more heavy gunfire and thick black smoke in the south. At 5:17, the soldiers allowed the frightened students to file out through the south side of the square, making them run a gauntlet of truncheons and fists. The students straggled past the Kentucky Fried Chicken outlet and then north. As they turned west onto the Avenue of Eternal Peace, they saw a row of tanks lined up between them and the square. A retreating student hurled a curse. Suddenly, one of the tanks roared to life and mowed down eleven marchers from behind, killing seven instantly.

Afterwards, the government denied that tanks had crushed students at Tiananmen Square. But there were too many eyewitnesses, including an AP reporter. Eventually I tracked down two of the four survivors. One was a Beijing Sports Institute student whose legs were crushed when he pushed a classmate out of the tank's path. Another was a young factory technician whose right ear was torn off and right arm crushed. When I found him six months later, he was still afraid to leave his home because he knew he was a living contradiction of the government's Big Lie.

Dawn broke cold and gray on Sunday, June 4. As convoys of trucks and tanks rumbled in from the east, people frantically tried to push a bus into their path. One young man ran out and tossed a rock at the tanks. At 5:30, another convoy of a jeep and nine trucks went by, firing at random. People cowered in the bushes. At 5:36, a convoy of thirty trucks entered the square, followed by twenty armored personnel carriers and three tanks. At 5:47, two soldiers dismounted and started shooting their AK-47s into the crowd. I saw many fall to the ground, but I couldn't tell who had been hit and who was simply trying to take cover.

As Beijing awoke, ordinary people streamed toward the square, even as the pedicabs brought out more casualties. I saw a little girl and her parents take refuge behind a gray pick-up truck in the Beijing Hotel parking lot. The thick smoke from a burning bus gave some protective cover. By now, I was aware of the bullets whistling past. Still, it seemed unthinkable to stay inside. Over the next hour, I counted dozens of armored personnel carriers and tanks. It was overkill. Whom were they fighting now? Some of the tank drivers seemed lost. I saw three make U-turns, change their minds, then turn around again.

With daylight, I could see better. At 6:40, a tank plowed into the Goddess of Democracy, sending her plaster torso smashing to the ground. I saw flames and lots of smoke. Chai Ling, in a dramatic video released in Hong Kong, later testified: "Tanks began running over students who were sleeping in tents. Then the troops poured gasoline on tents and bodies and torched them." (This turned out to be false. The tents *were* set on fire, but apparently no one was in them.) By 6:47, dozens of tanks had lined up in formation at the north end of Tiananmen Square. From a distance, the square looked solid green. The army had finally retaken the square. The broadcast stopped.

Cathy switched on the early-morning newscast. Through the open balcony door, we could still hear gunfire. "A small minority of hoodlums created chaos in Beijing," the government announcer said. "The army came in, but not to suppress the students and the masses." I left Cathy, an insomniac, to take notes of the broadcast while I fell into an exhausted stupor on the bed. I had been working day and night without a break for more than seven weeks, and had had almost no sleep in the past seventy-two hours. I awoke with a start a short while later as three military helicopters roared by our window on their way to the square to pick up wounded soldiers, casualties of friendly fire. More ambulances whizzed by. From the balcony, I recorded a lull as a crowd massed outside the hotel. Fifteen minutes later, the soldiers charged forward, firing directly into the crowd. Bodies littered the ground. I saw a couple of people use their own blood to smear slogans on a sheet of plywood propped against a barricade at the intersection. "Kill Li Peng!" said one slogan. "Blood debts will be repaid with blood," read another.

By then, I was numb. It seems strange in hindsight – perhaps it was my Chinese starvation genes – but I felt I had to eat. I could tell it was going to be a long, bloody Sunday, and without some food, I knew I would not last the day. When I suggested we try to get breakfast downstairs in the hotel dining room, neither Cathy nor Norman objected. We left Simon Long behind to take notes.

Downstairs, I discovered that many other journalists had spent the night on their balconies and seemed to have the same surreal craving for scrambled eggs. Mitch Farkas, a husky soundman for CNN, told us that we had just missed a fight. When the Chinese waitresses announced there was only coffee, no food, because the chef was too upset to cook, a couple of reporters became unhinged and started yelling that they would cook their own breakfast. Suddenly the chef appeared in the dining room. He was crying. "I've seen too many people killed last night," he said, his shaking hand resting on a doorknob. Everyone stared at the ground, ashamed of the boorish behavior of their colleagues. A waitress broke the silence. "We are all Chinese," she said. "We love our country." Everyone began apologizing to everyone else, Mitch said, and the cook pulled himself together and announced that he would feed the reporters because "you are telling the world what happened."

As he recounted this, Mitch himself started crying. Like us, he was physically and mentally drained. When he broke down, Cathy and I did, too. I – who cried at the drop of a hat, when Beijing University was going to expel me, when I couldn't hack the labor at Big Joy Farm – realized that I hadn't shed a single tear all night. The enormity of the massacre hit home. So many people had been killed. Although it had been years since I was a Maoist, I still had harbored some small hope for China. Now even that was gone. I sat there weeping as the waitresses passed out plates of toast and fried eggs. None of us could eat.

By the time we returned to Cathy's room, it was after nine in the morning. A French tourist asked if she could look from our balcony. Tens of thousands of enraged people were streaming toward Tiananmen Square, and a huge crowd gathered at the intersection in front of the hotel. It was such an extraordinary moment, and yet they looked so ordinary. The men wore shorts and sandals. Some of the women carried purses. A few people even brought their children, because Chinese never use babysitters. In the background, city buses smoldered. Two blocks away, a double line of soldiers sat cross-legged, facing them, along the northeast edge of the square, backed by rows of tanks.

At 9:46, the crowd suddenly began stampeding away from the square. I couldn't figure out why. Then I saw that the soldiers had knelt into a shooting position and were taking aim. As the people ran, the soldiers fired into their backs. More than a dozen bodies lay on the ground. When the shooting stopped, there was absolute silence. Some of the wounded began to crawl to the edge of the road. To my amazement, the crowd began to creep *back* toward the square. At 10:09, another murderous barrage sent them racing down the street toward the hotel. They crept back toward the square *again*. At 10:22, there was another volley, lasting three minutes. I watched in horror as the soldiers advanced, shooting into the backs of fleeing civilians. The wounded lay, beyond reach of rescuers, as the soldiers kept up their heavy fire. The French tourist began shriek-ing hysterically, "They are crazy! Simply crazy!"

A Chinese friend had invited Norman to Sunday lunch. Just as I oddly had wanted to go for breakfast, he wanted to keep his date. I told him it would be insane to bicycle across town during a mas-sacre. When he wouldn't listen to me, I suggested he phone his friend.

"A nine-year-old girl was killed and they've just brought her body back," his friend said in a flat, emotionless tone. "I don't think it's a good idea to make the trip out here."

After the third barrage, I counted more than twenty bodies. One cyclist was shot in the back right below our balcony. There were two big puddles of blood on the Avenue of Eternal Peace. People carried the body of a little girl toward the back of the hotel. After twenty-three more minutes, a few people gathered up enough courage to approach the wounded. The soldiers let loose another blast, sending the would-be rescuers scurrying for cover. The crowd was enraged. I grimly kept track of the time. An hour later, the wounded were still on the ground, bleeding to death.

For the rest of the morning, and throughout the afternoon, this scene repeated itself again and again. In all, I recorded eight long murderous volleys. Dozens died before my eyes. By midafternoon, the crowd was down to about five hundred maniacs who stood on the corner screaming, "Kill Li Peng! Kill Li Peng!" Only when a steady rain began to fall at 4:15 did they finally drift away. The rain cleansed the street of the blood. When it stopped, the crowds returned, and the soldiers fired again, and again, and many more people died.

I thought how strange it was that Beijingers didn't want to get wet, but they weren't afraid of getting killed.

15

End of the Snitch Dynasty

Top: A lone man stops a column of tanks from Tiananmen Square. He was variously reported to have later been arrested and even executed, but this was never confirmed. In fact, it seems that authorities had no idea who he was. He presumably remains anonymous — and free.

Photo: AP/Jeff Widener

Bottom: Deng Xiaoping congratulating military officers for a job well done after the Tiananmen Massacre. This photo was published in a Chinese propaganda brochure.

"You'd better get out here," Norman said. It was noon on Monday, June 5, 1989. I dashed onto the balcony. A young man had leaped in front of a convoy of tanks. "Oh, no!" I cried. I held my breath. I was convinced he was going to die. My eyes filled with tears. Miraculously, the lead tank stopped. Standing underneath its giant muzzle, the young man looked like a kitten under a car fender. Annoyed at myself for crying so easily, I brushed away my tears so I could see clearly.

The tank twisted left, then right. Each time, the man stepped lightly in front. After a few feints, the tank switched off its engine. The whole street fell silent. The young man seemed to know his way around a tank. He scrambled onto its caterpillar treads and up its sloping sides. A shot cracked. He didn't flinch. He clambered onto the gun turret. Was he trying to reason with them? Another heart-stopping moment later, he climbed back down. *Now run!* I urged silently. But he didn't. The tank cranked up its motor and edged forward. Again, the man stepped in front and blocked it. By then a few people on the sidelines had regained their wits and they hustled him to safety. The convoy continued rumbling down the Avenue of Eternal Peace.

Who was he? Some overseas reports claimed he was a nineteen-year-old student named Wang Weilin and that he was later executed. Another report said he had been sentenced to ten years. Neither story was ever verified. My own theory was that authorities had no idea who he was, either. In 1994, a Chinese journalist confirmed my hunch. She told me that her bosses at the Xinhua News Agency had tried in vain to find the mystery tank man. "They wanted to show him to the world to prove that China doesn't kill people," she said.

In the excitement, everyone forgot the other hero. The driver of the lead tank had exercised extraordinary restraint. And although the Chinese government belatedly made propaganda hay out of this, my bet is the tank driver was secretly punished for losing the government so much face.

After the television footage of that dramatic confrontation made it clear that foreign journalists were holed up in the Beijing Hotel, the police came searching for us. Unfortunately, the documents we needed to obtain a room identified us as journalists. The police kicked out anyone they could find and confiscated notebooks and film. Before they got to Cathy's room, I asked Norman, who had a businessman's visa because he was working for Sun Microsystems, to rent one in his name. By simply hanging a Do Not Disturb sign on the door, I kept out the hotel staff for days. Each time I left the room, I hid my notes under the minibar fridge and inside the bathroom light fixture.

That Monday, tanks assumed a defensive position at the Jianguomen intersection, sparking rumors of civil war. The airport was pandemonium as most foreigners tried to flee. All the gas stations shut down. I stopped driving the old Toyota to save my half tank of fuel for an emergency. Taxi drivers began charging $500 or more for a ride to the airport. Chinese soldiers stopped one vanload of Americans, relieving them of their money, plane tickets, luggage *and* vehicle. When the Canadian Embassy rescued its students trapped on campuses, its convoy was stopped at gunpoint and forced to detour through the back roads of the countryside to avoid roadblocks on the main highways.

The now-deserted Beijing Hotel felt creepy. It closed its dining rooms, doused the lobby lights and issued special passes to the handful of remaining guests. For a few nights, even the streetlights in front were out. Crouching on my darkened balcony, I peeked at gun-toting soldiers scouring the shrubbery for civilians as if they were on a jungle reconnaissance mission. When the tanks rumbled by, I was so angry I wanted to hurl down a hotel chair, or at least a tea cup, like the residents at Muxidi the night of the massacre. Norman restrained me, a good thing, too, because one afternoon a trigger-happy soldier fired his AK-47 through the hotel's plate-glass doors.

The capital of China looked like a war zone. Bullet holes pock-marked lampposts and subway entrances. Charred buses littered the streets. Torn fences, concrete lane dividers, smashed dumpsters and overturned tractors – futile barricades against the army's onslaught – clogged roads all over the city. On the road leading north to the Great Wall, the carbonized hulks of tanks were still warm to the touch, like a backyard barbecue after the guests have left. Tank treads had chewed up the asphalt. Five years after the government repaved the roads, I could still feel the ridges as I drove along the Avenue of Eternal Peace.

Absurdly, Norman wanted to go to work that Monday and tried tempting me with the promise of eyewitness reports from the other side of the city. "It's too dangerous," I said flatly, refusing to let him go. "The army is shooting at anything that moves." I didn't take my own advice. With another reporter, I drove to Beijing University, where someone was reading out the names of slain students over the loudspeakers. Every person I saw was wearing a black armband. Many were weeping. As I walked around the familiar campus, I cried, too. I had spent so many years here, and now it had come to this: I was counting the dead at my alma mater.

At the National Minorities Institute, the front entrance was draped with crepe. The gate's walls were pasted with photos of slain students. Funeral music swelled from campus loudspeakers. At the University of Politics and Law, students had just finished holding a memorial service. Black and white banners said, "An eternal injustice" and "Tragic beyond compare in this world." A half hour earlier, a dead youth, crushed by a tank, had lain on a block of ice. The floor was still wet where the ice had melted. His face had been unrecognizable, someone said, like raw hamburger. His blood-soaked corpse, one of four unidentified victims, was being transported to

Qinghua University as a stand-in at another funeral. "We can't find our own classmates' bodies so we're using these," explained one exhausted female student, her eyes red and swollen.

At People's University, where Mao's grandson was enrolled, seven had died – five students and two children of faculty members. The pine trees at the front entrance were covered with white tissue chrysanthemums. On a branch, someone had hung a bloodstained khaki coat, the kind the students wrapped themselves in to keep warm at night. At one dorm, weeping students were conducting a memorial service for a slain classmate. Her ID card lay on top of a clean bedsheet. Two candles were burning. A tape recorder played a scratchy version of the now ubiquitous funeral music. I felt wrung out, utterly exhausted. I went back to the hotel and had a long cry. Then I wrote my stories.

The next day, two army units faced off near the Military Museum, intensifying rumors of civil war. Feelings were running high after the 27th Army's armored division had accidentally crushed some soldiers from the 38th. That Tuesday morning, I dropped by Wangfujing Street for my daily bullet-hole check of the *Globe's* Toyota. It was gone. It was just a car, an old one at that, and not even mine, but I was disconsolate. My getaway car, my security blanket, had disappeared. I felt utterly depressed, out of all proportion to the loss.

For seven weeks, I had been working nineteen-hour days. Radio and television stations in Canada and the U.S. had been calling at all hours of the night (their day) for quick updates. Norman had learned to pick up the phone in his sleep and pass it to me without a word. I didn't even bother sitting up or switching on the light. In the morning, I couldn't remember who called or what I said. Once, while filing a pre-dawn story to the *Globe,* I fell asleep at my desk. I awoke to find my modem on and the phone line still open to Toronto – at $250 an hour.

Many reporters were at their breaking point. Even before the massacre, Kathy Wilhelm, of the Associated Press, got so run-down covering the protests she was evacuated to Hong Kong and hospitalized. A BBC reporter collapsed. Several journalists dissolved into hysterical tears and couldn't function. Andrew Higgins of the

Independent was still shell-shocked after crawling on his belly through the bushes back to the Beijing Hotel the night of the massacre. A couple of days later, he remained convinced that he would be hit by a stray bullet and refused to stand upright in my hotel room, actually crawling along the carpet while he talked to me.

For years, I had weighed a constant 124 pounds, but as a result of the Tiananmen diet – lots of missed meals and little sleep – I lost 14 pounds. After the theft of the *Globe's* car, I decided to cheer myself up with my first real meal in three days. Norman and I chose the nearby swank Palace Hotel, which, despite roadblocks, massacres and martial law, managed to offer a lavish daily buffet because it was partly owned by the People's Liberation Army.

Norman and I had just stepped out of our hotel at noon when we heard the telltale roar of an approaching convoy. I ducked behind some cedar shrubs in the parking lot to count tanks. Perhaps they didn't like me taking inventory: the soldiers opened fire. We hit the ground, just like in the movies. We were so close the bullets didn't whistle. Only six yards, the skimpy shrubs and a wrought-iron fence separated us from them. I noticed Norman's head was up and realized with a jolt that he was still counting tanks.

"Get down!" I screamed. When he ignored me, as husbands do, I hissed, "If they don't kill you now, I'm going to kill you later!" He got down. The shooting seemed to go on for an eternity. I couldn't tell if they were firing in the air, at someone else or at us. Something smashed into my right elbow. I screamed, "I've been hit!" After the convoy passed, I got up and checked myself. I had been struck by a ricocheting stone. "You're always screaming before you even know if you're hurt," said Norman disgustedly, but he looked relieved.

At the Palace, the suave maître d' ignored our head-to-toe grime. I suppose he was just thankful we didn't have gunshot wounds. One of his waiters had been grazed by a bullet and was serving lunch with a bandaged arm.

By Wednesday, China seemed on the brink of civil war. A doctor, exhausted from caring for the wounded, tried to check himself into his own hospital with a bleeding ulcer. It refused to take him, citing secret orders to clear the beds for possible bombing victims. The

Canadian Embassy hastily dusted off contingency plans to move into its bomb-shelter basement. Officers at the People's Armed Police headquarters in Beijing began stockpiling food. For a few days, frantic diplomats were unable to rouse anyone at the Ministry of Foreign Affairs.

Just about the time we hit the ground in the hotel parking lot, the PLA was firing on the Jianguomenwai Diplomatic Compound. Two daughters of Sidney Rittenberg, one of our old China Hand friends, cowered on the floor as bullets ripped into their ceiling. Soldiers stormed the compound searching for a sniper they claimed had killed an infantryman. Hysterical diplomats and their families took refuge in their embassies and, after a sleepless night, fled to the airport at dawn, their national flags taped to their cars.

I panicked, too. Some foreign correspondents, especially those with children, had already left for Hong Kong or Tokyo. Ann Rauhala, my foreign editor, said the decision to stay or go was completely up to me. After five days of random killing, I was terrified the soldiers would raid the Beijing Hotel and murder us in our rooms. I started shivering uncontrollably. Troops had beaten up several television crews and smashed their equipment on the night of the massacre. At one point, they blindfolded a Reuters correspondent and threatened to kill him. A French reporter had been shot in the arm. A Taiwanese journalist was hit in the mouth. The bullet smashed his teeth, went clean through his throat and just missed his spinal cord. He spent a year in a wheelchair, but survived.

"What should I do?" I asked Norman, all but wringing my hands.

"Well, if I were a housewife, I'd go to Hong Kong," he said dryly. "But if I were a journalist, you couldn't pry me out of here."

He was right. I calmed down and never thought about leaving again. Instead, I calculated how much telephone wire I needed if I tossed the phone out my office window and walked it across a construction site to the Canadian Embassy's basement. I wanted to be sure I could keep filing stories.

Canada sent special planes to evacuate its citizens. The embassy urged me to get on one, but allowed me to give my seat to a friend. A skeletal staff stayed behind, including the ambassador, Earl Drake, and his wife, Monica Gruder Drake. Although she wasn't much older than I, Monica acted as my surrogate mother, cheerfully ordering me to call in daily so she wouldn't worry. She also promised me some of her canned goods in the event of civil war.

Sun Microsystems evacuated all its expatriate staff to Hong Kong, but Norman refused to go. A couple of days later, when he was the only one left in the Beijing office, the U.S. computer company offered to fly us "anywhere, any class." I thought longingly of first-class tickets to Paris. By the end of the week, Sun was threatening to fire Norman if he didn't leave immediately. He gallantly declared he would stay as long as his wife did, dashing my dreams of croissants and café au lait. Finally, Sun's lawyers in Silicon Valley faxed him a release form to sign, absolving them of liability should he be maimed or killed.

By this time, there didn't seem to be any more point in counting tanks in the square. I decided it was time to move back to our apartment. The taxis had stopped running, as had city buses. Our only remaining means of transportation was the *Globe's* old Forever bike. With our apartment a forty-minute ride away, I called the Canadian Embassy for advice on which routes through the city were safe. A military attaché came on the phone.

"This is Jan Wong," I said.

"Do you look Chinese?" he asked.

"Well, yes."

"Do you have a T-shirt with a Canadian flag?"

I was wearing an Irish green T-shirt, a freebie from the sports department of the *Boston Globe*. It had a cartoon of a football player that said, "The Globe's here." But I didn't think the military attaché wanted to know all that. No, I told him, I didn't have a T-shirt with a Canadian flag.

"Tie a scarf over your head," he advised brusquely and hung up.

Great, I thought. *I'll look like a Chinese in a stupid T-shirt wearing a scarf in a 95-degree heat wave.* I didn't have a scarf, either. So I slung the *Globe's* laptop computer around my neck and climbed onto the unpadded rear rack of Norman's bike. He pedaled, and I swayed, yelping every time we hit a hole. And that, with the recent urban warfare, occurred about every four yards.

On Thursday, June 8, Deng Xiaoping ordered the leaders of the warring 27th and 38th Armies, and their supporters, to a meeting where he forced them to shake hands. As quickly as the rumors of civil war had started, they died down.

That afternoon, I went with a friend to the Beijing Union Medical Hospital. Hysterical relatives, clutching pictures of loved ones, were besieging the front gate. Hospital staff were turning away all reporters. My friend, who had once worked there, steered me to an unguarded staff entrance at the back, and we slipped through unnoticed. As we walked down the dim hall, she remarked on the sweet, musty odor that filled the corridors.

"Smell that?" my friend said. "That's the smell of death. I think they must be sprinkling lime over the bodies."

She knocked on a door. Inside, she introduced me to a middle-aged doctor. He was nervous about talking. "I have a lot of opinions on what happened," he said, "but I won't say what I think until this is all over." The morgue was jammed with more than a hundred bodies, he said. The hospital had obtained extra refrigerated cases that held four corpses each, but that still wasn't enough. That Saturday night he had been called out of bed and had worked until dawn trying to bandage shattered bodies.

How did he feel? I asked. Had he been affected?

"Not at all," he said. But I noticed his leg twitched uncontrollably and that he smiled at all the wrong times. "Everyone is terrified," he conceded. "The government has stationed its own people in the hospital. All the wounded have been placed under guard in a special ward. The guards tell us who to treat, when we can see our patients, even when we can change a dressing."

At People's Hospital across the city, doctors were forced to carry their patients on stretchers to police interrogations. Only one young man, the factory technician who had been run over by a tank, was excused. As a special favor, his father was allowed to submit to the interrogation in his place.

Each night, I sat glued to the television set, horrified and fascinated by the evening news. For two hours, up from the normal thirty minutes, I watched footage of helmeted soldiers handcuffing "counter-revolutionary thugs" to trees or tossing them into trucks. Close-ups showed the detainees' swollen, bruised faces. Ten days after the massacre, the government issued a Most Wanted list of twenty-one student leaders. Within a few weeks, thirty people were summarily executed for "counter-revolutionary crimes" ranging from torching a military vehicle to taking guns abandoned by the soldiers.

The universities were closed to outsiders, but it was easy for me to slip past the guards. In a Qinghua University dorm, I was interviewing a student leader, Li Xiaolong, when his class Party secretary burst into the room. "I understand you've been giving interviews to the *Globe and Mail*," the cadre barked. My heart beat wildly. Li was already under investigation for his leadership role in the hunger strike. Now I was going to get him arrested and myself expelled. I shoved my notebook under a pillow on one of the bunkbeds and turned my face to the wall. I picked up a book – it was an English grammar – and prayed the Party secretary would ignore me. Li kept his cool.

"I've never met the *Globe and Mail* reporter," he lied smoothly.

"We have reports. We know you've been seeing the foreign journalist."

"It's not true. It's unfounded gossip," Li said. After interrogating him for several minutes more, the Party secretary gave up and left. Li resumed telling me about four of his schoolmates who died in the massacre, but it took me several minutes to start breathing normally.

The government opened eighteen snitch hotlines. Millions of Beijingers had joined in the demonstrations. Were people flooding the switchboard with calls? I dialed the hotline to see if I got a busy signal. An operator answered on the first ring.

"So how does this work?" I asked.

"We want concrete information. The more concrete, the better," she said enthusiastically. "We guarantee you anonymity."

"Have many people called in?" I asked. She hesitated. When I asked if she was getting useful information, she smelled a reporter and hung up.

The hotline idea backfired. Some callers let loose a stream of invective. Others reported the names of two mass murderers – Deng

272 RED CHINA BLUES

Xiaoping and Premier Li Peng. It was a turning point. Ever since the Song dynasty (960–1279), Chinese society had been organized on the *Bao-Jia* system, a feudal method of collective responsibility and control in which the security of each household was directly tied to that of ninety-nine others. If one household created a problem, the others would all be punished. Inevitably, it created a culture of snitching.

In the People's Republic, betrayal had once been so common that a single anonymous letter could spark a lengthy inquiry. The Chinese had a saying: "A four-fen stamp buys three years' investigation." The massive demonstrations at Tiananmen Square, the people power, the calls for democracy, all were watershed events, but to me the hotline fiasco symbolized the beginning of the end of feudal repression. No longer would people abet their oppressors. There were still isolated cases of betrayal, of course, but I was startled and gladdened by the universal revulsion. As someone who had twice ratted on others, I rejoiced at the end of the "snitch dynasty."

Beijing was like an occupied city. With many student leaders on the run, the army set up checkpoints throughout the capital. One night, gun-toting soldiers flagged down Jim Munson, Beijing bureau chief for the CTV television network. Munson had left his journalist's identification at home. Thinking fast, he pulled out his American Express card. The young soldier examined the profile of the helmeted Roman gladiator on the credit card, sized up Munson's Big Nose – and waved him on. "Don't leave home without it," Munson yelled as he drove off.

After the theft of the *Globe's* Toyota, I went everywhere on bike or by foot. Two and a half weeks after the massacre, I was strolling home late one sunny afternoon when I noticed a car and a motorcycle trailing me on the bike path. They slowed to a stop. Three rough looking men in their late twenties made a bee-line for me. I thought they were muggers. Bracing for a fight, I slipped both arms through the straps of my backpack.

"Miss, we have something to discuss with you," one of them said with a sneer. Before I could answer, two of them gripped my arms, and the third propelled me across the sidewalk to the car.

One man pushed my head down as the others tried to stuff me into the back seat.

As I struggled, rush-hour bicycle traffic came to a stop. A few weeks earlier, dozens of cyclists might have leaped to my aid. But the post-Tiananmen crackdown was already well under way. The terror was too great. Everyone just watched. For a split second, I couldn't decide whether to scream in English or Chinese. Fu the Enforcer had ingrained in me a fear of incorrect tones. I knew I would get them wrong in my panic.

"Help! Help!" I screamed, in English.

The men abruptly stopped trying to cram me into the car. Still gripping my arms, they conferred briefly with one another. I didn't register what they said. As suddenly as they had grabbed me, they dropped me. They got back in the car. I collected myself sufficiently to note it was a brown Volkswagen Santana. I concentrated on memorizing the license plate. But as the car pulled away, I saw that it had none.

Half a dozen soldiers on martial-law duty in front of the nearby Australian Embassy had heard my screams and stepped onto the bicycle path for a better look. I stumbled over to them.

"Some men in that brown car tried to grab me," I said, still trembling. "Could you radio for help on your walkie talkie and tell the police to stop the car?"

"What car?" said a soldier sarcastically. His buddies laughed.

I must have been the only person on the street too dumb to realize my would-be kidnappers were plainclothes police. Maybe they knew I was a reporter and were trying to scare me. More likely, they thought I was a Chinese student, and when I yelled in English, they realized their mistake. Too bad, I thought later, after I calmed down. I should have gone with them. It would have been a much better story.

I never had nightmares after Tiananmen, but I found myself crying at the oddest moments. In the middle of doing something, I would suddenly have a flashback. Once, Yan Yan and I were in a restaurant eating lunch when we both gradually dissolved into tears.

After Tiananmen, one of the first questions I set out to answer was, Why had the massacre happened at all? The students had already voted to leave the square. Most had drifted back to campus. To any neutral observer, it was clear that the protests were winding down. Why didn't the government let hot weather and boredom take their toll? Why did the army launch a full-scale invasion of Beijing? Use anti-aircraft guns? Tanks? Armor-piercing bullets? I couldn't just go on to the next story. I needed to understand what had happened, both as a reporter and for myself. Gradually, I pieced the puzzle together.

The Tiananmen Massacre was part of an old-fashioned power struggle. After the massive demonstrations that spring, which must have reminded Deng Xiaoping of the worst days of the Cultural Revolution, he became convinced that further liberalization would weaken the Communist Party – and his own grip on power. But his dapper, golf-playing heir apparent, Zhao Ziyang, still endorsed Deng's original thesis that Marxist dogma handcuffed the profit motive and that without reform, the Party was doomed.

Yet China's paramount leader wanted a yes-man, not someone who thought for himself. When Deng decided to use the army to suppress the demonstrations, Zhao alone among the Politburo members objected, his final act of disobedience. The bloody massacre that followed Zhao's purge had a two-fold objective: to force his many supporters in the government and Party into total surrender, and to crush the fledgling democracy movement.

In forty years of Communist rule, no one, not even Mao, had ever dared bring tanks into the capital. So that there would be no finger-pointing afterward, Deng decided everyone had to have blood on their hands. He ordered every single military region to *biao tai,* or demonstrate their attitude, with a tangible show of loyalty. Many commanders dragged their feet, but Deng waited, and lobbied. Those who didn't go along were arrested and eventually court-martialed. It took fifteen tense days, from the declaration of martial law to the start of the massacre, for him to bring every general on side.

Because I had once admired my soldier classmates so much, I became obsessed with trying to understand how and why China's 3.5-million-member army had changed. When the Museum of Military History opened a post-massacre exhibit extolling the army for its "glorious" performance, I looked there for a rank-and-file soldier to interview on Chinese Army Day, August 1, 1989.

The museum's parking lot displayed a dozen burned-out tanks. Inside, fourteen plaster busts of "martyred" soldiers, including the two who had been immolated, dominated the main exhibition room. I approached a young man in civilian clothes whose brush cut indicated he was a soldier. He turned out to be a junior officer in the People's Armed Police. When I whispered that I was a reporter, he didn't recoil, and even offered to show me around.

I'll call him Yang. As we looked at some bloodstained uniforms and tattered banners, I told him I'd heard that Beijingers were treating the People's Armed Police and the People's Liberation Army like occupying armies. Two soldiers had been garroted near where I lived, I said. Another was stabbed to death. The military had issued commemorative watches to soldiers who had participated in the massacre, but few dared wear them. Instead, the watches almost immediately appeared in Beijing's flea markets, where foreigners snapped them up as souvenirs. I remembered how my soldier classmates had once proudly worn their uniforms, even when off-duty. I asked Yang, who was wearing a blue T-shirt, sandals and white dungarees, if I was imagining that off-duty soldiers avoided wearing their uniforms these days.

"Now it is a badge of shame," he said. When martial law was declared, he said, waitresses sometimes refused to serve soldiers. But since the massacre, civilians had been elaborately polite. "It's their way of telling you how much they hate you," he said.

Based in a city a thousand miles away, Yang, twenty-six, had arrived in Beijing on an unrelated mission the day after martial law was declared. He had often gone to Tiananmen Square to listen to speeches. On the night of the massacre, he had lain awake in his army hostel, listening to the crackle of gunfire. The shooting had been so close he could smell the gunpowder.

"They shot a lot of people, didn't they?" he said hesitantly. With a nervous smile, he added a horrifying detail. "Some soldiers sang as they shot people."

"What song?" I asked, morbidly curious.

" 'Our Army Is Marching toward the Sun,'" Yang said.

I was sorry I had asked. It was the pep song I remembered my soldier classmates singing back in my Maoist days.

At People's Armed Police headquarters, he had picked up some gossip. Deng Xiaoping himself had given the order to shoot, delicately phrased as "use all necessary measures," in his role as chairman of the Central Military Commission. Few soldiers dared talk about what happened, Yang said. Some felt they had been used in a power struggle. Many felt intense guilt. "But what we feel in our hearts and carrying out orders are two different things."

Yang suddenly pulled two tickets out of his pocket. "It's for an Army Day dance at the Beijing Officers Club," he said. "Would you like to go with me?" We strolled over to the club, right next to the museum, flashed our tickets at the armed guard and walked into a cool oasis of privilege. In the ballroom, festooned with Christmas lights, we took a spin on the parquet floor. White-haired, heavy-set officers in shirts and ties danced with lithe young women in dresses and high-heels. "Look," said Yang. "No one is wearing an army uniform."

If morale was bad among the rank and file, what did senior officers think? Did they support Deng? A few months later, I arranged through a friend to interview a top general in one of China's seven military regions. The general, whom I'll call Fu, had joined the Communists in the 1930s to fight the Japanese invaders. The son of poor peasants, he had been intensely loyal his whole career – until June 4, 1989. "He can't accept that the army fired on people," his daughter told me.

For the first time in his fifty-year career, General Fu had lost the faith. Even during the Cultural Revolution, when he was exiled to the provinces, his belief in communism had never wavered. But now he, too, had joined the ranks of the disillusioned. "Of course there was a problem with the government," said General Fu, who had neatly cropped gray hair and an erect military bearing. "Otherwise, why all of a sudden did so many people come out on the streets?"

We were sitting in his austere living room, sipping jasmine tea. Later he hosted me at a simple dinner. Because of his rank, he had a chauffeured car, traveled by "soft berth" on trains and lived in a magnificent home by Chinese standards – eleven bright, airy rooms. A soldier had been assigned full time to cook, clean, wash the laundry and fetch boiling water for the general's tea habit. Otherwise, he lived simply, as army officers had been exhorted to do in Maoist times. His floors were bare, the walls whitewashed. His furniture was army issue – a heavy, scarred desk, steel beds and inexpensive rattan chairs. His only luxury was a large Chinese-made color television. He stuck to his old-fashioned baggy clothing, and looked askance at his fashion-conscious daughter in her black leather miniskirt and bomber jacket.

Despite his high rank, General Fu wasn't politically invulnerable. He chose his words with care, his voice lowered. When the soldier-servant came in the room, the general fell silent. He agreed to talk to me in part because he was anxious to hear first-hand what had happened in Beijing. He confessed that he no longer believed his own government. During the pro-democracy protests, the army had issued a specific order banning soldiers from listening to Voice of America broadcasts. He had tuned in every day. As he pumped me for details of Tiananmen, I realized that even senior army offi-cers had been kept in the dark. He listened gravely as I described the soldiers shooting again and again into the backs of fleeing demonstrators.

"Deng Xiaoping didn't handle it properly," said General Fu. "It didn't have to be handled that way. It was a mistake." He looked steadily at me. "How many died in all?"

"I'm not sure," I said. "I'm still not sure."

How many died was a question that particularly obsessed me. Even if I wanted to forget, I couldn't. Everywhere I went as a reporter in China, when people learned I had been there, they asked: How many died? At first, Beijing asserted that no one died in Tiananmen Square. In the face of universal disbelief, it then announced a death toll of 323, but contended that many of the victims were soldiers. It didn't specify how they had died, but considering the protesters were unarmed, it's likely many were killed by friendly fire.

Foreign media estimates of the death toll ranged from several hundred to several thousand. Like other reporters, I visited hospitals in the days after the massacre, but their numbers counted only those who died there. Many victims who were patched up and sent home might not have survived. And many others who died in the streets were never taken to hospital. I know of several cases where bodies were turned directly over to their families.

As the government began cracking down, keeping records, or even acknowledging their existence, became a dangerous political act. One couple had to search for two harrowing weeks through forty-six hospitals before they found the body of their son. While some Beijing residents had taken the precaution of slipping a note with their names and addresses in their pockets before going out that night, many demonstrators were illiterate migrant workers who may have died in anonymity. Their families back in the village would know only that some time after mid-1989, they were never heard from again. Few relatives were foolhardy enough to come to the capital asking troubling questions.

After much research, I believe the death toll was about three thousand, based partly on a Chinese Red Cross report, issued a day after the massacre, of 2,600 dead. Under intense government pressure, the Chinese Red Cross almost immediately retracted the figure, but the Swiss ambassador, acting in the name of the International Red Cross, quietly confirmed that initial number and passed it on to other ambassadors in Beijing. What's more, if several hundred soldiers died in friendly fire, then many, many more civilians must have died trying to block the army's approach. Several Western military attachés who witnessed the massacre also concur with the estimate of three thousand dead, based on crowd density, troop size, volume of firing and the use of combat-type ammunition.

Will we ever know the true number? Many think not. I disagree. Like all preceding Chinese governments, Beijing's mania for record-keeping is obvious. If the government can tell us that "before the rains on May 18, 1989, the Municipal Public Transport Company drove seventy-eight buses and the Bureau of Goods and Materials sent four hundred thick wooden sheets to the square to protect students from the downpour," then they also know how many died. They are the ones with access to cemetery and crematorium records.

One day, a new government may launch an investigation of the Tiananmen Massacre. Then, perhaps, the truth will finally be told. Still, it is sobering to remember that, twenty years after the first Tiananmen crackdown in 1976, few details have emerged. That earlier death toll remains shrouded in mystery. How long will it take – fifty years? a hundred? – before we will finally know how many people died that June at Tiananmen Square.

16
Professor Ding's List

Top left: Professor Ding with her husband. They are standing beside a cabinet holding the ashes of their teenaged son, one of the first people killed during the Tiananmen Massacre. Photo: Jan Wong

Top right: Wei Jingsheng, during a brief period of freedom in September, 1993, after serving nearly fifteen years in prison. He was subsequently accused of trying to overthrow the government, and sentenced to fourteen more years in December, 1995. Photo: AP/Greg Baker

Bottom: Zhang Lin with his grandfather, outside the adobe cottage where he grew up in Anhui province. Photo: Jan Wong/ Globe and Mail

The guns at Tiananmen Square killed my last illusions about China. Long after I stopped being a Maoist, I had tried to make allowances. China was, after all, a developing country struggling to come to grips with enormous problems of poverty and overpopulation. But my disillusionment had been an inexorable process, ever since my fifth day in China, in 1972, when Guide Bai berated the hapless auto mechanic on the steps of the Overseas Chinese Hotel.

Like the Chinese themselves, I misjudged how hard-line the regime really was. In 1988, when I arrived back as a reporter, I had tried giving the benefit of the doubt to Deng Xiaoping's unique combination – an iron fist ruling a capitalist-style economy. I had thought that because so many other things had changed, the Communist leaders must have changed, too. Many Chinese reinforced this sense, especially young people, who had been mere babies during the Cultural Revolution. Like the post–Vietnam War generation in the States, young Chinese had no sense of history. Millions of ordinary citizens also miscalculated the risks. Caught up in the euphoria of the first anti-government demonstrations in Chinese Communist history, they believed they could make a difference. How innocently we had all stuffed hankies in our pockets before going to the square.

In a single hot June night, that innocence was lost. When Chinese realized those next to them were falling in a bloody heap, they were shocked to the core. For them, and for me, the Chinese Communist Party had forfeited its Mandate of Heaven, its moral right to rule. In future, I knew that people would expect nothing more from the Party. The next time they battled in the streets, they would not go undisguised or unarmed. They were no longer naive, and neither was I.

For a full year and four months, I found it impossible to write a story that wasn't related in some way to Tiananmen. It wasn't just that I was obsessed. The reality was that no important aspect of life in China had been untouched by the tragedy. In 1970, when four student protesters were shot dead at Kent State University, the intense American reaction helped end the Vietnam War. In China, so many, many more had died. Every key university in Beijing had become a Kent State, with four, five or seven of its students shot dead that night. Tiananmen affected economics, politics, education, science, the arts, foreign relations and, of course, the military.

I had grossly misjudged the importance of dissent. In the 1970s, I had been startled by the first protest posters at Democracy Wall, but I considered them an isolated phenomenon. By1988, I had been dismissive, almost condescending, toward activists like Ren Wanding. I thought their time had passed. They seemed like relics from a bygone era, ignored even by the government they were trying to subvert. After doing a few stories on dissidents, I had left them to my American colleagues, many of whom seemed fixated on cold war politics. But after the Tiananmen Massacre when Ren was sentenced to seven years in prison on charges of counter-revolutionary propaganda and incitement, I felt I had made a huge mistake. And when authorities sentenced one of the ink throwers to life in prison – *life*, for lobbing a bag of ink at a Mao portrait – I knew I had to start paying attention.

By 1993 I was paying so much attention that when Wei Jingsheng was released after serving fourteen and a half years of a fifteen-year sentence, I invited him to my home. "Guess who's coming to dinner?" I told the staff. They were in a tizzy. Despite a domestic-news blackout, they had all heard of the man who had

dared call Deng a fascist dictator. I had no idea what to feed someone who had spent one-third of his life in the gulag. Most Chinese
were revolted by bloody slices of beef and considered raw lettuce an
invitation to dysentery. But I figured Wei Jingsheng wasn't an average Chinese. I suggested to Mu Xiangheng, the *Globe*'s chef, that he
make rare filet of beef, french fries and a green salad.

Wei arrived dressed against the November chill in a bulky
sweater, a black leather vest, baggy pants and tan construction boots.
His hair, which he cropped short, had not gone white, as some early
reports had said. But his face was puffy, and he had lost more than
half his teeth, replaced by an unnervingly beautiful false set. His
hand was soft and cool when I shook it. I had invited several foreign friends who spoke Chinese because Wei, who was forty-three,
spoke no English. I introduced Cook Mu as he passed around platters of beef.

"This is Wei Jingsheng," I said. "This is Cook Mu. He's a
Communist Party member." Wei jumped to his feet and pumped
Cook Mu's free hand.

"We're all one big family," Wei said warmly. "I nearly became a
Party member myself at one point."

"Yes, I heard that," said Cook Mu, clearly dazzled. Here was a
law-abiding Party member greeting China's most prominent dissident like he was a rock star. If this was how people at the grassroots
felt, Deng Xiaoping was in trouble.

I asked Wei about his puffy face.

"I suspect authorities added hormones to my rice. They wanted
me to gain weight because they were planning to release me in
early 1989. Then Fang Lizhi [the dissident astrophysicist] and others got wind of it, and started a petition so they could claim credit
for my release. The demonstrations that spring, and later the
Tiananmen crackdown, sealed my fate. I had already been transferred to a salt farm as a transition, but I had to spend four years
more there."

Wei staged six hunger strikes in jail. "I wanted newspapers, pen
and paper, a radio, better food for political prisoners," he said. One
strike lasted a hundred days. "I took only water," he said. When he
was down to skin and bones, authorities gave in to all his demands,

except for a radio. "They were afraid I'd tune in to the enemy stations" – the BBC and the Voice of America. During another prolonged hunger strike, his jailers held him down and stuffed a feeding tube up his nose. "The guard deliberately raked it back and forth. It was excruciating," said Wei. It was strange to be talking about such things over dinner, but the discussion didn't dampen his appetite.

Wei Jingsheng was the eldest of four children of a senior Communist Party official in Beijing. At twelve, his father made him memorize a page of Mao's works each day or go without dinner. An excellent student, Wei entered the prestigious middle school attached to People's University, graduating at the start of the Cultural Revolution. In 1966, at age sixteen, he joined millions of other Red Guards tramping around the country, "planting the seeds of revolution." Until then, Wei Jingsheng, whose name meant Born in the Capital, had led a sheltered existence in Beijing. At one rural train station, he was shocked to see a naked woman, smeared with mud and soot, begging for food. It was a revelation, the first time he realized that China was not a socialist utopia.

Wei spent several years laboring in the countryside in his ancestral village in Anhui province, one of China's poorest. Later, like many children of elite Communist Party officials, he was able to escape a life of unremitting toil by joining the army, at the time considered a prestigious assignment. After he was demobilized, Wei was given a state job as an electrician at the Beijing Zoo. He often failed to show up for his shift, and instead spent his time discussing politics with his friends.

I remembered how fearless he had seemed at Democracy Wall in 1979. In one of his Big Character posters, he called Marxism-Leninism Mao Zedong Thought "an even more brilliant piece of quackery than any of the old itinerant pox doctors' panaceas." Wei was not naive about the horrors awaiting him. Among the daring articles he published in *Explorations*, his samizdat, was an Amnesty International report on the treatment of Chinese prisoners. Had he been afraid back then? I asked.

"I called a meeting of all the activists," he recalled, "and drew my finger across my throat. I told them that they must realize their activities could mean they would die. I said that if they weren't prepared for it, or if they had to think about their parents or their wives or their children, they should back off. By the end of the meeting, there were just three people left." He smiled wryly. "All three of us served time in prison."

At his trial, the prosecutor accused Wei of leaking military secrets, including telling a foreign journalist the name of China's commander-in-chief during its 1979 war with Vietnam. "Whoever has heard of a victory being won because the commander-in-chief's name was not revealed?" Wei mocked, speaking in his own defense because no Chinese lawyer would offer an innocent plea on his behalf. "Conversely, whoever has heard of defeat being suffered simply because the enemy knew the name of one's own commander-in-chief?"

Back then, when he first opposed the government at Democracy Wall, few Chinese even knew how to say dissident, clumsily rendered in six characters – *chi bu tong zheng jian zhe,* or one who holds differing political views. The government decided to make an example of its first prominent dissident, a classic technique of killing the chicken to scare the monkeys.

Instead, like a reverse domino effect, Wei's arrest, trial and harsh sentence created more heroes. A fellow dissident who refused to testify against him was punished with a six-year jail term. Someone else who published a transcript of Wei's secret trial was arrested and spent more than ten years behind bars. That same person's younger brother became an activist, too. When still another person protested all their arrests, *he* was sentenced to fifteen years in prison.

Through his network of elite friends, Wei subsequently learned how his sentence had been decided. "The Politburo met. Some wanted to execute me. Others argued it was not necessary. Deng Xiaoping sat there grimly," said Wei. "Finally, Vice-Premier Li Xiannian came up with a compromise. 'Don't execute him, but give him a heavy sentence.' The order was handed down to the Beijing Communist Party secretary in charge of law and order. He scratched his head. 'I know what *don't execute* means, but what does *heavy sentence* mean?' He ordered an aide to find out, but the aide said, 'That's not necessary. You know what *heavy sentence* means.'

The Party secretary said, 'Fifteen years?' His assistant nodded. And that's how I got fifteen years," said Wei.

He was first sent to death row at the Beijing Lock-up. In a densely populated country, space, or the lack thereof, was used to reward and punish people. Sun Yat-sen's widow, who supported the Communists, had a bathroom the size of a small garage. But prisoners were sometimes shut away in windowless cells so small they couldn't lie down or stand up. "I was in a punishment cell about the size of this," he said, pointing to our dining table. After eight months, he was transferred from the Lock-up to the Beijing Number One Prison, a forbidding maze of barbed wire and gray walls on the southwest edge of the city. In 1983, he was shipped to Tanggemu, a notorious labor camp in the Qinghai gulag. In late 1988, he was sent to his last camp, the Nanpu New Life Salt Farm, near Tangshan.

His summary conviction and harsh sentence were eclipsed by an avalanche of stories about China's economic boom. In a Politburo meeting eight years later, Deng gloated over the world's inattention. "We put Wei Jingsheng in jail, didn't we? Did that damage China's reputation? We haven't released him, but China's image has not been tarnished by that. Our reputation improves day by day." Deng gloated too soon. Wei's refusal to recant eventually made him the symbol of human rights repression in China.

As Cook Mu poured coffee and served his mouth-puckering lemon tart, someone asked if Wei had ever been beaten or tortured. "The guards never beat me. They sent in other convicts to beat me instead." He stirred three spoonfuls of sugar into his coffee. "And it depends what you mean by torture," he continued. "To never be allowed out for air and sunshine is a form of torture. My gums swelled up and my teeth fell out. That is a form of torture. Fourteen and a half years in solitary is a form of torture."

"Is it true that you had a mental breakdown in prison?" I asked.

He smiled and said, "Do I look like I had a mental breakdown? I tried to keep my mind active. I did math puzzles. I even tried to figure a way to tow icebergs from Antarctica to the Middle East as a fresh-water supply. I wrote to the Chinese Academy of Sciences with my idea, but they never answered me. I never kept a diary. I knew they'd take it from me. I relied on this," he said, tapping his head. Wei was in solitary so long that he forgot how to talk. But at Tanggemu he was allowed to watch television. He forced himself to talk back to it, cursing the news, debating the propaganda shows and bantering with pop singers. Maybe that's how the rumors of his mental breakdown started.

As Wei lit up his tenth Marlboro of the evening, one of my guests, Bill Hinton, the brother of Joan Hinton, could contain himself no longer. "You people want democracy for China, but you smoke *American* cigarettes. You're poisoning yourself with *American* cigarettes," he sputtered. At six foot two inches tall with a booming voice, blue eyes and a thatch of pure white hair, Bill was a seventy-five-year-old unreconstructed Maoist. The author of several classics on China, he had worked there in the 1940s for the Communists. He returned to the States in the 1950s and turned to farming after he was hounded from his mechanic's job for union organizing and the State Department confiscated his passport and his book notes. At one point, he allowed the Black Panthers to use his Pennsylvania farm for target practice.

"I take whatever is the best from each culture," said Wei, unruffled. "Marlboros are the best cigarettes. I don't drink red wine. I drink Shaoxing rice wine. It's the best wine."

"Well, you survived prison, but those cigarettes will kill you," said Bill, shaking his head.

"At least I have the freedom to choose what I want," replied Wei.

At the word *freedom*, Bill gagged. "You think that bourgeois democracy is going to solve China's ills? It won't. You'll just get fascism. The only solution for China is the collective road."

Wei laughed. "The collective road leads to fascism. China has proved that."

For the next hour, the two of them hotly debated Maoism and Chinese history, shouting over the head of one guest until she gave up and pushed her chair back from the table. Bill said Mao's 1950s collectivization movement was the first time many peasants had owned land. Wei retorted that they never really owned it; the Party grabbed back the land a few years later when it organized the People's Communes. To Bill, Wei was a young whippersnapper who hadn't a clue what a lousy system Western democracy was. To Wei, Bill was an old fogy who hadn't a clue what a lousy system social- ism was. Only two things united the American Marxist and the Chinese democrat: their love for China and their contempt for Deng. At the end of the evening, Bill graciously stood up, shook Wei's hand and said, "I really respect you."

I had one last question. Had Western pressure helped Wei at all? In 1993, the Gleitsman Foundation in Malibu, California, had named Wei a co-recipient, with Nelson Mandela, of its International Activist Award, an honor that came with a $50,000 grant for each. I wanted to know if naming names made a difference. Wei looked at me as if I were an idiot. "If it wasn't for pressure from the West," he said, "I wouldn't be sitting here now. I'd be dead."

His release, he said, had nothing to do with China's 1993 bid to host the 2000 Olympics, as was widely believed. "That was a face-saving pretext," he said, and recounted another tantalizing story from his elite contacts. Some Chinese leaders feared time was run- ning out if they were going to gain any political points for letting Wei out early. But because Deng had ordered his arrest, no one dared take responsibility for his release. So the Politburo deputized Deng's youngest daughter, Deng Maomao, to broach the subject with her father. "He refused at first. Finally, after two hours, he nod- ded. Deng Maomao rushed back to the Politburo. 'Father has nod- ded,' she said. And that's how I got out."

But why would Deng's daughter care? I asked. Wei lit another Marlboro. "After he dies, his kids still have to survive in China," he said, blowing the smoke in my face. "The friend who told me also said, 'If something happens, you must remember what she did for you.' "

A month after my dinner party, I went to see Wei, who had moved back into his old room in his father's apartment. It was sparsely furnished with a white telephone, two bamboo armchairs and a narrow single bed. On the wall was a glossy poster of a Dalmatian sitting among ten black-and-white spotted cats. In English, it said, "In a world full of copycats ... Be an original!" I asked how he was spending the $50,000 from the Gleitsman Foundation. Wei laughed, and lit a Japanese cigarette.

"The first time I tried to get the money, the Bank of China confiscated it," he said. When the money finally came through, he hired a secretary, purchased a photocopier for a fellow activist and bought a computer, which he hadn't yet learned to use. Wei had quickly become a magnet for the dissident community, which lionized him for emerging unbowed from the gulag. I asked if he knew anyone who was organizing workers and peasants who also dared to meet with foreign journalists. I wanted to write a story about dissent in the countryside, where the majority of Chinese lived. He told me he'd think about it.

"Let's meet for lunch today," the caller said, without giving his name.

"Fine," I agreed, and hung up. By prior agreement, Wei Jingsheng was telling me that he had found a pro-democracy organizer willing to talk, and that I and several colleagues should meet him the *next* day at the Holiday Inn near his home.

I discreetly notified three other reporters, Cathy Sampson of The *Times*, the BBC's James Miles and the *Washington Post*'s Lena Sun. We rented a room at the hotel, and at the appointed time, there was a light tap on the door. Wei Jingsheng walked in, trailed by a slight man with hooded eyelids, a wispy mustache and a goatee.

"This is Zhang Lin," Wei said.

Zhang (pronounced *Jaang*) was from Bengbu, a transportation hub on the banks of the Huai, China's third-largest river. At thirty-one, he was already hardened by five stints in jail. We listened in amazement to his claim that he was agitating among workers and peasants in Anhui province right under the nose of the Communist Party.

"Can we visit you?" Lena asked eagerly.

"Of course," Zhang said. "I'll arrange everything."

Such a trip would be illegal. Anhui authorities had rejected my applications several times before. Even though we risked being expelled from the country if caught, Lena and I thought the story on rural unrest was too important. James and Cathy agreed that we could go first because, as ethnic Chinese, we had a better chance of avoiding detection. We booked our flights without using the telephones and instead sent Lena's Canadian assistant to buy them in person. A couple of weeks later, we took a bumpy propeller plane to Bengbu.

I had known Lena since the late 1970s. The American-born daughter of the prominent Overseas Chinese novelist Yu Lihua, Lena had spent her junior year abroad, studying at Beijing University. I liked traveling with her because she had a great sense of humor, an eye for a good story and was a thoughtful, seasoned journalist who could browbeat the most recalcitrant hotel staff into changing the dirty sheets when we checked in.

In Bengbu, on his own turf, Zhang Lin exuded the charisma of a Latin American guerrilla leader. Indeed, he had once tried organizing a band of armed rebels in the Yunnan mountains of southwest China. He referred to other activists as "my *bu xia*," or underlings, and they ran his errands and carried out his orders. Zhang said we could use his real name because the police already knew him well, but everyone else in his circle had to remain anonymous. "Ordinary people don't think it's worth the sacrifice to go to jail for democracy," he said. "I do."

He and his pregnant young wife, Ji Xiao, lived in a single whitewashed room, without heat or plumbing, down a dirt alley too narrow for cars. On his wall, he had pasted a small photo of Wei Jingsheng, with a handwritten caption: "Democracy Fighter." As Zhang held forth on politics, Ji Xiao made lunch on a small coal stove in the yard. "My democratic work is the most important thing in my life," he said. "My wife and unborn child come second."

To reduce our chances of being discovered, Zhang had arranged for his aides to take us to Yuan Village, a godforsaken hamlet of several hundred mud huts where he was organizing the peasants. The next morning we set out in a battered minibus. At Yuan Village, eleven nervous peasants, some of them Party members, were waiting for us inside an adobe cottage. Lena and I were jittery, too. As ethnic Chinese, we risked being beaten first and asked questions later. We could also be charged with spying since we weren't authorized to be there. The consequences for Zhang's aides were even worse.

The peasants gave us a copy of their denunciation. I knew that Party members were no longer models of moral rectitude, but I was not ready for Shen Shaoxi. The Communist Party secretary of Yuan

Village was a rapist, an embezzler, a tyrant and a thief. The denunciation accused Shen, among other things, of lechery, fornication, assault and using China's one-child policy to reward his friends and punish his enemies. Each charge was meticulously documented with the date of the alleged incident, the place, and the accuser's name and thumbprint in bright red ink. I felt sick as I scanned the petition. As the village's main broker in an illegal wife trade, Shen helped kidnap women for sale as brides to the local peasants. He also took the feudal overlord's ancient right of first night. At night, when a light burned late in his office, the peasants knew their Party secretary was raping the abducted women. "All the kidnapped women must spend the first night with him in his office. The next morning, after the deal has been reached with the buyer, firecrackers are lit at the office doorway, and the new bride is conveyed home," the petition said. The wife trade was so brisk that local villagers dubbed his office the Commodity Exchange.

It was odd how spectacularly wrong Mao had been when it came to running China and how right he had been on so much else. He once warned that if the Chinese Communist Party did not police itself, it would turn into a fascist dictatorship. He had been prescient. The Party, once cherished as the liberator of the Chinese people in the 1940s, had become their oppressor in the 1990s. Where wealthy landlords once tyrannized the peasants, the local despot was now the Communist Party secretary. Was Party Secretary Shen typical? In 1994, Xinhua, the official news agency, reported that corruption was endemic in Anhui province, with one in five cadres on the take.

Shen Shaoxi typified the thousands of petty tyrants who made life miserable for millions of peasants in the Chinese countryside. As Party secretary for the past fifteen years, he wielded absolute power over Yuan Village's three hundred families. Although he had only a third-grade education, he was village mayor, police chief, prosecutor, judge, jury, welfare dispenser and father confessor rolled into one. He could, and did, label his critics counter-revolutionaries, and used the local militia to suppress them. When our minibus stopped to pick up three peasants to interview, a rumor flashed through the village that Shen had abducted them.

Most galling of all to the peasants, he selectively enforced China's tough one-child policy. "If you're close to him, you can have six children with no problem," said one. Shen's closest ally, the village accountant, had five, and never paid a fine. And three-fourths of the families in Yuan Village had three or more children, including Party Secretary Shen himself. But after one peasant accused Shen of corruption, he ordered the village militia to drag the man's daughter-in-law, then pregnant with her third child, to the county hospital for a forced abortion. And for good measure, he bulldozed her home while she was gone.

Yuan Village was so poor it lacked running water. It had no commerce, if you didn't count the wife trade. But in 1991 when the mighty Huai River overflowed its banks, causing the worst flooding in China in decades, Shen, who was in his forties, saw a get-rich-quick opportunity. He fenced relief grain from Beijing, embezzled emergency construction funds and divided up special shipments of cooking oil, sweet dates and fertilizer among eight of his cronies. He also gave eight sacks of flour, intended for the neediest families, to the village accountant. "It rotted before he could eat it, so he fed it to his pigs," one peasant said bitterly. Another said angrily, "Even the Party secretary's pigsty is better than our homes."

Three times that year, the villagers rode into the county town in a convoy of bicycles and belching tractors, demanding justice. They kowtowed before the county officials, trying to present their petition. Nobody cared. Two-thirds of the families in Yuan Village were forced to leave home to go begging. A handicapped bachelor in his fifties nicknamed Lu the Deaf starved to death. Three years later, many villagers were still living in temporary shelters.

Lena and I went on a quick walking tour of the desolate village. In front of one lean-to, a tearful old woman told us that she had nothing to feed her grandchildren that day. Others were living in the ruins of their destroyed homes. We decided we had to see where Party Secretary Shen lived. It was the grandest house in the village, with a high courtyard wall, a snug tile roof and a cement foundation. And the peasant had been right; Shen's pigsty was made of brick while the villagers' homes were made of mud. A bent old woman, perhaps his mother, suddenly emerged from the house. We froze. One of Zhang's quick-thinking associates thrust his hands behind his back, assumed an official air, and strode up, scowling and gesturing at the home's blank walls.

"We're inspecting slogans," he said importantly. "Your home doesn't have any slogans about family planning."

"So sorry," the old woman said hastily. "We'll fix it right away."

Emboldened, we strolled over to the village accountant's home and walked in without knocking. Only an old man was in. Our "city official" dismissed him with a perfunctory wave. I couldn't believe my eyes. Inside one large room were four giant straw bins, each the size of a chest-high hot tub. They were overflowing with grain. I felt a wave of anger as I thought of the old woman whose grandchildren had gone hungry that day. I thought of Lu the Deaf, who had starved to death a few years earlier. And I remembered the class-struggle exhibits I had seen as a revolutionary tourist so long ago – the evil landlord hoarding food while the masses starved.

Party Secretary Shen learned of our visit a few hours after we left. The village militia, led by his brother, beat up three of the peasants who had talked to us and seized and interrogated two others. A sixth peasant, who evaded capture by hiding in the fields, managed to smuggle out a statement, thumbprinted by eleven villagers, testifying to the reprisals. Party Secretary Shen had no idea who we were, but the village accountant swore that if we ever returned he would break our legs.

We caught up with Zhang Lin in nearby Big Temple Village, where his grandfather now lived alone. It was in this simple thatched-roof cottage that Grandfather Zhang had taught his precocious grandson the Confucian classics, rewarding every correct recitation with a piece of candy. In 1979, the old man had been so proud when his grandson became the first person from the Bengbu region ever admitted to Qinghua University. In 1989, when Zhang was arrested for his pro-democracy activities, his grandfather went into shock. For six months, he wore a rope around his waist, planning to commit suicide the moment he confirmed his grandson's execution.

At Qinghua, Zhang Lin wanted to study literature, but central planners assigned him to nuclear physics. Bored and alienated, he began cutting classes to listen to dissidents like Wei Jingsheng at Democracy Wall. After graduation, Zhang went back to Bengbu, where he organized a democracy discussion group and supported himself by washing dishes and selling sweaters. He would have rejected the comparison, but Zhang reminded me of a young Mao Zedong. Seventy years earlier, Mao, too, had traveled the backroads of his native province, leading peasant uprisings against cruel despots.

Back in Beijing, we kept in touch, meeting at prearranged spots. Whenever he was late, I feared he had been arrested. When his wife gave birth to a baby girl in the spring of 1994, she warned him to stay away because their home was being watched. Zhang never saw his baby daughter. A few days later, he was arrested at midnight when police raided the safe house he was staying at in Beijing.

I mailed Zhang's wife a package of baby clothes. I dared not contact Grandfather Zhang in case the family had not told him what happened. After I returned to Toronto, I learned that Zhang Lin had been sentenced to three years of hard labor in a coal mine. At last report, he had gone on a hunger strike. Among his crimes was giving interviews to the *Globe and Mail*.

On April 1, 1994, Wei Jingsheng, too, was rearrested by police as he made his way to a press conference with foreign reporters. Authorities were furious that he had refused to halt his pro-democracy activities. The last straw had been a secret meeting with John Shattuck, the top human rights official in the U.S. State Department.

In 1995, Wei was nominated for the Nobel Peace Prize. Late that year, after nearly twenty months in detention, he was formally charged with attempting to overthrow the Chinese government. Authorities refused to disclose where they were keeping him. On December 13, 1995, as the first snowfall of the season dusted the bleak streets of Beijing, Wei was convicted of conspiracy to subvert the government and sentenced to fourteen more years in prison.

Soon after Wei Jingsheng's rearrest, I slipped onto the campus of People's University. Walking right past the plainclothes agents surrounding a modest three-room apartment, I knocked on the door.

"Everyone is afraid," said Professor Ding Zilin softly, shutting the door behind me.

It was a tense time, just a few weeks before the fifth anniversary of the Tiananmen Square massacre. The fifty-seven-year-old philosophy professor peered through the lace curtains of her ground-floor apartment. "They're still there. They can see right in. Are you afraid?" I shook my head. Foreign reporters hadn't been beaten up in more than a year. Professor Ding was the one in danger. The government tapped her phone, confiscated her mail and tailed her whenever she went out grocery shopping. For the past six months, an anonymous caller had threatened to trash her home. It was clear why authorities were so afraid of her. But why was she not afraid of them?

"What have I got to lose?" she said quietly. She patted the small black briefcase beside her containing some neatly folded receipts and a mailing list. "I've made arrangements for someone to continue this work in case I am arrested." With her gray hair, tailored white silk blouse and charcoal trousers, she hardly seemed like a dangerous subversive. But Ding Zilin was living up to her name, which meant Gentle Rain. With the quiet persistence of a drizzle that never lets up, she was compiling the most comprehensive list in existence of the dead and wounded of Tiananmen Square. When she found them, or their next-of-kin, she passed on financial aid from donors overseas. More important, perhaps, she reassured the families they were not alone. Gentle Rain Ding was the government's Chinese Water Torture.

The first name on her list was Jiang Jielian, a top student who had turned seventeen the day before he died. He was an ace badminton player, president of his high-school class and an avid supporter of the pro-democracy demonstrations. He was also Professor Ding's youngest child. His death had devastated her. For weeks, she had lain bedridden, unable to move. She left his desk intact, his athletic and scholarly awards and his favorite books displayed just as he had left them. To hold the ashes, her husband built a camphor cabinet and placed it in a corner of their bedroom. Above it, Professor Ding hung an oil painting based on a precious last photo of him taken during the protests. It depicted him in a headband, smiling and holding aloft a pro-democracy banner.

It took two years for her to evolve from broken-hearted mother to fearless subversive. On April 9, 1991, she was watching a televised press conference with Premier Li Peng when Lena Sun raised her hand and asked: "When will the government release a list of names of those who died at Tiananmen Square?" The premier allowed himself a tight smile. "The family members of the dead are reluctant to have their names disclosed because they view the event as an anti-government riot. We must respect their wishes."

Professor Ding, a Communist Party member, was stunned. A few weeks later, she gave her first interview to a foreign reporter. Looking straight into the television camera, she declared how proud she was that her son had marched for democracy. She described how she had tried so hard to keep him home that fateful night, and how he had insisted on trying to stop the troops from reaching Tiananmen Square. She recalled with a faint smile how he kissed her, how he mischievously locked himself in the bathroom, and then how he quietly slipped out the window. She wept as she repeated his playful last words: "We are parting forever."

With a classmate, Jiang Jielian headed for Muxidi. A huge crowd was blocking the path of thousands of heavily armed soldiers. They opened fire. "I think I've been hit," Jiang cried out. He had been shot in the back. His classmate lifted him onto the back of a pedi-cab, then got him into a taxi. Jiang died on the operating table of the nearby Beijing Children's Hospital, the first of more than fifty deaths there that night. At home, Professor Ding waited anxiously. Her husband kept a vigil by the school gate, the distant roar of tanks and gunfire freezing his heart. At dawn, their son's hysterical class-mate returned to campus, his clothes stained with blood. Professor Ding's husband went to the hospital to claim their son's body.

After the interview was broadcast in Canada and the U.S., reprisals were swift. People's University banned her from teaching and slashed her pay. The Party expelled her. (Technically speaking, Professor Ding had already quit by refusing to pay her monthly dues after her son's death.) When her husband, head of the Esthetics Institute at People's University, gave his own interview to Voice of America, he, too, was dismissed.

Professor Ding should have felt fear. Instead she felt liberated.

With time on her hands, and nothing more to lose, she began to write articles about her son for publications abroad. Donations began trickling in. She knew several victims' families and decided they needed the money more. They in turn passed on other names. Professor Ding began compiling her list. To start with, seven young men and women from People's University had died. Gradually, she transformed her tiny apartment into a nerve center. She served tea to bereft families in her living room. Her son's empty bedroom became her office. A donation from Chinese students at Stanford University paid for a computer. And a Chinese man who had attended the same high school as their son nearly a quarter century earlier bought Professor Ding a Canon copier. His name was Wei Jingsheng.

At first, Professor Ding's neighbors and colleagues were supportive. "But as the government increased the pressure on me, friends I've known for decades turned the other way. Now I only speak to people when they speak to me first. But I walk with my head high. I've done nothing wrong. I'm doing humanitarian work."

The more families she met, the less isolated Professor Ding felt. She kept her records in a safe house, promising both donors and recipients confidentiality. If she determined that the family had lost its main breadwinner, she made additional payments. Occasionally the money ran out. Once, a young man, disabled from his wounds, knocked on her door. "All I could do was invite him to dinner," she said regretfully. Her list included victims who lived as far away as Ningxia in the northwest and Hainan Island in the south. Her dogged detective work unearthed harrowing stories. A medical student one month short of graduation was shot in the throat as she rescued others. A coal miner was forbidden to leave his city in the provinces to retrieve the ashes of his nineteen-year-old son in Beijing.

Only one family betrayed her. Two days after the massacre, their eight-year-old son had taunted the troops. A soldier aimed his AK-47 at him and squeezed off a round. As the boy crawled, bleeding, along the road, the soldier refused to let anyone help him. An agitated bystander pulled out his identity card and said, "I support the suppression, but this is an innocent child. Please let me take him to the hospital. I will leave my ID here as a guarantee." The soldier relented. The boy survived, but lost a kidney, a rib and his spleen.

Professor Ding telephoned the boy's family. But when she learned they lived at Muxidi, where her own son had been killed, she couldn't bear to go. Instead, a volunteer delivered the money. By then, the father had had a change of heart. "How do I know you're not the police?" he said, pushing the volunteer out of his home. The shaken woman wrote Professor Ding's name on the back of a business card and handed it to him. The father grew angrier. "I'm polite to you. At least I didn't search your bag," he said. He later turned the business card over to the police.

"The father was trying to prove his loyalty," said Professor Ding. "What's happened to his son has already happened. The father was worried about the future. I'm not angry at him. I just pity him, and especially his son."

Most recipients were deeply moved by her letters and the money she passed along. One of them was Fang Zheng, the student at the Beijing Sports Institute whose legs were crushed by a tank. After his school expelled him, he moved to Hainan Island, where he earned a meager living selling cigarettes by the roadside. Fang began lifting weights in his wheelchair. He discovered he was good at discus, shot put and javelin. Within a couple of years, he became China's national disabled discus champion. In 1994, Hainan chose him for its team at the Far East and South Pacific Disabled Games. As soon as Fang arrived in Beijing for training, he phoned Professor Ding. "Seeing me will only hurt your career. Just concentrate on winning," she advised him. He did as she asked.

Some foreign journalists invited to cover the Disabled Games inquired whether China's teams included anyone injured at Tiananmen Square. Fang suddenly became a public-relations liability. An official from the Sports Commission told him he would have to go. Fang argued that he was the national discus champion. The official said the event was canceled. What about javelin and shot put? Fang asked. "You're not number one," he was told. "Go home."

Deng Pufang, Deng Xiaoping's handicapped eldest son, tried to intervene. The two young men, both victims of China's violent political upheavals, faced one another in their wheelchairs. In his role as chairman of the China Welfare Fund for the Disabled, Deng Pufang offered Fang a deal: he could stay and compete on condition he not tell anyone how he lost his legs. The shot-put champion agreed. But a few days later, Sports Commission officials overruled Deng's son.

Fang Zheng decided he had to meet Professor Ding before he left. She told him that plainclothes agents still ringed her home. "I'm coming anyway," he said. He arrived late that afternoon, his wheelchair towed by a friend on a bicycle. Professor Ding cooked dinner for him. Afterward, she pushed his wheelchair to the front gate as eight plainclothes police snapped photographs and barked into walkie talkies. "Five years ago, they cut off his legs," she said to me. "Now it's as if they have cut off his arms."

By mid-1995, Professor Ding was working on new leads. She had already contacted more than 130 families in which someone had been killed at Tiananmen Square. That fall, the New York Academy of Sciences honored her with its Human Rights Award. Perhaps to prevent her from physically receiving the award, authorities temporarily detained Professor Ding and her husband. But just as Wei Jingsheng's arrest a generation earlier created more heroes, the couple's detention prompted others to come forward. For the first time since the Tiananmen Massacre, sixteen relatives of those killed or wounded dared to speak out, signing a petition demanding the couple's release.

In fact, Professor Ding had no intention of going to New York. In an acceptance speech written before her arrest, she thanked the academy but said she dared not leave China for fear of not being allowed back in. "In the past," she wrote, "the overwhelming majority of those who had been treated with injustice, including those whose family members were slaughtered or persecuted to death, carried their burdens in silence and in humiliation, and waited patiently for the authorities to 'right the wrongs and restore their reputations' for them. This amounts to the victims surrendering their dignity and integrity as ransom for the second time. It is high time the Chinese people close the chapter on submitting themselves to humiliation in a slavish manner.

"In the years since [Tiananmen], I have simply done what a mother's love and an intellectual's conscience drove me to do. Each and every citizen living in this land not only should have the freedom from fear, adversity and misery but should have the right to choose the kind of society, political system and individual lifestyle that is compatible with human dignity. These were the dreams of those who gave their lives at Tiananmen Square. These are the goals for which we, the living, strive."

17

China's Gulag

Top: An inmate operating a milling machine at Beijing Number One Prison, a model facility. Photo: Jan Wong/*Globe and Mail*

Bottom: Police and judicial authorities recording the details just after a mass execution of drug dealers in Yunnan province.

Photo: Max Photo/*Globe and Mail*

One by one, Wei Jingsheng, Zhang Lin and Professor Ding Zilin had all been in and out of China's gulag. Many activists like them had spent years in jails and labor camps. Some had been tortured. Some had endured solitary confinement. Others had been tossed into overcrowded cells full of rapists and murderers. A few had had show trials, but most had been locked up for years without formality.

As a starry-eyed Maoist, I had not given it much thought when "counter-revolutionaries" were bundled off after a struggle meeting. And even when the slogan shouting and denunciations seemed cruel, I tried to suppress any pity I felt because I thought that caring about class enemies was hopelessly bourgeois. Only at Big Joy Farm had I begun to think my first subversive thoughts: was China just one big prison camp?

After Mao's death, as people unburdened themselves at Democracy Wall, my friends began talking openly for the first time about the gulag. Later, as a news assistant for the *New York Times*, I started probing the underside of China in earnest. Now, as a reporter for the *Globe and Mail*, I asked questions, lots of them, and I no longer cared what Teacher Dai or anybody thought.

I began noticing that I was sometimes followed. The first sign would be the officer from State Security, China's KGB, at my compound gate, picking up the phone as I drove out. A block later, an unmarked car or, occasionally, a motorcycle, would ease out from a side street. It would follow me, always staying one or two vehicles behind. I became adept at flushing them out, by circling a traffic rotary several times to see who stayed on the merry-go-round, or by abruptly slowing to a crawl to see who ducked behind a bus. While it was easy to spot them, it was hard to shake them. State Security stationed plainclothes "spotters" at key intersections across the city. As you passed one, he would stare hard at you, talking into his collar, presumably warning the next spotter you were on your way.

At first I was rattled. Later, I took a childish delight in trying to lose them. Eventually, I got so used to being followed that it hardly bothered me. I even caught myself feeling inordinately flattered when my "tail" was a big black Mercedes and deflated when it was a mere Volkswagen. Always, there were four men inside: a driver and a spotter in front, and two men in back to follow me on foot if I got out of my car.

In the provinces, the tails seemed particularly crude and inept. At the Fuzhou airport, on the east coast, two plainclothes agents, a male and a female, persisted in snapping pictures of Lena Sun and me with cameras secreted inside shoulder bags – until Lena took out her camera and began photographing *them*. In Qinghai, the Chinese province infamous for its labor camps, I got so sick of being followed on foot that I turned around and chased my tail all the way down the street.

In one sense, the surveillance was a blessing. It reminded me never to be careless. I talked obliquely on the telephone and avoided sensitive topics at home, in my office and in my car. If I obtained a secret document, I wrote the story without making it clear whether I had actually seen the document, then destroyed it before filing my story. When I saw I was being followed, I altered plans to meet friends or contacts. Occasionally I didn't notice and was once horrified to bump into one of my tails on the street just outside a friend's apartment building. Luckily, they never figured out exactly whom I was seeing inside.

After the Tiananmen Square massacre, I was haunted by a compulsion, an *obligation*, to examine the darkest side of China's police state. I knew I had to stare it in the face, in a way I might not have done before, in order to exorcise the ghosts of my past. In Canada, academics complained that my harsh reports hurt their scholarly exchanges. Businessmen muttered about ruined trade prospects. In Montreal, my mother scolded: "Don't tell people the bad stuff. That's just what *lo fan*" – foreigners – "want to hear."

I agonized over the question of fairness. Was I overcompensating for having been a youthful apologist for the regime? Was I going overboard for fear of being duped again? At the *Boston Globe*, I had never felt any twinges when I wrote exposés of money laundering at New England banks. Now my job was to write about a country in flux. I concluded that China deserved the same treatment as any other beat. If you don't like bad publicity, I figured, don't shoot people in cold blood. After Tiananmen, I began an investigation that would take me to half a dozen prisons, a death rally and an execution ground. To my dismay, the wildest rumors turned out to be true.

One cool spring day, I flew into the heart of the Chinese gulag. For centuries, emperors had exiled traitorous officials to a living death in Qinghai, a landlocked northwestern province of snow-capped mountains and high-altitude plains. A little-known policy called forced job placement doomed many convicts to remain in the gulag long after their prison terms ended. By the 1990s, one-fourth of Qinghai's 4.3 million population were prisoners, ex-prisoners or their families.

"I call Qinghai China's Siberia," said Harry Wu, who spent nineteen years in Chinese labor camps after criticizing the Soviet invasion of Hungary. When I talked to him by telephone from Beijing, he had just published a ground-breaking book, *Laogai, the Chinese Gulag*, and was planning to testify before the U.S. Congress.

Wu, who emigrated to California in 1985, seemed to live a charmed life. Twice in 1991, he daringly returned to China. Variously posing as a local Chinese, a policeman and a Chinese-American businessman, he documented prison-camp life and surreptitiously filmed inmates in a tannery standing waist-deep in toxic fluids. In

1994, he returned to help the BBC film a documentary about harvesting organs from executed prisoners. His luck ran out in June 1995, when he was arrested on his fourth fact-finding trip. By then a U.S. citizen, he was charged with spying. That August, he was sentenced to fifteen years and expelled with the warning that if he ever returned, he would have to serve his sentence in full.

In the mid-1990s, Beijing claimed a nationwide prison population of 1.26 million, or one inmate per one thousand citizens, a figure that would put China on a par with many European nations. Harry Wu – and Amnesty International – estimated the prison population at 20 million. If true, China would have the most inmates per capita of any country in the world, sixteen or seventeen prisoners per one thousand people, compared with five or six per one thousand in second-place Russia, itself reeling from a post-Communist crime wave, and five per one thousand in third-place United States.

Just as the Inuit have many words for snow, so the Chinese have a rich and varied penal vocabulary. There were *jian yu* (prisons), *kan shou suo* (lock-up pens) and *shou rong suo* (detention centers), not to mention half a dozen kinds of labor camps. You could disappear for months or even years if you were *ju liu* (detained), *shou rong shen cha* (taken in for investigation) or *ge li shen cha* (isolated for investigation). In the meantime, Chinese officials could play semantics. If anyone asked, they could deny with a straight face that you had been *dai bu* (formally arrested).

Every Chinese understood the fine distinctions. A nasty "reform-through-labor farm" was much worse than a "re-education-through-labor camp." But a policeman could toss anyone into one of these re-education camps for up to three years without a formal charge or trial. And if the victim was imprudent enough to object, the police could tack on a fourth year for bad behavior.

Qinghai (pronounced *Ching-hi*) was normally closed to foreign journalists. To my astonishment, they agreed to let Caroline Straathof, a Dutch reporter for *De Volkskrant*, and me in after we applied to write about tourism and economic investment. (I subsequently kept my promise, albeit slightly tongue-in-cheek: a regional gastronomic specialty was yak penis and a local guest house beside Qinghai Lake was a former torpedo test site.)

Xining, the provincial capital, was filled with prison factories and ringed by labor camps. At a visit to an ordinary factory, Caroline casually asked the manager what the prison facility "up the road" manufactured. He rattled off four or five different jails, uncertain which one she meant – until our handler from the provincial Foreign Affairs office glared at him.

Although inmates in the West also worked, several countries banned imports of Chinese prison-made products because of Beijing's forced-labor policy for political detainees. While Beijing didn't deny that it used prison labor, it claimed that it didn't export the products. But in Xining, along an extraordinary street lined with prison-factory outlets, we found a number of items that appeared designed for export. I bought a set of toy police equipment in a package showing two Caucasian boys playing cops and robbers. It said, in English: "SPECIAL AGENT. Fun! Safe! For ages 3 and up. Made in China."

"It's made in the Qinghai Number One Prison," the shop clerk said to me as I paid for it. "Don't tell the foreigner," she added, glancing at Caroline, who pretended to be engrossed in some toy machine guns.

Like Treblinka, Auschwitz and Dachau, which in their time were secret, Chinese prison camps weren't marked on local maps. The actual number of prisoners in Qinghai was also a state secret, although the official number was a suspiciously round "ten thousand," low even by China's already low national figure of 1.26 million. "Every country has its secrets. Our prisons are our secret," said Dong Maicang, deputy chief of Qinghai's Labor Reform Bureau, in his first interview ever with journalists, foreign or Chinese.

A local resident with a friend in Tanggemu, the notorious labor camp where Wei Jingsheng once talked back to his television, told us that inmates in solitary confinement were locked inside a metal box so small they had to crouch. "You can't sit or stand. There are no toilet breaks. They make you soil your pants."

Deputy Chief Dong denied such bleak conditions existed. "Solitary confinement means the prisoner can choose the television channel he wants to watch," he said with a wide smile. When we asked about forced labor, he replied, "Criminals who meet production quotas are paid cash bonuses."

One afternoon, Caroline and I strolled into the retail outlet of the Qinghai Hide and Leather Garment Factory. Harry Wu and others had tipped us off that the innocuously named factory was actually a prison. Its three thousand inmates apparently included Tibetans – Qinghai, which borders Tibet, has a sizable Tibetan population – because the shop displayed photographs of traditional blue and white canvas tents. As we browsed among the crudely made leather jackets and miniskirts, Caroline, pretending she didn't speak Chinese, asked through me to see some of the Tibetan tents. I duly translated, and the clerk, an old man, assumed she was a bona fide Western tourist.

"Would you like to go into the warehouse?" he asked helpfully. We nodded, hardly believing our luck. He led us down the street and through the factory's outer gates. Caroline and I exchanged glances. Several dozen police cars filled the parking lot. The inner entrance, invisible from the street, was flanked by a watchtower and a guardhouse. A uniformed soldier cradling a semi-automatic rifle on a catwalk above us stared down in surprise. As we walked through, four or five people rushed out of the guardhouse, shouting.

"They're customers," the clerk explained.

As they berated him for being such a numskull, I drank in every detail. A sign ordered visitors to remove their sunglasses and produce identification. All cars had to stop and open their trunks. The actual prison, fifty yards farther down a narrow alley, was blocked by a solid iron gate topped with spikes. Another watchtower loomed.

"You're not supposed to be here," said a young man in plain clothes, shooing us out. "You must wait in the store. He will bring the tents to you." While the chastened clerk continued into the factory, the young man escorted us back to the shop. On the way, he whispered to me: "You can't go in the factory. There are prisoners there."

"I've heard that," I said, nodding conspiratorially.

Back at the shop, he handed me a perfumed business card of pale iridescent pink and blue stripes. It identified him as Zhao Lixin of the sales department and helpfully included the prison's bank account number so buyers could wire payments. I guess Deng Xiaoping had figured out from personal experience that there was nothing mind-reforming about labor. Convicts still had to work, but now they toiled for Gulag Inc. In the West prisons drained tax dollars; in China they produced revenue. Convicts had always paid for their own food. Now, under Deng's get-rich-quick philosophy, the camps and prisons had been given a green light to make a profit. The harder they drove the prisoners, the more money there was for bonuses, pensions and cattle prods. Torn between the need for secrecy and the pressure for profits, some prison enterprises were abandoning discretion.

"Would the leather jackets and miniskirts appeal to foreigners?" Zhao Lixin asked. "We've had a hard time finding export markets. Can you help us?"

I dutifully translated for Caroline, who widened her blue eyes and said innocently, "I think there are bans in Western countries on goods made with forced labor. My country, Holland, would have a problem with prison-made goods."

"No problem," said Zhao Lixin. "We can change the labels."

Suddenly, a uniformed policeman walked in. We froze. Had we been followed here? But Zhao Lixin introduced the policeman as his team leader. We relaxed.

"How about a wholesale discount?" I asked.

"I can't give you better than five percent," the policeman said. "The price of hides has been going up."

To follow the gulag story to its inevitable conclusion, I had to find an execution ground. Armed only with some vague, outdated directions, I spent an afternoon in Beijing's outlying areas getting lost with Lena Sun. A friend had told me to look for a certain section of the dry, stony bed of the Yongding River, but the local peasants directed me instead to a secluded hillside. Apparently, someone had decided that shooting people in public was bad for China's image.

A twelve-foot-high gray brick wall topped with barbed wire rose from the side of a scrub-covered hill. A black and white sign identified it as Beijing Supreme Court Project 86, blandly named for the year it was built. Even though it was a warm spring afternoon, I felt chilled. We had found Beijing's secret killing field. Project 86 was about as isolated as it was possible to be in a city of eleven million.

Behind the wall, an unseen guard dog barked. There was no other sign of life. In the distance I saw the perpetual haze from the smoke-stacks of Capital Iron and Steel. The nearest village was beyond the next hill. The only people in sight were two peasants scavenging steel rods from chunks of discarded reinforced concrete.

"Anybody executed here lately?" I asked. In the context, it seemed a perfectly normal question.

"They shot a bunch of people here about ten days ago," said one of the peasants.

"What did you see?"

"We're never allowed to watch," he said, pausing to look me over. "They always shut down the entire area. Impose a curfew. No one is allowed near. We can only hear the shots." The soldiers had AK-47 assault rifles, he said, and would fan across the mountain sealing off the area as a precaution against last-minute rescue attempts. Then the condemned would arrive in a speeding convoy of jeeps and trucks.

In the distance, Lena spotted a security guard wearing sunglass-es, a blue padded coat and a red armband. The peasant saw him, too, and abruptly fell silent. The guard, still several hundred yards away, blocked the path back to my Jeep. "Let's go farther up," I whispered.

At the top, we had an even better view of Project 86. Looking down, I saw that it was an irregular hexagonal wall surrounding a dusty field. There was nothing aside from some corrugated tin-roofed shacks, a circular dirt road in the center and a long line of concrete V shapes at the base of the hill that reminded me of a row of giant books, opened in the middle and propped upright. We took turns standing in a half crouch to snap some photos. Below, the security guard was still waiting. I emptied my camera and dropped the roll of film down my shirt, annoyed I had forgotten to bring an extra roll as a decoy. Then Lena and I crawled down the far side of the hill, through thorn bushes and weeds, into a dusty gully and back over a couple of steep hills, eventually reaching the main road, and my Jeep.

Only after interviewing several people involved in executions did I understand what we had seen. The circular dirt road had been worn down by trucks carrying prisoners. The condemned knelt against the concrete Vs so that stray bullets lodged safely in the slope of the hill. After I developed the photos, I counted the Vs. There were thirty.

I was not against the death penalty in principle. But in China, state executions were more like wholesale slaughter. Not only was the Chinese justice system an abyss of perfunctory trials, near-certain conviction and rejected appeals, the death penalty was used for a vast array of offenses, from cattle rustling to copyright infringement. By the 1990s, the Beijing regime led the world in per capita executions. With 22 percent of the world's population, China accounted for 63 percent of the world's executions. Each year it executed about seven thousand people, compared with a few hundred a year during the Qing dynasty (1644–1911), according to Bernard Luk, a history professor at Toronto's York University. Even allowing for a tripling of the population since Qing times, Communist China's rulers are far more bloodthirsty than the feudal emperors they replaced.

"At this stage in our history, we need the death penalty. We can't afford not to have it," Xiao Yang, the governor of Sichuan province, told me, citing the soaring crime rate sparked by a growing gap between the haves and have-nots.

When Lena and I requested an interview with a judicial official to ask about the death penalty, a spokeswoman for the Beijing Supreme Court snapped, "That is not within the acceptable realm of reporting." On our own, we interviewed justice officials, ex-prisoners and a former execution-ground worker and, from their accounts, pieced together a picture of the final hours of a condemned convict's life.

Holidays, the traditional time for settling accounts in China, are also the most common time for executions. On death row, the footsteps come just before dawn. As the condemned sits shackled to the floor, police make a final identification check. Name? Work unit? Age? Crime? Sentence? A jailer takes mug shots. If the prisoner's organs are to be used for transplants, a medic gives an injection of anticoagulant. Another officer checks the locks on the handcuffs and leg irons to make sure they can retrieve their hardware afterwards. Other officers truss the prisoner like "a pig for slaughter," in the words of one witness. That way, a sharp jerk of the rope throttles any prisoner who tries to shout anti-government slogans. Someone binds the shoes so they don't fall off if the prisoner has to be dragged along the ground at the end. Then someone ties the pants at the ankles with twine to prevent a mess in case the prisoner loses control of his or her bodily functions. "Otherwise, it would look too pathetic," said a government official who witnessed thirty-two executions.

After being shackled and trussed, the condemned are loaded onto military jeeps, right behind the executioner and between the soldiers who will march them to their deaths. There are no blind-folds, no masks, no sanitized rituals as in the West, where the message is that the prisoner is being killed not by a person but by the state. The feelings of the Chinese guards and executioners, all rank-and-file soldiers rotated through the task, aren't considered. Carrying out an execution is supposed to be an honorable task, a glorious blow dealt to a class enemy.

In the early days of the People's Republic, citizens were urged to attend public executions: "If you really love the people, then you must hate the people's enemies." By the 1990s, death rallies had replaced public executions. Scheduled just before executions, the rallies are usually held in sports arenas. "They are supposed to edu-cate the living," one court official said. While the prisoners and guards wait for the invitation-only seats to fill up, they mingle like actors backstage. No one has had time for breakfast. The guards sometimes munch steamed cornpone grabbed from the prison can-teen. Because the hands of the condemned are manacled behind, a guard may offer to feed them, an intimacy so raw compared to the anonymity of executions in the West.

At the death rally, the condemned wear placards around their necks identifying their crimes: "rapist," for instance, or "drug dealer". The placards also bear their names crossed out by a big X, indicat-ing they are about to die. Dissent, not normally a capital offense, is labeled "counter-revolutionary crime." Led by an emcee, the audi-ence shouts slogans such as "Shoot to death the rapist Wang!" Then the prisoners are loaded back into the jeep and driven to the exe-cution ground. Three soldiers frog-march each prisoner to a con-crete V. Last statements are forbidden. "Once a young man started singing the pop song 'Good-bye, Mama!' " said another official. "He got badly beaten up. Then they shot him."

When more than one prisoner is being executed, a squad leader coordinates the shooting with a flag. "Sometimes they beg us, 'Please shoot accurately,' " an official who took part in more than a hundred executions told me. "Often, the soldiers miss the first time. They're standing very close, aiming at the back of the head, but maybe they're nervous."

Afterwards, a medic checks for a pulse, and sometimes orders a second bullet. A police photographer snaps pictures of the wound and the face, even if there is not much of it left. To stop excessive bleeding, a soldier might toss a shovelful of dirt over the wound. A clerk notes the date, the time and the names of the executioners and presiding officers. The jailers, wearing gloves to protect them from the gore, unlock the handcuffs and shackles and toss them into the jeep. Soldiers wrap the corpses in bags or stuff them into gray coffins. Then a truck hauls the remains to the crematorium. It is all over in fifteen minutes.

For a long time, death sentences that stripped a person of "political rights for life" confused me. If the person was dead, what rights remained? Finally, a Chinese friend explained: Authorities can remove organs with impunity. No one can accuse the government of mutilating a corpse.

Harvesting inmates' organs is a taboo subject. Asia Watch, a human rights group, obtained a secret 1984 document issued by the Ministries of Justice, Health and Public Security that stated: "The use of the corpses or organs of executed criminals must be kept strictly secret. Security must always be tight." A friend who is a military surgeon in Beijing confirmed that China performs thousands of kidney transplants a year. But he backed off instantly when I asked whether prisoners were the source. "Don't even touch that," he warned and refused to say anything more.

However, in 1989, the official *Legal Daily* publicly confirmed the practice: "Since in China there are relatively few donors of human organs, some medical units and people's courts get together and use ... organs of executed prisoners without obtaining the agreement of prisoners' families. By so doing, they can obtain relatively healthy human organs and they do not need to spend money. This method is incorrect from a legal point of view."

"We do remove organs, but only when the family gives permis-

316 RED CHINA BLUES

sion," said Governor Xiao Yang of Sichuan. In a speech in Geneva, China's ambassador to the United Nations also confirmed the practice. But Ambassador Jin Yongjian insisted it happened "in rare instances" and "with the consent of the individual."

Amnesty International estimates that executed criminals are the source of 90 percent of transplant organs. The government official who witnessed thirty-two executions said that because organs deteriorate rapidly, doctors hook up the corpses to mechanical ventilators or remove organs at the execution ground. Wei Jingsheng, who spent eight months in a punishment cell on death row, said prisoners sometimes had their organs removed *before* execution. "The prison would phone up the hospital each time an execution was planned [to find out what organs were needed]. They would give the prisoner an injection, remove the organ, stitch him up and shoot him in the head."

To be sure, from one perspective, harvesting organs is smart recycling of a scarce resource. "Some of the criminals are quite young and in good health," a Chinese legal scholar told Lena. But because transplant operations are expensive, recipients tend to be senior officials. That raises the question: Is the rate of executions up because important people need organs? Perhaps. Prisoners are usually executed with a bullet to the back of the head. But several sources said that when a hospital wants corneas, the prisoner is shot through the heart.

China uses a bullet, not because it is more humane than the gas chamber or the electric chair but because it is cheap. Still, it seems unimaginably cruel to bill families for the bullets. The practice, which originated during the Cultural Revolution when heartlessness was politically correct, persists today, according to several friends. I didn't believe them. Then someone told me a family in Yunnan province had shown the receipt for the bullet that killed their son to Nick Driver, a UPI reporter. I called Nick and asked him to describe it.

"It was a small slip of paper printed with the Chinese characters *zi dan fei*, [bullet fee]," said Nick. "It was dated 1991, and was issued by the local police station. The charge was 50 fen."

I did the math. Fifty fen was equal to 6 cents.

18

Chasing the Dragon

Top: An addict's wife in Handeng village, near the Burmese border, labors to water a rice crop, which has already been sold to buy opium for her husband. The couple has not been told that he is dying of AIDS.

Photo: Jan Wong/ *Globe and Mail*

Bottom: Bought bride Forest Plum Ma and her husband, Wang Chengguo, outside their house in Dragon Hamlet.

Photo: Jan Wong/ *Globe and Mail*

What first attracted me to Mao's China was its absolute purity. It was a country where evil had seemingly been eliminated by fiat. In a historically unprecedented mass campaign, the Communists had rounded up opium addicts, prostitutes and beggars and transformed them with strong doses of hard labor and Mao Zedong Thought. In the 1950s, with the help of a dermatologist from Buffalo, N.Y., named George Hatem, the Chinese had essentially eradicated venereal disease inside their borders. This was no idle propaganda claim. Sexually transmitted diseases were so rare that, in the 1970s, many young Chinese doctors had never seen an actual case of VD.

But by the 1990s, all the old evils were making a comeback, and then some. The absolutism and fervor of the early years, the deprivation and self-sacrifice, had all been for nothing. As China grappled with child labor, pollution, gambling, high crime rates and horrific industrial accidents, I felt compelled to explore this side of the country. In the 1970s, I had sometimes deliberately heard no evil, seen no evil and spoken no evil. Now, in a small way, I wanted to make amends. What's more, many Chinese were eager to help me understand the plethora of social problems, explaining that the best way to attack problems was to expose them.

I found it especially depressing, as a Chinese-Canadian woman, to see that prostitution was flourishing again. My assistant, Yan Yan, and I had gone on a reporting trip to Hainan Island, China's newest province. In Haikou, its free-for-all frontier capital, cars ignored one-way signs and everyone ignored venereal disease. At night, we watched desperate streetwalkers pluck at the sleeves of passing men. We peered into the darkened windows of seedy massage parlors. We even paid 7 yuan (90 cents) each to squeeze into a makeshift cinema to watch a badly made porno film in which the plot consisted of Lin Biao's son holding beauty contests and screwing the contestants. In our hotel, I noticed women in stretch lace tops with spangles in their hair, but assumed it was merely the local bad taste. Only after a series of phone calls kept me awake the first night did I realize our hotel was crawling with prostitutes and johns.

I knew that blending in gave me an edge as a reporter, but I didn't realize how useful my camouflage would be until I went to Xian, an ancient city famous for its vast collection of terra cotta warriors. Yan Yan burst into my hotel room one night clutching a small piece of folded paper. "Guess what!" she said. Inside was a bit of tan powder. I looked at her, puzzled.

"Opium!" she hissed. "Our taxi driver knows where there's an opium den." I stared at her. *Opium?* An opium *den?* In China? In *1989*?

"Let's go," I said.

I had booked Taxi Driver Pu (not his real name) for the four days we would be in Xian. As we drove through the darkened streets, my mind was reeling. Surely opium, once the scourge of old China, had been abolished under Communist rule. Taxi Driver Pu parked in the shadows. "Don't tell them you're a reporter," he cautioned as he led the way up the darkened stairs of a low-rise brick apartment building, past bunches of drying leeks and untidy heaps of pressed coal-dust lumps. At the top floor, he paused, critically eyeing my baggy cotton trousers.

"You don't look like the type. Let her do the talking," he said, jerking his head at Yan Yan, who was wearing tight stonewashed jeans. He rapped on the scarred yellow door.

"Who is it?" a wary male voice called.

"Me," said Taxi Driver Pu.

That was how Chinese always answered. No one ever said, "Zhao, here," or "It's Wang." They just said, "Me." The man inside unbolted the door. He was skinny, with a scrawny mustache, and appeared to be in his twenties.

"They're with me," said Taxi Driver Pu.

I guess I expected an opium den to have divans, candles and burgundy velvet curtains. Instead, we were in an ordinary run-down Chinese apartment with whitewashed walls and a bare bulb dangling from the ceiling. I spoke as little as possible. What if they discovered I was a reporter? What if we got raided? I knew China executed drug dealers and sent addicts for hard labor in re-education camps. What about reporters caught in opium dens?

Two young women lounged on a double bed covered with a grimy flowered sheet. An older man sat on a wooden chair. Taxi Driver Pu, who was in his forties, stood in a corner. Yan Yan and I took the remaining two chairs. The skinny young man who had let us in resumed smoking opium. In between inhalations, he gulped tea from an oversized enamel mug. His eyes slightly unfocused, he stared at a small black-and-white television, which was showing a movie with lots of Chinese running around in Mao suits.

"What *is* this movie?" he asked.

"It's an old one from the fifties," said Yan Yan, who knew everything.

A few minutes later, he asked again, and Yan Yan repeated her answer. A little later, he asked a third time.

"Shut up," snapped one of the young women. She was dressed in a schoolgirlish plaid skirt and a cream blouse, with a black wool sweater tied over her shoulders. Her face was hard, and she swore like a longshoreman. She was, Taxi Driver Pu told me later, a "public bus," local slang for a prostitute because lots of customers rode her. She put a pinch of Big Dirt, as they called it, on a piece of foil and lit a match underneath. The brownish powder liquefied and gave off a wisp of white smoke, which she expertly sucked up through a straw. She lit and relit the powder, each time greedily inhaling the wisp of smoke. Between puffs, she sucked on an orange. To my surprise, everyone seemed as addicted to fresh fruit as to opium.

"Why are you eating fruit?" I blurted out.

"Your mouth gets too dry," the young man explained.

I didn't know that they were smoking low-grade heroin. Few people at the time were aware that traffickers were shipping heroin from Burma's Golden Triangle overland through China to Hong Kong and from there to North America, Europe and Australia. Three years later, when Beijing finally admitted that it had a drug problem, I interviewed doctors in rehabilitation clinics and realized that the addicts in Xian had been "chasing the dragon," addict parlance for sucking up the wisp of heroin smoke.

After fifteen minutes of smoking, the prostitute fell back with a deep sigh against a folded quilt. "I'm hot," she said. "Open the window."

"No," said the older man sharply. He switched on an electric fan.

The skinny young man, a drug dealer, moved the heroin from Lanzhou, the capital of northwest Gansu province, to Xian, the ancient terminus of the fabled Silk Road.

"It's hard to get this stuff in Beijing," I said, awkwardly trying to make conversation.

"We can do a deal," he said instantly. "I'll ship it to Beijing. You handle it from there. You can be the distributor."

I smiled weakly. I did not need to do that kind of first-person story.

A tall, gaunt man in his late thirties walked in. His cheekbones were hollow, his long stringy hair hung down his neck. Even his mustache was thin. He wore baggy pants, a cheaply made Western-style suit jacket and heavy beige leather shoes. It turned out he was a dealer and an addict, and we were in his apartment. The man, whom I'll call Sheng, squatted down on his haunches, put a pinch of powder on a piece of foil and lit a match underneath, simultaneously sucking in the smoke. Then he cut himself a slice of apple to nibble on while he prepared his next dose. Using a cigarette, he lit match after match and chased the dragon. Sheng suddenly stared at me. His pupils were dilated. It had just dawned on him where we were from.

"What really happened in Beijing?" he asked. "Did they really shoot people?"

"What do you think?" I asked.

"Of course they shot people."

"How many do you think died?" I asked.

"Seven thousand," he said flatly.

I told him the official government estimate was about three hundred dead but that some foreign embassies put the death toll at three thousand. "Do you believe the government?" I asked.

"Are you kidding?" He snorted. "Not at all."

Sheng, who had been jailed in Beijing for theft, had escaped and now ran a restaurant in Xian and sold drugs to support his thousand-dollar-a-month habit. "Want to try some?" he said, offering me some on a piece of foil.

"No, thanks," I said, realizing I sounded absurdly polite. To my horror, Yan Yan accepted. As she handed over 50 yuan, the equivalent of $6, I scowled at her. She ignored me. Sheng helped her hold a match under the powder. Using a straw, she clumsily sucked up the smoke, missing half. She started giggling. Having spent my youth as a Maoist, not a dopehead, I knew nothing about drugs. I was terrified she would get addicted after one try. Later she told me the smoke left a sweet taste on the tongue and that, after a few minutes, she felt completely relaxed. "It was like walking on cotton puffs."

About a half hour later, Sheng insisted on driving his older friend home – in Taxi Driver Pu's car.

"Uh, why don't you drive," I said to Pu as we all piled into the car.

"He doesn't know the way. I'll drive," insisted Sheng, clearly high as a kite. He turned on the ignition, put the car in first gear and drove shakily down the lane.

"Watch out for that bicycle!" Pu warned. I closed my eyes, and regretted not chasing the dragon myself.

Reading *Das Kapital* in the 1970s wasn't a total waste because it helped me understand China in the 1990s. What Marx had predicted for capitalist society – the concentration of economic wealth in fewer and fewer hands and a widening gap between rich and poor – was actually occurring in a Communist system. China was now a capitalist country under a Communist dictatorship, or a Communist country with a capitalist economy.

The gap between rich and poor was distinctly regional. Under Deng's laissez-faire policies, the wealthy coastal regions were booming while the vast interior remained mired in poverty. But it wasn't until I went to Gansu that I saw the terrible face of hunger and disease. Much of China's poorest province was off-limits to foreigners, but I was able to get there thanks to an invitation from Canadian diplomats, who ran aid projects there and had special access.

Gansu, which borders Qinghai province, Outer Mongolia and the Uighur region of Xinjiang in northwest China, was an arid moonscape of barren gullies and mountains. On the same latitude as Kansas, its annual rainfall was so sparse that peasants blanketed their fields with stones to slow evaporation. Leprosy, dysentery, high infant mortality, malnutrition and tuberculosis plagued the province. But the worst curse of all was mental retardation.

About 1.2 percent of Gansu's 22 million people were retarded, the highest rate in China. In 1989, the province passed its first eugenics law. "Insane, dull-witted and idiotic people must first complete sterilization operations before they can register for marriage. Some people say this is inhumane, but we think just the opposite is true," said Jia Zhijie, Gansu's governor, adding that there were instances in which children of mentally retarded parents died of neglect.

The new law shocked many in the West. Yet not so long ago, at least sixteen American states and two Canadian provinces used to sterilize people with mental illness, low IQs, epilepsy and, sometimes, syphilis and alcoholism. In 1972, by the time the province of Alberta repealed its 1920s Sexual Sterilization Act, more than 2,800 Albertans had been sterilized.

At Luo Family Mill Village, it was obvious why a eugenics law was needed. Seventy-eight villagers, or one out of every three, were retarded. Many suffered from cretinism, a form of mental retardation caused by iodine deficiency in the fetus. Others were dwarf-like and retarded from Kashin-Beck disease, contracted from eating fungus-infected grain. Still others had become retarded after drinking water contaminated by heavy metals.

In mid-November, I shivered in my down coat. The children in this muddy hamlet wore only rags. Some lacked socks. An elderly woman, hunched over a cane, had an untreated goiter the size of a cantaloupe. A teenaged girl lay half-naked on the icy ground cramming dirt in her mouth while her retarded mother chuckled. Pigs and sheep and horses defecated into the creek, the only water supply. There was no school, store or clinic.

I knocked on the open door of a mud hut. In the darkness, I saw a man lying on an earthen *kang*, the coal-heated brick bed of north China, eating a bowl of cold boiled potatoes. "Want a potato?" Zhang De said hospitably, proffering his bowl. It was all he had. Chinese considered potatoes a poor substitute for wheat or rice, but Zhang's grain bins were nearly empty. I didn't see how he would get through the long winter. Nor did he. Although he was bedridden with back pain, he was anxious to get back to his fields. At forty-five, Zhang De was the only able-bodied person in his family.

"I was so poor I couldn't afford a dowry," he said, explaining that he had married a retarded mute no one else wanted for a wife. He pointed to his wife, sitting silently in the corner. She was a placid-faced woman, with a soiled blue scarf wrapped around her head. They had three daughters. Two were retarded mutes like their mother. The third had left home at age sixteen to marry. "I'm the only one in my family who's clear up here," he said, tapping his temple. His wife tried to help with the housework, but accomplished very little. "She doesn't know anything," he said, without rancor.

I felt utterly depressed. The ragged petitioners who had flooded into Beijing in 1979 had opened my eyes to the poverty in China, but I had never imagined there were whole wretched villages like Luo Family Mill. In 1995, China disclosed for the first time that 80 million of its people were so poor they did not have enough food or clothing. The World Bank put its own estimate at 100 million to 110 million. Deng Xiaoping's philosophy was to allow a few people to get rich first, hoping they would drag along the rest of the country. Now, some parts of China were booming, but Gansu remained mired in poverty. Deng's trickle-down economics had

326 RED CHINA BLUES

done zip for Luo Family Mill. Yet I couldn't see any other way. Maoism had been the great leveler – and everyone had been equally poor.

Another old evil was rebounding in Deng Xiaoping's China: trafficking in women. It was the rawest indication yet that the Maoist morality I once knew was gone forever. For the first time I felt personally at risk. Chinese friends warned me to be careful and to avoid traveling alone in the provinces. After weathering the post-Tiananmen kidnapping attempt, I realized anything was now possible, and I took their warnings seriously.

Many women were sold by their own relatives. But professional gangs also operated far-flung networks. They duped rural women with bogus job offers in remote provinces or drugged them or used brute force. Often, they raped the women before selling them. The victims would wake up in some remote village, already sold into marriage or forced into prostitution. Equipped with walkie talkies, cellular telephones and fleets of cars, the traffickers easily outmaneuvered the police.

Bride trafficking flourished because of a huge demand by unloved men and an equally huge supply of vulnerable females. Deng's economic reforms had created "bachelor armies" as women in the poorest villages left to find paying jobs elsewhere, or at least tried to marry up and out. Female infanticide – in part a reaction to China's strict family-planning policies – only worsened the sex imbalance. In some poor regions, as many as one in six families bought wives, the Chinese press reported.

One peasant woman who had been sterilized was resold four times by disgruntled husbands who couldn't understand why she failed to conceive. Some families dealt with a reluctant bride by holding her down while the husband raped her, according to the official *China Youth* newspaper. "Many peasant families ignore the resistance and tears," it said. "They think that after a while, she'll get used to it. They believe that she'll cry a little, but after she has a baby she'll be obedient." Escapees were punished, locked in latrines or beaten. After one victim repeatedly tried to escape, her husband, a Shandong peasant, gouged out her eyes.

If the women managed to return home, they were often treated like "broken shoes," or whores who had been tried on by too many customers. No one wanted to marry them. If there were children, the offspring had to stay behind with the man's side. Not surprisingly, many victims stayed where they were. Authorities turned a blind eye. "If a woman is sold, and she puts up with it, it is legal under the Marriage Law," said an official of the Chongqing Women's Federation, a Party-controlled organization.

Authorities needed the wife trade to keep restive men down on the farm. For years, the punishment for traffickers was less than five years, the same for the theft of two cows. Rescue attempts were often difficult and risky. Qu Weijia, a Beijing filmmaker who took part in one attempt, told me that even with the help of the local police and the women's association, the rescuers barely escaped with the victim, a high-school girl who had been abducted and married off to a peasant. "Everybody is related in the same village. Who cares about some woman from the outside?" he said. "Party officials don't want to offend fellow villagers. Nor do they have a strong sense of the law."

Although the wife trade was flourishing, authorities refused to allow any interviews on the subject. Apparently, its very existence was too great a loss of face for China. After trying in vain for two years to go through official channels, the only way foreign journalists were authorized to conduct interviews, Lena Sun and I decided to report the story on our own. Receiving a tip from a friend, we drove east for two hours from Beijing and found a peasant I'll call Farmer Wang. He was a combination village errand boy, deal maker, seeker of foreign investment and glib promoter of local tourist attractions, of which there were none of note. At twenty-six, he had a pinched face and a crooked jaw, and spoke with a slight lisp. When we found him, he was living with his mother because his wife had just walked out on him. I explained to Farmer Wang that we were foreign reporters. I wondered how to delicately broach the subject of wife buying.

"Anybody here bought a wife lately?" I asked.

"Loads," he said. "Otherwise, nobody could find a wife. The women in our village all want to marry someone in the city."

Lena asked if we could meet someone who had bought a bride.

"No problem," he said. One of his neighbors had bought a wife the year before for their deaf, mildly retarded son. The young woman had recently run away. Farmer Wang proposed taking us to meet the family right away. After so many fruitless applications for official interviews, we were thrilled. But we suddenly had the identical thought. It had been hours since we left home.

"Uh, do you have a toilet?" I asked, dreading the answer.

"Outside," he said.

We found an open-air latrine in the front yard, shielded by corn stalks and vines. There were some rickety wooden slats to stand on. It wasn't too bad by rural standards, but Lena looked dubious.

"You go first," the intrepid *Washington Post* reporter said.

I had just finished when some ferocious snorting erupted behind me.

"Look out!" Lena screamed. I shot out of the latrine, my pants still around my ankles, huge jaws snapping at my derrière. It turned out that the Wang family outhouse doubled as a pigsty. Chinese sows aren't cute, pink, cuddly North American pigs. They are huge black excrement-eating monsters with enormous snouts and sharp fangs.

Lena decided she didn't have to go after all. Instead, we went with Farmer Wang to visit his neighbors, who were in the midst of lunch. While the son continued eating, the mother bustled about pouring cups of "white tea" – plain hot water – which she politely set in front of Wang and the *Globe*'s driver, Liu Xinyong. Lena and I glanced at one another. In this household, females didn't even rate a glass of water.

"They want to know about Little Orchid," said Farmer Wang, using the errant wife's name, as mother and son resumed eating lunch. It was a sensitive topic.

"We paid 2,600 yuan [$325] to her matchmaker," the mother said, the anger welling up in her voice. "They fought from the beginning. She was stubborn and had a bad temper. They never got along. They had fistfights."

Little Orchid had been sold against her will by her own brother-in-law. Her survival technique was to make her new family more miserable than they made her. When they gave her laundry to wash, she ripped the clothes. When they asked her to wash the dishes, she smashed the plates. "Once she ripped the hearts out of all our cabbages, out of sheer spite, just to ruin them," the mother complained.

Her ultimate weapon was withholding sex. The family was so poor they shared one big room, the parents on one side, Little Orchid and the retarded son on the other. When he made advances, she punched him and ran outside to sit in the yard. "If she doesn't sleep with me, what do I want her for?" the son had whined, according to a neighbor. He finally agreed to a divorce so he could remarry, but when they went to the county office to fill out forms, Little Orchid was furious to discover she couldn't obtain one on the spot. She tore up her marriage certificate, then excused herself to go to the toilet. They never saw her again.

After we left, Lena told Farmer Wang that we really wanted to meet some brides.

"Some men from Dragon Hamlet, my mother's ancestral village, recently went on a wife-buying expedition to the south. They bought eight women, including a bride for my cousin. I'll take you. It's not far."

He brushed off our profuse thanks. When we got back to his house, we discovered we had been snookered into providing a taxi service for Farmer Wang's sixty-two-year-old mother. She was waiting, her bags already packed. "My father is ninety," explained Guixian (Cassia). "I want to see him one more time before he dies."

"Not far" in peasant parlance meant a four-hour drive – on the other side of Beijing. We had no choice but to take Farmer Wang and Cassia back with us to the city so we could start early the next morning. Lena and I agreed to split the costs of putting them in a budget hotel. We all piled into the *Globe*'s Jeep. After four minutes on the road, Cassia turned green and began to gasp and clutch at her mouth.

"She's throwing up!" Lena shouted. Driver Liu screeched to the side of the road. Lena, who was sitting in the middle, reached over the retching woman to roll down her window.

"She dribbled on my arm!" Lena cried.

"My mother's never ridden in a car before," said Farmer Wang, as Cassia leaned out the window.

"Lena," I said, "I really appreciate your sitting in the middle."

"Shut up," she said.

We rode along in silence, as Cassia hung her head out the window. It started to rain. Then it poured. After a while, we began to discuss which hotel to put them in.

"Aiya!" said Farmer Wang in the front seat, slapping his forehead. "We didn't bring our *shen fen zheng!*" My heart sank. It was too late to turn back to fetch their government-issued identification cards. But since the Tiananmen Massacre, tightened security measures made it impossible to check into a hotel without one. One of us would have to put them up for the night. I knew that since Lena had already been dribbled on, it was my turn to suffer.

"Don't you have anywhere to stay in Beijing?" I beseeched Farmer Wang.

"We can stay with Third Elder Brother," he said.

I brightened. "You have relatives in Beijing?"

"My daughter-in-law doesn't like us," said Cassia.

Suddenly, my concern about oppressed daughters-in-law evaporated. "How nice!" I said brightly. "A family visit! You can see your son *and* your father."

"But we don't have his address," said Farmer Wang.

"We have a flat tire," Driver Liu announced.

While he changed the tire in the pouring rain, with Lena holding an umbrella over him, I tried to jog Cassia's memory about Third Elder Brother's address. By the time the driver had finished, I had narrowed the target area to a neighborhood of only one million people in southwest Beijing. We drove randomly around in the rain until Cassia recognized a landmark – the local greasy chopstick joint – and assured us she could find Third Elder Brother's home from there.

The next morning we picked up Farmer Wang and Cassia at dawn. We rode in silence, warily keeping an eye on her until she assured us she hadn't eaten breakfast. After three hours, Farmer Wang, with the nanosecond timing of a person who has never driven a car, cried, "Turn here!" Driver Liu slammed on the brakes.

"Here" was a rock-strewn slope leading down to a rushing brook. Driver Liu ordered us out and carefully eased the Jeep down the slope, across the stream and up the other side. Ahead rocky, barren mountains loomed in the shadow of the Great Wall. For another hour we wheezed in low gear before reaching Dragon Hamlet, a village of just eleven stone huts.

"Nothing's changed. It can't change," said Cassia, gloomily surveying the village where she grew up. The surrounding mountains were so steep that, for forty days each winter, the villagers never saw the sun. Most were so poor that they tasted meat just once a month. It was easy to see why no woman willingly married into Dragon Hamlet.

The wife of Farmer Wang's cousin was home alone when we arrived. Although the marriage had taken place only seven months earlier and the red paper Double-Happiness symbols were still on the wall, Ma Linmei (Forest Plum Ma) couldn't recall her wedding date. She hadn't known any of the 150 guests, except for her father, a moonshiner. He had accompanied her to Dragon Hamlet. Although he was shocked by the poverty, he stuck with the deal, which had paid him 2,000 yuan, or $250. Before he left, he gave his twenty-year-old daughter a green windbreaker and 10 yuan, or $1.25.

Forest Plum played nervously with the zipper of her windbreaker and ducked her head so that her long bangs hid her sad eyes. She was understandably wary of us, since her husband's relative had introduced us. At a signal from Lena, I lured Farmer Wang into the courtyard so she could talk alone with Plum Forest.

"I want to escape," she told Lena, "but if I tried, they would beat me." There was no need to lock her up. Dragon Hamlet was her prison. Forest Plum didn't speak the local dialect, she was surrounded by her husband's clan and, because she was illiterate, all her letters had to go through her husband.

She had only one weapon left. As Lena gently probed, Forest Plum said she refused to have sex with her husband. The female chattel of China, it seemed, were on strike. "He sleeps here. I sleep there," she said, motioning to opposite ends of the *kang*. But she was afraid the family might lose patience with her and sell her to someone worse.

Farmer Wang and I were discussing the intricacies of making beancurd when his cousin arrived home. He was a slight man with a pinched, angular face and bushy hair prematurely streaked with gray, a sign of malnutrition. Because Farmer Wang had introduced me, he didn't take offense at my questions. As he untied a sack of pig feed from his bike, I asked why he had gone more than a thousand miles to the south to Yunnan province to buy a wife.

"I tried for two years to find someone around here. People said I was too scrawny," said Cousin Wang, who was twenty-five. Apparently, no one wanted a weakling in an agrarian society that depended on brawn. Yet he couldn't understand why Forest Plum wasn't thrilled. She was so unhappy and homesick that she had lost a lot of weight and was now barely healthy enough to bear a child, he complained. And although she had cost four times as much as the cassette deck in his bedroom, she was turning out to be a poor bargain. She refused to work in the fields and spent most of her time lying on the *kang*.

Just then, Lena and Forest Plum came out. I asked if I could take a photo of the couple. As I focused my camera, Cousin Wang tried to put his arm around his wife, but she shied away like a nervous colt. The picture I snapped showed him smirking, hands proudly tucked behind him, with Forest Plum, hollow-cheeked, staring straight ahead.

I felt depressed as I left Dragon Hamlet. I had the urge to do something useful, like rescuing Forest Plum, or paying off her husband and setting her free, instead of merely jotting down notes and taking photographs. It was hard for me, with my old Maoist baggage and my Chinese ethnic roots, to stay detached and objective in the face of so much human suffering. After I had been a foreign correspondent in China for a while, I learned to always take a stack of exercise books and a bag of pencils and a couple of soccer balls along whenever I visited a rural school. But what good would a bit of stationery do? There were so many wretched villages like Luo Family Mill, so many women trapped like Forest Plum. China's problems seemed vast, daunting, insoluble.

Part IV

PARADISE REGAINED?

19

Workers of the World United

Top left: Housekeeper Ma with Ben, when he was seven months old.

Top right: Nanny Ma with Sam, our second son, when he was one.

Bottom: Cook Mu made this cake for Ben's first birthday.

All photos: Jan Wong

After witnessing so much death and destruction at Tiananmen, some might have concluded the world was too horrible for children. I felt the opposite. I had postponed children for my career, and I was now thirty-seven. I realized, when the dust settled, that I was lucky to be alive, and my first instinct was to bring new life into the world. But I was a bit taken aback when my doctor told me my due date was the first anniversary of the massacre.

In fact, Ben arrived two weeks early. At first, I planned to have him in China, and I went for check-ups at the special foreigners' ward in the Sino-Japanese Friendship Hospital. "Your *gu pen* is too small," the Chinese gynecologist said one day. She spoke fluent English but, like many Chinese who dealt with foreigners, insisted on speaking Chinese to me because I looked Chinese. Like the guard at the compound gate, she assumed I was a fake foreign devil putting on airs.

"My what?" I asked.

"Your *gu pen*!" she snapped, reminding me of Fu the Enforcer.

I racked my brain. "What is a *gu pen*," I finally asked.

"You're having a *baby* and you don't know what a *gu pen* is?" she sputtered. Shaking her head at my colossal ignorance, she disdainfully uttered the word in English: *pelvis*. That's when I considered going to Hong Kong. I wasn't worried about my undersized pelvis. (It turned out to be normal sized, anyway.) I just didn't want to be scolded for my vocabulary when I was in labor.

My resolve hardened when a Yugoslav journalist friend, Zorana Bakovic, told me that as she was rolled into the operating room for an emergency cesarean, the Chinese doctor asked, "Are you a Communist Party member?" Zorana panicked. She was, but couldn't decide whether they'd treat her better or worse. It seemed that China deliberately made childbirth as unpleasant as possible. Perhaps it was a diabolical family-planning plot to ensure the memories were so bad you'd be put off having any more babies. Two women in labor, for instance, sometimes shared a single gurney, one's head next to the other's feet. And anesthetic was banned for all childbirth except cesarean sections.

Like many Chinese of the nineties, I saw no virtue in deprivation. I no longer had any desire to haul pig manure or overhaul my ideology. I lusted after creature comforts like anesthetic. So I decided to go to Hong Kong to have Ben.

I had originally gone to China to escape shopping malls. But like the other 1.2 billion Chinese, I found I now suffered from massive pent-up consumer desire. Living a thousand miles from the closest Toys "Я" Us made me, a first-time mother, nervous. I had no idea what babies needed. So, on a home leave just before Ben's birth, I had cleverly bought everything: orthodontically correct pacifiers, teething rings, formula bottles, powdered formula, a baby-food processor, an electronic baby monitor, diaper safety pins, plain cloth diapers, two dozen ducky-printed flannel diapers with Velcro closures, a diaper-changing bag, plastic outer pants, diaper detergent, disinfectant and softener, paper diaper liners, diaper rash cream, baby sunscreen, shampoo, oil, cream and wipes, Q-Tips, infant Tylenol, three types of baby thermometers, five parenting books and baby manicure scissors. Oh yes, and baby clothes and shoes, baby blankets, stuffed animals, baby books, a crib mobile, a crib bumper, baby back and arm carriers, a portable crib, a high chair, a Jolly Jumper, two strollers and a safety-tested car seat.

"Boy, are you ever insecure," my mother said as she watched me trying to jam everything into my suitcase in Montreal. Back in

Beijing, our nanny, Ma Naiying, watched me unpack. "I thought foreign countries had disposable diapers," she said suspiciously. They did, I admitted. But I figured that, with all my household help, I could be environmentally virtuous without having to wash a single diaper myself. Nanny Ma soon set me straight.

"These will get really stiff and uncomfortable, and take hours to dry," she said, poking suspiciously at the very expensive ducky-printed, Velcro-closing cloth diapers I had just carried across the Pacific. "Why don't you use disposable ones." It was a command, not a question. The problem was, I could barely carry in the basic equipment, never mind thousands of disposable diapers. And China didn't make diapers, disposable or otherwise. At the fancy Palace Hotel drugstore, imported Pampers sold for the equivalent of a dollar apiece. At that rate, I calculated Ben would be going through $4,000 worth a year.

As a compromise, Nanny Ma suggested we *ba* Ben. *Ba* meant to hold a baby gently by the hips over a potty or by the edge of the road and whistle softly to imitate the tinkle of urine. Chinese babies and toddlers didn't wear diapers at all, not even cloth ones. Instead, they always wore *kai dang ku*, literally open-crotch pants. Cotton, water and soap were all scarce items. People weren't. Someone was always available to *ba* a Chinese baby.

Parents began to *ba* as early as one month. Incredibly, most babies were toilet-trained by six months – at least during waking hours. By the time they could walk, usually at twelve to fourteen months, they knew to squat down in their open-crotch pants whenever they felt the urge. In winter, their tiny bums were as rosy as their other cheeks. Cathy McGregor, an American trying to toilet train her own daughter, watched in amazement once as teachers prepared fifteen toddlers for a turn on the trampoline in a Beijing park.

"The teachers went around and said, " '*Niao, niao, niao*' – 'Pee, pee, pee,' " said Cathy. "I thought, how could they all have to go at the same time? But they all squatted down."

Still, the system had its drawbacks. Older children, even ten-year-olds, had to be woken every four hours at night, or they would wet their beds. Nanny Ma was confident she could *ba* Ben. Having read the five parenting books, I mumbled something incoherent about the emotional scarring of over-early toilet training. I didn't tell her Norman and I were lousy whistlers and that we dreaded waking Ben twice each night until he went to college. Notwithstanding my huge investment, it did occur to me that cloth diapers *were* silly. After all, who used cloth toilet paper? So Nanny Ma and I agreed on disposable diapers, meaning that I agreed to import thousands of them.

Outsiders were always impressed that I could have a baby and work as a foreign correspondent. They didn't realize that in grand *Globe* tradition, I had a cook, a driver, a housekeeper, a news assistant and a nanny. As an ex-Maoist, though, I felt awkward having people wait on me hand and foot. At first, Driver Liu tried to open the car door for me chauffeur-style, until I set him straight. And unlike some foreigners, I refused to sit in the back seat – the battered Globemobile wasn't a limousine, after all. At mealtimes, I found it discomfiting to be served. Before Norman arrived, I ate in solitary splendor in the *Globe*'s large dining room while the cook hovered in the kitchen. Just like the old days at Beijing University, I tried to help clean up afterwards.

For their part, the Chinese staff had never worked for anyone who spoke their language, in more ways than one. I knew, for instance, all the words to that Cultural Revolution ditty "Sailing the Seas Depends on the Helmsman." It made us closer that I, like them, had once been a Maoist who had worked in the paddy fields. They always enjoyed it when a stranger dropped by the bureau and couldn't figure out which one of us was the foreign correspondent.

My colleagues at home were understandably envious when they heard about the bureau set-up. Some even started taking Chinese lessons. What they didn't realize was that my staff belonged to a powerful union I dubbed Workers of the World United. If I "fired" one of the staff, they returned to the Diplomatic Service Bureau, a wing of the Foreign Ministry, where they simply waited for another assignment. Short of a brush with the law, they had "iron rice bowls," a guaranteed job for life.

Besides their regular duties, the staff was supposed to spy on us. That was easy because emptying the trash and hanging around were in their job description. In addition to regular tattle meetings, the staff also had to attend special brainwashing sessions because working for Westerners was likened to working in a "vat of dye"; they had to cleanse themselves of the stain of foreign contact. For this, the Diplomatic Service Bureau charged us ten times the market rate and skimmed off most of the money for itself.

But especially after Tiananmen, morale was so bad that people openly balked at going to these meetings. To boost attendance, the Diplomatic Service resorted to giving out door prizes of enamel pots and frozen carp. By the 1990s, about all that remained of the old system was a set of forty-two secret rules, which covered everything from receiving foreigners in your home (absolutely banned) to receiving gifts from foreigners (absolutely banned).

It was poetic justice that an ex-Maoist like me be condemned to manage four Commie servants. I paid their salaries, and they bossed me around. On Monday mornings, Nanny Ma clucked her tongue if she found even a hint of rash on Ben's behind.

"You didn't change his diaper fast enough," she scolded.

"I'm really sorry," I apologized. "I'll try not to let it happen again."

When Ben went through his terrible twos and refused to eat a perfectly delicious meal, I tried to impose a modicum of discipline. "Fine. Starve," I said. At the first sign of tears, Cook Mu would sweep Ben up in his arms, take him into the kitchen and share his bowl of food with him. I never gave away my old Cultural Revolution clothes to the staff, in mistress-of-the-manor fashion. Instead, Nanny Ma, who preferred silk, gave me *her* hand-me-downs.

We lived in a brand-new diplomatic compound of an architectural style best described as Post-Stalinist Instant Decrepitude. Pagoda Garden, as our dreary cluster of concrete highrises was called, didn't have a pagoda or, at first, even a garden. For the first three years, our front yard was an expanse of mud studded with the occasional dead rat. Our backyard was the midnight gravel dump for the new Canadian Embassy, which, like the rest of Beijing, seemed to be endlessly under construction.

We paid more than $4,000 each month for an office and a three-bedroom apartment. For that money, we got the same whitewashed walls, drafty windows and scary elevators as ordinary Chinese flats. It was possible to have the apartment painted, but there was no guarantee the paint wouldn't be lead-based, and it meant having to suffer through a dozen workmen lounging around your home for weeks. One of my predecessors, Norman Webster, decided to get his wooden floors refinished. A team arrived, strapped sandpaper to their running shoes and skated around his living room for days.

But at least we had Western-style bathrooms, sort of. The bathroom doors came with picture windows and the toilets sometimes flushed hot water. The shower ran either ice cold or scalding hot, with nothing in between. I remembered Pagoda Garden's mystery plumbing every time Premier Li Peng assured investors and environmentalists that the gigantic Three Gorges dam China was building on the Yangtze River was completely safe.

What I loved – well, maybe *love* is too strong a word – what I *liked* about Pagoda Garden were the quirky touches so revealing of the national psyche. In a nation that once tried to outlaw private property, every single door in our apartment, including the kitchen pantry, the linen closet and the fuse box, came with a lock and key. The locks were of such poor quality that they regularly seized up, sometimes trapping us inside the room. Whenever I fretted about electronic bugs, the quality of Pagoda Garden's locks always reassured me.

To me, our smoke detectors epitomized China's crass new materialism. I was impressed we had them at all, until an inspection team dropped by, armed with a lit cigarette and an eight-foot length of bamboo. Norman and I watched one man blow cigarette smoke up the hollow pole while the other aimed it at our dining-room smoke detector. They prepared to leave.

"But I haven't heard a thing," Norman protested.

The smoker looked at him as if he were stupid. "The alarm sounds in *our* office," he said. No one cared if *we* burned to a crisp. Big Brother just wanted to know if his real estate was okay.

My staff exploded many myths I held about China. I'm sure I did the same for theirs about foreigners. I had to laugh when Westerners asked for etiquette tips on dealing with the inscrutable, polite and highly civilized Chinese.

"What's that on your nose?" Cook Mu asked one day as he set a dish of steaming dumplings on the table. I just *knew* he would ask. I was having a bout of complexion problems during pregnancy.

With as much dignity as I could muster, I replied, "A pimple."

"Gee, it looks pretty bad," he said, standing there with his arms folded over his white apron. I grunted assent, and busied myself with the delicious dumplings, hoping he would take the hint and go back inside the kitchen. But he stood there, scrutinizing my nose.

"Bet it hurts, too," he said, finally.

I stopped chewing and put down my chopsticks. "Yes," I said, "it hurts."

Another time, Yan Yan met me at the airport when I came back from a trip. "Wow," my news assistant said by way of greeting. "Who cut your hair? Looks like a dog bit it off." My old teacher, Fu the Enforcer, had made similar remarks. But somehow they bothered me less in the early days when I was enamored of Maoism and willing to put up with a lot.

Cook Mu exploded the myth that Chinese food was healthy. A former peasant who had learned to cook in the army, he didn't stir-fry meat so much as boil it in oil. His real training was in French cooking – airy spinach soufflés, homemade strawberry ice cream and rosy filets of beef with buttery mashed potatoes. He even made bagels. At Christmas, he roasted a goose in traditional English style, stuffing it with forcemeat and sage. More than once, I ignored broad hints from the other staff that my weekly grocery bill exceeded Deng Xiaoping's monthly pay. I suspected Cook Mu of inflating receipts, but I kept him on because, really, how many times in life could you find someone who made perfect roast chicken? Besides, I appreciated his comments on my acne.

"My wife is fooling around with Cook Mu," the caller said. I sat up straight at my desk and, as was my phone habit in China, began to jot down notes. He said he was the husband of my housekeeper, Ma Baoying. "Since she started working at your place, we fight all the time. Several nights last month, she didn't come home. She is having *relations* with the cook. She's painting her *nails*."

"What do you want me to do about it?" I said. I had never met Housekeeper Ma's husband, who installed radiators.

"You are the boss," said the caller. "It's your job to stop them."

"How?" I said.

"Fire her. Separate her from the cook. Then she will be assigned another job."

I demurred, but the caller was adamant. "You are the work unit. You must stop them," he said. "I'm an ordinary worker. I kneel down before you. I beg you to help me save my marriage."

"I'll look into it," I said uncertainly, and hung up. What business was it of mine if the cook and housekeeper were indulging in hanky panky? I had done enough meddling in my time, and I certainly wasn't going to do any more.

Cook Mu was a Communist Party member. Despite everything I now knew about China, I still couldn't shake the feeling that Party members should be more honorable than the average person. Could he really be two-timing his wife, a peasant on the outskirts of Beijing whom he saw only a few times a year? I secretly started observing the two of them. Like many Beijing women in their thirties, Housekeeper Ma frizzed her hair, used lipstick, tattooed her brows and, for a while, even wore a wig. But so what? She often joked with Cook Mu, and he teased her back. While there was camaraderie, there was zero electricity.

One afternoon, the caller telephoned again.

"My wife is sleeping with Cook Mu," he said. "She was caught in his dormitory room this week. You have to stop them."

"Thank you for letting me know," I said, and hung up.

I was beginning to doubt the caller was Housekeeper Ma's husband. If she really had been caught in Cook Mu's dormitory, Chinese officials would have dealt with it. Yet nothing happened.

One morning an official from the Diplomatic Services Bureau called. "Housekeeper Ma won't be going to work today."

"When will she be coming back?" I asked politely, knowing that, as the person who paid the salary, I had the least say in Housekeeper Ma's schedule.

"We'll send over another cleaner," he said.

I was taken aback. "Why?"

"The police are interrogating Housekeeper Ma. She won't be working for you any more."

"Is it because of me?" I blurted. I lived with every journalist's fear of getting someone into trouble.

"It's nothing to do with you," the official said blandly.

Housekeeper Ma phoned me the next morning. "I'm not working for you any more," she said nervously.

"I know. Are you okay?" I asked.

"I'm fine, but I want to collect a few things I left in the office. And I don't want to see the others," she said.

I wondered if she was in trouble because she really was fooling around with Cook Mu. But he seemed perfectly normal; if it were true, he'd be in hot water, too. I met her a few days later in an alley. When she saw me, she started to cry.

"I've been fired," she said. Two days earlier, police had interrogated her. "They told me to confess," she said, wiping away her tears. "I had no idea what they were talking about. They kept telling me to confess."

That was standard operating procedure in China. The police already had the goods on you, but they wanted to see what else you coughed up. Housekeeper Ma had racked her brains. After ten hours, a policeman dropped the first hint. It had to do, he said, with pornography. She finally understood. Four years earlier, when she was a cleaner at the Polish Embassy, several drivers and maids got together to watch porno films on a VCR. One of the drivers had recently been arrested on unrelated charges, and when police tried the fishing-expedition tactics on him, he told them about the porno-film club.

"I supplied one of the cassettes," said Housekeeper Ma, reddening in shame. She began to cry again. I hastily assured her I watched porno movies all the time.

"The police wanted to know where I got the film," she said, "but I refused to name names. I'm not like that turtle's egg driver. I would never turn anyone in."

After fifteen hours of interrogation, the police released her with a warning. Then the Diplomatic Service Bureau fired her.

"What are you going to do?" I said.

"I'm going into business for myself," she said defiantly.

I felt bad. I knew she would fail. I mean, Housekeeper Ma just wasn't all that smart. And where would she get the start-up capital?

"If you need seed money, I can help," I said.

She shook her head, thanked me for everything I had done and asked me to give Ben a hug. Lamely, I thanked her, too. Then she bicycled off.

Seventeen months later, Housekeeper Ma phoned to invite everyone to lunch at Pizza Hut. "Are you sure?" I said. "It's pretty expensive."

"No problem," she said. "Make sure everyone comes: Cook Mu, Nanny Ma, Driver Liu, Ben and Fat Paycheck Shulman." Pizza Hut was a big hit among Beijing's up-and-coming middle class. It was clean, served an exotic concoction called cheese and offered a non-smoking section. The Chinese thought that was cute, since everybody smoked.

Housekeeper Ma was waiting for us outside. She had gained a little weight and was wearing an expensive gray sweater embroidered with silver beads. She gathered Ben into her arms and won his heart when she gave him a toy police car with a siren, flashing lights and doors that opened and shut. Considering her recent trauma, I couldn't understand why she had picked a toy like that. But the Chinese, who hate living in a police state as much as the next person, loved dressing their toddlers in soldier uniforms. By the time we left China, Ben had amassed the largest collection of toy tanks and machine guns of any four-year-old I knew.

Like a proper Chinese hostess, Housekeeper Ma ordered for her guests. "Three extra-large deep-dish meat pizzas," she told the waitress.

"Two are enough," I whispered.

Housekeeper Ma ignored me.

"Six orders of spaghetti," she continued. "We're all having the salad bar. Soup. Seven ice creams. And Coke for everyone."

The bill came to nearly 300 yuan, or more than a month's pay for state workers like Driver Liu. I felt terrible. I told her it was too expensive and that she should let me treat.

"I expected to pay 400 yuan," she said airily.

I finally understood. Housekeeper Ma was redeeming her pride after her ignominious departure. As a correct hostess, she had ordered more than we could possibly finish (and by now I knew better than to try to clean my plate). But she also wanted us to know that she was just fine, thank you. She had opened a tiny convenience store selling soy sauce, cigarettes, toilet paper and instant noodles. Each month, she netted ten times what she had earned at the Diplomatic Service Bureau. The state had tossed Housekeeper Ma out like an old shoe. A year and a half later, she was part of China's up-and-coming middle class.

After that lunch, Driver Liu was openly envious. He had thought many times of ditching his iron rice bowl and striking out on his own. Housekeeper Ma's success was especially galling, for he had always looked down on her. When she was fired, he told me he suspected all along that she was a lowlife.

"Why do you say that?" I asked, annoyed at the rush to judgment.

"She has *two* VCRs at home," he said triumphantly, as if that was proof of a porno ring. And in China, it probably often was.

Liu Xinyong was born in 1953 in Beijing, one of seven children in a poor, working-class family. During the Cultural Revolution, he was sent to a bleak state farm near the Soviet border. In 1974, he won the district's only scholarship to Beijing University. We would have been schoolmates, but the local Communist Party secretary bumped him in favor of his own son. The next year, Liu managed to win the only slot to a technical school, but the same anti-Deng political campaign that ruined my studies obliterated his.

Driver Liu was a Party member but, like Cook Mu, he never revealed that to me himself. (Disclosing Party membership to foreigners was another no-no, according to the forty-two secret rules of conduct.) His brush cut and square-jawed face matched his plain-spoken personality. Whereas other drivers napped whenever they weren't driving, he was never idle. Besides polishing our car until it sparkled, he cheerfully took charge of paying bills, banking, developing film, mailing letters and buying supplies, all time-consuming chores in a Third World country.

Driver Liu was also one of the best drivers in Beijing which, I guess, wasn't saying much. At any rate, he never had an accident. But we did seem to attract more than our share of people hitting us. Once, a cyclist, zipping through lanes of traffic, broadsided *us*. He bounced off, picked himself up with an embarrassed grin and disappeared, leaving us stunned, and with a fresh dent in the driver's door. Another time, in 1990, we were stopped at a red light on the Second Ring Road when a white minibus crashed into the rear of our brand-new Jeep Cherokee, which I had just bought to replace the stolen Toyota. I turned around in time to see the minibus bounce back, rear up and smash into us again. For a split second, I thought plainclothes police were trying out a new way to kill us.

Driver Liu's sunglasses flew off. So did Yan Yan's earrings. I was in my eighth month of pregnancy, but my seatbelt saved me, and Ben. The back seat buckled under the impact, and the force of the crash pushed us several yards forward. Luckily, Driver Liu had the hand brake on, or we would have flattened a few pedestrians. Three peasants emerged from the white van, shaken but unhurt. Their brakes had failed, they explained apologetically. I asked if they had insurance. They didn't. But they said they were pretty good at repairs and offered to fix our Jeep, free. I declined.

A few weeks later, Norman and Driver Liu were on the way to the repair shop to handle some paperwork when they suddenly spotted our old tan Toyota parked at a traffic circle. It looked exactly the same … except for the red police lights strapped across the roof and its special police plates. "I think that's our car," Norman said. "Can I see the serial numbers?" The uniformed policeman sitting inside ignored him.

The next morning, I hurried down to the special police station for foreigners. I had very little time because the following day I was scheduled to board a plane for Hong Kong to have Ben. On the way to the station, Driver Liu coached me on strategy.

"Now don't lose your temper," he warned. "Don't accuse them of stealing your car. Don't even say the word *steal*. Just say, 'Sorry. Excuse me, but I believe you might have our car.' You'll never get the car back if you lose your temper."

The problem would be keeping a straight face. It was a delicious moment, catching the Reds red-handed. That morning, I faithfully stuck to Driver Liu's script. I also produced the import documents my predecessors had meticulously filed away a decade earlier. Eventually, two tough-looking men in leather jackets walked in, introducing themselves as special detectives. I repeated my story for the umpteenth time and apologized for bothering them that day. I had little choice, I added, glancing down at my bulging belly. A look of panic flickered across their faces.

"Do you have a car?" said one, not realizing the irony of his question.

We piled into the *Globe*'s newly repaired Jeep and headed for their headquarters. "No matter what we do," one of the detectives muttered, "it's going to look bad. There's no good explanation for this one."

At headquarters, they conferred some more. The thieves turned out to be the police at the Eastern Peace precinct. Their alibi: they didn't know who owned it. I refrained from pointing out it was the same police station where I had initially reported the theft. The police not only didn't apologize, they announced they would keep our Toyota another month. They needed it, they explained, as an extra squad car during the tense run-up to the first anniversary of Tiananmen Square. On June 5, 1990, we got our Toyota back, a year less a day after the police had stolen it. The gas tank was empty, the odometer was broken, the cigarette lighter was gone and cigarette butts and Popsicle sticks littered the interior. As Norman cleaned out the debris, he came across a receipt for our 1989 road tax. It said: "Paid by the *Globe and Mail* of Canada."

A couple of years later, when thieves stole the Jeep Cherokee of Deng's eldest daughter, police recovered her car in record time.

In 1993, I decided to take the whole family to Hong Kong for the birth of our second son, Sam. "Take me with you, too," urged Nanny Ma. "I can look after Ben while you're in the hospital and help you with everything." I treasured Nanny Ma. She was the smartest person in the bureau, myself included. Were it not for the Cultural Revolution, which truncated her education, I'm sure she would have been running a bank.

She was in her forties and had small crinkly eyes, a stubborn jaw and delicate hands and feet. Like all my staff, her childhood had been marked by poverty. Born in a village in coastal Shandong province, she had to feign illness as a child to get a precious egg. Now, in one generation, she had made the leap from famine to fat. In attempts to shed a few extra pounds, she sipped special "thinning" teas and went on weird diets, sometimes refusing to eat even a single grain of rice.

"She has the airs of a duchess and the fate of a scullery maid," snorted Cook Mu in disgust, after she declined to sample a dish of his delectable fatty pork.

Nanny Ma made Ben tiny, rose-bedecked cakes out of Play-Doh. On warm summer days, she taught him how to catch dragonflies. In winter, she knitted him little wool mitts, with the thumbs missing so he could suck his thumb. And she brought him the baby quilt she had made years earlier for her own son. Ben loved Nanny Ma with all his heart. She was convinced it was destiny when at four months he developed a tiny mole in the middle of his nose that exactly matched the beauty spot on hers.

More than one friend hinted they would love to inherit her when we left. I told them not to hold their breath. Nanny Ma was coming with me to Canada. It was her idea, not mine. She assured me she could temporarily leave behind her husband and teenaged son. When I realized she was serious, I applied to bring her into Canada under a special foreign-domestics program that would eventually enable the rest of her family to emigrate to Canada.

I knew it would be expensive to take her to Hong Kong, but she would help ease Sam's arrival into our family. And I knew it was also a rare chance for her to see the outside world. She brushed off my worries about a visa. "Lots of nannies have gone there. It's easy," she said.

It turned out she didn't know a single nanny who had ever been to Hong Kong. I found myself ensnarled in months of red tape. As our departure date drew near, she asked for a week off "to rest and pack." By then, I was very pregnant, very busy and very irritable. When I refused, she asked if she could fly down alone a week later. I nixed that idea, too. The reason I was bringing her, I testily explained, was so that I could work.

But we both knew who was boss. She took the last day off despite my objections. I was so busy shutting down the office, paying last-minute bills, taking care of Ben and packing that I canceled a much-postponed haircut. I showed up at the airport the next day with my regular dog-bitten-off hairdo. Nanny Ma was relaxed and smiling. She looked great. I asked how her day off had been.

"Great," she said. "I got my hair done."

For a person who had never left China, Nanny Ma suffered remarkably little culture shock. On weekends, she eagerly struck out on her own in Hong Kong, taking the subway, wandering through department stores, chatting to strangers on the street and taking in the occasional movie.

Thanks to her membership in Workers of the World United, she figured we were all on a camping trip together and everybody ought to pitch in. I soon found myself doing the laundry, the grocery shopping and most of the cooking, while continuing to work.

After Sam was born, it dawned on me that I didn't have to spend my maternity leave in smoggy, sweltering Beijing. "We've decided to go back to Montreal for the summer," I told Nanny Ma. "I've checked. There's a perfect flight for you back to Beijing. It leaves two hours after our flight for Montreal."

Nanny Ma flushed. "You should see *me* off first," she said.

I was taken aback. I remembered how she had wanted to fly down on her own. I reassured her she would have no problem waiting at the Hong Kong airport, a bilingual model of efficiency. I pointed out that she had been roaming around on her own for nearly a month. When I realized she was truly insecure, I promised to book her a business-class seat, give her extra cash for an emergency and leave the phone numbers of Hong Kong friends in case disaster struck in those two hours.

"I help you, but you don't help me," she said, storming into her room and slamming the door. I took a deep breath and followed her in. She was lying on her bed, dabbing at her eyes with a fluffy white bath towel.

"Sam will be just one month old when we leave. I have to breast-feed him every two or three hours. Ben has just turned three. He's still in diapers. We have to get on an eighteen-hour flight through thirteen time zones," I explained through gritted teeth. "We just can't go to the airport two hours early to see you off first."

"You saw your sister off to the airport, but you won't take me," said Nanny Ma. "What if I get lost? What if I can't find the plane? What if the luggage never makes it to Beijing?" She started sobbing. Decades of cradle-to-grave socialism had rendered her incapable of handling anything on her own, or at least it had convinced her she couldn't.

That same cradle-to-grave socialism had turned me into a raging member of the bourgeoisie. I wanted to scream: "You work for me, remember?" Just then, Norman, who loses his temper about once every ten years, stomped into the room. I left. Through the door I could hear them shouting. Norman told her she was being ridiculous. Neither of us had ever talked to her like that before. It was too traumatic for words.

"This just isn't done," Nanny Ma said angrily. "According to custom, if you ask someone to do a job, you must escort them all the way home again. You just can't abandon them." Norman retorted that if we treated her the way foreign companies treated Chinese workers, we would make her take the train to save money. It was a mistake.

"Take the *train*?" she yelled. "I'd be glad to. I'd *walk* back if I could. What if you took me to Canada and did this to me? Do you expect me to swim back?" She burst into tears anew. Norman walked out, throwing his arms in the air. After a moment, Nanny Ma emerged from her room, ignored us completely, and with great dignity told Ben she was taking him for a walk.

I looked at Norman. He looked at me. We had forgotten our place. He meekly changed her flight to one that would leave before ours. By the time Nanny Ma returned with Ben, Norman was hiding in our bedroom.

"It's all fixed," I said politely. "You'll go before us. Don't worry about Fat Paycheck Shulman. He sometimes speaks bluntly."

"No, no. I will go *after* you," she said icily. For ten minutes, we had that ritually polite Chinese conversation that caused traffic jams at entrances. Nanny Ma was bitterly determined we should go first, even though she remained unconvinced she would make it back to Beijing alive. I finally hit upon the perfect solution.

"Well, I *am* a half-wit anyway," she said, when I told her my plan.

Dragonair provided escort services for unaccompanied children, very old people and anyone who was ill. But how to get them to take care of a middle-aged, healthy woman? I called them up and explained: My friend has to fly back on her own. The problem is, I said, she is mildly retarded.

"She can talk and all that, but, well, you know ..."

The person on the other end of the line said smoothly, "Don't worry, ma'am. We'll take good care of her." And that was how Nanny Ma got back to Beijing.

Nanny Ma eventually forgave us for mistreating her in Hong Kong. After three months, she even began speaking again to Norman. I assumed she was still interested in the chance at a better life, or at least the chance to give her only son that opportunity. I was wrong. She never again mentioned the plan to go with us to Canada.

At first, I thought we had fatally offended her by not seeing her off first. But it turned out that her twenty-two-year-old son had no desire to leave the motherland. He enjoyed hanging out with his friends at home. After failing the entrance exam to senior high school, he worked briefly as a hotel cook, then quit and refused to show up for other jobs his parents wangled for him. Whenever Nanny Ma lost her temper with her son, she would call him a lout and threaten to go to Canada. He would then fall to his knees and beg her to stay. The erstwhile Golden Mountain, as the earliest Chinese immigrants called North America, had gone from being the promised land to the bogeyman.

Life, it seemed, was getting very good in China. Nanny Ma's husband was deputy chief of the Beijing Municipal Taxation Bureau, an ideal get-rich-quick job under Deng's reforms. I watched as their standard of living soared. The tax bureau assigned him a car and a driver. It installed a phone in their home. Nanny Ma bought a freezer. And she hired a cleaning woman. If I needed any more evidence of China's economic boom, I had it. Even my maid had a maid.

20

Ferrari Li

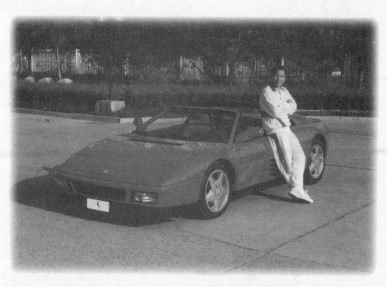

Top: The felicitously named Dr. Long.

Photo: Jan Wong/*Globe and Mail*

Bottom: Li Xiaohua, an ex-labor camp convict and the first Chinese to own a Ferrari.

Photo courtesy Li Xiaohua

t was impossible to ignore the fact that for many, many people like Nanny Ma, life was improving dramatically. Seemingly overnight, cheap yellow minibuses flooded the streets of Beijing, making taxis affordable for the masses for the very first time. Despite a steep hook-up charge – about half a year's pay for a state worker - many friends began installing home phones.

Retro-hardship became hip. People flocked to nostalgic eateries like Beijing's Remembering Bitterness Restaurant to listen to blind accordion players while sampling famine-era menus of fried locusts and boiled weeds. Photography studios rented flouncy wedding dresses so brides could be queen for a minute. And pet dogs, as opposed to the stir-fried variety, became a hot status symbol despite a continuing Maoist ban on dogs. (Rabies is rendered in Chinese as "mad dog disease.") While the middle class had to content itself with renting dogs – 10 yuan, or $1.25, for ten minutes – the rich flaunted pedigreed Pekingese and shih tzus. To deal with the illegal fad, special police squads swept through neighborhoods, strangling dogs with steel wire looped at the end of metal poles. As Muffy and Maoism faced off, I remembered Fragrance, my old dog-beating roommate, and was not surprised Muffy lost.

The new middle class still didn't have hot running water at home, but public bathhouses began offering specialty soaks scented with milk or Shaoxing rice wine. I sampled the Nescafé bath, which the attendant promised would perk me up. It didn't. Although Nescafé's agent in Beijing could not tell me the manufacturer's recommended amount for a bath, he was thrilled to hear the Chinese were wallowing in his product.

Having lived through the days when I had to shop daily for perishables, I was cheered that people could now afford refrigerators. But some conspicuous consumption raised eyebrows. Yan Yan showed up for work one day with tattooed boomerangs in place of her eyebrows. When Housekeeper Ma also arrived with an air of permanent surprise, I knew it was a trend. For a month's pay, Beijing clinics also sliced and stitched eyelids to create a second fold, transforming almond shapes into Round Eyes.

After forty years of deprivation, people were lavishing money on themselves, often literally. Some women opted for bigger breasts and some men decided to get bigger penises. I personally thought that was going a bit overboard, but I had never let excess get in the way of a good story. When the official Xinhua News Agency published a small item on China's first penis-extension doctor, Lena Sun and I rushed to Wuhan, a gritty industrial port on the Yangtze River, to interview him.

"First, before I say anything, are you both married?" asked Dr. Long Daochou, chief of plastic surgery at Hubei Medical College's Number One Affiliated Hospital. We had invited the felicitously named Dr. Long to a get-to-know-you dinner, hoping he would let us visit his penis clinic. He turned out to be a jolly, libidinous fellow with friendly puppy-dog eyes who loved discussing racially linked penis sizes, vaginal elasticity and various combinations of interracial marriage – provided you weren't a virgin.

"We're both married," I quickly assured him. "We each have a son, and our husbands are both foreigners, white."

"Then you must be very satisfied," he said, beaming, as Lena choked on her rice. Dr. Long was a firm believer in length. He continued to expound on his favorite subject in a hearty voice, oblivious to the knot of fascinated waitresses hovering nearby. "Chinese women have the smallest vaginas, just like Chinese men have the smallest penises. White people have bigger penises. The longer the penis, the greater the sexual satisfaction for the woman. It doesn't much change for the man."

The Long Dong Silver episode of the Anita Hill–Clarence Thomas hearings was all over CNN at the time, but Dr. Long hadn't heard about the sexual-harassment controversy dogging the U.S. Supreme Court nominee. "The bigger the better, the longer the better," he boomed as other diners glanced our way. "Blacks have longer and bigger penises than whites."

"I thought that was a big myth," I said, fretting that I would never get racially-linked penis sizes into the paper.

"I saw it myself," insisted Dr. Long, who was fifty-seven. "I was part of a volunteer Chinese medical team in Algeria from 1968 to 1971. As a doctor, I got to see everything." Unerect, Asians averaged five inches and Caucasians six or seven inches, he told us. "Blacks are even longer."

Some of his patients had been sent by their wives. Others got on his waiting list after their fiancées saw the goods and broke off the engagement. I remembered how my classmates had buried their burning faces in their laps during a population-control lecture at Big Joy Farm, and was glad that Chinese women had become more assertive. "Twenty years ago, if sexual relations were bad, women suffered their whole lives," he continued. "But today, if a young woman isn't happy, she just says, 'Bye-bye.' " He said the "bye-bye" part in English. The waitresses tittered behind their hands. Dr. Long invited us to visit his clinic the next morning.

"Lena," I said back at the hotel that night, "we need a specialized vocabulary list."

"I'm not calling *my* interpreter," she said.

I called Norman. "Tell me the Chinese words for orgasm, oral sex and premature ejaculation."

"Orgasm is *extreme joy*, oral sex is *mouth perversion* and premature ejaculation is *early leaking*," he said. "Why?"

I wanted to tell him that Wuhan was a really swinging town. Instead I told him what Dr. Long had said about Chinese penis sizes and asked if he had ever paid attention back when he used public bathhouses.

"I never noticed any difference," he said, "but then I never ran around with a ruler."

The next day, Dr. Long met us wearing a white surgical cap, a white coat and a broad smile. In his office we paged through before-and-after photos, lovingly displayed in blue brocade albums. After admiring his handiwork, we dipped into a shoebox full of fan mail. Then it was time to visit the ward.

"Pretend you're medical students," said Dr. Long, thrusting a couple of white lab coats at us. We scurried after him, pulling on the coats as we clutched our notebooks and cameras. He barged into a ward and, without warning, flipped the quilt off the patient nearest the door. The man was naked from the waist down. A small teepee-like frame protected his penis, which was partially wrapped in thick white bandages.

"We operated on him yesterday. He used to be one inch," said Dr. Long. Whipping a small metal ruler from his breast pocket, the doctor took a quick measure. "See? Three point seven inches." Patient and doctor beamed. Now *this* was China reconstructs.

"I wasn't normal. I was always afraid to find a girlfriend," said the patient, a twenty-one-year-old security guard from Manchuria. He glanced down at his member, still swollen from surgery, and grinned. "Now I can."

The next patient was a twenty-two-year-old metalworker from northwest China. He was awaiting surgery. "Drop your pants," Dr. Long ordered. I couldn't help myself. I stared in fascination. He had no pubic hair, and his penis was a mere half inch long.

"Look," said Dr. Long, fingering the tiny protuberance. "It's only skin, nothing else. He was born like that. It's a micro-penis. He never developed. We're going to have to lengthen it *and* thicken it." This humiliating synopsis brought back memories of Fu the Enforcer telling me I was so flat I looked like a boy. I searched for a neutral question.

"How will you pay for the operation?" I asked.

The patient burst into tears. "My father is retired," he sobbed, "but he managed to save the money for me. I'm his only son."

Dr. Long patted him on the shoulder and told him to pull up his pants. "Don't worry. We'll fix you up."

Dr. Long charged a couple of hundred dollars an operation, or about three to four months' pay for a state worker. He rejected anyone with impotence, ejaculation problems or a penis five inches or longer. Dr. Long didn't extend so much as excavate, uncovering the base of the penis the way you might scoop out the earth around a building to expose the basement to light and air.

"The penis extends deep inside the body," he said. "We cut the suspensory ligaments at the side of the pubic bone so the entire length can be used. No one has lost sensitivity or the ability to have an erection." Dr. Long claimed to have performed more than two hundred such operations, with an average extension of three inches. Caucasians and blacks got better results because, relatively speaking, their buried part was longer, he said.

I understood why his waiting list was so full when Dr. Long introduced the third patient, a twenty-five-year-old peasant from central China. He was meekly waiting for us with his pants down. His operation was scheduled for the following week.

"It's because of this I've never married," he said. He looked down and pointed to his … *nothing*.

"A dog bit it off when he was three months old," explained Dr. Long. "In the village, children just squat down wherever they are. There are always lots of dogs and pigs, and they fight to eat the feces. Sometimes in the commotion, they end up biting off the penis." The vast majority of his patients, he said, were maimed as toddlers in open-crotch pants. I had a flashback of the Jurassic Park latrine at Farmer Wang's, and shuddered. China desperately needed a Pampers factory, or at least a dog-food industry.

Dr. Long had launched his penis-extending career in 1984 by fixing up one of those dog-bite victims. Although doctors had sewn the little boy's penis back on at the time, it remained toddler-sized. Now the boy had become a young man and he wanted to get married. Dr. Long suggested a prosthesis, but the patient refused. He wanted a real penis.

"I said I couldn't do it. Then his father got down on his knees and said to me, 'He's my only son. Please do something so we can have grandsons to carry on the family line.' " Dr. Long called a meeting of Wuhan's top urologists and reconstructive surgeons.

Nobody had any ideas. He began dissecting corpses and pondered the suspensory ligaments. The son agreed to be the first guinea pig, and the operation was a success. With the suspensory ligaments severed, the newly extended penis was nearly four inches long when flaccid and more than five inches long when erect. "He married two years later," said Dr. Long, with a thousand-watt smile. "They wrote me a letter to tell me they had a baby girl the following year."

I didn't believe Dr. Long about racially linked penis sizes. When I got back to Beijing, I phoned Seattle-based PATH, an affiliate member of the United Nations task force on condom sizes, part of the International Standards Organization. Did blacks really have bigger penises than whites? Were Asians the smallest of them all? "It still has an emotional edge and is considered to be mythology, but we know this is probably true," said Dr. Michael Free, PATH's vice-president and a reproductive physiologist. He told me that the World Health Organization made a special condom with a circumference of 106 millimeters for Africa, compared with a standard 104-millimeter size in North America and Europe. PATH itself supplied a 98-millimeter condom to Asia, and had helped build a factory in China that manufactured condoms in four sizes, from 104 millimeters to 90 millimeters.

Ninety millimeters?

Dr. Free assured me I hadn't heard wrong. "It's the smallest size PATH is aware of in the world," he said.

Mao had always railed against "sugar-coated bullets." What he meant was that post-victory decadence could kill a communist as surely as real ammunition could. Now, after so many years of intense Maoism, the Chinese were in hot pursuit of those sugar-coated bullets. Besides tattooed brows and bigger penises, they seemed to be embracing the worst parts of Western civilization. They bought pin-up calendars of busty blondes. They re-recorded "The East Is Red" to a disco beat. And they snacked on Kentucky Fried Chicken at the Great Wall.

In April 1992, when the world's biggest McDonald's opened in Beijing, I felt as though a great civilization was taking a Great Leap Backward. But who was I to judge? After all, I had dreamed of greasy french fries down at Big Joy Farm. I dutifully went to cover the opening. "I wanted to be the first Chinese in Beijing to taste a Big Mac," said Dong Jie, a serious-faced college student who had waited in line since 4 a.m. When the doors finally opened at 8:36, he and hundreds of others stampeded into the marble and glass building.

"Put on the music," a manager shouted.

"Stand back," a McDonald's executive warned.

There was no breakfast menu. Dong Jie raced to one of the twenty-nine cash registers and ordered a Big Mac and a hot chocolate. He struggled with the white plastic lid. "How do you open this?" he wondered out loud. Before anyone could stop him, he plunged in the straw provided by an overzealous server and took a sip, scalding his tongue. Gamely, he took a bite of his Big Mac, called a *Ju Han Bao*, or a giant hamburger. "It's delicious," he said.

American executives surveyed the feeding frenzy with glee. "Did you see the people out there!" cried James Cantalupo, president of McDonald's international division. Pressed against the wall of the staircase by the crush, he had the glazed-eye look of a capitalist who just realized that a billion Chinese will eat burgers for breakfast.

"What time does lunch start here?" he said, glancing at his watch. He burst out laughing when he realized it was just 9:30 a.m.

It wasn't all that funny to me. This was the site, three years earlier, where people had died trying to keep the army from Tiananmen Square. After the massacre, while other corporations dithered, McDonald's pounced on the prime location, just across from the Beijing Hotel. The two-story, seven-hundred-seat restaurant was seven times bigger than the average U.S. McDonald's.

At the press conference on opening day, I sat in the front row and listened to a speech by Xing Chunhua, the Chinese chairman of Beijing McDonald's. He had a round face, thinning hair and a look of great importance. On the lapel of his dark pinstriped suit, he wore a McDonald's icon where I presumed he once had pinned a Mao button. "This is not just a restaurant opening," enthused Chairman Xing (pronounced *Sing*), "but the culmination of the fruits of labor between two partners who share the same vision and values."

"The same vision and values?" McDonald's and Dengism? I liked that quote. When I went home and showed Norman the elaborate press kit, he let out a yelp. "What's wrong?" I said.

"It's Old Xing!" he said.

"What are you talking about?"

"Old Xing is chairman of the board of *McDonald's*," Norman said, choking with laughter.

I had seen him talk. I had jotted down a physical description in my notebook. I had even read his biography, supplied by McDonald's publicists on recycled paper. But never once did it occur to me that he was Old Xing, Joan and Sid's former Party secretary. When Norman and I used to bike to the Red Star Commune every weekend in the 1970s, he would drop by to chat about wheat yields and dialectics. I just didn't recognize him without his faded Mao suit. The hand-out said he had worked for "a large state-run company where he devoted himself to administrative management." I guess that was McDonald-speak for "Communist Party secretary of the Red Star Commune."

While the new middle class sampled Big Macs, the new rich supped at Maxim's. On Valentine's Day 1994, I lolled among the silken cushions at Pierre Cardin's *luxe* restaurant to watch Beijing's Beautiful People having an end-of-the-Party party. Soong Huai-kuei, Maxim's *soignée* manager, jumped up constantly from her plate of poached vegetables to air-kiss guests and snap their photos with a tiny flash camera. Maxim's lobby was already plastered with celebrity snapshots. One showed the French designer frowning as he fitted Deng Lin, Deng's roly-poly artist daughter, with a battle-ship-gray muumuu. It was hard to say whether the sour expression on Cardin's face was due to a mouthful of pins or because he knew she was going to make his creation look like hell.

A group of fifteen Chinese walked in, creating a stir. Intrigued, I asked a waiter who they were. He patiently pointed out Jiang Wen, the handsome star of *Beijingers in New York*, a hit mini-series about émigré life in the Big Apple, and Xie Yuan, star of the hit movie *I Love You Without Question*. One of the young women, wearing a fur-trimmed jacket, posed prettily for Madame Soong's camera. And who was she?

"That's Cheng Fangyuan!" the waiter exclaimed, in the same incredulous tone someone might say "Madonna!" "She emceed last year's *entire* Lunar New Year show on Central Television." I tried to look suitably impressed as I sipped my Dragon Seal chardonnay. I didn't tell him that *I* had hosted the 1980 show.

At 10 p.m., a fourteen-piece orchestra began playing Viennese waltzes. As several couples twirled on the parquet floor, I thought of the languid ballroom scene in Bertolucci's film *The Last Emperor*. Were they dancing the century away while others starved? I knew rationally that snatching the *foie gras* out of the mouths of the rich wouldn't solve the problem of mental retardation in Gansu. But a part of the old me felt disheartened by all the extravagance. It was as if the revolution had never happened. In the 1970s, no one would have guessed that Luo Ning, my plain-living classmate, was the daughter of a marshal. In the 1990s, China's Communist elite was no longer afraid to flaunt its privilege and perks.

In 1992, a friend invited me to lunch to meet the daughter of deposed Party chief Zhao Ziyang. Wang Yannan (Amaranth Wang) arrived late, looking glamorous in a silk print dress and a string of good pearls. At thirty-seven, she was a willowy beauty with ivory skin, a perfect carriage and satin hair caught at the nape of her neck. She had learned English at the prestigious Foreign Languages Institute in Canton while her father was running Guangdong province. Two years of studying hotel management in Hawaii in the mid-1980s had given her an American accent.

My friend had picked a restaurant specializing in Chaozhou-style food, a sprightly offshoot of Cantonese cuisine. We ordered baby oysters in congee, aromatic sautéed chicken with deep-fried parsley, braised hearts of bok choy and duck consommé scented with dried lemons. As I watched Amaranth nibbling on a baby oyster, I was struck by how much China had changed. In the old days, the children of powerful people suffered immensely after their parents' downfall. But despite the purge of Zhao Ziyang, Amaranth had kept her high-profile job as deputy general manager of the Great Wall Sheraton, where she was chauffeured to work in a Mercedes.

"Do you know where I can get an old typewriter?" she asked me out of the blue. "Or an old phone?"

"I just bought some touch-tone phones for my office. You can have the old black phone the *Globe* has used since the sixties," I said, a bit puzzled.

"Is it a crank-handled one?" Amaranth asked excitedly.

"Dial," I said. She looked disappointed. It turned out she collected antique machines as a hobby. She asked about sewing machines.

"Several of my friends have treadle ones," I said, trying to be helpful. Then I remembered they were still using them. China's Communist elite lived in a world of its own. The gap between Amaranth and the masses was so great that she considered their ordinary household items to be antiques.

I met her several times after our first lunch, usually to trade videos. She lent me an old James Bond movie. I lent her *Cookie*, a comedy about a Mafia boss's daughter who protects her father during an internal Mob power struggle. I'll bet ex–Party chief Zhao watched the movie, too, but if he saw any parallels with his own predicament, Amaranth never said.

Although the police had stopped watching her by 1992, she remained understandably wary. One day when we met for afternoon tea in the Sheraton's atrium, I asked how her father was doing "His health is fine. But he can't travel," she said. "His spirits are good, and he hopes to work." Until Tiananmen, Amaranth had lived with him inside Zhongnanhai, along with her brigadier-general husband and their ten-year-old son. When her father was put under house arrest in a traditional old courtyard home in central Beijing, she moved her family out to join him.

A month after the massacre, Amaranth quietly applied for a visitor's visa to Canada. Like many Western governments, Ottawa was eager to accept the children of senior officials in order to build up a network of future contacts. Of course, Amaranth lied on the form about who her father was. But even though she arrived for her interview in her Mercedes, an obtuse Canadian visa officer rejected her, noting on the file that she seemed like the type to overstay a visitor's visa.

You could hardly blame the officer for failing to be impressed by Amaranth's Mercedes. Beijing's roads were now clogged with luxury cars as the new rich took a great leap into the driver's seat. My neighborhood seafood restaurant acquired a two-tone Rolls to ferry around Premier Li Peng's son and other favored customers. In 1994 alone, Mercedes-Benz, BMW, Ferrari and Rolls-Royce all opened dealerships in Beijing. Business was so brisk that Rolls-Royce adapted its cars to China's leaded fuel. A company spokesman told me that mainland buyers preferred the Silver Spur, which was four inches longer than the Silver Shadow and cost $250,000.

In 1993, at a solemn ceremony at Beijing's ancient Temple of Heaven, a former labor-camp convict was handed the keys to the first Ferrari ever sold in China. When I told Driver Liu I was going to meet the famous ex-con, he was so excited that I invited him to sit in on the interview. I began by asking Li Xiaohua when he had first dreamed of owning a car.

"While harvesting wheat in northeast China behind an 'East Is Red' tractor," he said.

"What did you grow?" Driver Liu broke in.

"Wheat and soybeans."

"Me, too!" said Liu.

It turned out that in 1969 they had both been sent to state farms near the Soviet border. Listening to them compare notes on the Cultural Revolution was like attending a Big Chill reunion of Red Guards. In the late 1970s, they both managed to get back to Beijing. While Driver Liu worked for various state companies, Li became a canteen cook. Then their paths diverged. Li closed a deal on some digital watches. Like the ration-coupon trader at the Number One Machine Tool Factory, he was sent to a labor camp for the crime of *tou ji dao ba*, a Maoist pejorative for buying low and selling high. "Nowadays, you could sell a whole trainload of watches and nobody would blink," Li said with a sardonic laugh.

He emerged from labor camp at the beginning of Deng's reforms and assiduously courted a general's daughter. She threatened to kill herself unless her parents let her marry him. Using his new father-in-law's clout, Li obtained a duty-free permit to buy a used Toyota from a Libyan diplomat. In 1981, he became one of only twenty Beijingers to own a private car.

Having finally achieved his driving ambition, he smooth-talked his way into becoming the exclusive Japanese distributor of Formula 101, the baldness tonic created by millionaire Zhao Zhangguang. Li invested the profits in Hong Kong real estate, just as property prices plunged following the 1989 Tiananmen Massacre. Two years later, when values bounced back, he became a multi-millionaire at the age of forty.

Li spotted lucrative opportunities in China and returned to Beijing. Flashing a newly acquired Japanese passport, he moved into the Jianguomenwai Diplomatic Compound, where the guards kept his fellow Chinese at bay. "I was sick of everyone pestering me for investments and donations," he said. "Besides, I needed a place to park my cars." He owned seven, including a Mazda sportscar, three Mercedes-Benzes and the bright red Ferrari Testarossa. His wife, who stopped by to say hello, reminded me of a Chinese Dolly Parton, with her cascading country-and-western hairdo, generous bosom, snug black dress and high-heeled mules. She even had false eyelashes and a huge diamond solitaire.

Li rarely drove his Ferrari, for which he had paid $134,888 (eight is a lucky number in Chinese because it rhymes with wealth). Alas, the car was too high-strung and too low-slung for Beijing's bumpy roads, not to mention that he ran a high risk of uninsured peasants smashing into him when their brakes failed. A rough-edged man with eyes that absorbed everything at a glance, Li proudly showed us a photo of himself in Ferrari's glossy yearbook. He was the only mainland Chinese in it and, surely, the only former labor-camp convict among dozens of European princes and Arab sheiks. As he passed us a copy of *Car Fan*, a new Chinese magazine, which had put him and his Ferrari on the cover, neither Driver Liu nor I could miss the flash of his solid-gold Rolex watch. Its entire face was encrusted with diamonds and rubies. Liu and I had recently priced a similar one at $40,000 in a local department store.

My driver was starting to sweat. I could see the beads forming on his scalp through his short-cropped brush cut. I knew he was upset. As I was winding down the interview, Li suddenly turned to my driver. "You know, I could use a guy like you. I have ten thousand people working for me, but I'm not strong on management. After all, I used to be a canteen cook. Maybe you should work for me."

Driver Liu was speechless. So was I. Raiding my prize employee right under my nose? Li took his silence for assent. "You could manage the other drivers. Think about it. We'll talk." Liu managed to croak, "Okay. Fine."

On the way home, he was strangely silent. I didn't want to lose Driver Liu, but I also didn't want him to lose the opportunity of a lifetime. "If you want to work for Li Xiaohua, feel free," I said finally. "You must do what you want."

Driver Liu glanced at me, and narrowly missed an errant cyclist. Maybe, I thought to myself, we should discuss his career back at the office. But he wanted to talk. To my surprise, he was disgusted by Li. "Things aren't very fair," he said vehemently. "Some people become billionaires. Some people work their whole lives for nothing." As we pulled into Pagoda Garden, he cut the engine, got out and slammed the door. "I don't want to work for someone like that," he said. "He got where he is by using his wife's connections, by doing shady stuff. It would be risky to work for him."

Anger at corruption and privilege had helped spark the massive Tiananmen demonstrations. The subsequent military crackdown had silenced the complaints but did nothing to reassure people like Driver Liu that anything was being done about the problems. When I had left Beijing in 1980, China had been an unrelentingly pure country. Government officials had refused to take even a chocolate bar from a foreigner. But a decade later, cadres were demanding bribes of cash, fancy cars and college tuition overseas for their children.

A Dutch businessman who ran an import-export company in China said it was now virtually impossible to do business without paying off Chinese officials. "The normal kickback is 0.5 percent to 1.5 percent of the deal. In one recent case, a white-haired gentle grandmother-type walked in and asked for a 4 percent commission. She dressed very simply, very ordinarily, just like the grandmothers you see on the street. She was a former section chief at the Ministry of Foreign Economic Relations and Trade."

He said he was in the midst of his worst case of bribery. A well-connected man in his twenties was demanding a 25 percent kickback, or $200,000 in cash, in exchange for brokering an $800,000 deal being financed by the World Bank. The businessman shrugged as if to say he had no choice but to acquiesce. "China ultimately pays. But because the loan has very low interest, it means that tax-payers in the U.S., Canada and Europe are subsidizing the loan."

If you had told me back in the 1970s that little old ladies would one day be demanding bribes, or that Old Xing would be chairman of McDonald's, or that the daughter of a deposed Party chief would go to work in a Mercedes, or that a former labor-camp convict would be the first Chinese to buy a Ferrari, I would have accused you of having had too many cups of *maotai*. It seemed bewildering that all these changes were taking place before, not after, the collapse of communism. Even more remarkable, the man presiding over all these changes was one of the original Long Marchers, the ancient patriarch of communism himself, Comrade Deng Xiaoping, an ail-ing leader now entering his tenth decade. And some of the biggest wheeler-dealers in the new economy were his own five children. To me and the other one billion ex-Maoists, the high-flying Deng children were the ultimate outrage.

Mao was right about those capitalist roaders. He had predicted that without continuous class struggle, the "landlords, rich peasants, counter-revolutionaries, bad elements and monsters" would all "crawl out," and "it would not take long, perhaps only several years ... before a counter-revolutionary restoration occurred." In his *Little Red Book of Quotations*, he warned: "To win country-wide vic-tory is only the first step in a long march of ten thousand *li* ... The comrades must be helped to preserve the style of plain living and hard struggle."

Mao's drastic antidote, the Great Proletarian Cultural Revolution, had failed to block the rise of a parasitic, privileged new class. By the 1990s, the children of China's leaders had become the new robber barons. This small group of Red Princelings and Princesses made obscene profits from insider information and monopolies. They ran large state enterprises like fiefdoms. With no shareholders to answer to, they dipped into company coffers for limousines, banquets and trips abroad. Still others got rich through *guan dao*, literally official profiteering, buying scarce commodities like steel at artificially low state prices, then flipping them at a huge mark-up.

The five Deng children constituted the very top layer of an extremely thin upper crust. Fearing the Party might soon be over, Deng's children concentrated on salting money away for the lean days ahead. They knew what had happened to the Great Helmsman's offspring: his daughter Li Na, once a deputy Party chief of Beijing, now lived in a humble apartment and shopped herself for oil, salt, rice and other daily needs; one of his grandsons, New World's cousin, worked as a lowly hotel clerk.

The net worth of Deng & Co. was impossible to calculate. The children worked through layers of holding companies and investment firms, mostly in Hong Kong. And like smart money everywhere, they leaned toward the safety of diversification. Deng Lin, the eldest daughter, was China's most commercially successful artist. Her husband, a graduate of an obscure mining school, was deputy general manager of China Non-Ferrous Metals Corporation, a huge state-owned conglomerate. Deng Pufang, the paralyzed son, ran China's cash-rich Welfare Fund for the Disabled. Deng Nan, the third child, was vice-minister of the powerful State Science and Technology Commission and a partner in China Venture Capital, which owned sizable stakes in at least four Hong Kong companies. Deng Maomao was imperial lip reader and her father's biographer. Her husband was a key player in China's international arms sales. Deng Zhifang, the youngest, had multi-million-dollar interests in real estate, shipping, investment and construction in Shanghai and Hong Kong.

Cynics charged that Deng Lin's paintings provided a genteel cover for influence peddling. At any rate, her canvases often fetched $45,000. Five of her works were acquired by Hong Kong tycoon Li Ka-shing, who had extensive business interests in mainland China and who, according to *Forbes*, was the tenth-richest person in the world. Few insiders were surprised when China subsequently reneged on one of its long-term leases for McDonald's, at the prime spot in Beijing, after Li Ka-shing made it known that he wanted it.

Perhaps it was because Deng Lin managed her father's household budget, but foreign investors seemed anxious to curry favor with her. On a recent trip to America, she stayed with an artist I knew in Boston. On the last day, Deng Lin invited her hostess to lunch at

Quincy Market, a local tourist attraction. "When it came time to pay," my friend recalled, "Deng Lin pulled out a credit card and said, 'Occidental Petroleum gave this to me.'"

In 1992, a one-woman show of Deng Lin's latest works opened at the Beijing Fine Arts Museum, the biggest ever by a living artist in its history. The black and white silk tapestries, hand-woven to her specifications by a rug factory in coastal Jiangsu province, reminded me of nothing more than giant eyeballs and fishbones. But others apparently loved them. I could hardly fight my way through the thicket of congratulatory bouquets, potted plants and floral stands from art lovers such as the Shenzhen Taxation Bureau.

Local officials knew better than to refuse her brother, Deng Pufang, when he arrived on fund-raising trips, carried sedan-style in his wheelchair by panting aides. (Virtually no buildings in China have handicap access.) A chain-smoker who favored three-piece pinstriped suits and red silk ties, Deng Pufang might well have been heir apparent. But his suicide attempt killed his political career; the Chinese are deeply prejudiced against any kind of disability. Once, during an interview with a Chinese friend, he leaned over in his wheelchair and snapped off the recorder. "If I weren't paralyzed, there would be no need to train the third generation of leaders. *I* would be the successor."

As the "donations" poured in to the welfare fund, Deng Pufang shoveled the cash into a shady conglomerate called Kang Hua Development Corp. He named himself chief executive. In 1989, as rumors of corruption grew, the company was disbanded in disgrace. Only his exalted pedigree saved Deng Pufang from being investigated.

Of all the children, Deng Maomao seemed most adept at deciphering her father's Delphic utterances. So it was not surprising that many people wooed her, too. Although the first volume of her 1995 book, *Deng Xiaoping, My Father*, was a strong contender for the world's most boring biography, others saw it as a business opportunity. Media mogul Rupert Murdoch, who was eyeing the Chinese satellite market, snapped up the English rights.

To please Beijing, which preferred that the masses didn't see stories about dissidents, he had already yanked the BBC World Service from his STAR television broadcasts into China. He flew Maomao to the U.S. on a lavish book tour. In New York, accompanied by her personal secretary and her teenaged daughter, she stayed at the Waldorf Astoria. Her daughter went shopping and took in a Broadway show, *Beauty and the Beast*. In Washington, they stayed at the Four Seasons Hotel, where a standard room cost $325. In Beverly Hills, Murdoch invited the first-time author to dinner at his home. No doubt, he was breathlessly awaiting volume two.

Deng Zhifang was the youngest and the richest of the five children. Back in 1981, I had cornered him in a library carrel at the University of Rochester, where he was a doctoral student in quantum optics. I was researching a story for my journalism degree about the first trickle of Chinese students into America. As I approached, I saw him slip a copy of *Newsweek* under his desk. Remembering how the Chinese post office had once confiscated my own copies, I introduced myself and joked, "Did you know you're reading a counter-revolutionary magazine?"

"I read *Newsweek* to improve my English," he stammered.

My comment hadn't been a terrific ice-breaker, and he didn't want to talk to me. Ten years later, in 1991, he formed a huge real estate firm and teamed up with Li Ka-shing, his sister's billionaire art fan.

"I am involved with Deng's son," Li exulted at an annual shareholders meeting in Hong Kong. "And I will be involved in more partnerships with him."

The Cultural Revolution had taught the five Deng children that political power was ephemeral. After the Tiananmen Massacre, they especially worried about life after their father's death. They knew he had given the order to shoot to kill and feared the people might vent their fury on them. Deng Maomao had already persuaded her father to release dissident Wei Jingsheng six months early.

In 1995, she made another conciliatory move, publicly acknowledging that Tiananmen had been a "tragedy." It was the first important deviation from the official government hard line. To me, and to many ordinary Chinese, it was an intriguing sign that history would be rewritten one day.

21

Middle-Class Kingdom

Top: Maternity-ward nurse with newborn baby.

Photo: Jan Wong/ *Globe and Mail*

Bottom: Amaranth Wang, daughter of deposed party chief, Zhao Ziyang, on duty at the Great Wall Sheraton, as Foreign Minister Wu Xueqian meets the foreign minister of the United Arab Emirates.

What with the spectacular economy and a country poised on the brink of major political change, it was tempting to stay in China forever. With two young children, it didn't hurt to have a cook, nanny, housekeeper and driver, either. But six years as a student, followed by six more years as a reporter, were finally enough. Norman had already quit working for Sun Microsystems because he didn't want to get stuck in the area of pre-sales technical support for the rest of his life. And after the Tiananmen Massacre, he didn't feel right about working for a Chinese government organization like the Academy of Science, either. My husband had put his career on hold long enough. And I didn't want my children growing up in an atmosphere of smog and telephone taps.

When my editor told me I should return to Toronto by the summer of 1994, just six months away, I wanted to find out what had happened to the people I had known back in Mao's time. And to placate my editors, who began asking for a swan song, I also began to think long and hard about where China was headed.

For old times' sake, I wanted to visit the Number One Machine Tool Factory. I invited Teacher Dai to accompany me, and she readily agreed. As we walked into the same dilapidated red brick gatehouse, memories of struggle meetings and pneumatic drills flooded back. A cadre named Zhao Zirong, who had been a young worker when I toiled there twenty-one years earlier, ushered us into an air-conditioned reception room. The old Mao portrait was gone, replaced by a rooster-shaped clock composed of tiny seashells glued on black velvet. (I preferred the Mao portrait.) I asked Zhao about the Iron Women's Team.

"It lasted a few years after you left, but then it was disbanded," he said. "Women can drill, but not for long. Better to let men do it." That annoyed me, but so much annoyed me now in China.

The original five-thousand-member work force had shrunk to sixteen hundred. The factory, still the top lathe maker in China, now sold 15 percent of its output to Asia and North America. "Back then, we exported to, uh, you know" – he grinned in embarrassment – "socialist countries."

In 1973, the factory had virtually been in the farm fields. Now it was prime property, right across from Maxim's in the glittering World Trade Center, Beijing's tallest skyscraper. As we walked through the dank workshops where I had spent fifty days trying to reform my thinking, Zhao wanted to talk about real estate, not epistemology. "We're going to tear down all these buildings and put up skyscrapers," he said. "The subway will stop right underneath us."

Several workers chuckled in disbelief when he introduced me as someone who had been there for "open-door schooling." Zhao mentioned that the workers now averaged 10,000 yuan ($1,200) a year in salary.

"How wonderful!" said Teacher Dai, as upbeat as ever. "I don't even make half that."

"Everyone here would rather be teachers," Zhao said sourly. "These salaries are just middling to low. At least you people can moonlight by tutoring."

I showed Zhao my ten-page "ideological summing-up," written just after I left Number One. It was the kind of soul-searching confession every Chinese wrote after a long stint of labor, except that I actually meant it. He stared at it as if it were a moon rock. "I hoped that through physical labor," I had written, "I could change my bourgeois world outlook to that of a proletarian world outlook."

On one of my last reporting trips, to Hangzhou, I decided to look up my old geisha classmates. Pearl had recently written a long, but very proper, reminiscence about the Chairman, which had been published in the Zhejiang provincial newspaper. But my other class-mates warned me that Center, now chairman of the provincial Zither Association, remained hyper-sensitive about her secret rela-tionship with Mao. Alas, both Pearl and Center were out of town at meetings. But I tracked down Center's husband, who sent her a telegram, and she flew back a day early. That evening, they arrived at my hotel, bearing a tin of Dragon Well tea and a bag of traditional rice dumplings wrapped in fragrant palm leaves.

Except for some fine lines around her eyes and mouth, she was unchanged. At fifty-one, she looked like a petite Chinese version of Audrey Hepburn. She was still a fragile beauty, tiny-waisted in an olive silk blouse and mid-calf beige skirt, her hair swept back in an elegant chignon of black silk. Center didn't realize that I now knew about her and Mao.

After half an hour of chitchat, I broached the subject. "Why were you and Pearl the only ones from our class selected to attend his funeral? And why were you two the only ones from Beijing University to help build his mausoleum?"

Center stiffened and blushed. Her husband, a former baritone, stared off into space. "We represented the whole history department at Beijing University," she said in a flat voice, her tone closing off that avenue of discussion. It was too late. Now I couldn't tell her I knew, after pretending I didn't. We went downstairs for dinner. As the waitress poured us Cokes, I edged toward the topic one last time. Had Center ever visited the Mao Mausoleum? I asked.

"No," she said. "I never have time. On business trips, I'm always so rushed."

In 1988, when I first returned to China, I avoided Cadre Huang and Teacher Fu. I knew my status as a reporter would only make them nervous, and I wasn't dying to have my tones corrected. After the Tiananmen Massacre, when half a dozen of its students had made the Most Wanted list, my alma mater was even more phobic about foreign journalists. On sensitive political anniversaries, plainclothes police patrolled the campus while armed soldiers and more police ringed the perimeter.

I knew that Beijing University had changed over the years. It now taught such bourgeois subjects as sociology, psychology and even women's studies. Nobody did hard labor any more. And students no longer vied to eat steamed sawdust. In 1994, when I knew I would be leaving China, curiosity got the better of me. Had Fu the Enforcer mellowed? What had happened to Party Secretary Pan? Chancellor Zhou? I phoned Cadre Huang.

"It's Bright Precious Wong," I said.

"Aiya! Why do you never call? Why do you never come to visit?" he shouted, even though the new imported phone lines were crystal clear.

"As a matter of fact, I thought I'd drop by to see you. How about tomorrow?"

I heard a strangled giggle over the phone. The next day he was waiting in his office dressed in a Western suit and red tie. He was a mere four years away from retirement, but his hair was still coal black, and he still had an unruly cowlick. His narrow face, sharp chin, piercing eyes and sallow complexion hadn't changed at all. At fifty-six, he was now chief of the Foreign Students Office, in charge of more than fifteen hundred students in six buildings.

"So sudden," he said apologetically. "No one is around." Fu had just left for a three-month teaching job in France. Dai was in Japan, also teaching. Party Secretary Pan had gone to the airport to meet a foreign delegation. And Chancellor Zhou had recently died, at the age of ninety-one. I told Huang that Fat Paycheck Shulman and I now had two little boys. He laughed his embarrassed whinny, putting his hand up to shield his mouth.

"I can't *believe* the stupid things I did," he said. He squinted at me. "I can hardly remember. Let's see. Did your father tell us to try to stop it?" I shook my head, and said nothing.

"I remember we had a big fight. You were very upset. I was very sad," he said with another humorless laugh. He repeated this twice more, as if trying to convince himself. I changed the subject. I knew that my alma mater had recently banned kissing.

"How are things at Beijing University?" I asked.

"No time to play ping-pong," he said, with another giggle. "And no one has a Chinese roommate any more."

I suddenly felt nostalgic about wheat harvests. "Is there any more open-door schooling?"

He burst out laughing. "Now foreign students want comfort. Factories want to make money. It's not like before."

I felt a bit sad. As difficult and crazy as my years at Beijing University had been, I had had a unique experience. Now, the students coming after me were having such a conventional time they might as well have been studying in Singapore or Taipei or Hong Kong.

"Before you leave, we'll get everybody together," said Cadre Huang. "And you must bring Fat Paycheck Shulman."

We waited and waited for Fu the Enforcer to return from Paris, but she kept extending her stay. She was now a good three months past her scheduled return date. I would be leaving China in two weeks, and we could wait no longer. Cadre Huang scheduled a farewell banquet at the campus restaurant. When I arrived, I couldn't resist asking, "So, has Teacher Fu defected?" Cadre Huang burst into nervous laughter. For a moment, I thought she had, but he assured me she would return any day now.

He had invited Erica's old roommate, now a professor in the Chinese department, Teacher Dai, who was just back from Japan, and Party Secretary Pan. I knew it was my last chance to ask Pan why he had never passed on my wedding invitation, but I decided that he no longer deserved to be embarrassed. My classmates told me that in 1989 he had marched to Tiananmen Square and had even encouraged foreign students to join the protests. The university had punished him with a demotion, which is why he now spent his days hanging around airport waiting rooms. If Lacking Virtue Pan could change, anybody could.

The food was far better than in the 1970s. We had a dozen cold appetizers: dark, woodsy Chinese mushrooms, paper-thin slices of smoked pork, chicken with crushed chilies and Sichuan peppercorns, and slivered, blanched green peppers tossed in sesame oil. A parade of hot dishes followed: wok-fried jumbo shrimp and broccoli, steamed whole fish, spicy squid with crackling rice, a soothing crab and corn chowder and numerous varieties of savory dumplings. The sweet cassia wine loosened people's tongues. Cadre Huang, who was sitting on my left, turned to me.

"We used to recall the bitterness of the past to savor the sweetness of the present," he said, swallowing a mouthful of shrimp. "Well, now when we talk about recalling bitterness, we don't mean before Liberation. We mean the 1970s. Do you recall I was so poor I didn't even own a watch when you first knew me?"

I didn't. Back then nobody ever hinted life was hard. But I did remember the day he accidentally threw out a month's worth of his family's rice ration coupons. "You turned white," I said. "But all the teachers shared theirs with you, and you were able to get through the month."

Inevitably, the talk turned to the massacre. Every conversation did, even five years later. Cadre Huang repeated the government line. "No one died in Tiananmen Square," he said. I refused to rise to the bait. Why get emotional? I now understood he was just another Party hack doing his job. Still, I had to say something. In an even voice I told him I had been there that night and had seen the army shoot into the crowds over and over again. There was an awkward silence. Party Secretary Pan stared at his plate. Teacher Dai and Erica's roommate giggled uncomfortably.

Did they have any news from Erica? I asked. I hadn't seen her since we parted in 1973, twenty-one years earlier. Cadre Huang told me she had returned twice after earning a Ph.D. in mathematics in the States. "She's upset with how Beijing University has changed. She misses the old days." He laughed his humorless whinny. "We stuffed you two full of revolutionary thinking. Her problem is that she left too soon. She never experienced what happened after."

He stopped and cleared his throat. He looked at a spot on the wall above my head. In a low voice he said that thirty-six university students had been killed at Tiananmen Square. "Three were from Beijing University."

I nodded expressionlessly. Anything more would have embarrassed him. But for a fleeting moment, I wanted to hug him. Even Cadre Huang had changed.

The fact that I now had two sons made a deep impression on Cadre Huang. In urban China, almost no Chinese my age had more than one child – unless they were lucky enough to have twins. I felt guilty whenever I walked down the street pushing Sam in a stroller with Ben toddling beside. "Look, she has *two* children," people would whisper, nudging one another. "Two *sons!*"

As I pondered China's future for my final dispatches, I began to think about the long-term repercussions of Beijing's one-child policy. In rural areas, where three out of four Chinese lived, many families had several children. But in the cities, where the one-child policy was strictly enforced, millions of onlies were growing up sibling-free, doted on by two parents and four grandparents. I saw six-year-olds still spoon-fed, ten-year-olds who couldn't dress themselves. In a Beijing department store, my sister witnessed a three-year-old throwing a temper tantrum. "The parents and the grandparents were all crowding around, trying to get him to stop crying. They kept offering him toys, and he kept screaming louder. Finally, the father pulled out a pack of cigarettes and gave him one."

Many parents of the nineties were part of the Lost Generation of the Cultural Revolution. After suffering so much themselves, they were determined not to deprive their only child. Beijing's biggest toy store was always jammed with parents buying toddler-sized fake fur coats, imported baby shampoo and red Porsche pedal cars. "My wife squanders her entire salary buying things for our son. She spends 50 yuan" – $6 – "on a shirt for him. For a *kid!*" complained Driver Liu, who usually spent one-fifth that amount on a shirt for himself. "She has to get him a famous brand name. Ordinary clothes won't do. When they go out, they always go to Kentucky Fried Chicken. Then they're so tired they take a *taxi* home!" he sputtered.

Nanny Ma always saved the choicest fruit for *her* only son. When he was a teenager, he still took the best for himself and said, in all seriousness, "But, Mom, you *like* bruised fruit." As he was growing up, she never let anyone, not even her husband, reprimand him. At sixteen, when her son was addicted to video games, she wanted him to eat some juicy grapes but didn't want to interrupt him or get his fingers sticky. So she peeled him one and popped it into his mouth. Then another, and another. He glared at her. "Not so fast," he snapped. "Can't you see I have to spit out the seeds?" By the time he was in his early twenties, her son refused to make his bed. He always left a scrap of food on the plate so he could stick it back in the refrigerator unwashed. When he began bringing his girlfriend home for the night, Nanny Ma finally put her foot down. That's when he pulled a knife on her.

Many people thought that a country populated with Little Emperors was headed for disaster. I disagreed. Granted, it might be unpleasant to live in a nation of me-first onlies, yet I saw a social revolution in the making. For generations, Chinese society had emphasized the family, the clan, the collective over the individual. Now, for the first time in four thousand years of history, the relationship was reversed. Pampered onlies were growing up to be self-centered, strong-willed, knife-wielding individualists like, well, Americans. Where the Mao generation failed, the Me generation just might succeed. "It's China's salvation," said Michael Crook, a British friend who was born and raised in Beijing. "If you have a population of Little Emperors, you can't have little slaves. Everyone will want to tell everyone else what to do. You'll have *democracy*."

In the late 1980s, a team of Chinese psychologists conducted a study of the only child with the help of Dr. T. Berry Brazelton, a Harvard pediatrician and chief of the child development unit at Boston Children's Hospital Medical Center. Researchers picked 360 children, half with siblings, half without, and asked them to rate each other. Factors such as age, income and rural or urban backgrounds didn't affect the outcome. Onlies did whatever best served their own interests. None voluntarily shared toys.

"Their peers always rated them as more selfish, less modest and less helpful in group activities," said Dr. Brazelton. The study's results boded ill for the collectivism espoused by the Chinese Communist Party. At a meeting to discuss the results, Dr. Brazelton found himself sitting next to the wife of Premier Li Peng. She turned to him and said with a frown, "This will never work for communism, will it?"

After Tiananmen, after the fall of the Berlin Wall, after the collapse of the Soviet Union, the intriguing question was how long Chinese communism would last. And many Chinese also wondered how long Deng Xiaoping himself would endure. His health, of course, was a state secret. The official word was always that he was just fine. His eldest son even told reporters that Deng watched fifty of the fifty-two televised soccer matches during the 1990 World Cup.

But Deng rarely left his gray brick residence at Rice Granary Alley, in the heart of Beijing. Although he had quit smoking his favorite Panda cigarettes, he was still said to play his beloved bridge every day. By 1994, his eyesight had failed and others had to read to him. By then, he had retired from all his positions except honorary chairman of the Chinese Bridge Association. Despite his poor health and the lack of any formal post, Deng continued to wield supreme power. To honor him, the Party struck an 18-karat gold-plated medallion in his likeness and inscribed it with a new title, the Great Architect.

On February 19, 1997, Deng Xiaoping died of advanced Parkinson's disease in a military hospital in Beijing. He was 92, and hadn't been seen publicly for three years. The Communist Party announced his death four hours later, in the middle of the night, so that people heard as they awoke the next day. Across the country, flags flew at half-mast. But except for loud sobs captured on state television, most citizens went about their business as usual. On the fifth day, Deng's body was cremated, and on the sixth, soldiers sealed off Tiananmen Square during the funeral service in the Great Hall of the People. No foreigners were allowed to attend.

So much had changed after the Great Helmsman's death in 1976. What would happen now that the Great Architect had passed away? Deng had sown the seeds of instability by creating a Communist-capitalist hybrid. Many Chinese fervently hoped the country would remain stable, but the new emphasis on profits was setting off an explosive reaction. As money-losing industries went bust, restive state workers were learning they had nothing to lose but their chains. Everyone knew Deng had failed to anoint a true successor. Few people were willing to bet that either Party Chief Jiang Zemin, a grinning yes-man appointed after Tiananmen, or Premier Li Peng, who had a reputation for stupidity and cruelty, could retain power.

The ethnic forces that tore asunder the Soviet Union do not exist in China. The fault lines are economic. In a frank report, the Chinese Academy of Science predicted a post-Deng power struggle between Beijing and the provinces. It warned that China could disintegrate like a "post-Tito Yugoslavia" unless drastic steps were taken to halt mounting regionalism. Rich provinces like coastal Guangdong have nothing in common with landlocked, impoverished Gansu. Already, wealthy regions balk at remitting taxes to the central government. Poor regions are voting with their feet. About 110 million peasants, the biggest migration in world history, have flooded the cities in search of work. Unlike in Maoist times, they are under no one's control, a nightmarish problem for the central government.

Is there a Gorbachev or a Yeltsin waiting in the wings? It is impossible to say. In any dictatorship, the smart players keep their heads down until the coast is clear. But whoever ultimately seizes the reins of power has to confront Deng's contradictory legacy. Is the solution to abandon Marxist controls – to unleash economic growth? Or clamp down – and stifle the economy? Either way, the Communist Party is in trouble.

I have no idea what is going to happen next in China. Nobody does. Most people agree that in the short term there is a high risk of chaos. The elite is certainly worried, which is why it is frantically transferring its money out. Dynastic change has rarely come smoothly in the Middle Kingdom. In the 1920s, powerful warlords carved China into fiefdoms. In the absence of a strong central power, some think it can happen again, this time with the rich south and coastal areas trying to break free from the impoverished, backward northwest. If the country degenerates into civil war, the military might step in and play king maker. It might even take over for a few years and try to roll back Deng's economic reforms.

A peasant revolt, the perennial catalyst for dynastic change, is another strong possibility. "In a very short time," Mao predicted, "in China's central, southern and northern provinces, several hundred million peasants will rise like a mighty storm, like a hurricane, a force so swift and violent that no power, however great, will be able to hold it back ... They will sweep all the imperialists, warlords, corrupt officials, local tyrants and evil gentry into their graves."

Mao was forecasting peasant unrest in the 1920s, but he could as easily have been sketching a scenario for the next millennium. A critical question is how much longer the peasants in Yuan Village will wait. "We're not afraid of getting our heads chopped off," one of them told me. "We have a saying: If I fall in battle, others will follow in my footsteps." What if the peasants in Yuan Village one day rebel against Party Secretary Shen and, tasting success, decide to keep on going? The Communists came to victory on the heels of one peasant rebellion. They can go down to defeat in another.

The old Maoist in me would once have cheered an old-fashioned peasant rebellion. But I know now that overthrowing tyrants only repeats the endless cycle of dynastic history. There would be bloodshed and suffering, and eventually a new emperor would sit upon the throne of China, and the rot and corruption would begin anew. My perspective has changed. I am now middle class and middle-aged, and I am beginning to see an alternative revolution, one that is brewing among China's own up-and-coming middle class.

What impressed me most in my final months was that many Chinese were becoming content, no, *happy* to stay in China. For the first time anyone could remember, they didn't necessarily want to join the traditional diaspora. After making a fortune in Japan and Hong Kong, Ferrari owner Li Xiaohua chose to return to the country that once tossed him into a labor camp. Driver Liu told me he planned to go into business when his younger brother came *back* from Germany. And Amaranth Wang came home to China after the Great Wall Sheraton sent her for training to Hong Kong and Brussels. (So much for the Canadian visa officer's assessment.)Life was so good for the Party elite that even when some of its members were down and out, there didn't seem to be much point in leaving. With its booming economy and alluringly primitive income-tax system, China was the new Land of Opportunity. Two decades after I snitched on people who begged me to help them escape, I couldn't *beg* Nanny Ma to leave China. For me, it was a stunning change.

Despite the possibility of short-term chaos, my hunch is that the key to China's future lies with its new middle class. By staying instead of leaving, these people will transform the country. It will not be simple, and it may not be especially tasteful, but it could be fast. China has already telescoped the industrial revolution and a century of development into a couple of decades.

This first generation of entrepreneurs is going on a wild, pent-up spending spree that has Western companies panting, but eventually it will stop bingeing, calm down and accumulate wealth. Then, like its counterparts elsewhere, the new middle class will be pushed by its own self-interest to invest in the future. Because it needs a free flow of information to do business, it will operate newspapers and television stations. Because it requires a skilled, healthy work force, it will support education and health care. When the masses of Chinese peasants see an economic reason for their children to stay in school, they will. And the more educated people become, the fewer babies they will want. Then, for the first time in history, it may be possible to extricate China from poverty.

My viewpoint might strike the China-watching community as naive. But I am convinced that the strongest proponent of democracy in China today is its middle class. At Tiananmen Square, it was Beijing's new shopkeepers who deluged the student strikers with free blankets and bread. It was the Flying Tigers, entrepreneurs rich enough to buy motorcycles, who roared around gathering intelligence on troop movements.

There is every indication China's middle class will continue to grow exponentially. Former peasants now run airline companies, jade-carving factories and fast-food franchises. Dissidents are getting rich by running bars and restaurants. Ex-convicts monopolize the stalls in Silk Alley, the best open-air market in Beijing. Across China, millions of entrepreneurs are opening florists, private schools, book stalls, video stores and beauty salons. Their factories manufacture virtually everything we buy in the West, from silk underwear to steering-wheel locks. I like to think that some of the budding entrepreneurs making Christmas decorations labeled Made in China were among the 400 million viewers watching when my friends and I sang "Jingle Bells" so long ago.

Many pundits abroad feel China isn't ready for democracy and human rights, that the mainland is too poor, too vast, too backward for anything but an iron dictatorship. The Chinese, the classic argument goes, need discipline. They yearn for authority. Democracy is too inherently messy, too chaotic for them. Again, I disagree. The Chinese may not use our terminology, but ask a peasant in Yuan Village if he would like a way to dump Party Secretary Shen, preferably without bloodshed, and you will get a resounding yes.

But can the middle class succeed where the Communist Party failed? Can it end China's age-old curse of too many people and too little food? By the Party's own admission, one out of every fourteen Chinese does not have enough to eat or wear. The World Bank believes the number is more like one in ten. Meanwhile, traditional graves, erosion and sprawling industrial zones shrink the amount of arable land. The Party, which swept to power on a pledge to eradicate poverty and inequality, is obsessed not with these problems but with staying in power. Yet the Chinese Communist Party is terminally ill. In my last five years in China, I scarcely met a soul who was interested in joining. Its death will probably be messy, but it could also be quick and painless.

China has changed more in the past two decades than it has in the preceding two centuries. Perhaps it is crazy to think that in my lifetime I will see the end of Chinese feudalism. It has, after all, persisted for four thousand years and, when I recall the abject poverty of places like Gansu, it's easy to sink into despair. But my optimism returns when I see how energetic and enterprising the Chinese people can be, how quickly Housekeeper Ma picked herself out of the gutter and paid our bill at Pizza Hut. The Chinese are natural entrepreneurs. They may behave like sloths under socialism, but when they can work for themselves, they make money hand over fist. A generation that has never experienced capitalism somehow knows instinctively about things like profit margins and opportunity costs. When Deng Xiaoping said "To get rich is glorious," it was only the second time in Chinese history that a leader has given capitalism a fighting chance. The previous time was during the Southern Song dynasty, nearly nine hundred years ago. For the first time in centuries, a growing middle class offers a ray of hope that China may one day become a true Middle Kingdom.

I have to admit that China's future looks very different from the one I had envisioned in the 1970s. Back then, I thought it was going to be the first country in the world where everyone would be equal, where there would be no unemployment, no exploitation, no crime, no ill will, not even a headache. Now I understand that the future of China may be the West's past. The Chinese are working very hard, but for their own sakes now, the way people in the West did during the industrial revolution, before they decided they wanted a forty-hour work week, labor unions and a minimum wage. Canadian Senator Richard Doyle, a former managing editor of the *Globe and Mail*, told me how he once had to lead a delegation of

Chinese visitors across a boisterous picket line of *Globe* employees.

"They're on strike," Doyle explained.

"Can't you just send them back to work?" a Chinese official asked in astonishment.

The Western world, especially Canada, is far more socialistic than China has ever been, with its free public education, universal medicare, unemployment insurance, old-age pensions and government funding for television ads against domestic violence. Living in China has made me appreciate my own country, with its tiny, ethnically diverse population of unassuming donut-eaters. I had gone all the way to China to find an idealistic, revolutionary society when I already had it right at home.

Yet I do not regret for a moment that I spent the best years of my life in China. I do not regret that I dug ditches or mixed cement or harvested rice – or that I studied Mao and Lenin and Marx. I *am* glad I never had Mao's image tattooed on my bicep, the way an admiring Mike Tyson did while serving time for rape in an Indiana prison. I was duped, conned, suckered by Maoism. But I do not feel ashamed or sad or even angry that my youthful devotion was betrayed. To paraphrase Tennyson, 'tis better to have believed and lost than never to have believed at all. Those years taught me about who I am, and what kind of world I want to live in. They taught me about life in a way that would have been impossible had I stayed safely at home. If you tell someone in Toronto that you think freedom and democracy are wonderful, they give you a strange look, as if you are raving about how nice oxygen is.

My disillusion with the workers' paradise has not made me more cynical, just less patient. Having been there myself, I can no longer tolerate dogma in any form. I'm suspicious of anything that's too theoretically tidy, too black and white. If I adhere to any creed today, it's a belief in human dignity and strength. Anything I do believe in today has to stand up to reason – and be explainable to my five-year-old son.

I have had a long time to think my second thoughts. I had once planned to live like the original Maoist missionaries. But in the end I took a different Long March. China had changed, and so had I.

EPILOGUE
Long Live Chairman Mao

Gu Yue, who specializes in playing Mao Zedong in films.

In the 1990s, I often went to the Mao Mausoleum. I liked lining up among the sunburned peasants from the provinces to eavesdrop on their conversations. I would shuffle through the dimly lit vault, guarded by statue-like PLA soldiers, and catch a quick glimpse of his rouged, waxen face. On the way out, I enjoyed the raucous in-your-face gauntlet of souvenir stands, which I suspected were a ploy by Deng to get Mao to turn over in his crystal sarcophagus. I always bought something – a Mao key chain, some slides of the Helmsman lying in state or a cigarette lighter that played "The East Is Red."

As the one-hundredth anniversary of the Great Helmsman's birth approached, organizing officials began to fret. To attack Maoism was tantamount to admitting that the first half of Deng's own career had been a mistake. But fulsome praise was unseemly, too. Deng could not be eclipsed by his old nemesis. Mao's centenary had to be marked, but no one should get carried away. In Beijing, the sole commemorative activity on December 26, 1993, was a formal meeting in the Great Hall of the People.

I was among the ten thousand invited guests. Most foreign correspondents considered the anniversary so unnewsworthy that they declined. But my life had been shaped by the Great Helmsman, so

I pinned on a small Mao badge, for old times' sake, and went an hour early.

My Mao badge didn't set off the metal detector. A female soldier inspected my backpack and waved me through. As I waited in my balcony seat, four military choirs filed in and began belting out competing revolutionary songs, as if they were at a college football rally. Below me, the stage was draped with enormous red silk flags and banked with pots of kumquats and miniature tangerines. Mao hated bourgeois trappings like potted plants, and he would have despised these. Kumquats and tangerines symbolized golden ingots. The more fruit there was, so the superstition went, the richer and luckier you'd be in the new year.

At 9 a.m. I watched a parade of Mao's old enemies totter on stage. They had come not to praise Mao but to bury him in the dust heap of history. There was General Yang Shangkun, a surprisingly hearty eighty-six-year-old, who was caught bugging Mao's office and private railway car in the 1960s. There was Rong Yiren, now seventy-seven, a dapper Shanghai capitalist who lost his immense textile-mill fortune under Mao and remade it under Deng. And there was Bo Yibo, now eighty-five, whom Mao purged as a vice-premier during the Cultural Revolution. Bo Yibo spent the first half hour of the memorial meeting ignoring the ceremonies, and instead chatted animatedly to Ding Guangen, Deng's bridge partner. General Yang Shangkun was passed a note as the meeting began. He glanced at the note, walked out and never returned. Had he arranged this in advance?

Deng himself was conspicuous by his absence. He had been well enough to vote in a municipal election just a few days earlier, but no one really expected him to show up. Mao, after all, had purged him twice. And no doubt Deng held Mao responsible for the crippling of his eldest son.

As Communist Party Chief Jiang Zemin droned on and on, I suddenly realized he was no longer talking about Mao. He was praising Deng. Our Great Architect, he said, had the wisdom to recognize that class struggle was outdated by 1978 and to open China to foreign investment. He hailed Deng as the true successor of Mao

Zedong Thought. The final indignity came when he called on people to study Deng's *Selected Works*.

Party Chief Jiang reminded me of a grinning panda, with his
rounded, black-rimmed glasses, his broad smile and his snugly tailored Mao suit. Under a gigantic portrait of Mao, he read his twen-
ty-eight-page speech smoothly, his voice rising in a crescendo like
a carnival barker's to indicate appropriate moments to applaud. The
audience dutifully clapped nine times. Only once was Jiang disappointed – when he attacked corruption among high officials. Then
there was silence.

As he droned on, I scanned the choice first rows of the vast auditorium with my binoculars. I couldn't spot Jade Phoenix. I knew
that to mark the centenary, she had gone to Beijing University a
few weeks earlier to speak to an invitation-only audience about
Mao. It was nothing titillating, just about how hard he had worked
in his later years, but everyone had been curious to see what Mao's
mistress was like.

As I peered through my binoculars, I noted without surprise that
Mao's descendants had not been allowed to sit on the stage.
Seventeen years after the Great Helmsman's death, Deng still kept a
tight rein on them. I spotted them in the first three rows. Mao's
three surviving children were all there, his mentally ill son, Mao
Anqing, in his wheelchair in the aisle, his two matronly daughters,
Li Na and Li Min, in the first row. The four grandchildren, including the hotel clerk, sat in the second two rows. New World Mao was
slumped over in the third row. He looked like he was trying not to
fall asleep.

A military band closed the meeting with a rousing rendition of
the "Internationale," still one of my favorite songs. "Arise, ye prisoners of starvation, Arise, ye wretched of the earth," I sang softly in
Chinese, as some of the foreign correspondents around me gave me
strange looks. I suddenly realized I was the only one actually singing
in the Great Hall of the People. Even the four choirs were silent. I
took off my Mao badge, and went home.

INDEX

Fat Paycheck Shulman. *See* Shulman, Norman

FBI (Federal Bureau of Investigation), 205-6

female infanticide, 326

Feng, Center. *See* Feng Jizhong

Feng Jizhong (Center), 135-9, 379
  on Mao's death, 174, 175, 379

Fermi, Enrico, 196

Festival for Tending Graves (Qing Ming), 167-8, 171

feudalism, 389; and sexual relations, 131, 152, 327

Flying Tigers, entrepreneurs, 232, 239, 388

Fonda, Jane, 16, 206

Fong Shee (maternal grandmother), 27-9

food, abundance of, 82, 94, 109, 208, 343, 365, 381-2; scarcity of, 24, 30-1, 42-3, 98-9, 102, 107, 127, 189, 286, 325; oddities, 49, 308; western, 109, 346, 362-4

foot-binding, 27, 33, 98

forced job placement, 307. *See also* prisons

foreign journalists, 77, 251, 258-9, 264
  and Beijing University, 379-80; danger in Beijing, 268; and Mao's centenary, 393

Foreign Languages Institute (Canton), 365

Foreign Languages Press, 156, 157, 173, 174, 178-9; Fragrant Hills faction, 157-8

Foreign Students Office (Beijing University), 48-9, 51, 85, 110, 380; and access to material in English, 74

foreigners, dual-price policy, 214, 215, 341; double standard at Beijing University, 182; forty-two secret rules of conduct, 62, 341, 347; Friendship Store, 42; and kickbacks, 369; liaisons with, 119; special treatment of, 154; surveillance of, 52-3, 73, 211, 213, 305-6; and Tiananmen Square massacre, 240, 250, 259-60

Free, Michael, 362

Friendship Store, 42

From Society Back to Society Movement, 144, 182

Fu Min (Fu the Enforcer), 44, 57-60, 73, 76, 78-9, 82-4, 86, 88, 95, 98, 101, 152-3, 379-81; and Ye Xuanping, 105; and Zhao Lihai, 110; and Betty Zheng, 152

Fu the Enforcer. *See* Fu Min

Fu Yuehua, 189-90

Fuxing Hospital, 248

Fuzhou airport, 306

G

Gang of Four, 51-2, 166-7, 169-171, 175-6
  arrest of, 176-8; denunciation of, 181

Gansu province, 324-6, 365, 385

Gaobei (North Marsh), 215-6

gays, and marriage, 181

geishas, of Mao, 135-139, 174-5, 177, 379

Gilmartin, Peter, 193

Gleitsman Foundation, 290

Globe and Mail, 76, 192, 206, 235, 238, 266, 271, 296, 305, 389-90; Beijing bureau, 207; Chinese staff at, 340; Forever bike, 269; Jeep Cherokee, 328-9, 348-9; Tiananmen Square massacre, 248-60; Toyota, 209, 240-41, 249, 266-7, 348-9 *See also* Wong, Jan

Goddess of Democracy, 244, 247, 250, 257

Gorbachev, Mikhail, summit, 220, 230-4

Great Architect, Deng Xiaoping as, 385, 394

Great Depression, 33, 99

Great Hall of the People, 227, 228, 233, 247, 256
  Mao's body lying in state, 175; and Mao's centenary, 393-5; Tiananmen Square incident (1976), 169-70

Great Helmsman. *See* Mao Zedong

Great Leap Forward, (1958), 15, 30, 97; and Deng Xiaoping, 104

Great Proletarian Cultural Revolution. *See* Cultural Revolution

Great Wall Sheraton hotel, 207-8, 220, 365-6, 387

Gu, Future. *See* Gu Weiming

Gu Weiming (Future), 142-5, 172, 174, 180

Guangdong province, 17-20, 23-35, 365, 385
  Ye Xuanping as governor, 105

Guixian (Cassia) 329-31

gulag. *See* prisons

Guomindang Party, 28, 110, 124, 174, 196

H

Hainan Island, 300, 320

Hangzhou (city), 135, 137, 139, 379

Hansson, Anders, 77-82, 85, 87, 89, 150

Hard Rock Café (Beijing), 65

Hatem, George, 319

He Shen, 45

health 18, 96, 142, 388; acupuncture anesthesia, 37-8; in childbirth, 338

height requirements, 212

heroin, 322

Higgins, Andrew, 235, 251, 266-267

Hinton, Bill, 196, 289-90

Hinton, Joan (Cold Spring), 156, 195-99,364

About the Author

An award-winning journalist, Jan Wong was the Beijing correspondent for *The Globe and Mail* from 1988 to 1994. She is a graduate of McGill University and the Columbia University Graduate School of Journalism, and is the recipient of the George Polk Award, and other honours for her reporting. Wong has written for the Montreal *Gazette*, *The New York Times*, *The Boston Globe* and *The Wall Street Journal*. She is the author of three other books: *Lunch with Jan Wong*, *Jan Wong's China* and *Beijing Confidential*. She lives with her family in Toronto, where she is a reporter for *The Globe and Mail*.